# THE LOST ROAD
## AND OTHER WRITINGS

# THE HISTORY OF MIDDLE-EARTH

## I
### THE BOOK OF LOST TALES, PART ONE

## II
### THE BOOK OF LOST TALES, PART TWO

## III
### THE LAYS OF BELERIAND

## IV
### THE SHAPING OF MIDDLE-EARTH
#### THE QUENTA, THE AMBARKANTA AND
#### THE ANNALS

## V
### THE LOST ROAD
#### AND OTHER WRITINGS

## VI
### THE RETURN OF THE SHADOW
#### THE HISTORY OF THE LORD OF THE RINGS, PART ONE
(in preparation)

J. R. R. TOLKIEN

# THE LOST ROAD
## AND OTHER WRITINGS

Language and Legend
before
'The Lord of the Rings'

Edited by Christopher Tolkien

BOSTON
HOUGHTON MIFFLIN COMPANY
1987

Copyright © 1987 by Frank Richard Williamson and Christopher Reuel Tolkien
as Executors of the Estate of J.R.R. Tolkien

**Library of Congress Cataloging-in-Publication Data**
Tolkien, J.R.R. (John Ronald Reuel), 1892–1973.
The lost road and other writings.

(The History of Middle-earth; 5)
Includes index.
1. Middle Earth (Imaginary place) — Literary
collections.   2. Fantastic literature, English.
I. Tolkien, Christopher.   II. Title.   III. Series:
Tolkien, J.R.R. (John Ronald Reuel), 1892–1973.
History of Middle-earth; 5.
PR6039.O32L64   1987     823'.912     87-16926
ISBN 0-395-45519-7

Printed in the United States of America

S 10 9 8 7 6 5 4 3 2 1

# CONTENTS

# PREFACE

This fifth volume of *The History of Middle-earth* completes the presentation and analysis of my father's writings on the subject of the First Age up to the time at the end of 1937 and the beginning of 1938 when he set them for long aside. The book provides all the evidence known to me for the understanding of his conceptions in many essential matters at the time when *The Lord of the Rings* was begun; and from the *Annals of Valinor*, the *Annals of Beleriand*, the *Ainulindalë*, and the *Quenta Silmarillion* given here it can be quite closely determined which elements in the published *Silmarillion* go back to that time, and which entered afterwards. To make this a satisfactory work of reference for these purposes I have thought it essential to give the texts of the later 1930s in their entirety, even though in parts of the *Annals* the development from the antecedent versions was not great; for the curious relations between the *Annals* and the *Quenta Silmarillion* are a primary feature of the history and here already appear, and it is clearly better to have all the related texts within the same covers. Only in the case of the prose form of the tale of Beren and Lúthien have I not done so, since that was preserved so little changed in the published *Silmarillion*; here I have restricted myself to notes on the changes that were made editorially.

I cannot, or at any rate I cannot yet, attempt the editing of my father's strictly or narrowly linguistic writings, in view of their extraordinary complexity and difficulty; but I include in this book the general essay called *The Lhammas* or Account of Tongues, and also the *Etymologies*, both belonging to this period. The latter, a kind of etymological dictionary, provides historical explanations of a very large number of words and names, and enormously increases the known vocabularies of the Elvish tongues – as they were at that time, for like everything else the languages continued to evolve as the years passed. Also hitherto unknown except by allusion is my father's abandoned 'time-travel' story *The Lost Road*, which leads primarily to Númenor, but also into the history and legend of northern and western Europe, with the associated poems *The Song of Ælfwine* (in the stanza of *Pearl*) and *King Sheave* (in alliterative verse). Closely connected with *The Lost Road* were the earliest forms of the legend of the

Drowning of Númenor, which are also included in the book, and the first glimpses of the story of the Last Alliance of Elves and Men.

In the inevitable *Appendix* I have placed three works which are not given complete: the *Genealogies*, the *List of Names*, and the second 'Silmarillion' Map, all of which belong in their original forms to the earlier 1930s. The *Genealogies* only came to light recently, but they add in fact little to what is known from the narrative texts. The *List of Names* might have been better included in Vol. IV, but this was again a work of reference which provides very little new matter, and it was more convenient to postpone it and then to give just those few entries which offer new detail. The second Map is a different case. This was my father's sole 'Silmarillion' map for some forty years, and here I have redrawn it to show it as it was when first made, leaving out all the layer upon layer of later accretion and alteration. The *Tale of Years* and the *Tale of Battles*, listed in title-pages to *The Silmarillion* as elements in that work (see p. 202), are not included, since they were contemporary with the later *Annals* and add nothing to the material found in them; subsequent alteration of names and dates was also carried out in a precisely similar way.

In places the detailed discussion of dating may seem excessive, but since the chronology of my father's writings, both 'internal' and 'external', is extremely difficult to determine and the evidence full of traps, and since the history can be very easily and very seriously falsified by mistaken deductions on this score, I have wished to make as plain as I can the reasons for my assertions.

In some of the texts I have introduced paragraph-numbering. This is done in the belief that it will provide a more precise and therefore quicker method of reference in a book where the discussion of its nature moves constantly back and forth.

As in previous volumes I have to some degree standardized usage in respect of certain names: thus for example I print *Gods*, *Elves*, *Orcs*, *Middle-earth*, etc. with initial capitals, and *Kôr*, *Tûn*, *Eärendel*, *Númenórean*, etc. for frequent *Kôr*, *Tûn*, *Earendel*, *Numenórean* of the manuscripts.

The earlier volumes of the series are referred to as I (*The Book of Lost Tales Part I*), II (*The Book of Lost Tales Part II*), III (*The Lays of Beleriand*), and IV (*The Shaping of Middle-earth*). The sixth volume now in preparation will concern the evolution of *The Lord of the Rings*.

The tables illustrating *The Lhammas* are reproduced with the permission of the Bodleian Library, Oxford, who kindly supplied photographs.

I list here for convenience the abbreviations used in the book in reference to various works (for a fuller account see pp. 107–8).

*Texts in Vol. IV:*

**S**    The *Sketch of the Mythology* or 'earliest Silmarillion'.

**Q**    The *Quenta* ('*Quenta Noldorinwa*'), the second version of 'The Silmarillion'.

**AV 1**    The earliest *Annals of Valinor*.

**AB 1**    The earliest *Annals of Beleriand* (in two versions, the second early abandoned).

*Texts in Vol. V:*

**FN**    *The Fall of Númenor* (**FN I** and **FN II** referring to the first and second texts).

**AV 2**    The second version of the *Annals of Valinor*.

**AB 2**    The second version (or strictly the third) of the *Annals of Beleriand*.

**QS**    The *Quenta Silmarillion*, the third version of 'The Silmarillion', nearing completion at the end of 1937.

Other works (*Ambarkanta, Ainulindalë, Lhammas, The Lost Road*) are not referred to by abbreviations.

In conclusion, I take this opportunity to notice and explain the erroneous representation of the Westward Extension of the first 'Silmarillion' Map in the previous volume (*The Shaping of Middle-earth* p. 228). It will be seen that this map presents a strikingly different appearance from that of the Eastward Extension on p. 231. These two maps, being extremely faint, proved impossible to reproduce from photographs supplied by the Bodleian Library, and an experimental 'reinforcement' (rather than re-drawing) of a copy of the Westward Extension was tried out. This I rejected, and it was then found that my photocopies of the originals gave a result sufficiently clear for the purpose. Unhappily, the rejected 'reinforced' version of the Westward Extension map was substituted for the photocopy. (Photocopies were also used for diagram III on p. 247 and map V on p. 251, where the originals are in faint pencil.)

# PART ONE

# THE FALL OF NÚMENOR

## AND

# THE LOST ROAD

# I
# THE EARLY HISTORY OF THE LEGEND

In February 1968 my father addressed a commentary to the authors of an article about him (*The Letters of J. R. R. Tolkien* no. 294). In the course of this he recorded that 'one day' C. S. Lewis said to him that since 'there is too little of what we really like in stories' they would have to try to write some themselves. He went on:

We agreed that he should try 'space-travel', and I should try 'time-travel'. His result is well known. My effort, after a few promising chapters, ran dry: it was too long a way round to what I really wanted to make, a new version of the Atlantis legend. The final scene survives as *The Downfall of Númenor*.*

A few years earlier, in a letter of July 1964 (*Letters* no. 257), he gave some account of his book, *The Lost Road*:

When C. S. Lewis and I tossed up, and he was to write on space-travel and I on time-travel, I began an abortive book of time-travel of which the end was to be the presence of my hero in the drowning of Atlantis. This was to be called *Númenor*, the Land in the West. The thread was to be the occurrence time and again in human families (like Durin among the Dwarves) of a father and son called by names that could be interpreted as Bliss-friend and Elf-friend. These no longer understood are found in the end to refer to the Atlantid-Númenórean situation and mean 'one loyal to the Valar, content with the bliss and prosperity within the limits prescribed' and 'one loyal to friendship with the High-elves'. It started with a father-son affinity between Edwin and Elwin of the present, and was supposed to go back into legendary time by way of an Eädwine and Ælfwine of circa A.D.918, and Audoin and Alboin of Lombardic legend, and so to the traditions of the North Sea concerning the coming of corn and culture heroes, ancestors of kingly lines, in boats (and their departure in funeral ships). One such Sheaf, or Shield Sheafing, can actually be made out as one of the remote ancestors of the present Queen. In my tale we were to come at last to Amandil and Elendil leaders of the loyal party in Númenor, when it fell under the dominion of Sauron. Elendil 'Elf-friend' was the founder of the Exiled kingdoms in Arnor and Gondor. But I found my real

---

*This is *Akallabêth, The Downfall of Númenor*, posthumously published in *The Silmarillion*, pp. 259–82.

interest was only in the upper end, the *Akallabêth* or *Atalantie**
('Downfall' in Númenórean and Quenya), so I brought all the stuff I
had written on the originally unrelated legends of Númenor into
relation with the main mythology.

I do not know whether evidence exists that would date the conversation
that led to the writing of *Out of the Silent Planet* and *The Lost Road*, but
the former was finished by the autumn of 1937, and the latter was
submitted, so far as it went, to Allen and Unwin in November of that
year (see III.364).

The significance of the last sentence in the passage just cited is not
entirely clear. When my father said 'But I found my real interest was only
in the upper end, the *Akallabêth* or *Atalantie*' he undoubtedly meant that
he had not been inspired to write the 'intervening' parts, in which the
father and son were to appear and reappear in older and older phases of
Germanic legend; and indeed *The Lost Road* stops after the introductory
chapters and only takes up again with the Númenórean story that was to
come at the end. Very little was written of what was planned to lie
between. But what is the meaning of '*so* I brought all the stuff I had
written on *the originally unrelated legends of Númenor* into relation with
the main mythology'? My father seems to be saying that, having found
that he only wanted to write about Númenor, he therefore and only then
(abandoning *The Lost Road*) appended the Númenórean material to 'the
main mythology', thus inaugurating the Second Age of the World. But
what was this material? He cannot have meant the Númenórean matter
contained in *The Lost Road* itself, since that was already fully related to
'the main mythology'. It must therefore have been something else, already
existing when *The Lost Road* was begun, as Humphrey Carpenter assumes
in his *Biography* (p. 170): 'Tolkien's legend of Númenor . . . was probably
composed some time before the writing of "The Lost Road", perhaps in
the late nineteen-twenties or early thirties.' But, in fact, the conclusion
seems to me inescapable that my father erred when he said this.

The original rough workings for *The Lost Road* are extant, but they are
very rough, and do not form a continuous text. There is one complete
manuscript, itself fairly rough and heavily emended in different stages;
and a professional typescript that was done when virtually all changes
had been made to the manuscript.† The typescript breaks off well before

---

*It is a curious chance that the stem *talat* used in Q[uenya] for 'slipping,
sliding, falling down', of which *atalantie* is a normal (in Q) noun-formation,
should so much resemble Atlantis. [Footnote to the letter.] – See the
*Etymologies*, stem TALÁT. The very early Elvish dictionary described in I.246 has
a verb *talte* 'incline (transitive), decline, shake at foundations, make totter, etc.'
and an adjective *talta* 'shaky, wobbly, tottering – sloping, slanting.'

†This typescript was made at Allen and Unwin, as appears from a letter from
Stanley Unwin dated 30th November 1937: '*The Lost Road*: We have had this
typed and are returning the original herewith. The typed copy will follow when
we have had an opportunity of reading it.' See further p. 73 note 14.

the point where the manuscript comes to an end, and my father's emendations to it were very largely corrections of the typist's errors, which were understandably many; it has therefore only slight textual value, and the manuscript is very much the primary text.

*The Lost Road* breaks off finally in the course of a conversation during the last days of Númenor between Elendil and his son Herendil; and in this Elendil speaks at length of the ancient history: of the wars against Morgoth, of Eärendel, of the founding of Númenor, and of the coming there of Sauron. *The Lost Road* is therefore, as I have said, entirely integrated with 'the main mythology' – and this is true already in the preliminary drafts.

Now as the papers were found, there follows immediately after the last page of *The Lost Road* a further manuscript with a new page-numbering, but no title. Quite apart from its being so placed, this text gives a strong physical impression of belonging to the same time as *The Lost Road*; and it is closely associated in content with the last part of *The Lost Road*, for it tells the story of Númenor and its downfall – though this second text was written with a different purpose, to be a complete if very brief history: it is indeed the first fully-written draft of the narrative that ultimately became the *Akallabêth*. But it is *earlier* than *The Lost Road*; for where that has *Sauron* and *Tarkalion* this has *Sûr* and *Angor*.

A second, more finished manuscript of this history of Númenor followed, with the title (written in afterwards) *The Last Tale: The Fall of Númenor*. This has several passages that are scarcely different from passages in *The Lost Road*, but it seems scarcely possible to show for certain which preceded and which followed, unless the evidence cited on p. 74, note 25, is decisive that the second version of *The Fall of Númenor* was the later of the two; in any case, a passage rewritten very near the time of the original composition of this version is certainly later than *The Lost Road*, for it gives a later form of the story of Sauron's arrival in Númenor (see pp. 26–7).

It is therefore clear that the two works were intimately connected; they arose at the same time and from the same impulse, and my father worked on them together. But still more striking is the existence of a single page that can only be the original 'scheme' for *The Fall of Númenor*, the actual first writing down of the idea. The very name *Númenor* is here only in process of emergence. Yet in this primitive form of the story the term *Middle-earth* is used, as it never was in the *Quenta*: it did not appear until the *Annals of Valinor* and the *Ambarkanta*. Moreover the form *Ilmen* occurs, which suggests that this 'scheme' was later than the actual writing of the *Ambarkanta*, where *Ilmen* was an emendation of *Ilma* (earlier *Silma*): IV.240, note 3.

I conclude therefore that 'Númenor' (as a distinct and formalised conception, whatever 'Atlantis-haunting', as my father called it, lay behind) arose in the actual context of his discussions with C. S. Lewis in (as seems probable) 1936. A passage in the 1964 letter can be taken to say precisely that: 'I began an abortive book of time-travel of which the end was to be the presence of my hero in the drowning of Atlantis. *This was to be called Númenor, the Land in the West.*' Moreover, 'Númenor' was from the outset conceived in full association with 'The Silmarillion'; there never was a time when the legends of Númenor were 'unrelated to the main mythology'. My father erred in his recollection (or expressed himself obscurely, meaning something else); the letter cited above was indeed written nearly thirty years later.

# II

# THE FALL OF NÚMENOR

## (i)

### The original outline

The text of the original 'scheme' of the legend, referred to in the previous chapter, was written at such speed that here and there words cannot be certainly interpreted. Near the beginning it is interrupted by a very rough and hasty sketch, which shows a central globe, marked *Ambar*, with two circles around it; the inner area thus described is marked *Ilmen* and the outer *Vaiya*. Across the top of *Ambar* and cutting through the zones of *Ilmen* and *Vaiya* is a straight line extending to the outer circle in both directions. This must be the forerunner of the diagram of the World Made Round accompanying the *Ambarkanta*, IV.247. The first sentence of the text, concerning Agaldor (on whom see pp. 78–9) is written separately from the rest, as if it were a false start, or the beginning of a distinct outline.

Agaldor chieftain of a people who live upon the N.W. margin of the Western Sea.

The last battle of the Gods. Men side largely with Morgoth. After the victory the Gods take counsel. Elves are summoned to Valinor. [*Struck out*: Faithful men dwell in the Lands]
Many men had not come into the old Tales. They are still at large on earth. The Fathers of Men are given a land to dwell in, raised by Ossë and Aulë in the great Western Sea. The Western Kingdom grows up. *Atalantë*. [*Added in margin*: Legend so named it afterward (the old name was *Númar* or *Númenos*) *Atalantë* = The Falling.] Its people great mariners, and men of great skill and wisdom. They range from Tol-eressëa to the shores of Middle-earth. Their occasional appearance among Wild Men, where Faithless Men also [?ranged corrupting them]. Some become lords in the East. But the Gods will not allow them to land in Valinor – and though they become long-lived because many have been bathed in the radiance of Valinor from Tol-eressëa – they are mortal and their span brief. They murmur against this decree. Thû comes to Atalantë, heralded [*read* heralding] the approach of Morgoth. But Morgoth cannot come except as a

spirit, being doomed to *dwell* outside the Walls of Night. The Atalanteans fall, and rebel. They make a temple to Thû-Morgoth. They build an armament and assail the shores of the Gods with thunder.

The Gods therefore sundered Valinor from the earth, and an awful rift appeared down which the water poured and the armament of Atalantë was drowned. They globed the whole earth so that however far a man sailed he could never again reach the West, but came back to his starting-point. Thus new lands came into being beneath the Old World; and the East and West were bent back and [?water flowed all over the round] earth's surface and there was a time of flood. But Atalantë being near the rift was utter[ly] thrown down and submerged. The remnant of [*struck out at time of writing*: Númen the Lie-númen] the Númenóreans in their ships flee East and land upon Middle-earth. [*Struck out*: Morgoth induces many to believe that this is a natural cataclysm.]

The [?longing] of the Númenóreans. Their longing for life on earth. Their ship burials, and their great tombs. Some evil and some good. Many of the good sit upon the west shore. These also seek out the Fading Elves. How [*struck out at time of writing*: Agaldor] Amroth wrestled with Thû and drove him to the centre of the Earth and the Iron-forest.

The old line of the lands remained as a plain of air upon which only the Gods could walk, and the Eldar who faded as Men usurped the sun. But many of the Númenórië could see it or faintly see it; and tried to devise ships to sail on it. But they achieved only ships that would sail in Wilwa or lower air. Whereas the Plain of the Gods cut through and traversed Ilmen [in] which even birds cannot fly, save the eagles and hawks of Manwë. But the fleets of the Númenórië sailed round the world; and Men took them for gods. Some were content that this should be so.

As I have said, this remarkable text documents the beginning of the legend of Númenor, and the extension of 'The Silmarillion' into a Second Age of the World. Here the idea of the World Made Round and the Straight Path was first set down, and here appears the first germ of the story of the Last Alliance, in the words 'These also seek out the Fading Elves. How [Agaldor >] Amroth wrestled with Thû and drove him to the centre of Earth' (at the beginning of the text Agaldor is named as the chief of a people living on the North-west coasts of Middle-earth). The longevity of the Númenóreans is already present, but (even allowing for the compression and distortion inherent in such 'outlines' of my father's, in which he attempted to seize and dash onto paper a bubbling up of new ideas) seems to have far less significance than it would afterwards attain; and is ascribed, strangely, to 'the radiance of Valinor', in which the mariners of Númenor were 'bathed' during their visits to Tol-eressëa, to which they were permitted to sail. Cf. the *Quenta*, IV.98: 'Still therefore is the light of Valinor more great and fair than that of the other lands, because there the Sun and Moon together rest a while before they go upon their dark journey under the world'; but this does not seem a sufficient or satisfactory explanation of the idea (see further p. 20). The mortuary culture of the Númenóreans does indeed appear, but it arose among the survivors of Númenor in Middle-earth, after the Downfall; and this remained into more developed forms of the legend, as did the idea of the flying ships which the exiles built, seeking to sail on the Straight Path through *Ilmen*, but achieving only flight through the lower air, *Wilwa*.*

The sentence 'Thû comes to Atalantë, herald[ing] the approach of Morgoth' certainly means that Thû *prophesied* Morgoth's return, as in subsequent texts. The meaning of 'But Morgoth cannot come except as a spirit' is made somewhat clearer in the next version, §5.

(ii)

*The first version of The Fall of Númenor*

The preliminary outline was the immediate precursor of a first full narrative – the manuscript described above (p. 9), placed with *The Lost Road*. This was followed by further versions, and I shall refer to the work as a whole (as distinct from the *Akallabêth*, into which it was afterwards transformed) as *The Fall of Númenor*, abbreviated 'FN'; the first text has no title, but I shall call it 'FN I'.

FN I is rough and hasty, and full of corrections made at the time of composition; there are also many others, mostly slight, made later and moving towards the second version FN II. I give it as it was written, without the second layer of emendations (except in so far as these make small necessary corrections to clarify the sense). As explained in the Preface, here as elsewhere I have introduced paragraph numbers into the text to make subsequent reference and comparison easier. A commentary, following the paragraphing of the text, follows at its end.

§1   In the Great Battle when Fionwë son of Manwë over-threw Morgoth and rescued the Gnomes and the Fathers of Men, many mortal Men took part with Morgoth. Of these those that were not destroyed fled into the East and South of the World, and the servants of Morgoth that escaped came to them and guided

---

*Although this text has the final form *Ilmen*, beside *Silma* > *Ilma* > *Ilmen* in the *Ambarkanta*, *Wilwa* was replaced in the *Ambarkanta* by *Vista*.

them; and they became evil, and they brought evil into many places where wild Men dwelt at large in the empty lands. But after their victory, when Morgoth and many of his captains were bound, and Morgoth was thrust again into the Outer Darkness, the Gods took counsel. The Elves were summoned to Valinor, as has been told, and many obeyed, but not all. But the Fathers of Men, who had served the Eldar, and fought against Morgoth, were greatly rewarded. For Fionwë son of Manwë came among them and taught them, and gave them wisdom, power and life stronger than any others of the Second Kindred.

§2    And a great land was made for them to dwell in, neither part of Middle-earth nor wholly separate from it. This was raised by Ossë out of the depths of Belegar, the Great Sea, and established by Aulë, and enriched by Yavanna. It was called Númenor, that is Westernesse, and Andúnië or the Sunsetland, and its chief city in the midmost of its western coasts was in the days of its might called Númar or Númenos; but after its fall it was named in legend Atalantë, the Ruin.

§3    For in Númenórë a great people arose, in all things more like the First Kindred than any other races of Men that have been, yet less fair and wise than they, though greater in body. And above all their arts the people of Númenor nourished shipbuilding and sea-craft, and became mariners whose like shall never be again, since the world was diminished. They ranged from Tol-eressëa, where for many ages they still had converse and dealings with the Gnomes, to the shores of Middle-earth, and sailed round to the North and South, and glimpsed from their high prows the Gates of Morning in the East. And they appeared among the wild Men, and filled them with wonder and also with fear. For many esteemed them to be Gods or sons of Gods out of the West, and evil men had told them lies concerning the Lords of the West. But the Númenóreans tarried not long yet in Middle-earth, for their hearts hungered ever westward for the undying bliss of Valinor. And they were restless and pursued with desire even at the height of their glory.

§4    But the Gods forbade them to sail beyond the Lonely Isle, and would not permit any save their kings (once in each life before he was crowned) to land in Valinor. For they were mortal Men, and it was not in the power and right of Manwë to alter their fate. Thus though the people were long-lived, since their land was more nigh than other lands to Valinor, and many had looked long on the radiance of the Gods that came faintly to Tol-eressëa, they remained mortal, even their kings, and their span brief in the eyes of the Eldar. And they murmured against this decree. And a great discontent grew among them; and their masters of lore sought unceasingly for the secrets that should prolong their lives, and they sent spies to seek these in Valinor. And the Gods were angered.

§5   And in time it came to pass that Sûr (whom the Gnomes called Thû) came in the likeness of a great bird to Númenor and preached a message of deliverance, and he prophesied the second coming of Morgoth. But Morgoth did not come in person, but only in spirit and as a shadow upon the mind and heart, for the Gods shut him beyond the Walls of the World. But Sûr spake to Angor the king and Istar his queen, and promised them undying life and lordship of the Earth. And they believed him and fell under the shadow, and the greatest part of the people of Númenor followed them. Angor raised a great temple to Morgoth in the midst of the land, and Sûr dwelt there.

§6   But in the passing of the years Angor felt the oncoming of old age, and he was troubled; and Sûr said that the gifts of Morgoth were withheld by the Gods, and that to obtain plenitude of power and undying life he must be master of the West. Wherefore the Númenóreans made a great armament; and their might and skill had in those days become exceedingly great, and they had moreover the aid of Sûr. The fleets of the Númenóreans were like a great land of many islands, and their masts like a forest of mountain-trees, and their banners like the streamers of a thunderstorm, and their sails were black. And they moved slowly into the West, for all the winds were stilled and the world lay silent in the fear of that time. And they passed Tol-eressëa, and it is said that the Elves mourned and grew sick, for the light of Valinor was cut off by the cloud of the Númenóreans. But Angor assailed the shores of the Gods, and he cast bolts of thunder, and fire came upon the sides of Taniquetil.

§7   But the Gods were silent. Sorrow and dismay were in the heart of Manwë, and he spoke to Ilúvatar, and took power and counsel from the Lord of All; and the fate and fashion of the world was changed. For the silence of the Gods was broken suddenly, and Valinor was sundered from the earth, and a rift appeared in the midst of Belegar east of Tol-eressëa, and into this chasm the great seas plunged, and the noise of the falling waters filled all the earth and the smoke of the cataracts rose above the tops of the everlasting mountains. But all the ships of Númenor that were west of Tol-eressëa were drawn down into the great abyss and drowned, and Angor the mighty and Istar his queen fell like stars into the dark, and they perished out of all knowledge. And the mortal warriors that had set foot in the land of the Gods were buried under fallen hills, where legend saith that they lie imprisoned in the Forgotten Caves until the day of Doom and the Last Battle. And the Elves of Tol-eressëa passed through the gates of death, and were gathered to their kindred in the land of the Gods, and became as they; and the Lonely Isle remained only as a shape of the past.

§8 But Ilúvatar gave power to the Gods, and they bent back the edges of the Middle-earth, and they made it into a globe, so that however far a man should sail he could never again reach the true West, but came back weary at last to the place of his beginning. Thus New Lands came into being beneath the Old World, and all were equally distant from the centre of the round earth; and there was flood and great confusion of waters, and seas covered what was once the dry, and lands appeared where there had been deep seas. Thus also the heavy air flowed round all the earth in that time, above the waters; and the springs of all waters were cut off from the stars.

§9 But Númenor being nigh upon the East to the great rift was utterly thrown down and overwhelmed in sea, and its glory perished. But a remnant of the Númenóreans escaped the ruin in this manner. Partly by the device of Angor, and partly of their own will (because they revered still the Lords of the West and mistrusted Súr) many had abode in ships upon the east coast of their land, lest the issue of war be evil. Wherefore protected for a while by the land they avoided the draught of the sea, and a great wind arose blowing from the gap, and they sped East and came at length to the shores of Middle-earth in the days of ruin.

§10 There they became lords and kings of Men, and some were evil and some were of good will. But all alike were filled with desire of long life upon earth, and the thought of Death was heavy upon them; and their feet were turned east but their hearts were westward. And they built mightier houses for their dead than for their living, and endowed their buried kings with unavailing treasure. For their wise men hoped ever to discover the secret of prolonging life and maybe the recalling of it. But it is said that the span of their lives, which had of old been greater than that of lesser races, dwindled slowly, and they achieved only the art of preserving uncorrupt for many ages the dead flesh of men. Wherefore the kingdoms upon the west shores of the Old World became a place of tombs, and filled with ghosts. And in the fantasy of their hearts, and the confusion of legends half-forgotten concerning that which had been, they made for their thought a land of shades, filled with the wraiths of the things of mortal earth. And many deemed this land was in the West, and ruled by the Gods, and in shadow the dead, bearing the shadows of their possessions, should come there, who could no more find the true West in the body. For which reason in after days many of their descendants, or men taught by them, buried their dead in ships and set them in pomp upon the sea by the west coasts of the Old World.

§11     For the blood of the Númenóreans was most among the men of those lands and coasts, and the memory of the primeval world remained most strongly there, where the old paths to the West had of old set out from Middle-earth. And the spell that lay there was not wholly vain. For the old line of the world remained in the mind of the Gods and in the memory of the world as a shape and a plan that has been changed, but endures. And it has been likened to a plain of air, or to a straight vision that bends not to the hidden curving of the earth, or to a level bridge that rises imperceptibly but surely above the heavy air of earth. And of old many of the Númenóreans could see or half see the paths to the True West, and believed that at times from a high place they could descry the peaks of Taniquetil at the end of the straight road, high above the world.

§12     But the most, that could not see this, scorned them, and trusted in ships upon the water. But they came only to the lands of the New World, and found them to be as those of the Old; and they reported that the world was round. But upon the straight road only the Gods and the vanished Elves could walk, or such as the Gods summoned of the fading Elves of the round earth, who became diminished in substance as Men usurped the sun. For the Plain of the Gods being straight, whereas the surface of the world was bent, and the seas that lay upon it, and the heavy airs that lay above, cut through the air of breath and flight, and traversed Ilmen, in which no flesh can endure. And it is said that even those of the Númenóreans of old who had the straight vision did not all comprehend this, and they tried to devise ships that would rise above the waters of the world and hold to the imagined seas. But they achieved only ships that would sail in the air of breath. And these ships flying came also to the lands of the New World and to the East of the Old World; and they reported that the world was round. And many abandoned the Gods, and put them out of their legends, and even out of their dreams. But Men of Middle-earth looked on them with wonder and great fear, and took them to be gods; and many were content that this should be so.

§13   But not all the hearts of the Númenóreans were crooked; and the lore of the old days descending from the Fathers of Men, and the Elf-friends, and those instructed by Fionwë, was preserved among some. And they knew that the fate of Men was not bounded by the round path of the world, nor destined for the straight path. For the round is crooked and has no end but no escape; and the straight is true, but has an end within the world, and that is the fate of the Elves. But the fate of Men, they said, is neither round nor ended, and is not within the world. And they remembered from whence the ruin came, and the cutting off of Men from their just portion of the straight path; and they avoided the shadow of Morgoth according to their power, and hated Thû. And they assailed his temples and their servants, and there were wars of allegiance among the mighty of this world, of which only the echoes remain.

§14   But there remains still a legend of Beleriand: for that land in the West of the Old World, although changed and broken, held still in ancient days to the name it had in the days of the Gnomes. And it is said that Amroth was King of Beleriand; and he took counsel with Elrond son of Eärendel, and with such of the Elves as remained in the West; and they passed the mountains and came into inner lands far from the sea, and they assailed the fortress of Thû. And Amroth wrestled with Thû and was slain; but Thû was brought to his knees, and his servants were dispelled; and the peoples of Beleriand destroyed his dwellings, and drove him forth, and he fled to a dark forest, and hid himself. And it is said that the war with Thû hastened the fading of the Eldar, for he had power beyond their measure, as Felagund King of Nargothrond had found in the earliest days; and they expended their strength and substance in the assault upon him. And this was the last of the services of the older race to Men, and it is held the last of the deeds of alliance before the fading of the Elves and the estrangement of the Two Kindreds. And here the tale of the ancient world, as the Elves keep it, comes to an end.

*Commentary on the first version of The Fall of Númenor*

§1   As Q §18 was first written (IV. 158), it was permitted by Fionwë that 'with the Elves should those of the race of Hador and Bëor alone be suffered to depart, if they would. But of these only Elrond was now left . . .' On this extremely puzzling passage see the commentary, IV. 200, where I suggested that obscure as it is it represents 'the first germ of the story of the departure of the Elf-friends to Númenor.' It was removed in the rewriting, Q II §18, where there appears a reference to Men of Hithlum who 'repentant of their evil servitude did deeds of valour, and many beside of Men new come out of the East', but now no mention of the Elf-friends. A final hasty revision of the passage (IV. 163, notes 2 and 3) gave:

> And it is said that *all that were left of the three Houses of the Fathers of Men* fought for Fionwë, and to them were joined some of the Men of Hithlum who repenting of their evil servitude did deeds of valour . . . But most Men, and especially those new come out of the East, were on the side of the Enemy.

This is very close to, and no doubt belongs in fact to the same time as, the corresponding passage in the following version of 'The Silmarillion' (QS*, p. 328 §16), which however omits the reference to the Men of Hithlum. I have little doubt that this development came in with the emergence of Númenor.

§2    Here first appear the names *Andúnië* (but as a name of the island, translated 'the Sunsetland'), and *Númenor* itself (which does not occur in the preliminary outline, though the people are there called *Númenórië* and *Númenóreans*). The chief city is called *Númar* or *Númenos*, which in the outline were the names of the land. The name *Belegar* was emended later, here and in §7, to *Belegaer*.

After the words *enriched by Yavanna* the passage concerning names was early replaced as follows:

> It was called by the Gods Andor, the Land of Gift, but by its own folk Vinya, the Young; but when the men of that land spake of it to the men of Middle-earth they named it Númenor, that is Westernesse, for it lay west of all lands inhabited by mortals. Yet it was not in the true West, for there was the land of the Gods. The chief city of Númenor was in the midmost of its western coasts, and in the days of its might it was called Andúnië, because it faced the sunset; but after its fall it was named in the legends of those that fled from it Atalantë the Downfall.

Here first appears *Andor*, Land of Gift, and also the name given to the land by the Númenóreans, *Vinya*, the Young, which did not survive in the later legend (cf. *Vinyamar*, *Vinyalondë*, Index to *Unfinished Tales*); *Andúnië* now becomes the name of the chief city. In the text as originally written the name *Atalantë* could refer either to the land or the city, but in the rewriting it can only refer to the city. It seems

---

*Throughout this book the abbreviation 'QS' (*Quenta Silmarillion*) is used for the version interrupted near the end of 1937; see pp. 107–8.

unlikely that my father intended this; see the corresponding passage in
FN II and commentary.

§3    The permission given to the Númenóreans to sail as far west as Tol-
eressëa, found already in the original outline, contrasts with the
*Akallabêth* (pp. 262–3), where it is told that they were forbidden 'to
sail so far westward that the coasts of Númenor could no longer be
seen', and only the most keen-sighted among them could descry far off
the tower of Avallónë on the Lonely Isle.

The *Gates of Morning* reappear, remarkably, from the *Lost Tales*
(I. 216). In the original astronomical myth the Sun passed into the
Outer Dark by the Door of Night and re-entered by the Gates of
Morn; but with the radical transformation of the myth that entered
with the *Sketch of the Mythology* (see IV. 49), and is found in the
*Quenta* and *Ambarkanta*, whereby the Sun is drawn by the servants of
Ulmo beneath the roots of the Earth, the Door of Night was given a
different significance and the Gates of Morn no longer appear (see IV.
252, 255). How the reference to them here (which survives in the
*Akallabêth*, p. 263) is to be understood I am unable to say.

In this paragraph is the first occurrence of the expression *The Lords
of the West*.

§4    The words *save their kings (once in each life before he was crowned)*
were early placed in square brackets. In the conclusion of QS (p. 326
§§8–9) the prohibition appears to be absolute, not to be set aside for
any mortal; there Mandos says of Eärendel 'Now he shall surely die,
for he has trodden *the forbidden shores*', and Manwë says 'To Eärendel
I remit *the ban*, and the peril that he took upon himself.' Later (as
noted under §3 above) the Ban extended also, and inevitably, to Tol-
eressëa ('easternmost of the Undying Lands', the *Akallabêth*, p. 263).

The ascription of the longevity of the Númenóreans to the light of
Valinor appeared already in the original outline, and I cited (p. 13) the
passage from the *Quenta* where it is said that the light of Valinor was
greater and fairer than in the other lands 'because there the Sun and
Moon together rest a while.' But the wording here, 'the radiance of the
Gods that came faintly to Tol-eressëa', surely implies a light of a
different nature from that of the Sun and Moon (which illumine the
whole world). Conceivably, the further idea that appears in the
corresponding passage in QS (§79) is present here: 'moreover the
Valar store the radiance of the Sun in many vessels, and in vats and
pools for their comfort in times of dark.' The passage was later
enclosed in brackets, and it does not appear in FN II; but at a
subsequent point in the narrative (§6) the Elves of Tol-eressëa
mourned 'for the light of Valinor was cut off by the cloud of the
Númenóreans', and this was not rejected. Cf. the *Akallabêth* (p. 278):
'the Eldar mourned, for *the light of the setting sun* was cut off by the
cloud of the Númenóreans.'

§5    With what is said here of Morgoth's not returning 'in person', for he was shut beyond the Walls of the World, 'but only in spirit and as a shadow upon the mind and heart', cf. the *Quenta* (IV. 164): 'Some say also that Morgoth at whiles secretly as a cloud that cannot be seen or felt . . . creeps back surmounting the Walls and visiteth the world' (a passage that survived in QS, pp. 332–3 §30).

§7    The concluding sentence concerning the Elves of Tol-eressëa was an addition, but one that looks as if it belongs with the writing of the text. It is very hard to interpret. The rift in the Great Sea appeared *east* of Tol-eressëa, but the ships that were *west* of the isle were drawn down into the abyss; and it might be concluded from this that Tol-eressëa also was swallowed up and disappeared: so the Elves who dwelt there 'passed through the gates of death, and were gathered to their kindred in the land of the Gods', and 'the Lonely Isle remained only as a shape of the past.' But this would be very strange, for it would imply the abandonment of the entire story of Ælfwine's voyage to Tol-eressëa in ages after; yet Ælfwine as recorder and pupil was still present in my father's writings after the completion of *The Lord of the Rings*. On the diagram of the World Made Round accompanying the *Ambarkanta* (IV. 247) Tol-eressëa is marked as a point on the Straight Path. Moreover, much later, in the *Akallabêth* (pp. 278–9), the same is told of the great chasm: it opened 'between Númenor and the Deathless Lands', and all the fleets of the Númenóreans (which had passed on to Aman and so were west of Tol-eressëa) were drawn down into it; but 'Valinor and Eressëa were taken from [the world] into the realm of hidden things.'

§8    The concluding sentence ('Thus also the heavy air . . .') is a marginal addition which seems certainly to belong with the original text. It has no mark for insertion, but must surely be placed here.

§10    The desire to prolong life was already a mark of the Númenóreans (§4), but the dark picture in the *Akallabêth* (p. 266) of a land of tombs and embalming, of a people obsessed with death, was not present. At this stage in the evolution of the legend, as already in the preliminary outline, the tomb-culture arose among the Númenóreans who escaped the Downfall and founded kingdoms in the 'Old World': whether of good or evil disposition 'all alike were filled with desire of long life upon earth, and the thought of Death was heavy upon them'; and it was the life-span of the Exiles, as it appears, that slowly dwindled. There are echoes of the present passage in the *Akallabêth* account of Númenor after the Shadow fell upon it in the days of Tar-Atanamir (cf. *Unfinished Tales* p. 221); but in the very different context of the original story, when this culture arose among those who survived the Cataclysm and their descendants, other elements were present: for the Gods were now removed into the realm of the unknown and unseen, and they became the 'explanation' of the mystery of death, their dwelling-place in the far West the region to which the dead passed with their possessions.

In 'The Silmarillion' the Gods are 'physically' present, because (whatever the actual mode of their own being) they inhabit the same physical world, the realm of the 'seen'; if, after the Hiding of Valinor, they could not be reached by the voyages sent out in vain by Turgon of Gondolin, they were nonetheless reached by Eärendel, sailing from Middle-earth in his ship Wingelot, and their physical intervention of arms changed the world for ever through the physical destruction of the power of Morgoth. Thus it may be said that in 'The Silmarillion' there is no 'religion', because the Divine is present and has not been 'displaced'; but with the physical removal of the Divine from the World Made Round a religion arose (as it had arisen in Númenor under the teachings of Thû concerning Morgoth, the banished and absent God), and the dead were despatched, for religious reasons, in burial ships on the shores of the Great Sea.

§12  'But upon the straight road only the Gods and the vanished Elves could walk, or such as the Gods summoned of the fading Elves of the round earth, who became diminished in substance as Men usurped the sun.' Cf. the *Quenta*, IV. 100–1, as emended (a passage that goes back to the *Sketch of the Mythology*, IV. 21):

In after days, when because of the triumph of Morgoth Elves and Men became estranged, as he most wished, those of the Eldalië that still lived in the world faded, and Men usurped the sunlight. Then the Eldar wandered in the lonelier places of the Outer Lands, and took to the moonlight and the starlight, and to the woods and caves, and became as shadows, wraiths and memories, such as set not sail unto the West and vanished from the world.

This passage survived very little changed in QS (§87).

I believe that the story of the flying ships built by the exiled Númenóreans, found already in the preliminary draft (p. 12), is the sole introduction of aerial craft in all my father's works. No hint is given of the means by which they rose and were propelled; and the passage did not survive into the later legend.

§13  It is a curious feature of the original story of Númenor that there is no mention of what befell Thû at the Downfall (cf. the *Akallabêth* p. 280); but he reappears here as a master of temples (cf. the *Lay of Leithian* lines 2064–7), dwelling in a fortress (§14), an object of hatred to those of the survivors of Númenor who retained something of the ancient knowledge.

§14  In the *Quenta* (IV. 160–1) it is told that in the Great Battle

the Northern regions of the Western world were rent and riven, and the sea roared in through many chasms, and there was confusion and great noise; and the rivers perished or found new paths, and the valleys were upheaved and the hills trod down, and Sirion was no more. Then Men fled away . . . and long was it ere they came back over the mountains to where Beleriand once had been.

The last words of the earliest *Annals of Beleriand* (IV. 310) are 'So ended the First Age of the World and Beleriand was no more.' It is also said in the *Quenta* (IV. 162) that after the War was ended 'there was a mighty building of ships on the shores of the Western Sea, and especially upon the great isles, which in the disruption of the Northern world were fashioned of ancient Beleriand.'

In FN a rather different conception is suggested. Though Beleriand had been 'changed and broken', it is spoken of as 'that land', it was still called *Beleriand*, and it was peopled by Men and Elves, able to form an alliance against Thû. I would suggest (though hesitantly) that with the emergence, here first glimpsed, of a Second Age of Middle-earth consequent on the legend of Númenor, the utter devastation of Beleriand, suitable to the finality of the conclusion of the earlier conception, had been diminished.* Moreover it seems that at this time my father did not conceive of any further destruction of Beleriand at the time of the Downfall of Númenor, as he would do later (see p. 32).

At this stage there is no mention of a first and founder king of Númenor. Elrond was still the only child of Eärendel and Elwing; his brother Elros has appeared only in late additions to the text of Q (IV. 155), which were inserted after the Númenórean legend had begun to develop. In the oldest conception in the *Sketch of the Mythology* (IV. 38) Elrond 'bound by his mortal half elects to stay on earth' (i.e. in the Great Lands), and in Q (IV. 158) he 'elected to remain, being bound by his mortal blood in love to those of the younger race'; see my remarks on the Choice of the Half-elven, IV. 70. Elrond is here, as it seems, a leader of the Elves of Beleriand, in alliance with Amroth, predecessor of Elendil. The Last Alliance leading to the overthrow of Thû is seen as the last intervention of the Elves in the affairs of the World of Men, in itself hastening their inevitable fading. The 'dark forest' to which Thû fled (cf. the 'Iron-forest' in the original outline) is doubtless Mirkwood. In *The Hobbit* all that had been told of the Necromancer was that he dwelt in a dark tower in the south of Mirkwood.†

(iii)

*The second version of The Fall of Númenor*

FN II is a clear manuscript, made by my father with FN I before him and probably soon after it. It has many emendations made in the act of

---

*The passages cited here from Q were rather surprisingly retained almost unaltered in QS: see p. 337.

†Cf. *Letters* no. 257, referring to *The Hobbit*: 'the (originally) quite casual reference to the Necromancer, whose function was hardly more than to provide a reason for Gandalf going away and leaving Bilbo and the Dwarves to fend for themselves, which was necessary for the tale.'

composition, and none that seem to have been made after any significant interval, apart from the title, which was inserted later in pencil, and the rejection of a sentence in §7. In contrast to my father's common tendency to begin a new text keeping close to the antecedent but then to diverge ever more strongly as he proceeded, in this case the earlier part is much changed and expanded whereas the latter is scarcely altered, other than in very minor improvements to the run of sentences, until the end is reached. To give the whole of FN II is therefore unnecessary. Retaining the paragraph numbering of FN I, I give §§1–5 and 14 in full, and of the remainder only such short passages as were significantly altered.

### THE LAST TALE: THE FALL OF NÚMENOR

§1   In the Great Battle when Fionwë son of Manwë overthrew Morgoth and rescued the Exiles, the three houses of the Men of Beleriand fought against Morgoth. But most Men were allies of the Enemy; and after the victory of the Lords of the West those that were not destroyed fled eastward into Middle-earth; and the servants of Morgoth that escaped came to them, and enslaved them. For the Gods forsook for a time the Men of Middle-earth, because they had disobeyed their summons and hearkened to the Enemy. And Men were troubled by many evil things that Morgoth had made in the days of his dominion: demons and dragons and monsters, and Orcs, that are mockeries of the creatures of Ilúvatar; and their lot was unhappy. But Manwë put forth Morgoth, and shut him beyond the world in the Void without; and he cannot return again into the world, present and visible, while the Lords are enthroned. Yet his Will remaineth, and guideth his servants; and it moveth them ever to seek the overthrow of the Gods and the hurt of those that obey them.

But when Morgoth was thrust forth, the Gods held council. The Elves were summoned to return into the West, and such as obeyed dwelt again in Eressëa, the Lonely Island, which was renamed Avallon: for it is hard by Valinor. But Men of the three faithful houses and such as had joined with them were richly rewarded. For Fionwë son of Manwë came among them and taught them; and he gave them wisdom, power, and life stronger than any others have of the mortal race.

§2   And a great land was made for them to dwell in, neither part of Middle-earth nor wholly separate from it. It was raised by Ossë out of the depths of the Great Sea, and established by Aulë and enriched by Yavanna; and the Eldar brought thither flowers and fountains out of Avallon and wrought gardens there of great beauty, in which the Gods themselves at times would walk. That land was called by the Valar Andor, the Land of Gift, and by its own folk it was at first called Vinya, the Young; but in the days of its pride they named it Númenor, that is Westernesse, for it lay west of all lands inhabited by mortals; yet it was far from the true West, for that is Valinor, the land of the Gods. But its glory fell and its name perished; for after its ruin it was named in the legends of those that fled from it Atalantë, the Downfallen. Of old its chief city and haven was in the midst of its western coasts, and it was called Andúnië, because it faced the sunset. But the high place of its king was at Númenos in the heart of the land. It was built first by Elrond son of Eärendel, whom the Gods and Elves chose to be the lord of that land; for in him the blood of the houses of Hador and Bëor was mingled, and with it some part of that of the Eldar and Valar, which he drew from Idril and from Lúthien. But Elrond and all his folk were mortal; for the Valar may not withdraw the gift of death, which cometh to Men from Ilúvatar. Yet they took on the speech of the Elves of the Blessed Realm, as it was and is in Eressëa, and held converse with the Elves, and looked afar upon Valinor; for their ships were suffered to sail to Avallon and their mariners to dwell there for a while.

§3    And in the wearing of time the people of Númenor grew great and glorious, in all things more like the Firstborn than any other races of Men that have been; yet less fair and wise than the Elves, though greater in stature. For the Númenóreans were taller even than the tallest of the sons of Men in Middle-earth. Above all their arts they nourished shipbuilding and sea-craft, and became mariners whose like shall never be again, since the world has been diminished. They ranged from Eressëa in the West to the shores of Middle-earth, and came even into the inner seas; and they sailed about the North and the South, and glimpsed from their high prows the Gates of Morning in the East. And they appeared among the wild Men and filled them with wonder and dismay, and some esteemed them to be Gods or the sons of Gods out of the West; and the Men of Middle-earth feared them, for they were under the shadow of Morgoth, and believed the Gods to be terrible and cruel. The Númenóreans taught them such of the truth as they could comprehend, but it became only as a distant rumour little understood; for as yet the Númenóreans came seldom to Middle-earth and did not tarry there long. Their hearts were set westward, and they began to hunger for the undying bliss of Valinor; and they were restless and pursued by desire as their power and glory grew.

§4   For the Gods forbade them to sail beyond the Lonely Isle, and would not permit any to land in Valinor, because the Númenóreans were mortal; and though the Lords had rewarded them with long life, they could not take from them the weariness of the world that cometh at last; and they died, even their kings of the seed of Eärendel, and their span was brief in the eyes of the Elves. And they began to murmur against this decree; and a great discontent grew among them. Their masters of knowledge sought unceasingly for secrets that should prolong their lives; and they sent spies to seek forbidden lore in Avallon. But the Gods were angered.

§5   And it came to pass that Sauron, servant of Morgoth, grew mighty in Middle-earth; and the mariners of Númenor brought rumour of him. Some said that he was a king greater than the King of Númenor; some said that he was one of the Gods or their sons set to govern Middle-earth. A few reported that he was an evil spirit, perchance Morgoth himself returned. But this was held to be only a foolish fable of the wild Men. Tar-kalion was King of Númenor in those days, and he was proud; and believing that the Gods had delivered the dominion of the earth to the Númenóreans, he would not brook a king mightier than himself in any land. Therefore he purposed to send his servants to summon Sauron to Númenor, to do homage before him. The Lords sent messages to the king and spake through the mouths of wise men and coun-selled him against this mission; for they said that Sauron would work evil if he came; but he could not come to Númenor unless he was summoned and guided by the king's messengers. But Tar-kalion in his pride put aside the counsel, and he sent many ships.

Now rumour of the power of Númenor and its allegiance to the Gods came also to Sauron, and he feared lest the Men of the West should rescue those of Middle-earth from the Shadow; and being cunning and filled with malice he plotted in his heart to destroy Númenor, and (if he might) to bring grief upon the Gods. Therefore he humbled himself before the messengers, and came by ship to Númenor. But as the ships of the embassy drew nigh to the land an unquiet came upon the sea, and it arose like a mountain and cast the ships far inland; and the ship whereon Sauron stood was set upon a hill. And Sauron stood upon the hill and preached a message of deliverance from death to the Númenóreans; and he beguiled them with signs and wonders. And little by little he turned their hearts toward Morgoth, his master; and he pro-phesied that ere long he would come again into the world. And

Sauron spake to Tar-kalion the king, and to Tar-ilien his queen, and promised them life unending and the dominion of the earth, if they would turn unto Morgoth. And they believed him, and fell under the Shadow, and the greatest part of their people followed them. And Tar-kalion raised a great temple to Morgoth upon the Mountain of Ilúvatar in the midst of the land; and Sauron dwelt there and all Númenor was under his vigilance.

[The greater part of §5 was replaced by the following shorter version:]

And it came to pass that Sauron, servant of Morgoth, grew strong in Middle-earth; and he learned of the power and glory of the Númenóreans, and of their allegiance to the Gods, and he feared lest coming they should wrest the dominion of the East from him and rescue the Men of Middle-earth from the Shadow. And the king heard rumour of Sauron; and it was said that he was a king greater than the King of Númenor. Wherefore, against the counsel of the Gods, the king sent his servants to Sauron, and bade him come and do homage. And Sauron, being filled with cunning and malice, humbled himself and came; and he beguiled the Númenóreans with signs and wonders. But little by little Sauron turned their hearts towards Morgoth; and he prophesied that ere long he would come again into the world. And Sauron spake to Tar-kalion King of Númenor and to Tar-ilien his queen . . .

For the remainder of FN II, until the final paragraph, I note only the few differences from FN I that are of any substance. The changes of *Sûr*, *Angor*, and *Istar* to *Sauron*, *Tar-kalion*, and *Tar-ilien* are not noticed.

§6 'And they passed Eressëa' > 'And they encompassed Avallon'; 'fire came upon the sides of Taniquetil' > 'fire came upon Kôr and smokes rose about Taniquetil.'

§7 In FN II the paragraph opens: 'But the Gods made no answer. Then many of the Númenóreans set foot upon the forbidden shores, and they camped in might upon the borders of Valinor.'

'Angor the mighty and Istar his queen' > 'Tar-kalion the golden and bright Ilien his queen'; 'the Forgotten Caves' > 'the Caves of the Forgotten'.

The mysterious concluding sentence concerning the Elves of Eressëa (see the commentary on FN I) was retained but struck out later in pencil.

§8 The concluding sentence does not appear; see the commentary on FN I.

§9 'Partly by the [desire >] command of Tar-kalion, and partly by their own will (because some still revered the Gods and would not go with war into the West) many had remained behind, and sat in their ships . . .'

There is now no mention of the great wind that arose.

§10   The paragraph now opens: 'There, though shorn of their former power, and few in number and scattered, they after became lords and kings of Men. Some were evil and forsook not Sauron in their hearts; and some were of good will and retained memory of the Gods. But all alike . . .'

In 'the span of their lives, which had of old been greater than that of the lesser races' the words 'greater than' > 'thrice'.

The concluding sentence reads: 'For which reason in after days they would bury their dead in ships, or set them in pomp . . .'

§11   'And the spell that lay there was not wholly vain' > 'And this was not wholly fantasy', but this was struck out.

'For the ancient line of the world remained in the mind of Ilúvatar and in the thought of the Gods, and in the memory of the world . . .'

At the end of the paragraph is added: 'Therefore they built very high towers in those days.'

§12   The paragraph now begins: 'But most, who could not see this or conceive it in thought, scorned the builders of towers, and trusted to ships that sailed upon water. But they came only to the lands of the New World, and found them like to those of the Old, and subject to death; and they reported that the world was round. But upon the Straight Road only the Gods could walk, and only the ships of the Elves of Avallon could journey. For the Road being straight, whereas the surface of the earth was bent . . .'

The paragraph concludes: 'Therefore many abandoned the Gods, and put them out of their legends. But Men of Middle-earth looked up with wonder upon them, and with great fear, for they descended out of the air; and they took the Númenóreans to be Gods, and some were content that this should be so.'

§13   The paragraph begins: 'But not all the hearts of the Númenóreans were crooked; and the knowledge of the days before the ruin, descending from their fathers and the Elf-friends, and those that had held converse with the Gods, was long preserved among the wise. And they said that the fate of Men . . .'

'But the fate of Men . . . is not complete within the world.'

'there were wars of faith among the mighty of Middle-earth'

§14   But there remains still a legend of Beleriand: for that land in the West of the North of the Old World, where Morgoth had been overthrown, was still in a measure blessed and free from his shadow; and many of the exiles of Númenor had come thither. Though changed and broken it retained still in ancient days the name that it had borne in the days of the Gnomes. And it is said that in Beleriand there arose a king, who was of Númenórean race, and he was named Elendil, that is Elf-friend. And he took counsel with the Elves that remained in Middle-earth (and these abode then mostly in Beleriand); and he made a league with Gil-galad the Elf-king who was descended from Fëanor. And their armies were joined, and passed the mountains and came into inner lands far from the Sea. And they came at last even to Mordor the Black Country, where Sauron, that is in the Gnomish tongue named Thû, had rebuilt his fortresses. And they encompassed the stronghold, until Thû came forth in person, and Elendil and Gil-galad wrestled with him; and both were slain. But Thû was thrown down, and his bodily shape destroyed, and his servants were dispelled, and the host of Beleriand destroyed his dwelling; but Thû's spirit fled far away, and was hidden in waste places, and took no shape again for many ages. But it is sung sadly by the Elves that the war with Thû hastened the fading of the Eldar, decreed by the Gods; for Thû had power beyond their measure, as Felagund, King of Nargothrond, had found aforetime; and the Elves expended their strength and substance in the assault upon him. And this was the last of the services of the Firstborn to Men, and it is held the last of the deeds of alliance before the fading of the Elves and the estrangement of the Two Kindreds. And here endeth the tale of the ancient world as it is known to the Elves.

*Commentary on the second version of The Fall of Númenor*

§1　On 'Orcs, that are mockeries of the creatures of Ilúvatar' see QS §18 and commentary. – It was said in FN I §5 that Morgoth 'did not come in person, but only in spirit, and as a shadow upon the mind and heart.' Now the idea of his 'return' in any sense seems to be denied; but there appears the concept of his malevolent and guiding Will that remains always in the world.

　　'such as obeyed dwelt again in Eressëa': in FN I 'the Elves were summoned to Valinor, as has been told, and many obeyed, but not all.' In the *Quenta* (IV. 162) 'the Gnomes and Dark-elves rehabited for the most part the Lonely Isle . . . But some returned even unto Valinor, as all were free to do who willed' (retained in QS, pp. 331–2 §27). The name *Avallon* ('for it is hard by Valinor') appears, but as a new name for Tol Eressëa; afterwards, in the form *Avallónë* ('for it is of all cities the nearest to Valinor'), it became the name of a haven in the isle: *Akallabêth* p. 260.

§2　At first my father preserved exactly the rewriting of FN I given in the commentary on FN I §2, whereby *Atalantë* is the name of the city Andúnië after the Downfall. I have suggested that he did not in fact intend this; at any rate he corrected it here, so that *Atalantë* again becomes the name of Númenor drowned. *Númenos* now reappears from FN I §2 as originally written, where it was the name of the western city, but becomes the name of the high place of the king in the centre of the land (afterwards *Armenelos*).

Elrond (see the commentary on FN I §14) now becomes the first King of Númenor and the builder of Númenos; his brother Elros has still not emerged.

The statement here that the Númenóreans 'took on the speech of the Elves of the Blessed Realm, as it was and is in Eressëa' suggests that they abandoned their own Mannish tongue; and that this is the meaning is shown in *The Lost Road* (p. 68). In the *Lhammas* it is said (p. 179) that 'already even in [Húrin's father's] day Men in Beleriand forsook the daily use of their own tongue and spoke and gave even names unto their children in the language of the Gnomes.' The words 'as it was and is in Eressëa' would contradict any idea that the Lonely Isle was destroyed in the Downfall (see the commentary on FN I §7). But the difficult passage which suggests it was preserved in the present text, §7 (though subsequently struck out).

§4    The association of the longevity of the Númenóreans with the radiance of Valinor (see the commentary on FN I §4) is abandoned, and is attributed solely to the gift of the Valar.

§5    In all probability the name *Sauron* (replacing *Súr* of FN I) first occurs here or in the closely related passage in *The Lost Road* (p. 66). Its first occurrence in the 'Silmarillion' tradition is in QS §143. The story of Sauron's coming to Númenor is changed from that in FN I, and it is explicit that he could not have come had he not been summoned. The story as told in the first version here, in which the ships returning from Middle-earth were cast upon Númenor far inland by a great wave, and Sauron stood upon a hill and 'preached a message of deliverance', is told in more detail in *The Lost Road*; but the second version in FN II, omitting the element of the great wave, looks as if it were substituted for the first almost immediately (on the significance of this see p. 9).

The temple to Morgoth is now raised upon the Mountain of Ilúvatar in the midst of the land, and this (or in *The Lost Road*) is the first appearance of the Meneltarma. The story was later rejected: in the *Akallabêth* 'not even Sauron dared to defile the high place', and the temple was built in Armenelos (pp. 272–3).

§11   The addition in FN II, 'Therefore they built very high towers in those days', must be the first reference to the White Towers on Emyn Beraid, the Tower Hills. Cf. *The Lord of the Rings* Appendix A (I. iii), where it is told of the *palantír* of Emyn Beraid that 'Elendil set it there so that he could look back with "straight sight" and see Eressëa in the vanished West; but the bent seas below covered Númenor for ever.' Cf. also *Of the Rings of Power* in *The Silmarillion*, p. 292. But when the present text was written the *palantíri* had not (so far as one can tell) been conceived.

§14  The rewriting of the passage concerning Beleriand reinforces the suggestion in FN I that it remained a country less destroyed after the Great Battle than is described in the other texts: it was 'still in a measure blessed' – and moreover the Elves who remained in Middle-earth 'abode mostly in Beleriand'. Here Elendil 'Elf-friend' appears, displacing Amroth of FN I. It might be thought from the words 'in Beleriand there arose a king, who was of Númenórean race' that he was not a survivor of the Downfall; but this is clearly not the case. In *The Lost Road*, closely connected with FN II, Elendil (the father in the Númenórean incarnation of 'Elwin-Edwin') is a resolute foe of Sauron and his dominance in Númenor; and though *The Lost Road* breaks off before the sailing of Tar-kalion's fleet, Elendil must have been among those who 'sat in their ships upon the east coast of the land' (FN §9) and so escaped the Downfall.

Here is certainly the first appearance of Gil-galad, the Elf-king in Beleriand, descended from Fëanor (it would be interesting to know his parentage), and the story of the Last Alliance moves a stage further; and there seems no question but that it was in this manuscript that the name *Mordor*, the Black Country, first emerged in narrative.

(iv)

*The further development of The Fall of Númenor*

FN II was followed by a typescript made on my father's typewriter of that period, but not typed by him. This is seen from its being an exact copy of FN II after all corrections had been made to it, and from two or three misreadings of the manuscript. I have no doubt that the typescript was made soon afterwards. In itself it has no textual value, but my father used it as the basis for certain further changes.

Associated with it is a loose manuscript page bearing passages that relate closely to changes made to the typescript. There is here a textual development that has important bearings on the dating in general.

Two passages are in question. The first concerns §8 (which had remained unchanged from FN I, apart from the omission in FN II of the concluding sentence). The loose page has here two forms of a new version of the paragraph, of which the first, which was struck through, reads as follows:

Then Ilúvatar cast back the Great Sea west of Middle-earth and the Barren Land east of Middle-earth and made new lands and new seas where aforetime nought had been but the paths of the Sun and Moon. And the world was diminished; for Valinor and Eressëa were taken into the Realm of Hidden Things, and thereafter however far a man might sail he could never again reach the True West. For all lands old and new were equally distant from the centre of the earth. There was [flood and great confusion of waters, and seas covered what once was dry, and lands appeared where there had been deep seas,] and Beleriand fell into the sea in that time, all save the land where Beren and Lúthien had dwelt for a while, the land of Lindon beneath the western feet of the [*struck out*: Ered] Lunoronti.

(The section enclosed in square brackets is represented in the manuscript by a mark of omission, obviously meaning that the existing text was to be followed.) Here the words '[the Gods] bent back the edges of the Middle-earth' have disappeared; it is the Great Sea in the West and 'the Barren Land' in the East that are 'cast back' by Ilúvatar. It is now said that the new lands and new seas came into being 'where aforetime nought had been but the paths of the Sun and Moon' (i.e. at the roots of the world, see the *Ambarkanta* diagrams IV. 243, 245). This was in turn lost in the further rewriting (below), where the final and very brief statement found in the *Akallabêth* (p. 279) is reached.

This passage is very notable, since the drowning of all Beleriand west of Lindon is here ascribed to the cataclysm of the Downfall of Númenor; see the commentaries on FN I and II, §14. The name *Lunoronti* of the Blue Mountains has not occurred previously (but see the *Etymologies*, stem LUG²); and this is perhaps the first occurrence of the name *Lindon* for the ancient Ossiriand, or such of it as remained above the sea (see the commentary on QS §108).

The second form of this revised version of §8 follows immediately in the manuscript:

Then Ilúvatar cast back the Great Sea west of Middle-earth, and the Empty Land east of it, and new lands and new seas were made; and the world was diminished: for Valinor and Eressëa were taken from it into the realm of hidden things. And thereafter however a man might sail, he could never again reach the True West, but would come back weary at last to the place of his beginning; for all lands and seas were equally distant from the centre of the earth, and all roads were bent. There was flood and great confusion of waters in that time, and sea covered much that in the Elder Days had been dry, both in the West and East of Middle-earth.

Thus the passage concerning the drowning of Beleriand at the time of the Númenórean cataclysm and the survival of Lindon was again removed. In this form my father then copied it onto the typescript, with change of *Empty Land* to *Empty Lands*. (If this region, called in the first version *the Barren Land*, is to be related to the *Ambarkanta* map V (IV. 251) it must be what is there called *the Burnt Land of the Sun*; perhaps also *the Dark Land*, which is there shown as a new continent, formed from the southern part of *Pelmar* or Middle-earth (map IV) after the vast extension of the former inland sea of Ringil at the time of the breaking of

Utumno). – The expression *Elder Days* is not found in any writing of my father's before this.

The second passage is the concluding paragraph in FN II §14, concerning Beleriand and the Last Alliance. Here a few pencilled changes were made to the typescript: *Thû* was changed to *Sauron* except in the sentence 'that is in the Gnomish tongue named Thû', where *Thû* > *Gorthû* (see p. 338); 'in Beleriand there arose a king' > 'in Lindon . . .'; and Gil-galad is descended from Finrod, not Fëanor. The passage in the typescript was then struck through, with a direction to introduce a substitute. This substitute is found on the reverse of the loose page giving the two forms of the rewriting of §8, and was obviously written at the same time as those. It reads as follows:

But there remains a legend of Beleriand. Now that land had been broken in the Great Battle with Morgoth; and at the fall of Númenor and the change of the fashion of the world it perished; for the sea covered all that was left save some of the mountains that remained as islands, even up to the feet of Eredlindon. But that land where Lúthien had dwelt remained, and was called Lindon. A gulf of the sea came through it, and a gap was made in the Mountains through which the River Lhûn flowed out. But in the land that was left north and south of the gulf the Elves remained, and Gil-galad son of Felagund son of Finrod was their king. And they made Havens in the Gulf of Lhûn whence any of their people, or any other of the Elves that fled from the darkness and sorrow of Middle-earth, could sail into the True West and return no more. In Lindon Sauron had as yet no dominion. And it is said that the brethren Elendil and Valandil escaping from the fall of Númenor came at last to the mouths of the rivers that flowed into the Western Sea. And Elendil (that is Elf-friend), who had aforetime loved the folk of Eressëa, came to Lindon and dwelt there a while, and passed into Middle-earth and established a realm in the North. But Valandil sailed up the Great River Anduin and established another realm far to the South. But Sauron dwelt in Mordor the Black Country, and that was not very distant from Ondor the realm of Valandil; and Sauron made war against all Elves and all Men of Westernesse or others that aided them, and Valandil was hard pressed. Therefore Elendil and Gil-galad seeing that unless some stand were made Sauron would become lord of [?all] Middle-earth they took counsel together, and they made a great league. And Gil-galad and Elendil marched into the Middle-earth [?and gathered force of Men and Elves, and they assembled at Imladrist].

Towards the end the text degenerates into a scribble and the final words are a bit doubtful. If the name *Imladrist* is correctly interpreted there is certainly a further letter after the *s*, which must be a *t*. Cf. *The Tale of*

*Years* in *The Lord of the Rings* (Appendix B): Second Age 3431 'Gil-galad and Elendil march east to Imladris.'

All this passage was in turn struck through, and not copied into the typescript. It will be seen that it brings in the new matter concerning Beleriand and Lindon which appeared in the first form of the revision of §8 but was then removed (pp. 31–2); and in addition many important new elements have entered. Gil-galad is the son of Felagund; it is now explicit that Elendil was one of the survivors of Númenor, and he has a brother named Valandil (the name of his father in *The Lost Road*); the river Lhûn appears, and its gulf, and the gap in the Blue Mountains through which it flowed; the Elves of Lindon built havens on the Gulf of Lhûn; Elendil established a kingdom in the North, east of the mountains, and Valandil, sailing up the Anduin, founded his realm of Ondor not far from Mordor.

Now there is no question that the entire conception of Gondor arose in the course of the composition of *The Lord of the Rings*. Moreover my father pencilled the following notes (also struck through) at the end of the typescript:

> More of this is told in *The Lord of the Rings*
> Only alteration required is this:
> (1)  Many Elves remained behind
> (2)  Beleriand was all sunk except for a few islands = mountains, and part of Ossiriand (called Lindon) where Gil-galad dwelt.
> (3)  Elrond remained with Gil-galad. Or else sailed back to Middle-earth. The Half-elven.

The second of these is decisive, since the passage last given clearly contains a working-up of this note; and it is clear that all the rewritings of the second version of *The Fall of Númenor* considered here come from several years later. FN II represents the form of the work at the time when *The Lord of the Rings* was begun. On the other hand, these revisions come from a time when it was a long way from completion, as is seen by the form *Ondor*, and by the brothers Elendil and Valandil, founders of the Númenórean kingdoms in Middle-earth.

Apart from these major passages of revision there were few other changes made to the typescript copy of FN II, and those very minor, save for the substitution of *Elros* for *Elrond* at both occurrences in §2. This belongs to the pre-*Lord of the Rings* period, as is seen from the appearance of Elros in the conclusion of QS (see p. 337, commentary on §28).*

---

*The third 'alteration' required (in the notes on the typescript of FN II), that 'Elrond remained with Gil-galad, or else sailed back to Middle-earth', presumably takes account of this change, and means that my father had not yet determined whether or not Elrond originally went to Númenor with his brother Elros.

My father next wrote a fine new manuscript incorporating the changes made to the typescript of FN II – but now wholly omitting the concluding passage (§14) concerning Beleriand and the Last Alliance, and ending with the words 'there were wars among the mighty of Middle-earth, of which only the echoes now remain.' This version, improved and altered in detail, shows however very little further advance in narrative substance, and clearly belongs to the same period as the revisions studied in this section.

# III

# THE LOST ROAD

## (i)

### The opening chapters

For the texts of *The Lost Road* and its relation to *The Fall of Númenor* see pp. 8–9. I give here the two completed chapters at the beginning of the work, following them with a brief commentary.

## Chapter I

### *A Step Forward. Young Alboin**

'Alboin! Alboin!'

There was no answer. There was no one in the play-room.

'Alboin!' Oswin Errol stood at the door and called into the small high garden at the back of his house. At length a young voice answered, sounding distant and like the answer of someone asleep or just awakened.

'Yes?'

'Where are you?'

'Here!'

'Where is "here"?'

'Here: up on the wall, father.'

Oswin sprang down the steps from the door into the garden, and walked along the flower-bordered path. It led after a turn to a low stone wall, screened from the house by a hedge. Beyond the stone wall there was a brief space of turf, and then a cliff-edge, beyond which outstretched, and now shimmering in a calm evening, the western sea. Upon the wall Oswin found his son, a boy about twelve years old, lying gazing out to sea with his chin in his hands.

'So there you are!' he said. 'You take a deal of calling. Didn't you hear me?'

'Not before the time when I answered,' said Alboin.

'Well, you must be deaf or dreaming,' said his father. 'Dream-

---

*The title was put in afterwards, as was that of Chapter II; see p. 78.

ing, it looks like. It is getting very near bed-time; so, if you want any story tonight, we shall have to begin at once.'

'I am sorry, father, but I was thinking.'

'What about?'

'Oh, lots of things mixed up: the sea, and the world, and Alboin.'

'Alboin?'

'Yes. I wondered why Alboin. Why am I called Alboin? They often ask me "Why Alboin?" at school, and they call me All-bone. But I am not, am I?'

'You look rather bony, boy; but you are not all bone, I am glad to say. I am afraid I called you Alboin, and that is why you are called it. I am sorry: I never meant it to be a nuisance to you.'

'But it is a *real* name, isn't it?' said Alboin eagerly. 'I mean, it means something, and *men* have been called it? It isn't just invented?'

'Of course not. It is just as real and just as good as Oswin; and it belongs to the same family, you might say. But no one ever bothered me about Oswin. Though I often used to get called Oswald by mistake. I remember how it used to annoy me, though I can't think why. I was rather particular about my name.'

They remained talking on the wall overlooking the sea; and did not go back into the garden, or the house, until bed-time. Their talk, as often happened, drifted into story-telling; and Oswin told his son the tale of Alboin son of Audoin, the Lombard king; and of the great battle of the Lombards and the Gepids, remembered as terrible even in the grim sixth century; and of the kings Thurisind and Cunimund, and of Rosamunda. 'Not a good story for near bed-time,' he said, ending suddenly with Alboin's drinking from the jewelled skull of Cunimund.

'I don't like that Alboin much,' said the boy. 'I like the Gepids better, and King Thurisind. I wish they had won. Why didn't you call me Thurisind or Thurismod?'

'Well, really mother had meant to call you Rosamund, only you turned up a boy. And she didn't live to help me choose another name, you know. So I took one out of that story, because it seemed to fit. I mean, the name doesn't belong only to that story, it is much older. Would you rather have been called Elf-friend? For that's what the name means.'

'No-o,' said Alboin doubtfully. 'I like names to mean something, but not to say something.'

'Well, I might have called you Ælfwine, of course; that is the

Old English form of it. I might have called you that, not only after Ælfwine of Italy, but after all the Elf-friends of old; after Ælfwine, King Alfred's grandson, who fell in the great victory in 937, and Ælfwine who fell in the famous defeat at Maldon, and many other Englishmen and northerners in the long line of Elf-friends. But I gave you a latinized form. I think that is best. The old days of the North are gone beyond recall, except in so far as they have been worked into the shape of things as we know it, into Christendom. So I took Alboin; for it is not Latin and not Northern, and that is the way of most names in the West, and also of the men that bear them. I might have chosen Albinus, for that is what they sometimes turned the name into; and it wouldn't have reminded your friends of bones. But it is too Latin, and means something in Latin. And you are not white or fair, boy, but dark. So Alboin you are. And that is all there is to it, except bed.' And they went in.

But Alboin looked out of his window before getting into bed; and he could see the sea beyond the edge of the cliff. It was a late sunset, for it was summer. The sun sank slowly to the sea, and dipped red beyond the horizon. The light and colour faded quickly from the water: a chilly wind came up out of the West, and over the sunset-rim great dark clouds sailed up, stretching huge wings southward and northward, threatening the land.

'They look like the eagles of the Lord of the West coming upon Númenor,' Alboin said aloud, and he wondered why. Though it did not seem very strange to him. In those days he often made up names. Looking on a familiar hill, he would see it suddenly standing in some other time and story: 'the green shoulders of Amon-ereb,' he would say. 'The waves are loud upon the shores of Beleriand,' he said one day, when storm was piling water at the foot of the cliff below the house.

Some of these names were really made up, to please himself with their sound (or so he thought); but others seemed 'real', as if they had not been spoken first by him. So it was with Númenor. 'I like that,' he said to himself. 'I could think of a long story about the land of Númenor.'

But as he lay in bed, he found that the story would not be thought. And soon he forgot the name; and other thoughts crowded in, partly due to his father's words, and partly to his own day-dreams before.

'Dark Alboin,' he thought. 'I wonder if there is any Latin in me. Not much, I think. I love the western shores, and the *real* sea – it is quite different from the Mediterranean, even in stories. I wish there was no other side to it. There were darkhaired people who were not Latins. Are the Portuguese Latins? What is Latin? I wonder what kind of people lived in Portugal and Spain and Ireland and Britain in old days, very old days, before the Romans, or the Carthaginians. Before anybody else. I wonder what the man thought who was the first to see the western sea.'

Then he fell asleep, and dreamed. But when he woke the dream slipped beyond recall, and left no tale or picture behind, only the feeling that these had brought: the sort of feeling Alboin connected with long strange names. And he got up. And summer slipped by, and he went to school and went on learning Latin.

Also he learned Greek. And later, when he was about fifteen, he began to learn other languages, especially those of the North: Old English, Norse, Welsh, Irish. This was not much encouraged – even by his father, who was an historian. Latin and Greek, it seemed to be thought, were enough for anybody; and quite old-fashioned enough, when there were so many successful modern languages (spoken by millions of people); not to mention maths and all the sciences.

But Alboin liked the flavour of the older northern languages, quite as much as he liked some of the things written in them. He got to know a bit about linguistic history, of course; he found that you rather had it thrust on you anyway by the grammar-writers of 'unclassical' languages. Not that he objected: sound-changes were a hobby of his, at the age when other boys were learning about the insides of motor-cars. But, although he had some idea of what were supposed to be the relationships of European languages, it did not seem to him quite all the story. The languages he liked had a definite flavour – and to some extent a similar flavour which they shared. It seemed, too, in some way related to the atmosphere of the legends and myths told in the languages.

One day, when Alboin was nearly eighteen, he was sitting in the study with his father. It was autumn, and the end of summer holidays spent mostly in the open. Fires were coming back. It was the time in all the year when book-lore is most attractive (to those who really like it at all). They were talking 'language'. For Errol encouraged his boy to talk about anything he was interested in; although secretly he had been wondering for some time whether Northern languages and legends were not taking up more time and energy than their practical value in a hard world justified. 'But I had better know what is going on, as far as any father can,' he thought. 'He'll go on anyway, if he really has a bent – and it had better not be bent inwards.'

Alboin was trying to explain his feeling about 'language-atmosphere'. 'You get echoes coming through, you know,' he said, 'in odd words here and there – often very common words in their own language, but quite unexplained by the etymologists; and in the general shape and sound of all the words, somehow; as if something was peeping through from deep under the surface.'

'Of course, I am not a philologist,' said his father; 'but I never could see that there was much evidence in favour of ascribing language-changes to a *substratum*. Though I suppose underlying ingredients do have an influence, though it is not easy to define, on the final mixture in the case of peoples taken as a whole, different national talents and temperaments, and that sort of thing. But races, and cultures, are different from languages.'

'Yes,' said Alboin; 'but very mixed up, all three together. And after all, language goes back by a continuous tradition into the past, just as much as the other two. I often think that if you knew the living faces of any man's ancestors, a long way back, you might find some queer things. You might find that he got his nose quite clearly from, say, his mother's great-grandfather; and yet that something about his nose, its expression or its set or whatever you like to call it, really came down from much further back, from, say, his father's great-great-great-grandfather or greater. Anyway I like to go back – and not with race only, or culture only, or language; but with all three. I wish I could go back with the three that are mixed in us, father; just the plain Errols, with a little house in Cornwall in the summer. I wonder what one would see.'

'It depends how far you went back,' said the elder Errol. 'If you went back beyond the Ice-ages, I imagine you would find nothing in these parts; or at any rate a pretty beastly and uncomely race, and a tooth-and-nail culture, and a disgusting language with no echoes for you, unless those of food-noises.'

'Would you?' said Alboin. 'I wonder.'

'Anyway you can't go back,' said his father; 'except within the limits prescribed to us mortals. You can go back in a sense by honest study, long and patient work. You had better go in for archaeology as well as philology: they ought to go well enough together, though they aren't joined very often.'

'Good idea,' said Alboin. 'But you remember, long ago, you said I was not *all-bone*. Well, I want some mythology, as well. I want myths, not only bones and stones.'

'Well, you can have 'em! Take the whole lot on!' said his father laughing. 'But in the meanwhile you have a smaller job on hand. Your Latin needs improving (or so I am told), for school purposes. And scholarships are useful in lots of ways, especially for folk like you and me who go in for antiquated subjects. Your first shot is this winter, remember.'

'I wish Latin prose was not so important,' said Alboin. 'I am really much better at verses.'

'Don't go putting any bits of your *Eressëan*, or *Elf-latin*, or whatever you call it, into your verses at Oxford. It might scan, but it wouldn't pass.'

'Of course not!' said the boy, blushing. The matter was too private, even for private jokes. 'And don't go blabbing about *Eressëan* outside the partnership,' he begged; 'or I shall wish I had kept it quiet.'

'Well, you did pretty well. I don't suppose I should ever have heard about it, if you hadn't left your note-books in my study. Even so I don't know much about it. But, my dear lad, I shouldn't dream of blabbing, even if I did. Only don't waste too much time on it. I am afraid I am anxious about that schol[arship], not only from the highest motives. Cash is not too abundant.'

'Oh, I haven't done anything of that sort for a long while, at least hardly anything,' said Alboin.

'It isn't getting on too well, then?'

'Not lately. Too much else to do, I suppose. But I got a lot of jolly new words a few days ago: I am sure *lōmelindë* means *nightingale*, for instance, and certainly *lōmë* is *night* (though not *darkness*). The verb is very sketchy still. But –' He hesitated. Reticence (and uneasy conscience) were at war with his habit of what he called 'partnership with the pater', and his desire to unbosom the secret anyway. 'But, the real difficulty is that another language is coming through, as well. It seems to be related but quite different, much more – more Northern. *Alda* was a *tree* (a word I got a long time ago); in the new language it is *galadh*, and *orn*. The Sun and Moon seem to have similar names in both: *Anar* and *Isil* beside *Anor* and *Ithil*. I like first one, then the other, in different moods. *Beleriandic* is really very attractive; but it complicates things.'

'Good Lord!' said his father, 'this is serious! I will respect unsolicited secrets. But do have a conscience as well as a heart, and – moods. Or get a Latin and Greek mood!'

'I do. I have had one for a week, and I have got it now; a Latin one luckily, and Virgil in particular. So here we part.' He got up. 'I am going to do a bit of reading. I'll look in when I think you ought to go to bed.' He closed the door on his father's snort.

As a matter of fact Errol did not really like the parting shot. The affection in it warmed and saddened him. A late marriage had left him now on the brink of retirement from a schoolmaster's small pay to his smaller pension, just when Alboin was coming of University age. And he was also (he had begun to feel, and this year to admit in his heart) a tired man. He had never been a strong man. He would have liked to accompany Alboin a great deal further on the road, as a younger father probably would have done; but he did not somehow think he would be going very far. 'Damn it,' he said to himself, 'a boy of that age ought not to be thinking such things, worrying whether his father is getting enough rest. Where's my book?'

Alboin in the old play-room, turned into junior study, looked out into the dark. He did not for a long time turn to books. 'I wish life was not so short,' he thought. 'Languages take such a time, and so do all the things one wants to know about. And the pater, he is looking tired. I want him for years. If he lived to be a hundred I should be only about as old as he is now. and I should still want him. But he won't. I wish we could stop getting old. The pater could go on working and write that book he used to talk about, about Cornwall; and we could go on talking. He always plays up, even if he does not agree or understand. Bother *Eressëan*. I wish he hadn't mentioned it. I am sure I shall dream tonight; and it is so exciting. The Latin-mood will go. He is very decent about it, even though he thinks I am making it all up. If I were, I would stop it to please him. But it comes, and I simply can't let it slip when it does. Now there is Beleriandic.'

Away west the moon rode in ragged clouds. The sea glimmered palely out of the gloom, wide, flat, going on to the edge of the world. 'Confound you, dreams!' said Alboin. 'Lay off, and let me do a little patient work at least until December. A schol[arship] would brace the pater.'

He found his father asleep in his chair at half past ten. They went up to bed together. Alboin got into bed and slept with no shadow of a dream. The Latin-mood was in full blast after breakfast; and the weather allied itself with virtue and sent torrential rain.

## Chapter II

### *Alboin and Audoin*

Long afterwards Alboin remembered that evening, that had marked the strange, sudden, cessation of the Dreams. He had got a scholarship (the following year) and had 'braced the pater'. He had behaved himself moderately well at the university – not too many side-issues (at least not what he called too many); though neither the Latin nor the Greek mood had remained at all steadily to sustain him through 'Honour Mods.' They came back, of course, as soon as the exams were over. They would. He had switched over, all the same, to history, and had again 'braced the pater' with a 'first-class'. And the pater had needed bracing. Retirement proved quite different from a holiday: he had seemed just to slip slowly out. He had hung on just long enough to see Alboin into his first job: an assistant lecturership in a university college.

Rather disconcertingly the Dreams had begun again just before 'Schools', and were extraordinarily strong in the following vacation – the last he and his father had spent together in Cornwall. But at that time the Dreams had taken a new turn, for a while.

He remembered one of the last conversations of the old pleasant sort he had been able to have with the old man. It came back clearly to him now.

'How's the Eressëan Elf-latin, boy?' his father asked, smiling, plainly intending a joke, as one may playfully refer to youthful follies long atoned for.

'Oddly enough,' he answered, 'that hasn't been coming through lately. I have got a lot of different stuff. Some is beyond me, yet. Some might be Celtic, of a sort. Some seems like a very old form of Germanic; pre-runic, or I'll eat my cap and gown.'

The old man smiled, almost raised a laugh. 'Safer ground, boy, safer ground for an historian. But you'll get into trouble, if you let your cats out of the bag among the philologists – unless, of course, they back up the authorities.'

'As a matter of fact, I rather think they do,' he said.

'Tell me a bit, if you can without your note-books,' his father slyly said.

'*Westra lage wegas rehtas, nu isti sa wraithas.*' He quoted that, because it had stuck in his mind, though he did not understand it. Of course the mere sense was fairly plain: *a straight road lay westward, now it is bent.* He remembered waking up, and feeling it was somehow very significant. 'Actually I got a bit of plain Anglo-Saxon last night,' he went on. He thought Anglo-Saxon would please his father; it was a real historical language, of which the old man had once known a fair amount. Also the bit was very fresh in his mind, and was the longest and most connected he had yet had. Only that very morning he had waked up late, after a dreamful night, and had found himself saying the lines. He jotted them down at once, or they might have vanished (as usual) by breakfast-time, even though they were in a language he knew. Now waking memory had them secure.

> 'Thus cwæth Ælfwine Wídlást:
> Fela bith on Westwegum werum uncúthra
> wundra and wihta, wlitescéne land,
> eardgeard elfa, and ésa bliss.
> Lýt ǽnig wát hwylc his longath síe
> thám the eftsíthes eldo getwǽfeth.'

His father looked up and smiled at the name Ælfwine. He translated the lines for him; probably it was not necessary, but the old man had forgotten many other things he had once known much better than Anglo-Saxon.

'Thus said Ælfwine the far-travelled: "There is many a thing in the West-regions unknown to men, marvels and strange beings, a land fair and lovely, the homeland of the Elves, and the bliss of the Gods. Little doth any man know what longing is his whom old age cutteth off from return."'

He suddenly regretted translating the last two lines. His father looked up with an odd expression. 'The old know,' he said. 'But age does not cut us off from going away, from – from *forthsith*. There is no *eftsith*: we can't go back. You need not tell me that. But good for Ælfwine-Alboin. You could always do verses.'

Damn it – as if he would make up stuff like that, just to tell it to the old man, practically on his death-bed. His father had, in fact, died during the following winter.

On the whole he had been luckier than his father; in most ways, but not in one. He had reached a history professorship fairly early; but he had lost his wife, as his father had done, and had been left with an only child, a boy, when he was only twenty-eight.

He was, perhaps, a pretty good professor, as they go. Only in a small southern university, of course, and he did not suppose he would get a move. But at any rate he wasn't tired of being one; and history, and even teaching it, still seemed interesting (and fairly important). He did his duty, at least, or he hoped so. The boundaries were a bit vague. For, of course, he had gone on with the other things, legends and languages – rather odd for a history professor. Still there it was: he was fairly learned in such book-lore, though a lot of it was well outside the professional borders.

And the Dreams. They came and went. But lately they had been getting more frequent, and more – absorbing. But still tantalizingly linguistic. No tale, no remembered pictures; only the feeling that he had seen things and heard things that he wanted to see, very much, and would give much to see and hear again – and these fragments of words, sentences, verses. *Eressëan* as he called it as a boy – though he could not remember why he had felt so sure that that was the proper name – was getting pretty complete. He had a lot of Beleriandic, too, and was beginning to understand it, and its relation to Eressëan. And he had a lot of unclassifiable fragments, the meaning of which in many cases he did not know, through forgetting to jot it down while he knew it. And odd bits in recognizable languages. Those might be explained away, of course. But anyway nothing could be done about them: not publication or anything of that sort. He had an odd feeling that they were not essential: only occasional lapses of forgetfulness which took a linguistic form owing to some peculiarity of his own mental make-up. The real thing was the feeling the Dreams brought more and more insistently, and taking force from an alliance with the ordinary professional occupations of his mind. Surveying the last thirty years, he felt he could say that his most permanent mood, though often overlaid or suppressed, had been since childhood the desire *to go back*. To walk in Time, perhaps, as men walk on long roads; or to survey it, as men may see the world from a mountain, or the earth as a living map beneath an airship. But in any case to see with eyes and to hear with ears: to see the lie of old and even forgotten lands, to behold ancient men walking, and hear their languages as they spoke them, in the days before the days, when tongues of forgotten lineage were heard in kingdoms long fallen by the shores of the Atlantic.

But nothing could be done about that desire, either. He used to be able, long ago, to talk about it, a little and not too seriously, to his father. But for a long while he had had no one to talk to about that sort of thing. But now there was Audoin. He was growing up. He was sixteen.

He had called his boy Audoin, reversing the Lombardic order.
It seemed to fit. It belonged anyway to the same name-family, and
went with his own name. And it was a tribute to the memory of his
father – another reason for relinquishing Anglo-Saxon Eadwine,
or even commonplace Edwin. Audoin had turned out remarkably
like Alboin, as far as his memory of young Alboin went, or his
penetration of the exterior of young Audoin. At any rate he
seemed interested in the same things, and asked the same questions; though with much less inclination to words and names, and
more to things and descriptions. Unlike his father he could draw,
but was not good at 'verses'. Nonetheless he had, of course,
eventually asked why he was called Audoin. He seemed rather
glad to have escaped Edwin. But the question of meaning had not
been quite so easy to answer. Friend of fortune, was it, or of fate,
luck, wealth, blessedness? Which?

'I like *Aud*,' young Audoin had said – he was then about thirteen
– 'if it means all that. A good beginning for a name. I wonder what
Lombards looked like. Did they all have Long Beards?'

Alboin had scattered tales and legends all down Audoin's
childhood and boyhood, like one laying a trail, though he was not
clear what trail or where it led. Audoin was a voracious listener, as
well (latterly) as a reader. Alboin was very tempted to share his
own odd linguistic secrets with the boy. They could at least have
some pleasant private fun. But he could sympathize with his own
father now – there was a limit to time. Boys have a lot to do.

Anyway, happy thought, Audoin was returning from school
tomorrow. Examination-scripts were nearly finished for this year
for both of them. The examiner's side of the business was decid-
edly the stickiest (thought the professor), but he was nearly
unstuck at last. They would be off to the coast in a few days,
together.

There came a night, and Alboin lay again in a room in a house
by the sea: not the little house of his boyhood, but the same sea. It
was a calm night, and the water lay like a vast plain of chipped and
polished flint, petrified under the cold light of the Moon. The path
of moonlight lay from the shore to the edge of sight.

Sleep would not come to him, although he was eager for it. Not
for rest – he was not tired; but because of last night's Dream. He
hoped to complete a fragment that had come through vividly that
morning. He had it at hand in a note-book by his bed-side; not that
he was likely to forget it once it was written down.

| *ar* | *sauron* | *tūle* | *nahamna* | ... | *lantier* | *turkildi* |
|------|----------|--------|-----------|-----|-----------|------------|
| and | ? | came | ? | ... | they-fell | ? |

| *unuhuine* | ... | *tarkalion* | *ohtakāre* | *valannar* ... |
|------------|-----|-------------|-----------|----------------|
| under-Shadow | ... | ? | war-made | on-Powers ... |

| *herunūmen* | *ilu* | *terhante* | ... | *ilūvatāren* | ... | *ëari* |
|-------------|-------|------------|-----|-------------|-----|--------|
| Lord-of-West | world | broke | ... | of-Ilúvatar | ... | seas |

| *ullier* | *kilyanna* | ... | *nūmenōre* | *ataltane* ... |
|----------|------------|-----|-----------|----------------|
| poured | in-Chasm | ... | Númenor | down-fell ... |

Then there had seemed to be a long gap.

| ... | *malle* | *tēra* | *lende* | *nūmenna* | *ilya* | *sī* | *maller* |
|-----|---------|--------|---------|-----------|--------|------|----------|
| ... | road | straight | went | Westward | all | now | roads |

| *raikar* | ..... | *turkildi* | *rōmenna* ... | *nuruhuine* | *mel-lumna* |
|----------|-------|------------|---------------|------------|-------------|
| bent | ..... | ? | eastward ... | Death-shadow | us-is-heavy |

| ... | *vahāya* | *sin* | *atalante.* |
|-----|----------|-------|-------------|
| ... | far-away | now | ? |

There were one or two new words here, of which he wanted to discover the meaning: it had escaped before he could write it down this morning. Probably they were names: *tarkalion* was almost certainly a king's name, for *tār* was common in royal names. It was curious how often the remembered snatches harped on the theme of a 'straight road'. What was *atalante*? It seemed to mean *ruin* or *downfall*, but also to be a name.

Alboin felt restless. He left his bed and went to the window. He stood there a long while looking out to sea; and as he stood a chill wind got up in the West. Slowly over the dark rim of sky and water's meeting clouds lifted huge heads, and loomed upwards, stretching out vast wings, south and north.

'They look like the eagles of the Lord of the West over Númenor,' he said aloud, and started. He had not purposed any words. For a moment he had felt the oncoming of a great disaster long foreseen. Now memory stirred, but could not be grasped. He shivered. He went back to bed and lay wondering. Suddenly the old desire came over him. It had been growing again for a long time, but he had not felt it like this, a feeling as vivid as hunger or thirst, for years, not since he was about Audoin's age.

'I wish there was a "Time-machine",' he said aloud. 'But Time is not to be conquered by machines. And I should go back, not forward; and I think backwards would be more possible.'

The clouds overcame the sky, and the wind rose and blew; and in his ears, as he fell asleep at last, there was a roaring in the leaves of many trees, and a roaring of long waves upon the shore. 'The storm is coming upon Númenor!' he said, and passed out of the waking world.

In a wide shadowy place he heard a voice.
'Elendil!' it said. 'Alboin, whither are you wandering?'
'Who are you?' he answered. 'And where are you?'
A tall figure appeared, as if descending an unseen stair towards him. For a moment it flashed through his thought that the face, dimly seen, reminded him of his father.
'I am with you. I was of Númenor, the father of many fathers before you. I am Elendil, that is in Eressëan "Elf-friend", and many have been called so since. You may have your desire.'
'What desire?'
'The long-hidden and the half-spoken: to go back.'
'But that cannot be, even if I wish it. It is against the law.'
'It is against the *rule*. Laws are commands upon the will and are binding. Rules are conditions; they may have exceptions.'
'But are there ever any exceptions?'
'Rules may be strict, yet they are the means, not the ends, of government. There are exceptions; for there is that which governs and is above the rules. Behold, it is by the chinks in the wall that light comes through, whereby men become aware of the light and therein perceive the wall and how it stands. The veil is woven, and each thread goes an appointed course, tracing a design; yet the tissue is not impenetrable, or the design would not be guessed; and if the design were not guessed, the veil would not be perceived, and all would dwell in darkness. But these are old parables, and I came not to speak such things. The world is not a machine that makes other machines after the fashion of Sauron. To each under the rule some unique fate is given, and he is excepted from that which is a rule to others. I ask if you would have your desire?'
'I would.'
'You ask not: how or upon what conditions.'
'I do not suppose I should understand how, and it does not seem to me necessary. We go forward, as a rule, but we do not know how. But what are the conditions?'
'That the road and the halts are prescribed. That you cannot return at your wish, but only (if at all) as it may be ordained. For

you shall not be as one reading a book or looking in a mirror, but as one walking in living peril. Moreover you shall not adventure yourself alone.'

'Then you do not advise me to accept? You wish me to refuse out of fear?'

'I do not counsel, yes or no. I am not a counsellor. I am a messenger, a permitted voice. The wishing and the choosing are for you.'

'But I do not understand the conditions, at least not the last. I ought to understand them all clearly.'

'You must, if you choose to go back, take with you Herendil, that is in other tongue Audoin, your son; for you are the ears and he is the eyes. But you may not ask that he shall be protected from the consequences of your choice, save as your own will and courage may contrive.'

'But I can ask him, if he is willing?'

'He would say yes, because he loves you and is bold; but that would not resolve your choice.'

'And when can I, or we, go back?'

'When you have made your choice.'

The figure ascended and receded. There was a roaring as of seas falling from a great height. Alboin could still hear the tumult far away, even after his waking eyes roamed round the room in the grey light of morning. There was a westerly gale blowing. The curtains of the open window were drenched, and the room was full of wind.

He sat silent at the breakfast-table. His eyes strayed continually to his son's face, watching his expressions. He wondered if Audoin ever had any Dreams. Nothing that left any memory, it would appear. Audoin seemed in a merry mood, and his own talk was enough for him, for a while. But at length he noticed his father's silence, unusual even at breakfast.

'You look glum, father,' he said. 'Is there some knotty problem on hand?'

'Yes – well no, not really,' answered Alboin. 'I think I was thinking, among other things, that it was a gloomy day, and not a good end to the holidays. What are you going to do?'

'Oh, I say!' exclaimed Audoin. 'I thought you loved the wind. I do. Especially a good old West-wind. I am going along the shore.'

'Anything on?'

'No, nothing special – just the wind.'

'Well, what about the beastly wind?' said Alboin, unaccountably irritated.

The boy's face fell. 'I don't know,' he said. 'But I like to be in it, especially by the sea; and I thought you did.' There was a silence.

After a while Audoin began again, rather hesitatingly: 'Do you remember the other day upon the cliffs near Predannack, when those odd clouds came up in the evening, and the wind began to blow?'

'Yes,' said Alboin in an unencouraging tone.

'Well, you said when we got home that it seemed to remind you of something, and that the wind seemed to blow through you, like, like, a legend you couldn't catch. And you felt, back in the quiet, as if you had listened to a long tale, which left you excited, though it left absolutely no *pictures* at all.'

'Did I?' said Alboin. 'I can remember feeling very cold, and being glad to get back to a fire.' He immediately regretted it, and felt ashamed. For Audoin said no more; though he felt certain that the boy had been making an opening to say something more, something that was on his mind. But he could not help it. He could not talk of such things to-day. He felt cold. He wanted peace, not wind.

Soon after breakfast Audoin went out, announcing that he was off for a good tramp, and would not be back at any rate before tea-time. Alboin remained behind. All day last night's vision remained with him, something different from the common order of dreams. Also it was (for him) curiously unlinguistic – though plainly related, by the name Númenor, to his language dreams. He could not say whether he had conversed with Elendil in Eressëan or English.

He wandered about the house restlessly. Books would not be read, and pipes would not smoke. The day slipped out of his hand, running aimlessly to waste. He did not see his son, who did not even turn up for tea, as he had half promised to do. Dark seemed to come unduly early.

In the late evening Alboin sat in his chair by the fire. 'I dread this choice,' he said to himself. He had no doubt that there was really a choice to be made. He would have to choose, one way or another, however he represented it to himself. Even if he dismissed the Dream as what is called 'a mere dream', it would be a choice – a choice equivalent to *no*.

'But I cannot make up my mind to *no*,' he thought. 'I think, I am almost sure, Audoin would say *yes*. And he will know of my choice sooner or later. It is getting more and more difficult to hide my thoughts from him: we are too closely akin, in many ways besides blood, for secrets. The secret would become unbearable, if I tried to keep it. My desire would become doubled through feeling that *I might have*, and become intolerable. And Audoin would probably feel I had robbed him through funk.

'But it is dangerous, perilous in the extreme – or so I am warned. I don't mind for myself. But for Audoin. But is the peril any greater than fatherhood lets in? It is perilous to come into the world at any point in Time. Yet I feel the shadow of this peril more heavily. Why? Because it is an exception to the rules? Or am I experiencing a choice backwards: the peril of fatherhood repeated? Being a father twice to the same person would make one think. Perhaps I am already moving back. I don't know. I wonder. Fatherhood is a choice, and yet it is not wholly by a man's will. Perhaps this peril is my choice, and yet also outside my will. I don't know. It is getting very dark. How loud the wind is. There is storm over Númenor.' Alboin slept in his chair.

He was climbing steps, up, up on to a high mountain. He felt, and thought he could hear, Audoin following him, climbing behind him. He halted, for it seemed somehow that he was again in the same place as on the previous night; though no figure could be seen.

'I have chosen,' he said. 'I will go back with Herendil.'

Then he lay down, as if to rest. Half-turning: 'Good night!' he murmured. 'Sleep well, Herendil! We start when the summons comes.'

'You have chosen,' a voice said above him. 'The summons is at hand.'

Then Alboin seemed to fall into a dark and a silence, deep and absolute. It was as if he had left the world completely, where all silence is on the edge of sound, and filled with echoes, and where all rest is but repose upon some greater motion. He had left the world and gone out. He was silent and at rest: a point.

He was poised; but it was clear to him that he had only to will it, and he would move.

'Whither?' He perceived the question, but neither as a voice from outside, nor as one from within himself.

'To whatever place is appointed. Where is Herendil?'

'Waiting. The motion is yours.'

'Let us move!'

Audoin tramped on, keeping within sight of the sea as much as he could. He lunched at an inn, and then tramped on again, further than he had intended. He was enjoying the wind and the rain, yet he was filled with a curious disquiet. There had been something odd about his father this morning.

'So disappointing,' he said to himself. 'I particularly wanted to have a long tramp with him to-day. We talk better walking, and I really must have a chance of telling him about the Dreams. I can talk about that sort of thing to my father, if we both get into the mood together. Not that he is usually at all difficult – seldom like to-day. He usually takes you as you mean it: joking or serious; doesn't mix the two, or laugh in the wrong places. I have never known him so frosty.'

He tramped on. 'Dreams,' he thought. 'But not the usual sort, quite different: very vivid; and though never quite repeated, all gradually fitting into a story. But a sort of phantom story with no explanations. Just pictures, but not a sound, not a word. Ships coming to land. Towers on the shore. Battles, with swords glinting but silent. And there is that ominous picture: the great temple on the mountain, smoking like a volcano. And that awful vision of the chasm in the seas, a whole land slipping sideways, mountains rolling over; dark ships fleeing into the dark. I want to tell someone about it, and get some kind of sense into it. Father would help: we could make up a good yarn together out of it. If I knew even the name of the place, it would turn a nightmare into a story.'

Darkness began to fall long before he got back. 'I hope father will have had enough of himself and be chatty to-night,' he thought. 'The fireside is next best to a walk for discussing dreams.' It was already night as he came up the path, and saw a light in the sitting-room.

He found his father sitting by the fire. The room seemed very still, and quiet – and too hot after a day in the open. Alboin sat, his head rested on one arm. His eyes were closed. He seemed asleep. He made no sign.

Audoin was creeping out of the room, heavy with disappointment. There was nothing for it but an early bed, and perhaps better luck tomorrow. As he reached the door, he thought he heard the chair creak, and then his father's voice (far away and rather strange in tone) murmuring something: it sounded like *herendil*.

He was used to odd words and names slipping out in a murmur

from his father. Sometimes his father would spin a long tale round
them. He turned back hopefully.

'Good night!' said Alboin. 'Sleep well, Herendil! We start when
the summons comes.' Then his head fell back against the chair.

'Dreaming,' thought Audoin. 'Good night!'

And he went out, and stepped into sudden darkness.

### Commentary on Chapters I and II

Alboin's biography sketched in these chapters is in many respects closely
modelled on my father's own life – though Alboin was not an orphan, and
my father was not a widower. Dates pencilled on the covering page of the
manuscript reinforce the strongly biographical element: Alboin was
born on February 4, (1891 >) 1890, two years earlier than my father.
Audoin was born in September 1918.

'Honour Mods.' (i.e. 'Honour Moderations'), referred to at the begin-
ning of Chapter II, are the first of the two examinations taken in the
Classical languages at Oxford, after two years (see Humphrey Carpenter,
*Biography*, p. 62); 'Schools', in the same passage, is a name for the final
Oxford examinations in all subjects.

Alboin's father's name *Oswin* is 'significant': *ós* 'god' and *wine* 'friend'
(see IV. 208, 212); Elendil's father was *Valandil* (p. 60). That *Errol* is to
be associated in some way with *Eriol* (the Elves' name for Ælfwine the
mariner, IV. 206) must be allowed to be a possibility.*

### The Lombardic legend

The Lombards ('Long-beards': Latin *Langobardi*, Old English *Long-
beardan*) were a Germanic people renowned for their ferocity. From
their ancient homes in Scandinavia they moved southwards, but very
little is known of their history before the middle of the sixth century. At
that time their king was *Audoin*, the form of his name in the *Historia
Langobardorum* by the learned Paul the Deacon, who died about 790.
*Audoin* and Old English *Éadwine* (later *Edwin*) show an exact correspondence, are historically the same name (Old English *ēa* derived from
the original diphthong *au*). On the meaning of *ēad* see p. 46, and cf.
*Éadwine* as a name in Old English of the Noldor, IV. 212.

Audoin's son was *Alboin*, again corresponding exactly to Old English
*Ælfwine* (*Elwin*). The story that Oswin Errol told his son (p. 37) is
known from the work of Paul the Deacon. In the great battle between the
Lombards and another Germanic people, the Gepids, Alboin son of
Audoin slew Thurismod, son of the Gepid king Thurisind, in single
combat; and when the Lombards returned home after their victory they

---

*It is worth mentioning that Osin Errol's frequent address to Alboin as 'boy' is
not intended to suggest an aloofly schoolmasterish tone. My father frequently
used it to his sons as a term of friendship and affection.

asked Audoin to give his son the rank of a companion of his table, since it was by his valour that they had won the day. But this Audoin would not do, for, he said, 'it is not the custom among us that the king's son should sit down with his father before he has first received weapons from the king of some other people.' When Alboin heard this he went with forty young men of the Lombards to king Thurisind to ask this honour from him. Thurisind welcomed him, invited him to the feast, and seated him at his right hand, where his dead son Thurismod used to sit.

But as the feast went on Thurisind began to think of his son's death, and seeing Alboin his slayer in his very place his grief burst forth in words: 'Very pleasant to me is the seat,' he said, 'but hard is it to look upon him who sits in it.' Roused by these words the king's second son Cunimund began to revile the Lombard guests; insults were uttered on both sides, and swords were grasped. But on the very brink Thurisind leapt up from the table, thrust himself between the Gepids and the Lombards, and threatened to punish the first man who began the fight. Thus he allayed the quarrel; and taking the arms of his dead son he gave them to Alboin, and sent him back in safety to his father's kingdom.

It is agreed that behind this Latin prose tale of Paul the Deacon, as also behind his story of Alboin's death, there lies a heroic lay: as early a vestige of such ancient Germanic poetry as we possess.

Audoin died some ten years after the battle, and Alboin became king of the Lombards in 565. A second battle was fought against the Gepids, in which Alboin slew their king Cunimund and took his daughter Rosamunda captive. At Easter 568 Alboin set out for the conquest of Italy; and in 572 he was murdered. In the story told by Paul the Deacon, at a banquet in Verona Alboin gave his queen Rosamunda wine to drink in a cup made from the skull of king Cunimund, and invited her to drink merrily with her father ('and if this should seem to anyone impossible,' wrote Paul, 'I declare that I speak the truth in Christ: I have seen [Radgisl] the prince holding the very cup in his hand on a feastday and showing it to those who sat at the table with him.')

Here Oswin Errol ended the story, and did not tell his son how Rosamunda exacted her revenge. The outcome of her machinations was that Alboin was murdered in his bed, and his body was buried 'at the going up of the stairs which are near to the palace,' amid great lamentation of the Lombards. His tomb was opened in the time of Paul the Deacon by Gislbert *dux Veronensium*, who took away Alboin's sword and other gear that was buried with him; 'wherefore he used to boast to the ignorant with his usual vanity that he has seen Alboin face to face.'

The fame of this formidable king was such that, in the words of Paul, 'even down to our own day, among the Bavarians and the Saxons and other peoples of kindred speech, his open hand and renown, his success and courage in war, are celebrated in their songs.' An extraordinary testimony to this is found in the ancient English poem *Widsith*, where occur the following lines:

Swylce ic wæs on Eatule mid Ælfwine:
se hæfde moncynnes mine gefræge
leohteste hond lofes to wyrcenne,
heortan unhneaweste hringa gedales,
beorhta beaga, bearn Eadwines.

(I was in Italy with Alboin: of all men of whom I have heard he had the hand most ready for deeds of praise, the heart least niggard in the giving of rings, of shining armlets, the son of Audoin.)*

In my father's letter of 1964 (given on pp. 7–8) he wrote as if it had been his intention to find one of the earlier incarnations of the father and son in the Lombard story: 'It started with a father-son affinity between Edwin and Elwin of the present, and was supposed to go back into legendary time by way of an Eädwine and Ælfwine of circa A.D. 918, *and Audoin and Alboin of Lombardic legend . . .*' But there is no suggestion that at the time this was any more than a passing thought; see further pp. 77–8.

*The two Englishmen named Ælfwine* (p. 38). King Alfred's youngest son was named Æthelweard, and it is recorded by the twelfth century historian William of Malmesbury that Æthelweard's sons Ælfwine and Æthelwine both fell at the battle of Brunanburh in 937.

Years later my father celebrated the Ælfwine who died at Maldon in *The Homecoming of Beorhtnoth*, where Torhthelm and Tídwald find his corpse among the slain: 'And here's Ælfwine: barely bearded, and his battle's over.'

*Oswin Errol's reference to a 'substratum'* (p. 40). Put very simply, the *substratum* theory attributes great importance, as an explanation of linguistic change, to the influence exerted on language when a people abandons their own former speech and adopts another; for such a people will retain their habitual modes of articulation and transfer them to the new language, thus creating a *substratum* underlying it. Different *substrata* acting upon a widespread language in different areas is therefore regarded as a fundamental cause of divergent phonetic change.

*The Old English verses of Ælfwine Wídlást* (p. 44). These verses, in identical form except for certain features of spelling, were used in the title-pages to the *Quenta Silmarillion* (p. 203); see also p. 103.

*The generous heart of Alboin, the hand ready for deeds of praise, made a different impression on the stricken population of Italy in the sixth century. From the walls of Rome Pope Gregory the Great watched men being led away by 'the unspeakable Lombards', tied together at the neck to be sold as slaves; and in one of his letters he welcomed the advent of bubonic plague, for 'when we consider the way in which other men have died we find a solace in reflecting on the form of death that threatens us. What mutilations, what cruelties we have seen inflicted upon men, for which death is the only cure, and in the midst of which life is a torture!'

*Names and words in the Elvish languages.* Throughout, the term *Eressëan* was a replacement of *Númenórean*. Perhaps to be compared is FN II, §2: 'Yet they [the Númenóreans] took on the speech of the Elves of the Blessed Realm, as it was and is in Eressëa.' The term 'Elf-latin', applied by Alboin to 'Eressëan' (pp. 41, 43), is found in the *Lhammas* (p. 172). There it refers to the archaic speech of the First Kindred of the Elves (the Lindar), which 'became early fixed . . . as a language of high speech and of writing, and as a common speech among all Elves; and all the folk of Valinor learned and knew this language.' It was called *Qenya*, the Elvish tongue, *tarquesta* high-speech, and *parmalambë* the book-tongue. But it is not explained in *The Lost Road* why Alboin should have called the language that 'came through' to him by this term.

*Amon-ereb* (p. 38): the rough draft of this passage had *Amon Gwareth*, changed more than once and ending with *Amon Thoros*. *Amon Ereb* (the Lonely Hill) is found in the *Annals of Beleriand* (p. 143, annal 340) and in QS §113.

'The shores of *Beleriand*' (p. 38): the draft has here 'the rocks of the *Falassë*.' The form *Falassë* occurs on the *Ambarkanta* map IV (IV. 249).

'*Alda* was a *tree* (a word I got a long time ago)' (p. 41). *Alda* 'tree' is found in the very early 'dictionary' (I. 249), where also occurs the word *lómë*, which Alboin also refers to here, with the meanings 'dusk, gloom, darkness' (I. 255).

*Anar*, *Isil*, and *Anor*, *Ithil* (p. 41): in QS §75 the names of the Sun and Moon given by the Gods are *Urin* and *Isil*, and by the Elves *Anar* and *Rana* (see the commentary on that passage).

The Eressëan fragment concerning the Downfall of Númenor and the Straight Road (p. 47) is slightly different in the draft text:

Ar Sauron lende nūmenorenna...lantie nu huine...ohtakárie valannar...manwe ilu terhante. eari lantier kilyanna nūmenor atalante...malle tēra lende nūmenna, ilya si maller raikar. Turkildi rómenna...nuruhuine me lumna.
And Sauron came to-Númenor...fell under Shadow...war-made on-Powers... ? ? broke. seas fell into-Chasm. Númenor down-fell. road straight went westward, all now roads bent. ? eastward. Death-shadow us is-heavy.

The name *Tar-kalion* is here not present, but *Sauron* is (see p. 9), and is interpreted as being a name. Most notably, this version has *manwe* (which Alboin could not interpret) for *herunúmen* 'Lord-of-West' of the later; on this see p. 75.

On the name *Herendil* (= Audoin, Eadwine) see the *Etymologies*, stem KHER.

(ii)

*The Númenórean chapters*

My father said in his letter of 1964 on the subject that 'in my tale *we were to come at last* to Amandil and Elendil leaders of the loyal party in Númenor, when it fell under the dominion of Sauron.' It is nonetheless plain that he did not reach this conception until *after* the extant narrative had been mostly written, or even brought to the point where it was abandoned. At the end of Chapter II the Númenórean story is obviously just about to begin, and the Númenórean chapters were originally numbered continuously with the opening ones. On the other hand the decision to postpone Númenor and make it the conclusion and climax to the book had already been taken when *The Lost Road* went to Allen and Unwin in November 1937.

Since the Númenórean episode was left unfinished, this is a convenient point to mention an interesting note that my father presumably wrote while it was in progress. This says that when the first 'adventure' (i.e. Númenor) is over 'Alboin is still precisely in his chair and Audoin just shutting the door.'

With the postponement of Númenor the chapter-numbers were changed, but this has no importance and I therefore number these 'III' and 'IV'; they have no titles. In this case I have found it most convenient to annotate the text by numbered notes.

## Chapter III

Elendil was walking in his garden, but not to look upon its beauty in the evening light. He was troubled and his mind was turned inward. His house with its white tower and golden roof glowed behind him in the sunset, but his eyes were on the path before his feet. He was going down to the shore, to bathe in the blue pools of the cove beyond his garden's end, as was his custom at this hour. And he looked also to find his son Herendil there. The time had come when he must speak to him.

He came at length to the great hedge of *lavaralda*[1] that fenced the garden at its lower, western, end. It was a familiar sight, though the years could not dim its beauty. It was seven twelves of years[2] or more since he had planted it himself when planning his garden before his marriage; and he had blessed his good fortune. For the seeds had come from Eressëa far westward, whence ships came seldom already in those days, and now they came no more. But the spirit of that blessed land and its fair people remained still in the trees that had grown from those seeds: their long green leaves were golden on the undersides, and as a breeze off the water stirred them they whispered with a sound of many soft voices, and glistened like sunbeams on rippling waves. The flowers were pale with a yellow flush, and laid thickly on the branches like a sunlit snow; and their odour filled all the lower garden, faint but clear. Mariners in the old days said that the scent of *lavaralda* could be felt on the air long ere the land of Eressëa could be seen, and that it brought a desire of rest and great content. He had seen the trees in flower day after day, for they rested from flowering only at rare intervals. But now, suddenly, as he passed, the scent struck him with a keen fragrance, at once known and utterly strange. He seemed for a moment never to have smelled it before: it pierced the troubles of his mind, bewildering, bringing no familiar content, but a new disquiet.

'Eressëa, Eressëa!' he said. 'I wish I were there; and had not been fated to dwell in Númenor³ half-way between the worlds. And least of all in these days of perplexity!'

He passed under an arch of shining leaves, and walked swiftly down rock-hewn steps to the white beach. Elendil looked about him, but he could not see his son. A picture rose in his mind of Herendil's white body, strong and beautiful upon the threshold of early manhood, cleaving the water, or lying on the sand glistening in the sun. But Herendil was not there, and the beach seemed oddly empty.

Elendil stood and surveyed the cove and its rocky walls once more; and as he looked, his eyes rose by chance to his own house among trees and flowers upon the slopes above the shore, white and golden, shining in the sunset. And he stopped and gazed: for suddenly the house stood there, as a thing at once real and visionary, as a thing in some other time and story, beautiful, beloved, but strange, awaking desire as if it were part of a mystery that was still hidden. He could not interpret the feeling.

He sighed. 'I suppose it is the threat of war that maketh me look upon fair things with such disquiet,' he thought. 'The shadow of fear is between us and the sun, and all things look as if they were already lost. Yet they are strangely beautiful thus seen. I do not know. I wonder. A Númenórë! I hope the trees will blossom on your hills in years to come as they do now; and your towers will stand white in the Moon and yellow in the Sun. I wish it were not hope, but assurance – that assurance we used to have before the Shadow. But where is Herendil? I must see him and speak to him, more clearly than we have spoken yet. Ere it is too late. The time is getting short.'

'Herendil!' he called, and his voice echoed along the hollow shore above the soft sound of the light-falling waves. 'Herendil!'

And even as he called, he seemed to hear his own voice, and to mark that it was strong and curiously melodious. 'Herendil!' he called again.

At length there was an answering call: a young voice very clear came from some distance away – like a bell out of a deep cave.

'*Man-ie, atto, man-ie?*'

For a brief moment it seemed to Elendil that the words were strange. '*Man-ie, atto?* What is it, father?' Then the feeling passed.

'Where art thou?'

'Here!'

'I cannot see thee.'

'I am upon the wall, looking down on thee.'

Elendil looked up; and then swiftly climbed another flight of stone steps at the northern end of the cove. He came out upon a flat space smoothed and levelled on the top of the projecting spur of rock. Here there was room to lie in the sun, or sit upon a wide stone seat with its back against the cliff, down the face of which there fell a cascade of trailing stems rich with garlands of blue and silver flowers. Flat upon the stone with his chin in his hands lay a youth. He was looking out to sea, and did not turn his head as his father came up and sat down on the seat.

'Of what art thou dreaming, Herendil, that thy ears hear not?'

'I am thinking; I am not dreaming. I am a child no longer.'

'I know thou art not,' said Elendil; 'and for that reason I wished to find thee and speak with thee. Thou art so often out and away, and so seldom at home these days.'

He looked down on the white body before him. It was dear to him, and beautiful. Herendil was naked, for he had been diving from the high point, being a daring diver and proud of his skill. It seemed suddenly to Elendil that the lad had grown over night, almost out of knowledge.

'How thou dost grow!' he said. 'Thou hast the makings of a mighty man, and have nearly finished the making.'

'Why dost thou mock me?' said the boy. 'Thou knowest I am dark, and smaller than most others of my year. And that is a trouble to me. I stand barely to the shoulder of Almáriel, whose hair is of shining gold, and she is a maiden, and of my own age. We hold that we are of the blood of kings, but I tell thee thy friends' sons make a jest of me and call me *Terendul*⁴ – slender and dark;

and they say I have Eressëan blood, or that I am half-Noldo. And that is not said with love in these days. It is but a step from being called half a Gnome to being called Godfearing; and that is dangerous.'[5]

Elendil sighed. 'Then it must have become perilous to be the son of him that is named *elendil*; for that leads to Valandil, God-friend, who was thy father's father.'[6]

There was a silence. At length Herendil spoke again: 'Of whom dost thou say that our king, Tarkalion, is descended?'

'From Eärendel the mariner, son of Tuor the mighty who was lost in these seas.'[7]

'Why then may not the king do as Eärendel from whom he is come? They say that he should follow him, and complete his work.'

'What dost thou think that they mean? Whither should he go, and fulfil what work?'

'Thou knowest. Did not Eärendel voyage to the uttermost West, and set foot in that land that is forbidden to us? He doth not die, or so songs say.'

'What callest thou Death? He did not return. He forsook all whom he loved, ere he stepped on that shore.[8] He saved his kindred by losing them.'

'Were the Gods wroth with him?'

'Who knoweth? For he came not back. But he did not dare that deed to serve Melko, but to defeat him; to free men from Melko, not from the Lords; to win us the earth, not the land of the Lords. And the Lords heard his prayer and arose against Melko. And the earth is ours.'

'They say now that the tale was altered by the Eressëans, who are slaves of the Lords: that in truth Eärendel was an adventurer, and showed us the way, and that the Lords took him captive for that reason; and his work is perforce unfinished. Therefore the son of Eärendel, our king, should complete it. They wish to do what has been long left undone.'

'What is that?'

'Thou knowest: to set foot in the far West, and not withdraw it. To conquer new realms for our race, and ease the pressure of this peopled island, where every road is trodden hard, and every tree and grass-blade counted. To be free, and masters of the world. To escape the shadow of sameness, and of ending. We would make our king Lord of the West: *Nuaran Númenóren*.[9] Death comes here slow and seldom; yet it cometh. The land is only a cage gilded to look like Paradise.'

'Yea, so I have heard others say,' said Elendil. 'But what knowest thou of Paradise? Behold, our wandering words have come unguided to the point of my purpose. But I am grieved to find thy mood is of this sort, though I feared it might be so. Thou art my only son, and my dearest child, and I would have us at one in all our choices. But choose we must, thou as well as I – for at thy last birthday thou became subject to arms and the king's service. We must choose between Sauron and the Lords (or One Higher). Thou knowest, I suppose, that all hearts in Númenor are not drawn to Sauron?'

'Yes. There are fools even in Númenor,' said Herendil, in a lowered voice. 'But why speak of such things in this open place? Do you wish to bring evil on me?'

'I bring no evil,' said Elendil. 'That is thrust upon us: the choice between evils: the first fruits of war. But look, Herendil! Our house is one of wisdom and guarded learning; and was long revered for it. I followed my father, as I was able. Dost thou follow me? What dost thou know of the history of the world or Númenor? Thou art but four twelves,[10] and wert but a small child when Sauron came. Thou dost not understand what days were like before then. Thou canst not choose in ignorance.'

'But others of greater age and knowledge than mine – or thine – have chosen,' said Herendil. 'And they say that history confirmeth them, and that Sauron hath thrown a new light on history. Sauron knoweth history, all history.'

'Sauron knoweth, verily; but he twisteth knowledge. Sauron is a liar!' Growing anger caused Elendil to raise his voice as he spoke. The words rang out as a challenge.

'Thou art mad,' said his son, turning at last upon his side and facing Elendil, with dread and fear in his eyes. 'Do not say such things to me! They might, they might . . .'

'Who are *they*, and what might they do?' said Elendil, but a chill fear passed from his son's eyes to his own heart.

'Do not ask! And do not speak – so loud!' Herendil turned away, and lay prone with his face buried in his hands. 'Thou knowest it is dangerous – to us all. Whatever he be, Sauron is mighty, and hath ears. I fear the dungeons. And I love thee, I love thee. *Atarinya tye-meláne.*'

*Atarinya tye-meláne*, my father, I love thee: the words sounded strange, but sweet: they smote Elendil's heart. 'A *yonya inye tye-méla*: and I too, my son, I love thee,' he said, feeling each syllable strange but vivid as he spoke it. 'But let us go within! It is too late to bathe. The sun is all but gone. It is bright there westwards in the gardens of the Gods. But twilight and the dark are coming here, and the dark is no longer wholesome in this land. Let us go home. I must tell and ask thee much this evening – behind closed doors, where maybe thou wilt feel safer.' He looked towards the sea, which he loved, longing to bathe his body in it, as though to wash away weariness and care. But night was coming.

The sun had dipped, and was fast sinking in the sea. There was fire upon far waves, but it faded almost as it was kindled. A chill wind came suddenly out of the West ruffling the yellow water off shore. Up over the fire-lit rim dark clouds reared; they stretched out great wings, south and north, and seemed to threaten the land.

Elendil shivered. 'Behold, the eagles of the Lord of the West are coming with threat to Númenor,' he murmured.

'What dost thou say?' said Herendil. 'Is it not decreed that the king of Númenor shall be called Lord of the West?'

'It is decreed by the king; but that does not make it so,' answered Elendil. 'But I meant not to speak aloud my heart's foreboding. Let us go!'

The light was fading swiftly as they passed up the paths of the garden amid flowers pale and luminous in the twilight. The trees were shedding sweet night-scents. A *lómelindë* began its thrilling bird-song by a pool.

Above them rose the house. Its white walls gleamed as if moonlight was imprisoned in their substance; but there was no moon yet, only a cool light, diffused and shadowless. Through the clear sky like fragile glass small stars stabbed their white flames. A voice from a high window came falling down like silver into the pool of twilight where they walked. Elendil knew the voice: it was the voice of Fíriel, a maiden of his household, daughter of Orontor. His heart sank, for Fíriel was dwelling in his house because Orontor had departed. Men said he was on a long voyage. Others said that he had fled the displeasure of the king. Elendil knew that he was on a mission from which he might never return, or return too late.[11] And he loved Orontor, and Fíriel was fair.

Now her voice sang an even-song in the Eressëan tongue, but made by men, long ago. The nightingale ceased. Elendil stood still to listen; and the words came to him, far off and strange, as some melody in archaic speech sung sadly in a forgotten twilight in the beginning of man's journey in the world.

*Ilu Ilúvatar en káre eldain a fírimoin*
*ar antaróta mannar Valion: númessier.* . . . .

The Father made the World for elves and mortals, and he gave
it into the hands of the Lords, who are in the West.

So sang Fíriel on high, until her voice fell sadly to the question
with which that song ends: *man táre antáva nin Ilúvatar,*
*Ilúvatar, enyáre tar i tyel íre Anarinya qeluva?* What will
Ilúvatar, O Ilúvatar, give me in that day beyond the end, when
my Sun faileth?'[12]

'*E man antaváro?* What will he give indeed?' said Elendil; and
stood in sombre thought.

'She should not sing that song out of a window,' said Herendil,
breaking the silence. 'They sing it otherwise now. Melko cometh
back, they say, and the king shall give us the Sun forever.'

'I know what they say,' said Elendil. 'Do not say it to thy father,
nor in his house.' He passed in at a dark door, and Herendil,
shrugging his shoulders, followed him.

## Chapter IV

Herendil lay on the floor, stretched at his father's feet upon a
carpet woven in a design of golden birds and twining plants with
blue flowers. His head was propped upon his hands. His father sat
upon his carved chair, his hands laid motionless upon either arm
of it, his eyes looking into the fire that burned bright upon the
hearth. It was not cold, but the fire that was named 'the heart of
the house' (*hon-maren*)[13] burned ever in that room. It was moreover a protection against the night, which already men had begun
to fear.

But cool air came in through the window, sweet and flower-
scented. Through it could be seen, beyond the dark spires of still
trees, the western ocean, silver under the Moon, that was now
swiftly following the Sun to the gardens of the Gods. In the night-
silence Elendil's words fell softly. As he spoke he listened, as if to
another that told a tale long forgotten.[14]

'There[15] is Ilúvatar, the One; and there are the Powers, of
whom the eldest in the thought of Ilúvatar was Alkar the Radiant;[16]
and there are the Firstborn of Earth, the Eldar, who perish not
while the World lasts; and there are also the Afterborn, mortal
Men, who are the children of Ilúvatar, and yet under the rule of
the Lords. Ilúvatar designed the World, and revealed his design

to the Powers; and of these some he set to be Valar, Lords of the World and governors of the things that are therein. But Alkar, who had journeyed alone in the Void before the World, seeking to be free, desired the World to be a kingdom unto himself. Therefore he descended into it like a falling fire; and he made war upon the Lords, his brethren. But they established their mansions in the West, in Valinor, and shut him out; and they gave battle to him in the North, and they bound him, and the World had peace and grew exceeding fair.

'After a great age it came to pass that Alkar sued for pardon; and he made submission unto Manwë, lord of the Powers, and was set free. But he plotted against his brethren, and he deceived the Firstborn that dwelt in Valinor, so that many rebelled and were exiled from the Blessed Realm. And Alkar destroyed the lights of Valinor and fled into the night; and he became a spirit dark and terrible, and was called Morgoth, and he established his dominion in Middle-earth. But the Valar made the Moon for the Firstborn and the Sun for Men to confound the Darkness of the Enemy. And in that time at the rising of the Sun the Afterborn, who are Men, came forth in the East of the world; but they fell under the shadow of the Enemy. In those days the exiles of the Firstborn made war upon Morgoth; and three houses of the Fathers of Men were joined unto the Firstborn: the house of Bëor, and the house of Haleth, and the house of Hador. For these houses were not subject to Morgoth. But Morgoth had the victory, and brought all to ruin.

'Eärendel was son of Tuor, son of Huor, son of Gumlin, son of Hador; and his mother was of the Firstborn, daughter of Turgon, last king of the Exiles. He set forth upon the Great Sea, and he came at last unto the realm of the Lords, and the mountains of the West. And he renounced there all whom he loved, his wife and his child, and all his kindred, whether of the Firstborn or of Men; and he stripped himself.[17] And he surrendered himself unto Manwë, Lord of the West; and he made submission and supplication to him. And he was taken and came never again among Men. But the Lords had pity, and they sent forth their power, and war was renewed in the North, and the earth was broken; but Morgoth was overthrown. And the Lords put him forth into the Void without.

'And they recalled the Exiles of the Firstborn and pardoned them; and such as returned dwell since in bliss in Eressëa, the Lonely Isle, which is Avallon, for it is within sight of Valinor and the light of the Blessed Realm. And for the men of the Three Houses they made Vinya, the New Land, west of Middle-earth in the midst of the Great Sea, and named it Andor, the Land of Gift; and they endowed the land and all that lived thereon with good beyond other lands of mortals. But in Middle-earth dwelt lesser men, who knew not the Lords nor the Firstborn save by rumour; and among them were some who had served Morgoth of old, and were accursed. And there were evil things also upon earth, made by Morgoth in the days of his dominion, demons and dragons and mockeries of the creatures of Ilúvatar.[18] And there too lay hid many of his servants, spirits of evil, whom his will governed still though his presence was not among them. And of these Sauron was the chief, and his power grew. Wherefore the lot of men in Middle-earth was evil, for the Firstborn that remained among them faded or departed into the West, and their kindred, the men of Númenor, were afar and came only to their coasts in ships that crossed the Great Sea. But Sauron learned of the ships of Andor, and he feared them, lest free men should become lords of Middle-earth and deliver their kindred; and moved by the will of Morgoth he plotted to destroy Andor, and ruin (if he might) Avallon and Valinor.[19]

'But why should we be deceived, and become the tools of his will? It was not he, but Manwë the fair, Lord of the West, that endowed us with our riches. Our wisdom cometh from the Lords, and from the Firstborn that see them face to face; and we have grown to be higher and greater than others of our race – those who served Morgoth of old. We have knowledge, power, and life stronger than they. We are not yet fallen. Wherefore the dominion of the world is ours, or shall be, from Eressëa to the East. More can no mortals have.'

'Save to escape from Death,' said Herendil, lifting his face to his father's. 'And from sameness. They say that Valinor, where the Lords dwell, has no further bounds.'

'They say not truly. For all things in the world have an end, since the world itself is bounded, that it may not be Void. But Death is not decreed by the Lords: it is the gift of the One, and a gift which in the wearing of time even the Lords of the West shall envy.[20] So the wise of old have said. And though we can perhaps no longer understand that word, at least we have wisdom enough to know that we cannot escape, unless to a worse fate.'

'But the decree that we of Númenor shall not set foot upon the shores of the Immortal, or walk in their land – that is only a decree of Manwë and his brethren. Why should we not? The air there giveth enduring life, they say.'

'Maybe it doth,' said Elendil; 'and maybe it is but the air which those need who already have enduring life. To us perhaps it is death, or madness.'

'But why should we not essay it? The Eressëans go thither, and yet our mariners in the old days used to sojourn in Eressëa without hurt.'

'The Eressëans are not as we. They have not the gift of death. But what doth it profit to debate the governance of the world? All certainty is lost. Is it not sung that the earth was made for us, but we cannot unmake it, and if we like it not we may remember that we shall leave it. Do not the Firstborn call us the Guests? See what this spirit of unquiet has already wrought. Here when I was young there was no evil of mind. Death came late and without other pain than weariness. From Eressëans we obtained so many things of beauty that our land became well nigh as fair as theirs; and maybe fairer to mortal hearts. It is said that of old the Lords themselves would walk at times in the gardens that we named for them. There we set their images, fashioned by Eressëans who had beheld them, as the pictures of friends beloved.

'There were no temples in this land. But on the Mountain we spoke to the One, who hath no image. It was a holy place, untouched by mortal art. Then Sauron came. We had long heard rumour of him from seamen returned from the East. The tales differed: some said he was a king greater than the king of Númenor; some said that he was one of the Powers, or their offspring set to govern Middle-earth. A few reported that he was an evil spirit, perchance Morgoth returned; but at these we laughed.[21]

'It seems that rumour came also to him of us. It is not many years – three twelves and eight[22] – but it seems many, since he came hither. Thou wert a small child, and knew not then what was happening in the east of this land, far from our western house. Tarkalion the king was moved by rumours of Sauron, and sent forth a mission to discover what truth was in the mariners' tales. Many counsellors dissuaded him. My father told me, and he was one of them, that those who were wisest and had most knowledge of the West had messages from the Lords warning them to beware. For the Lords said that Sauron would work evil; but he could not come hither unless he were summoned.[23] Tarkalion was grown proud, and brooked no power in Middle-earth greater than his own. Therefore the ships were sent, and Sauron was summoned to do homage.

'Guards were set at the haven of Mariondë in the east of the land,[24] where the rocks are dark, watching at the king's command without ceasing for the ships' return. It was night, but there was a bright Moon. They descried ships far off, and they seemed to be sailing west at a speed greater than the storm, though there was little wind. Suddenly the sea became unquiet; it rose until it became like a mountain, and it rolled upon the land. The ships were lifted up, and cast far inland, and lay in the fields. Upon that ship which was cast highest and stood dry upon a hill there was a man, or one in man's shape, but greater than any even of the race of Númenor in stature.

'He stood upon the rock[25] and said: "This is done as a sign of power. For I am Sauron the mighty, servant of the Strong" (wherein he spoke darkly). "I have come. Be glad, men of Númenor, for I will take thy king to be my king, and the world shall be given into his hand."

'And it seemed to men that Sauron was great; though they feared the light of his eyes. To many he appeared fair, to others terrible; but to some evil. But they led him to the king, and he was humble before Tarkalion.

'And behold what hath happened since, step by step. At first he revealed only secrets of craft, and taught the making of many things powerful and wonderful; and they seemed good. Our ships go now without the wind, and many are made of metal that sheareth hidden rocks, and they sink not in calm or storm; but they are no longer fair to look upon. Our towers grow ever stronger and climb ever higher, but beauty they leave behind upon earth. We who have no foes are embattled with impregnable fortresses – and mostly on the West. Our arms are multiplied as if for an agelong war, and men are ceasing to give love or care to the making of other things for use or delight. But our shields are impenetrable, our swords cannot be withstood, our darts are like thunder and pass over leagues unerring. Where are our enemies? We have begun to slay one another. For Númenor now seems narrow, that was so large. Men covet, therefore, the lands that other families have long possessed. They fret as men in chains.

'Wherefore Sauron hath preached deliverance; he has bidden our king to stretch forth his hand to Empire. Yesterday it was over the East. To-morrow – it will be over the West.

'We had no temples. But now the Mountain is despoiled. Its trees are felled, and it stands naked; and upon its summit there is a Temple. It is of marble, and of gold, and of glass and steel, and is

wonderful, but terrible. No man prayeth there. It waiteth. For
long Sauron did not name his master by the name that from old is
accursed here. He spoke at first of the Strong One, of the Eldest
Power, of the Master. But now he speaketh openly of Alkar,[26] of
Morgoth. He hath prophesied his return. The Temple is to be his
house. Númenor is to be the seat of the world's dominion.
Meanwhile Sauron dwelleth there. He surveys our land from the
Mountain, and is risen above the king, even proud Tarkalion, of
the line chosen by the Lords, the seed of Eärendel.

'Yet Morgoth cometh not. But his shadow hath come; it lieth
upon the hearts and minds of men. It is between them and the
Sun, and all that is beneath it.'

'Is there a shadow?' said Herendil. 'I have not seen it. But I have
heard others speak of it; and they say it is the shadow of Death.
But Sauron did not bring that; he promiseth that he will save us
from it.'

'There is a shadow, but it is the shadow of the fear of Death, and
the shadow of greed. But there is also a shadow of darker evil. We
no longer see our king. His displeasure falleth on men, and they go
out; they are in the evening, and in the morning they are not. The
open is insecure; walls are dangerous. Even by the heart of the
house spies may sit. And there are prisons, and chambers underground. There are torments; and there are evil rites. The woods at
night, that once were fair – men would roam and sleep there for
delight, when thou wert a babe – are filled now with horror. Even
our gardens are not wholly clean, after the sun has fallen. And now
even by day smoke riseth from the temple: flowers and grass are
withered where it falleth. The old songs are forgotten or altered;
twisted into other meanings.'

'Yea: that one learneth day by day,' said Herendil. 'But some of
the new songs are strong and heartening. Yet now I hear that some
counsel us to abandon the old tongue. They say we should leave
Eressëan, and revive the ancestral speech of Men. Sauron teacheth
it. In this at least I think he doth not well.'

'Sauron deceiveth us doubly. For men learned speech of the
Firstborn, and therefore if we should verily go back to the
beginnings we should find not the broken dialects of the wild men,
nor the simple speech of our fathers, but a tongue of the Firstborn.
But the Eressëan is of all the tongues of the Firstborn the fairest,
and they use it in converse with the Lords, and it linketh their
varied kindreds one to another, and them to us. If we forsake it, we
should be sundered from them, and be impoverished.[27] Doubtless

that is what he intendeth. But there is no end to his malice. Listen now, Herendil, and mark well. The time is nigh when all this evil shall bear bitter fruit, if it be not cut down. Shall we wait until the fruit be ripe, or hew the tree and cast it into the fire?'

Herendil got suddenly to his feet, and went to the window. 'It is cold, father,' he said; 'and the Moon is gone. I trust the garden is empty. The trees grow too near the house.' He drew a heavy embroidered cloth across the window, and then returned, crouching by the fire, as if smitten by a sudden chill.

Elendil leant forward in his chair, and continued in a lowered voice. 'The king and queen grow old, though all know it not, for they are seldom seen. They ask where is the undying life that Sauron promised them if they would build the Temple for Morgoth. The Temple is built, but they are grown old. But Sauron foresaw this, and I hear (already the whisper is gone forth) that he declareth that Morgoth's bounty is restrained by the Lords, and cannot be fulfilled while they bar the way. To win life Tarkalion must win the West.[28] We see now the purpose of the towers and weapons. War is already being talked of – though they do not name the enemy. But I tell thee: it is known to many that the war will go west to Eressëa: and beyond. Dost thou perceive the extremity of our peril, and the madness of the king? Yet this doom draws swiftly near. Our ships are recalled from the [?corners] of the earth. Hast thou not marked and wondered that so many are absent, especially of the younger folk, and in the South and West of our land both works and pastimes languish? In a secret haven to the North there is a building and forging that hath been reported to me by trusty messengers.'

'Reported to thee? What dost thou mean, father?' asked Herendil as if in fear.

'Even what I say. Why dost thou look on me so strangely? Didst thou think the son of Valandil, chief of the wise men of Númenor, would be deceived by the lies of a servant of Morgoth? I would not break faith with the king, nor do I purpose anything to his hurt. The house of Eärendel hath my allegiance while I live. But if I must choose between Sauron and Manwë, then all else must come after. I will not bow unto Sauron, nor to his master.'

'But thou speakest as if thou wert a leader in this matter – woe is me, for I love thee; and though thou swearest allegiance, it will not save thee from the peril of treason. Even to dispraise Sauron is held rebellious.'

'I am a leader, my son. And I have counted the peril both for myself and for thee and all whom I love. I do what is right and my right to do, but I cannot conceal it longer from thee. Thou must choose between thy father and Sauron. But I give thee freedom of choice and lay on thee no obedience as to a father, if I have not convinced thy mind and heart. Thou shalt be free to stay or go, yea even to report as may seem good to thee all that I have said. But if thou stayest and learnest more, which will involve closer counsels and other [?names] than mine, then thou wilt be bound in honour to hold thy peace, come what may. Wilt thou stay?'

'*Atarinya tye-meláne*,' said Herendil suddenly, and clasping his father's knees he laid his [?head there] and wept. 'It is an evil hour that [?putteth] such a choice on thee,' said his father, laying a hand on his head. 'But fate calleth some to be men betimes. What dost thou say?'

'I stay, father.'

The narrative ends here. There is no reason to think that any more was ever written. The manuscript, which becomes increasingly rapid towards the end, peters out in a scrawl.

### Notes on the Númenórean chapters of The Lost Road

1 *Lavaralda* (replacing *lavarin*) is not mentioned in *A Description of Númenor* (*Unfinished Tales* p. 167) among the trees brought by the Eldar from Tol-eressëa.

2 *seven twelves of years* is an emendation of *four score of years* (first written *three score of years*); see note 10.

3 *Vinya* is written above *Númenor* in the manuscript; it occurs again in a part of the text that was rewritten (p. 64), rendered 'the New Land'. The name first appeared in an emendation to FN I (p. 19, §2).

4 For *Terendul* see the *Etymologies*, stem TER, TERES.

5 As the text was originally written there followed here:
Poldor called me *Eärendel* yesterday.'
Elendil sighed. 'But that is a fair name. I love the story above others; indeed I chose thy name because it recalleth his. But I did not presume to give his name even to thee, nor to liken myself to Tuor the mighty, who first of Men sailed these seas. At least thou canst answer thy foolish friends that Eärendel was the chief of mariners, and surely that is still held worthy of honour in Númenor?'
'But they care not for Eärendel. And neither do I. We wish to do what he left undone.'
'What dost thou mean?'
'Thou knowest: to set foot in the far West . . .' (&c. as on p. 60).

6   This is the earliest appearance of a Númenórean named *Valandil*.
    In later rewriting of FN II Valandil is Elendil's brother, and they
    are the founders of the Númenórean kingdoms in Middle-earth
    (pp. 33–4). The name was afterwards given to both an earlier
    Númenórean (the first Lord of Andúnië) and a later (the youngest
    son of Isildur and third King of Arnor): Index to *Unfinished Tales*,
    entries *Valandil* and references.

7   In the *Quenta* (IV. 151) it is not told that Tuor was 'lost'. When he felt
    old age creeping on him 'he built a great ship Eärámë, Eagle's Pinion,
    and with Idril he set sail into the sunset and the West, and came no
    more into any tale or song.' Later the following was added (IV. 155):
    'But Tuor alone of mortal Men was numbered among the elder race,
    and joined with the Noldoli whom he loved, and in after time dwelt
    still, or so it hath been said, ever upon his ship voyaging the seas of the
    Elven-lands, or resting a while in the harbours of the Gnomes of Tol
    Eressëa; and his fate is sundered from the fate of Men.'

8   This is the final form in the *Quenta* of the story of Eärendel's
    landing in Valinor, where in emendations made to the second text
    Q II (IV. 156) Eärendel 'bade farewell to all whom he loved upon
    the last shore, and was taken from them for ever,' and 'Elwing
    mourned for Eärendel yet found him never again, and they are
    sundered till the world endeth.' Later Elendil returns more fully to
    the subject (p. 64). In QS the story is further changed, in that
    Elwing entered Valinor (see pp. 324–5 §§1–2, and commentary).

9   *Nuaran Númenóren*: the letters *ór* were scratched out in the type-
    script (only).

10  *Thou art but four twelves* replaced *Thou art scarce two score and
    ten*. As in the change recorded in note 2, a duodecimal counting
    replaces a decimal; but the number of years is in either case very
    strange. For Herendil has been called a 'boy', a 'lad', and a 'youth',
    and he is 'upon the threshold of early manhood' (p. 58); how then
    can he be forty-eight years old? But his age is unequivocally stated,
    and moreover Elendil says later (p. 66) that it is 44 years since
    Sauron came and that Herendil was then a small child; it can only
    be concluded therefore that at this time the longevity of the
    Númenóreans implied that they grew and aged at a different rate
    from other men, and were not fully adult until about fifty years old.
    Cf. *Unfinished Tales* pp. 224–5.

11  Orontor's mission, from which he might never return, seems like a
    premonition of the voyage of Amandil into the West, from which he
    never returned (*Akallabêth* pp. 275–6).

12  The manuscript (followed by the typescript) is here confused, since
    in addition to the text as printed the whole song that Fíriel sang is
    given as well, with translation; thus the two opening and the two
    closing lines and their translations are repeated. It is clear however
    from pencilled markings on the manuscript that my father moved at

once to a second version (omitting the greater part of the song) without striking out the first. The text of the song was emended in three stages. Changes made probably very near the time of writing were *Valion númenyaron* (translated 'of the Lords of the West') > *Valion: númessier* in line 2, and *hondo-ninya* > *indo-ninya* in line 9; *Vinya* was written above *Númenor* as an alternative in line 8 (cf. note 3). Before the later emendations the text ran thus:

Ilu Ilúvatar en kárẹ eldain a fírimoin
ar antaróta mannar Valion: númessier.
Toi aina, mána, meldielto – enga morion:
talantie. Mardello Melko lende: márie.
Eldain en kárier Isil, nan hildin Úr-anar.
Toi írimar. Ilqainen antar annar lestanen
Ilúvatáren. Ilu vanya, fanya, eari,
i-mar, ar ilqa ímen. Írima ye Númenor.
Nan úye sére indo-ninya símen, ullume;
ten sí ye tyelma, yéva tyel ar i-narqelion,
írẹ ilqa yéva nótina, hostainiéva, yallume:
ananta úva táre fárea, ufárea!
Man táre antáva nin Ilúvatar, Ilúvatar
enyárẹ tar i tyel, írẹ Anarinya qeluva?

The Father made the World for Elves and Mortals, and he gave it into the hands of the Lords. They are in the West. They are holy, blessed, and beloved: save the dark one. He is fallen. Melko has gone from Earth: it is good. For Elves they made the Moon, but for Men the red Sun; which are beautiful. To all they gave in measure the gifts of Ilúvatar. The World is fair, the sky, the seas, the earth, and all that is in them. Lovely is Númenor. But my heart resteth not here for ever; for here is ending, and there will be an end and the Fading, when all is counted, and all numbered at last, but yet it will not be enough, not enough. What will the Father, O Father, give me in that day beyond the end when my Sun faileth?

Subsequently *Mardello Melko* in line 4 was changed to *Melko Mardello*, and lines 5–6 became

En kárielto eldain Isil, hildin Úr-anar.
Toi írimar. Ilyain antalto annar lestanen

Then, after the typescript was made, *Melko* was changed to *Alkar* in text and translation; see note 15.

The thought of lines 5–6 of the song reappears in Elendil's words to Herendil later (p. 64): 'But the Valar made the Moon for the Firstborn and the Sun for Men to confound the Darkness of the Enemy.' Cf. QS §75 (*The Silmarillion* p. 99): 'For the Sun was set as a sign for the awakening of Men and the waning of the Elves; but the Moon cherishes their memory.'

13 For *hon-maren* 'heart of the house' see the *Etymologies*, stem KHO-N.
14 Here the typescript made at Allen and Unwin (p. 8, footnote) ends. The publishers' reader (see p. 97) said that 'only the preliminary two chapters . . . and one of the last chapters . . . are written.' It might be supposed that the typescript ended where it does because no more had been written at that time, but I do not think that this was the reason. At the point where the typescript breaks off (in the middle of a manuscript page) there is no suggestion at all of any interruption in the writing, and it seems far more likely that the typist simply gave up, for the manuscript here becomes confused and difficult through rewriting and substitutions.

In the previous parts of *The Lost Road* I have taken up all corrections to the manuscript, however quickly and lightly made, since they all appear in the typescript. From this point there is no external evidence to show when the pencilled emendations were made; but I continue to take these up into the text as before.
15 Elendil's long tale to Herendil of the ancient history, from 'There is Ilúvatar, the One' to 'and ruin (if he might) Avallon and Valinor' on p. 65, is a replacement of the original much briefer passage. This replacement must be later than the submission of *The Lost Road* to Allen and Unwin, for Morgoth is here called *Alkar* as the text was first written, not *Melko*, whereas in the song sung by Fíriel in the previous chapter *Melko* was only changed in pencil to *Alkar*, and this was not taken up into the typescript. The original passage read thus:

He spoke of the rebellion of Melko [*later* > Alkar *and subsequently*], mightiest of the Powers, that began at the making of the World; and of his rejection by the Lords of the West after he had wrought evil in the Blessed Realm and caused the exile of the Eldar, the firstborn of the earth, who dwelt now in Eressëa. He told of Melko's tyranny in Middle-earth, and how he had enslaved Men; of the wars which the Eldar waged with him, and were defeated, and of the Fathers of Men that had aided them; how Eärendel brought their prayer to the Lords, and Melko was overthrown and thrust forth beyond the confines of the World.

Elendil paused and looked down on Herendil. He did not move or make a sign. Therefore Elendil went on. 'Dost thou not perceive then, Herendil, that Morgoth is a begetter of evil, and brought sorrow upon our fathers? We owe him no allegiance except by fear. For his share of the governance of the World was forfeit long ago. Nor need we hope in him: the fathers of our race were his enemies; wherefore we can look for no love from him or any of his servants. Morgoth doth not forgive. But he cannot return into the World in present power and form while the Lords are enthroned. He is in the Void, though his Will remaineth and guideth his servants. And his will is to overthrow the Lords, and return, and wield dominion, and have vengeance on those who obey the Lords.

'But why should we be deceived . . .' (&c. as on p. 65).

The closing sentences ('But he cannot return into the World . . .') closely echo, or perhaps rather are closely echoed by (see note 25) a passage in FN II (§1).

16    In QS §10 it is said that Melko was 'coëval with Manwë'. The name *Alkar* 'the Radiant' of Melko occurs, I believe, nowhere outside this text.

17    See note 8. The reference to Eärendel's *child* shows that Elros had not yet emerged, as he had not in FN II (p. 34).

18    'mockeries of the creatures of Ilúvatar': cf. FN II §1 and commentary.

19    Here the long replacement passage ends (see note 15), though as written it continued in much the same words as did the earlier form ('For Morgoth cannot return into the World while the Lords are enthroned . . .'); this passage was afterwards struck out.

20    The words 'a gift which in the wearing of time even the Lords of the West shall envy' were a pencilled addition to the text, and are the first appearance of this idea: a closely similar phrase is found in a text of the *Ainulindalë* written years later (cf. *The Silmarillion* p. 42: 'Death is their fate, the gift of Ilúvatar, which as Time wears even the Powers shall envy.')

21    Cf. FN II §5: 'Some said that he was a king greater than the King of Númenor; some said that he was one of the Gods or their sons set to govern Middle-earth. A few reported that he was an evil spirit, perchance Morgoth himself returned. But this was held to be only a foolish fable of the wild Men.'

22    This duodecimal computation is found in the text as written; see note 10.

23    Cf. FN II §5: 'for [the Lords] said that Sauron would work evil if he came; but he could not come to Númenor unless he was summoned and guided by the king's messengers.'

24    The name *Moriondë* occurs, I think, nowhere else. This eastern haven is no doubt the forerunner of Rómenna.

25    This is the story of the coming of Sauron to Númenor found in FN II §5, which was replaced soon after by a version in which the lifting up of the ships by a great wave and the casting of them far inland was removed; see pp. 9, 26–7. In the first FN II version the sea rose like a *mountain*, the ship that carried Sauron was set upon a *hill*, and Sauron stood upon the hill to preach his message to the Númenóreans. In *The Lost Road* the sea rose like a *hill*, changed in pencil to *mountain*, Sauron's ship was cast upon a *high rock*, changed in pencil to *hill*, and Sauron spoke standing on the rock (left unchanged). This is the best evidence I can see that of these two companion works (see notes 15, 21, 23) *The Lost Road* was written first.

26  *Alkar*: pencilled alteration of *Melko*: see note 15.

27  On Eressëan ('Elf-latin', Qenya), the common speech of all Elves, see p. 56. The present passage is the first appearance of the idea of a linguistic component in the attack by the Númenórean 'government' on Eressëan culture and influence; cf. *The Line of Elros* in *Unfinished Tales* (p. 222), of Ar-Adûnakhôr, the twentieth ruler of Númenor: 'He was the first King to take the sceptre with a title in the Adûnaic tongue . . . In this reign the Elven-tongues were no longer used, nor permitted to be taught, but were maintained in secret by the Faithful'; and of Ar-Gimilzôr, the twenty-third ruler: 'he forbade utterly the use of the Eldarin tongues' (very similarly in the *Akallabêth*, pp. 267–8). But of course at the time of *The Lost Road* the idea of Adûnaic as one of the languages of Númenor had not emerged, and the proposal is only that 'the ancestral speech of Men' should be 'revived'.

28  This goes back to FN I §6: 'Sûr said that the gifts of Morgoth were withheld by the Gods, and that to obtain plenitude of power and undying life he [the king Angor] must be master of the West.'

There are several pages of notes that give some idea of my father's thoughts – at a certain stage – for the continuation of the story beyond the point where he abandoned it. These are in places quite illegible, and in any case were the concomitant of rapidly changing ideas: they are the vestiges of thoughts, not statements of formulated conceptions. More important, some at least of these notes clearly preceded the actual narrative that was written and were taken up into it, or replaced by something different, and it may very well be that this is true of them all, even those that refer to the latter part of the story which was never written. But they make it very clear that my father was concerned above all with the relation between the father and the son, which was cardinal. In Númenor he had engendered a situation in which there was the potentiality of anguishing conflict between them, totally incommensurate with the quiet harmony in which the Errols began – or ended. The relationship of Elendil and Herendil was subjected to a profound menace. This conflict could have many narrative issues within the framework of the known event, the attack on Valinor and the Downfall of Númenor, and in these notes my father was merely sketching out some solutions, none of which did he develop or return to again.

An apparently minor question was the words 'the Eagles of the Lord of the West': what did they mean, and how were they placed within the story? It seems that he was as puzzled by them as was Alboin Errol when he used them (pp. 38, 47). He queries whether 'Lord of the West' means the King of Númenor, or Manwë, or whether it is the title properly of Manwë but taken in his despite by the King; and concludes 'probably the latter'. There follows a 'scenario' in which Sorontur King of Eagles is sent by Manwë, and Sorontur flying against the sun casts a great shadow on the ground. It was then that Elendil spoke the phrase, but he was overheard, informed upon, and taken before Tarkalion, who declared that the title was his. In the story as actually written Elendil speaks the words to Herendil (p. 62), when he sees clouds rising out of the West in the evening sky and stretching out 'great wings' – the same spectacle as made Alboin Errol utter them, and the men of Númenor in the *Akallabêth* (p. 277); and Herendil replies that the title has been decreed to belong to the King. The outcome of Elendil's arrest is not made clear in the notes, but it is said that Herendil was given command of one of the ships, that Elendil himself joined in the great expedition because he followed Herendil, that when they reached Valinor Tarkalion set Elendil as a hostage in his son's ship, and that when they landed on the shores Herendil was struck down. Elendil rescued him and set him on shipboard, and 'pursued by the bolts of Tarkalion' they sailed back east. 'As they approach Númenor the world bends; they see the land slipping towards them'; and Elendil falls into the deep and is drowned.* This group of notes ends with references to the coming of the Númenóreans to Middle-earth, and to the 'later stories'; 'the flying ships', 'the painted caves', 'how Elf-friend walked on the Straight Road'.

Other notes refer to plans laid by the 'anti-Saurians' for an assault on the Temple, plans betrayed by Herendil 'on condition that Elendil is spared'; the assault is defeated and Elendil captured. Either associated with this or distinct from it is a suggestion that Herendil is arrested and imprisoned in the dungeons of Sauron, and that Elendil renounces the Gods to save his son.

My guess is that all this had been rejected when the actual narrative was written, and that the words of Herendil that conclude it show that my father had then in mind some quite distinct solution, in which Elendil and his son remained united in the face of whatever events overtook them.†

In the early narratives there is no indication of the duration of the realm of Númenor from its foundation to its ruin; and there is only one named king. In his conversation with Herendil, Elendil attributes all the evils that have befallen to the coming of Sauron: they have arisen therefore in a quite brief time (forty-four years, p. 66); whereas in the *Akallabêth*, when a great extension of Númenórean history had taken

---

*It would be interesting to know if a tantalisingly obscure note, scribbled down in isolation, refers to this dimly-glimpsed story: 'If either fails the other they perish and do not return. Thus at the last moment Elendil must prevail on Herendil to hold back, otherwise they would have perished. At that moment he sees himself as Alboin: and realises that Elendil and Herendil had perished.'

†I have suggested (p. 31) that since Elendil of Númenor appears in FN II (§14) as king in Beleriand he must have been among those who took no part in the expedition of Tar-kalion, but 'sat in their ships upon the east coast of the land' (FN §9).

place, those evils began long before, and are indeed traced back as far as the twelfth ruler, Tar-Ciryatan the Shipbuilder, who took the sceptre nearly a millennium and a half before the Downfall (*Akallabêth* p. 265, *Unfinished Tales* p. 221).

From Elendil's words at the end of *The Lost Road* there emerges a sinister picture: the withdrawal of the besotted and aging king from the public view, the unexplained disappearance of people unpopular with the 'government', informers, prisons, torture, secrecy, fear of the night; propaganda in the form of the 'rewriting of history' (as exemplified by Herendil's words concerning what was now said about Eärendel, p. 60); the multiplication of weapons of war, the purpose of which is concealed but guessed at; and behind all the dreadful figure of Sauron, the real power, surveying the whole land from the Mountain of Númenor. The teaching of Sauron has led to the invention of ships of metal that traverse the seas without sails, but which are hideous in the eyes of those who have not abandoned or forgotten Tol-eressëa; to the building of grim fortresses and unlovely towers; and to missiles that pass with a noise like thunder to strike their targets many miles away. Moreover, Númenor is seen by the young as over-populous, boring, 'over-known': 'every tree and grass-blade is counted', in Herendil's words; and this cause of discontent is used, it seems, by Sauron to further the policy of 'imperial' expansion and ambition that he presses on the king. When at this time my father reached back to the world of the first man to bear the name 'Elf-friend' he found there an image of what he most condemned and feared in his own.

(iii)

*The unwritten chapters*

It cannot be shown whether my father decided to alter the structure of the book by postponing the Númenórean story to the end before he abandoned the fourth chapter at Herendil's words 'I stay, father'; but it seems perfectly possible that the decision in fact led to the abandonment. At any rate, on a separate sheet he wrote: '*Work backwards* to Númenor and make that last', adding a proposal that in each tale a man should utter the words about the Eagles of the Lord of the West, but only at the end would it be discovered what they meant (see pp. 75–6). This is followed by a rapid jotting down of ideas for the tales that should intervene between Alboin and Audoin of the twentieth century and Elendil and Herendil in Númenor, but these are tantalisingly brief: 'Lombard story?'; 'a Norse story of ship-burial (Vinland)'; 'an English story – of the man who got onto the Straight Road?'; 'a Tuatha-de-Danaan story, or Tir-nan-Og' (on which see pp. 81–3); a story concerning 'painted caves'; 'the Ice Age – great figures in ice', and 'Before the Ice Age: the Galdor story'; 'post-Beleriand and the Elendil and Gil-galad story of the

assault on Thû'; and finally 'the Númenor story'. To one of these, the
'English story of the man who got onto the Straight Road', is attached a
more extended note, written at great speed:

> But this would do best of all for introduction to the Lost Tales: How
> Ælfwine sailed the Straight Road. They sailed on, on, on over the sea;
> and it became very bright and very calm, – no clouds, no wind. The
> water seemed thin and white below. Looking down Ælfwine suddenly
> saw lands and mt [*i.e.* mountains *or* a mountain] down in the water
> shining in the sun. Their breathing difficulties. His companions dive
> overboard one by one. Ælfwine falls insensible when he smells a
> marvellous fragrance as of land and flowers. He awakes to find the ship
> being drawn by people walking in the water. He is told very few men
> there in a thousand years can breathe air of Eressëa (which is Avallon),
> but *none* beyond. So he comes to Eressëa and is told the Lost Tales.

Pencilled later against this is 'Story of Sceaf or Scyld'; and it was only
here, I think, that the idea of the Anglo-Saxon episode arose (and this
was the only one of all these projections that came near to getting off the
ground).

This note is of particular interest in that it shows my father combining
the old story of the voyage of Ælfwine to Tol-eressëa and the telling of the
*Lost Tales* with the idea of the World Made Round and the Straight Path,
which entered at this time. With the words about the difficulty of
breathing cf. FN §12, where it is said that the Straight Path 'cut through
the air of breath and flight [Wilwa, Vista], and traversed Ilmen, in which
no flesh can endure.'

My father then (as I judge) roughed out an outline for the structure of
the book as he now foresaw it. Chapter III was to be called *A Step
Backward: Ælfwine and Eadwine*\* – the Anglo-Saxon incarnation of the
father and son, and incorporating the legend of King Sheave; Chapter
IV 'the Irish legend of Tuatha-de-Danaan – and oldest man in the
world'; Chapter V 'Prehistoric North: old kings found buried in the ice':
Chapter VI 'Beleriand'; Chapter VIII (presumably a slip for VII)
'Elendil and Herendil in Númenor'. It is interesting to see that there is
now no mention of the Lombard legend as an ingredient: see p. 55.

This outline structure was sent to Allen and Unwin with the manuscript and was incorporated in the typescript made there.

Apart from the Anglo-Saxon episode, the only scrap of connected
writing for any of the suggested tales is an extremely obscure and
roughly-written fragment that appears to be a part of 'the Galdor story'
(p. 77). In this, one *Agaldor* stands on a rocky shore at evening and sees
great clouds coming up, 'like the very eagles of the Lord of the West'. He
is filled with a formless foreboding at the sight of these clouds; and he

---

\*I think it almost certain that the titles of Chapters I and II were put in at this
time: as the manuscript was written they had no titles.

turns and climbs up the beach, passing down behind the land-wall to the houses where lights are already lit. He is eyed doubtfully by men sitting at a door, and after he has gone by they speak of him.

'There goes Agaldor again, from his speech with the sea: earlier than usual,' said one. 'He has been haunting the shores more than ever of late.' 'He will be giving tongue soon, and prophesying strange things,' said another; 'and may the Lords of the West set words more comforting in his mouth than before.' 'The Lords of the West will tell him naught,' said a third. 'If ever they were on land or sea they have left this earth, and man is his own master from here to the sunrise. Why should we be plagued with the dreams of a twilight-walker? His head is stuffed with them, and there let them bide. One would think to hear him talk that the world had ended in the last age, not new begun, and we were living in the ruins.'

'He is one of the old folk, and well-nigh the last of the long-lived in these regions,' said another. 'Those who knew the Eldar and had seen even the Sons of the Gods had a wisdom we forget.' 'Wisdom I know not,' said the other, 'but woe certainly in abundance if any of their tales are true. I know not (though I doubt it). But give me the Sun. That is glory . . . I would that the long life of Agaldor might be shortened. It is he that holds [??nigh] this sea-margin – too near the mournful water. I would we had a leader to take us East or South. They say the land is golden in the [??domains] of the Sun.'

Here the fragment ends. Agaldor has appeared in the original outline for *The Fall of Númenor*: 'Agaldor chieftain of a people who live upon the N.W. margin of the Western Sea' (p. 11), and later in that text it was Agaldor who wrestled with Thû, though the name was there changed at the time of writing to Amroth (p. 12). That this is a fragment of 'the Galdor story' seems to be shown by a pencilled and partly illegible scrawl at the head of the page, where *Galdor* appears; but the story is here significantly different.

Galdor is a good man [?among] the exiles (not a Númenórean) – not a long-liver but a prophet. He prophesies [?coming] of Númenóreans and [?salvation] of men. Hence holds his men by sea. This foreboding passage heralds the Ruin and the Flood. How he escapes in the flood . . . . . of land. The Númenóreans come – but appear no longer as good but as rebels against the Gods. They slay Galdor and take the chieftainship.

There is very little to build on here, and I shall not offer any speculations. The story was abandoned without revealing how the Ælfwine-Eadwine element would enter.

Turning now to 'the Ælfwine story', there are several pages of very rough notes and abandoned beginnings. One of these pages consists of increasingly rapid and abbreviated notes, as follows:

Ælfwine and Eadwine live in the time of Edward the Elder, in North Somerset. Ælfwine ruined by the incursions of Danes. Picture opens with the attack (c. 915) on *Portloca* (Porlock) and *Wæced*. Ælfwine is awaiting Eadwine's return at night. (The attack actually historically took place in autumn, *æt hærfest*). Conversation of Ælfwine and Eadwine. Eadwine is sick of it. He says the Danes have more sense; always pressing on. They go *west*. They pass round and go to Ireland; while the English sit like *Wealas* waiting to be made into slaves.

Eadwine says he has heard strange tales from Ireland. A land in the North-west filled with ice, but fit for men to dwell – holy hermits have been driven out by Norsemen. Ælfwine has Christian objections. Eadwine says the holy Brendan did so centuries ago – and lots of others, [as] Maelduin. And they came back – not that he would want to. *Insula Deliciarum* – even Paradise.

Ælfwine objects that Paradise cannot be got to by ship – there are deeper waters between us than Garsecg. *Roads are bent*: you come back in the end. No escape by ship.

Eadwine says he does not think it true – and hopes it isn't. At any rate their ancestors had won new lands by ship. Quotes story of *Sceaf*.

In the end they go off with ten neighbours. Pursued by Vikings off Lundy. Wind takes them out to sea, and persists. Eadwine falls sick and says odd things. Ælfwine dreams too. Mountainous seas.

The Straight Road . . . . . water (island of Azores?) . . . . . off. Ælfwine [?restores ?restrains] Eadwine. Thinks it a vision of delirium. The vision of Eressëa and the sound of voices. Resigns himself to die but prays for Eadwine. Sensation of falling. They come down in [?real] sea and west wind blows them back. Land in Ireland (implication is they *settle* there, and this leads to Finntan).

I add some notes on this far-ranging outline. Edward the Elder, eldest son of King Alfred, reigned from 900 to 924. In the year 914 a large Viking fleet, coming from Brittany, appeared in the Bristol Channel, and began ravaging in the lands beyond the Severn. According to the *Anglo-Saxon Chronicle* the leaders were two *jarls* ('earls') named Ohtor and Hroald. The Danes were defeated at Archenfield (Old English *Ircingafeld*) in Herefordshire and forced to give hostages in pledge of their departure. King Edward was in arms with the forces of Wessex on the south side of the Severn estuary, 'so that', in the words of the *Chronicle*, 'they did not dare to attack the land anywhere on that side. Nonetheless they twice stole inland by night, on one occasion east of Watchet and on the other at Porlock (*æt oþrum cierre be eastan Wæced, and æt oþrum cierre æt Portlocan*). Each time they were attacked and only those escaped who swam out to the ships; and after that they were out on the island of Steepholme, until they had scarcely any food, and many died of hunger. From there they went to Dyfed [South Wales] and

from there to Ireland; and that was in the autumn (*and þis wæs on hærfest*).'
Porlock and Watchet are on the north coast of Somerset; the island of Steepholme lies to the North-east, in the mouth of the Severn. My father retained this historical mise-en-scène in the draft of a brief 'Ælfwine' narrative given below, pp. 83–4, and years later in *The Notion Club Papers* (1945).

*Wealas*: the British (as distinct from the English or Anglo-Saxons); in Modern English *Wales*, the name of the people having become the name of the land.

'A land in the North-west filled with ice, but fit for men to dwell – holy hermits have been driven out by Norsemen.' It is certain that by the end of the eighth century (and how much earlier cannot be said) Irish voyagers had reached Iceland, in astounding journeys achieved in their boats called *curachs*, made of hides over a wooden frame. This is known from the work of an Irish monk named Dicuil, who in his book *Liber de Mensura Orbis Terrae* (written in 825) recorded that

It is now thirty years since certain priests who lived in that island from the first day of February to the first day of August told me that not only at the summer solstice, but also in the days before and after, the setting sun at evening hides itself as if behind a little hill, so that it does not grow dark even for the shortest period of time, but whatever task a man wishes to perform, even picking the lice out of his shirt, he can do it just as if it were broad daylight.

When the first Norsemen came to Iceland (about 860) there were Irish hermits living there. This is recorded by the Icelandic historian Ari the Learned (1067–1148), who wrote:

At that time Christian men whom the Norsemen call *papar* dwelt here; but afterwards they went away, because they would not live here together with heathen men, and they left behind them Irish books, bells, and croziers; from which it could be seen that they were Irishmen.

Many places in the south of Iceland, such as Papafjörðr and the island of Papey, still bear names derived from the Irish *papar*. But nothing is known of their fate: they fled, and they left behind their precious things.

*Brendan; Maelduin; Insula Deliciarum.* The conception of a 'blessed land' or 'fortunate isles' in the Western Ocean is a prominent feature of the old Irish legends: *Tir-nan-Og*, the land of youth; *Hy Bresail*, the fortunate isle; *Insula Deliciosa*; etc. *Tir-nan-Og* is mentioned as a possible story for *The Lost Road*, p. 77.

*The holy Brendan* is Saint Brendan called the Navigator, founder of the Abbey of Clonfert in Galway, and the subject of the most famous of the tales of seavoyaging (*imrama*) told of early Irish saints. Another is the *Imram Maelduin*, in which Maelduin and his companions set out from Ireland in a *curach* and came in their voyaging to many islands in succession, where they encountered marvel upon marvel, as did Saint Brendan.

My father's poem *Imram*, in which Saint Brendan at the end of his life recalls the three things that he remembers from his voyage, was published in 1955, but it originally formed a part of *The Notion Club Papers*. Many years before, he had written a poem (*The Nameless Land*) on the subject of a paradisal country 'beyond the Shadowy Sea', in which Brendan is named. This poem and its later forms are given in a note at the end of this chapter, pp. 98 ff.; to the final version is attached a prose note on Ælfwine's voyage that relates closely to the end of the present outline.

*Garsecg:* the Ocean. See II. 312 and note 19; also the Index to Vol. IV, entry *Belegar*.

*Sceaf:* see pp. 7, 78, and 85 ff.

*Lundy:* an island off the west coast of Devon.

It is unfortunate that the last part of this outline is so illegible. The words following 'The Straight Road' could be interpreted as 'a world like water'. After the mysterious reference to the Azores the first word is a noun or name in the plural, and is perhaps followed by 'driven'.

*Finntan:* An isolated note elsewhere among these papers reads: 'See Lit. Celt. p. 137. Oldest man in the world *Finntan* (*Narkil* White Fire).' The reference turns out to be to a work entitled *The Literature of the Celts*, by Magnus Maclean (1906). In the passage to which my father referred the author wrote of the history of Ireland according to mediaeval Irish annalists:

Forty days before the Flood, the Lady Cæsair, niece or granddaughter of Noah – it is immaterial which – with fifty girls and three men came to Ireland. This, we are to understand, was the first invasion or conquest of that country. All these were drowned in the Deluge, except Finntan, the husband of the lady, who escaped by being cast into a deep sleep, in which he continued for a year, and when he awoke he found himself in his own house at Dun Tulcha. . . . At Dun Tulcha he lived throughout many dynasties down to the sixth century of our era, when he appears for the last time with eighteen companies of his descendants engaged in settling a boundary dispute. Being the oldest man in the world, he was *ipso facto* the best informed regarding ancient landmarks.

After the Flood various peoples in succession stepped onto the platform of Irish history. First the Partholans, then the Nemedians, Firbolgs, Tuatha de Danaan, and last of all the Milesians, thus carrying the chronology down to the time of Christ. From the arrival of the earliest of these settlers, the Fomorians or 'Sea Rovers' are represented as fighting and harassing the people. Sometimes in conjunction with the plague, at other times with the Firbolgs and Gaileoin and Fir-Domnann, they laid waste the land. The Partholans and Nemedians were early disposed of. And then appeared from the north of Europe, or from heaven, as one author says, the Tuatha de Danann, who at the great battle of Moytura South overcame the Firbolgs, scattering them to the islands of Aran, Islay, Rathlin, and the Hebrides, and afterwards defeating the Fomorians at Moytura North, thus gaining full possession of the land.

The Tuatha de Danann are twice mentioned (pp. 77–8) as a possible narrative element in *The Lost Road*.

The only actual narrative concerning Ælfwine from this time (apart from some beginnings abandoned after a few lines) is brief and roughly scrawled; but it was to be used afterwards, and in places quite closely followed, in *The Notion Club Papers*.

Ælfwine awoke with a start – he had been dozing on a bench with his back to a pillar. The voices poured in on him like a torrent. He felt he had been dreaming; and for a moment the English speech about him sounded strange, though mostly it was the soft speech of western Wessex. Here and there were men of the Marches, and a few spoke oddly, using strange words after the manner of those among whom the Danes dwelt in the eastern lands. He looked down the hall, looking for his son Eadwine. He was due on leave from the fleet, but had not yet come.

There was a great crowd in the hall, for King Edward was here. The fleet was in the Severn sea, and the south shore was in arms. The jarls had been defeated far north at Irchenfield, but the Danish ships were still at large on the Welsh coast; and the men of Somerset and Devon were on guard.

Ælfwine looked down the hall. The faces of the men, some old and careworn, some young and eager, were dim, not only because the torchlight was wavering and the candles on the high table were guttering. He looked beyond them. There was a wind blowing, surging round the house; timbers creaked. The sound brought back old longings to him that he had thought were long buried. He was born in the year the Danes wintered in Sheppey, and he had sailed many seas and heard many winds since then. The sound of the west wind and the fall of seas on the beaches had always been a challenging music to him. Especially in spring. But now it was autumn, and also he was growing old. And the seas were wide, beyond the power of man to cross – to unknown shores: wide and dangerous. The faces of the men about him faded and the clamour of their voices was changed. He heard the crash of waves on the black cliffs and the sea-birds diving and crying; and snow and hail fell. Then the seas opened pale and wide; the sun shone on the land and the sound and smell of it fell far behind. He was alone going west towards the setting sun with fear and longing in his heart, drawn against his will.

His dream was broken by calls for the minstrel. 'Let Ælfwine sing!' men were crying. The king had sent to bid him sing something. He lifted up his voice and chanted aloud, but as one speaking to himself alone:

> Monað modes lust mid mereflode
> forð to feran, þæt ic feor heonan
> ofer hean holmas, ofer hwæles eðel
> elþeodigra eard gesece.
> Nis me to hearpan hyge ne to hringþege
> ne to wife wyn ne to worulde hyht
> ne ymb owiht elles nefne ymb yða gewealc.

'The desire of my spirit urges me to journey forth over the flowing sea, that far hence across the hills of water and the whale's country I may seek the land of strangers. No mind have I for harp, nor gift of ring, nor delight in women, nor joy in the world, nor concern with aught else save the rolling of the waves.'

Then he stopped suddenly. There was some laughter, and a few jeers, though many were silent, as if feeling that the words were not spoken to their ears – old and familiar as they were, words of the old poets whom most men had heard often. 'If he has no mind to the harp he need expect no [?wages],' said one. 'Is there a mortal here who has a mind?' 'We have had enough of the sea,' said another. 'A spell of Dane-hunting would cure most men's love of it.' 'Let him go rolling on the waves,' said another. 'It is no great sail to the . . . Welsh country, where folk are strange enough – and the Danes to talk to as well.'

'Peace!' said an old man sitting near the threshold. 'Ælfwine has sailed more seas than you have heard of; and the Welsh tongue is not strange to him . . . . . His wife was of Cornwall. He has been to Ireland and the North, and some say far to the west of all living lands. Let him say what his mood bids.' There was a short silence.

The text ends here. The historical situation is slightly filled out, with mention of the Viking *jarls* and their defeat at *Irchenfield* (Archenfield), on which see p. 80. Ælfwine 'was born in the year the Danes wintered in Sheppey' (the isle of Sheppey off the north coast of Kent). The *Anglo-Saxon Chronicle* records under the year 855: *Her hæþne men ærest on Sceapige ofer winter sætun* (In this year heathen men for the first time stayed in Sheppey ['Sheep-isle'] over the winter); but an earlier wintering on Thanet is recorded under 851. These winterings by Vikings were ominous of what was to come, a sign of the transition from isolated raids followed by a quick departure to the great invasions in the time of Æthelred and Alfred. – Ælfwine was therefore approaching sixty at this time.

The verses that Ælfwine chanted are derived from the Old English poem known as *The Seafarer*, with the omission of five lines from the original after line 4, and some alterations of wording. The third line is an addition (and is enclosed, both in the Old English and in the translation, in square brackets in the manuscript).

With the reference to Ælfwine's wife who came from Cornwall cf. the old tale of *Ælfwine of England*, where his mother came 'from the West, from Lionesse' (II. 313).

It seems to me certain that what was to follow immediately on the end of this brief narrative was the legend of *King Sheave*, which in one of the three texts is put into Ælfwine's mouth (and which follows here in *The Notion Club Papers*, though it is not there given to Ælfwine). There is both a prose and a verse form of *King Sheave*; and it may well be that the prose version, which I give first, belongs very closely with the Ælfwine narrative; there is no actual link between them, but the two manuscripts are very similar.

To the shore the ship came and strode upon the sand, grinding upon the broken shingle. In the twilight as the sun sank men came down to it, and looked within. A boy lay there, asleep. He was fair of face and limb, dark-haired, white-skinned, but clad in gold. The inner parts of the boat were gold-adorned, a vessel of gold filled with clear water was at his side, [*added*: at his right was a harp,] beneath his head was a sheaf of corn, the stalks and ears of which gleamed like gold in the dusk. Men knew not what it was. In wonder they drew the boat high upon the beach, and lifted the boy and bore him up, and laid him sleeping in a wooden house in their burh. They set guards about the door.

In the morning the chamber was empty. But upon a high rock men saw the boy standing. The sheaf was in his arms. As the risen sun shone down, he began to sing in a strange tongue, and they were filled with awe. For they had not yet heard singing, nor seen such beauty. And they had no king among them, for their kings had perished, and they were lordless and unguided. Therefore they took the boy to be king, and they called him *Sheaf*; and so is his name remembered in song. For his true name was hidden and is forgotten. Yet he taught men many new words, and their speech was enriched. Song and verse-craft he taught them, and rune-craft, and tillage and husbandry, and the making of many things; and in his time the dark forests receded and there was plenty, and

corn grew in the land; and the carven houses of men were filled
with gold and storied webs. The glory of King Sheaf sprang far
and wide in the isles of the North. His children were many and
fair, and it is sung that of them are come the kings of men of the
North Danes and the West Danes, the South Angles and the East
Gothfolk. And in the time of the Sheaf-lords there was peace in
the isles, and ships went unarmed from land to land bearing
treasure and rich merchandise. And a man might cast a golden
ring upon the highway and it would remain until he took it up
again.

Those days songs have called the golden years, while the great
mill of Sheaf was guarded still in the island sanctuary of the
North; and from the mill came golden grain, and there was no
want in all the realms.

But it came to pass after long years that Sheaf summoned his
friends and counsellors, and he told them that he would depart.
For the shadow of old age was fallen upon him (out of the East)
and he would return whence he came. Then there was great
mourning. But Sheaf laid him upon his golden bed, and became as
one in deep slumber; and his lords obeying his commands while
he yet ruled and had command of speech set him in a ship. He lay
beside the mast, which was tall, and the sails were golden.
Treasures of gold and of gems and fine raiment and costly stuffs
were laid beside him. His golden banner flew above his head. In
this manner he was arrayed more richly than when he came among
them; and they thrust him forth to sea, and the sea took him, and
the ship bore him unsteered far away into the uttermost West out
of the sight or thought of men. Nor do any know who received him
in what haven at the end of his journey. Some have said that that
ship found the Straight Road. But none of the children of Sheaf
went that way, and many in the beginning lived to a great age, but
coming under the shadow of the East they were laid in great tombs
of stone or in mounds like green hills; and most of these were by
the western sea, high and broad upon the shoulders of the land,
whence men can descry them that steer their ships amid the
shadows of the sea.

This is a first draft, written at speed and very roughly; but the form in
alliterative verse is very finished, so far as it goes (it does not extend to the
departure of Sheaf, or Sheave, and was not added to for its inclusion in
*The Notion Club Papers*). There are two texts of the verse form: (i) a
clear manuscript in which the poem is written out as prose, and (ii) a
more hasty text in which it is written out in verse-lines. It is hard to

decide which of the two came first, but the poem is in any case almost identical in the two versions, which were obviously closely contemporary. I print it here in lines, with breaks introduced from the paragraphs of the 'prose' form. Version (i) has a formal title, *King Sheave*; (ii) has a short narrative opening, which could very well follow the words 'There was a short silence' on p. 84.

Suddenly Ælfwine struck a note on his harp. 'Lo!' he cried, loud and clear, and men stiffened to attention. 'Lo!' he cried, and began to chant an ancient tale, yet he was half aware that he was telling it afresh, adding and altering words, not so much by improvisation as after long pondering hidden from himself, catching at the shreds of dreams and visions.

> In days of yore out of deep Ocean
> to the Longobards, in the land dwelling
> that of old they held amid the isles of the North,
> a ship came sailing, shining-timbered
> without oar and mast, eastward floating.
> The sun behind it sinking westward
> with flame kindled the fallow water.
> Wind was wakened.   Over the world's margin
> clouds greyhelméd climbed slowly up
> wings unfolding wide and looming,                              10
> as mighty eagles moving onward
> to eastern Earth omen bearing.
> Men there marvelled, in the mist standing
> of the dark islands in the deeps of time:
> laughter they knew not, light nor wisdom;
> shadow was upon them, and sheer mountains
> stalked behind them stern and lifeless,
> evilhaunted.   The East was dark.
>
> The ship came shining to the shore driven
> and strode upon the strand, till its stem rested       20
> on sand and shingle.   The sun went down.
> The clouds overcame the cold heavens.
> In fear and wonder to the fallow water
> sadhearted men swiftly hastened
> to the broken beaches the boat seeking,
> gleaming-timbered in the grey twilight.
> They looked within, and there laid sleeping
> a boy they saw breathing softly:
> his face was fair, his form lovely,

his limbs were white, his locks raven                    30
golden-braided.   Gilt and carven
with wondrous work was the wood about him.
In golden vessel gleaming water
stood beside him; strung with silver
a harp of gold neath his hand rested;
his sleeping head was soft pillowed
on a sheaf of corn shimmering palely
as the fallow gold doth from far countries
west of Angol.   Wonder filled them.

The boat they hauled and on the beach moored it          40
high above the breakers; then with hands lifted
from the bosom its burden.   The boy slumbered.
On his bed they bore him to their bleak dwellings
darkwalled and drear in a dim region
between waste and sea.   There of wood builded
high above the houses was a hall standing
forlorn and empty.   Long had it stood so,
no noise knowing, night nor morning,
no light seeing.   They laid him there,
under lock left him lonely sleeping                       50
in the hollow darkness.   They held the doors.
Night wore away.   New awakened
as ever on earth early morning;
day came dimly.   Doors were opened.
Men strode within, then amazed halted;
fear and wonder filled the watchmen.
The house was bare, hall deserted;
no form found they on the floor lying,
but by bed forsaken the bright vessel
dry and empty in the dust standing.                      60

The guest was gone.   Grief o'ercame them.
In sorrow they sought him, till the sun rising
over the hills of heaven to the homes of men
light came bearing.   They looked upward
and high upon a hill hoar and treeless
the guest beheld they: gold was shining
in his hair, in hand the harp he bore;
at his feet they saw the fallow-golden
cornsheaf lying.   Then clear his voice
a song began, sweet, unearthly,                          70

words in music woven strangely,
in tongue unknown.  Trees stood silent
and men unmoving marvelling hearkened.

Middle-earth had known for many ages
neither song nor singer; no sight so fair
had eyes of mortal, since the earth was young,
seen when waking in that sad country
long forsaken.  No lord they had,
no king nor counsel, but the cold terror
that dwelt in the desert, the dark shadow                    80
that haunted the hills and the hoar forest.
Dread was their master.  Dark and silent,
long years forlorn, lonely waited
the hall of kings, house forsaken
without fire or food.

           Forth men hastened
from their dim houses.  Doors were opened
and gates unbarred.  Gladness wakened.
To the hill they thronged, and their heads lifting
on the guest they gazed.  Greybearded men
bowed before him and blessed his coming                      90
their years to heal; youths and maidens,
wives and children welcome gave him.
His song was ended.  Silent standing
he looked upon them.  Lord they called him;
king they made him, crowned with golden
wheaten garland, white his raiment,
his harp his sceptre.  In his house was fire,
food and wisdom; there fear came not.
To manhood he grew, might and wisdom.

Sheave they called him, whom the ship brought them,    100
a name renowned in the North countries
ever since in song.  For a secret hidden
his true name was, in tongue unknown
of far countries where the falling seas
wash western shores beyond the ways of men
since the world worsened.  The word is forgotten
and the name perished.

           Their need he healed,
and laws renewed long forsaken.

Words he taught them wise and lovely –
their tongue ripened in the time of Sheave          110
to song and music.   Secrets he opened
runes revealing.   Riches he gave them,
reward of labour, wealth and comfort
from the earth calling, acres ploughing,
sowing in season seed of plenty,
hoarding in garner golden harvest
for the help of men.   The hoar forests
in his days drew back to the dark mountains;
the shadow receded, and shining corn,
white ears of wheat, whispered in the breezes          120
where waste had been.   The woods trembled.

Halls and houses hewn of timber,
strong towers of stone steep and lofty,
golden-gabled, in his guarded city
they raised and roofed.   In his royal dwelling
of wood well-carven the walls were wrought;
fair-hued figures filled with silver,
gold and scarlet, gleaming hung there,
stories boding of strange countries,
were one wise in wit the woven legends          130
to thread with thought.   At his throne men found
counsel and comfort and care's healing,
justice in judgement.   Generous-handed
his gifts he gave.   Glory was uplifted.
Far sprang his fame over fallow water,
through Northern lands the renown echoed
of the shining king, Sheave the mighty.

At the end of (ii) occur eight lines which seem to have been added to the
text; they were also inserted in pencil to the 'prose' text (i), here written
in as verse-lines, with a further eight lines following (the whole passage of
sixteen lines was struck through, but it was used afterwards in *The
Notion Club Papers*, in the form of an addition to the poem proper).

Seven sons he begat, sires of princes,
men great in mind, mighty-handed
and high-hearted.   From his house cometh          140
the seeds of kings, as songs tell us,
fathers of the fathers, who before the change
in the Elder Years the earth governed,
Northern kingdoms named and founded,

shields of their peoples: Sheave begat them:
Sea-danes and Goths, Swedes and Northmen,
Franks and Frisians, folk of the islands,
Swordmen and Saxons, Swabes and English,
and the Langobards who long ago
beyond Myrcwudu a mighty realm                        150
and wealth won them in the Welsh countries
where Ælfwine Eadwine's heir
in Italy was king.    All that has passed.

## Notes on King Sheave

References in the following notes are given to the lines of the poem.

1–3    On the association of Sheave with the Longobards (Lombards)
        see p. 93.

7        The word *fallow* ('golden, golden-brown') is used several times
        in this poem of water, and once of gold (38); the corn sheaf is
        fallow-golden (68). See III. 369.

8–12    The 'eagle-clouds' that precede Sheave's coming in the poem
        do not appear in the prose version.

39       *Angol*: the ancient home of the English before their migration
        across the North Sea. See I. 24, 252 (entry *Eriol*).

142–3   I am at a loss to say what is referred to in these lines, where the
        'fathers of the fathers' who founded kingdoms in the North, the
        descendants of Sheave, 'governed the earth *before the change
        in the Elder Years*'.

148      *Swordmen*: it is evident that this is intended as the name of a
        people, but it is not clear to me which people. Conceivably, my
        father had in mind the *Brondingas*, ruled by Breca, Beowulf's
        opponent in the swimming-match, for that name has been
        interpreted to contain the word *brond* (*brand*) 'sword'.
        *Swabes*: this reading seems clear (*Swabians* in *The Notion
        Club Papers*). The Old English form was *Swæfe*: thus in
        *Widsith* is found *Engle ond Swæfe*, and *Mid Englum ic wæs
        ond mid Swæfum*. The *Suevi* of Roman historians, a term used
        broadly to cover many Germanic tribes, but here evidently
        used as in *Widsith* to refer particularly to Swabians dwelling in
        the North and neighbours of the Angles.

150      *Myrcwudu* (Old English): 'Mirkwood'. This was an ancient
        Germanic legendary name for a great dark boundary-forest,
        found in various quite different applications. The reference
        here is to the Eastern Alps (see note to line 151).

151      *Welsh*: 'foreign' (Roman). My father used the word here in the
        ancient sense. The old Germanic word *walhoz* meant 'Celtic or
        Roman foreigner'; whence in the plural the Old English *Walas*

(modern *Wales*), the Celts of Britain. So in *Widsith* the Romans are called *Rūm-walas*, and Caesar ruled over the towns and riches of *Wala rice*, the realm of the *Walas*. A line in *King Sheave* rejected in favour of 150–1 reads *Wide realms won them beyond the Welsh Mountains*, and these are the Alps. The ancient meaning survives in the word *walnut*, 'nut of the Roman lands'; also in *Wallace, Walloon*.

152–3    See pp. 54–5.

The roots of *King Sheave* lie far back in Northern Germanic legend. There are three primary sources: *Beowulf*, and the statements of two later chroniclers writing in Latin, Æthelweard (who died about the year 1000), and William of Malmesbury (who died in 1143). I give those of the historians first.

In Æthelweard's Chronicle the genealogy of the English kings ends with the names *Beo – Scyld – Scef* (which mean Barley, Shield, and Sheaf; Old English *sc* = 'sh'); and of *Scef* he says:

This Scef came in a swift boat, surrounded by arms, to an island of the ocean called Scani, and he was a very young boy, and unknown to the people of that country; but he was taken up by them, and they watched over him attentively as one of their own kin, and afterwards chose him to be their king.

William of Malmesbury (a writer notable for his drawing on popular stories and songs) has likewise in his genealogy the three figures *Beowius – Sceldius – Sceaf*, and he tells this of *Sceaf*:

He, as they say, was brought as a child in a boat without any oarsman to Scandza, a certain island of Germany.... He was asleep, and by his head was placed a handful of corn, on which account he was called 'Sheaf'. He was regarded as a marvel by the people of that country, and carefully fostered; when he was grown he ruled in the town which was then called Slaswic, but now Haithebi. That region is called Old Anglia, whence the Angli came to Britain.

The prologue, or as my father called it the *exordium*, to *Beowulf*, I give from his prose translation of the poem.

Lo! the glory of the kings of the people of the Spear-Danes in days of old we have heard tell, how those princes deeds of valour wrought. Oft Scyld Scefing robbed the hosts of foemen, many peoples of the seats where they drank their mead, laid fear upon men, who first was found in poverty; comfort for that he lived to know, mighty grew under heaven, throve in honour, until all that dwelt nigh about over the sea where the whale rides must hearken to him and yield him tribute – a good king was he!

To him was an heir afterwards born, a young child in his courts whom God sent for the comfort of the people: perceiving the dire need which they long while endured aforetime being without a prince. To him therefore the Lord of Life who rules in glory granted honour among men: Beowulf was renowned, far and wide his glory sprang – the heir of Scyld in Scedeland. Thus doth a young man bring it to pass with good deed and gallant gifts, while he dwells in his father's bosom, that after in his age there cleave to him loyal knights of his table, and the people stand by him when war shall come. By worthy deeds in every folk is a man ennobled.

Then at his allotted hour Scyld the valiant passed into the keeping of the Lord; and to the flowing sea his dear comrades bore him, even as he himself had bidden them while yet their prince he ruled them with his words – beloved lord of the land, long was he master. There at the haven stood with ringéd prow, ice-hung, eager to be gone, the prince's bark; they laid then their beloved king, giver of rings, in the bosom of the ship, in glory by the mast. There were many precious things and treasures brought from regions far away; nor have I heard tell that men ever in more seemly wise arrayed a boat with weapons of war and harness of battle; on his lap lay treasures heaped that now must go with him far into the dominion of the sea. With lesser gifts no whit did they adorn him, with treasures of that people, than did those that in the beginning sent him forth alone over the waves, a little child. Moreover, high above his head they set a golden standard and gave him to Ocean, let the sea bear him. Sad was their heart and mourning in their soul. None can report with truth, nor lords in their halls, nor mighty men beneath the sky, who received that load.

There is also a reference to a king named Sheaf (*Sceafa*) in *Widsith*, where in a list of rulers and the peoples they ruled occurs *Sceafa [weold] Longbeardum*, 'Sheaf ruled the Lombards'; at the beginning of the poem *King Sheave* it is to the Lombards that the boat bearing the child comes.

This is obviously not the place to enter into elaborate discussion of so intricate a subject as that of *Scyld Scefing*: 'a most astonishing tangle', my father called it. His lectures at Oxford during these years devote many pages to refined analysis of the evidences, and of competing theories concerning them. The long-fought argument concerning the meaning of 'Shield Sheafing' in *Beowulf* – does 'Sheafing' mean 'with a sheaf' or 'son of Sheaf', and is 'Shield' or 'Sheaf' the original ancestor king? – could in my father's opinion be settled with some certainty. In a summarising statement of his views in another lecture (here very slightly edited) he said:

*Scyld* is the eponymous ancestor of the *Scyldingas*, the Danish royal house to which Hrothgar King of the Danes in this poem belongs. His name is simply 'Shield': and he is a 'fiction', that is a name derived from the 'heraldic' family name *Scyldingas* after they became famous. This process was aided by the fact that the Old English (and Germanic) ending *-ing*, which could mean 'connected with, associated with, provided with', etc., was also the usual patronymic ending. The

invention of this eponymous 'Shield' was probably Danish, that is
actually the work of Danish dynastic historians (*þylas*) and alliterative
poets (*scopas*) in the lifetime of the kings of whom we hear in *Beowulf*,
the certainly historical Healfdene and Hrothgar.

As for *Scēfing*, it can thus, as we see, mean 'provided with a sheaf,
connected in some way with a sheaf of corn', or son of a figure called
Sheaf. In favour of the latter is the fact that there *are* English
traditions of a *mythical* (not the same as eponymous and fictitious)
ancestor called *Sceaf*, or *Sceafa*, belonging to ancient culture-myths
of the North; and of his special association with Danes. In favour of
the former is the fact that Scyld comes out of the unknown, a babe, and
the name of his father, if he had any, could not be known by him or the
Danes who received him. But such poetic matters are not strictly
logical. Only in *Beowulf* are the two divergent traditions about the
Danes blended in this way, the heraldic and the mythical. I think the
poet meant (Shield) Sheafing as a patronymic. He was blending the
vague and fictitious warlike glory of the eponymous ancestor of the
conquering house with the more mysterious, far older and more
poetical myths of the mysterious arrival of the babe, the corn-god or
the culture-hero his descendant, at the beginning of a people's history,
and adding to it a mysterious Arthurian departure, *back into the
unknown*, enriched by traditions of ship-burials in the not very remote
heathen past – to make a magnificent and suggestive *exordium*, and
background to his tale.

*Beowulf*, son of Scyld Scefing, who appears in the *exordium* (to every
reader's initial confusion, since he is wholly unconnected with the hero of
the poem) my father held to be a corruption of *Beow* ('Barley') – which is
the name found in the genealogies (p. 92).

To my mind it is overwhelmingly probable [he wrote] that the *Beowulf*
name properly belongs *only* to the story of the bear-boy (that is of
Beowulf the Geat); and that it is a fairy-tale name, in fact a 'kenning'
for *bear*: 'Bee-wolf', that is 'honey-raider'. Such a name would be very
unlikely to be transferred to the Scylding line by the poet, or at any
time while the stories and legends which are the main fabric of the
poem had any existence independent of it. I believe that *Beow* was
turned into *Beowulf* after the poet's time, in the process of scribal
tradition, either deliberately (and unhappily), or merely casually and
erroneously.

Elsewhere he wrote:

A complete and entirely satisfactory explanation of the peculiarities of
the *exordium* has naturally never been given. Here is what seems to me
the most probable view.

The exordium is poetry, not (in intent) history. It was composed for
its present place, and its main purpose was to glorify Scyld and his
family, and so enhance the background against which the struggle of
Grendel and Beowulf takes place. The choice of a marvellous legend,

rather than a mere dynastic invention, was therefore natural. That our author was working principally on the blended form: *Beow < Scyld < Sceaf* [found in the genealogies, see p. 92] is shown by his retention of the patronymic *Scefing*. This title has indeed little point in his version, and certainly would not have appeared, had he really drawn on a story in which it was *Scyld* that came in a boat; while certain points in his account (the little destitute child) belong clearly to the Sheaf-Barley legends.

Why then did he make *Scyld* the child in the boat? – plainly his own device: it occurs nowhere else. Here are some probable reasons: (a) He was concentrating all the glamour on *Scyld* and the *Scylding* name.

(b)   A departure over sea – a sea-burial – was already associated with northern chieftains in old poems and lore, possibly already with the name of Scyld. This gains much in power and suggestiveness, if the same hero arrives and departs in a boat. The great heights to which Scyld climbed is also emphasized (explicitly) by the contrast thus made with his forlorn arrival.

(c)   Older and even more mysterious traditions may well still have been current concerning Danish origins: the legend of Ing who came and went back over the waves [see II. 305]. Our poet's *Scyld* has (as it were) replaced *Ing*.

Sheaf and Barley were after all in origin only rustic legends of no great splendour. But their legend here catches echoes of heroic traditions of the North going back into a remote past, into what philologists would call Primitive Germanic times, and are at the same time touched with the martial glories of the House of the Shield. In this way the poet contrives to clothe the lords of the golden hall of Hart with a glory and mystery, more archaic and simple but hardly less magnificent than that which adorns the king of Camelot, Arthur son of Uther. This is our poet's way throughout, seen especially in the exaltation among the great heroes that he has achieved for the Bear-boy of the old fairy-tale, who becomes in his poem Beowulf last king of the Geatas.

I give a final quotation from my father's lectures on this subject, where in discussing the concluding lines of the *exordium* he wrote of

the suggestion – it is hardly more; the poet is not explicit, and the idea was probably not fully formed in his mind – that Scyld went back to some mysterious land whence he had come. He came out of the Unknown beyond the Great Sea, and returned into It: a miraculous intrusion into history, which nonetheless left real historical effects: a new Denmark, and the heirs of Scyld in Scedeland. Such must have been his feeling.

In the last lines 'Men can give no certain account of the havens where that ship was unladed' we catch an echo of the 'mood' of pagan times in which ship-burial was practised. A mood in which the *symbolism* (what we should call the *ritual*) of a departure over the sea whose further shore was unknown; and an actual belief in a magical land or otherworld located 'over the sea', can hardly be distinguished – and for neither of these elements or motives is conscious symbolism, or real belief, a true description. It was a *murnende mōd*, filled with doubt and darkness.

There remains to notice an element in my father's legend of Sheaf which was not derived from the English traditions. This is found only in the prose version (p. 86), where in the account of the great peace in the Northern isles in the time of 'the Sheaf-lords' (so deep a peace that a gold ring lying on the highway would be left untouched) he wrote of 'the great mill of Sheaf', which 'was guarded still in the island sanctuary of the North.' In this he was drawing on (and transforming) the Scandinavian traditions concerned with Freyr, the god of fruitfulness, and King Fróthi the Dane.

I cite here the story told by the Icelander Snorri Sturluson (c. 1179–1241) in his work known as the *Prose Edda*, which is given to explain the meaning of the 'kenning' *mjöl Fróða* ('Fróthi's meal') for 'gold'. According to Snorri, Fróthi was the grandson of *Skjöldr* (corresponding to Old English *Scyld*).

Fróthi succeeded to the kingdom after his father, in the time when Augustus Caesar imposed peace on the whole world; in that time Christ was born. But because Fróthi was the mightiest of all kings in the Northlands the peace was named after him wherever the Danish tongue was spoken, and men call it the Peace of Fróthi. No man injured another, even though he met face to face with the slayer of his father or of his brother, free or bound; and there was no thief or robber in those days, so that a gold ring lay long on *Ialangrsheiði* [in Jutland]. King Fróthi went to a feast in Sweden at the court of a king named Fjölnir. There he bought two bondwomen called Fenia and Menia; they were big and strong. At that time there were in Denmark two millstones so huge that no man was strong enough to turn them; and the nature of these stones was such that whatever he who turned them asked for was ground out by the mill. This mill was called Grótti. King Fróthi had the bondwomen led to the mill, and he bade them grind gold; and they did so, and at first they ground gold and peace and happiness for Fróthi. Then he gave them rest or sleep no longer than the cuckoo was silent or a song could be sung. It is said that they sang the song which is called the Lay of Grótti, and this is its beginning:

> Now are come to the king's house
> The two foreknowing ones, Fenia and Menia;
> They are by Fróthi, son of Frithleif,
> The mighty maidens, as bondslaves held.

And before they ended their song they ground out a host against Fróthi, so that on that very night the sea-king named Mýsing came, and slew Fróthi, and took much plunder; and then the Peace of Fróthi was ended.

Elsewhere it is said that while the Danes ascribed the peace to Fróthi the Swedes ascribed it to Freyr; and there are close parallels between them. Freyr (which itself means 'the Lord') was called *inn Fróði*, which almost certainly means 'the Fruitful One'. The legend of the great peace, which in my father's work is ascribed to the time of Sheaf and his sons, goes back to very ancient origins in the worship of a divinity of fruitfulness in the great sanctuaries of the North: that of Freyr the Fruitful Lord at the great temple of Uppsala, and (according to an extremely plausible theory) that on the island of Zealand (Sjælland). Discussion of this would lead too far and into evidences too complex for the purpose of this book, but it may be said at least that it seems beyond question that Heorot, hall of the Danish kings in *Beowulf*, stood where is now the village of Leire, about three miles from the sea on the north coast of Zealand. At Leire there are everywhere huge grave mounds; and according to an eleventh-century chronicler, Thietmar of Merseburg, there was held at Leire in every ninth year (as also at Uppsala) a great gathering, in which large numbers of men and animals were sacrificed. A strong case can be made for supposing that the famous sanctuary described by Tacitus in his *Germania* (written near the end of the first century A.D.) where the goddess Nerthus, or *Mater Terra*, was worshipped 'on an island in the ocean', was indeed on Zealand. When Nerthus was present in her sanctuary it was a season of rejoicing and peace, when 'every weapon is laid aside.'*

In my father's legend of Sheaf these ancient echoes are used in new ways and with new bearings; and when Sheaf departed on his last journey his ship (as some have said) found the Straight Road into the vanished West.

A brief but perceptive report on *The Lost Road*, dated 17 December 1937, was submitted by a person unknown invited by Allen and Unwin to read the text. It is to be remembered that the typescript that had been made extended only to the beginning of the fourth chapter (p. 73 note 14) – and also, of course, that at this time nothing concerning the history of Middle-earth, of the Valar and Valinor, had been published. The reader described it as 'immensely interesting as a revelation of the personal enthusiasms of a very unusual mind', with 'passages of beautiful descriptive prose'; but found it 'difficult to imagine this novel when completed receiving any sort of recognition except in academic circles.' Stanley

---

*In Norse mythology the name of the goddess Nerthus survives in that of the god Njörth, father of Freyr. Njörth was especially associated with ships and the sea; and in very early writing of my father's *Neorth* briefly appears for Ulmo (II. 375, entry *Neorth*).

Unwin, writing to my father on 20 December 1937, said gently that he had no doubt of its being a *succès d'estime*, but while he would 'doubtless want to publish it' when complete, he could not 'hold out any hope of commercial success as an inducement to you to give the finishing of it prior claim upon your time.' He wrote this on the day after my father had written to say that he had finished the first chapter of 'a new story about Hobbits' (see III. 366).

With the entry at this time of the cardinal ideas of the Downfall of Númenor, the World Made Round, and the Straight Road, into the conception of 'Middle-earth', and the thought of a 'time-travel' story in which the very significant figure of the Anglo-Saxon Ælfwine would be both 'extended' into the future, into the twentieth century, and 'extended' also into a many-layered past, my father was envisaging a massive and explicit linking of his own legends with those of many other places and times: all concerned with the stories and the dreams of peoples who dwelt by the coasts of the great Western Sea. All this was set aside during the period of the writing of *The Lord of the Rings*, but not abandoned: for in 1945, before indeed *The Lord of the Rings* was completed, he returned to these themes in the unfinished *Notion Club Papers*. Such as he sketched out for these parts of *The Lost Road* remain, as it seems to me, among the most interesting and instructive of his unfinished works.

*Note on the poem 'The Nameless Land' and its later form*

*The Nameless Land** is written in the form of the mediaeval poem *Pearl*, with both rhyme and alliteration and partial repetition of the last line of one stanza in the beginning of the next. I give it here in the form in which it was published; for *Tir-nan-Og* the typescripts have *Tír na nÓg*.

## THE NAMELESS LAND

There lingering lights do golden lie
    On grass more green than in gardens here,
On trees more tall that touch the sky
    With silver leaves a-swinging clear:
By magic dewed they may not die
    Where fades nor falls the endless year,
Where ageless afternoon goes by
    O'er mead and mound and silent mere.

---

*The Nameless Land* was published in *Realities: an Anthology of Verse*, edited by G. S. Tancred (Leeds, at the Swan Press; London, Gay and Hancock Ltd.; 1927). A note on one of the typescripts states that it was written in May 1924 in the house at Darnley Road, Leeds (Carpenter, *Biography*, p. 107), and was 'inspired by reading *Pearl* for examination purposes'.

There draws no dusk of evening near,
    Where voices move in veiléd choir,
Or shrill in sudden singing clear.
    And the woods are filled with wandering fire.

The wandering fires the woodland fill,
    In glades for ever green they glow,
In dells that immortal dews distill
    And fragrance of all flowers that grow.
There melodies of music spill,
    And falling fountains plash and flow,
And a water white leaps down the hill
    To seek the sea no sail doth know.
Its voices fill the valleys low,
    Where breathing keen on bent and briar
The winds beyond the world's edge blow
    And wake to flame a wandering fire.

That wandering fire hath tongues of flame
    Whose quenchless colours quiver clear
On leaf and land without a name
    No heart may hope to anchor near.
A dreamless dark no stars proclaim,
    A moonless night its marches drear,
A water wide no feet may tame,
    A sea with shores encircled sheer.
A thousand leagues it lies from here,
    And the foam doth flower upon the sea
'Neath cliffs of crystal carven clear
    On shining beaches blowing free.

There blowing free unbraided hair
    Is meshed with light of moon and sun,
And tangled with those tresses fair
    A gold and silver sheen is spun.
There feet do beat and white and bare
    Do lissom limbs in dances run,
Their robes the wind, their raiment air –
    Such loveliness to look upon
Nor Bran nor Brendan ever won,
    Who foam beyond the furthest sea
Did dare, and dipped behind the sun
    On winds unearthly wafted free.

Than Tir-nan-Og more fair and free,
    Than Paradise more faint and far,
O! shore beyond the Shadowy Sea,
    O! land forlorn where lost things are,

O! mountains where no man may be!
The solemn surges on the bar
Beyond the world's edge waft to me;
I dream I see a wayward star,
Than beacon towers in Gondobar
More fair, where faint upon the sky
On hills imagineless and far
The lights of longing flare and die.

My father turned again later to *The Nameless Land*, and altered the title first to *Ælfwine's Song calling upon Eärendel* and then to *The Song of Ælfwine (on seeing the uprising of Eärendel)*. There are many texts, both manuscript and typescript, of *The Song of Ælfwine*, forming a continuous development. That development, I feel certain, did not all belong to the same time, but it seems impossible to relate the different stages to anything external to the poem. On the third text my father wrote afterwards 'Intermediate Version', and I give this here; my guess is – but it is no more than a guess – that it belongs to about the time of *The Lost Road*. Following it are two further texts which each change a few lines, and then a final version with more substantial changes (including the loss of a whole stanza) and an extremely interesting prose note on Ælfwine's voyage. This is certainly relatively late: probably from the years after *The Lord of the Rings*, though it might be associated with the *Notion Club Papers* of 1945 – with the fifth line of the last verse (a line that entered only in this last version) 'The white birds wheel; there flowers the Tree!' compare the lines in the poem *Imram* (see p. 82), of the Tree full of birds that Saint Brendan saw:

The Tree then shook, and flying free
from its limbs the leaves in air
as white birds rose in wheeling flight
and the lifting boughs were bare.

Of course the *imrama* of Brendan and Ælfwine are in any case closely associated. – There follow the texts of the 'intermediate' and final versions.


## THE SONG OF ÆLFWINE

(on seeing the uprising of Eärendel)

There lingering lights still golden lie
on grass more green than in gardens here,
On trees more tall that touch the sky
with swinging leaves of silver clear.
While world endures they will not die,
nor fade nor fall their timeless year,

As morn unmeasured passes by
  o'er mead and mound and shining mere.
When endless eve undimmed is near,
  o'er harp and chant in hidden choir
A sudden voice upsoaring sheer
  in the wood awakes the Wandering Fire.

The Wandering Fire the woodland fills:
  in glades for ever green it glows,
In dells where immortal dew distils
  the Flower that in secret fragrance grows.
There murmuring the music spills,
  as falling fountain plashing flows,
And water white leaps down the hills
  to seek the Sea that no sail knows.
Through gleaming vales it singing goes,
  where breathing keen on bent and briar
The wind beyond the world's end blows
  to living flame the Wandering Fire.

The Wandering Fire with tongues of flame
  with light there kindles quick and clear
The land of long-forgotten name:
  no man may ever anchor near;
No steering star his hope may aim,
  for nether Night its marches drear,
And waters wide no sail may tame,
  with shores encircled dark and sheer.
Uncounted leagues it lies from here,
  and foam there flowers upon the Sea
By cliffs of crystal carven clear
  on shining beaches blowing free.

There blowing free unbraided hair
  is meshed with beams of Moon and Sun,
And twined within those tresses fair
  a gold and silver sheen is spun,
As fleet and white the feet go bare,
  and lissom limbs in dances run,
Shimmering in the shining air:
  such loveliness to look upon
No mortal man hath ever won,
  though foam upon the furthest sea
He dared, or sought behind the Sun
  for winds unearthly flowing free.

O! Shore beyond the Shadowy Sea!
  O! Land where still the Edhil are!

O! Haven where my heart would be!
　the waves that beat upon thy bar
For ever echo endlessly,
　　when longing leads my thought afar,
And rising west of West I see
　　beyond the world the wayward Star,
Than beacons bright in Gondobar
　more clear and keen, more fair and high:
O! Star that shadow may not mar,
　nor ever darkness doom to die!

In the final version of the poem that now follows the prose note concerning Ælfwine's voyage is linked by an asterisk to the name *Ælfwine* in the title.

## THE SONG OF ÆLFWINE
### on seeing the uprising of Eärendil

Eressëa! Eressëa!

There elven-lights still gleaming lie
　On grass more green than in gardens here,
On trees more tall that touch the sky
　With swinging leaves of silver clear.
While world endures they will not die,
　Nor fade nor fall their timeless year,
As morn unmeasured passes by
　O'er mead and mount and shining mere.
When endless eve undimmed is near,
　O'er harp and chant in hidden choir
A sudden voice up-soaring sheer
　In the wood awakes the wandering fire.

With wandering fire the woodlands fill:
　In glades for ever green it glows;
In a dell there dreaming niphredil
　As star awakened gleaming grows,
And ever-murmuring musics spill,
　For there the fount immortal flows:
Its water white leaps down the hill,
　By silver stairs it singing goes
To the field of the unfading rose,
　Where breathing on the glowing briar
The wind beyond the world's end blows
　To living flame the wandering fire.

The wandering fire with quickening flame
　Of living light illumines clear

That land unknown by mortal name
  Beyond the shadow dark and drear
And waters wild no ship may tame.
  No man may ever anchor near,
To haven none his hope may aim
  Through starless night his way to steer.
Uncounted leagues it lies from here:
  In wind on beaches blowing free
Neath cliffs of carven crystal sheer
  The foam there flowers upon the Sea.

O Shore beyond the Shadowy Sea!
  O Land where still the Edhil are!
O Haven where my heart would be!
  The waves still beat upon thy bar,
The white birds wheel; there flowers the Tree!
  Again I glimpse them long afar
When rising west of West I see
  Beyond the world the wayward Star,
Than beacons bright in Gondobar
  More fair and keen, more clear and high.
O Star that shadow may not mar,
  Nor ever darkness doom to die.

Ælfwine (Elf-friend) was a seaman of England of old who, being
driven out to sea from the coast of Erin [*ancient name of Ireland*],
passed into the deep waters of the West, and according to legend by
some strange chance or grace found the 'straight road' of the Elvenfolk
and came at last to the Isle of Eressëa in Elvenhome. Or maybe, as
some say, alone in the waters, hungry and athirst, he fell into a trance
and was granted a vision of that isle as it once had been, ere a West-
wind arose and drove him back to Middle-earth. Of no other man is it
reported that he ever beheld Eressëa the fair. Ælfwine was never again
able to rest for long on land, and sailed the western seas until his death.
Some say that his ship was wrecked upon the west shores of Erin and
there his body lies; others say that at the end of his life he went forth
alone into the deeps again and never returned.

   It is reported that before he set out on his last voyage he spoke these
verses:

> Fela bið on Westwegum werum uncúðra
> wundra and wihta, wlitescýne lond,
> eardgeard Ylfa and Ésa bliss.
> Lýt ænig wát hwylc his longað sý
> þám þe eftsíðes yldu getwæfeð.

'Many things there be in the West-regions unknown to Men, many
wonders and many creatures: a land lovely to behold, the homeland of

the Elves and the bliss of the Valar. Little doth any man understand what the yearning may be of one whom old age cutteth off from returning thither.'

Here reappears the idea seen at the end of the outline for the Ælfwine story in *The Lost Road* (p. 80), that after seeing a vision of Eressëa he was blown back again by a wind from the West. At the time when the outline was written the story that Ælfwine actually came to Tol-eressëa and was there told 'the Lost Tales' was also present (p. 78), and in the same way it seems from the present passage that there were the two stories. The idea that Ælfwine never in fact reached the Lonely Isle is found in a version of the old tale of *Ælfwine of England*, where he did not leap overboard but returned east with his companions (II. 332–3).

The verses that he spoke before his last voyage are those that Alboin Errol spoke and translated to his father in *The Lost Road* (p. 44), and which were used also in the title-pages to the *Quenta Silmarillion* (p. 203).

The retention of the name *Gondobar* right through from *The Nameless Land* is notable. It is found in the late version of the poem *The Happy Mariners*, which my father afterwards dated '1940?' (II. 274–5): 'O happy mariners upon a journey far, / beyond the grey islands and past Gondobar'. Otherwise *Gondobar* 'City of Stone' is one of the Seven Names of Gondolin (II. 158, 172; III. 145–6).

# PART TWO

---

## VALINOR AND MIDDLE-EARTH BEFORE THE LORD OF THE RINGS

# I
# THE TEXTS AND THEIR
# RELATIONS

In the fourth volume of this History were given the *Quenta Noldorinwa*
(**Q**) or History of the Gnomes, which can be ascribed to the year 1930
(IV. 177–8); the earliest *Annals of Beleriand* (**AB**), which followed Q
but is not itself dateable to a year, and the beginning of a new version
(AB II); the earliest *Annals of Valinor* (**AV**), which followed the first
version of AB but preceded the second (IV. 327); and the *Ambarkanta*
or Shape of the World. The *Lay of Leithian*, given in Vol. III, was
abandoned when far advanced in 1931.

I have described in III. 364 ff. how in November 1937 a new though
unfinished version of 'The Silmarillion' was delivered to Allen and
Unwin; while the first draft of the first chapter of *The Lord of the Rings*
was written between 16 and 19 December 1937. Between 1930 and the
end of 1937 must be placed the texts following Q in Vol. IV, and in
addition these others which are given in this book (as well as *The Fall of
Númenor* and *The Lost Road*):

(1) *Ainulindalë*, a new version of the original 'Lost Tale' of *The Music
of the Ainur*. This is certainly later than AV, since in it the First Kindred
of the Elves is named *Lindar*, not *Quendi*, and the old name *Noldoli* has
given place to *Noldor*.

(2) A new version of the *Annals of Valinor*, again with the forms
*Lindar* and *Noldor*. This version I shall call the *Later Annals of Valinor*,
referring to it by the abbreviation **AV 2**, while the earliest version given
in Vol. IV will be **AV 1**.

(3) A new version of the *Annals of Beleriand*, which looks to be a close
companion text to AV 2. This I shall refer to similarly as **AB 2**, the *Later
Annals of Beleriand*. In this case there are two antecedent versions,
mentioned above, and called in Vol. IV AB I and AB II. These, to keep
the parallel with the *Annals of Valinor*, can be referred to collectively as
**AB 1** (since in writing AB 2 my father followed AB II so far as it went and
then followed AB I).

(4) The *Lhammas* or Account of Tongues. This, extant in three
versions, seems to have been closely related to the composition of the
*Quenta Silmarillion*.

(5) The new version of 'The Silmarillion' proper, a once very fine
manuscript whose making was interrupted when the material went to the
publishers. To distinguish this version from its predecessor the *Quenta*

*Noldorinwa* or simply the *Quenta*, I use throughout the abbreviation **QS**, i.e. *Quenta Silmarillion* or History of the Silmarils.

These five works form a later group (though I do not mean to imply that there was any significant gap in time between them and the earlier); a convenient defining mark of this is that they have *Noldor* where the earlier have *Noldoli*.

Although I have said (IV. 262) that there seems no way of showing whether the *Ambarkanta* was earlier or later than the earliest version of the *Annals of Valinor*, it now seems clear to me that the *Ambarkanta* belongs with the later group of texts. This is shown, I think, by the fact that its title-page is closely similar in form to those of the *Ainulindalë* and the *Lhammas* (all three bear the Elvish name of the work in *tengwar*); moreover the reappearance in the *Ambarkanta* of *Utumna* as the name of Melko's original fortress (see IV. 259–60) seems to place it later than AB 2, which still names it *Angband* (but AV 2 has *Utumna*).

On the whole, I would be inclined to place these texts in the sequence AB 2, AV 2, *Lhammas*, QS; the *Ambarkanta* at any rate after AB 2, and the *Ainulindalë* demonstrably before QS. *The Fall of Númenor* was later than the *Ambarkanta* (see p. 9 and IV. 261). But a definitive and demonstrable sequence seems unattainable on the evidence; and the attempt may in any case be somewhat unreal, for my father did not necessarily complete one before beginning another. Certainly he had them all before him, and as he progressed he changed what he had already written to bring it into line with new developments in the stories and in the names.

# II

# THE LATER ANNALS OF VALINOR

The second version of the *Annals of Valinor* (AV 2) is a fluent and legible manuscript in my father's ordinary handwriting of that time, with very little alteration during composition and very few subseqeunt changes in the early period – as opposed to wholesale rewriting of the earlier annals in the time after *The Lord of the Rings*: this being the initial drafting of the major later work, the *Annals of Aman*, and at almost all points clearly distinct from the emendations made many years before.

AV 2 shows no great narrative evolution from AV 1 (IV. 262 ff.), as that text was emended; on the other hand there are some noteworthy developments in names and conceptions. A curious feature is the retention of the original dates between the destruction of the Trees and the rising of the Sun and Moon, which in AV 1 were greatly accelerated by later pencilled changes: see IV. 273–4 and the commentary on annal 2992 below. Thus for example in AV 1 as originally written, and in AV 2, some ten years of the Sun (one Valian Year) elapsed between the Battle of Alqualondë and the utterance of the Prophecy of the North, whereas in AV 1 as emended only one year of the Sun passed between the two events.

In the brief commentary I treat AV 1 as including the emendations to it, fully recorded in IV. 270–4, and discussed in the commentary on that text. Later changes of the early period are recorded in the notes; these are few, mostly aspects of the progressive movement of names, and are merely referred forward to the place where they appear in original writing. Towards the end AV 2 becomes scarcely more than a fair copy of AV 1, but I give the text in full in order to provide within the same covers complete texts of the *Annals* and *Quenta* 'traditions' as they were when *The Lord of the Rings* was begun.

AV 2 is without any preamble concerning authorship, but there is a title-page comprising this and the closely similar later version of the *Annals of Beleriand* (AB 2):

*The Silmarillion*

2  Annals of Valinor

3  Annals of Beleriand

With this compare the title-pages given on p. 202, where 'The Silmarillion' is the comprehensive title of the tripartite (or larger) work.

## SILMARILLION

II

## ANNALS OF VALINOR

Here begin the Annals of Valinor and speak of the foundation of the World.

At the beginning Ilúvatar, that is Allfather, made all things. Afterwards the Valar, or Powers, came into the world. These are nine: Manwë, Ulmo, Aulë, Oromë, Tulkas, Ossë, Mandos, Lórien, and Melko. Of these Manwë and Melko were most puissant, and were brethren; and Manwë is lord of the Valar, and holy. But Melko turned to lust and pride, and to violence and evil, and his name is accursed, and is not uttered, but he is called Morgoth. Oromë, Tulkas, Ossë, and Lórien were younger in the thought of Ilúvatar, ere the world's devising, than the other five; and Oromë was born of Yavanna, who is after named, but he is not Aulë's son.

The queens of the Valar were Varda, Manwë's spouse, and Yavanna, whom Aulë espoused after in the world, in Valinor; Vana the fair was the wife of Oromë; and Nessa the sister of Oromë was Tulkas' wife; and Uinen, the lady of the seas, was wife of Ossë; Vairë the weaver dwelt with Mandos, and Estë the pale with Lórien. No spouse hath Ulmo or Melko. No lord hath Nienna the mournful, queen of shadows, Manwë's sister and Melko's.

With these great ones came many lesser spirits, beings of their own kind but of smaller might; these are the Vanimor, the Beautiful. And with them also were later numbered their children, begotten in the world, but of divine race, who were many and fair; these are the Valarindi.

Of the beginning of the reckoning of Time and the foundation of Valinor.

Time was not measured by the Valar, until the building of Valinor was ended; but thereafter they counted time by the ages of Valinor, whereof each hath 100 years of the Valar, and each Valian year is as ten years of the Sun now are.

**Valian Years 500**    It is said that the Valar came into the world 30,000 Sun-years ere the first rising of the Moon, that is thirty ages ere the beginning of our time; and that Valinor was built five ages after their coming. In the long time before the fortifying of the West, Aulë made great lamps for the lighting of the world and set them upon pillars wrought by Morgoth. But Morgoth was already moved with hatred and jealousy and his pillars were made with deceit. Wherefore the Lamps fell and growth that had begun with the gathering of light was arrested; but the Gods assailed by many waters withdrew into the West. There they began the building of their land and mansions, between the Encircling Sea and the Great Sea of the West, upon whose shore they piled high mountains. But Morgoth departed to the North of the world. The symmetry of earth and water was first broken in those days.

**V.Y.1000**  In this Valian Year, after Valinor was made, and Valmar built, the city of the Gods, the Valar brought into being the Two Trees, Laurelin and Silpion, of gold and silver, whose bloom gave light to Valinor. All this while Morgoth dwelt in Middle-earth, and he made his fortress at Utumna in the North; but he held sway with violence and the lands were yet more broken in that time.

**V.Y.1000–2000**  A thousand Valian Years of bliss and splendour followed the kindling of the Trees in Valinor, but Middle-earth was in darkness. Thither came Yavanna at times, and the slow growth of the forests was begun. Of the Valar only Oromë came ever there, and he hunted in the dark woods of the ancient earth, when he was weary of the shining lands. Morgoth withdrew before his horn.

**V.Y.1900**  Yavanna often reproached the Valar for their neglected stewardship; wherefore on a time Varda began the fashioning of the stars, and she set them aloft. Thereafter the night of the world was beautiful, and some of the Vanimor strayed into Middle-earth. Among these was Melian, whose voice was renowned in Valmar. She was of Lórien's house, but she returned not thither for many years, and the nightingales sang about her in the dark woods of the western lands.

**V.Y.1950**  The mightiest of the works of Varda, lady of the stars, was that constellation which is called by the Elves the Sickle of the Gods, but by Men of the ancient North it was named the Burning Briar, and by later Men it has been given many names beside. This sign of the sickle Varda hung above the North as a threat to Morgoth and an omen of his fall. At its first shining the Elder Children of Ilúvatar awoke in the midmost of Middle-earth. They are the Elves.[1] Hence they are called also the children of the stars.[2]

**V.Y.1980–1990** Oromë found the Elves and befriended them; and the most part of that folk marched under his guidance west and north to the shores of Beleriand, being bidden by the Gods to Valinor. But first Morgoth was overcome with war and bound and led captive and imprisoned under Mandos. In that war of the Gods the lands were rent anew.

**V.Y.2000** From this time was counted the imprisonment of Morgoth. By the doom of Manwë he should be confined in punishment for seven ages, 700 Valian Years, after which time he should be given grace of repentance and atonement.

The Valian Year 2000 from the entry of the Gods into the world, and 1000 from the kindling of the Trees, is accounted the Noontide of the Blessed Realm, and the full season of the mirth of Valinor. In that time all the earth had peace.

In that year the first kindreds of the Elves came to the Western Shore and entered into the light of the Gods. The Eldar are all those Elves called who obeyed the summons of Oromë. Of these there are three kindreds, the Lindar, the Noldor, and the Teleri. The Lindar and the Noldor came first to Valinor, and they built the hill of Kôr in a pass of the mountains nigh to the sea-shore, and upon it upraised the city of Tûn³ and the tower of Ingwë their king.

**V.Y.2000–2010** But the Teleri, who came after them, waited in the meanwhile for ten Valian Years upon the shores of Beleriand, and some never departed thence. Wherefore they were called Ilkorindi, for they came never unto Kôr. Of these most renowned was Tindingol or Thingol,⁴ brother of Elwë, lord of the Teleri. Melian enchanted him in the woods of Beleriand; and he after wedded her and dwelt as a king in the western twilight. But while he slept under the spells of Melian his people sought him in vain, and ere he awoke most of the Teleri had departed. For they were drawn upon an island by Ulmo and so passed the sea as the Lindar and Noldor had done before.

[It is told that a company of the Noldor, whose leader was Dan, forsook the host of Finwë, lord of the Noldor, early upon the westward march, and turned south. But they found the lands barren and dark, and turned again north, and marched west once more with much wandering and grief. Of these some, under Denithor⁵ son of Dan, came at last, about the year of the Valar **2700**, over Eredlindon, and dwelt in Ossiriand, and were allies of

Thingol.[6] This have I, Pengolod, added here, for it was not known unto Rúmil.]

**V.Y.2010–2110** By the deeds of Ossë, as is elsewhere recounted, the Teleri came not at once into Valinor, but during this time dwelt upon Tol-eressëa, the Lonely Isle, in the Great Sea, within sight of Valinor.

**V.Y.2111** In this year the Teleri came in their ships to Valinor, and dwelt upon its eastern strands; and there they made the town and haven of Alqualondë, that is Swanhaven, thus named because they moored there their swans and their swan-shaped boats.[7]

**V.Y.2500** The Noldor had at this time invented gems, and they fashioned them in many myriads. At length, about five ages after the coming of the Noldor to Valinor, Fëanor the Smith, eldest son of Finwë, chief of the Noldor, devised the thrice-renowned Silmarils, about whose fate these tales are woven. They shone of their own light, being filled with the radiance of the Two Trees, the holy light of Valinor, which was blended therein to a marvellous fire.

**V.Y.2700** In this time Morgoth sued for pardon; and at the prayers of Nienna his sister, and by the clemency of Manwë his brother, but against the wish of Tulkas and Aulë and Oromë, he was released; and he feigned humility and repentance, obeisance to the Valar, and love and friendship for the Elves, and dwelt in Valinor in ever-increasing freedom. He lied and dissembled, and most he cozened the Noldor, for he had much to teach, and they had an overmastering desire to learn; but he coveted their gems and lusted for the Silmarils.[8]

**V.Y.2900** During two more ages the bliss of Valinor remained, yet a shadow began to gather in many hearts; for Morgoth was at work with secret whisperings and crooked counsels. Most he prevailed upon the Noldor, and he sowed the seeds of dissension between the proud sons of Finwë, lord of Gnomes, Fëanor, Fingolfin, and Finrod, and distrust was born between Noldor and Valar.

About this time, because of the feuds that began to awake, the Gods held council, and by their doom Fëanor, eldest son of Finwë, and his household and following, were deprived of the leadership of the Gnomes. Wherefore the house of Fëanor was after called the Dispossessed, for this, and because Morgoth later robbed them of their treasure. Finwë and Fëanor departed from the city of Tûn and dwelt in the north of Valinor; but Morgoth hid himself, and appeared only to Fëanor in secret, feigning friendship.

**V.Y.2950**   The Gods heard tidings of Morgoth, and sent to apprehend him, but he fled over the mountains into the shadows of Arvalin, and abode there long, plotting evil, and gathering the strength of darkness unto him.

**V.Y.2990**   Morgoth now completed his designs, and with the aid of Ungoliantë out of Arvalin he stole back into Valinor, and destroyed the Trees. Thence he escaped in the gathering dark northward, and he sacked the dwellings of Finwë and Fëanor, and carried off a host of jewels, and stole the Silmarils. There he slew Finwë before his doors, and many Elves, and defiled thus Valinor and began murder in the world. This reward had Finwë and Fëanor for their friendship.

Morgoth was hunted by the Valar, but he escaped into the North of Middle-earth, and re-established there his strong places, and bred and gathered once more his evil servants, Orcs and Balrogs.

[Then fear came into Beleriand, which for many ages had dwelt in starlit peace. But Thingol with his ally Denithor of Ossiriand for a long while held back the Orcs from the South. But at length Denithor son of Dan was slain, and Thingol made his deep mansions in Menegroth, the Thousand Caves, and Melian wove magic of the Valar about the land of Doriath; and most of the Elves of Beleriand withdrew within its protection, save some that lingered about the western havens, Brithombar and Eglorest beside the Great Sea, and the Green-elves of Ossiriand who dwelt still behind the rivers of the East, wherein the power of Ulmo ran. This have I, Pengolod, added to the words of Rúmil of Valinor.]

**V.Y.2990–3000**   Of the last years before the Hiding of Valinor.

**V.Y.2991**   Valinor lay now in great gloom, and darkness, save only for the stars, fell on all the western world. Then Fëanor, against the will of the Valar, returned to Tûn, and claimed the kingship of the Noldor after Finwë; and he summoned all that people unto Kôr. There Fëanor spoke unto them. Fëanor was the mightiest Gnome of all that have been, wordcrafty and hand-crafty, fair and strong and tall, fiery of mood and thought, hardtempered, undaunted, master of the wills of others. Songs have been made of his deeds that day. His speech was like to flame. Though his heart was hot with hatred for the slayer of his father and the robber of his gems, and he spoke much of vengeance, yet he echoed Morgoth unwitting, and his words were strong with the lies of Morgoth, and rebel[lion] against Manwë. The most part of the Noldor he persuaded that day to follow him out of Valinor and recover their realms on earth, lest they be filched by the Younger Children of Ilúvatar. At that assembly Fëanor and his seven sons swore their dreadful oath to slay or pursue with hate any so ever that held a Silmaril against their will.

**V.Y.2992** The great march of the Gnomes was long preparing. The Gods forbade but did not hinder, for Fëanor had accused them of keeping the Elves captive against their wills. At length the host set out, but under divided leadership, for Fingolfin's house held him for king.

The host had not gone far, ere it came into Fëanor's heart that all these mighty companies, both warriors and others, and great store of goods, would never make the vast leagues unto the North save with the help of ships. Now they went north both because they purposed to come at Morgoth, and because northward the Sundering Seas grew narrow; for Tûn beneath Taniquetil is upon the girdle of the earth, where the Great Sea is measurelessly wide. But the Teleri alone had ships, and they would not give them up, nor lend them, against the will of the Valar.

Thus befell in this year of dread the grievous battle about Alqualondë, and the kinslaying evilly renowned in song, wherein the Noldor distraught furthered Morgoth's work. But the Noldor overcame the Teleri, and took their ships, and fared thence slowly along the rocky coasts in great peril, and amid dissensions. Many marched on foot, and others manned the vessels.

**V.Y.2993** About this time the Noldor came unto a place, nigh unto the northern confines of Valinor, where a high rock stands above the shore, and there stood either Mandos himself or his messenger, and spoke the Doom of Mandos. For the kinslaying he cursed the house of Fëanor, and to a less degree all those who followed them or shared in their enterprise, unless they would return to abide the doom of the Valar. But if they would not, then should evil fortune and disaster befall them, and ever should this come most to pass through treachery of kin towards kin; and their oath should turn against them, hindering rather than aiding the recovery of the jewels. A measure of mortality should visit the Noldor, and they should be slain with weapons, and with torments, and with sorrow, and in the long end they should fade upon Middle-earth and wane before the younger race. Much else he foretold darkly that after befell, and he warned them that the Valar would fence Valinor against their return.

But Fëanor hardened his heart and held on, and with him went still, but reluctantly, Fingolfin's folk, feeling the constraint of their kinship and of the will of Fëanor; they feared also the doom of the Gods, for not all of Fingolfin's people had been guiltless of the kinslaying. Inglor (who was after surnamed Felagund, Lord of Caves) and the other sons of Finrod went forward also; for they had aforetime had great friendship, Inglor with the sons of Fingolfin, and his brothers Orodreth, Angrod, and Egnor with Celegorm and Curufin, sons of Fëanor.[9] But the lords of the house of Finrod were less grim and of kinder mood than the others, and they had no part in the kinslaying; yet they did not escape its curse who now refused to turn back. Finrod himself returned and many of his people with him, and came at last once more unto Valinor and received the pardon of the Gods. But Aulë their ancient friend smiled on them no more, and the Teleri were estranged.

Here endeth that which Rúmil wrote.

Here followeth the continuation of Pengolod.

**V.Y.2994** The Noldor came at length into the bitter North, and further along the land they could not go by ship; for there is a strait between the Westworld, whereon Valinor is built, that curveth eastward, and the coast of Middle-earth, which beareth westward, and through these narrows the chill waters of the Encircling Sea and the waves of the Great Sea flow together, and there are vast mists of deathly cold, and the sea-streams are filled with clashing hills of ice, and the grinding of ice submerged. This strait was named Helkaraksë.

The ships that remained, many having been lost, were too few to carry all across, save with many a passage and return. But none were willing to abide upon the coast, while others sailed away, for trust was not full between the leaders, and quarrel arose between Fëanor and Fingolfin.

Fëanor and his folk seized all the ships and sailed east across the sea, and they took none of the other companies save Orodreth,[10] Angrod, and Egnor, whom Celegorm and Curufin loved. And

Fëanor said: 'Let the murmurers whine their way back to the shadows of Valmar!' And he burned the ships upon the eastern shore, and so great was its fire that the Noldor[11] left behind saw the redness afar off.

**V.Y.2995** In this year of the Valar Fëanor came unto Beleriand and the shores beneath Eredlómin, the Echoing Mountains; and his landing was at the narrow inlet, Drengist, that runs into Dorlómen. The Gnomes came thence into Dorlómen and about the north of the Mountains of Mithrim, and camped in the land of Hithlum in that part that is named Mithrim, and north of the great lake that hath the same name.

In the land of Mithrim they fought the first of the battles of the long war of the Gnomes and Morgoth. For an army of Orcs came forth aroused by the burning of the ships and the rumour of their advance; but the Gnomes were victorious and drove away the Orcs with slaughter, and pursued them beyond Eredwethion into the plain of Bladorion. That battle is the First Battle of Beleriand, and is called Dagor-os-Giliath,[12] the Battle under Stars; for all was yet dark.

But the victory was marred by the fall of Fëanor. He advanced unwarily upon Bladorion, too hot in pursuit, and was surrounded when the Balrogs turned to bay in the rearguard of Morgoth. Very great was the valour of Fëanor, and he was wrapped in fire; but at length he fell mortally wounded by the hand of Gothmog, Lord of Balrogs. But his sons bore him back to Mithrim, and he died there, reminding them of their oath. To this they added now an oath of vengeance for their father.

**V.Y.2996** Maidros, eldest son of Fëanor, was caught in the snares of Morgoth. For Morgoth feigned to treat with him, and Maidros feigned to be willing, and either purposed evil to the other; and each came with force to the parley, but Morgoth with the more, and Maidros was made captive.

Morgoth held Maidros as a hostage, and swore only to release him if the Noldor would march away, either to Valinor if they could, or else from Beleriand and away to the South of the world. But if they would not, he would torment Maidros. But the sons of Fëanor believed not that he would release their brother, if they departed, nor were they willing to depart, whatever he might do.

**V.Y.2997** Morgoth hung Maidros by the right wrist in a band of hellwrought steel above a precipice upon Thangorodrim, where none could reach him.

**V.Y.2998–3000**   Now Fingolfin and Inglor, son of Finrod, won their way at last with grievous losses and with minished might into the North of Middle-earth. This is accounted among the most valiant and desperate of the deeds of the Gnomes; for they came perforce over Helkaraksë, being unwilling to retrace their way to Valinor, and having no ships. But their agony in that crossing was very great, and their hearts were filled with bitterness.

Even as Fingolfin set foot in Middle-earth the First Ages of the World were ended, for they had tarried long in despair upon the shores of the West, and long had been their bitter journey.

The First Ages are reckoned as 30000 years, or 3000 years of the Valar; whereof the first Thousand was before the Trees, and Two thousand save nine were the Years of the Trees or of the Holy Light, which lived after, and lives yet, only in the Silmarils; and the nine are the Years of Darkness, or the Darkening of Valinor.

Towards the end of these nine years, as is elsewhere told, the Gods made the Moon and Sun, and sent them forth over the world, and light came into the Hither Lands. The Moon was the first to go forth.

Men, the Younger Children of Ilúvatar, awoke in the East of the world at the first Sunrise;[13] hence they are also called the Children of the Sun. For the Sun was set as a sign of the waning of the Elves, but the Moon cherisheth their memory.

With the first Moonrise Fingolfin set foot upon the North, for the Moonrise came ere the Dawn, even as Silpion of old bloomed ere Laurelin and was the elder of the Trees.

**Year of the Sun 1**   But the first Dawn shone upon Fingolfin's march, and his blue and silver banners were unfurled, and flowers sprang under his marching feet; for a time of opening and growth, sudden, swift, and fair, was come into the world, and good of evil, as ever happens.

Then Fingolfin marched through the fastness of Morgoth's land, that is Dor Daideloth,[14] the Land of Dread; and the Orcs fled before the new light, amazed, and hid beneath the earth; and the Elves smote upon the gates of Angband, and their trumpets echoed in Thangorodrim's towers.

Now, being wary of the wiles of Morgoth, Fingolfin withdrew from the doors of hell and turned unto Mithrim, so that the Shadowy Mountains, Eredwethion, might be his guard, while his folk rested. But there was little love between Fingolfin's following and the house of Fëanor; and the sons of Fëanor removed and camped upon the southern shore, and the lake lay between the peoples.

From this time are reckoned the Years of the Sun, and these things happened in the first year. Now measured time came into the world, and the growth, changing, and ageing of all things was hereafter more swift, even in Valinor, but most swift in the Hither Lands upon Middle-earth, the mortal regions between the seas of East and West. And all living things spread and multiplied in those days, and the Elves increased, and Beleriand was green and filled with music. There many things afterward came to pass, as is recorded in the *Annals of Beleriand*, and in the *Quenta*, and in other songs and tales.

## NOTES

All the changes to the original text recorded here belong certainly to the 'early period', as distinct from alterations made after the completion of *The Lord of the Rings*.

1 *They are the Elves* > *They are the Quendi or Elves.* See *Lhammas* §1 and commentary.

2 *the children of the stars* > *Eldar, the children of the stars.* See *Lhammas* §2 and commentary.

3 *Tûn* > *Túna* (and in annals 2900 and 2992). See *Lhammas* §5, QS §39, and commentaries.

4 *Tindingol or Thingol* > *Sindo the Grey, later called Thingol.* See *Lhammas* §6 and commentary.

5 *Denithor* > *Denethor* (and in annal 2990). See *Lhammas* §7 and commentary.

6 Added here: *These were the Green-elves*.

7 The words *swans, and their* are a careful addition, probably made at the time of writing; but it seems odd, since my father can hardly have wished to say that the Teleri 'moored' their swans at Alqualondë.

8 Added here, perhaps at the time of composition of the *Annals*: [*Here the Danians came over Eredlindon and dwelt in Ossiriand*.] On the term *Danians* see commentary on *Lhammas* §7.

9 This sentence changed to read: *for they had aforetime had great friendship, Inglor and Orodreth with the sons of Fingolfin, and his brothers Angrod and Egnor with Celegorn and Curufin, sons of Fëanor.* See QS §42 and commentary. – *Celegorm* > *Celegorn* again in annal 2994; see commentary on QS §41.

10 *Orodreth* struck out; see note 9, and QS §73 and commentary.

11 *Noldor* was changed from *Noldoli*: see commentary on annal 2000.

12 *Dagor-os-Giliath* > *Dagor-nuin-Giliath*. See QS §88 and commentary.

13    *Men . . . awoke in the East of the world at the first Sunrise* > *At the
      Sunrise Men . . . awoke in Hildórien in the midmost regions of the
      world.* See QS §82 and commentary.
14    *Dor-Daideloth* > *Dor-Daedeloth.* See QS §91 and commentary.

## Commentary on the Later Annals of Valinor

**Opening section**    The mixture of tenses, already present in AV 1,
becomes now slightly more acute with *Manwë is* for *Manwë was* lord of
the Valar; see p. 208.

The sentence concerning Oromë, Tulkas, Ossë, and Lórien, who were
'younger in the thought of Ilúvatar, ere the world's devising' than the
other five Valar, is not in AV 1, nor is anything similar said in any text of
the *Quenta* tradition (though there does appear in QS §6 the statement
that Mandos was the *elder* and Lórien the *younger* of the Fanturi; cf. also
*The Lost Road* p. 63, where Alkar (Melko) is called 'the *eldest* in the
thought of Ilúvatar'). The statements in AV 2 that 'Aulë espoused
Yavanna after in the world, in Valinor', and that Oromë is Yavanna's son
but not Aulë's, are likewise absent from AV 1 and from the whole *Quenta*
tradition.

Two of the fragments of Ælfwine's Old English translations of the
*Annals* given in Vol. IV bear on this. In the brief version III (IV. 291)
the statement concerning the relative 'youth' of certain of the Valar
appears, but it is confined to Tulkas and Oromë; and there also it is said,
as here, that Aulë and Yavanna became husband and wife (*wurdon to
sinhíwan*) after the Valar entered the world. That this text derives from
the post-*Lord of the Rings* period is suggested but not proved by the form
*Melkor*, not *Melko* (on this point see p. 338, commentary on §30). The
other Old English passage in question, a hastily-written scrap (IV. 293),
has the statement found in AV 2 that Oromë was not Aulë's son, but lacks
that concerning the later union of Yavanna and Aulë.*

The opening of AV 2 was long after extensively changed and rewritten; but one alteration in the present passage looks as if it were made
during the earlier time. The sentence 'and Oromë was born of Yavanna,
who is after named, but he is not Aulë's son' was changed to this notable
statement:

> and Oromë was the offspring of Yavanna, who is after named, but not
> as the Children of the Gods born in this world, for he came of her
> thought ere the world was made.

This is associated with development in the idea of the lesser beings who
came into the world with the Valar, which underwent several changes
(ultimately emerging into the conception of the Maiar). In Q (IV. 78)

---

*The uninterpretable mark following the name Oromë in this passage, which
I explained to mean 'and Tulkas', may in fact be a shorthand for 'Oromë, Tulkas,
Ossë, and Lórien', as in AV 2, with which this Old English fragment evidently
belongs.

these spirits are mentioned but not given any name, and the same remains the case in QS (§2). In AV 1 (IV. 263) a distinction is made between the children of the Valar on the one hand and 'beings of their own kind but of less might' on the other; but all entered the world with the Valar, and all are called *Valarindi*. In AV 2 the distinction is enlarged: the lesser spirits, 'beings of their own kind but of smaller might', who came with the Valar, are the *Vanimor*, 'the Beautiful', and the Children of the Valar, who did not enter the world with them but were *begotten in the world*, are the *Valarindi*; these were 'later numbered with' the *Vanimor*. In the Old English fragment referred to above the same is said, though the name *Valarindi* is not there given to the Children of the Valar (IV. 293).

**Annal 500**   The story (going back to the *Lost Tales*) that Morgoth devised the pillars of the Lamps out of ice is told in the *Ambarkanta* (IV. 238) and indicated in AV 1 (IV. 263: 'Morgoth destroyed *by deceit* the Lamps which Aulë made'). In the other tradition, QS (§11) retains the wording of Q (IV. 80), in which it is only said that Morgoth overthrew the Lamps, and does not suggest the story of his deceit.

**Annal 1000**   On the appearance here of *Utumna*, a reversion to the *Lost Tales*, as the name of Melko's original fortress see p. 108. This is an indication that AV 2 followed AB 2, where (in the opening passage in both texts) *Angband* was retained.

**Annal 1000–2000**   The phrase 'and the slow growth of the forests was begun' is surprising. In S and Q (IV. 12, 82) the primaeval forests already grew in Middle-earth at the time of the downfall of the Lamps, and this is repeated in QS (§18). The present passage seems at variance with that under V.Y.500 ('the Lamps fell and growth that had begun with the gathering of light was arrested'), and to revert to the old story of the *Lost Tales*: cf. the commentary on the tale of *The Chaining of Melko* (I. 111): 'In this earliest narrative there is no mention of the beginning of growth during the time when the Lamps shone, and the first trees and low plants appeared with Yavanna's spells in the twilight after their overthrow.'

**Annal 1900**   This is the first appearance of the idea that the Valar, withdrawn behind their mountain-wall, 'neglected their stewardship' of Middle-earth, and that it was the reproaches of Yavanna that led to Varda's making of the stars. The idea of the two starmakings was not yet present.

For *Vanimor* AV 1 has *Valarindi*: see the commentary on the opening section.

**Annal 2000**   The form *Noldor* for *Noldoli* first occurs in these Annals and in AB 2 (in that for V.Y. 2994 my father still inadvertently wrote *Noldoli* before changing it to *Noldor*); and in the present passage is the first appearance of the name *Lindar* of the First Kindred, replacing earlier *Quendi* of S, Q, and AV 1 (*Lindar* occurs in the earlier texts by emendation at this later time). This change implies also that the application of *Quendi* had shifted, to its final meaning of 'all Elves' (this being in fact a reversion to a nomenclature that appeared briefly long before, I. 234–5); and indeed by an early change to the manuscript (note 1 above) 'They are the Elves' became 'They are the Quendi or Elves'. With this shift went the narrowing of meaning, first found here, of the term *Eldar* to those Elves who obeyed the summons of Oromë (although in the early change given in note 2 *Eldar* seems to be used as a simple equivalent of *Quendi*); see the commentary on *Lhammas* §2.

**Annal 2000–2010**   This is the first indication of a new meaning given to *Ilkorindi*, narrowing it from the old sense of 'Dark-elves' in general (IV. 85) to those of the Teleri who remained in Beleriand; see the commentary on *Lhammas* §2.

The conclusion of the annal is enclosed in square brackets in the manuscript, and this is no doubt original. It closely followed the pencilled addition to AV 1 (IV. 270–1), where it is not however said that this was an addition by Pengolod to Rúmil's work; for the preamble to AV 1 states that the *Annals of Valinor* were written in their entirety by Pengolod. This had now been changed, with Pengolod becoming the continuator of Rúmil's annals. See the commentary on annals 2990 and 2993. – The coming of the 'Danians' over Eredlindon in V.Y.2700 is referred to again in an addition to the annal for that year (note 8).

**Annal 2700**   Oromë is not named in the other texts as opposed to the release of Melko. In Q (IV. 90) and in QS (§48) it was Ulmo and Tulkas who doubted its wisdom; in AV 1 Aulë and Tulkas are named as opposers.

**Annal 2900**   On the evolution of the story of Morgoth's movements at this time see IV. 277–8.

**Annal 2990**   On the probable meaning of the sentence 'This reward had Finwë and Fëanor for their friendship' see IV. 278.

The phrase 'bred and gathered once more his evil servants, Orcs and Balrogs', retained from AV 1, shows the conception still present that the Orcs were first brought into being long before Morgoth's return to Middle-earth, in contrast to the opening of AB 2.

The conclusion of this annal, like that in annal 2000–2010, is enclosed in square brackets in the manuscript, and like the former passage is closely based on (though re-ordered from) interpolations to AV 1 (IV. 271), but with the addition attributing it to Pengolod.

**Annal 2992**   The accusation of Fëanor against the Valar is not in AV 1. – As first written AV 1 has 'Thus about 2992 of Valian Years befell . . .', which was changed to 'Thus in the dread Year of the Valar 2999 (Sun

Year 29991)' (IV. 273). The fact that my father partially adopted the revised phrasing ('the dread Year', 'this year of dread') suggests perhaps that the revised dating in AV 1, greatly accelerating the succession of events, was before him, and he rejected it.

That some went on foot up the coast while others manned the ships is not told in AV 1, but goes back to the *Lost Tales* (see IV. 48).

**Annal 2993**  In the phrase in the Doom of Mandos 'they should be slain with weapons' my father first put 'they should be lightly slain', as in AV 1, but struck out the word *lightly* as he wrote; see IV. 278–9.

After 'warned them that the Valar would fence Valinor against their return' he put 'Here endeth that which Rúmil wrote' (words added in pencil at this point in AV 1, IV. 271 note 20), but at once struck them out and set them at the end of the annal, as printed in the text. While the preamble to AV 1 states that the Annals were the work of Pengolod alone, a second version of the preamble (IV. 292) says that they 'were written first by Rúmil the Elfsage of Valinor, and after by [i.e. continued by] Pengolod the Wise of Gondolin'; and I have suggested (IV. 292–3) that Rúmil was one of the Noldor who returned to Valinor with Finrod, and that this would explain why the end of his part in the Annals was moved further on in AV 2 – 'his part ends with the actual record of Finrod's return, and the reception that he and those with him received.' Cf. the passages in annals 2000–2010 and 2990 where insertions are made by Pengolod into Rúmil's text.

In this annal (and in AB 2 annal 50) *Felagund* is for the first time rendered 'Lord of Caves'. He was called *Inglor Felagund* in the Old English version of AB (IV. 339, 341).

**Annal 2998–3000**  With the words 'For the Sun was set as a sign of the waning of the Elves, but the Moon cherisheth their memory' (repeated in QS §75) cf. *The Lost Road*, p. 72 (note 12).

# III

# THE LATER ANNALS OF BELERIAND

The manuscript of this version, **AB 2**, of the *Annals of Beleriand* is closely similar to that of AV 2, and obviously belongs to very much the same time. As with AV 2, the manuscript was in its earlier part heavily corrected and overwritten years later – the first stage in the development of the final version of these chronicles, the *Grey Annals*. In this case, however, there was far more revision in the earlier period than with AV 2, and in some places it is hard to separate the 'early' from the 'late'; reference to QS will usually decide the point, but doubt remains in cases where QS was itself altered at an indeterminable time.

I give the text as it was originally written (admitting a few additions or corrections that were clearly made at or very soon after the time of composition), but make an exception in the case of dates. Here it is less confusing and easier for subsequent reference to give the emended dates in square brackets after the original ones. These major alterations in the chronology took place during the writing of QS, and are discussed on pp. 257–8. Changes others than those to dates, where I feel sufficiently certain that they belong to the pre-*Lord of the Rings* period, are recorded in the notes; the great majority of them reflect movement of names and narrative that had come in when QS was written (or in some cases entered in the course of the writing of QS), and I do not discuss them in the commentary on AB 2.

As already noted (p. 107), the two earlier versions of these Annals given in Vol. IV (AB I and AB II) are here referred to as **AB 1**; as far as annal 220 the comparison being with AB II, and after that point with AB I. As with AV 2, in the commentary I treat AB 1 as including the emendations made to those manuscripts (fully recorded in IV. 310–13, 323–3), and do not take up again points discussed in the commentaries in Vol. IV.

In content AB 2 remains in general close to AB 1, but it is not only fuller in matter but also more finished in manner; the *Annals of Beleriand* was becoming an independent work, and less (as I described AB 1 in IV. 294) a 'consolidation of the historical structure in its internal relations and chronology' in support of the *Quenta* – but it is still annalistic, retaining the introductory *Here* of the year-entries (derived from the *Anglo-Saxon Chronicle*), and lacking connection of motive between events. And since, most unhappily, my father abandoned the *Grey Annals* at the end of the story of Túrin, the conclusion of AB 2 contains the last account in the *Annals* tradition of the fourth (becoming the sixth) century of the Sun and of the Great Battle. Both AV 2 and AB 2 only came to light very recently (I was not aware of their existence when *The Silmarillion* was prepared for publication).

# SILMARILLION

## III

## ANNALS OF BELERIAND

**Before the uprising of the Sun**    Morgoth fled from the land of the Valar and carried off the Silmarils, the holy gems of Fëanor. He returned into the northern regions of the West of Middle-earth, and rebuilt his fortress of Angband, beneath the black Mountains of Iron, where their highest peak Thangorodrim towers. He brought forth Orcs and Balrogs; and set the Silmarils in his iron crown. Thingol and Denithor[1] resisted the inroads of the Orcs, but Denithor was slain, and Thingol withdrew to Menegroth, and Doriath was closed.

Here the Dispossessed came into the North, and Fëanor led them, and with him came his seven sons, Maidros, Maglor, Celegorm,[2] Curufin, Cranthir, Damrod, and Díriel, and with them their friends, the younger sons of Finrod. They burned the Telerian ships upon the coast, where it is since called Losgar, nigh to the outlet of Drengist. Soon after they fought that battle with the host of Morgoth that is named Dagor-os-Giliath;[3] and Fëanor had the victory, but he was mortally wounded by Gothmog, and died in Mithrim.

Maidros, Fëanor's son, was ambushed and captured by Morgoth, and hung upon Thangorodrim; but his brethren were camped about Lake Mithrim, behind Eredwethion, the Shadowy Mountains.

**Years of the Sun**

1    Here the Moon and Sun, made by the Valar after the death of the Two Trees, first appeared. At this time the Fathers of Men awoke first in the East of the world. Here Fingolfin, and with him Inglor son of Finrod, led the second host of the Gnomes over Helkaraksë, the Grinding Ice, into the Hither Lands. With the first Moonrise they set foot upon Middle-earth, and the first Sunrise shone upon their march.

At the coming of Day Morgoth withdrew, dismayed, into his deepest dungeons; and there he smithied in secret, and sent forth black smoke. Fingolfin blew his trumpets in defiance before the gates of Angband, and came thence into Mithrim; but the sons of Fëanor withdrew to the southern shore, and there was feud between the houses, because of the burning of the ships, and the lake lay between them.

**2** [5]   Here Fingon, Fingolfin's son, healed the feud; for he sought after Maidros, and rescued him with the help of Thorndor,[4] King of Eagles.

**1–50**   Now the Gnomes wandered far and wide over Beleriand, exploring the land, and settling it in many places, from the great sea Belegar unto Eredlindon, that is the Blue Mountains; and they took all Sirion's vale to dwell in, save Doriath in the midmost of the land, which Thingol and Melian held, both the forest of Region and the forest of Neldoreth on either side of Esgalduin.

**20**   Here was held the Feast of Reuniting, that is Mereth-Aderthad in Gnomish speech. In Nan-Tathrin,[5] the Vale of Willows, near the mouths of Sirion, were gathered the Elves of Valinor, of the three houses of the Gnomes, and many of the Dark-elves, both those of the woods and of the havens of the West, and some of the Green-elves of Ossiriand; and Thingol sent ambassadors from Doriath. But Thingol came not himself, nor would he open his kingdom, nor remove the enchantment that fenced it in, for he trusted not in the restraint of Morgoth to last long. Yet a time of peace, of growth and blossoming, and of prosperous mirth followed.

**50**   Here unquiet and troubled dreams came upon Turgon son of Fingolfin, and Inglor his friend, son of Finrod; and they sought in the land for places of strength and refuge, lest Morgoth burst from Angband, as their dreams foreboded. Inglor found the caves of Narog, and began there to establish a stronghold and armouries, after the fashion of Thingol's abode in Menegroth; and he called his deep halls Nargothrond. Wherefore the Gnomes called him anew Felagund, lord of caverns, and that name he bore till death.

But Turgon journeyed alone, and by the grace of Ulmo discovered the hidden valley of Gondolin, but of this he told no one as yet.

**51** [60]   Here Morgoth made trial of the strength and watchfulness of the Noldor. His might was moved once more on a sudden, and there were earthquakes in the North, and fire came from the mountains, and the Orcs raided Beleriand, and bands of robbers were abroad far and wide in the land. But Fingolfin and Maidros gathered great force of their own folk, and of the Dark-elves, and they destroyed all the wandering Orcs; and they pursued the main host unto Bladorion, and there surrounded it, and destroyed it utterly within sight of Angband. This was the Second Battle, Dagor Aglareb, the Glorious Battle.

Now was set the Siege of Angband,[6] and it lasted more than two [> four] hundred years; and Fingolfin boasted that Morgoth could never burst again from the leaguer of his foes. Yet neither could the Gnomes take Angband or regain the Silmarils. But war never ceased utterly in all this time, for Morgoth was secretly forging new weapons, and ever anon he would make trial of his enemies; moreover he was not encircled upon the uttermost North.

**52**  Here[7] Turgon was troubled anew and yet more grievously in sleep; and he took a third part of the Gnomes of Fingolfin's people, and their goods and their womenfolk, and departed south, and vanished, and none knew whither he was gone; but he came to Gondolin and built there a city and fortified the surrounding hills.

In this fashion the other chieftains beleaguered Angband. In the West were Fingolfin and Fingon, and they dwelt in Hithlum, and their chief fortress was at Sirion's Well, Eithel Sirion, where the river hath its source on the eastern slopes of Eredwethion. And all Eredwethion they manned and watched Bladorion thence, and their cavalry rode upon the plain even to the feet of the mountains of Morgoth, and their horses multiplied, for the grass was good. Of those horses many of the sires came from Valinor, and were given back to Fingolfin by the sons of Fëanor at the settlement of the feud.[8]

The sons of Finrod held the land from Eredwethion unto the eastern end of the Taur-na-Danion,[9] the Forest of Pines, from the northward slopes of which they also held watch over Bladorion. Here were Angrod and Egnor, and Orodreth was nighest to the sons of Fëanor in the East.[10] Of these Celegorm and Curufin held the land between the rivers Aros and Celon, from the borders of Doriath to the pass of Aglon, that is between Taur-na-Danion and the Hill of Himling;[11] and this pass and the plain beyond they guarded. Maidros had his stronghold upon Himling, and those lower hills that lie from the Forest of Pines unto the foothills of Eredlindon were called the Marches of Maidros. Thence he rode often into East Bladorion, the plains to the north, but he held also the woods south between Celon and Gelion. Maglor lay to the east again about the upper waters of Gelion, where the hills are low or fail; and Cranthir ranged beneath the shadows of the Blue Mountains. And all the folk of Fëanor kept watch by scout and outrider towards the North-east.

To the south the fair land of Beleriand, west and east of Sirion, was apportioned in this manner. Fingolfin was King of Hithlum, and he was Lord of the Falas or Western Shore, and overlord of the Dark-elves as far south as Eglorest and west of the river Eglor. Felagund, lord of caverns, was King of Narog, and his brothers were the lords of Taur-na-Danion and his vassals;[12] and he possessed the lands both east and west of the river Narog, as far south as the mouths of Sirion, from Eglor's banks in the West, east to the banks of Sirion, save only for a portion of Doriath that lay west of Sirion, between the river Taiglin and Umboth-Muilin.[13] But between Sirion and the river Mindeb no one dwelt; and in Gondolin, to the south-west of Taur-na-Danion, was Turgon, but that was not yet known.

Now King Felagund had his seat in Nargothrond far to the south, but his fort and place of battle was in the north, in the wide pass between Eredwethion and Taur-na-Danion, through which Sirion flows to the south. There was an isle amid the waters of Sirion, and it was called Tolsirion, and there Felagund built a mighty watchtower.[14]

South of Taur-na-Danion was a wide space untenanted, between the precipices into which those highlands fall, and the fences of Melian, and here many evil things fled that had been nurtured in the dark of old, and sought refuge now in the chasms and ravines. South of Doriath and east, between Sirion and Aros and Gelion, was a wide land of wood and plain; this was East Beleriand, and it was wild and wide. Here few came and seldom, save Dark-elves wandering, but this land was held to be under the lordship of the sons of Fëanor, and Damrod and Díriel hunted in its borders and came seldom to the affrays in the northern siege. Ossiriand, the Land of Seven Rivers, that lies between Eredlindon and the river Gelion, and is watered by the streams of Ascar, Thalos, Legolin, Brilthor, Duilwen, and Adurant, was not subject to Maidros. Here dwelt the Green-elves, but they took no king after the death of Denithor, until Beren came among them. Into East Beleriand the Elf-lords, even from afar, would ride at times for hunting in the wild woods; but none passed east over Eredlindon, save only the Green-elves, for they had kindred that were yet in the further lands.

**52–255** [60–455] The time of the Siege of Angband was a time of bliss, and the world had peace under the new light. Beleriand became exceedingly fair, and was filled with beasts and birds and flowers. In this time Men waxed and multiplied, and spread; and they had converse with the Dark-elves of the East, and learned much of them. From them they took the first beginnings of the many tongues of Men. Thus they heard rumour of the Blessed Realms of the West and the Powers that dwelt there, and many of the Fathers of Men in their wanderings moved ever westward.

**65** Here Brithombar and Eglorest were built to fair towns, and the Tower of Tindobel was set up upon the cape west of Eglorest, to watch the Western Sea. Here some of the folk of Nargothrond built new ships with the help of the people of the havens, and they went forth and dwelt upon the great isle of Balar that lieth in the Bay of Balar into which Sirion flows.

**102** About this time the building of Nargothrond and of Gondolin was complete.

**104** [154] About this time the Gnomes climbed Eredlindon and gazed eastward, but they did not pass into the lands beyond. In those mountains the folk of Cranthir came first upon the Dwarves, and there was yet no enmity between them, and nonetheless little love. It was not known in those days whence the Dwarves had origin, save that they were not of Elf-kin or of mortal kind, nor yet of Morgoth's breeding. But it is said by some of the wise in Valinor, as I have since learned,[15] that Aulë made the Dwarves long ago, desiring the coming of the Elves and of Men, for he wished to have learners to whom he could teach his crafts of hand, and he could not wait upon the designs of Ilúvatar. But the Dwarves have no spirit indwelling, as have the Children of the Creator, and they have skill but not art; and they go back into the stone of the mountains of which they were made.[16]

In those days and regions the Dwarves had great mines and cities in the east of Eredlindon, far south of Beleriand, and the chief of these cities were Nogrod and Belegost. But the Elves went not thither, and the Dwarves trafficked into Beleriand; and they made a great road, which came north, east of the mountains, and thence it passed under the shoulders of Mount Dolm,[17] and followed thence the course of Ascar, and crossed Gelion at the ford Sarn-Athrad, and so came unto Aros. But the Dwarves came that way seldom after the coming of the Gnomes, until the power of Maidros fell in the Third Battle.

**105** [155]   Here Morgoth endeavoured to take Fingolfin at unawares, and he sent forth an army into the white North, and it turned then west, and again south, and came by the coast west of Eredlómin. But it was destroyed and passed not into Hithlum, and the most part was driven into the sea at Drengist. This is not reckoned among the great battles. Thereafter there was peace for many years, and no Orcs issued forth to war. But Morgoth took new counsel in his heart, and thought of Dragons.

**155** [260]   Here Glómund the first of Dragons came forth from Angband's gate by night; and he was yet young and but half grown. But the Elves fled before him to Eredwethion and Taur-na-Danion in dismay, and he defiled Bladorion. Then Fingon, prince of Gnomes, rode up against him with his horsed archers, and Glómund could not yet withstand their darts, being not yet come to his full armoury; and he fled back to hell, and came not forth again for a long time.

**170** [370]   Here Bëor, Father of Men, was born in the East.

**188** [388]   Here Haleth the Hunter was born.

**190** [390]   Here was born Hádor[18] the Goldenhaired.

**200** [400]   Here Felagund hunting in the East with the sons of Fëanor came upon Bëor and his men, new come into Beleriand. Bëor became a vassal of Felagund, and went back with him into the West.[19] In East Beleriand was born Bregolas son of Bëor.

**202** [402]   Here there was war on the East Marches, and Bëor was there with Felagund. Barahir son of Bëor was born.

**213** [413]   Hundor son of Haleth was born.

**217** [417]   Gundor son of Hádor was born.

**219** [419]   Gumlin son of Hádor was born, beneath the shadows of Eredlindon.[20]

**220** [420]   Here Haleth the Hunter came into Beleriand. In the same year came also Hádor the Goldenhaired, with his great companies of men. Haleth remained in Sirion's vale, and his folk wandered much, owning allegiance to none, but they held most to the woods[21] between Taiglin and Sirion. Hádor became a vassal of Fingolfin, and he strengthened much the armies of the king, and was given lands in Hithlum. There was great love between Elves and the Men of Hádor's house, and the folk of Hádor abandoned their own tongue and spoke with the speech of the Gnomes.

**222** [422]   In this time the strength of Men being added to the Gnomes hope grew high, and Morgoth was straitly enclosed. Fingolfin pondered an assault upon Angband, for he knew that they lived in danger while Morgoth was free to labour in the dark; but because the land was so fair most of the Gnomes were content with matters as they were, and his designs came to naught.

The Men of the three houses grew now and multiplied, and they learned wisdom and crafts of the Gnomes, and were gladly subject to the Elf-lords. The Men of Bëor were dark or brown of hair, but fair of face, with grey eyes; of shapely form, having courage and endurance, yet they were little greater in stature than the Elves of that day. The people of Hádor were yellow-haired and blue-eyed, for the most part (not so was Túrin, but his mother was of Bëor's house), and of greater strength and stature. Like unto them were the woodmen of Haleth, but somewhat less tall and more broad.

**224** [424]   Baragund, son of Bregolas son of Bëor, was born in Taur-na-Danion.

**228** [428]   Belegund his brother was born.

**232** [432]   Beren, after surnamed Ermabuin, the One-handed, or Mablosgen, the Empty-handed, son of Barahir son of Bëor, was born.[22]

**241** [441]   Húrin the Steadfast, son of Gumlin son of Hádor, was born in Hithlum. In the same year was born Handir, son of Hundor son of Haleth.

**244** [444]   Huor, brother of Húrin, was born.

**245** [445]   Morwen Eledwen[23] (Elfsheen) was born to Baragund. She was the fairest of all mortal maidens.

**250** [450]   Rian, daughter of Belegund, mother of Tuor, was born. In this year Bëor the Old, Father of Men, died of old age. The Elves saw then for the first time the death of weariness, and they sorrowed over the short span allotted to Men. Bregolas thereafter ruled the people of Bëor.

★   **255** [455]   Here came an end of peace and mirth. In the winter of this year Morgoth unloosed his long-prepared forces, and he sought to break into Beleriand and destroy the wealth of the

Gnomes. The battle began suddenly on a night of mid-winter, and
fell first most heavily on the sons of Finrod. This is Dagor Húr-
Breged,[24] the Battle of Sudden Fire. Rivers of flame ran from
Thangorodrim. Here Glómund the Golden, father of Dragons,
came forth in his full might. The green plains of Bladorion were
turned into a great desert without growing thing; and thereafter
they were called Dor-na-Fauglith, Land of Gasping Thirst. In
this war Bregolas was slain and a great part of the warriors of
Bëor's folk. Angrod and Egnor, sons of Finrod, fell. But Barahir
son of Bëor with his chosen companions saved King Felagund and
Orodreth, and Felagund swore an oath of help and friendship in
all need to Barahir and his kin and seed. Barahir ruled the remnant
of the house of Bëor.

**256** [456]    Fingolfin and Fingon marched to the aid of Felagund and his folk, but they were driven back with grievous loss.
Hádor now aged fell defending his lord Fingolfin, and with him
fell Gundor his son. Gumlin took the lordship of the house of
Hádor.

The sons of Fëanor were not slain, but Celegorm and Curufin
were defeated, and fled unto Orodreth in the west of Taur-na-
Danion.[25] Maidros did deeds of valour, and Morgoth could not as
yet take the heights of Himling, but he broke through the passes[26]
to the east and ravaged far into East Beleriand, and the Gnomes of
Fëanor's house, for the most part, fled before him. Maglor joined
Maidros, but Cranthir, Damrod, and Díriel fled into the South.

Turgon was not in that battle, nor Haleth, nor any but few of
Haleth's folk. It is said that about this time[27] Húrin son of Gumlin
was being fostered by Haleth, and that Haleth and Húrin hunting
in Sirion's vale came upon some of Turgon's folk, and espied their
secret entrance into the valley of Gondolin. But they were taken
and brought before Turgon, and looked upon the hidden city,
whereof of those outside none yet knew save Thorndor King of
Eagles. Turgon welcomed them, for messages and dreams sent by
Ulmo Lord of Waters up the streams of Sirion warned him that
the aid of mortal Men was necessary for him. But Haleth and
Húrin swore oaths of secrecy, and never revealed Gondolin; yet at
this time they learned something of the counsels of Turgon,
though they kept them hidden in their hearts. It is said that
Turgon had great liking for the boy Húrin, and wished to keep
him in Gondolin; but grievous tidings of the great battle came,
and they departed to the succour of their folk.

When Turgon learned of the breaking of the leaguer he sent

secret messengers to the mouths of Sirion and to the Isle of Balar, and there was a building of swift ships. Many a messenger set sail thence seeking for Valinor, there to ask for aid and pardon, but none reached the West, or none returned.[28]

Fingolfin saw now the ruin of the Gnomes and the defeat of all their houses, and he was filled with wrath and despair; and he rode alone to the gates of Angband, and in his madness challenged Morgoth to single combat. Morgoth slew Fingolfin, but Thorndor recovered his body, and set it under a cairn on the mountains north of Gondolin. There was sorrow in Gondolin when those tidings were brought by Thorndor, for the folk of the hidden city were of Fingolfin's folk. Fingon now ruled the royal house of the Gnomes.

**257** [457]   Morgoth attacked now the west passes, and pierced them, and passed into the Vale of Sirion; and he took Tolsirion and made it into his own watchtower, and set there Thû the Wizard, his most evil servant, and the isle became a place of dread, and was called Tol-na-Gaurhoth, Isle of Werewolves. But Felagund and Orodreth retreated, and went unto Nargothrond, and strengthened it and dwelt in hiding. With them were Celegorm and Curufin.[29]

Barahir would not retreat but defended still the remnant of his lands in Taur-na-Danion. But Morgoth hunted his people down, and he turned all that forest into a region of great dread and dark enchantment, so that it was after called Taur-na-Fuin, which is Forest of Night, or Gwathfuin-Daidelos,[30] which is Deadly Nightshade. At length only Barahir and his son Beren, and his nephews Baragund and Belegund, sons of Bregolas, were left, with a few men yet faithful. Of these Gorlim, Radros,[31] Dagnir and Gildor are named. They were a desperate band of outlaws, for their dwellings were destroyed, and their wives and children were captured or slain, save Morwen Eledwen daughter of Baragund and Rian daughter of Belegund. For the wives of the sons of Bregolas were of Hithlum, and were sojourning there when war broke out, and Hithlum was not yet overthrown. But no help now came thence, and Barahir and his men were hunted like wild beasts.

**258** [458]   Haleth and his folk dwelt now on the west marches of Doriath, and fought with the Orcs that came down Sirion. Here with the help of Beleg of Doriath they took an Orc-legion at unawares, and were victorious, and the Orcs came not afterwards for a long while into the land between Taiglin and Sirion: that is the forest of Brethil.[32]

**261** [460]    There was a high lake in the midst of Taur-na-Fuin, and here there was much heath, and there were many tarns; but the ground was full of deceit, and there was much fen and bog. In this region Barahir made his lair; but Gorlim betrayed him, and he was surprised and slain with all his company, save Beren only. Beren pursued the Orcs, and slew his father's murderer, and regained the ring of Felagund. Beren became now a solitary outlaw, and did many deeds of singlehanded daring, and Morgoth put a great price on his head.

**262** [462]    Here Morgoth renewed his assaults; and the invasion of the Orcs encompassed Doriath, both west down Sirion, and east through the passes beyond Himling. And Morgoth went against Hithlum, but was driven back as yet; but Gumlin was slain in the siege of the fortress of Fingon at Eithel Sirion. Húrin his son was new come to manhood, but he was mighty in strength, and he ruled now the house of Hádor, and served Fingon. In this time Beren was driven south and came hardly into Doriath.

**263** [463]    Here the Swarthy Men first came into Beleriand in the East. They were short and broad, long and strong in the arm, growing much hair on face and breast, and their locks were dark, as were their eyes; their skins were swart, yet their countenances were not uncomely for the most part, though some were grim-looking and illfavoured. Their houses were many, and some had liking rather for the Dwarves of the mountains, of Nogrod and Belegost, than for the Elves. But Maidros seeing the weakness of the Noldor, and the growing power of the armies of Morgoth, made alliance with these Men, and with their chieftains Bor and Ulfand.[33] The sons of Bor were Borlas and Boromir and Borthandos, and they followed Maidros and Maglor and were faithful. The sons of Ulfand the Swart were Uldor the Accursed, and Ulfast, and Ulwar,[34] and they followed Cranthir the Dark and swore allegiance to him, and proved faithless.

**263–4** [463–4]    Here began the renowned deeds of Beren and Lúthien Tinúviel, Thingol's daughter, of Doriath.

**264** [464]    Here King Felagund and Beren son of Barahir were emprisoned in Tol-na-Gaurhoth by Thû, and King Felagund was slain in combat with Draugluin the Werewolf; but Lúthien and

Huan, the hound of Valinor, slew Draugluin and overthrew Thû, who fled to Taur-na-Fuin. Orodreth took now the kingship of Nargothrond and broke friendship with Celegorm and Curufin, who fled to their kinsfolk in the East; but Nargothrond was closely hidden.

Húrin son of Gumlin wedded Morwen Elfsheen of the house of Bëor in Hithlum.

**265** [465]   Beren and Lúthien went unto Angband and took a Silmaril from the crown of Morgoth. This is the most renowned deed of these wars. Carcharoth, the wolfwarden of the gate, bit off Beren's hand, and with the Silmaril in his belly burst in madness into Doriath. Then there was made the Wolfhunt, and Huan slew Carcharoth and the Silmaril was regained, but Carcharoth slew both Huan and Beren.

Beren was recalled from the Dead by Lúthien, and they passed from the knowledge of Men and Gnomes, and dwelt a while by the green waters of Ossiriand, Land of Seven Rivers. But Mandos foretold that Lúthien should be subject hereafter to death, together with Beren, whom she rescued for a time.

In the winter of this year Túrin son of Húrin was born with sad omens.

**265-70** [465-70]   In this time was begun the Union of Maidros; for Maidros, taking heart from the deeds of Beren and Lúthien, planned the reuniting of the Elvish forces and the liberation of Beleriand. But because of the deeds of Celegorm and Curufin, Thingol would not aid him, and small help came from Nargothrond. There the Gnomes sought to guard their dwelling by stealth and secrecy. But Maidros had the help of the Dwarves in the smithying of many weapons, and there was much traffick between Beleriand and the mountains in the East; and he gathered again all the Gnomes of Fëanor's house, and he armed them; and many Dark-elves were joined to him; and the men of Bor and Ulfand were marshalled for war, and summoned yet more of their kindred out of the East.

Fingon prepared for war in Hithlum; and tidings came also to Turgon the hidden king, and he prepared for war in secret. Haleth's folk gathered also in the woods of Brethil, and made ready for battle.

**267** [467]   Dior the Beautiful was born to Beren and Lúthien in Ossiriand.

**268** [468]   Now the Orcs were driven back once more out of Beleriand, east and west, and hope was renewed; but Morgoth took counsel against the uprising of the Elves, and he sent spies and secret emissaries far and wide among Elves and Men. Here Haleth, last of the Fathers of Men, died in the woods; and Hundor his son ruled over his folk.

**271** [471]   Here Isfin, sister of Turgon, strayed out of Gondolin, and was lost; but Eöl the Dark-elf took her to wife.

★  **272** [472]   This is the Year of Sorrow. Maidros planned now an assault upon Angband from West and East. With the main host he was to march from the East across Dor-na-Fauglith, and as soon as he gave the signal then Fingon should come forth from Eredwethion; for they thought to draw the host of Morgoth from its walls and take it between their two armies.

Huor son of Hádor wedded Rian daughter of Belegund upon the eve of battle, and marched with Húrin his brother in the army of Fingon.

Here was fought the Fourth Battle, Nirnaith Dirnoth,[35] Un-numbered Tears, upon the plains of Dor-na-Fauglith, before the pass of Sirion. The place was long marked by a great hill in which the slain were piled, both Elves and Men. Grass grew there alone in Dor-na-Fauglith. There Elves and Men were utterly defeated, and the ruin of the Gnomes was accomplished. For Maidros was hindered on the road by the machinations of Uldor the Accursed, whom the spies of Morgoth had bought. Fingon attacked without waiting, and he drove in Morgoth's feinted onslaught, and came even unto Angband. The companies of Nargothrond, such as Orodreth suffered to depart to the aid of Fingon, were led by Gwindor son of Guilin, a very valiant prince, and they were in the forefront of battle; and Gwindor and his men burst even within Angband's gates, and their swords slew in the halls of Morgoth. But they were cut off, and all were taken captive; for Morgoth released now a countless host that he had withheld, and he drove back the Gnomes with terrible slaughter.

Hundor son of Haleth, and most of the Men of the woods, were slain in the rearguard in the retreat across the sands of Dor-na-Fauglith.[36] But the Orcs came between Fingon and the passes of Eredwethion that led into Hithlum, and they withdrew towards Tolsirion.

Then Turgon and the army of Gondolin sounded their horns, and issued out of Taur-na-Fuin. They were delayed by the deceit and evil of the forest, but came now as help unlooked for. The meeting between Húrin and Turgon was very joyful, and they drove back the Orcs.

Now the trumpets of Maidros were heard in the East, and hope was renewed. It is said that the Elves would yet have had the victory, but for the deeds of Uldor; but very mighty was Glómund. For Morgoth sent forth now all the dwellers in Angband, and hell was emptied. There came a hundred thousand Orcs, and a thousand Balrogs, and in the van was Glómund the Dragon; and Elves and Men withered before him. Thus did Morgoth prevent the union of the forces of Maidros and Fingon. And Uldor went over to Morgoth with most of the Men of Ulfand, and they fell upon the right flank of the sons of Fëanor.

Cranthir slew Uldor, but Ulfast and Ulwar slew Bor and his three sons, and many faithful Men; and the host of Maidros was scattered to the winds, and the remnant fled far into hiding into East Beleriand and the South, and wandered there in sorrow.

Fingon fell in the West, surrounded by a host of foes, and flame sprang from his helm, as he was smitten down by the Balrogs. But Húrin, and Huor his brother, and the Men of the house of Hádor, stood firm, and the Orcs could not yet gain the pass of Sirion. The stand of Húrin is the most renowned deed of Men among the Elves; for Húrin held the rear, while Turgon with part of his battle, and some of the remnants of the host of Fingon, escaped down Sirion into the dales and mountains. They vanished once more, and were not found again by Elf or Man or spy of Morgoth, until Tuor's day. Thus was the victory of Morgoth marred, and his anger was very great.

Huor fell pierced with a venomed arrow, but Húrin fought until he alone was left. He threw away his shield, and wielded an axe, and he slew well nigh a hundred Orcs; but he was taken alive by Morgoth's command, and dragged to Angband. But Húrin would not reveal whither Turgon was gone, and Morgoth cursed him, and he was chained upon Thangorodrim; and Morgoth gave him sight to see the evil that befell his kindred in the world. Morwen his wife went with child, but his son Túrin was now well nigh seven years old.

The Orcs now piled the slain, and poured into Beleriand. No tidings came to Hithlum of the battle, wherefore Rian went forth, and her child Tuor was born to her in the wild. He was taken to nurture by Dark-elves; but Rian went to the Mound of Slain[37] and laid her there and died.

**273** [473]   Morgoth was now lord of Beleriand, save Doriath, and he filled it with roving bands of Orcs and wolves. But he went not yet against the gates of Nargothrond in the far South, and of Gondolin he could discover nothing. But the northern kingdom was no more. For Morgoth broke his pledges to the sons of Ulfand, and denied them the reward of their treachery; and he drove these evil Men into Hithlum, and forbade them to wander from that land. But they oppressed the remnant of the folk of Hádor, and took their lands and goods and their womenfolk, and enslaved their children. Such as remained of the Elves of Hithlum Morgoth took to the mines of Angband, and they became his thralls, save few that lived perilously in the woods.

In the beginning of this year Nienor the Sorrowful was born in Hithlum, daughter of Húrin and Morwen; but Morwen sent Túrin to Doriath, begging for Thingol's fostering and aid; for she was of Beren's kindred. Two old men she had, Gethron and Grithron, and they undertook the journey, as Túrin's guides. They came through grievous hardship and danger, and were rescued on the borders of Doriath by Beleg. Gethron died in Doriath, but Grithron returned to Morwen.

**281** [481]   The power of Morgoth grew now very great, and Doriath was cut off, and no tidings of the lands without came thither. Túrin was now but in his sixteenth year; but he took to war, and fought against the Orcs on the marches of Doriath in the company of Beleg.

**284** [484]   Here Túrin slew Orgof, kinsman of Thingol, at the king's board, and fled from Menegroth. He became an outlaw in the woods, and gathered a desperate band, and plundered on the marches of Doriath.

**287** [487]   Here Túrin's companions captured Beleg, but Túrin released him, and renewed his fellowship with him, and they adventured together beyond Doriath, making war upon the Orcs.

Tuor son of Huor came unto Hithlum seeking his kindred, but they were no more, and he lived as an outlaw in the woods about Mithrim.

**288** [488]   Here Halmir[38] Orodreth's son of Nargothrond was trapped and hung on a tree by Orcs.

**289** [489]   Here Gwindor son of Guilin escaped from the mines of Angband. Blodrin Ban's son betrayed the camp of Túrin and Beleg, and Túrin was taken alive, but Beleg was left for dead. Beleg was healed of his wounds by Melian, and followed the trail of the captors of Túrin. He came upon Gwindor bewildered in Taur-na-Fuin, and together they rescued Túrin; but Túrin slew Beleg by misadventure.

**290** [490]   Túrin was healed of his madness at Ivrineithel, and was brought at last by Gwindor to Nargothrond. They were admitted to the secret halls at the prayer of Finduilas, daughter of Orodreth, who had before loved Gwindor.

**290–5** [490–5]   During this time Túrin dwelt in Nargothrond. Beleg's sword, wherewith he was slain, was reforged for Túrin; and Túrin rejected his former name, and he called himself Mormael, Black-sword, but his sword he named Gurtholfin,[39] Wand of Death. Finduilas forgot her love of Gwindor and loved Túrin, and he loved her, but spoke not, for he was faithful to Gwindor. Túrin became a captain of the host of Nargothrond, and persuaded the Gnomes to abandon stealth and ambush and make open war. He drove the Orcs out of all the land between Narog and Sirion and Doriath to the east, and west to Eglor and the sea, and north to Eredwethion; and he let build a bridge over Narog. The Gnomes of Nargothrond allied themselves with Handir of Brethil and his men. Thus Nargothrond was revealed to the wrath of Morgoth.

**292** [492]   Meglin son of Eöl was sent by Isfin to Gondolin, and was received as his sister's son by Turgon.

**294** [494]   In this time when the power of Morgoth was stayed in the West, Morwen and Nienor departed from Hithlum and came to Doriath, seeking tidings of Túrin. There many spake of the prowess of Mormael, but of Túrin no man had heard, since the Orcs took him.

★ **295** [495]   Here Glómund passed into Hithlum and did great evil, and he came over Eredwethion with a host of Orcs, and came into the realm of Narog. And Orodreth and Túrin and Handir went up against him, and they were defeated in the field of Tum-halad between Narog and Taiglin; and Orodreth was slain, and Handir; and Gwindor died, and refused the succour of Túrin. Túrin gathered the remnants of the Gnomes and hastened to Nargothrond, but it was sacked ere his coming; and Túrin was deceived and bound in spell by Glómund. Finduilas and the women of Nargothrond were taken as thralls, but Túrin forsook them, and deceived by the lies of Glómund went to Hithlum to seek Morwen.

Tidings of the fall of Nargothrond came to Doriath, and Mormael was revealed as Túrin.

Tuor son of Huor departed from Hithlum by a secret way under the leading of Ulmo, and journeying down the coast he passed the ruined havens of Brithombar and Eglorest, and came to the mouths of Sirion.

**295–6** [495–6]   Túrin found that Morwen had departed from Hithlum. He slew Brodda in his hall and escaped from Hithlum. He took now the name of Turambar, Conqueror of Fate,[40] and joined the remnant of the Woodmen in Brethil; and he became their lord, since Brandir son of Handir was lame from childhood.

**296** [496]   Here Tuor met the Gnome Bronweg at the mouths of Sirion. Ulmo himself appeared to Tuor in Nantathrin, and Tuor went thence up Sirion, and guided by Ulmo found the entrance to Gondolin. There Tuor spake the embassy of Ulmo; but Turgon would not now harken to it, and Meglin urged him to this against Tuor. But Tuor was held in honour in Gondolin for his kindred's sake.

Glómond returned unto Nargothrond, and lay upon the treasure of Felagund in the caves.

Morwen Eledwen went to Nargothrond seeking tidings of Túrin, and Nienor against her bidding rode in disguise among her escort of Elves. But Glómund laid a spell upon the company and dispersed it, and Morwen was lost in the woods; and a great darkness of mind came upon Nienor.

Turambar found Nienor hunted by Orcs. He named her Níniel the tearful, since she knew not her own name.

**297–8** [497–8]   Níniel dwelt with the Woodmen, and was loved both by Turambar and by Brandir the Lame.

**298** [498]   Turambar wedded Níniel.

**299** [499]   Glómund sought out the dwelling of Túrin Turambar; but Túrin smote him mightily with Gurtholfin, and fell aswoon beside him. There Níniel found him; but Glómund ere death released her from spells and declared her kindred. Nienor cast herself over the waterfall in that place which was then called Celebros, Silver Rain, but afterwards Nen-girith, Shuddering Water.

Brandir brought the tidings to Túrin, and was slain by him, but Túrin bade Gurtholfin slay him; and he died there.

Húrin was released from Angband, and he was bowed as with great age; but he departed and sought for Morwen.

Tuor wedded Idril Celebrindal, Turgon's daughter, of Gondolin; and Meglin hated him.

**300** [500]    Here was born Eärendel the Bright, star of the Two Kindreds, unto Tuor and Idril in Gondolin. In this year was born also Elwing the White, fairest of all women save Lúthien, unto Dior son of Beren in Ossiriand.

Húrin gathered men unto him, and they came to Nargothrond, and slew the dwarf Mîm, who had taken the treasure unto himself. But Mîm cursed the treasure. Húrin brought the gold to Thingol in Doriath, but he departed thence again with bitter words, and of his fate and the fate of Morwen thereafter no sure tidings were ever heard.

**301** [501]    Thingol employed Dwarvish craftsmen to fashion his gold and silver and the treasure of Nargothrond; and they made the renowned Nauglamír, the Dwarf-necklace, whereon was hung the Silmaril. Enmity awoke between Dwarves and Elves, and the Dwarves were driven away unrewarded.

**302** [502]    Here the Dwarves[41] came in force from Nogrod and from Belegost and invaded Doriath; and they came within by treachery, for many Elves were smitten with the accursed lust of the gold. Thingol was slain and the Thousand Caves were plundered; and there hath been war between Elf and Dwarf since that day. But Melian the Queen could not be slain or taken, and she departed to Ossiriand.

Beren and the Green-elves overthrew the Dwarves at Sarn-Athrad as they returned eastward, and the gold was cast into the river Ascar, which was after called Rathloriel, the Bed of Gold. But Beren took the Nauglamír and the Silmaril. Lúthien wore the Silmaril upon her breast. Dior their son ruled over the remnants of the Elves of Doriath.

**303** [503]    Here Beren and Lúthien departed out of the knowledge of Elves and Men, and their deathday is not known; but at night a messenger brought the necklace to Dior in Doriath, and the Elves said: 'Lúthien and Beren are dead as Mandos doomed.'

**304** [504]    Dior son of Beren, Thingol's heir, was now king in Doriath, and he re-established it for a while. But Melian went back to Valinor and Doriath had no longer her protection. Dior wore the Nauglamír and the Silmaril upon his breast.

**305** [505]   The sons of Fëanor heard tidings of the Silmaril in the East, and they gathered from wandering, and held council together. Maidros sent unto Dior and summoned him to give up the jewel.

**306** [506]   Here Dior Thingol's heir fought the sons of Fëanor on the east marches of Doriath, but he was slain. This was the second kinslaying, and the fruit of the oath. Celegorm fell in that battle, and Curufin, and Cranthir. The young sons of Dior, Elboron and Elbereth,[42] were taken captive by the evil men of Maidros' following, and they were left to starve in the woods; but Maidros lamented the cruel deed, and sought unavailingly for them.

The maiden Elwing was saved by faithful Elves, and they fled with her to the mouths of Sirion, and they took with them the jewel and the necklace, and Maidros found it not.

Meglin was taken in the hills, and he betrayed Gondolin to Morgoth.

**307** [507]   Here Morgoth loosed a host of dragons over the mountains from the North and they overran the vale of Tumladin, and besieged Gondolin. The Orcs sacked Gondolin, and destroyed King Turgon and most of his people; but Ecthelion of the Fountain slew there Gothmog, Lord of Balrogs, ere he fell.

Tuor slew Meglin. Tuor escaped with Idril and Eärendel by a secret way devised before by Idril, and they came with a company of fugitives to the Cleft of Eagles, Cristhorn, which is a high pass beneath the cairn of Fingolfin in the north of the surrounding mountains. They fell into an ambush there, and Glorfindel of the house of the Golden Flower of Gondolin was slain, but they were saved by Thorndor, and escaped at last into the vale of Sirion.

**308** [508]   Here the wanderers from Gondolin reached the mouths of Sirion and joined there the slender company of Elwing. The Silmaril brought blessing upon them, and they were healed, and they multiplied, and built a haven and ships, and dwelt upon the delta amid the waters. Many fugitives gathered unto them.

**310** [510]   Maidros learned of the upspringing of Sirion's Haven, and that the Silmaril was there, but he forswore his oath.

**324** [524]   Here the unquiet of Ulmo came upon Tuor, and he built the ship Eärámë, Eagle's wing, and he departed with Idril into the West, and was heard of no more. Eärendel wedded Elwing the White, and was lord of the folk of Sirion.

325 [525] Torment fell upon Maidros and his brethren, because of their unfulfilled oath. Damrod and Díriel resolved to win the Silmaril, if Eärendel would not give it up willingly. But the unquiet had come also upon Eärendel, and he set sail in his ship Wingelot, Flower of the Foam, and he voyaged the far seas seeking Tuor, and seeking Valinor. But he found neither; yet the marvels that he did were many and renowned.[43] Elrond the Half-elfin,[44] son of Eärendel, was born while Eärendel was far at sea.

The folk of Sirion refused to surrender the Silmaril, both because Eärendel was not there, and because they thought that their bliss and prosperity came from the possession of the gem.

329 [529] Here Damrod and Díriel ravaged Sirion, and were slain. Maidros and Maglor were there, but they were sick at heart. This was the third kinslaying. The folk of Sirion were taken into the people of Maidros, such as yet remained; and Elrond was taken to nurture by Maglor. But Elwing cast herself with the Silmaril into the sea, and Ulmo bore her up, and in the shape of a bird she flew seeking Eärendel, and found him returning.

330 [530] Eärendel bound the Silmaril upon his brow, and with Elwing he sailed in search of Valinor.

333 [533] Eärendel came unto Valinor, and spake on behalf of the two races, both Elves and Men.

340 [540] Maidros and Maglor, sons of Fëanor, dwelt in hiding in the south of Eastern Beleriand, about Amon Ereb, the Lonely Hill, that stands solitary amid the wide plain. But Morgoth sent against them, and they fled to the Isle of Balar. Now Morgoth's triumph was complete, and all that land was in his hold, and none were left there, Elves or Men, save such as were his thralls.

333–343 [533–543] Here the sons of the Gods prepared for war, and Fionwë son of Manwë was their leader. The Light-elves marched under his banners, but the Teleri did not leave Valinor; but they built a countless multitude of ships.

347 [547] Here the host of Fionwë was seen shining upon the sea afar, and the noise of his trumpets rang over the waves and

echoed in the western woods. Thereafter was fought the battle of Eglorest, where Ingwiel son of Ingwë, prince of all the Elves, made a landing, and drove the Orcs from the shore.

Great war came now into Beleriand, and Fionwë drove the Orcs and Balrogs before him; and he camped beside Sirion, and his tents were as snow upon the field. He summoned now all Elves, Men, Dwarves, beasts and birds unto his standard, who did not elect to fight for Morgoth. But the power and dread of Morgoth was very great and many did not obey the summons.

★ **350** [550]    Here Fionwë fought the last battle of the ancient world, the Great or Terrible Battle. Morgoth himself came forth from Angband, and passed over Taur-na-Fuin, and the thunder of his approach rolled in the mountains. The waters of Sirion lay between the hosts; and long and bitterly they contested the passage. But Fionwë crossed Sirion and the hosts of Morgoth were driven as leaves, and the Balrogs were utterly destroyed; and Morgoth fled back to Angband pursued by Fionwë.

From Angband Morgoth loosed the winged dragons, which had not before been seen; and Fionwë was beaten back upon Dor-na-Fauglith. But Eärendel came in the sky and overthrew Ancalagon the Black Dragon, and in his fall Thangorodrim was broken.

The sons of the Gods wrestled with Morgoth in his dungeons, and the earth shook, and gaped, and Beleriand was shattered and changed, and many perished in the ruin of the land. But Morgoth was bound.

This war lasted fifty years from the landing of Fionwë.

**397** [597]    In this year Fionwë departed and went back to Valinor with all his folk, and with them went most of the Gnomes that yet lived and the other Elves of Middle-earth. But Elrond the Half-elfin remained, and ruled in the West of the world.

Now the Silmarils were regained, for one was borne in the airs by Eärendel, and the other two Fionwë took from the crown of Melko; and he beat the crown into fetters for his feet. Maidros and Maglor driven by their oath seized now the two Silmarils and fled; but Maidros perished, and the Silmaril that he took went into the bosom of the earth, and Maglor cast his into the sea, and wandered ever after upon the shores of the world in sorrow.

Thus ended the wars of the Gnomes, and Beleriand was no more.

# NOTES

From the end of annal 257 (457) the manuscript was very little changed, either before *The Lord of the Rings* or after, and while the addition of 200 years to every date was carried through to the end the alteration of names became more superficial, and instances were ignored or missed. This is obviously of no significance, but in the notes that follow I refer only to the first occurrence of the change.

1   *Denithor > Denethor* (as in AV 2, note 5).

2   *Celegorm > Celegorn* (as in AV 2, note 9).

3   *Dagor-os-Giliath > Dagor-nuin-Giliath* (as in AV 2, note 12).

4   *Thorndor > Thorondor.* See commentary on QS §§96–7.

5   *Nan-Tathrin > Nan-Tathren.* See commentary on QS §109.

6   *Now was set the Siege of Angband > But after this the chieftains of the Gnomes took warning, and drew closer their leaguer, and strengthened their watch; and they set the Siege of Angband*

7   This first paragraph of annal 52 was struck out; see note 8.

8   New matter was added here, taking up that of the cancelled first paragraph of annal 52 (note 7). The date of Dagor Aglareb was at the same time changed from 51 to 60.

> But Turgon held the land of Nivros [> Nivrost], between Eredwethion and the sea, south of Drengist; and his folk were many. But the unquiet of Ulmo was upon him, and a few years after the Dagor Aglareb he gathered his folk together, even to a third of the Gnomes of Fingolfin's house, and their goods and wives, and departed eastward in secret, and vanished from his kindred. And none knew whither he was gone; but he came to Gondolin and built there a hidden city.

Against this is written the date 64. On *Nivros(t)* see QS §100 and commentary; and on the changed chronology, as throughout, see pp. 257–8.

9   *Taur-na-Danion > Taur-na-Thanion > Dorthanion > Dorthonion. Taur-na-Danion* is emended at every occurrence, but hardly ever in the same way; in addition, *Taur-na-Donion* and *Taur-na-Thonion* are found (see IV. 211). The precise details are scarcely material, and I do not notice these competing forms any further.

10   The sentence beginning *Here were Angrod and Egnor* changed to read:

> Inglor and Orodreth held the pass of Sirion, but Angrod and Egnor held the northern slopes of Dorthanion, as far as Aglon where the sons of Fëanor lay.

See note 14 and commentary on QS §117.

11   *Himling > Himring.* This change is found also in late emendations to Q.

12   The passage beginning *Fingolfin was King of Hithlum* changed to read:

Fingolfin was King of Hithlum and Nivrost, and overlord of all the Gnomes. Felagund, lord of caverns, was King in Nargothrond, and his brothers Angrod and Egnor were the lords of Dorthanion and his vassals;
By this change Fingolfin ceases to be Lord of the Western Havens; see note 13.

13  Added here (see commentary on QS §109):
And he was held also to be overlord of the Falas, and of the Dark-elves of the havens of Brithombar and Eglorest.

14  Added after *a mighty watchtower*:
Inglormindon; but after the founding of Nargothrond this was in the keeping of Orodreth.
Subsequently *Inglormindon > Minnastirith*, and that in turn to *Minastirith*. See QS §117 and commentary.

15  *as I have since learned > as we have since learned*. See commentary on QS §123.

16  The passage beginning *But the Dwarves* changed to read:
And the Noldor believed that the Dwarves have no spirit in-dwelling, as have the Children of the Creator, and they have skill but not art; and that they go back into the stone of the mountains of which they were made. Yet others say that Aulë cares for them, and that Ilúvatar will accept from him the work of his desire, so that the Dwarves shall not perish.
See the *Lhammas* §9 and QS §123, and commentaries.

17  *a great road, which came north, east of the mountains, and thence it passed under the shoulders of Mount Dolm > a great road, which passed under the shoulders of Mount Dolmed*. At the same time, no doubt, the words *far south of Beleriand* earlier in the paragraph were struck out; see commentary on QS §122.

18  *Hádor > Hador* or *Hădor* sporadically, where noticed; see IV. 317.

19  Annal 200 to this point changed to read:
400   Here Felagund hunting in the East with the sons of Fëanor passed into Ossiriand, and came upon Bëor and his men, new come over the mountains. Bëor became a vassal of Felagund, and went back with him into the West, and dwelt with him until death. But Barahir his son dwelt in Dorthanion.

20  The three annals recording the births of Hundor, Gundor, and Gumlin were misplaced after annal 220, as in AB 1, but a direction moves them to their proper place, as I have done in the text printed.
*Gundor > Gumlin the Tall; Gumlin > Gundor*. See QS §140 and commentary.

21  *the woods > the woods of Brethil*. *Brethil* occurs under the year 258 in the text as written (and subsequently); see the commentary on that annal.

22  *Ermabuin > Erchamion* (but first to *Erchamui*), and *Mablosgen > Camlost*. See p. 405. After this annal a new one was added:

436 Hundor son of Haleth wedded Glorwendel daughter of Hador. On this see p. 310 (§13) and note 36 below.

23 *Eledwen > Eledhwen*.

24 *Dagor Húr-breged > Dagor Vregedúr*. The latter occurs in QS §134.

25 *Celegorm and Curufin were defeated, and fled unto Orodreth in the west of Taur-na-Danion > Celegorn and Curufin were defeated, and fled south and west, and took harbour at last with Orodreth in Nargothrond*. See commentary on QS §§117, 141.

26 *the passes > the passes of Maglor*.

27 *about this time > in the autumn before the Sudden Fire*. Cf. QS §153.

28 *or none returned > and few returned*. Cf. QS §154.

29 The passage from *But Felagund and Orodreth retreated* changed to read:

> Orodreth, brother of Felagund, who commanded Minnastirith, escaped hardly and fled south. There Felagund had taken refuge in the stronghold he had prepared against the evil day; and he strengthened it, and dwelt in secret. Thither came Celegorn and Curufin.

See commentary on QS §§117, 141.

30 *Gwathfuin-Daidelos > Deldúwath*. See QS §138.

31 *Radros > Radruin*. In QS §139 the name is spelt *Radhruin*.

32 Added here:

> Húrin of Hithlum was with Haleth; but he departed afterward since the victory had made the journey possible, and returned to his own folk.

See QS §§153 and 156 (footnote to the text). Subsequently *afterward > soon after*, and the words *since the victory had made the journey possible* removed.

33 *Bor > Bór*, and *Ulfand > Ulfang*. See QS §151 and commentary.

34 *Ulwar > Ulwarth*. See QS §151 and commentary.

35 *Nirnaith Dirnoth > Nirnaith Arnediad*. See IV. 312 note 38.

36 Added here: *Glorwendel his wife died in that year of grief*. See note 22.

37 *the Mound of Slain > Cûm-na-Dengin the Mound of Slain*. See IV. 312 note 42.

38 *Halmir > Haldir* (the name of Orodreth's son in the *Etymologies*, stem SKAL¹).

39 *Gurtholfin > Gurtholf*. See p. 406.

40 *Conqueror of Fate > Master of Fate*.

41 *Dwarves > Dwarfs* (the only occurrence of the change in the text). See commentary on QS §122.

42 *Elboron and Elbereth > Elrûn and Eldûn* (a hasty pencilled change). See IV. 325–6 and the *Etymologies*, stem BARATH.

43 Added here: *Chief of these was the slaying of Ungoliantë*. See the commentary on annal 325.

44  *Elrond the Half-elfin* > *Elrond Beringol, the Half-elven.* See the
commentary on annal 325.

## Commentary on the Later Annals of Beleriand

**Before the uprising of the Sun**   I take the words 'rebuilt his fortress of
Angband' to mean that that was the name of Melko's original stronghold;
see the commentary on AV 2, annal 1000.

The statement that Melko 'brought forth Orcs and Balrogs' after his
return to Middle-earth is retained from AB 1 (where the word *devised*
was used), in contrast to AV 1 and 2, where 'he bred and gathered *once
more* his evil servants, Orcs and Balrogs'; see my discussion of this,
IV. 314.

The sentence concerning Thingol and Denithor enters from the AV
tradition (annal 2990).

The name *Losgar* of the place where the Telerian ships were burnt
occurs here for the first time (and the only time in the texts of this
period). The name had been used long before in the old tale of *The
Cottage of Lost Play*, where it meant 'Place of Flowers', the Gnomish
name of *Alalminórë* 'Land of Elms' in Tol-eressëa, and where it was
replaced by *Gar Lossion* (I. 16, 21).

**Annal 1–50**   Here are the first occurrences of the names *Region* and
*Neldoreth* (which were also marked in on the initial drawing of the
Second Map, p. 409).

**Annal 20**   The presence of Green-elves at Mereth Aderthad is not
mentioned in AB 1.

**Annal 52**   In AB 1 (IV. 329) the departure of Turgon to Gondolin is
placed in annal 51 (as is all that follows concerning the regions over which
the Noldorin princes ruled during the Siege).

The return of the horses to Fingolfin at the settlement of the feud is a
new element in the story.

In the third paragraph of this annal is a clear reference to 'Maglor's
Gap' (unnamed). The region where 'the hills are low or fail', shown
clearly on the Second Map (though the name was never written in),
is implied by the lines on the Eastward Extension of the First Map
(IV. 231).

In the passage at the end of the annal concerning the Green-elves new
elements in their history appear: that they were kingless after the death of
Denithor, and that they had kindred who remained east of the Blue
Mountains. The speech of the two branches of this people will have an
important place in the linguistic history expounded in the *Lhammas*.

**Annal 52–255**   The earliest references in my father's writings to the
origin of speech among Men are in outlines for *Gilfanon's Tale*, I. 236–7,
where it is told that the Dark Elf Nuin 'Father of Speech', who awakened
the first Men, taught them 'much of the Ilkorin tongue'. In S (IV. 20)

and Q (IV. 99) it is told, as here, that the first Men learned speech from the Dark-elves.

The reference to '*many of* the Fathers of Men' wandering westward suggests a different application of the term, which elsewhere seems always to be used specifically of Bëor, Hador, and Haleth; so in annal 268, recording the death of Haleth, he is 'last of the Fathers of Men'.

**Annal 65** The matter of this entry is not dated to a separate year in AB 1 (IV. 331), but is contained in the annal 51–255, of the Siege of Angband. It is said there only that 'some went forth and dwelt upon the great isle of Balar.'

**Annal 104** In this annal (combining matter concerning the Dwarves from the old entries 51–255 and 104) is the first emergence of the legend of Aulë's making of the Dwarves, forestalling the plan of Ilúvatar, in longing to have those whom he might teach; but the old hostile view of them (see IV. 174) finds expression in the remarkable assertion that they 'have no spirit indwelling, as have the Children of the Creator, and they have skill but not art.' With the words 'they go back into the stone of the mountains of which they were made' cf. the reference in Appendix A (III) to *The Lord of the Rings* to 'the foolish opinion among Men . . . that the Dwarves "grow out of stone".'

**Annal 105** The phrase 'sent forth an army into the white North, and it turned then west', which is not in the earlier form of the annal, makes the route of this army clearer; see QS §103, and the note on the northern geography pp. 270–1.

**Annal 220** The second version of AB 1 comes to an end with the beginning of this annal – a hasty note concerning the unfriendliness of the sons of Fëanor towards Men, which was not taken up into AB 2. We here go back to the earlier version of AB 1 (IV. 297), the dates in AB 2 being of course a hundred years later.

There is here the first mention of the abandonment of their own tongue by the Men of Hador's house; cf. the *Lhammas*, §10. Afterwards the idea became important that they retained their own language; in *The Silmarillion* (p. 148), whereas in the house of Hador 'only the Elven-tongue was spoken', 'their own speech was not forgotten, and from it came the common tongue of Númenor (see further *Unfinished Tales*, p. 215 note 19). But at this time the large linguistic conception did not include the subsequent development of Adûnaic. In the second version of *The Fall of Númenor* (§2) the Númenóreans 'took on the speech of the Blessed Realm, as it was and is in Eressëa', and in *The Lost Road* (p. 68) there is talk in Númenor of 'reviving the ancestral speech of Men'.

**Annal 222** With this allusion to Túrin's dark hair, not in AB 1, cf. the *Lay of the Children of Húrin* (III. 17): *the black-haired boy / from the beaten people.*

**Annal 255**   On the story repeated from AB 1, that Barahir rescued Orodreth as well as Felagund in the Battle of Sudden Fire see under Annal 256.

**Annal 256**   In AB 1 the date 155 is repeated here (see IV. 319). The date 256 in AB 2 is presumably because the Battle of Sudden Fire began at midwinter of the year 255.

The confusion in the story of Orodreth at this point is not less than that in the earlier *Annals*. In AB 1 Orodreth with his brothers Angrod and Egnor dwelt in Taur-na-Danion (in the second version, IV. 330, Orodreth is specifically placed furthest east and nearest to the sons of Fëanor); thus when Celegorm and Curufin were defeated in the Battle of Sudden Fire they 'fled with Orodreth' (annal 155), which must mean that they took refuge with Felagund on Tol Sirion, for two years later, when Morgoth captured Tol Sirion, all four went south to Nargothrond (annal 157). Obviously in contradiction to this story, however, is the statement earlier in 155 that Barahir and his men rescued Felagund *and Orodreth* in the Battle of Sudden Fire; see my discussion, IV. 319.

In AB 2 (annal 255) it is again said that Barahir rescued Orodreth as well as Felagund, apparently contradicting the statement in annal 52 that Orodreth dwelt furthest east on Taur-na-Danion. But where AB 1 says that Celegorm and Curufin, defeated, 'fled with Orodreth', in AB 2 (annal 256) they 'fled *unto* Orodreth in the *west* of Taur-na-Danion' (the word *west* being perfectly clear). In annal 257 AB 2 agrees with AB 1 that all four retreated together to Nargothrond. It does not seem possible to deduce a coherent narrative from AB 2. Alterations to the manuscript given in notes 10, 14, 25 and 29 show the later story.

The story of the sojourn of Haleth and Húrin in Gondolin scarcely differs from that in AB 1, except in the point that in the older version the men 'came upon some of Turgon's folk, and were brought into the secret vale of Gondolin', whereas here they 'espied their secret entrance'.

It is not said in AB 1 that Turgon's messengers went also to the Isle of Balar (where, according to annal 65 in AB 2, Elves from Nargothrond dwelt), nor that the messengers were to ask for 'aid and pardon'.

**Annal 257**   The puzzling statement in AB 1, that 'Felagund and Orodreth, together with Celegorm and Curufin, retreated to Nargothrond, and made there a great hidden palace', is now clarified, or anyway made consistent with the earlier annals. I suggested (IV. 319) that the meaning might be that 'though Nargothrond had existed for more than a hundred years as a Gnomish stronghold it was not until after the Battle of Sudden Fire that it was made into a great subterranean dwelling or "palace", and the centre of Felagund's power'; and the words of AB 2 here ('went unto Nargothrond, and strengthened it') support this.

The named members of Barahir's band are now increased by *Gildor*, who was not included in the addition to AB 1 (IV. 311 note 23).

The concluding sentences of this annal introduce the story that

Morwen and Rian only escaped because they were staying in Hithlum at the time, with their mothers' people; for the wives of Baragund and Belegund were of Hador's house. In AB 1 they were sent into Hithlum at the taking of Taur-na-Danion by Morgoth.

**Annal 258** This is the first appearance of the story (*The Silmarillion* p. 157) of the defeat of the Orcs in Brethil by the people of Haleth and Beleg of Doriath; and this is the first occurrence of *Brethil* in a text as written.

**Annal 261** To this corresponds in AB 1 annal 160, not 161; but when (in the course of writing QS) my father lengthened the Siege of Angband by a further 200 years, and then entered the revised dates on the AB 2 manuscript, he changed 261 to 460, not 461.

**Annal 263** AB 1 does not name the sons of Bor, nor state that they followed Maidros and Maglor. Bor's son Boromir is the first bearer of this name. Afterwards the Boromir of the Elder Days was the father of Bregor father of Bregolas and Barahir.

**Annal 263–4** The matter of the much longer annal 163–4 in AB 1 is in AB 2 distributed into annals 264 and 265.

**Annal 264** It is strange that my father should have written here that Felagund was slain by Draugluin (who himself survived to be slain by Huan). Of this there is no suggestion elsewhere – it is told in the *Lay of Leithian* that Felagund slew the wolf that slew him in the dungeon (III. 250, line 2625), and still more emphatically in the prose tale: 'he wrestled with the werewolf, and slew it with his hands and teeth' (*The Silmarillion* p. 174).

**Annal 273** *Gethron* and *Grithron*: the two old men are not named in Q or AB 1; in S (IV. 28) they are Halog and Mailgond, their names in the second version of the *Lay of the Children of Húrin*. Later their names were *Gethron* and *Grithnir*, and it was Grithnir who died in Doriath, Gethron who went back (*Unfinished Tales* pp. 73–4).

**Annal 287** It might seem from the statement here (not found in AB 1) that Tuor '*came unto Hithlum* seeking his kindred' that he was born after Rian had crossed the mountains, wandering towards the battlefield, and that fifteen years later he came back; but there is no suggestion of this anywhere else. In AB 1, annal 173, it is said that 'Tuor grew up wild among fugitive Elves nigh the shores of Mithrim', and though this is omitted in AB 2 the idea was undoubtedly present; the explanation of the words 'came unto Hithlum' is then that Mithrim and Hithlum were distinct lands, even if the one is comprised within the other (cf. QS §§88, 106).

**Annal 290–5** As AB 1 was first written here, it was as a result of the loss of the 'ancient secrecy' of Nargothrond in Túrin's time that Morgoth 'learned of the stronghold'; but this was early changed (IV. 313 note 53) to 'learned of the growing strength of the stronghold', which looks as if my father was retreating from the idea that Nargothrond had till then been wholly concealed from Morgoth. AB 2 is explicit that Nargothrond was 'revealed' to him by Túrin's policy of open war. See IV. 323–4.

**Annal 292**   In Q (IV. 140) Isfin and Meglin went to Gondolin together. AB 1 is not explicit: 'Meglin comes to Gondolin'. AB 2 reverts to the old story in S (IV. 35), that Meglin was sent to Gondolin by his mother.

**Annal 295**   It is now said expressly, what is implied in AB 1, that Glómund approached Nargothrond by way of Hithlum, with the addition that he 'did great evil' there; see IV. 324. Here first appears the name *Tum-halad*, but the site of the battle, to which the name refers, was still east of Narog, not between Narog and Ginglith.

For an explanation of why the havens of Brithombar and Eglorest were in ruins see IV. 324.

**Annal 296**   It was said also in AB 1 that Glómund returned to Nargothrond in the year following the sack, though I did not there remark on it. I cannot explain this. There is no suggestion elsewhere that after Túrin had departed on his journey to Hithlum Glómund did other than crawl back into the halls of Nargothrond and lie down upon the treasure.

**Annal 299**   *Celebros*, here rendered 'Silver Rain', has previously been translated 'Foam-silver', 'Silver Foam'; see the *Etymologies*, stem ROS[1].

**Annal 325**   The early addition made to this annal (note 43), 'Chief of these was the slaying of Ungoliantë', is notable. This story goes back through S and Q (§17) to the very beginning (II. 254, etc.), but it does not appear again. It is told in S and Q (§4) that when Morgoth returned with Ungoliantë to Middle-earth she was driven away by the Balrogs 'into the uttermost South', with the addition in Q (and QS §62) 'where she long dwelt'; but in the recasting and expansion of this passage made long after it is reported as a legend that 'she ended long ago, when in her uttermost famine she devoured herself at last' (*The Silmarillion* p. 81).

The surname given to Elrond in another addition (note 44), *Beringol*, is not found again, but the form *Peringol* appears in the *Etymologies*, stem PER, of which *Beringol* is a variant (see p. 298, note on *Gorgoroth*). It is convenient to notice here a later, hastily pencilled change, which altered the passage to read thus:

The *Peringiul*, the Half-elven, were born of Elwing wife of Eärendel,
     while Eärendel was at sea, the twin brethren Elrond and Elros.

The order was then inverted to 'Elros and Elrond'. No doubt at the same time, in annal 329 'Elrond was taken' was changed to 'Elros and Elrond were taken'. Elros has appeared in late additions to the text of Q (IV. 155), which were inserted after the arising of the legend of Númenor, and by emendation to the second version of *The Fall of Númenor* (p. 34), where he replaces Elrond as the first ruler.

**Annal 340** It is not told in AB 1 that Maidros and Maglor and their people fled in the end from Amon Ereb to the Isle of Balar. In Q nothing is told of the actual habitation of Maidros and Maglor during the final years.

**Annal 350** Some new (and unique) elements appear in the account in AB 2 of the invasion out of the West. The camp of Fionwë beside Sirion (annal 347) does not appear in AB 1 (nor in Q or QS, where nothing is said of the landing of Fionwë or of the Battle of Eglorest), nor is it said there that Morgoth crossed Taur-na-Fuin and that there was a long battle on the banks of Sirion where the host of Valinor attempted to cross; in the second version of the story in Q §18 (repeated in QS, p. 329) it is indeed strongly suggested that Morgoth never left Angband until he was dragged out in chains.

After the words 'many perished in the ruin of the land' my father pencilled in the following sentence:

and the sea roared in and covered all but the tops of the mountains, and only part of Ossiriand remained.

This addition is of altogether uncertain date, but it bears on matters discussed earlier in this book and may be conveniently considered here.

What little was ever told of the Drowning of Beleriand is very difficult to interpret; the idea shifted and changed, but my father never at any stage clearly expounded it. In the *Quenta* (cited on p. 22) and the *Annals* there is a picture of cataclysmic destruction brought about by 'the fury of the adversaries' in the Great Battle between the host of Valinor and the power of Morgoth. The last words of the *Annals*, retained in AB 2, are 'Beleriand was no more' (which could however be interpreted to mean that Beleriand as the land of the Gnomes and the scene of their heroic wars had no further history); in Q there remained 'great isles', where the fleets were built in which the Elves of Middle-earth set sail into the West – and these may well be the British Isles (see IV. 199). In the concluding passage (§14) of *The Fall of Númenor* the picture is changed (see p. 23), for there it is said (most fully in the second version, p. 28) that the name *Beleriand* was preserved, and that it remained a land 'in a measure blessed'; it was to Beleriand that many of the Númenórean exiles came, and there that Elendil ruled and made the Last Alliance with the Elves who remained in Middle-earth ('and these abode then mostly in Beleriand'). There is no indication here of the extent of Beleriand remaining above the sea – and no mention of islands; all that is said is that it had been 'changed and broken' in the war against Morgoth. Later (at some time during the writing of *The Lord of the Rings*) my father rewrote this passage (see pp. 33–4), and there had now entered the idea that the Drowning of Beleriand took place at the fall of Númenor and the World Made Round – a far more overwhelming cataclysm, surely, than even the battle of the divine adversaries:

Now that land had been broken in the Great Battle with Morgoth; and

*at the fall of Númenor and the change of the fashion of the world it
perished*; for the sea covered *all that was left* save some of the
mountains that remained as islands, even up to the feet of Eredlindon.
But that land where Lúthien had dwelt remained, and was called
Lindon.

Into these successive phases of the idea it is extremely difficult to find a
place for the sentence added to this annal in AB 2. On the one hand, it
describes the Drowning in the same way as does the later passage just
cited – a part of Ossiriand and some high mountains alone left above the
surface of the sea; on the other, it refers not to the time of the fall of
Númenor and the World Made Round, but to the Great Battle against
Morgoth. Various explanations are possible, but without knowing when
the sentence was written they can only be extremely speculative and fine-
spun, and I shall not rehearse them. It is in any case conceivable that this
addition is an example of the casual, disconnected emendations that my
father sometimes made when looking through an earlier manuscript –
emendations that were not part of a thoroughgoing preparation for a new
version, but rather isolated pointers to the need for revision. It may be
that he jotted down this sentence long after – perhaps when considering
the writing of the *Grey Annals* after *The Lord of the Rings* was completed,
and that its real reference is not to the Great Battle at all but to the time
after the fall of Númenor.

**Annal 397**   It is not said in AB 1 that the Iron Crown was beaten into
fetters. In Q (§18) it was made into a collar for Morgoth's neck.

# IV
# AINULINDALË

In all the works given in this history so far, there has been only one account of the Creation of the World, and that is in the old tale of *The Music of the Ainur*, written while my father was at Oxford on the staff of the Dictionary in 1918–20 (I. 45). The 'Sketch of the Mythology' (S) makes no reference to it (IV. 11); Q and AV 1 only mention in their opening sentences 'the making of the World', the making of 'all things' by Ilúvatar (IV. 78, 263); and AV 2 adds nothing further. But now, among the later writings of the 1930s (see pp. 107–8), he turned again to the tale told by Rúmil to Eriol in the garden of Mar Vanwa Tyaliéva in Kortirion, and wrote a new version; and it is remarkable that in this case he went back to the actual text of the original *Music of the Ainur*. The new version was composed with the 'Lost Tale' in front of him, and indeed he followed it fairly closely, though rephrasing it at every point – a great contrast to the apparent jump between the rest of the 'Valinórean' narrative in the *Lost Tales* and the 'Sketch', where it seems possible that he wrote out the condensed synopsis without re-reading them (cf. IV. 41–2).

The 'cosmogonical myth', as he called it long after (I. 45), was thus already, as it would remain, a separate work, independent of 'The Silmarillion' proper; and I believe that its separation can be attributed to the fact that there was no mention of the Creation in S, where the *Quenta* tradition began, and no account of it in Q. But QS has a new opening, a brief passage concerning the Great Music and the Creation of the World, and this would show that the *Ainulindalë* was already in existence, even were this not demonstrable on other grounds (see note 20).

But the *Ainulindalë* consists in fact of two separate manuscripts. The first, which simply for the purposes of this chapter I will call 'A', is extremely rough, and is full of changes made at the time of composition – these being for the most part readings from the old *Lost Tales* version which were written down but at once struck out and replaced. There is neither title-page nor title, but at the beginning my father later scribbled *The Music of the Ainur*. The second text, which I will here call 'B', is a fair copy of the first, and in its original form a handsome manuscript, without hesitations or changes in the act of writing; and although there are a great many differences between the two the great majority of them are minor stylistic alterations, improvements of wording and the fall of sentences. I see no reason to think that there was any interval between them; and I think therefore that A can be largely passed over here, and comparison of the substance made directly between the very finished second text B and the original *Tale of the Music of the Ainur*; noting however that in many details of expression A was closer to the old *Tale*. More substantial differences between A and B are given in the notes.

B has a title-page closely associated in form with those of the *Ambarkanta* and the *Lhammas*, works also ascribed to Rúmil; see p. 108.

*Ainulindalë*
The Music of the Ainur
This was written by Rúmil of Tûn

I give now the text of this version as it was originally written (the manuscript became the vehicle of massive rewriting many years later, when great changes in the cosmological conception had entered).

The Music of the Ainur
and the Coming of the Valar

These are the words that Rúmil spake to Ælfwine concerning the beginning of the World.[1]

There was Ilúvatar, the All-father, and he made first the Ainur, the holy ones, that were the offspring of his thought, and they were with him before Time. And he spoke to them, propounding to them themes of·music, and they sang before him, and he was glad. But for a long while they sang only each alone, or but few together, while the rest hearkened; for each comprehended only that part of the mind of Ilúvatar from which he came, and in the understanding of their brethren they grew but slowly. Yet ever as they listened they came to deeper understanding, and grew in unison and harmony.

And it came to pass that Ilúvatar called together all the Ainur, and declared to them a mighty theme, unfolding to them things greater and more wonderful than he had yet revealed; and the glory of its beginning and the splendour of its end amazed the Ainur, so that they bowed before Ilúvatar and were silent.

Then said Ilúvatar: 'Of the theme that I have declared to you, but only incomplete and unadorned, I desire now that ye make in harmony together a great music. And since I have kindled you with the Fire, ye shall exercise your powers in adorning this theme, each with his own thoughts and devices. But I will sit and hearken and be glad that through you great beauty has been wakened into song.'

Then the voices of the Ainur, like unto harps and lutes, and pipes and trumpets, and viols and organs, and like unto countless choirs singing with words, began to fashion the theme of Ilúvatar to a great music; and a sound arose of endless interchanging melodies, woven in harmonies, that passed beyond hearing both in the depths and in the heights, and the places of the dwelling of Ilúvatar were filled to overflowing, and the music and the echo of the music went out into the Void, and it was not void. Never was there before, nor has there since been, a music so immeasurable, though it has been said that a greater still shall be made before Ilúvatar by the choirs of the Ainur and the Children of Ilúvatar after the end of days.[2] Then shall the themes of Ilúvatar be played aright, and take being in the moment of their playing, for all shall then understand his intent in their part, and shall know the comprehension each of each, and Ilúvatar shall give to their thoughts the secret Fire, being well pleased.

But now the All-father sat and hearkened, and for a great while it seemed good to him, for the flaws in the music were few. But as the theme progressed, it came into the heart of Melko[3] to inter-weave matters of his own imagining that were not in accord with the theme of Ilúvatar; for he sought therein to increase the power and glory of the part assigned to himself. To Melko among the Ainur had been given the greatest gifts of power and knowledge, and he had a share in all the gifts of his brethren;[4] and he had gone often alone into the void places seeking the secret Fire that gives life. For desire grew hot within him to bring into being things of his own, and it seemed to him that Ilúvatar took no thought for the Void, and he was impatient of its emptiness.[5] Yet he found not the Fire, for it is with Ilúvatar, and he knew it not. But being alone he had begun to conceive thoughts of his own unlike those of his brethren.

Some of these he now wove into his music, and straightway discord arose about him, and many that sang nigh him grew despondent and their thought was disturbed and their music faltered; but some began to attune their music to his rather than to the thought which they had at first. And the discord of Melko spread ever wider and the music darkened, for the thought of Melko came from the outer dark whither Ilúvatar had not yet turned the light of his face. But Ilúvatar sat and hearkened, until all that could be heard was like unto a storm, and a formless wrath that made war upon itself in endless night.

Then Ilúvatar was grieved, but he smiled, and he lifted up his left hand, and a new theme began amid the storm, like and yet unlike the former theme, and it gathered power and had new

sweetness. But the discord of Melko arose in uproar against it, and
there was again a war of sound in which music was lost. Then
Ilúvatar smiled no longer, but wept, and he raised his right hand;
and behold, a third theme grew amid the confusion, and it was
unlike the others, and more powerful than all. And it seemed at
last that there were two musics progressing at one time before the
seat of Ilúvatar, and they were utterly at variance. One was deep
and wide and beautiful, but slow and blended with unquenchable
sorrow, from which its beauty chiefly came. The other had grown
now to a unity and system, yet an imperfect one, save in so far as it
derived still from the eldest theme of Ilúvatar; but it was loud, and
vain, and endlessly repeated, and it had little harmony, but rather
a clamorous unison as of many trumpets braying upon one note.
And it essayed to drown the other music by the violence of its
voice, but it seemed ever that its most triumphant notes were
taken by the other and woven into its pattern.[6]

   In the midst of this strife, whereat the halls of Ilúvatar shook
and a tremor ran through the dark places, Ilúvatar raised up both
his hands, and in one chord, deeper than the abyss, higher than
the firmament, more glorious than the sun, piercing as the light of
the eye of Ilúvatar, the music ceased.

   Then said Ilúvatar: 'Mighty are the Ainur, and mightiest
among them is Melko; but that he may know, and all the Ainur,
that I am Ilúvatar, those things that ye have sung and played, lo! I
have caused to be. Not in the musics that ye make in the heavenly
regions, as a joy to me and a play unto yourselves, but rather to
have shape and reality, even as have ye Ainur. And behold I shall
love these things that are come of my song even as I love the Ainur
who are of my thought. And thou, Melko, shalt see that no theme
may be played that has not its uttermost source in me, nor can any
alter the music in my despite. For he that attempts this shall but
aid me in devising things yet more wonderful, which he himself
has not imagined. Through Melko have terror as fire, and sorrow
like dark waters, wrath like thunder, and evil as far from my light
as the uttermost depths of the dark places come into the design. In
the confusion of sound were made pain and cruelty, devouring
flame and cold without mercy, and death without hope. Yet he
shall see that in the end this redounds only to the glory of the
world, and this world shall be called of all the deeds of Ilúvatar the
mightiest and most lovely.'

   Then the Ainur were afraid, and understood not fully what was said; and Melko was filled with shame and with the anger of shame. But Ilúvatar arose in splendour and went forth from the fair regions that he had made for the Ainur and came into the dark places; and the Ainur followed him.[7]

But when they came into the midmost Void they beheld a sight of surpassing beauty, where before had been emptiness. And Ilúvatar said: 'Behold your music! For of my will it has taken shape, and even now the history of the world is beginning. Each will find contained within the design that is mine the adornments that he himself devised; and Melko will discover there those things which he thought to bring out new from his own heart, and will see them to be but a part of the whole, and tributary to its glory. But I have given being unto all.'[8] And lo! the secret Fire burned in the heart of the World.

Then the Ainur marvelled seeing the world globed amid the Void, and it was sustained therein, but not of it. And looking upon light they were joyful, and seeing many colours their eyes were filled with delight; but because of the roaring of the sea they felt a great unquiet. And they observed the air and winds, and the matters whereof the middle-earth was made,[9] of iron and stone and silver and gold and many substances: but of all these water they most greatly praised. And it is said that in water there lives yet the echo of the Music of the Ainur more than in any substance else that is in the world, and many of the Children of Ilúvatar hearken still unsated to the voices of the sea, and yet know not for what they listen.

Now of water had that Ainu whom we call Ulmo mostly thought, and of all most deeply was he instructed by Ilúvatar in music. But of the airs and winds Manwë most had pondered, who was the noblest of the Ainur. Of the fabric of earth had Aulë thought, to whom Ilúvatar had given skill and knowledge scarce less than to Melko; but the delight and pride of Aulë was in the process of making, and in the thing made, and not in possession nor in himself, wherefore he was a maker and teacher and not a master, and none have called him lord.[10]

Now Ilúvatar spake to Ulmo and said: 'Seest thou not how Melko has made war upon thy realm? He has bethought him of biting cold without moderation, and has not destroyed the beauty of thy fountains, nor of thy clear pools. Behold the snow, and the cunning work of frost! Behold the towers and mansions of ice! Melko has devised heats and fire without restraint, and has not dried up thy desire, nor utterly quelled the music of the sea. Behold rather the height and glory of the clouds, and the ever-changing mists and vapours, and listen to the fall of rain upon the earth. And in these clouds thou art drawn yet nearer to thy brother Manwë whom thou lovest.'[11]

Then Ulmo answered: 'Yea, truly, water is become now fairer than my heart imagined, neither had my secret thought conceived the snow-flake, nor in all my music was contained the falling of the rain. Lo! I will seek Manwë, that he and I may make melodies for ever and ever to thy delight!' And Manwë and Ulmo have from the beginning been allied, and in all things served most faithfully the purpose of Ilúvatar.

And even as Ilúvatar spake to Ulmo, the Ainur beheld the unfolding of the world, and the beginning of that history which Ilúvatar had propounded to them as a theme of song. Because of their memory of the speech of Ilúvatar and the knowledge that each has of the music which he played the Ainur know much of what is to come, and few things are unforeseen by them. Yet some things there are that they cannot see, neither alone nor taking counsel together. But even as they gazed, many became en-amoured of the beauty of the world, and engrossed in the history which came there to being, and there was unrest among them. Thus it came to pass that some abode still with Ilúvatar beyond the world, and those were such as had been content in their playing with the thought of the All-father's design, caring only to set it forth as they had received it. But others, and among them were many of the wisest and fairest of the Ainur, craved leave of Ilúvatar to enter into the world and dwell there, and put on the form and raiment of Time.[12] For they said: 'We desire to have the guidance of the fair things of our dreams, which thy might has made to have a life apart, and we would instruct both Elves and Men in their wonder and uses, when the times come for thy Children to appear upon earth.' And Melko feigned that he desired to control the violence and turmoils, of heat and of cold, that he had caused within the world, but he intended rather to usurp the realms of all the Ainur and subdue to his will both Elves and Men; for he was jealous of the gifts with which Ilúvatar purposed to endow them.

For Elves and Men were devised by Ilúvatar alone, nor, since they comprehended not fully that part of the theme when it was propounded to them, did any of the Ainur dare in their music to add anything to their fashion; and for that reason these races are called the Children of Ilúvatar, and the Ainur are rather their elders and their chieftains than their masters. Wherefore in their meddling with Elves and Men the Ainur have endeavoured at times to force them, when they would not be guided, but seldom to good result, were it of good or evil intent. The dealings of the Ainur have been mostly with the Elves, for Ilúvatar made the Elves most like in nature to the Ainur, though less in might and stature; but to Men he gave strange gifts.

Knowing these things and seeing their hearts, Ilúvatar granted the desire of the Ainur, and it is not said that he was grieved. Then those that wished descended, and entered into the world. But this condition Ilúvatar made, or it is the necessity of their own love (I know not which), that their power should thenceforth be contained and bounded by the world, and fail with it; and his purpose with them afterward Ilúvatar has not revealed.

Thus the Ainur came into the world, whom we call the Valar, or the Powers, and they dwelt in many places: in the firmament, or in the deeps of the sea, or upon earth, or in Valinor upon the borders of earth. And the four greatest were Melko and Manwë and Ulmo and Aulë.

Melko for a long while walked alone, and he wielded both fire and frost, from the Walls of the World to the deepest furnaces that are under it, and whatsoever is violent or immoderate, sudden or cruel, is laid to his charge, and for the most part justly. Few of the divine race went with him, and of the Children of Ilúvatar none have followed him since, save as slaves, and his companions were of his own making: the Orcs and demons that long troubled the earth, tormenting Men and Elves.[13]

Ulmo has dwelt ever in the Outer Ocean, and governed the flowing of all waters, and the courses of all rivers, the replenishment of springs and the distilling of rain and dew throughout the world. In the deep places he gives thought to music great and terrible; and the echo thereof runs through all the veins of the world, and its joy is as the joy of a fountain in the sun whose wells are the wells of unfathomed sorrow at the foundations of the world.[14] The Teleri learned much of him, and for this reason their music has both sadness and enchantment. Salmar came with him, who made the conches of Ulmo;[15] and Ossë and Uinen, to whom he gave control of waves and of the inner seas; and many other spirits beside.

Aulë dwelt in Valinor, in the making of which he had most part, and he wrought many things both openly and in secret. Of him comes the love and the knowledge of the substances of earth, both tillage and husbandry, and the crafts of weaving and of beating metals and of shaping wood. Of him comes the science of earth and its fabric and the lore of its elements, their blending and mutation.[16] Of him the Noldor learned much in after days, and they are the wisest and most skilled of the Elves. But they added much to his teaching and delighted much in tongues and alphabets and in the figures of broidery, of drawing and carving. For art was the especial gift of the Children of Ilúvatar.[17] And the Noldor achieved the invention of gems, which were not in the world before them; and the fairest of all gems were the Silmarils, and they are lost.

But the highest and holiest of the Valar was Manwë Súlimo, and he dwelt in Valinor, sitting in majesty upon his throne; and his throne was upon the pinnacle of Taniquetil, which is the highest of the mountains of the world, and stands upon the borders of Valinor. Spirits in the shape of hawks and of eagles flew ever to and from his house, whose eyes could see to the depths of the sea and could pierce the hidden caverns under the world, whose wings could bear them through the three regions of the firmament beyond the lights of heaven to the edge of darkness;[18] and they brought word to him of well nigh all that passed: yet some things are hid even from the eyes of Manwë.

With him was Varda the most beautiful. Now the Ainur that came into the world took shape and form, such even as have the Children of Ilúvatar who were born of the world; but their shape and form is greater and more lovely and it comes of the knowledge and desire of the substance of the world rather than of that substance itself, and it cannot always be perceived, though they be present. And some of them, therefore, took form and temper as of female, and some as of male.[19] But Varda was the Queen of the Valar, and was the spouse of Manwë; and she wrought the stars, and her beauty is high and aweful, and she is named in reverence. The children of Manwë and Varda are Fionwë Úrion their son and Ilmar their daughter; and these are the eldest of the Children of the Gods.[20] They dwell with Manwë, and with them are a great host of fair spirits in great happiness. Elves and Men love Manwë most of all the Valar,[21] for he is not fain of his own honour, nor jealous of his own power, but ruleth all to peace. The Lindar[22] he loved most of all the Elves, and of him they received song and poesy; for poesy is the delight of Manwë, and the song of words is his music. Behold the raiment of Manwë is blue, and blue is the fire of his eyes, and his sceptre is of sapphire; and he is the king in this world of Gods and Elves and Men, and the chief defence against Melko.

After the departure of the Valar there was silence for an age, and Ilúvatar sat alone in thought. Then Ilúvatar spake, and he said: 'Behold I love the world, and it is a mansion for Elves and Men. But the Elves shall be the fairest of earthly creatures, and they shall have and shall conceive more beauty than all my children, and they shall have greater bliss in this world. But to Men I will give a new gift.'

Therefore he willed that the hearts of Men should seek beyond the world and find no rest therein; but they should have a virtue to fashion their life, amid the powers and chances of the world, beyond the Music of the Ainur, which is as fate to all things else. And of their operation everything should be, in shape and deed, completed, and the world fulfilled unto the last and smallest. Lo! even we, Elves, have found to our sorrow that Men have a strange power for good or ill, and for turning things aside from the purpose of Valar or of Elves; so that it is said among us that Fate is not master of the children of Men; yet are they blind, and their joy is small, which should be great.

But Ilúvatar knew that Men, being set amid the turmoils of the powers of the world, would stray often, and would not use their gift in harmony; and he said: 'These too, in their time, shall find that all they do redounds at the end only to the glory of my work.' Yet the Elves say that Men are often a grief even unto Manwë, who knows most of the mind of Ilúvatar.[23] For Men resemble Melko most of all the Ainur, and yet have ever feared and hated him.[24] It is one with this gift of freedom that the children of Men dwell only a short space in the world alive, and yet are not bound to it, nor shall perish utterly for ever. Whereas the Eldar remain until the end of days, and their love of the world is deeper, therefore, and more sorrowful. But they die not, till the world dies, unless they are slain or waste in grief – for to both these seeming deaths are they subject – nor does age subdue their strength, unless one grow weary of ten thousand centuries; and dying they are gathered in the halls of Mandos in Valinor, whence often they return and are reborn in their children. But the sons of Men die indeed. Yet it is said that they will join in the Second Music of the Ainur,[25] whereas

Ilúvatar has not revealed what he purposes for Elves and Valar after the world's end; and Melko has not discovered it.

## NOTES

1 There is nothing corresponding to this prefatory sentence in the draft text A. It is notable that Ælfwine still heard the story of the Music of the Ainur from Rúmil's own lips in Tol-eressëa, as he did in the *Lost Tales*.

2 The *Tale* has here: 'by the choirs of both Ainur *and the sons of Men* after the Great End.' Both texts of the new version have: 'by the choirs of the Ainur *and the Children of Ilúvatar* after the end of days.' On this see I. 63, where I suggested that the change in the present version may have been unintentional, in view of the last sentence of the text.

3 A has here: 'sitting upon the left hand of Ilúvatar'.

4 The *Tale* has here: '*some of the greatest* gifts of power and wisdom and knowledge'; A has '*many of the greatest* gifts of power and knowledge'. The statement in B that Melko had '*the greatest* gifts of power and knowledge' is the first unequivocal statement of the idea that Melko was the mightiest of all the Ainur; although in the *Tale* (I. 54) Ilúvatar says that 'among them [the Ainur] is Melko the most powerful in knowledge' (where the new version has 'mightiest among them is Melko' (p. 158)). In Q it is said (IV. 79) that 'Very mighty was he made by Ilúvatar, and some of the powers of all the Valar he possessed' (cf. QS §10). In *The Lost Road* (p. 63) he was 'the eldest in the thought of Ilúvatar', whereas in QS §10 he was 'coëval with Manwë'.

5 This sentence, from 'and it seemed to him', is not in A.

6 From this point a page is lost from the A manuscript. See note 7.

7 Here A takes up again after the missing page. It will be seen that in this passage B is very close to the *Tale* (I. 54–5), and A may be supposed to have been even closer.

8 The *Tale* has here: 'One thing only have I added, the fire that giveth Life and Reality'; A has: 'But this I have added: life.'

9 A has 'a middle-earth' (in the *Tale* 'the Earth'). The use of 'middle-earth' (which probably first appears in AV 1, IV. 264) here is curious and I cannot account for it; there seems no reason to specify the middle lands, between the seas, to the exclusion of the lands of the West and East. But the reading survived through the post-*Lord of the Rings* versions of the *Ainulindalë*; the change in *The Silmarillion* (p. 19) to 'the matters of which Arda was made' was editorial.

10 This sentence, from 'but the delight and pride of Aulë', is not in A.

11 Both A and B have Ilúvatar speak to Ulmo of 'thy brother Manwë'.

12 The words 'and put on the form and raiment of Time' are not in A.

13  This notable sentence ('Few of the divine race . . .') is not in A.

14  A still closely echoed the passage in the *Tale*: 'In the deeps he bethinks him of music great and strange, and yet full of sorrow (and in this he has aid from Manwë).' – On 'the veins of the world' see IV. 255.

15  Salmar appears here in the original *Music of the Ainur* and elsewhere in the *Lost Tales*, but in no subsequent text until now. This is the first mention of his being the maker of the conches of Ulmo.

16  This sentence is not in A.

17  A has here: 'For art was the especial gift of the Eldar.' The term *Eldar* is presumably used here in the old sense, i.e. 'Elves', as again also in the last paragraph of the text; cf. AV 2, annal 2000 and commentary.

18  This sentence, from 'whose wings could bear them', is not in A. For the three regions of the firmament (*Vista, Ilmen, Vaiya*) see the diagrams accompanying the *Ambarkanta*, IV. 243, 245.

19  This passage replaces the following briefer wording of A: 'Now the Ainur that came into the world took shape and form, such even as the Children of Ilúvatar who were born in the world; but greater and more beautiful, and some were in form and mind as women and some as men.' This is the first statement in my father's writings concerning the 'physical' (or rather 'perceptible') form of the Valar, and the meaning of gender as applied to them.

20  Fionwë *Úrion* reappears from the *Lost Tales*; in the previous texts of the 1930s he is Fionwë simply, as also in QS (§4). On his 'parentage' see IV. 68. – Where B has *Ilmar* A has *Ild Merildë Ildumë Ind Estë*, struck out one after the other, and then *Ilmar* (*Ild* and *Ind* are perhaps uncompleted names). This was obviously where the name *Ilmar(ë)* arose (replacing *Erinti* of the *Lost Tales*), and it is thus shown that the *Ainulindalë* preceded QS, which has *Ilmarë* as first written (§4). A final *-e* was added, probably early, to *Ilmar* in B. The occurrence of *Estë* among the rejected names in A is curious, since Estë already appears in the certainly earlier AV 1 as the wife of Lórien; presumably my father was momentarily inclined to give the name another application.

The statements that Fionwë and Ilmar(ë) are the eldest of the Children of the Gods, and that they dwell with Manwë, are not in A.

21  A retains the reading of the *Tale*, 'and Men love Manwë most of all the Valar.'

22  A has: 'The Lindar whom Ingwë ruled'; cf. the *Tale*: 'The Teleri whom Inwë ruled.'

23  A has: 'Yet the Eldar say that the thought of Men is often a grief to Manwë, and even to Ilúvatar.'

24  After 'feared and hated him' A (deriving closely from the *Tale*) has: 'And if the gift of freedom was the envy and amazement of the Ainur, the patience of Ilúvatar is beyond their understanding.'

25   This passage is somewhat different in A: 'whereas the Eldar remain
     until the end of days, unless they are slain or waste in grief – for to
     both these deaths they are subject – nor does age subdue their
     strength, unless one grow weary in a thousand centuries; and dying
     they are gathered in the halls of Mandos in Valinor, and some are
     reborn in their children. But the sons of Men will it is said join in the
     Second Music of the Ainur,' &c. In changing 'a thousand centuries'
     to 'ten thousand centuries' my father was going back to the *Tale*
     (I. 59).
         On the mention specifically of Men at the Second Music of the
     Ainur, which goes back to the *Tale*, see note 2.

It will be seen that while every sentence of the original *Tale of the Music
of the Ainur* was rewritten, and many new elements entered, the central
difference between the oldest version and that in the published *Silmarillion* still survived at this time: 'the Ainur's first sight of the World
was in its actuality, not as a Vision that was taken away from them and
only given existence in the words of Ilúvatar: *Eä!* Let these things Be!'
(I. 62).

# V

# THE LHAMMAS

There are three versions of this work, all good clear manuscripts, and I think that all three were closely associated in time. I shall call the first *Lhammas A*, and the second, developed directly from it, *Lhammas B*; the third is distinct and very much shorter, and bears the title *Lammasethen*. *Lhammas A* has now no title-page, but it seems likely that a rejected title-page on the reverse of that of *B* in fact belonged to it. This reads:

The *Lammas*
Or 'Account of Tongues' that Pengolod of Gondolin wrote afterward in Tol-eressëa, using in part the work of Rúmil the sage of Kôr

The title-page of *Lhammas B* reads:

The *'Lhammas'*
This is the 'Account of Tongues' which Pengoloð of Gondolin wrote in later days in Tol-eressëa, using the work of Rúmil the sage of Tûn. This account Ælfwine saw when he came into the West

At the head of the page is written: '3. *Silmarillion'*. At this stage the *Lhammas*, together with the *Annals*, was to be a part of 'The Silmarillion' in a larger sense (see p. 202).

The second version relates to the first in a characteristic way; closely based on the first, but with a great many small shifts of wording and some rearrangements, and various more or less important alterations of substance. In fact, much of *Lhammas B* is too close to *A* to justify the space required to give both, and in any case the essentials of the linguistic history are scarcely modified in the second version; I therefore give *Lhammas B* only, but interesting points of divergence are noticed in the commentary. The separate *Lammasethen* version is also given in full.

In order to make reference to the very packed text easier I divide it, without manuscript authority, into numbered sections (as with the *Quenta* in Vol. IV), and the commentary follows these divisions.

Associated with the text of *Lhammas A* and *B* respectively are two 'genealogical' tables, *The Tree of Tongues*, both of which are reproduced here (pp. 169–70). The later form of the *Tree* will be found to agree in almost all particulars with the text printed; differing features in the earlier form are discussed in the commentary.

Various references are made in the text to 'the Quenta'. In §5 the reference (made only in *Lhammas A*, see the commentary) is associated with the name *Kalakilya* (the Pass of Light), and this name occurs in QS but not in Q. Similarly in §6 'It is elsewhere told that Sindo brother of Elwë, lord of the Teleri, strayed from his kindred': the story of Thingol's disappearance and enchantment by Melian has of course been told elsewhere, but in Q he is not named Sindo, whereas in QS he is. It seems therefore that these references to the *Quenta* are to QS rather than to Q, though they do not demonstrate that my father had reached these passages in the actual writing of QS when he was composing the *Lhammas*; but that question is not important, since the new names themselves had already arisen, and therefore associate the *Lhammas* with the new version of 'The Silmarillion'.

There follows now the text of *Lhammas B*. The manuscript was remarkably little emended subsequently. Such few changes as were made are introduced into the body of the text but shown as such.

## Of the Valian Tongue and its Descendants

### 1

From the beginning the Valar had speech, and after they came into the world they wrought their tongue for the naming and glorifying of all things therein. In after ages at their appointed time the *Qendi* (who are the Elves) awoke beside Kuiviénen, the Waters of Awakening, under the stars in the midst of Middle-earth.

There they were found by Oromë, Lord of Forests, and of him they learned after their capacity the speech of the Valar; and all the tongues that have been derived thence may be called Oromian or Quendian. The speech of the Valar changes little, for the Valar do not die; and before the Sun and Moon it altered not from age to age in Valinor. But when the Elves learned it, they changed it from the first in the learning, and softened its sounds, and they added many words to it of their own liking and devices even from the beginning. For the Elves love the making of words, and this has ever been the chief cause of the change and variety of their tongues.

### 2

Now already in their first dwellings the Elves were divided into three kindreds, whose names are now in Valinorian form: the *Lindar* (the fair), the *Noldor* (the wise), and the *Teleri* (the last, for these were the latest to awake). The Lindar dwelt most

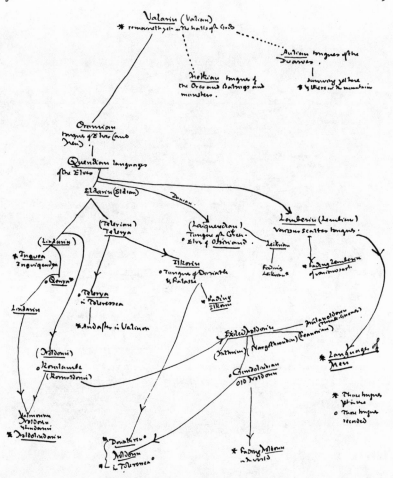

The Tree of Tongues (earlier form)

westerly; and the Noldor were the most numerous; and the Teleri
who dwelt most easterly were scattered in the woods, for even
from their awakening they were wanderers and lovers of freedom.
When Oromë led forth the hosts of the Elves on their march
westward, some remained behind and desired not to go, or heard
not the call to Valinor. These are named the *Lembi*, those that
lingered, and most were of Telerian race. / But those that followed
Oromë are called the *Eldar*, those that departed. [*This sentence
struck out and carefully emended to read:* But Oromë named the
Elves *Eldar* or 'star-folk', and this name was after borne by all that

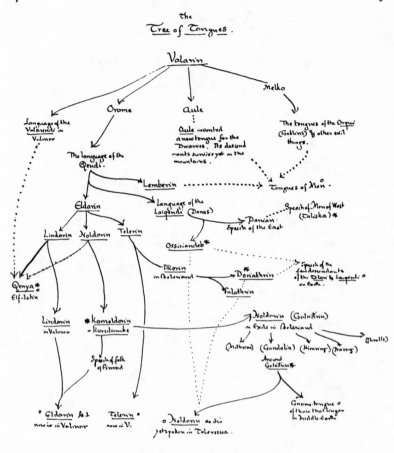

The Tree of Tongues (later form)

followed him, both the *Avari* (or 'departing') who forsook Middle-
earth, and those who in the end remained behind (*changed from*
who in the end remained in Beleriand, the Ilkorindi of Doriath
and the Falas).] But not all of the Eldar came to Valinor or to the
city of the Elves in the land of the Gods upon the hill of Kôr. For
beside the Lembi, that came never into the West of the Hither
Lands until ages after, there were the folk of the Teleri that
remained in Beleriand as is told hereafter, and the folk of the
Noldor that strayed upon the march and came also later into the

east of Beleriand. These are the *Ilkorindi* that are accounted among the Eldar, but came not beyond the Great Seas to Kôr while still the Two Trees bloomed. Thus came the first sundering of the tongues of the Elves, into *Eldarin* and *Lemberin*; for the Eldar and Lembi did not meet again for many ages, nor until their languages were wholly estranged.

## 3

On the march to the West the Lindar went first, and the chief house among them was the house of Ingwë, high-king of the Eldalië, and the oldest of all Elves, for he first awoke. His house and people are called the *Ingwelindar* or *Ingwi*. The march began when the Elves had dwelt for about thirty Valian years in the Hither Lands, and ten more Valian years passed, ere the first companies of the Lindar reached the Falassë, that is the western shores of the Hither Lands, where Beleriand lay of old. Now each Valian year in the days of the Trees was as ten years now are, but before the making of the Sun and Moon the change and growth of all living things was slow, even in the Hither Lands. Little difference, therefore, was found yet in the speeches of the three kindreds of the Eldalië. In the year 1950 of the Valar the Qendi awoke, and in the year 1980 they began their march, and in the year 1990 the Lindar came over the mountains into Beleriand; and in the year 2000 of the Gods the Lindar and the Noldor came over the seas unto Valinor in the west of the world and dwelt in the light of the Trees. But the Teleri tarried on the march, and came later, and they were left behind in Beleriand for ten Valian years, and lived upon the Falassë and grew to love the sea above all else. And thereafter, as is told in the *Quenta*, they dwelt, because of the deeds of Ossë, an age, which is 100 years of the Valar, on Toleressëa, the Lonely Isle, in the Bay of Faërie, before at last they sailed in their swan-ships to the shores of Valinor. The tongue of the Teleri became therefore sundered somewhat from that of the Noldor and Lindar, and it has ever remained apart though akin.

*Of the tongues of the Elves in Valinor*

## 4

For nine ages, which is nine hundred Valian years, the Lindar and Noldor dwelt in Valinor, ere its darkening; and for eight of those ages the Teleri dwelt nigh them, yet separate, upon the

shores and about the havens of the land of the Gods, while
Morgoth was in captivity and vassalage. Their tongues therefore
changed in the slow rolling of the years, even in Valinor, for the
Elves are not as the Gods, but are children of Earth. Yet they
changed less than might be thought in so great a space of time; for
the Elves in Valinor did not die, and in those days the Trees still
flowered, and the changeful Moon was not yet made, and there
was peace and bliss.

Nonetheless the Elves much altered the tongue of the Valar,
and each of their kindreds after their own fashion. The most
beautiful and the least changeful of these speeches was that of the
Lindar, and especially the tongue of the house and folk of Ingwë.*

It grew therefore to be a custom in Valinor, early in the days of
the abiding there of the Elves, for the Gods to use this speech in
converse with the Elves, and Elves of different kindred one with
another; and for long this language was chiefly used in inscriptions
or in writings of wisdom or poetry. Thus an ancient form of
Lindarin speech became early fixed, save for some later adoptions
of words and names from other dialects, as a language of high
speech and of writing, and as a common speech among all Elves;
and all the folk of Valinor learned and knew this language. It was
called by the Gods and Elves 'the Elvish tongue', that is *Qenya*,
and such it is usually now named, though the Elves call it also
*Ingwiqenya*, especially in its purest and highest form, and also
*tarquesta* high-speech, and *parmalambë* the book-tongue. This is
the Elf-latin, and it remains still, and all Elves know it, even such
as linger still in the Hither Lands. But the speech of daily converse
among the Lindar has not remained as Qenya, but has changed
therefrom, though far less than have Noldorin or even Telerin
from their own tongues in the ancient days of the Trees.

The Noldor in the days of their exile brought the knowledge of
the Elf-latin into Beleriand, and, though they did not teach it to
Men, it became used among all the Ilkorindi. The names of the
Gods were by all the Eldar preserved and chiefly used only in
Qenya form; although most of the Valar had titles and by-names,
different in different tongues, by which in daily use their high

*(*Footnote, added after the writing of the main text:*) But the Lindar
were soft-spoken, and at first altered the Elvish speech more than the
other peoples by the softening and smoothing of its sounds, especially the
consonants; yet in words [*struck out:* and forms] they were, as is
said, less changeful, and their grammar and vocabulary remained more
ancient than those of any other Elvish folk.

names were usually supplanted, and they were seldom heard save in solemn oath and hymn. It was the Noldor who in the early days of their sojourn in Valinor devised letters, and the arts of cutting them upon stone or wood, and of writing them with brush or pen; for rich as are the minds of the Elves in memory, they are not as the Valar, who wrote not and do not forget. But it was long ere the Noldor themselves wrote in books with their own tongue, and though they carved and wrote in those days many things in monument and document, the language they used was Qenya, until the days of Fëanor's pride.

## 5

Now in this way did the daily speeches of the Lindar and Noldor draw apart. At first, though they saw and marvelled at the light and bliss of Valinor, the Elves forgot not Middle-earth and the starlight whence they came, and they longed at times to look upon the stars and walk a while in shadow. Wherefore the Gods made that cleft in the mountain-wall which is called the Kalakilya the Pass of Light. Therein the Elves piled the green hill of Kôr, and built thereon the city of Tûn [> Túna],* and highest amid the city of Tûn [> Túna] was the white tower of Ingwë. And the thought of the lands of earth was deepest in the hearts of the Noldor, who afterward returned thither, and they abode in that place whence the outer shadows could be seen, and among the vales and mountains about Kalakilya was their home. But the Lindar grew soon to love more the tree-lit gardens of the Gods, and the wide and fertile plains, and they forsook Tûn [> Túna], and dwelt far away and returned seldom; and though Ingwë was ever held the high-king of all the Eldar, and none used his white tower, save such as kept aflame the everlasting lamp that burned there, the Noldor were ruled by Finwë, and became a people apart, busy with the making of many things, and meeting with their kin only at such times as they journeyed into Valinor for feast or council. Their converse was rather with the Teleri of the neighbouring shores than with the Lindar, and the tongues of Teleri and Noldor drew somewhat together again in those days.

Now as the ages passed and the Noldor became more numerous and skilled and proud, they took also to the writing and using in books of their own speech beside the Qenya; and the form in

*(Marginal note added at the same time as the change of Tûn to Túna:) Which the Gods called Eldamar.

which it was earliest written and preserved is the ancient Noldorin or *Kornoldorin*, which goes back to the days of the gem-making of Fëanor son of Finwë. But this Noldorin never became fixed, as was Qenya, and was used only by the Noldor, and its writing changed in the course of years with the change of speech and with the varying devices of writing among the Gnomes. For this old Noldorin, the *Korolambë* (tongue of Kôr) or *Kornoldorin*, besides its change by reason of passing time, was altered much by new words and devices of language not of Valian origin, nor common to all the Eldar, but invented anew by the Noldor. The same may be said of all the tongues of the Qendi, but in the invention of language the Noldor were the chief, and they were restless in spirit, even before Morgoth walked among them, though far more so afterwards, and changeful in invention. And the fruit of their spirit were many works of exceeding beauty, and also much sorrow and great grief.

Thus in Valinor, ere the end of the days of Bliss, there was the Elf-latin, the written and spoken Qenya, which the Lindar first made, though it is not the same as their own daily speech; and there was Lindarin the language of the Lindar; and Noldorin the language, both written and spoken, of the Noldor (which is in its ancient form named *Korolambë* or *Kornoldorin*); and the tongue of the Teleri. And over all was the *Valya* or *Valarin*, the ancient speech of the Gods, that changed not from age to age. But that tongue they used little save among themselves in their high councils, and they wrote it not nor carved it, and it is not known to mortal Men.

*Of the tongues of the Elves in Middle-earth, and of the Noldorin that returned thither*

**6**

It is elsewhere told how Sindo brother of Elwë, lord of the Teleri, strayed from his kindred and was enchanted in Beleriand by Melian and came never to Valinor, and he was after called Thingol and was king in Beleriand of the many Teleri who would not sail with Ulmo for Valinor but remained on the Falassë, and of others that went not because they tarried searching for Thingol in the woods. And these multiplied and were yet at first scattered far and wide between Eredlindon and the sea; for the land of Beleriand is very great, and the world was then still dark. In the course of ages the tongues and dialects of Beleriand became altogether estranged from those of the other Eldar in Valinor, though the learned in such lore may perceive that they were anciently sprung from Telerian. These were the Ilkorin speeches of Beleriand, and they are also different from the tongues of the Lembi, who came never thither.

In after days the chief of the languages of Beleriand was the tongue of Doriath and of the folk of Thingol. Closely akin thereto was the speech of the western havens Brithombar and Eglorest, which is *Falassian*, and of other scattered companies of the Ilkorindi that wandered in the land, but all these have perished; for in the days of Morgoth only such of the Ilkorindi survived as were gathered under the protection of Melian in Doriath. The speech of Doriath was much used in after days by Noldor and Ilkorindi alike, / for Thingol was a great king, and his queen Melian divine [*emended to:* among the survivors at Sirion's mouth, for Elwing their queen and many of their folk came from Doriath.]

**7**

About the year of the Valar 2700, and nearly 300 years of the Valar ere the return of the Gnomes, while the world was still dark, the Green-elves, that were called / in their own tongue *Danas* [*written over heavily struck out: Danyar* (. . . Qenya *Nanyar*)], the followers of Dan, came also into eastern Beleriand, and dwelt in that region which is called Ossiriand, the Land of Seven Rivers, beneath the western slopes of Eredlindon. This folk was in the beginning of Noldorin race, but is not counted among the Eldar, nor yet among the Lembi. For they followed Oromë at first, yet forsook the host of Finwë ere the great march had gone very far, and turned southwards. But finding the lands dark and barren, for in the eldest days the South was never visited by any of the Valar, and its sky was scanty in stars, this folk turned again north. Their first leader was Dan, whose son was Denethor; and Denethor led many of them at last over the Blue Mountains in the days of Thingol. For though they had turned back, the Green-elves had yet heard the call to the West, and were still drawn thither at times in unquiet and restlessness; and for this reason they are not among the Lembi. Nor was their tongue like the tongues of the Lembi, but was of its own kind, different from the tongues of Valinor and of Doriath and of the Lembi [*emended to:* different from the tongues of Valinor and of the Lembi, and most like that of Doriath, though not the same.]

But the speech of the Green-elves in Ossiriand became somewhat estranged from that of their own kindred that remained east of Eredlindon, being much affected by the tongue of Thingol's people. Yet they remained apart from the Telerian Ilkorins and remembered their kin beyond the mountains, with whom they had still some intercourse, and named themselves in common with these *Danas*. But they were called by others Green-elves, *Laiqendi*, because they loved the green wood, and green lands of fair waters; and the house of Denethor loved green above all colours, and the beech above all trees. They were allied with Thingol but not subject to him, until the return of Morgoth to the North, when after Denethor was slain many sought the protection of Thingol. But many dwelt still in Ossiriand, until the final ruin, and held to their own speech; and they were without a king, until Beren came unto them and they took him for lord. But their speech has now vanished from the earth, as have Beren and Lúthien.* Of their kindred that dwelt still east of the mountains few came into the history of Beleriand, and they remained in the Hither Lands after the ruin of the West in the great war, and have faded since or become merged among the Lembi. Yet in the overthrow of Morgoth they were not without part, for they sent many of their warriors to answer the call of Fionwë.

Of the tongues of the Lembi nought is known from early days, since these Dark-elves wrote not and preserved little; and now they are faded and minished. And the tongues of those that linger still in the Hither Lands show now little kinship one to another, save that they all differ from Eldarin tongues, whether of Valinor and Kôr or of lost Beleriand. But of Lembian tongues are come in divers ways, as is later said, the manifold tongues of Men, save only the eldest Men of the West.

## 8

Now we speak again of the Noldor; for these came back again from Valinor and dwelt in Beleriand for four hundred years of the Sun. In all about 500 years of our time passed from the darkening of Valinor and the rape of the Silmarils until the rescue of the remnant of the exiled Gnomes, and the overthrow of Morgoth by the sons of the Gods. For nigh 10 Valian years (which is 100 of our

---

*(*Footnote to the text:*) Yet this tongue was recorded in Gondolin, and it is not wholly forgotten, for it was known unto Elwing and Eärendel.

time) passed during the flight of the Noldor, five ere the burning of the ships and the landing of Fëanor, and five more until the reunion of Fingolfin and the sons of Fëanor; and thereafter wellnigh 400 years of warfare with Morgoth followed. And after the rising of the Sun and Moon and the coming into the Hither Lands of measured time, which had before lain under the moveless stars without night or day, growth and change were swift for all living things, most swift outside Valinor, and most swift of all in the first years of the Sun. The daily tongue of the Noldor changed therefore much in Beleriand, for there was death and destruction, woe and confusion and mingling of peoples; and the speech of the Gnomes was influenced also much by that of the Ilkorins of Beleriand, and somewhat by tongues of the eldest Men, and a little even by the speech of Angband and of the Orcs.

Though they were never far estranged, there came thus also to be differences in speech among the Noldor themselves, and the kinds are accounted five: the speech of Mithrim and of Fingolfin's folk; and the speech of Gondolin and the people of Turgon; the speech of Nargothrond and the house and folk of Felagund and his brothers; and the speech of Himring and the sons of Fëanor; and the corrupted speech of the thrall-Gnomes, spoken by the Noldor that were held captive in Angband, or compelled to the service of Morgoth and the Orcs. Most of these perished in the wars of the North, and ere the end was left only *múlanoldorin* [> *mólanoldorin*], or the language of the thralls, and the language of Gondolin, where the ancient tongue was kept most pure. But the folk of Maidros son of Fëanor remained, though but as a remnant, almost until the end; and their speech was mingled with that of all the others, and of Ossiriand, and of Men.

The Noldorin that lives yet is come in the most part from the speech of Gondolin. There the ancient tongue was preserved, for it was a space of 250 years from the founding of that fortress until its fall in the year of the Sun 307, and during most of that time its people held little converse with Men or Elves, and they dwelt in peace. Even after its ruin something was preserved of its books and traditions, and has survived unto this day, and in its most ancient form this is called *Gondolic* (*Gondolindeb* [> *Gondolindren*]) or Old [> Middle] Noldorin. But this tongue was the speech of the survivors of Gondolin at Sirion's mouth, and it became the speech of all the remnants of the free Elves in Beleriand, and of such as joined with the avenging hosts of Fionwë. But it suffered thus, after the fall of Gondolin, admixture from Falassian, and from Doriathrin most (for Elwing was there with the fugitives of Menegroth), and somewhat from Ossiriand, for Dior, father of Elwing, was the last lord of the Danas of Ossiriand.

Noldorin is therefore now the speech of the survivors of the wars of Beleriand that returned again to the West with Fionwë, and were given Tol-eressëa to dwell in. But still in the Hither Lands of the West there linger the fading remnants of the Noldor and the Teleri, and hold in secret to their own tongues; for there were some of those folk that would not leave the Middle-earth or the companionship of Men, but accepted the doom of Mandos that they should fade even as the younger Children of Ilúvatar waxed, and remained in the world, and are now, as are all those of Quendian race, but faint and few.

## 9

Of other tongues than the Oromian speeches, which have yet some relationship therewith, little will here be said. *Orquin*, or *Orquian*, the language of the Orcs, the soldiers and creatures of Morgoth, was partly itself of Valian origin, for it was derived from the Vala Morgoth. But the speech which he taught he perverted wilfully to evil, as he did all things, and the language of the Orcs was hideous and foul and utterly unlike the languages of the Qendi. But Morgoth himself spoke all tongues with power and beauty, when so he wished.

Of the language of the Dwarves little is known to us, save that its origin is as dark as is the origin of the Dwarvish race itself; and their tongues are not akin to other tongues, but wholly alien, and they are harsh and intricate, and few have essayed to learn them. (Thus saith Rúmil in his writings concerning the speeches of the earth of old, but I, Pengolod, have heard it said by some that Aulë first made the Dwarves, longing for the coming of Elves and Men, and desiring those to whom he could teach his crafts and wisdom. And he thought in his heart that he could forestall Ilúvatar. But the Dwarves have no spirit indwelling, as have Elves and Men, the Children of Ilúvatar, and this the Valar cannot give. Therefore the Dwarves have skill and craft, but no art, and they make no poetry.* Aulë devised a speech for them afresh, for his

---

*These two sentences were rewritten later, but very roughly; see the commentary on §9.

delight [is] in invention, and it has therefore no kinship with others; and they have made this harsh in use. Their tongues are, therefore, Aulian; and survive yet in a few places with the Dwarves in Middle-earth, and besides that the languages of Men are derived in part from them.)

But the Dwarves in the West and in Beleriand used, as far as they could learn it, an Elf-tongue in their dealings with the Elves, especially that of Ossiriand, which was nearest to their mountain homes; for the Elves would not learn Dwarvish speech.

## 10

The languages of Men were from their beginning diverse and various; yet they were for the most part derived remotely from the language of the Valar. For the Dark-elves, various folk of the Lembi, befriended wandering Men in sundry times and places in the most ancient days, and taught them such things as they knew. But other Men learned also wholly or in part of the Orcs and of the Dwarves; while in the West ere they came into Beleriand the fair houses of the eldest Men learned of the Danas, or Green-elves. But nought is preserved of the most ancient speeches of Men, save of the tongue of the folk of Bëor and Haleth and Hádor. Now the language of these folk was greatly influenced by the Green-elves, and it was of old named *Taliska*, and this tongue was known still to Tuor, son of Huor, son of Gumlin, son of Hádor, and it was in part recorded by the wise men of Gondolin, where Tuor for a while abode. Yet Tuor himself used this tongue no longer, for already even in Gumlin's day Men in Beleriand forsook the daily use of their own tongue and spoke and gave even names unto their children in the language of the Gnomes. Yet other Men there were, it seems, that remained east of Eredlindon, who held to their speech, and from this, closely akin to Taliska, are come after many ages of change languages that live still in the North of the earth. But the swarthy folk of Bor, and of Uldor the accursed, were not of this race, and were different in speech, but that speech is lost without record other than the names of these men.

## 11

From the great war and the overthrow of Morgoth by Fionwë and the ruin of Beleriand, which is computed to have happened about the year 397 of the Sun, are now very many ages passed; and the tongues of the waning Elves in different lands have changed beyond recognition of their kinship one to another, or to the languages of Valinor, save in so far as the wise among them use still Qenya, the Elf-latin, which remains in knowledge among them, and by means of which they yet at whiles hold converse with emissaries from the West. For many thousands of years have passed since the fall of Gondolin. Yet in Tol-eressëa, by the power of the Valar and their mercy, the old is preserved from fading, and there yet is Noldorin spoken, and the language of Doriath and of Ossiriand is held in mind; and in Valinor there flower yet the fair tongues of the Lindar and the Teleri; but the Noldor that returned and went not to war and suffering in the world are no longer separate and speak as do the Lindar. And in Kôr and in Tol-eressëa may still be heard and read the accounts and histories of things that befell in the days of the Trees, and of the Silmarils, ere these were lost.

[*The following passage was added to the manuscript:*]

The names of the Gnomes in the *Quenta* are given in the Noldorin form as that tongue became in Beleriand, for all those after *Finwë* father of the Noldor, whose name remains in ancient form. Likewise all the names of Beleriand and the regions adjacent (many of which were first devised by the Gnomes) dealt with in the histories are given in Noldorin form. Though many are not Noldorin in origin and only adjusted to their tongue, but come from Beleriandic, or from Ossiriandic or the tongues of Men. Thus from Beleriandic is the name *Balar*, and *Beleriand*, and the names *Brithombar*, *Eglorest*, *Doriath*, and most of the names of lakes and rivers.

## Commentary on the Lhammas

### 1

The use of *Quendi* to signify 'all Elves' has appeared in a correction to AV 2, and is in any case implied by the name *Lindar* which is used in AV 2 for the First Kindred, formerly called *Quendi*; see the commentary on annal 2000.

For much earlier references to the language of the Valar see I. 235. In the small part of *Gilfanon's Tale* that was written it is said expressly (I. 232) that 'the Eldar or Qendi had the gift of speech direct from Ilúvatar'. Now, in the *Lhammas*, the origin of all Elvish speech is the speech of the Valar (in both forms of the *Tree of Tongues* called *Valarin*, and in §5 also *Valya*), communicated to the Elves by the instruction of Oromë.

2

There is no mention in Q of Elves who would not leave the Waters of Awakening: the Ilkorindi or Dark-elves are there (§2) defined as those who were lost on the Great March. But in AV (both versions) it was only 'the most part' of the Elvenfolk who followed Oromë, and there are very early references to those who would not or did not leave Palisor (see I. 234, II. 64). These Elves are here for the first time given a name: the *Lembi*, those that lingered, opposed to the *Eldar*, those that departed – and at this stage the old term *Eldar* was to bear, not merely this reference, but this actual meaning: 'those that departed' (see p. 344).

The latter part of this section differs in *Lhammas A*:

These are called the *Lembi*, or those that were left. But the others were called the *Eldar*, those that departed. Thus came the first sundering of tongues, for the Eldar and Lembi met not again for many ages. With the Lembi were merged and are reckoned such of the three kindreds of the Eldar as fell out by the way, or deserted the host, or were lost in the darkness of the ancient world; save only the remnants of the Teleri and the folk of Thingol that lingered in Beleriand. These also are called Eldar, but surnamed *Ilkorindi*, for they came never to Valinor or the city of the Elves in the land of the Gods upon the hill of Kôr. The tongue of the Ilkorindi of Beleriand showed still in after ages its kinship with Telerian, and thus Quendian was divided into three: Eldarin, and Ilkorin, and Lemberin; but the last was scattered and diverse and never one.

This is very clear. The term *Eldar* has acquired its later significance of the Elves of the Great Journey (only), and it is not restricted to those who in the end went to Valinor, but includes the Elves of Beleriand: the *Eldar* are those who completed the journey from Kuiviénen to the country between Eredlindon and the Sea. On the other hand all Elves who did depart from Kuiviénen but who did not complete that journey are numbered among the *Lembi*. The term *Ilkorindi* is now used in a much narrower sense than previously: specifically the Eldar of Beleriand – the later *Sindar*, or Grey-elves. (These new meanings have in fact appeared, without elaboration, in AV 2 (annals 2000 and 2000–2010), where 'The Eldar are all those Elves called who obeyed the summons of Oromë', and where the Teleri who remained in Beleriand are called *Ilkorindi*.) Thus whereas in Q there is the simple scheme:

Eldar (all Elves)

Quendi     Noldoli     Teleri

Those lost on the Journey
Ilkorindi (Dark-elves)

in *Lhammas A* we have:

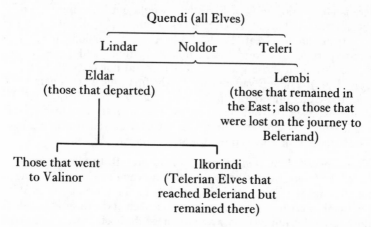

In *Lhammas B* (leaving aside for a moment the important emendation made to the text) there is now no mention of Elves who though they set out from Kuiviénen were lost on the road, and were merged with the Lembi; on the other hand, in addition to the Telerian Elves of Beleriand another people is included among the Ilkorindi – 'the folk of the Noldor that strayed upon the march and came also later into the east of Beleriand': the Green-elves of Ossiriand. It is also added in *Lhammas B* that most of the Lembi were of Telerian race (a statement not in fact consonant with what was said in one of the outlines for *Gilfanon's Tale* (I. 234), that the Elves who remained in Palisor were of the people of the Teleri, for the Teleri in the *Lost Tales* were the First Kindred, not the Third). The table just given for *Lhammas A* is changed to this extent, therefore:

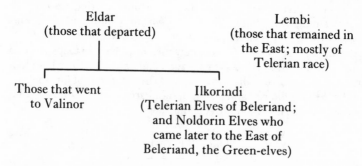

See further the commentaries on §§6, 7.

With the emendation made to *Lhammas B* we meet at last the ideas that it was Oromë who named the Elves *Eldar*, that *Eldar* meant 'Star-folk', and that Oromë's name was given to the Elves as a whole when he first found them, though it was only applied afterwards to those who set out on the Great Journey following him. (It is said in AV 2, annal 1950, that the Elves are called 'the children of the stars' on account of their awakening at the making of the stars, and this was later changed to '*Eldar*, the children of the stars'.) Here also appears for the first time the name *Avari*, taking over from *Eldar* the meaning 'Departing' (later, with the meaning changed to 'Unwilling', *Avari* was to replace *Lembi*). These movements are reflected in the *Etymologies* (see p. 344). The table must therefore now be further changed:

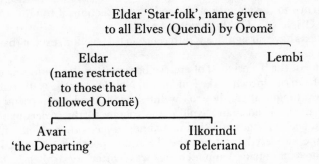

Eldar 'Star-folk', name given
to all Elves (Quendi) by Oromë

Eldar                                    Lembi
(name restricted
to those that
followed Oromë)

Avari                          Ilkorindi
'the Departing'              of Beleriand

The further change made to the emended passage, from 'remained in Beleriand, the Ilkorindi of Doriath and the Falas' to 'remained behind', was perhaps introduced because my father wished to allow for the Green-elves, who were Ilkorindi (and therefore Eldar), not Lembi.

We find here the first explanation of the name *Teleri* that has appeared ('the last, for these were the latest to awake'); see I. 267, entries *Telelli*, *Teleri*. Another new element in this section is the idea that the Three Kindreds were geographically separated in their first homes beside Kuiviénen – and the Noldor the most numerous of the three.

The fact that in *Lhammas B* the fundamental division of Elvish speech is twofold, *Eldarin* and *Lemberin*, whereas in *A* it is threefold, *Eldarin* and *Ilkorin* and *Lemberin*, does not, I think, represent any real difference in the linguistic conception. The primary division was twofold, for Eldarin and Lemberin speech began to move apart on separate paths from the time when the Eldar left Kuiviénen; but the division became threefold when the Ilkorindi were left behind in Beleriand.

### 3

The terms *Ingwi* and *Ingwelindar*, used here of the chief house of the Lindar, have not occurred before; but in the *Lost Tales* (see especially I. 115) the *Inwir* are the royal clan, the house of Inwë, among the First Kindred. It is now told that Ingwë was not only the high-king of the Eldalië, but was 'the oldest of all Elves, for he first awoke.'

The dates in this section agree precisely with the dates in AV 2 (which are those of AV 1 after emendation, IV. 272–3).

The form *Falassë* is found on the *Ambarkanta* map IV (IV. 249).

With what is said here about the slowness of change ('even in the Hither Lands') before the making of the Sun and Moon cf. the conclusion of AV 2:*

> Now measured time came into the world, and the growth, changing and ageing of all things was hereafter more swift, even in Valinor, but most swift in the Hither Lands upon Middle-earth, the mortal regions between the seas of East and West.

The reference to the *Quenta* at the end of this section, if to Q, is to IV. 87; if to QS, to §37. On this point see p. 168.

The two texts have no significant difference in this section, except that *Lhammas* A ends thus:

> The tongue of the Teleri on Tol-eressëa became therefore somewhat sundered from the speech of the Lindar and Noldor, and they adhered to their own tongue after; though dwelling many ages later in friendship nigh to the Lindar and Noldor the tongue of the Teleri progressed, in such changes as befell in Valinor, alike with its kindred, and became sundered far from the Telerian speech in Beleriand (where moreover outside Valinor change was swifter).

## 4

In writing 'nine ages' and 'eight ages' (found in both versions) at the beginning of this section my father seems for some reason to have been counting only to V.Y.2900; for the Lindar and Noldor dwelt in Valinor for 990 years (2000–2990) or nearly ten ages, and the Teleri dwelt on the shores for 880 years (2111–2990) or nearly nine ages, before the Darkening.

The complex linguistic development described in this section may be summarised thus:

Lindar: – *their early speech preserved* ('Elf-latin')    ⎤  Brought to
        – called *Qenya* (also *tarquesta, parmalabë*)   ⎥  Middle-earth
        – also called ('especially in its purest and    ⎥  by the Noldor
          highest form') *Ingwiqenya*    ⎬  and used by
        – used for *writing*, and also for converse with   ⎥  all the
          Elves of different speech and with the Gods  ⎦  Ilkorindi

Lindar: – *Lindarin*, later daily speech of the Lindar,
          changed from Qenya

The section in *Lhammas B* was changed in structure and substantially rewritten from that in *A*, but there is very little that materially changes

---

*Reference to the *Annals* is made to AV 2 and AB 2, the texts in this book, as being more convenient, whether or not the matter cited is found in the earlier versions given in Vol. IV.

the linguistic history as set out in the earlier version. At the end of the second paragraph, however, *Lhammas A* says of the speech of the Lindar:

> Least changed was the language of the Lindar, for they were closest to the Valar and most in their company; and most like Valian was the speech of Ingwë and his household.

In the next paragraph *A* makes no mention of *Ingwiqenya* (see the commentary on §5); and states that it was the Gods who called the 'Elf-latin' by the name *Qendya* (so spelt), 'Elfspeech', whereas the Elves called it *Eldarin*. This is an application of the term *Eldarin* different from its earlier use in *A* (see the commentary on §2) and from its use in *B* and in both versions of the *Tree of Tongues*.

Alboin Errol used the term 'Elf-latin' (or *Eressëan*, in contrast to *Beleriandic*); see p. 56. 'Elven-latin' is used of Quenya in Appendix F to *The Lord of the Rings*.

## 5

*Lhammas A* contains a reference to the *Quenta* which is omitted in B: 'wherefore, as is said in the *Qenta*, the Gods made that cleft in the mountain-wall which is Kalakilya the Pass of Light'; see p. 168.

The removal of the Lindar from Tûn is told in very similar terms in an addition to Q (IV. 89 note 7), where appears also the story that the Tower of Ingwë was not used afterwards except by those that tended the lamp – a story that was not told in later texts of 'The Silmarillion'.

*Lhammas B* follows the earlier version closely in this section, but there are one or two differences to be remarked. In the concluding paragraph, summarising all the tongues of Valinor, *Lhammas A* adds a reference to 'the noble dialect' of the speech of the Lindar, called *Ingwelindarin*, *Ingwëa*, or *Ingwiqendya* (see the commentary on §4); in *B* §4, on the other hand, *Ingwiqenya* is the 'purest and highest form' of the 'Elf-latin', *Qenya*. The earlier form of the *Tree of Tongues* illustrates the account of the matter in *Lhammas A*; the later form does not have any representation of it, nor does it mention the name *Ingwiqenya*.

In *Lhammas A* this section ends:

> And over all was *Valya* or *Valarin*, the Valian language, the pure speech of the Gods, and that changed little from age to age (and yet it did change, and swifter after the death of the Trees, for the Valar are not of the earth, yet they are in the world). But that tongue they used little save among themselves, for to Elves, and to such Men as knew it, they spoke the Qenya, and they wrote not nor carved in any letters the things which they spoke.

By emendations to *B* (as also in AV 2, note 3) Tûn becomes *Túna* – but it is still the name of the city, on the hill of Kôr; afterwards *Túna* was the hill, *Tirion* the city. In the added marginal note 'which the Gods called *Eldamar*' is the first occurrence of *Eldamar* since the *Lost Tales* (but the form *Eglamar* is found twice in drafts of the *Lay of Leithian*, in the line *from England unto Eglamar*, III. 157, 181). This was one of the original, foundation names of the mythology, occurring in the poem *The Shores of Faëry* (1915) and its prose preface (II. 262, 272). In the *Lost Tales* the name occurs very frequently, almost always with reference to the shores, or rocks, or bay of Eldamar. Now it becomes a name of the Elvish city itself, rather than of the regions in which the Elves dwelt and in which was situated their city on the hill. See QS §39 and commentary.

    This is a convenient place to mention an element in the second *Tree of Tongues* which is not explained by anything in the text of the *Lhammas*. An unbroken line is drawn from *Valarin* to *Language of the Valarindi in Valinor*, and from there a dotted line to *Qenya*. The *Valarindi* are the Children of the Valar; see pp. 110, 121. The meaning of the dotted and unbroken lines is defined in a note to a *Tree of Tongues* made later on: the dotted lines 'indicate lines of strong influence of one language upon another' [e.g. that of French upon English], while the unbroken lines 'denote inheritance and direct descent' [e.g. from Latin to French].

    A dotted line (originally drawn as unbroken) also runs from *Noldorin* to *Qenya*. This presumably illustrates the statement in the text (§4) that 'an ancient form of Lindarin speech became early fixed [i.e. as Qenya], save for some later adoptions of words and names from other dialects.'

## 6

In the *Lost Tales* (I. 120) the people of Tinwë Linto (Thingol) sought for him long when he was enchanted by Wendelin (Melian), but

> it was in vain, and he came never again among them. When therefore they heard the horn of Oromë ringing in the forest great was their joy, and gathering to its sound soon are they led to the cliffs, and hear the murmur of the sunless sea.

In Q (IV. 87) appears first the story that some of the Teleri were persuaded by Ossë 'to remain on the beaches of the world'; of Thingol's people all that is said in Q (IV. 85) is that 'they sought him in vain', and no more is added in QS (§32).

    With the reference here to the scattered Ilkorindi of Beleriand (i.e. those other than the folk of the Havens and Thingol's people) being gathered into Doriath at the time of Morgoth's return, cf. AV 2 (annal 2990, recounting the withdrawal after the fall of Denithor):

> Melian wove magic of the Valar about the land of Doriath; and most of the Elves of Beleriand withdrew within its protection, save some that lingered about the western havens, Brithombar and Eglorest beside the Great Sea, and the Green-elves of Ossiriand who dwelt still behind the rivers of the East.

    The reference to 'Sindo brother of Elwë, lord of the Teleri' is not in *Lhammas A*, which introduces the subject of the language of Beleriand differently:

Now in the courts of Thingol Valarin was known, for Melian was of the Valar; but it was used only by the king and queen and few of their household. For the tongue of Beleriand was the Eldarin speech of the Telerian Ilkorins, being the language of those that in the end would not sail with Ulmo, etc.

*Sindo the Grey* appears in AV 2, but as a correction of *Tindingol* (note 4); in QS §30 (again as *Sindo the Grey*) the name is present in the text from the first, as here in *Lhammas B*. With this name cf. *Singoldo* in the *Tale of Tinúviel* (II. 41), and *Sindingul* (> *Tindingol*) in AV 1 (IV. 264).

Where *Lhammas B* has 'These were the Ilkorin speeches of Beleriand, and they are also different from the tongues of the Lembi, who came never thither', *Lhammas A* has: 'These were the Ilkorin speeches of Beleriand, and they retained tokens of their kinship with Telerian, and they were different from the languages of the Lembi, for they saw none of these, until the Green-elves came from the East, as is later told.' That the Green-elves are reckoned as Lembi has been explicitly contradicted in *Lhammas B* §2, where they are Ilkorindi and counted among the Eldar; see the commentaries on §§2 and 7.

The emendation to *Lhammas B* at the end of the section modifies the linguistic history, but the implications of the change are not clear to me. As a result of it, it is no longer said that the Noldor and Ilkorindi in Beleriand used the speech of Doriath 'because Thingol was a great king', but, on the contrary, that the speech of Doriath was much used at Sirion's Haven. In §8 it was the Noldorin speech of Gondolin that was the speech of the Haven, influenced by that of Doriath because of the presence there of Elwing and fugitives from the Thousand Caves.

## 7

While the passage concerning the Green-elves very largely follows what has already been told in AV, there are some interesting details. It was said in AV that the Green-elves under their leader Dan found the southward lands barren and dark; but the barrenness and darkness are now explained: the Valar had neglected the South, and the skies had been less bountifully strewn with stars. The South was a dark region in the original myths: in the *Tale of the Sun and Moon* (I. 182) Manwë appointed the course of the Sun between East and West 'for Melko held the North and Ungweliant the South' – which as I noted (I. 200) 'seems to give Ungweliant a great importance and also a vast area subject to her power of absorbing light.'

It has not been told before that many of the Green-elves passed into Doriath after Morgoth's return; among these, much later, Túrin's enemy Saeros would be notorious (*Unfinished Tales* p. 77).

Other elements in the account in the *Lhammas* have already appeared in AB 2 (annal 52): that after the fall of Denethor the Green-elves had no king 'until Beren came among them', and also that they had kindred who remained east of Eredlindon, and whom they visited at times. In an early addition to annal 2700 in AV 2 (note 8) 'the *Danians* came over Eredlindon', and these Elves, on either side of the mountain-range, are called *Danians* also in *Lhammas A* (where B has *Danas*), with the further information that those who remained in the East were called *Leikvir*. In the earlier *Tree of Tongues* appears *Leikvian* where the later has *Danian speech of the East*.

In AV 1 the name of the Green-elves is *Laiqi* or *Laiqeldar* (IV. 270); in AV 2 no Elvish name is given; in *Lhammas A* they are *Laiqi* or *Laiqendi*, *Laiqendi* in B.

In *Lhammas A* the name *Denethor* is written over another name, very probably *Denilos*; in AV 1 *Denilos* > *Denithor* (IV. 270), in AV 2 *Denithor* > *Denethor* (note 5). In this connection there are some interesting pencilled alterations and additions in *Lhammas A* that were not taken up into B (or not made to it: it is not clear when these annotations were made):

> *ndan-* backwards, back. The turners-back. Thence the folk *ndăni̅*. *ndani-thārō* saviour of the Dani. Q[enya] *Nanisáro*. T[elerin] *Daintáro*. N[oldorin] *Dainthor*. D[oriathrin] *Denipor*.

(With this cf. the *Etymologies*, stems DAN, NDAN). At the same time, in 'This folk was in the beginning of Noldorin race' *Noldorin* was changed to *Lindarin*, and 'the host of Finwë' to 'the host of Ingwë'; cf. the conclusion of the *Lammasethen*.

The question again arises of whether the *Danas* were reckoned to be Eldar or not. *Lhammas A* is explicit that they were not Eldar but Lembi (commentary on §6); and again in the present section it is said in A that 'This folk was in the beginning of Noldorin race, but is not counted among the Eldar' – because they forsook the Great March. In *Lhammas B* on the other hand they are Ilkorindi and are counted among the Eldar (§2); yet in the present section the passage in A asserting that they were not Eldar reappears – with the addition that they were not Lembi either, because, although they turned back from the March, they were none-theless still drawn towards the West. I presume that my father changed his mind on this rather refined question as he wrote, and did not alter what he had written earlier. In any case, the Danas are sufficiently characterised as Elves of the Great March who abandoned it early on but who still felt a desire for the West, and the suggestion in B is clearly that it was this that ultimately brought a part of the people over the mountains. Their position is anomalous, and might equally well be classified either as Eldarin or as not Eldarin.

As a result, they introduce the possibility of a very distinct linguistic type among the Quendian tongues (it will be seen that in both forms of the *Tree of Tongues* their language is shown as branching from the Quendian line of descent between Lemberin and Eldarin). This type is characterised in an emendation to B as similar to the Ilkorin speech of Doriath (whereas in the text as first written it was said to be distinct from

Eldarin of Valinor, from Lemberin, and from the speech of Doriath). This emendation is rather puzzling. Why should the Danas show any particular linguistic affinity with the Elves of Doriath, who had completed the journey to Beleriand so very long before (some 700 Valian Years before)? Of course it is said immediately afterwards that the speech of the Danas *in Ossiriand* was 'much affected by the tongue of Thingol's people', but the emendation 'and most like that of Doriath, though not the same' presumably refers to this 'Danian' tongue in its original nature. See further the *Lammasethen* and commentary.

The sharp distinction made at the end of this section between all the Lemberin tongues on the one hand and all the Eldarin tongues (including those of the Ilkorindi of Beleriand) on the other is notable. It is implicit that long years of the Great Journey, followed by the utter separation of the Elves of Beleriand from those who remained in the East, rendered the Ilkorin speech at once quite isolated in development from any Lemberin tongue but also recognisably akin to Telerin of Valinor (at least to those 'learned in such lore', §6).

## 8

In this section *Lhammas B* followed *A* very closely, but one divergent passage in the earlier version may be cited. After the reference to *múlanoldorin* and the language of Gondolin as being the only forms of Noldorin speech in Middle-earth that survived 'ere the end', *A* has:

> First perished Fingolfin's folk, whose tongue was pure, save for some small influence from Men of the house of Hádor; and afterward Nargothrond. But the folk of Maidros son of Fëanor remained almost until the end, as also did the thrall-Noldor whose tongue was heard not only in Angband, but later in Mithrim and widely elsewhere. The tongue of Fëanor's sons was influenced largely by Men and by Ossiriand, but it has not survived. The Noldorin that lives yet, etc.

With the account in the first paragraph of the swiftness of change after the rising of the Sun and Moon cf. the commentary on §3. The reference here to 'the moveless stars' is reminiscent of the old *Tale of the Sun and Moon*, where it is said that certain of the stars 'abode where they hung and moved not': see I. 182, 200. – In the second paragraph the form *Himring* (for *Himling* in *Lhammas A*) appears for the first time other than by later emendation. – At the end of the third paragraph, 'somewhat from Ossiriand' in *B* should probably be 'somewhat from Ossiriandeb', as here in *A* and on the later form of the *Tree of Tongues*. – In the last paragraph the languages of those Eldarin Elves who remained in Middle-earth are in *A* called *Fading Noldorin* and *Fading Ilkorin*, terms that appear on the earlier *Tree of Tongues* (together with *Fading Leikvian*: see the commentary on §7).

The later dating pencilled into the manuscript AV 1 (whereby the events from the Battle of Alqualondë to the arrival of Fingolfin in

Middle-earth were contracted into a single Valian Year, IV. 273–4), not adopted in AV 2, was not adopted in the *Lhammas* either. The dates of the Sun-years are those of AB 2 (before they were changed), with the fall of Gondolin in 307 and the Great Battle at the end of the fourth century of the Sun.

The most noticeable feature of this section of the *Lhammas* in relation to the later conception is the absence of the story that a ban was placed by Thingol on the speech of the Noldor throughout his realm. In *The Silmarillion* it is said (p. 113) that already at the Feast of Reuniting in the year 20 'the tongue of the Grey-elves was most spoken even by the Noldor, for they learned swiftly the speech of Beleriand, whereas the Sindar were slow to master the tongue of Valinor'; and (p. 129) that after Thingol's ban 'the Exiles took the Sindarin tongue in all their daily uses, and the High Speech of the West was spoken only by the lords of the Noldor among themselves.' In the *Lhammas* it is indeed said (at the end of §6, before emendation) that 'the speech of Doriath was much used in after days by Noldor and Ilkorindi alike', and in the present section that 'the speech of the Gnomes was influenced much by that of the Ilkorins of Beleriand'; but it was Noldorin (from Gondolin) that was the language (influenced by other tongues) of Sirion's Haven and afterwards of Tol-eressëa. In its essential plan, therefore, though now much more complex, the linguistic evolution still derives from that in the *Lost Tales*; as I remarked in I. 51,

> In *The Silmarillion* the Noldor brought the Valinórean tongue to Middle-earth but abandoned it (save among themselves), and adopted instead the language of Beleriand, *Sindarin* of the Grey-elves who had never been to Valinor . . . In the *Lost Tales*, on the other hand, the Noldor still brought the Elvish speech of Valinor to the Great Lands, but they retained it, and there it itself changed and became wholly different ['Gnomish'].

There is no reference at the end of this section to any Gnomes returning to Valinor (as opposed to Tol-eressëa), as there is in Q (IV. 159, 162: 'But some returned even unto Valinor, as all were free to do who willed'; this is retained in QS, p. 332 §27). For those who did not depart into the West – the speakers of 'Fading Noldorin' and 'Fading Ilkorin' in *Lhammas A* – see the same passages in Q, again repeated in QS.

### 9

There appears here the first account of the origin of the Orc-speech: a wilful perversion of Valian speech by Morgoth. The further remarkable statement that Morgoth 'spoke all tongues with power and beauty, when so he wished' is not found in *Lhammas A*.

The legend of Aulë's making of the Dwarves has appeared in AB 2 (annal 104), in a passage strikingly similar to the present, and containing the same phrase 'the Dwarves have no spirit indwelling'. The passage in AB 2 was later modified (note 16) to make this not an assertion by the writer but a conception of the Dwarves entertained by the Noldor, and not the only opinion on the subject; in the *Lhammas* the passage was also changed, very hastily, and quite differently, thus:

> But the Dwarves derive their thought etc. (see *Quenta*). Therefore the works of the Dwarves have great skill and craft, but small beauty.

This reference to the *Quenta* is not to Q, which has nothing corresponding, but to QS, in which there is a chapter concerning the Dwarves. Here occurs the following (§123):

> Yet they *derive their thought* and being after their measure from only one of the Powers, whereas Elves and Men, to whomsoever among the Valar they chiefly turn, have kinship with all in some degree. Therefore the works of the Dwarfs *have great skill, but small beauty*, save where they imitate the arts of the Eldar . . .

Where *Lhammas B* has 'Of the language of the Dwarves little is known to us' *A* has 'known to me' (i.e. Rúmil).

## 10

In *Lhammas A* the origin and early history of the tongues of Men is somewhat differently described:

> For the Dark-elves . . . befriended wandering Men . . . and taught them such as they knew; and in the passing of the years the manifold tongues of Men developed from these beginnings, altered by time, and the invention of Men, and owning also the influence both of Dwarves and Orcs. But nought is preserved of the most ancient speech of Men, save [*struck out*: some words of] the tongues of Men of the West, who earliest came into Beleriand and spoke with the Elves, as is recorded in annals and accounts of those days by the Gnomes. Now the language of the three houses of Bëor, of Haleth, and of Hador, was *Taliska*, and this tongue was remembered still by Tuor, and recorded by the wise men of Gondolin. Yet Tuor himself used it no longer, for already ere [> in] his father Huor's day Men in Beleriand forsook the daily use of their own tongue, and spoke Noldorin, retaining some few words and names.

At the end of the section in *Lhammas A* my father added rapidly in pencil: 'But Taliska seems to have been derived largely from Danian'; see the commentary on the *Lammasethen*.

In the earlier *Tree of Tongues* the languages of Men are derived solely from Lemberin, agreeing with *Lhammas A* ('the manifold tongues of Men developed from these beginnings'), whereas the later *Tree* shows 'influence' (dotted lines) from Dwarf-speech, from Orc-speech, and from Lemberin (but no direct 'descent'), and 'influence' from the 'Danian speech of the East' on Taliska.

That the people of Hador abandoned their own language and adopted that of the Gnomes is told in AB 2 (annal 220). The account in *The Silmarillion* of the survival of the original tongue of the Edain, here called *Taliska*,* is quite different: see the commentary on AB 2 *ibid*.

The statement at the end of this section that the speech of the Swarthy Men 'is lost without record other than the names of these men' is not in accord with the *Etymologies* (stems BOR, ÚLUG), where the names of Bór and Ulfang and their sons are Elvish, given to them by the Noldor.

## 11

In the words of Rúmil here that 'many thousands of years have passed since the fall of Gondolin' an obliterated reading lies beneath 'many thousands of'; this was very probably '10,000', which is the reading of *Lhammas A*.

The statement in this section that 'the Noldor that returned [i.e. after hearing the Prophecy of the North] and went not to war and suffering in the world are no longer separate and speak as do the Lindar' is not in *Lhammas A*, but the earlier *Tree of Tongues* shows *Noldolindarin* as a coalescence of 'Valinorian Noldorin and Lindarin'; the later *Tree* similarly shows the 'speech of the folk of Finrod' (who returned to Valinor) coalescing with Lindarin, and becoming 'Eldarin as it now is in Valinor'.

The words '*in* Kôr' are not a simple slip, despite 'the Elves piled the green hill of Kôr, and built thereon the city of Tûn' in §5; see QS §29.

As regards the passage added at the end of *Lhammas B*, it may be noted that in Q (IV. 87) the names of the princes of the Noldoli are said to be given 'in form of Gnomish tongue as it was long spoken on the earth', and that there *Finn* (the form in S) was emended to *Finwë*. Of the place-names cited here as Beleriandic names accommodated to Noldorin, *Balar*, *Beleriand*, *Brithombar* and *Eglorest* appear in the *Etymologies* (stems BAL, BIRÍT, ELED) as Ilkorin names, but *Doriath* is Noldorin (stem GAT(H)).

## LAMMASETHEN

I give now the third, very short *Lhammas* text, which is I think certainly the latest of the three. At the head of it my father wrote in pencil *Sketch of a corrected version*, but then erased it. Its brief history is largely in agreement with that of *Lhammas B*, but it introduces a completely changed account of the origin of Quenya (so spelt).

### The shorter account of Pengolod: or *Lammasethen*
### Of the Elvish Tongues

The original Elvish or Quendian languages were derived from Oromë, and so from Valarin. But the Elves not only, already in the

---

*An historical grammar of *Taliska* is in existence.

brief period common to all, but especially in Eldarin, modified and softened the sounds, especially the consonants, of Valarin, but they began swiftly to invent new words and word-shapes, and developed a language of their own.

Apart from new inventions their language changed slowly. This was especially so in Valinor, but was true of all the tongues, for the Elves do not die. In this way it will be seen that Telerin, the last to leave Middle-earth, and isolated for an age and ten years of the Valar, first in Beleriand and after in Tol Eressëa, changed more than Koreldarin, but being after rejoined to its kindred in Valinor, remained closely akin to Noldorin and Lindarin. But its branch, spoken by the Teleri left in Beleriand for nearly 1000 Valian Years, changed more than the tongues of Valinor, and became very different from them. In some ways it grew like the Danian branch in Ossiriand.

Now the tongue of Noldor and Lindar was at first most akin. But the Lindar ceased after a time to dwell in Tûn or in close consort with the Noldor, and association was closer between Noldor and Teleri. Moreover the Lindar used a form of language which they took *afresh* from the Valar themselves in Valmar; and though they softened and altered this again it was in many ways quite different from the old Elvish or Quendian derived from Oromë. The Lindarin, which was a form of Quendian or Oromian, they used only among themselves, and never wrote. But their new tongue (Valinorian) became used by the Lindar in converse with the Gods, and in all their books of poetry, history, and wisdom. Moreover it was the first Elf-tongue to be written, and remained always the tongue used most in writing by Lindar, Teleri, and Noldor. It was used also by all Elves much in converse, especially among those of different kindred and dialect. The Gods, too, used this tongue, not pure Valarin, in their speech with all Elves. This tongue they called *Quenya* (that is *Elvish*). Quenya is the Elf-latin, and this name is given to its common form as used and written by all Elves. Therein are mixed some forms and words derived from other Elvish (Oromian) tongues. But a purer and more archaic form is used by Ingwë High-king of the Elves and his court and household, who never use the common Oromian Lindarin: this is *Ingwiqenya*.

Now ancient Noldorin, as first used, and written in the days of Fëanor in Tûn, remained spoken by the Noldor that did not leave Valinor at its darkening, and it abides still there, not greatly changed, and not greatly different from Lindarin. It is called

*Kornoldorin,* or *Finrodian* because Finrod and many of his folk returned to Valinor and did not go to Beleriand. But most of the Noldor went to Beleriand, and in the 400 years of their wars with Morgoth their tongue changed greatly. For three reasons: because it was not in Valinor; because there was war and confusion, and much death among the Noldor, so that their tongue was subject to vicissitudes similar to those of mortal Men; and because in all the world, but especially in Middle-earth, change and growth was very great in the first years of the Sun. Also in Beleriand the tongue and dialects of the Telerian Ilkorins was current, and their king Thingol was very mighty; and Noldorin in Beleriand took much from Beleriandic especially of Doriath. Most of the names and places in that land were given in Doriathrin form. Noldorin returned, after the overthrow of Morgoth, into the West, and lives still in Tol-eressëa, where it changes now little; and this tongue is derived mainly from the tongue of Gondolin, whence came Eärendel; but it has much of Beleriandic, for Elwing his wife was daughter of Dior, Thingol's heir; and it has somewhat of Ossiriand, for Dior was son of Beren who lived long in Ossiriand.

In Tol-eressëa are kept records of the ancient tongue of Ossiriand, which is no more; and also the tongue of the Western Men, the Elf-friends, whence came the mortal kindred of Eärendel. But this tongue is no more, and already in ancient days the Elf-friends spake mostly Noldorin, or Beleriandic; their own tongue was itself of Quendian origin, being learned east of the Mountains from a branch of the Danians, kindred of those Elves of Ossiriand which were called the Green-elves.

These are the Elvish tongues which are yet spoken, or of which writings are preserved.

| | | |
|---|---|---|
| Valinorian | { Ingwiqenya  Qenya (Elf-latin) } | Valarin |
| Oromian (a) | [ Lindarin  Kornoldorin——Noldorin  Telerin | } Eldarin |
| (b) | Doriathrin | |
| (c) | Danian——Ossiriandic  Taliskan (mortals) | } Ilkorin |
| (d) | Lembian (many scattered dialects) | Lemberin |

The Danians were of the Lindar [> Noldor] and began the march, but turned south and strayed, long ere Beleriand was reached. They did not come unto Beleriand, and then but in part, for many ages. Some reckon them Eldarin, some Lembian. In truth they are neither and have a middle place.

## Commentary on the Lammasethen

A further *Tree of Tongues* illustrates the *Lammasethen*, and is reproduced on p. 196. The starred languages are 'yet in use'.

The meaning of the passage concerning Quenya in this text is clearly that Quenya only arose after the separation of the Lindar from the Noldor, when the Noldor remained in Tûn but the Lindar retired into Valinor. There the Lindar retained their own spoken Eldarin tongue, not much different from the 'Finrodian' Noldorin of Tûn (*Kornoldorin*); but they also adopted and adapted a form of the Valarin language, and this 'Valinorian' tongue became *Quenya*. Much that is said of Quenya in the other versions is repeated in the *Lammasethen* – it was used by the Gods in converse with the Elves, by Elves in converse with Elves of different speech, and as the chief *written* language. The effect of this new conception is to withdraw Quenya from the various forms of Elvish (Quendian, Oromian) speech in Valinor and make it a language apart. *Ingwiqenya* remains as it became in *Lhammas B*, an especially pure and archaic form of Quenya used in the household of Ingwë; but it is now a pure and archaic form of 'Valinorian'. The differences between the conceptions are thus:

*Lhammas A* (commentary on §5):
- Early Lindarin speech preserved, and fixed as a high speech, a Common Speech, and a written tongue: *Quenya*
- *Later speech of the Lindar: Lindarin*
  'the noble dialect' of this: *Ingwiqendya* (*Ingwëa, Ingwelindarin*)
*Lhammas B* (§4):
- Early Lindarin speech preserved, and fixed as a high speech, a Common Speech, and a written tongue: *Quenya*
  Also called ('especially in its purest and highest form') *Ingwiqenya*
- Later speech of the Lindar: *Lindarin*
*Lammasethen:*
- The Lindar, after removal from Tûn, adopted anew the Valarin tongue; this 'Valinorian', a high speech, a Common Speech, and a written tongue, is *Quenya*
  A pure and archaic form of 'Valinorian': *Ingwiqenya*
- Original ('Quendian') speech of the Lindar, retained among themselves: *Lindarin*
There are a few other points to be noticed in the *Lammasethen*. The stage of *Koreldarin*, before the departure of the Lindar from Tûn upon Kôr, is marked on the third *Tree of Tongues*. – The Telerin speech of Beleriand (the speech of the Elves of Doriath and of the Havens of the Falas) is said to have 'grown like' (in some ways) the Danian tongue in

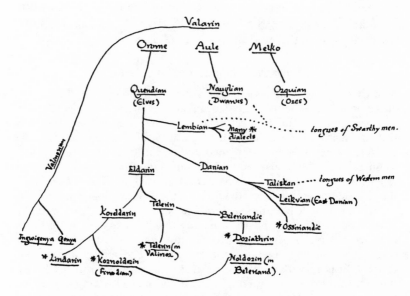

The Tree of Tongues (illustrating the *Lammasethen*)

Ossiriand; cf. the emendation in *Lhammas B* (§7) (the tongue of the Danians was 'most like that of Doriath, though not the same'), and my remarks on this in the commentary. – The Danians are said, as in *Lhammas B* §7, to be neither Eldar nor Lembi: they 'have a middle place'; though some will say one, and some the other. – The late emendation to *Lhammas A* (commentary on §7), making the Danians an originally Lindarin people, was adopted in the *Lammasethen*, but then rejected and replaced again by Noldorin.

Taliskan is said in the *Lammasethen* to be 'of Quendian origin', learned by the forefathers of the Western Men from Danian Elves east of Eredlindon; and in the list of tongues at the end of the text it is classed as an Ilkorin speech. In *B* (§10) the statements concerning Taliska are not perfectly clear: the Western Men 'learned of the Danas, or Green-elves', and their language was 'greatly influenced by the Green-elves'. In the third *Tree of Tongues* Taliskan is shown as deriving directly from Danian; cf. the addition to *Lhammas A* (commentary on §10): 'But Taliska seems to have been derived largely from Danian.' It is not clear to me why a dotted line (representing 'influence') leads from Taliskan to the 'tongues of Western Men'.

In the third *Tree* the name *Leikvian* reappears from the first, for the tongue of the Danians who remained east of Eredlindon (the *Leikvir* in

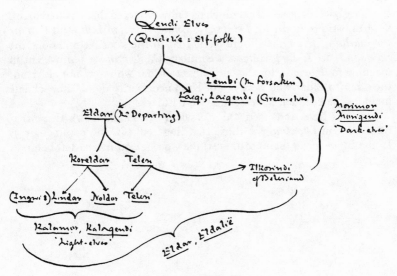

The Peoples of the Elves

*Lhammas A*, commentary on §7). The name *Nauglian* for the tongues of the Dwarves, used in the third *Tree*, does not appear in the *Lhammas* texts; in §9 they are called *Aulian*, as in the first *Tree*.

In conclusion, there is an interesting table of *the Elvish peoples* associated with the *Lhammas* papers, reproduced above. When my father made this table the *Eldar* were 'the Departing', as still in *Lhammas B* §2 before the emendation. The Green-elves, here *not* Eldar, are shown as a branch of the Quendi between Lembi and Eldar, just as in all three versions of the *Tree of Tongues* the language of the Green-elves (Danian) is shown as a branch from Quendian between Lemberin (Lembian) and Eldarin. The Lindar, Noldor, and Teleri are here placed as subdivisions of the Eldar, rather than as subdivisions of the Quendi before the Great Journey: in contrast to my table on p. 182, which is based on the express statement in *Lhammas A* and *B* (§2) that 'already in their first dwellings the Elves were divided into three kindreds, the Lindar, the Noldor, and the Teleri.'

An important new distinction appears in this table: *Morimor, Moriqendi* 'Dark-elves', and *Kalamor, Kalaqendi* 'Light-elves'. The Light-elves (a term formerly applied to the First Kindred) are now all those Elves who went to Valinor and saw the Light of the Trees; and the important overlap of nomenclature is introduced whereby the Ilkorindi of Beleriand are Eldar but also Dark-elves. The terms *Moriquendi* and *Calaquendi* of *The Silmarillion* here first appear. If this table is compared with that which I made for *The Silmarillion* ('The Sundering of the Elves') it will be seen that much had now emerged that was to remain, if we substitute *Avari* for *Lembi* and *Sindar* for *Ilkorindi* (and *Vanyar* for *Lindar*). The chief difference is that in the later formulations the *Laiquendi* are Eldar; while as a corollary the *Úmanyar* (equivalent in meaning to *Ilkorindi*, for the one refers to Eldar who were not of Aman, the other to Eldar who were not of Kôr) necessarily in the later scheme includes the Laiquendi, since they were Eldar.

*Lembi* is here translated 'the Forsaken'; in *Lhammas A* 'those that were left', in *Lhammas B* 'those that lingered' (§2 and commentary). In the *Etymologies* (stem LEB, LEM) the word *lemba* means 'left behind'.

# VI
# QUENTA SILMARILLION

As originally written, the *Quenta Silmarillion* (QS) was a beautiful and elegant manuscript; and when the first changes were made to it they were made with great care, usually by writing over erasures. It seems highly improbable that my father could have achieved this form without any intermediate texts developing it from the *Quenta Noldorinwa* (Q), and here and there in QS it appears in any case that he was copying, for words necessary to the sense were missed out and then put in above the line. But there is now, remarkably, no trace of any such material, until the tale of Beren and Lúthien is reached: from that point preliminary drafts do exist.

The manuscript became afterwards the vehicle of massive revisions, and was changed into a chaotic palimpsest, with layer upon layer of correction and wholesale rewriting, of riders and deletions. The great mass of this alteration and revision is firmly dateable to the period after the completion of *The Lord of the Rings*; but there is also an earlier phase of emendation in pencil to the opening chapters, which is in places substantial. From the manuscript thus emended my father made a typescript which was for most of its length almost an exact copy, but giving to the work a new title in addition to *Silmarillion*: *I·Eldanyárë*, 'The History of the Elves'. This new version did not proceed very far, however – no further in fact than the end of the chapter here numbered 3 (c). In order to understand the state of 'The Silmarillion' during the years when *The Lord of the Rings* was being written it is necessary to try to determine when it was made. It is in any case clear at once that it long preceded the major revision after *The Lord of the Rings* – the typescript, so far as it went, was indeed used for that revision, and was reduced to a shambles in the course of it.

In my father's letter to Stanley Unwin of 16 December 1937 – the day on which he received back the QS manuscript and other writings which he had submitted – he was still only 'promising to give thought and attention' to the question of 'a sequel or successor to *The Hobbit*' (*Letters* no. 19); but no more than three days later, on 19 December, he reported that he had written 'the first chapter of a new story about Hobbits – "A long expected party"' (*Letters* no. 20). It is certain, then, that he began work on the 'new story' at the very time that the QS manuscript came back into his possession; and I feel certain that when it did so he abandoned (for good, as it turned out) the new 'Silmarillion' narrative at

the point he had reached (for he had continued it in rougher form while
the manuscript was away, see pp. 293–4). But it is also clear that he did
not as yet abandon the work entirely. This is shown by some notes on a
scrap of paper to which my father fortunately and uncharacteristically
added a date:

Nov. 20 1937
*Note* when material returns
*Avari* are to be non-Eldarin = old *Lembi*
*Lembi* are to be Ilkorin Teleri
*Danians    Pereldar*
*Ilkorin*  :  *Alkorin* [struck out]
*hyarmen* for *harmen* south

The fact that the first three of these changes are among the early revisions
made to the QS manuscript (for their significance see pp. 218–19\*)
shows that he did do some further detailed work on it 'when the material
returned', i.e. after *The Lord of the Rings* was begun. It does not of course
show more precisely when that work was done or when the '*Eldanyárë*'
typescript was made, but here a second note with a date attached
provides evidence:

Feb. 3 1938
*Tintallë* Kindler can stand – but *tinwë* in Q[uenya] only = spark
(*tinta-* to kindle)
Therefore *Tinwerína > Elerína*
            *Tinwerontar > Elentári* (or *Tar-Ellion*)

Now the alterations of *Tinwerína* to *Elerína* and *Tinwerontar* to *Elentári*
were not made to the QS manuscript and do not appear in the typescript
(they were written in subsequently on the latter, only). This shows that
the typescript was made before 3 February 1938 – or more strictly, it had
at least reached the point where the name *Tinwerontar* occurs (chapter
3 (a), §19).

I conclude therefore that it was precisely at this crucial time (December 1937 – January 1938) that my father – entirely characteristically –
turned back again to the beginning of the *Quenta Silmarillion*, revising
the opening chapters and starting a new text in typescript ('*Eldanyárë*').
This soon petered out; and from that time the 'Silmarillion' narrative
remained unchanged for some thirteen years.

This conclusion determines the way in which the text of the first part
of the *Quenta Silmarillion* is presented in this book. In order to make the
contrast between 'The Silmarillion' of the earlier period and 'The
Silmarillion' after the major post-*Lord of the Rings* revision as clear in this
history as it was in fact, I give the text of the first five chapters (1 to 3 (c))
as it was *after* the first revision – which is the form of the typescript text as

---

\*For *Alkorin* beside *Ilkorin* see the *Etymologies*, stems AR², LA; for *Harmen*
> *Hyarmen* see p. 344.

it was originally made;* but important developments from the original form are given in the commentaries following each chapter. A great deal of this first rewriting was in fact a matter of improved expression rather than of narrative substance.

Although there are two texts for the first part of the work, I use the single abbreviation QS, distinguishing the manuscript and the typescript when necessary.

This is the title-page of the QS manuscript:

The
Quenta Silmarillion
Herein
is *Qenta Noldorinwa* or *Pennas inGeleidh*
or
History of the Gnomes

This is a history in brief drawn from many older tales; for all the matters that it contains were of old, and still are among the Eldar of the West, recounted more fully in other histories and songs. But many of these were not recalled by Eriol, or men have again lost them since his day. This Account was composed first by Pengolod of Gondolin, and Ælfwine turned it into our speech as it was in his time, adding nothing, he said, save explanations of some few names.

In this title, *inGeleidh* is an emendation made carefully over an erasure: the erased form was probably *na-Ngoelaidh* as in Q (IV. 77). The word *Silmarillion* was an addition; at first there stood simply *The Quenta*, as in Q.

In the preamble to Q only Eriol is named, and there is no mention of Pengolod; but in the preamble to AV 1 (IV. 263) it is said that both sets of *Annals*

> were written by Pengolod the Wise of Gondolin, before its fall, and after at Sirion's Haven, and at Tavrobel in Toleressëa after his return unto the West, and there seen and translated by Eriol of Leithien, that is Ælfwine of the Angelcynn.

The preamble to the QS manuscript is decisively different in its representation of the literary history from that of Q; for in Q the abridgement which that work is declared to be was *drawn from the Book of Lost Tales which Eriol wrote* after he had read the Golden Book in Kortirion, whereas in QS it was *written by Pengolod and translated by Eriol* (like

---

*Here and there my father made further very small alterations in wording as he typed (i.e. beyond changes marked on the manuscript), and these are of course included in the text given here. The relation between manuscript and typescript changes in chapter 3 (c); see p. 220.

the *Annals*) – the work being conceived by Pengolod as an epitome on a small scale against a background of 'histories and songs' in which the matters were recounted at greater length (but many of these are lost to us).

Associated with the QS typescript are no less than five sheets of title and preamble. The first of these is in manuscript, and reads thus:

### The Silmarillion

The history of the Three Jewels, the
Silmarils of Fëanor, in which is told
in brief the history of the Elves from
their coming until the Change of the
World

1. *Qenta Silmarillion*, or *Pennas Hilevril*
To which is appended
The houses of the princes of Men and Elves
The tale of years
The tale of battles

2. *The Annals of Valinor   Nyarna Valinóren*

3. *The Annals of Beleriand   Nyarna Valarianden*

4. The *Lhammas* or Account of Tongues

This manuscript page was then copied in typescript, with these differences: above *The Silmarillion* at the head stands *Eldanyárë*, and the *Lhammas* is not included. In both manuscript and typescript *Nyarna Valinóren* was changed to *Yénië Valinóren or Inias Valannor*; and *Nyarna Valarianden* to *Inias Veleriand*. (In Old English versions of the *Annals of Valinor* the Elvish name is *Valinórelúmien*, IV. 284, 290). Subsequently, in the typescript only, *Pennas Hilevril* > *Pennas Silevril*; *Inias Valannor* > *Inias Balannor*; *Inias Veleriand* > *Inias Beleriand*.

The next item is an elaborate and elegant page in red, blue, and black inks, which in its content is virtually the same as the typescript page just described; but here the name *I·Eldanyárë*, translated 'The History of the Elves', is explicitly an alternative: '*I·Eldanyárë* or *Silmarillion*'. The Elvish names of the *Annals* are the emended forms of the previous two pages: *Yénië Valinóren* or *Inias Valannor*, and *Inias Veleriand*, with the same later alterations of *Hilevril*, *Valannor*, and *Veleriand* to *Silevril*, *Balannor*, and *Beleriand* found on the typescript. On all three title-pages *Silmarillion* is a comprehensive title comprising within it not only the *Quenta Silmarillion* but also the two sets of *Annals*; cf. p. 109. The name *Qenta Noldorinwa* is not used.

Following these title-pages is a preamble comprising a note by

Ælfwine and a note by the Translator. Five lines of Old English verse by Ælfwine are the selfsame lines that Alboin Errol 'dreamed', and translated for his father, in *The Lost Road* (p. 44); they would reappear again once more in association with the poem *The Song of Ælfwine* (p. 103). This preamble is found both in manuscript and typescript. The manuscript form reads:

### Silmarillion

*Ælfwine's note*

These histories were written by Pengolod the Wise of Gondolin, both in that city before its fall, and afterwards at Tathrobel in the Lonely Isle, Toleressëa, after the return unto the West. In their making he used much the writings of Rúmil the Elfsage of Valinor, chiefly in the annals of Valinor and the account of tongues, and he used also the accounts that are preserved in the Golden Book. The work of Pengolod I learned much by heart, and turned into my tongue, some during my sojourn in the West, but most after my return to Britain.

> þus cwæþ Ælfwine Wídlást:
> Fela bið on Westwegum werum uncúðra,
> wundra ond wihta, wlitescyne lond,
> eardgeard ylfa ond ésa bliss.
> Lýt ǽnig wát hwylc his longað síe
> þám þe eftsíðes yldu getwǽfeð.

*Translator's note*

The histories are here given in English of this day, translated from the version of Eriol of Leithien, as the Gnomes called him, who was Ælfwine of Angelcynn. Such other matters as Ælfwine took direct from the Golden Book, together with his account of his voyage, and his sojourn in Toleressëa, are given elsewhere.

*Eriol* was altered to *Ereol* (cf. IV. 166, 283); and there is a pencilled annotation against the *Translator's note*:

Specimens (not here) are extant
    (a) of the original Eressëan form and script
    (b) of the annals as written by Ælfwine in ancient English

*Ælfwine's note* here is a development from the preamble to AV 1 (cited above p. 201); cf. also the second version of that preamble and my remarks about Rúmil's part in the *Annals* (p. 123). There is now no mention of Pengolod's having continued his work at Sirion's Haven after the fall of Gondolin. The form *Tathrobel* for *Tavrobel* occurs in Old English versions of AV 1 (IV. 282, 290). For the Golden Book see IV. 78, 274.

The typescript version of the preamble has some differences. The page is headed *Eldanyárë*, not *Silmarillion*, and *Ælfwine's note* is changed: the passage beginning 'after the return unto the West' reads here:

> after the Elves had returned into the West. In their making he used much the writings of Rúmil the Elf-sage of Valinor concerning other matters than the wars of Beleriand; and he used also the accounts that are preserved by the Elves of Eressëa in the Golden Book. The work of Pengolod I learned by heart . . .

In the *Translator's note* the spelling is *Ereol* and the words *that is now England* are added after *Angolcynn* (so spelt).

I give now the text of the *Quenta Silmarillion* as I think it stood when it was for long laid aside. As with *The Fall of Númenor* I have numbered the paragraphs, the numbers running continuously through the text; the paragraphing of the original is very largely retained. A commentary, related to the paragraphs, follows each chapter.

# QUENTA SILMARILLION*

Here begins the *Silmarillion* or history of the Silmarils

## I  OF THE VALAR

§1   In the beginning the All-father, who in Elvish tongue is named Ilúvatar, made the Ainur of his thought; and they made music before him. Of this music the World was made; for Ilúvatar gave it being, and set it amid the Void, and he set the secret fire to burn at the heart of the World; and he showed the World to the Ainur. And many of the mightiest of them became enamoured of its beauty, and desired to enter into it; and they put on the raiment of the World, and descended into it, and they are in it.

§2   These spirits the Elves name the Valar, which is the Powers, and Men have often called them Gods. Many lesser spirits of their own kind they brought in their train, both great and small; and some of these Men have confused with the Elves, but wrongly, for they were made before the World, whereas Elves and Men awoke first in the World, after the coming of the Valar. Yet in the making of Elves and of Men, and in the giving to each of their especial gifts, none of the Valar had any part. Ilúvatar alone was their author; wherefore they are called the Children of Ilúvatar.

§3   The chieftains of the Valar were nine. These were the

---

*In the manuscript (only) the word *Silmarillion* was an addition, as on the title-page (p. 201); but the heading 'Here begins the *Silmarillion* . . .' is original.

names of the Nine Gods in the Elvish tongue as it was spoken in Valinor; though they have other or altered names in the speech of the Gnomes, and their names among Men are manifold: Manwë and Melko, Ulmo, Aulë, Mandos, Lórien, Tulkas, Ossë, and Oromë.

§4   Manwë and Melko were brethren in the thought of Ilúvatar and mightiest of those Ainur who came into the World. But Manwë is the lord of the Gods, and prince of the airs and winds, and ruler of the sky. With him dwells as wife Varda the maker of the stars, immortal lady of the heights, whose name is holy. Fionwë and Ilmarë* are their son and daughter. Next in might and closest in friendship to Manwë is Ulmo, lord of waters, who dwells alone in the Outer Seas, but has the government of all water, seas and rivers, fountains and springs, throughout the earth. Subject to him, though he has often rebelled, is Ossë, the master of the seas about the lands of Men; and his wife is Uinen, the lady of the sea. Her hair lies spread through all the waters under skies.

*Marginal note to the text: Ilma is in the Quendian tongue starlight.

§5   Aulë has might but little less than Ulmo. He is the lord of earth. He is a smith and a master of crafts; and his spouse is Yavanna, the giver of fruits and lover of all things that grow. In majesty she is next to Varda among the queens of the Valar. She is fair and tall; and often the Elves name her Palúrien, the Lady of the Wide Earth.

§6   The Fanturi were brethren, and are named Mandos and Lórien. Nurufantur the elder was also called, the master of the houses of the dead, and the gatherer of the spirits of the slain. He forgets nothing, and knows all that shall be, save only what Ilúvatar has hidden, but he speaks only at the command of Manwë. He is the doomsman of the Valar. Vairë the weaver is his wife, who weaves all things that have been in time in her storied webs, and the halls of Mandos, that ever widen as the ages pass, are clothed therewith. Olofantur the younger of these brethren was also named, maker of visions and of dreams. His gardens in the land of the Gods are the fairest of all places in the world, and filled with many spirits. Estë the pale is his wife, who walks not by day, but sleeps on an island in the dark lake of Lórien. Thence his fountains bring refreshment to the folk of Valinor.

§7   Strongest of limb, and greatest in deeds of prowess, is

Tulkas, who is surnamed Poldórëa, the Valiant. He is unclothed in his disport, which is much in wrestling; and he rides no steed, for he can outrun all things that go on feet, and he is tireless. His hair and beard are golden, and his flesh ruddy; his weapons are his hands. He recks little of either past or future, and is of small avail as a counsellor, but a hardy friend. He has great love for Fionwë son of Manwë. His wife is Nessa, sister of Oromë, who is lissom of limb and fleet of foot, and dances in Valinor upon lawns of never-fading green.

§8 Oromë was a mighty lord, and little less in strength than Tulkas, though slower in wrath. He loved the lands of earth, while they were still dark, and he left them unwillingly and came last to Valinor; and he comes even yet at times east over the mountains. Of old he was often seen upon the hills and plains. He is a hunter, and he loves all trees; for which reason he is called Aldaron, and by the Gnomes Tauros, the lord of forests. He delights in horses and in hounds, and his horns are loud in the friths and woods that Yavanna planted in Valinor; but he blows them not upon the Middle-earth since the fading of the Elves, whom he loved. Vana is his wife, the queen of flowers, who has the beauty both of heaven and of earth upon her face and in all her works; she is the younger sister of Varda and Palúrien.

§9 But mightier than she is Nienna, Manwë's sister and Melko's. She dwells alone. Pity is in her heart, and mourning and weeping come to her; shadow is her realm and her throne hidden. For her halls are west of West, nigh to the borders of the World and the Darkness, and she comes seldom to Valmar, the city of the Gods, where all is glad. She goes rather to the halls of Mandos, which are nearer and yet more northward; and all those who go to Mandos cry to her. For she is a healer of hurts, and turns pain to medicine and sorrow to wisdom. The windows of her house look outward from the Walls of the World.

§10 Last do all name Melko. But the Gnomes, who suffered most from his evil deeds, will not speak his name, and they call him Morgoth, the Black God, and Bauglir, the Constrainer. Great might was given to him by Ilúvatar, and he was coëval with Manwë, and part he had of all the powers of the other Valar; but he turned them to evil uses. He coveted the world and all that was in it, and desired the lordship of Manwë and the realms of all the Gods; and pride and jealousy and lust grew ever in his heart, till he became unlike his brethren. Wrath consumed him, and he begot violence and destruction and excess. In ice and fire was his

delight. But darkness he used most in all his evil works, and
turned it to fear and a name of dread among Elves and Men.

### Commentary on Chapter 1

§1    There is nothing in Q concerning the Music of the Ainur; but the
new version of that work was now in existence (see note 20 to the
*Ainulindalë*).

§4    Though written in afterwards on the typescript, the marginal note
clearly belongs either with the original writing of the manuscript or
with the earliest changes. In the *Lhammas* (§1) *Quendian* is the term
for all the Elvish languages, derived from Oromë, as a group. In the
*Ambarkanta* (and on the diagrams associated with it) the 'middle
air' was *Ilma*, replaced throughout by *Ilmen* (the form in the early
Númenórean writings, pp. 9, 13); in the *Etymologies* both *Ilma* and
*Ilmen* appear, under the stem GIL: '*Ilma* starlight (cf. *Ilmare*)', '*Ilmen*
region above air where stars are'.

The children of Manwë and Varda are not mentioned here in Q: see
note 20 to the *Ainulindalë*.

§5    *Lady of the Wide Earth* was a carefully made alteration over an
erasure, the original reading being *Bosom of the Earth*, as in Q.

§6    *Nurufantur* was another early change like that in §5; here the erased
form was *Nefantur*, as in Q. This is the first appearance of these
elements in the character of Mandos: his knowledge of past and future,
and his speaking only when commanded so to do by Manwë (cf. I. 90,
111). Here also are the first characterisations of Vairë and of Estë, who
in AV are no more than names.

§7    This description of Tulkas, now first appearing, was largely retained in the ultimate form of this chapter, the *Valaquenta*, which like
the *Ainulindalë* became a separate and distinct element in the whole
work (see *The Silmarillion* pp. 28–9); but his great love for Fionwë is
not mentioned there. – The original reading in the manuscript was *He
had great love for Fionwë*; see the remarks on tenses at the end of this
commentary.

§9    In AV Nienna had become the sister of Manwë and Melko, as still
here; in the *Valaquenta* (p. 28) she is 'sister of the Fëanturi'.

The passage beginning 'For her halls are west of West' to the end of
the paragraph, not in Q, is retained in the *Valaquenta*. In the *Lost
Tales* the hall of Vefántur and Fui Nienna was 'beneath the roots of the
most cold and northerly of the Mountains of Valinor' (I. 76). I do not
certainly understand the statement that the windows of Nienna's
house 'look outward from the Walls of the World'; for if her house is
the extreme West of Valinor her windows must surely look into the
Chasm of Ilmen and through Vaiya *to* the Walls of the World (see the
*Ambarkanta* diagram and map IV. 243, 249, and cf. QS §12). But an
interpretation, admittedly rather forced, might be that from the

windows of her house the gaze passes unhindered through Ilmen and Vaiya, and the invisible Walls of the World, and in this sense 'looks outward from the Walls'.

§10    In Q Bauglir is translated 'Terrible'. In the published *Silmarillion* the name is not interpreted in the text; in the Index I translated it 'Constrainer' as here. In the *Etymologies*, stem MBAW, it is rendered 'tyrant, oppressor'.

### Past and Present Tense in Chapter 1

In Q the past tense is used throughout in the account of the Valar, but with exceptions in the cases of Ossë, Uinen, and Nienna. These present tenses would probably not have occurred had not my father been imposing the past tense on thought that was not in fact so definite. In the opening section of AV 1 there is a mixture of present and past which is slightly increased in that of AV 2. In QS the present tense is used, with very few exceptions, and of these 'Manwë and Melko *were* brethren' and 'The Fanturi *were* brethren' were probably fully intended (sc. they were brethren 'in the thought of Ilúvatar'). Tulkas '*had* great love for Fionwë' was early corrected (§7); and only 'Oromë *was* a mighty lord' remains – a repetition of the phrase in Q. – In §2 the manuscript has 'the Elves *named* the Valar'; the typescript has *name*.

## 2   OF VALINOR AND THE TWO TREES

§11    In the beginning of the overlordship of the Valar they saw that the World was dark, and that light was scattered over the airs and lands and seas. They made therefore two mighty lamps for the lighting of the World, and set them upon lofty pillars in the South and North of the Middle-earth. But most of the Valar dwelt upon an island in the seas, while they laboured at their first tasks in the ordering of the World. And Morgoth contested with them, and made war. He overthrew the lamps, and in the confusion of darkness he roused the seas against their island.

§12    Then the Gods removed into the West, where ever since their seats have been; but Morgoth escaped from their wrath, and in the North he built himself a fortress, and delved great caverns underground.* At that time the Valar could not overcome him or take him captive. Therefore they made their home in the uttermost West, and fortified it, and built many mansions in that land

---

*Marginal note to the text:* Melko builds Utumno.

upon the borders of the World which is called Valinor. It is bounded on the hither side by the Great Sea, and on the further side by the Outer Sea, which the Elves call Vaiya; and beyond that the Walls of the World fence out the Void and the Eldest Dark. Eastwards on the shores of the inner sea the Valar built the mountains of Valinor, that are highest upon earth.

§13   In that land they gathered all light and all fair things, and there are their houses, their gardens and their towers. In the midst of the plain beyond the mountains was the city of the Gods, Valmar the beautiful of many bells. But Manwë and Varda had halls upon the loftiest of the mountains of Valinor, whence they could look out across the earth even into the furthest East. Taniquetil the Elves name that holy mountain; and Oiolossë Everlasting Whiteness; Elerína Crowned with Stars; and many names beside. And the Gnomes spake of it in their later tongue as Amon Uilos; and in the language of this island of old Tindbrenting was its name, among those few that had ever descried it afar off.

§14   In Valinor Yavanna hallowed the mould with mighty song, and Nienna watered it with tears. In that time the Gods were gathered together, and they sat silent upon their thrones of council in the Ring of Doom nigh unto the golden gates of Valmar the Blessed; and Yavanna Palúrien sang before them and they watched.

§15   From the earth there came forth two slender shoots; and silence was over all the world in that hour, nor was there any other sound save the slow chanting of Palúrien. Under her song two fair trees uprose and grew. Of all things which the Gods made they have most renown, and about their fate all the tales of the Eldar are woven. The one had leaves of a dark green that beneath were as shining silver; and he bore white blossoms like the cherry, from which a dew of silver light was ever falling, so that the earth beneath was dappled with the dark dancing shadows of his leaves and the flickering white radiance of his flowers. The other bore leaves of young green like the new-opened beech; their edges were of glittering gold. Yellow flowers swung upon her branches like the hanging blossom of those trees Men now call Golden-rain; and from those flowers came forth warmth and a great light.

§16   Silpion the one was called in Valinor, and Telperion and Ninquelótë and many names in song beside; but the Gnomes name him Galathilion. Laurelin the other was called, and

Kulúrien and Malinalda, and many other names; but the Gnomes name her Galadlóriel.\*

§17    In seven hours the glory of each tree waxed to full and waned again to nought; and each awoke again to life an hour before the other ceased to shine. Thus in Valinor twice every day there came a gentle hour of softer light, when both Trees were faint, and their gold and silver beams were mingled. Silpion was the elder of the Trees, and came first to full stature and to bloom; and that first hour in which he shone alone, the white glimmer of a silver dawn, the Gods reckoned not into the tale of hours, but named it the Opening Hour, and counted therefrom the ages of their reign in Valinor. Therefore at the sixth hour of the First Day, and of all the joyous days afterward until the Darkening, Silpion ceased his time of flower; and at the twelfth hour Laurelin her blossoming. And each day of the Gods in Valinor contained, therefore, twelve hours, and ended with the second mingling of the lights, in which Laurelin was waning but Silpion was waxing.

### Commentary on Chapter 2

§12    The marginal note, with Utumno (not Angband) as the name of Melko's original fortress as in the *Ambarkanta* and AV 2, is an early addition, since in §§62, 105 *Utumno* is an early change from *Utumna*, whereas this is not the case in the note.

§13    The manuscript has 'named that holy mountain', but the typescript 'name'; cf. the note on tenses in the commentary on Chapter 1. In §16 both texts have 'the Gnomes name him', 'the Gnomes name her'.

*Elerína* is a change made to the typescript, which had *Tinwerína*, but it belongs to the earlier period (1938): see p. 200. The names *Oiolossë*, *Tinwerína*, *Amon Uilos* are replacements over erasures, the erased names being those found in Q (IV. 81), *Ialassë* (or perhaps rather *Iolossë*, see the *Etymologies*, stem EY), *Tinwenairin*, *Amon-Uilas*.

\**Footnote to the text:* Other names of Silpion among the Gnomes are Silivros glimmering rain (which in Elvish form is Silmerossë), Nimloth pale blossom, Celeborn tree of silver; and the image that Turgon made of him in Gondolin was called Belthil divine radiance. Other names of Laurelin among the Gnomes are Glewellin (which is the same as Laurelin song of gold), Lhasgalen green of leaf, Melthinorn tree of gold; and her image in Gondolin was named Glingal hanging flame.

§16    *Names of the Trees.* This is the first occurrence in the texts of *Telperion*, as also of *Ninquelótë*, *Kulúrien*, and *Malinalda*. The names *Galathilion* and *Galadlóriel* are replacements over erasures – i.e. of *Bansil* and *Glingol*, as in Q, or of *Belthil* and *Glingal*, as in the footnote.

The footnote was almost certainly added at the same time as these changes. In this note *Silmerossë* is called the 'Elvish' form as distinct from the Gnomish *Silivros*; later in QS (§25) the phrase 'The Lindar . . . who sometimes are alone called Elves' survived from Q (IV. 85), though it was struck out and does not appear in the typescript; in the present note, on the other hand, this old distinction between 'Elvish' and 'Gnomish' was retained in the typescript.

*Nimloth*, which now first appears, later became the name of the White Tree of Númenor, a seedling of the White Tree of Tol-eressëa. *Celeborn*, also now first appearing, was later the Tree of Tol-eressëa, derived from the Tree of Tirion. With *Lhasgalen* 'green of leaf' cf. *Eryn Lasgalen* 'Wood of Greenleaves', name of Mirkwood after the War of the Ring (*The Lord of the Rings*, Appendix B, III. 375).

*Belthil* and *Glingal* appear as late emendations of *Bansil* and *Glingol* in both the 'Lays of Beleriand' (III. 80–2, 195), where they are the names of the Trees of Valinor. The particular association of these names (in the earlier forms) with the Trees of Gondolin goes back to the old tale of *The Fall of Gondolin*, where however these Trees were not images but scions of the Trees of Valinor; but in Q (and in QS before the changes to *Galathilion* and *Galadlóriel*) they are the Gnomish names of Silpion and Laurelin. The present note is the first indication that the Trees of Gondolin were *images* made by Turgon.

§17    At the end of the chapter in the manuscript is a simplified form of the table of the periods of the Trees given in Q (IV. 83).

# 3 (a)    OF THE COMING OF THE ELVES

[In the QS manuscript the third chapter ('Of the Coming of the Elves') extends all the way through Chapters 3, 4 ('Of Thingol and Melian'), and 5 ('Of Eldamar and the Princes of the Eldalië') in the published work, though there is a sub-heading 'Thingol'. In the typescript text there are two emphatic breaks and subheadings, 'Of Thingol' and 'Of Kôr and Alqualondë' (which became 'Of Eldamar and the Princes of the Eldalië'), but they have no chapter-numbers; and after 'Of Kôr and Alqualondë' the typescript text comes to an end. It is convenient to treat the three parts here as separate chapters, numbering them 3 (a), 3 (b), and 3 (c).]

§18    In all this time, since Morgoth overthrew the lamps, the Middle-earth east of the Mountains of Valinor was without light. While the lamps were shining, growth began there, which now was checked, because all was again dark. But already the oldest living things had arisen: in the sea the great weeds, and on the earth the shadow of dark trees. And beneath the trees small things faint and silent walked, and in the valleys of the night-clad hills there were dark creatures old and strong. In such lands and forests Oromë would often hunt; and there too at times Yavanna came, singing sorrowfully; for she was grieved at the darkness of the Middle-earth and ill content that it was forsaken. But the other Valar came seldom thither; and in the North Morgoth built his strength, and gathered his demons about him. These were the first made of his creatures: their hearts were of fire, and they had whips of flame. The Gnomes in later days named them Balrogs. But in that time Morgoth made many monsters of divers kinds and shapes that long troubled the world; yet the Orcs were not made until he had looked upon the Elves, and he made them in mockery of the Children of Ilúvatar. His realm spread now ever southward over the Middle-earth.

§19   Varda looked out upon the darkness, and was moved. Therefore she took the silver dew that dripped from Silpion and was hoarded in Valinor, and therewith she made the stars. And for this reason she is called Tintallë, the Star-kindler, and Elentári, Queen of Stars. She strewed the unlit skies with these bright vessels, filled with silver flame; but high in the North, a challenge unto Morgoth, she set the crown of seven mighty stars to swing, the emblem of the Gods, and the sign of doom. Many names have these been called; but in the old days of the North both Elves and Men called them the Burning Briar, and some the Sickle of the Gods.

§20   It is told that at the opening of the first stars the children of the earth awoke, the Elder Children of Ilúvatar. Themselves they named the Quendi, whom we call Elves; but Oromë named them Eldar, Star-folk, and that name has since been borne by all that followed him upon the westward road. In the beginning they were greater and more strong than they have since become; but not more fair, for though the beauty of the Eldar in the days of their youth was beyond all other beauty that Ilúvatar has caused to be, it has not perished, but lives in the West, and sorrow and wisdom have enriched it. And Oromë looking upon the Elves was filled with love and wonder; for their coming was not in the Music of the Ainur, and was hidden in the secret thought of Ilúvatar. But Oromë came upon them by chance in his wandering, while they dwelt yet silent beside the starlit mere, Kuiviénen, Water of

Awakening, in the East of the Middle-earth. For a while he abode with them, and taught them the language of the Gods, from whence afterwards they made the fair Elvish speech, which was sweet in the ears of the Valar. Then swiftly Oromë rode back over land and sea to Valinor, filled with the thought of the beauty of the Elves, and he brought the tidings to Valmar. And the Gods were amazed, all save Manwë, to whom the secret thought of Ilúvatar was revealed in all matters that concern this world. Manwë sat now long in thought, and at length he spoke to the Valar, revealing to them the mind of the Father; and he bade them to return now to their duty, which was to govern the world for the Children of Ilúvatar, when they should appear, each kindred in its appointed time.

§21   Thus it came to pass that after long council the Gods resolved to make an assault upon the fortress of Morgoth in the North.* Morgoth did not forget that the Elves were the cause of his downfall. Yet they had no part in it; and little do they know of the riding of the power of the West against the North in the beginning of their days, and of the war and tumult of the first Battle of the Gods. In those days the shape of the Middle-earth was changed and broken and the seas were moved. It was Tulkas who at last wrestled with Morgoth and overthrew him, and bound him with the chain Angainor, and led him captive; and the world had peace for a long age. But the fortress of Morgoth had many vaults and caverns hidden with deceit far under earth, and these the Gods did not utterly destroy, and many evil things still lingered there; and others were dispersed and fled into the dark and roamed in the waste places of the world.

§22   The Gods drew Morgoth back to Valinor bound hand and foot and blindfold, and he was cast into prison in the halls of Mandos, from whence none have ever escaped save by the will of Mandos and of Manwë, neither Vala, nor Elf, nor Man. Vast are those halls and strong, and built in the North of Valinor.

§23   Then the Quendi, the people of the Elves, were summoned by the Gods to Valinor, for the Valar were filled with love of their beauty, and feared for them in the dangerous world amid the deceits of the starlit dusk; but the Gods as yet withheld the living light in Valinor. In this many have seen the cause of woes that after befell, holding that the Valar erred, and strayed from the

*Marginal note to the text: Utumno.

purpose of Ilúvatar, albeit with good intent. Yet such was the fate of the World, which cannot in the end be contrary to Ilúvatar's design. Nonetheless the Elves were at first unwilling to hearken to the summons; wherefore Oromë was sent unto them, and he chose from among them three ambassadors, and he brought them to Valmar. These were Ingwë and Finwë and Elwë, who after were kings of the Three Kindreds of the Eldar; and coming they were filled with awe by the glory and majesty of the Valar, and desired the light and splendour of Valinor. Therefore they returned and counselled the Elves to remove into the West, and the greater part of the people obeyed their counsel. This they did of their own free will, and yet were swayed by the power of the Gods, ere their wisdom was full grown. The Elves that obeyed the summons and followed the three princes are called the Eldar, by the name that Oromë gave them; for he was their guide, and led them at the last (save some that strayed upon the march) unto Valinor. Yet there were many who preferred the starlight and the wide spaces of the earth to the rumour of the glory of the Trees, and remained behind; and these are called the Avari, the Unwilling.

§24   The Eldar prepared now a great march from their first homes in the East. When all was ready, Oromë rode at their head upon his white horse shod with gold; and behind him the Eldalië was arrayed in three hosts.

§25   The first to take the road were led by Ingwë, the most high lord of all the Elvish race. He entered into Valinor, and sits at the feet of the Powers, and all Elves revere his name; but he never returned nor looked again upon the Middle-earth. The Lindar were his folk, the fairest of the Quendi; they are the High Elves, and the beloved of Manwë and Varda, and few among Men have spoken with them.

§26   Next came the Noldor. The Gnomes we may call them, a name of wisdom; they are the Deep Elves, and the friends of Aulë. Their lord was Finwë, wisest of all the children of the world. His kindred are renowned in song, and of them these tales have much to tell, for they fought and laboured long and grievously in the Northern lands of old.

§27   Third came the Teleri, for they tarried, and were not wholly of a mind to forsake the dusk; they are the Sea Elves, and the Soloneldi they were after named in Valinor, for they made music beside the breaking waves. Elwë was their lord, and his hair was long and white.

§28    The hindmost of the Noldor forsook the host of Finwë, repenting of the march, and they turned southward, and wandered long, and became a people apart, unlike their kin. They are not counted among the Eldar, nor yet among the Avari. Pereldar they are called in the tongue of the Elves of Valinor, which signifies Half-eldar. But in their own tongue they were called Danas, for their first leader was named Dân. His son was Denethor, who led them into Beleriand ere the rising of the Moon.

§29    And many others of the Eldar that set out upon the march were lost upon the long road, and they wandered in the woods and mountains of the world, and never came to Valinor nor saw the light of the Two Trees. Therefore they are called the Lembi, that is the Lingerers. And the Lembi and the Pereldar are called also the Ilkorindi, because though they began the journey they never dwelt in Kôr, the city which the Elves after built in the land of the Gods; yet their hearts were ever turned towards the West. But the Ilkorindi and the Avari are called the Dark Elves, because they never beheld the light of the Two Trees ere it was dimmed; whereas the Lindar and the Noldor and the Teleri are named the Light Elves, and remember the light that is no more.*

§30    The Lembi were for the most part of the race of the Teleri, and the chief of these were the Elves of Beleriand, in the West of the Middle-earth. Most renowned among them was that Elf who first was named Sindo, the Grey, brother of Elwë, but is called now Thingol in the language of Doriath.

*Footnote to the text : Other names in song and tale are given to these folk. The Lindar are the Blessed Elves, and the Spear-elves, and the Elves of the Air, the Friends of the Gods, the Holy Elves, and the Immortal, and the Children of Ingwë; they are the Fair Folk and the White. The Noldor are the Wise and the Golden, the Valiant, the Sword-elves, the Elves of the Earth, the Foes of Melko, the Skilled of Hand, the Lovers of Jewels, the Companions of Men, the Followers of Finwë. The Teleri are the Foam-riders, Musicians of the Shore, the Free, the Wanderers, and the Elves of the Sea, the Sailors, the Arrow-elves, Ship-friends, the Lords of the Gulls, the Blue Elves, the Pearl-gatherers, and the People of Elwë. The Danas are the Elves of the Woods, the Hidden Elves, the Green Elves, the Elves of the Seven Rivers, the Lovers of Lúthien, the Lost Folk of Ossiriand, for they are now no more.

*Commentary on Chapter 3 (a)*

[The names of the divisions of the Elves underwent extremely com-
plicated changes on the QS manuscript to reach the form in the
typescript text printed here, since the same names were moved into
different references and given different meanings. I do not refer to the
original names in the notes that follow, since the individual changes
would be extremely hard to follow if given piecemeal, but attempt an
explanation in a general note at the end of this commentary.]

§18   The original text of the passage concerning the demons of Morgoth
ran as follows:

   . . . in the North Morgoth built his strength, and gathered his
   demon-broods about him, whom the Gnomes after knew as
   Balrogs: they had whips of flame. The Úvanimor he made,
   monsters of divers kinds and shapes; but the Orcs were not
   made until he had looked upon the Elves.

The term *Úvanimor* occurs in the *Lost Tales*, I. 75 ('monsters, giants,
and ogres'), etc.; cf. *Vanimor* 'the Beautiful', p. 110. – On the question
of when the Orcs first came into being see p. 148 and commentary on
QS §62. It is said in *The Fall of Númenor* II (§1) that the Orcs are
'mockeries of the creatures of Ilúvatar' (cf. also *The Lost Road*, p. 65).
In QS §62 the idea that the Orcs were mockeries of the Elves is found
in the text as originally written.

§19   *Elentári* was changed on the typescript from *Tinwerontar*, but the
alteration belongs to the earlier period, like *Elerína* > *Tinwerína* in
§13; see p. 200. – *Tintallë* 'the Kindler' is found in *The Silmarillion*
(p. 48) – and in *The Lord of the Rings* – but is there the name of Varda
'out of the deeps of time': the name 'Queen of the Stars' (*Elentári*) was
given in reference to the second star-making, at the time of the
awakening of the Elves. This second star-making of *The Silmarillion*
was still in QS, as in AV 2 (annal 1900), the first.

§20   The sentence beginning 'but Oromë named them Eldar, "Star-
folk" . . .' is a footnote in the manuscript, a very early addition; in the
typescript it was taken up into the text. See the note on names at the
end of this commentary.

   The whole paragraph, from the words 'but not more fair', was
greatly extended and altered in the first rewriting to give the text
printed. As originally written it was almost an exact repetition of Q
(IV. 84):

   . . . yet not more fair. Oromë it was that found them, dwelling by
   the star-lit mere, Kuiviénen, Water of Awakening, in the East of
   Middle-earth. Swiftly he rode to Valinor filled with the thought of
   their beauty. When the Valar heard his tidings, they pondered long,
   and they recalled their duty. For they came into the world knowing
   that their office was to govern it for the Children of Ilúvatar, who
   should afterward come, each in the appointed time.

In addition to the statement in the rewriting that Oromë taught the Elves 'the language of the Gods' (see the *Lhammas* §1), the new passage introduces an extraordinary development into the thought of the *Ainulindalë*: the coming of the Children of Ilúvatar *was not in the Music of the Ainur*, the Valar were amazed at the news brought by Oromë, and Manwë then revealed to them the mind of Ilúvatar. What in the original text was their known duty ('For they came into the world knowing that their office was to govern it for the Children of Ilúvatar') is now (it seems) presented to them as a duty indeed, but one of which they had until then been ignorant. In the *Ainulindalë* version of this period (pp. 160–1) it is said:

> For Elves and Men were devised by Ilúvatar alone, nor, since they comprehended not fully that part of the theme when it was propounded to them, did any of the Ainur dare in their music to add anything to their fashion.

In the later, post-*Lord of the Rings* versions, while the conception is changed and the idea introduced of the Vision seen by the Ainur before the act of Creation, it is explicit that the Children of Ilúvatar 'came with the Third Theme' of the Music, and that the Ainur saw in the Vision the arising of Elves and Men.

§21   As originally written QS had 'symmetry' for 'shape', showing that my father had in mind the passage in the *Ambarkanta*: 'But the symmetry of the ancient Earth was changed and broken in the first Battle of the Gods' (IV. 239 and the map IV. 251).

§23   The passage from 'In this many have seen the cause of woes that after befell' is an addition to the original text, which had simply 'Oromë brought their ambassadors to Valmar.' Here the story of the three ambassadors, curiously absent from S and Q (IV. 68), re-emerges from the *Lost Tales* (I. 115–17); and the suggestion, first appearing in the rewriting of QS, that the Valar erred in summoning the Elves is also hinted at in the old tale: 'Maybe indeed had the Gods decided otherwise the world had been a fairer place and the Eldar a happier folk' (I. 117).

*Elwë* here, confusingly, is *not* Thingol, whose Quenya name is *Elwë* in *The Silmarillion*. In the *Lost Tales* Tinwelint (Thingol) was one of the three ambassadors; but the leader of the Third Kindred on the Great March (after the loss of Tinwelint) was 'one Ellu' (I. 120). In QS Thingol was *not* one of the ambassadors, and he never went to Valinor; the ambassador and the leader of the Third Host was Elwë (who was however the brother of Thingol). In *The Silmarillion* Thingol (Elwë Singollo) was again one of the ambassadors, while the leader of the Third Host (after the loss of Thingol) was his brother Olwë – a return therefore to the *Lost Tales*, with the addition that the two were brothers.

The original text of the passage following 'These were Ingwë and

Finwë and Elwë, who after were kings of the Three Kindreds of the Eldar' was thus:

> And returning they counselled that the Elves should remove into the West. This they did of their own free will, yet in awe of the power and majesty of the Gods. Most of the Elves obeyed the summons, and these are they who afterward came unto Valinor (save some who strayed), and are called the Eldar, the Departing.

This explanation of the name *Eldar* is the same as that in the *Lhammas* (§2 and commentary), and in both works it was overtaken by the translation 'Star-folk', the name given by Oromë: see under §20 above and the note on names at the end of this commentary.

§25 After 'The Lindar were his folk, the fairest of the Quendi' the original text added: 'who sometimes are alone called Elves'; see the commentary on §16.

*High Elves*: Q had here 'Light-elves'; subsequently (IV. 89 note 6) 'Light-elves' was emended to 'High-elves', and that in turn to 'Fair-elves'. The term 'Light Elves' was now differently employed: see §29, and p. 197.

§27 This is the first appearance of the idea that the Teleri were the last of the Three Kindreds because 'they tarried, and were not wholly of a mind to forsake the dusk'. In the *Lhammas* (§2) they were the last because they were 'the latest to awake'.

§28 For 'Pereldar they are called in the tongue of the Elves of Valinor, which signifies Half-eldar' the original reading was: 'No name had they in the tongue of Valinor.' See the note on names below.

§29 The words 'they never dwelt in Kôr, the city which the Elves after built' are a reversion to the original meaning of the name, the more puzzling in view of §39: 'On the top of the hill of Kôr the city of the Elves was built, the white walls and terraces of Tûn [> Túna]'. Similarly in the *Lhammas* §11 the words 'in Kôr' contradict the reference in §5 to Kôr as the hill on which Tûn [> Túna] was built.

§30 It is said also in the *Lhammas* (§2) that the Lembi were for the most part of Telerian race, but the meaning there is not precisely the same, since in the *Lhammas* the name *Lembi* still meant the Elves who never left the lands of their awakening. – On *Sindo the Grey* see the commentary on *Lhammas* §6.

### Note on the names of the divisions of the Elves

Several of the changes referred to below are found in the list of proposed alterations dated 20 November 1937 (p. 200).

As this chapter was originally written, the classification was:

(§23) *Eldar* 'the Departing', opposed to *Lembi* 'the Lingerers', those that remained behind. (This is the same formulation as in the *Lhammas* §2, before emendation.)

(§28) Those of the Noldor who repented of the journey and turned south, the *Danas*, are counted neither as *Eldar* or *Lembi*. (This agrees with the statement in the *Lhammas* §7 (but not with that in §2: on the contradictory views see p. 188 and the *Lammasethen*, pp. 194–5).

(§29)  Those of the Eldar who set out but 'were lost upon the long road' and never came to Kôr are called *Ilkorindi*. (This agrees with the *Lhammas* §2, except that there the Danas are included among the Ilkorindi.)

The earliest changes to the QS manuscript then brought in the ideas that *Eldar* meant 'Star-folk' and was a name given to all Elves by Oromë, but also that this name was 'borne by all that followed him upon the westward road'. The distinction was also introduced that those who actually crossed the Sea were called *Avari*, 'the Departing'. This new formulation was written in also to *Lhammas* §2 (see the commentary), doubtless at the same time.

The third layer of early change to this passage in the QS manuscript, giving the text printed, is not represented in the *Lhammas*. These are the changes referred to in the notes dated 20 November 1937. *Avari* was changed to mean 'the Unwilling', and replaced *Lembi* as the name for those who remained behind in the East (§23); the Danas were given the name 'in the tongue of Valinor' of *Pereldar* 'Half-eldar' (§28);* *Lembi* was now given to the Eldar who were lost on the road and never came to Kôr (§29); and while the name *Ilkorindi* was retained (an alternative to *Lembi*) it now included also the Danas (*Pereldar*) (§29) – to that extent agreeing with *Lhammas* §2. Thus (in contrast to the table on p. 183):

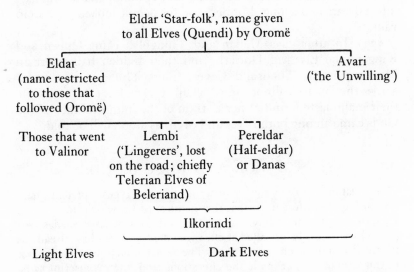

*In *The Lord of the Rings* the Sindarin form *Peredhil* has a totally different application: 'The sons of Eärendil were Elros and Elrond, the *Peredhil* or Half-elven', Appendix A I (i). An earlier name was *Peringol*, *Peringiul*: see the commentary on AB 2, annal 325.

## 3 (b)  OF THINGOL

§31   For this reason Thingol abode in Beleriand and came not to Valinor. Melian was a fay, of the race of the Valar. She dwelt in the gardens of Lórien, and among all his fair folk there were none more beautiful than she, nor more wise, nor more skilled in songs of magic and enchantment. It is told that the Gods would leave their business, and the birds of Valinor their mirth, that the bells of Valmar were silent, and the fountains ceased to flow, when at the mingling of the light Melian sang in the gardens of the God of dreams. Nightingales went always with her, and she taught them their song. She loved deep shadow, but she was akin, before the World was made, unto Yavanna, and often strayed from Valinor on long journey into the Hither Lands, and there she filled the silence of the dawning earth with her voice and with the voices of her birds.

§32   Thingol heard the song of the nightingales of Melian and a spell was laid upon him, and he forsook his folk, and was lost, following their voices amid the shadows of the trees. He came at last upon a glade open to the stars; and there Melian stood, and the light of Valinor was in her face. Nought she said, but being filled with love Thingol came to her and took her hand, and he was cast into a dream and a long slumber, and his people looked for him in vain.

§33   In after days Melian and Thingol became Queen and King of the Elves of Doriath, and their hidden halls were in Menegroth, the Thousand Caves. Thus Thingol came never across the Sea to Valinor, and Melian returned not thither while their realm lasted; and of her a strain of the immortal race of the Gods came among both Elves and Men, as after shall be told.


## 3 (c)  OF KÔR AND ALQUALONDË

[The relation between the manuscript and the typescript texts here becomes quite different, in that the manuscript (in which this is not a separate chapter or in any way marked off from what precedes, see p. 211) was scarcely emended at all, while the typescript has, already as typed, a great many changes from it. The explanation is presumably that in this case my father made the alterations from the manuscript as he typed without pencilling them in on the manuscript first. There is not in fact a great deal in the second text that seriously alters the narrative or nomenclature of the first, though certain new elements do enter. As hitherto, I follow the typescript text and record significant differences from the manuscript in the commentary. With *Of Kôr and Alqualondë* the typescript ceases.]

§34   In time the hosts of the Eldar came to the last western shores of the Hither Lands. In the North these shores, in the ancient days after the Battle of the Gods, sloped ever westward, until in the northernmost parts of the earth only a narrow sea divided the Outer Land, upon which Valinor was built, from the Hither Lands; but this narrow sea was filled with grinding ice, because of the violence of the frosts of Melko. Therefore Oromë did not lead the Eldar into the far North, but brought them to the fair lands about the River Sirion that afterwards were named Beleriand; and from those shores whence first the hosts of the Eldar looked in fear and wonder on the sea there stretched an ocean, wide and dark and deep, between them and the Mountains of Valinor.

§35   There they waited and gazed upon the dark waves. But Ulmo came from the Valar; and he uprooted the half-sunken island, upon which the Gods had dwelt in the beginning, but which now long had stood alone amid the sea, far from either shore; and with the aid of his servants he moved it, as it were a mighty ship, and anchored it in the bay into which Sirion pours his water.* Thereon he embarked the Lindar and the Noldor, for they had already assembled. But the Teleri were behind, being slower and less eager upon the march, and they were delayed also by the loss of Thingol; and they did not come until Ulmo had departed.

§36   Therefore Ulmo drew the Lindar and the Noldor over the sea to the long shores beneath the Mountains of Valinor, and they entered the land of the Gods and were welcomed to its bliss. But the Teleri dwelt long by the shores of the western sea, awaiting Ulmo's return; and they grew to love the sound of the waves, and they made songs filled with the music of water. Ossë heard them, and came thither; and he loved them, delighting in the music of their voices. Sitting upon a rock nigh to the margin of the sea he spoke to them and instructed them. Great therefore was his grief when Ulmo returned at length to bear them away to Valinor. Some he persuaded to remain on the beaches of the Middle-earth,

*Footnote to the text:* And some have told that the great isle of Balar, that lay of old in that bay, was the eastern horn of the Lonely Isle, that broke asunder and remained behind, when Ulmo removed that land again into the West.

and these were the Elves of the Falas that in after days had dwellings at the havens of Brithombar and Eglorest in Beleriand; but most of the Teleri embarked upon the isle and were drawn far away.

§37   Ossë followed them, and when they were come near to their journey's end he called to them; and they begged Ulmo to halt for a while, so that they might take leave of their friend and look their last upon the sky of stars. For the light of the Trees, that filtered through the passes of the hills, filled them with awe. And Ulmo was wroth with them, yet he granted their request, and left them for a while. Then Ossë seized the isle and chained it to the sea-bottom, far out in the Bay of Elvenhome, whence the Mountains of Valinor could only dimly be descried. And when Ulmo returned the island could not be moved or uprooted without peril to the Teleri; and it was not moved, but stood alone for many an age. No other land was near it, and it was called Tol Eressëa, or the Lonely Isle. There the Teleri long dwelt, and of Ossë they learned strange musics and sea-lore; and he made the sea-birds for their delight. By this long sojourn of the Teleri apart in the Lonely Isle was caused the sundering of their speech from the language of the Lindar and Noldor.

§38   To these the Valar had given a home and a dwelling. Even among the radiant flowers of the Tree-lit gardens of the Gods they longed still to see the stars at times. Therefore a gap was made in the encircling mountains, and there in a deep valley that ran down to the sea the green hill of Kôr was raised. From the West the light of the Trees fell upon it, and its shadow lay ever eastward, and to the East it looked towards the Bay of Elvenhome, and the Lonely Isle, and the Shadowy Seas. The light of the Blessed Realm streamed forth, kindling the waves with gleams of gold and silver, and it touched the Lonely Isle, and its western shore grew green and fair. There bloomed the first flowers that ever were east of the Mountains of the Gods.

§39   On the top of the hill of Kôr the city of the Elves was built, the white walls and terraces of Túna, and the highest of the towers of that city was the Tower of Ingwë, the Ingwemindon, whose silver lamp shone far out into the mists of the sea. Few are the ships of mortal Men that have seen its slender beam. In Túna* dwelt the Lindar and the Noldor.

*Footnote to the text: That is the Hill-city. This city the Gods called Eldamar (that is Elvenhome), and the Gnomes in their later speech Tûn or Eledûn. But the regions where the Elves dwelt, and whence

§40  Manwë and Varda loved most the Lindar, the High Elves, and holy and immortal were all their deeds and songs. The Noldor, the Gnomes, were beloved of Aulë, and of Mandos the wise; and great became their knowledge and their skill. Yet ever greater was their thirst for more knowledge, and their desire to make things wonderful and new. They were changeful in speech, for they had great love of words, and sought ever to find names more fit for all things that they knew or imagined. In Valinor they first contrived the fashioning of gems, and they made them of many kinds and hues in countless myriads; and they filled all Túna with them, and the halls of the Gods were enriched.

§41  The Noldor afterwards came back to the Middle-earth, and this tale tells mostly of their deeds; therefore the names and kinship of their princes may here be told, in that form which these names after had in the tongue of the Gnomes as it was in Beleriand upon the Middle-earth. Finwë was King of the Noldor. His sons were Fëanor, Fingolfin, and Finrod. Of these Fëanor was the mightiest in skill of word and of hand, more learned in lore than his brethren; in his heart his spirit burned as flame. Fingolfin was the strongest, the most steadfast, and the most valiant. Finrod was the fairest, and the most wise of heart. The seven sons of Fëanor were Maidros the tall; Maglor a musician and a mighty singer, whose voice carried far over land and sea; Celegorn the fair, and Cranthir the dark; and Curufin the crafty, who inherited most of his father's skill of hand; and the youngest Damrod and Díriel, who were twin brethren alike in mood and face. They afterwards were great hunters in the woods of the Middle-earth. A hunter also was Celegorn, who in Valinor was a friend of Oromë and followed oft the great god's horn.

§42  The sons of Fingolfin were Fingon, who was after King of the Gnomes in the North of the world; and Turgon of Gondolin; and their sister was Isfin the White. The sons of Finrod were Inglor the faithful (who afterwards was named Felagund, Lord of Caves), and Orodreth, and Angrod, and Egnor. Inglor and Orodreth were close in love, and they were friends of the sons of Fingolfin; but Angrod and Egnor were friends of the sons of Fëanor.

§43  Here must be told how the Teleri came at last to Valinor.

---

the stars could be seen, were called Elendë or Eldanor, that is Elfland. The pass through the mountains which led to Elendë was named the Kalakilya, Pass of Light.

For nigh on one hundred of the years of Valinor, which were each as ten of the years of the Sun that were after made, they dwelt in Tol Eressëa. But slowly their hearts were moved, and were drawn towards the light that flowed out over the sea unto their isle; and they were torn between the love of the music of the waves upon their shores, and desire to see again their kindred and to look upon the splendour of the Gods. Yet in the end desire of the light was the stronger. Therefore Ulmo taught them the craft of ship-building; and Ossë, submitting to Ulmo, brought them as his farewell gift the strong-winged swans. These they harnessed to their fleet of white ships, and thus they were drawn without the help of the winds to Valinor.

§44   There they dwelt upon the long shores of Elvenhome, and if they wished they could see the light of the Trees, and could visit the golden streets of Valmar and the crystal stairs of Túna upon Kôr. But most they sailed upon the waters of the Bay of Elvenhome, or danced in the waves with their hair gleaming in the light beyond the hill. Many jewels the Noldor gave them, opals and diamonds and pale crystals, which they strewed upon the shores and scattered in the pools. Marvellous were the beaches of Elendë in those days. And many pearls they won for themselves from the sea, and their halls were of pearl, and of pearl were the mansions of Elwë at the Haven of the Swans, lit with many lamps. For Alqualondë, the Haven of the Swans, was their chief town, and the harbour of their ships; and these were fashioned in the likeness of swans, white, and their beaks were of gold with eyes of gold and jet. The gate of that harbour was an arch of living rock sea-carven, and it lay upon the confines of Elfland, north of the Kalakilya, which is the Pass of Light wherein stood the hill of Kôr.

§45   As the ages passed the Lindar grew to love the land of the Gods and the full light of the Trees, and they forsook the city of Túna, and dwelt upon the mountain of Manwë, or about the plains and woods of Valinor, and became sundered from the Gnomes. But remembrance of the earth under stars remained in the hearts of the Noldor, and they abode in the Kalakilya, and in the hills and valleys within sound of the western sea; and though many of them went oft about the land of the Gods, making far journeys in search of the secrets of land and water and all living things, yet their intercourse was more with the Teleri than with the Lindar; and the tongues of Túna and Alqualondë drew together in those days. Finwë was King of Túna and Elwë of

Alqualondë; but Ingwë was ever held High-king of all the Elves. He dwelt at the feet of Manwë upon Taniquetil. Fëanor and his sons abode seldom in one place for long. They travelled far and wide within the confines of Valinor, going even to the borders of the Dark and the cold shores of the Outer Sea, seeking the unknown. Often they were guests in the halls of Aulë; but Celegorn went rather to the house of Oromë, and there he got great knowledge of all birds and beasts, and all their tongues he knew. For all living things that are or have been on this earth, save only the fell and evil creatures of Melko, lived then in Valinor; and there were many other creatures beautiful and strange that have not yet been seen upon the Middle-earth, and perchance never now shall be, since the fashion of the World was changed.

### Commentary on Chapter 3 (c)

§34   It is not told in the manuscript version where Oromë came to the coast of the Great Sea; but cf. the *Ambarkanta* map (IV. 249) on which the track of the March of the Elves is shown (and see IV. 257).

§35   The manuscript does not have the sentence 'and with the aid of his servants . . .' nor the footnote. The story of the origin of the Isle of Balar has not been told before.

In the last sentence of the paragraph the manuscript has only 'but the Teleri were behind and came not until he had gone.' In the typescript version enters the story that the loss of Thingol was one cause of the late arrival of the Teleri on the shores (though this idea was possibly present already in the original tale of *The Coming of the Elves*, I. 120); that they were less eager in any case has been said earlier in QS (§27).

§36   It has not been said expressly before that the Elves who were persuaded to remain by Ossë were the Elves of Brithombar and Eglorest.

§37   The story told here shows an interesting stage between Q and *The Silmarillion* (pp. 58–9). In QS, as in S and Q, the old story of Ossë's rebellious anchoring of Tol Eressëa still survives (see I. 120, 134; IV. 45); but there is now the element, found in *The Silmarillion*, that the Teleri hearing Ossë calling to them begged Ulmo to stay the voyage, and he did so, though in QS he was 'wroth with them'. In the final form of the story, however, not only did Ulmo do so willingly, but it was he himself who ordered Ossë to root the island to the sea-bottom, for he was opposed to the summoning of the Quendi to Valinor.

§39   The name *Ingwemindon* has not been used before. – The name *Tûn* in the body of the text was carefully altered to *Túna* in the manuscript at both occurrences in §39 and again in §§40, 44 (but not in §45: see the commentary), and the footnote clearly belongs to the same time. The name *Eldamar* is now used of the city itself, while the new names *Elendë* and *Eldanor* are given to the region. This is another case where my father altered the *Lhammas* in the same way and no doubt at the same time as he altered QS: in §5 *Tûn* was changed to *Túna*, with a marginal note 'which the Gods called Eldamar' (on the history of the name see the commentary on that section).

§40 The sentence about the changefulness of speech among the Noldor is not in the manuscript. Cf. the passage on this subject in the *Lhammas* §5.

§41 With the opening sentence concerning the form in which the names of the Noldorin princes are given cf. the passage added at the end of the *Lhammas* (§11): 'The names of the Gnomes in the *Quenta* are given in the Noldorin form as that tongue became in Beleriand, for all those after Finwë father of the Noldor, whose name remains in ancient form.' The manuscript has 'using the names in the form of the Gnomish tongue as it long was spoken on the earth', as in Q (IV. 87).

For 'in his heart his spirit burned as flame' the manuscript has 'he had a heart of fire'. Cf. the later interpretation of *Fëanáro* as 'Spirit of Fire', *The Silmarillion* p. 63 (in the *Etymologies*, stem PHAY, the name is translated 'radiant sun'). – *Celegorn* here and throughout QS until §141 was an early change on the manuscript from *Celegorm*, as also in AV 2 and AB 2. – The statement (not found in the manuscript version) that Damrod and Díriel were twins is now first made, though it is possible that they had always been conceived to be so (IV. 46).

§42 In AV 2 (annal 2993) the earlier idea of the alliances between the Noldorin princes still survived, with Inglor Felagund a friend of Fingon and Turgon, sons of Fingolfin, and his brothers Orodreth, Angrod, and Egnor friends especially of Celegorm and Curufin. This was changed in AV 2 to the story in QS, Orodreth becoming associated with Inglor in friendship with the sons of Fingolfin.

§44 The manuscript has 'Many pearls they made', as in Q (IV. 88). – The description of the ships of the Teleri is not in the manuscript; in the typescript text it re-emerges from the *Lost Tales*, I. 124–5.

§45 *Tûn* was not here emended to *Túna* in the manuscript, where there is a footnote to the text, added no doubt at the same time as that to §39: 'Which is therefore called hereafter by its name in the speech of the Gnomes' (i.e. because the Lindar had departed).

The conclusion of this chapter was much developed from the form in the manuscript, which has no mention of the drawing together of the tongues of Túna and Alqualondë after the departure of the Lindar (cf. the *Lhammas* §5), nor of Celegorn's knowledge of the tongues of birds and beasts, and it does not have the very curious concluding passage concerning the existence in Valinor of all living things that have ever been on earth, save only the creatures of Melko.

# 4 OF THE SILMARILS AND THE DARKENING OF VALINOR

[From this point, where the typescript version comes to an end, there seems to have been scarcely any emendation to the manuscript until the major revision was undertaken many years later. A few corrections, however, certainly belong to the early period, while some points are doubtful in this respect.]

§46 From this time, when the three kindreds of the Eldar were gathered at last in Valinor, began the Noontide of the Blessed Realm and its fullness of bliss and glory, which lasted many ages. In that time, five ages after the coming of the Noldor, when they had become full-grown in knowledge and skill, Fëanor, son of Finwë, began a long and marvellous labour; and he summoned all his lore, and power, and subtle skill; for he purposed to make things more fair than any of the Eldar had yet made, that should last beyond the end of all. Three jewels he made, and named them Silmarils. A living fire burned within them that was blended of the light of the Two Trees. Of their own radiance they shone even in the dark; yet all lights that fell upon them, however faint, they took and reflected in marvellous hues to which their own inner fire gave a surpassing loveliness. No mortal flesh, nor flesh unclean, could touch them, but was scorched and withered. These jewels the Elves prized beyond all their works, and Manwë hallowed them; but Varda foretold that the fate of the World was locked within them. And the heart of Fëanor was bound fast to these things that he himself had made.

§47 For two ages more the noontide of the glory of Valinor endured. For seven ages then, as the Gods had decreed, Melko had dwelt in the halls of Mandos, each age in lightened pain. When these ages were past, as they had promised, he was brought before their conclave. He looked upon the glory of the Valar, and greed and malice were in his heart; he looked upon the fair Children of Ilúvatar that sat at the feet of the Gods, and hatred filled him; he looked upon the wealth of gems and lusted for them; but he hid his thoughts and postponed his vengeance.

§48 Before the gates of Valmar Melko humbled himself at the feet of Manwë and sued for pardon, and Nienna his sister aided his prayer. But the Gods would not suffer him to depart from their sight and vigilance. He was given a humble dwelling within the gates of the city; but so fair-seeming were all his deeds and words that after a while he was permitted to go freely about all the land,

and both Gods and Elves had much help and profit from him. Yet Ulmo's heart misgave him, and Tulkas clenched his hands whenever he saw Morgoth, his foe, go by. For Tulkas is quick to wrath and slow to forgiveness.

§49    Most fair of all was Morgoth to the Elves, and he aided them in many works, if they would let him. The Lindar, the people of Ingwë, held him in suspicion; for Ulmo had warned them, and they heeded his words. But the Gnomes took delight in the many things of hidden knowledge that he could reveal to them, and some hearkened to words that it would have been better that they had never heard.* And when he saw his chance he sowed a seed of lies and suggestions of evil among such as these. Bitterly did the folk of the Noldor atone for their folly in after-days.

§50    Often Morgoth would whisper that the Gods had brought the Eldar to Valinor because of their jealousy, fearing that their marvellous skill and beauty and their magic would grow too strong for the Valar to control, as the Elves waxed and spread over the wide lands of the world. Visions he would conjure in their hearts of the mighty realms they might have ruled in power and freedom in the East. In those days, moreover, though the Valar knew of the coming of Men that were to be, the Elves knew yet nought of it; for the Gods had not revealed it, and the time was not yet near. But Morgoth spake to the Elves in secret of mortal Men, though he knew little of the truth. Manwë alone knew aught clearly of the mind of Ilúvatar concerning Men, and he has ever been their

*Footnote to the text:* It is said that among other matters Melko spoke of weapons and armour to the Gnomes, and of the power they give to him who is armed to defend his own (as he said). The Elves had before possessed only weapons of the chase, spears and bows and arrows, and since the chaining of Melko the armouries of the Gods had been shut. But the Gnomes now learned the fashioning of swords of tempered steel, and the making of mail; and they made shields in those days and emblazoned them with silver, gold, and gems. And Fëanor became greatly skilled in this craft, and he made store of weapons secretly, as jealousy grew between him and Fingolfin. Thus it was that the Noldor were armed in the days of their Flight. Thus, too, the evil of Melko was turned against him, for the swords of the Gnomes did him more hurt than anything under the Gods upon this earth. Yet they had little joy of Morgoth's teaching; for all the sorrows of the Gnomes came from their swords, both from the unjust battle at Alqualondë, and from many ill deeds afterwards. Thus wrote Pengolod.

friend. Yet Morgoth whispered that the Gods kept the Eldar captive, so that Men coming should defraud them of the kingdoms of Middle-earth; for the weaker and short-lived race the Valar saw would more easily be swayed by them. Small truth was there in this, and little have the Valar ever prevailed to sway the wills or fates of Men, and least of all to good. But many of the Elves believed, or half-believed, the evil words. Most of these were Gnomes.

§51    Thus, ere the Gods were aware, the peace of Valinor was poisoned. The Gnomes began to murmur against the Valar and their kindred; and many became filled with vanity, forgetting all that the Gods had given them and taught them. Most of all Morgoth fanned the flames of the eager heart of Fëanor, though all the while he lusted for the Silmarils. These Fëanor at great feasts wore on brow and breast, but at other times they were guarded close, locked in the deep hoards of Tûn, for though there were no thieves in Valinor, as yet, Fëanor loved the Silmarils with a greedy love, and began to grudge the sight of them to all save himself and his sons.

§52    The sons of Finwë were proud, but proudest was Fëanor. Lying Morgoth said to him that Fingolfin and his sons were plotting to usurp the leadership of Fëanor and his elder house, and to supplant him in the favour of their father and of the Gods. Of these lies quarrels were born among the children of Finwë, and of these quarrels came the end of the high days of Valinor and the evening of its ancient glory; for Fëanor spake words of rebellion against the Valar, and plotted to depart from Valinor back to the world without, and deliver, as he said, the Gnomes from thraldom.

§53    Fëanor was summoned before the Valar to the Ring of Doom, and there the lies of Morgoth were laid bare for all those to see who had the will. By the judgement of the Gods Fëanor was banished for a while from Tûn, since he had disturbed its peace. But with him went Finwë his father, who loved him more than his other sons, and many other Gnomes. Northward in Valinor in the hills near to the halls of Mandos they built a strong place and a treasury; and they gathered there a multitude of gems. But Fingolfin ruled the Noldor in Tûn; and thus in part Morgoth's words seemed justified (though Fëanor had wrought their fulfilment by his own deeds), and the bitterness that he sowed went on, though the lies were revealed, and long afterwards it lived still between the sons of Fëanor and Fingolfin.

§54     Straight from the midst of their council the Valar sent Tulkas to lay hands on Morgoth and bring him again to judgement, but Morgoth hid himself, and none could discover whither he had gone; and the shadows of all standing things seemed to grow longer and darker in that time. It is said that for a great while none saw Morgoth, until he appeared privily to Fëanor, feigning friendship with cunning argument, and urging him to his former thought of flight. But Fëanor shut now his doors, if not his heart; and Finwë sent word to Valmar, but Morgoth departed in anger.

§55     Now the Gods were sitting in council before their gates fearing the lengthening of the shadows, when the messenger came from Finwë, but ere Tulkas could set forth others came that brought tidings from Tûn. For Morgoth had fled over the passes of the mountains, and from Kôr the Elves saw him pass in wrath as a thunder-cloud. Thence he came into that region that is called Arvalin, which lies south of the Bay of Elfland, and is a narrow land beneath the eastern feet of the Mountains of Valinor. There the shadows are deepest and thickest in the world. In that land, secret and unknown, dwelt Ungoliantë, Gloomweaver, in spider's form. It is not told whence she came; from the Outer Darkness, maybe, that lies beyond the Walls of the World. In a ravine she lived, and spun her webs in a cleft of the mountains; for she sucked up light and shining things to spin them forth again in black nets of choking gloom and clinging fog. She hungered ever for more food.

§56     Morgoth met Ungoliantë in Arvalin, and with her he plotted his revenge; but she demanded a great and terrible reward, ere she would dare the perils of Valinor and the power of the Gods. She wove a great darkness about her for their protection, and black spider-ropes she span, and cast from rocky peak to peak; and in this way she scaled at last the highest pinnacle of the mountains south of Taniquetil. In this region the vigilance of the Valar was less, because the wild woods of Oromë lay in the south of Valinor, and the walls of the mountains looked there eastward upon untrodden land and empty seas; and the Gods held guard rather against the North where of old Morgoth had raised his throne and fortress.

§57     Now Ungoliantë made a ladder of woven ropes, and upon this Morgoth climbed, and sat beside her; and he looked down upon the shining plain, seeing afar off the domes of Valmar glittering in the mingling of the light. Then Morgoth laughed;

and swiftly he sped down the long western slopes with Ungoliantë at his side, and her darkness was about them.

§58   It was a day of festival, and most of the people of Valinor were upon the mountain of Manwë, singing before him in his halls, or playing in the upland pleasaunces upon the green slopes of Taniquetil. The Lindar were there and many of the Noldor. Valmar's streets were fallen silent, and few feet passed upon the stairs of Tûn; only upon the shores of Elvenhome the Teleri still sang and played, recking little of times or seasons or the fate that should befall. Silpion was waning and Laurelin had just begun to glow, when protected by fate Morgoth and Ungoliantë crept into the plain. With his black spear Morgoth stabbed each tree to its very core, and as their juices spouted forth Ungoliantë sucked them up; and the poison from her foul lips went into their tissues and withered them, leaf and branch and root. Ungoliantë belched forth black vapours as she drank their radiance; and she swelled to monstrous form.

§59   Then wonder and dismay fell on Valinor, when a sudden twilight and a mounting gloom came upon the land. Black clouds floated about the towers of Valmar, and darkness drifted down its streets. Varda looked down from Taniquetil and saw the trees drowned and hidden in a mist. Too late they ran from hill and gate. The Two Trees died and shone no more, while wailing throngs stood round them and called on Manwë to come down. Out upon the plain the horses of Oromë thundered with a thousand hooves, and fire started in the gloom about their feet. Swifter than they Tulkas ran before them, and the light of the anger of his eyes was as a beacon. But they found not what they sought. Wherever Morgoth went, a darkness and confusion was around him woven by Ungoliantë, so that their feet strayed and their eyes were blind, and Morgoth escaped the hunt.

### Commentary on Chapter 4

§46   The danger of the Silmarils to Men is increased: for the words of Q (IV. 88) 'no mortal flesh impure could touch them' are changed to 'no mortal flesh, nor flesh unclean, could touch them'.

§49   The long footnote on Gnomish arms (the content of which is entirely novel), if not written at the same time as the main text, was certainly an early addition. 'Thus wrote Pengolod' seems to have been written at the same time as the rest of the note, which is difficult to explain, if Pengolod was the author of the *Quenta Silmarillion* anyway; on this question see the commentary on §123.

§50    The words 'though the Valar knew of the coming of Men that were to be' are not at variance with the rewritten text of §20; for although it is said there that the coming of the Elves was not in the Music of the Ainur and was unknown to the Valar save Manwë, it is also told that at the awakening of the Elves Manwë 'spoke to the Valar, revealing to them the mind of the Father; and he bade them to return now to their duty, which was to govern the world for the Children of Ilúvatar, when they should appear, each kindred in its appointed time.'

§54    'But Feanor shut now his doors . . .': the story of Morgoth's going to the stronghold of Finwë and Fëanor at this juncture moves further towards the final form (see AV 2, annal 2900).

§55    'Bay of Elfland': in §§37–8, 44 the manuscript has 'Bay of Elfland' where the typescript has 'Bay of Elvenhome'.

§58    'With his black spear': 'With his black sword' Q (§4); cf. the story in the *Lost Tales*, I. 153.


5    OF THE FLIGHT OF THE NOLDOR

§60    This was the time of the Darkening of Valinor. In that day there stood before the gates of Valmar Gnomes that cried aloud, bearing evil tidings. For they told that Morgoth had fled northward, and with him went a thing before unseen that in the gathering night had seemed to be a spider of monstrous form. Suddenly they had fallen upon the treasury of Finwë. There Morgoth slew the King of the Noldor before his doors, and spilled the first Elvish blood that stained the earth. Many others he slew also, but Fëanor and his sons were not there. The Silmarils Morgoth took, and all the wealth of the jewels of the Noldor that were hoarded in that place. Great was the grief of Fëanor, both for his father and not less for the Silmarils, and bitterly he cursed the chance that had taken him on that evil day to Taniquetil, thinking in his folly that with his own hands and his sons he might have withstood the violence of Morgoth.

§61    Little is known of the paths of Morgoth after his dreadful deeds in Valinor. But it is told that escaping from the hunt he came at last with Ungoliantë over the Grinding Ice and so into the northern regions of the Middle-earth once more. Then Ungoliantë summoned him to give her the promised reward. The half of her pay had been the sap of the Trees. The other half was a full share in the plundered jewels. Morgoth yielded these, and she devoured them, and their light perished from the earth, but Ungoliantë grew yet darker and more huge and hideous in form. But Morgoth would give her no share in the Silmarils. That was the first thieves' quarrel.

§62   So great had Ungoliantë become that she enmeshed Morgoth in her choking nets, and his awful cry echoed through the shuddering world. To his aid there came the Balrogs that lived yet in the deepest places of his ancient fortress, Utumno in the North. With their whips of flame the Balrogs smote the webs asunder, and drove away Ungoliantë into the uttermost South, where she long remained. Thus Morgoth came back to his ancient habitation, and he built anew his vaults and dungeons and great towers, in that place which the Gnomes after knew as Angband. There countless became the hosts of his beasts and demons; and he brought into being the race of the Orcs, and they grew and multiplied in the bowels of the earth. These Orcs Morgoth made in envy and mockery of the Elves, and they were made of stone, but their hearts of hatred. Glamhoth, the hosts of hate, the Gnomes have called them. Goblins they may be called, but in ancient days they were strong and fell.

§63   And in Angband Morgoth forged for himself a great crown of iron, and he called himself the King of the World. In token of this he set the three Silmarils in his crown. It is said that his evil hands were burned black by the touch of those holy jewels; and black they have ever been since; nor was he ever afterward free from the pain of the burning, and the anger of the pain. That crown he never took from his head, though its weight was a deadly weariness; and it was never his wont to leave the deep places of his fortress, but he governed his vast armies from his northern throne.

§64   When it became at last clear that Morgoth had escaped, the Gods assembled about the dead Trees, and sat there in darkness for a long while silent, and they were filled with grief. Since the people of the Blessed Realm had been gathered for festival, all the Valar and their children were there, save Ossë who came seldom to Valinor, and Tulkas who would not leave the unavailing hunt; and with them the Lindar, the folk of Ingwë, stood and wept. But most of the Noldor returned to Tûn and mourned for the darkening of their fair city. Fogs and shadows now drifted in from the sea through the pass of Kôr, and all shapes were confused, as the light of the Trees perished. A murmur was heard in Elfland, and the Teleri wailed beside the sea.

§65   Then Fëanor appeared suddenly amid the Noldor and called on all to come to the high square upon the top of the hill of

Kôr beneath the tower of Ingwë; but the doom of banishment from Tûn which the Gods had laid upon him was not yet lifted, and he rebelled against the Valar. A vast concourse gathered swiftly, therefore, to hear what he would say, and the hill, and all the stairs and streets that climbed upon it, were lit with the light of many torches that each one that came bore in hand.

§66   Fëanor was a great orator with a power of moving words. That day he made before the Gnomes a mighty speech that has ever been remembered. Fierce and fell were his words and filled with wrath and pride, and they stirred the people to madness like the fumes of potent wine. His anger was most against Morgoth, yet most that he said was drawn from the very lies of Morgoth himself; but he was distraught with grief for the slaying of his father, and anguish for the rape of the Silmarils. He now claimed the kingship of all the Noldor, since Finwë was dead, and mocked the decree of the Valar. 'Why should we longer obey the jealous Gods,' he asked, 'who cannot keep us, nor their own realm, safe from their foe? And is not Melko the accursed one of the Valar?'

§67   He bade the Gnomes prepare for flight in the darkness, while the Valar were still wrapped in idle mourning; to seek freedom in the world, and of their own prowess to win there a new realm, since Valinor was no longer more bright and blissful than the lands outside; to pursue Morgoth and war with him for ever until they were avenged. 'And when we have regained the Silmarils,' he said, 'we shall be masters of the enchanted light, and lords of the bliss and beauty of the world.' Then he swore a terrible oath. His seven sons leaped staightway to his side and took the selfsame vow together, each with drawn sword. They swore an oath which none shall break, and none should take, by the name of the Allfather, calling the Everlasting Dark upon them, if they kept it not; and Manwë they named in witness, and Varda, and the Holy Mount, vowing to pursue with vengeance and hatred to the ends of the world Vala, Demon, Elf, or Man as yet unborn, or any creature great or small, good or evil, that time should bring forth unto the end of days, whoso should hold or take or keep a Silmaril from their possession.

§68   Fingolfin and his son Fingon spake against Fëanor, and there was wrath and angry words that came near to blows. But Finrod spake gently and persuasively, and sought to calm them, urging them to pause and ponder, ere deeds were done that could not be undone. But of his own sons Inglor alone spake with him; Angrod and Egnor took the part of Fëanor, and Orodreth stood aside. In the end it was put to the vote of the assembled people, and they being moved by the potent words of Fëanor, and filled with desire for the Silmarils, decided to depart from Valinor. Yet the Noldor of Tûn would not now renounce the kingship of Fingolfin; and as two divided hosts, therefore, they at length set forth upon their bitter road. The greater part marched behind Fingolfin, who with his sons yielded to the general voice against their wisdom, because they would not desert their people; and with Fingolfin were Finrod and Inglor, though they were loth to go. In the van marched Fëanor and his sons with lesser host, but they were filled with reckless eagerness. Some remained behind: both some that had been upon Taniquetil on the day of fate, and sat now with the Lindar at the feet of the Gods partaking of their grief and vigil; and some that would not forsake the fair city of Tûn and its wealth of things made by cunning hands, though the darkness had fallen upon them. And the Valar learning of the purpose of the Noldor sent word that they forbade the march, for the hour was evil and would lead to woe, but they would not hinder it, since Fëanor had accused them, saying that they held the Eldar captive against their will. But Fëanor laughed hardening his heart, and he said that sojourn in Valinor had led through bliss to sorrow; they would now try the contrary, to find joy at last through woe.

§69   Therefore they continued their march, and the house of Fëanor hastened ahead along the coast of Valinor, and they did not turn their eyes back to look upon Tûn. The hosts of Fingolfin followed less eagerly, and at the rear came sorrowing Finrod and Inglor and many of the noblest and fairest of the Noldor; and they looked often backward, until the lamp of Ingwë was lost in the gathering tide of gloom; and more than others they carried thence memories of the glory of their ancient home, and some even of the fair things there made with hands they took with them. Thus the folk of Finrod had no part in the dreadful deed that then was done; yet all the Gnomes that departed from Valinor came under the shadow of the curse that followed it. For it came soon into the heart of Fëanor that they should persuade the Teleri, their friends, to join with them; for thus in his rebellion he thought that the bliss of Valinor might be further diminished, and his power for war upon Morgoth be increased; moreover he desired ships. As his mind cooled and took counsel, he saw that the Noldor might hardly escape without many vessels; but it would need long to build so great a fleet, even were there any among the Noldor skilled in that craft. But there were none, and he brooked no delay, fearing lest many should desert him. Yet they must at some time cross the seas, albeit far to the North where they were narrower; for further still, to those places where the western land and Middle-earth touched nigh, he feared to venture. There he knew was Helkaraksë, the Strait of Grinding Ice, where the frozen hills ever broke and shifted, sundering and clashing again together.

§70   But the Teleri would not join the Noldor in flight, and sent back their messengers. They had never lent ear to Morgoth nor welcomed him among them. They desired now no other cliffs nor beaches than the strands of Elvenhome, nor other lord than Elwë, prince of Alqualondë; and he trusted that Ulmo and the great Valar would yet redress the sorrow of Valinor. And their white ships with their white sails they would neither give nor sell, for they prized them dearly, nor did they hope ever again to make others so fair and swift. But when the host of Fëanor came to the Haven of the Swans they attempted to seize by force the white fleets that lay anchored there, and the Teleri resisted them. Weapons were drawn and a bitter fight was fought upon the great arch of the Haven's gate, and upon the lamplit quays and piers, as is sadly told in the song of the Flight of the Gnomes. Thrice the folk of Fëanor were driven back, and many were slain upon either side; but the vanguard of the Noldor were succoured by the foremost of the people of Fingolfin, and the Teleri were over-come, and most of those that dwelt at Alqualondë were slain or cast into the sea. For the Noldor were become fierce and des-perate, and the Teleri had less strength, and were armed mostly with slender bows. Then the Gnomes drew away the white ships of the Teleri, and manned their oars as best they could, and took them north along the coast. And the Teleri cried to Ossë, and he came not, for he had been summoned to Valmar to the vigil and council of the Gods, and it was not decreed by fate nor permitted by the Valar that the flight of the Noldor should be waylaid. But Uinen wept for the slain of the Teleri; and the sea roared against the Gnomes, so that many of the ships were wrecked and those in them drowned.

§71   But most of them escaped and continued their journey, some by ship and some by foot; but the way was long and ever more evil going as they went on. After they had marched for a great while, and were come at length to the northern confines of the Blessed Realm – and they are mountainous and cold and look upon the empty waste of Eruman – they beheld a dark figure standing high upon a rock that looked down upon the shore. Some say it was the herald of the Gods, others that it was Mandos himself. There he spake in a loud voice, solemn and terrible, the curse and prophecy which is called the Prophecy of the North, warning them to return and ask for pardon, or in the end return only at last after sorrow and unspeakable misery. Much he foretold in dark words, which only the wisest of them understood, concerning things that after befell. But all heard the curse he uttered upon those that would not stay or seek the doom and pardon of the Valar, for the spilling of the blood of their kindred at Alqualondë and fighting the first battle between the children of earth unrighteously. For this the Noldor should taste death more often and more bitterly than their kindred, by weapon and by torment and by grief; and evil fortune should pursue the house of Fëanor, and their oath should turn against them, and all who now followed them should share their lot. And evil should come most upon them through treachery of kin to kin, so that in all their wars and councils they should suffer from treason and the fear of treason among themselves. But Fëanor said: 'He saith not that we shall suffer from cowardice, from cravens or the fear of cravens'; and that proved true also.

§72     Then Finrod and a few of his household turned back, and they came at last to Valinor again, and received the pardon of the Valar; and Finrod was set to rule the remnant of the Noldor in the Blessed Realm. But his sons went not with him; for Inglor and Orodreth would not forsake the sons of Fingolfin, nor Angrod and Egnor their friends Celegorn and Curufin; and all Fingolfin's folk went forward still, being constrained by the will of Fëanor and fearing also to face the doom of the Gods, since not all of them had been guiltless of the kinslaying at Alqualondë. Then all too swiftly the evil that was foretold began its work.

§73     The Gnomes came at last far to the North, and saw the first teeth of the ice that floated in the sea. They began to suffer anguish from the cold. Then many of them murmured, especially those that followed Fingolfin, and some began to curse Fëanor and name him as the cause of all the woes of the Eldar. But the ships were too few, many having been lost upon the way, to carry all across together, yet none were willing to abide upon the coast while others were transported; already fear of treachery was awake. Therefore it came into the heart of Fëanor and his sons to sail off on a sudden with all the ships, of which they had retained the mastery since the battle of the Haven; and they took with them only such as were faithful to their house, among whom were Angrod and Egnor. As for the others, 'we will leave the murmurers to murmur', said Fëanor, 'or to whine their way back to the cages of the Valar.' Thus began the curse of the kinslaying. When Fëanor and his folk landed on the shores in the west of the northern regions of Middle-earth, they set fire in the ships and made a great burning, terrible and bright; and Fingolfin and his people saw the light of it afar off red beneath the clouds. They saw then they were betrayed, and left to perish in Eruman or return; and they wandered long in misery. But their valour and endurance grew with hardship, for they were a mighty folk, but new come from the Blessed Realm, and not yet weary with the weariness of the earth, and the fire of their minds and hearts was young. Therefore led by Fingolfin, and Fingon, Turgon, and Inglor, they ventured into the bitterest North; and finding no other way they dared at last the terror of the Grinding Ice. Few of the deeds of the Gnomes after surpassed the perilous crossing in hardihood or in woe. Many there perished miserably, and it was with lessened host that Fingolfin set foot at last upon the northern lands. Small love for Fëanor or his sons had those that marched at last behind him, and came unto Beleriand at the rising of the sun.

## Commentary on Chapter 5

§60  Here first appears the story that Fëanor went to the festival, of which there is no suggestion in Q (IV. 92).

§62  Q has 'To his aid came the Orcs and Balrogs that lived yet in the lowest places of Angband', but Orcs are absent here in QS. Here and again in §105 *Utumno* is an early change from *Utumna*; see the commentary on §12. That the slightly ambiguous sentence 'he built anew . . .' means that he built Angband on the ruins of Utumno is seen from §105: 'Melko coming back into Middle-earth made the endless dungeons of Angband, the hells of iron, where of old Utumno had been.' See IV. 259–60.

In Q the passage about Morgoth's making of the Orcs, precursor of this in QS, is placed earlier (IV. 82), before the making of the stars and the awakening of the Elves; at the corresponding place in QS (§18) it is said that 'the Orcs were not made until he had looked upon the Elves.' In Q, at the place (IV. 93) corresponding to the present passage in QS, it is said that 'countless became the number of the hosts of his Orcs and demons' – i.e. the Orcs were already in existence before Morgoth's return (and so could come to his aid when they heard his cry); but there is a direction in Q at this point (IV. 93 note 8) to bring in the making of the Orcs here rather than earlier (the reason for this being the idea that the Orcs were made 'in mockery of the Children of Ilúvatar').

§68  That Orodreth 'stood aside', taking the part neither of Finrod and Inglor nor of Angrod and Egnor and the Fëanorians, is a new element in the story; see under §73 below.

§70  The account in QS of the Battle of Alqualondë, and of Fëanor's calculations before it, is given a better progression and is substantially expanded from that in Q (IV. 95), while the concluding passage of §70, recounting the calling of the Teleri upon Ossë and the storm raised by Uinen, is altogether absent from the earlier versions.

§71  *Eruman* is not used of this region in Q (where the name is applied to the land where Men first awoke in the East, IV. 99, 171), but it is found in this sense in the *Ambarkanta* (IV. 239; also on the maps, IV. 249, 251).

Some elements in this version of the Prophecy of the North not in Q (IV. 96) are found in AV annal 2993 (virtually the same in both versions), as 'their oath should turn against them', and 'they should be slain with weapons, and with torments, and with sorrow'. On the other hand the AV version has an element not in QS, the prophecy that the Noldor should 'in the long end fade upon Middle-earth and wane before the younger race' (see IV. 171–2).

§73  In AV 2 annal 2994 the story still went that Orodreth, as well as Angrod and Egnor, were taken by the Fëanorians in the ships; but with the separation of Orodreth from Angrod and Egnor in QS, making him instead a close associate of his brother Inglor Felagund (§42), his name was struck from the annal (AV 2 note 10). It is notable here that Orodreth is not named among the leaders in the passage of the second host across the Grinding Ice. This is to be associated, I think, with his 'standing aside' during the dissensions before the Flight of the Noldor (see §68); suggestions of the decline in his significance which I have described in III. 91, 246.

In QS §91 the first sun is said to have risen as Fingolfin marched into Mithrim; thus 'Beleriand' is here used in a very extended sense (as also in AV annal 2995: 'Fëanor came unto Beleriand and the shores beneath Eredlómin', repeated in QS §88). Similarly the Battle-under-Stars, fought in Mithrim, was the First Battle of Beleriand. But in QS §108 Beleriand 'was bounded upon the North by Nivrost and Hithlum and Dorthonion'.

# 6   OF THE SUN AND MOON AND THE HIDING OF VALINOR

§74  When the Gods learned that the Noldor had fled, and were come at last back into Middle-earth, they were aroused from their grief, and took counsel for the redress of the injuries of the world. And Manwë bade Yavanna to put forth all her power of growth and healing; and she put forth all her power upon the Trees, but it availed not to heal their mortal wounds. Yet even as the Valar listened in the gloom to her singing, Silpion bore at last upon a leafless bough one great silver bloom, and Laurelin a single golden fruit. These Yavanna took, and the Trees then died, and their lifeless stems stand yet in Valinor, a memorial of vanished joy. But the fruit and flower Yavanna gave to Aulë, and Manwë hallowed them, and Aulë and his folk made vessels to hold them and preserve their radiance, as is said in the song of the Sun and Moon. These vessels the Gods gave to Varda, that they might become lamps of heaven, outshining the ancient stars; and she gave them power to traverse the region of the stars, and set them to sail appointed courses above the earth. These things the Valar did, recalling in their twilight the darkness of the lands outside, and they resolved now to illumine Middle-earth, and with light to hinder the deeds of Melko; for they remembered the Dark-elves, and did not utterly forsake the exiled Gnomes; and Manwë knew that the hour of Men was drawing nigh.

§75   Isil the Sheen the Gods of old named the Moon in Valinor, and Úrin the Fiery they named the Sun; but the Eldar named them Răna, the wayward, the giver of visions, and Anar, the heart of flame, that awakens and consumes. For the Sun was set as a sign for the awakening of Men and the waning of the Elves; but the Moon cherishes their memory. The maiden chosen from among their own folk by the Valar to guide the ship of the Sun was named Arien; and the youth who steered the floating island of the Moon was Tilion.* In the days of the Trees Arien had tended the golden flowers in the gardens of Vana and watered them with the radiant dew of Laurelin. Tilion was a young hunter of the company of Oromë, and he had a silver bow. He loved Arien, but she was a holier spirit of greater power, and wished to be ever virgin and alone; and Tilion pursued her in vain. Tilion forsook then the woods of Oromë, and dwelt in the gardens of Lórien, sitting in dream beside the pools lit by the flickering light of Silpion.

§76   Răna was first wrought and made ready, and first rose into the region of the stars, and was the elder of the lights, as was Silpion of the Trees. Then for a while the world had moonlight,

---

*Marginal note to the text*: hyrned Æ.

and many creatures stirred and woke that had waited long in the dark; but many of the stars fled affrighted, and Tilion the bowman wandered from his path pursuing them; and some plunged in the chasm and sought refuge at the roots of the earth. The servants of Melko were amazed; and it is told that Fingolfin set foot upon the northern lands with the first moonrise, and the shadows of his host were long and black. Tilion had traversed the heaven seven times, and was thus in the furthest East when the ship of Arien was ready. Then Anar rose in glory and the snow upon the mountains glowed with fire, and there was the sound of many waterfalls; but the servants of Melko fled to Angband and cowered in fear, and Fingolfin unfurled his banners.

§77 Now Varda purposed that the two vessels should sail the sky and ever be aloft, but not together: each should journey from Valinor into the East and back, the one issuing from the West as the other turned from the East. Thus the first days were reckoned after the manner of the Trees from the mingling of the lights when Arien and Tilion passed above the middle of the earth. But Tilion was wayward and uncertain in speed, and held not to his appointed course; and at times he sought to tarry Arien, whom he loved, though the flame of Anar withered the sheen of Silpion's bloom, if he drew too nigh, and his vessel was scorched and darkened. Because of Tilion, therefore, and yet more because of the prayers of Lórien and Nienna, who said that all night and sleep and peace had been banished from the earth, Varda changed her design, and allowed a time wherein the world should still have shadow and half-light. The Sun rested, therefore, a while in Valinor, lying upon the cool bosom of the Outer Sea. So Evening, which is the time of the descent and resting of the Sun, is the hour of greatest light and joy in Valinor. But soon the Sun is drawn down into Vaiya by the servants of Ulmo, and brought in haste to the East, and mounts the sky again, lest night be overlong and evil strengthened. But the waters of Vaiya are made hot and glow with coloured fires, and Valinor has light for a while after the passing of Arien; yet as she goes under the earth and draws towards the East the glow fades and Valinor is dim, and the Gods mourn then most for the death of Laurelin. At dawn the shadows of their mountains of defence lie heavy on the land of the Valar.

§78 Varda commanded the Moon to rise only after the Sun had left heaven, but he travels with uncertain pace, and still pursueth her, so that at times they both are in the sky together, and still at times he draws nigh to her, and there is a darkness amid the day. But Tilion tarries seldom in Valinor, loving rather the great lands; and mostly he passes swiftly over the western land, either Arvalin or Eruman or Valinor, and plunges into the chasm between the shores of the earth and the Outer Sea, and pursues his way alone among the grots at the roots of the earth. There sometimes he wanders long, and stars that have taken hiding there flee before him into the upper air. Yet it happens at times that he comes above Valinor while the Sun is still there, and he descends and meets his beloved, for they leave their vessels for a space; then there is great joy, and Valinor is filled with silver and gold, and the Gods laugh recalling the mingling of the light long ago, when Laurelin flowered and Silpion was in bud.

§79   Still therefore the light of Valinor is greater and fairer than upon Middle-earth, because the Sun resteth there, and the lights of heaven draw nearer to the land in that region; moreover the Valar store the radiance of the Sun in many vessels, and in vats and pools for their comfort in times of dark. But the light is not the light which came from the Trees before the poisoned lips of Ungoliantë touched them. That light lives now only in the Silmarils. Gods and Elves, therefore, look forward yet to a time when the Elder Sun and Moon, which are the Trees, may be rekindled and the ancient joy and glory return. Ulmo foretold to them that this would only come to pass through the aid, frail though it might seem, of the second race of earth, the Younger Children of Ilúvatar. But Manwë alone heeded his words at that time; for the Valar were still wroth because of the ingratitude of the Noldor, and the cruel slaying at the Haven of the Swans. Moreover all save Tulkas for a while were in doubt, fearing the might and cunning of Morgoth. Therefore at this time they fortified all Valinor anew, and set a sleepless watch upon the mountain-walls, which now they raised, east, north, and south, to sheer and dreadful height. Their outer sides were dark and smooth, without ledge or foothold for aught save birds, and fell in precipices with faces hard as glass; their tops were crowned with ice. No pass led through them save only at the Kalakilya wherein stood the mound of Kôr. This they could not close because of the Eldar who were faithful; for all those of Elvish race must breathe at whiles the outer air of Middle-earth, nor could they wholly sunder the Teleri from their kin. But the Eldar were set to guard that pass unceasingly: the fleet of the Teleri kept the shore, the remnant of the Gnomes dwelt ever in the deep cleft of the mountains, and upon the plain of Valmar, where the pass issues into Valinor, the Lindar were camped as sentinels, that no bird nor beast nor Elf nor Man, nor any creature beside that came from Middle-earth could pass the leaguer.

§80   In that time, which songs call the Hiding of Valinor, the Enchanted Isles were set, and filled with shadows and bewilderment, and all the seas about were filled with shadows; and these isles were strung across the Shadowy Seas from north to south before Tol Eressëa, the Lonely Isle, is reached, sailing west; and hardly might any vessel come between them in the gloom or win through to the Bay of Elvenhome. For a great weariness comes upon mariners in that region, and a loathing of the sea; but all such as set foot upon those islands are there entrapped and wound in everlasting sleep. Thus it was that the many emissaries of the Gnomes in after days never came to Valinor – save one, the mightiest mariner of song or tale.

### Commentary on Chapter 6

§74   In the extremely brief account in Q (IV. 97) there is no mention of Aulë as having played any part in the making of the Sun and Moon, and QS reverts in this to the original story in the *Lost Tales* (I. 185–6, 191–2).

Of the passage beginning 'These vessels the Gods gave to Varda' there is only a trace in Q. Varda appears as the deviser of the motions of the Sun and Moon in the *Ambarkanta* (IV. 236).

§75   In Q the Moon is called *Rána* (without translation), and this name is said to have been given by the Gods (so also in the *Lost Tales*, I. 192). In QS the Gods' name is *Isil* 'the Sheen' (cf. the Elves' name *Sil* 'the Rose' in the *Lost Tales*, *ibid*.) and *Rǎna* 'the wayward' that of the Eldar. – In Q the name of the Sun, given by the Gods, is *Úr* (in the *Lost Tales*, I. 187, this was the Elvish name, meaning 'fire'; the Gods called the Sun *Sári*). In QS the Gods' name is *Úrin* 'the Fiery', and the Eldarin name *Anar*. – In *The Lost Road* (p. 41) the names of the Sun and Moon that 'came through' to Alboin Errol were *Anar* and *Isil* (and also *Anor* and *Ithil* in 'Beleriandic' – which presumably here means Exilic Noldorin: see the *Etymologies*, stems ANÁR and SIL).

Almost the same words of the Sun and Moon in relation to Men and Elves are used in AV 2 (annal 2998–3000 and commentary).

In Q the Sun-maiden was named *Úrien*, emended throughout to *Árien*. As QS was first written the name was still spelt *Árien*, but changed throughout to *Ärien, Arien*. This seems to have been a very early change and I therefore read *Arien* in the text.

On 'the floating island of the Moon' see IV. 171. The marginal gloss by Ælfwine (see the preamble to QS on p. 201) is certainly contemporary with the writing of the manuscript. Old English *hyrned* 'horned'; cf. the *Etymologies*, stem TIL.

From 'He loved Arien, but she was a holier spirit of greater power' to
the end of §76 there is nothing corresponding in Q, except the
reference (IV. 97) to Tilion's pursuit of the stars. In Q Tilion is rather
the rival of Arien, as was Ilinsor in the *Lost Tales* (I. 195); but cf. the
*Ambarkanta* (where Arien and Tilion are not referred to): 'it happens
at times that he [the Moon] comes above Valinor ere the Sun has left it,
and then he descends and meets his beloved' (IV. 237) – a passage
closely echoed in QS §78.

§76   'plunged in the chasm': the Chasm of Ilmen (see the *Ambarkanta*,
      IV. 236). – This is the first appearance of the image of the long
      shadows cast by Fingolfin's host as the Moon rose in the West behind
      them. – In this sentence the word *amazed* is used in an archaic and
      much stronger sense: overwhelmed with wonder and fear.

§77   'his vessel was scorched and darkened': no explanation is offered in
      Q for the markings on the Moon (for the old story concerning this see
      I. 191, 194). It is said in the *Ambarkanta* that the Moon 'pursues ever
      after the Sun, and overtakes her seldom, and then is consumed and
      darkened in her flame.'

§§77–8   While a great deal of the description of the motions of the Sun
      and Moon in these paragraphs is not found in Q, a passage in the
      *Ambarkanta* (IV. 237), while briefer and without any reference to the
      change in the divine plan, corresponds quite closely to QS in many
      features. The QS account introduces an explanation of solar eclipses
      ('still at times he draws nigh to her, and there is a darkness amid the
      day'), and of meteors ('stars that have taken hiding there flee before
      him into the upper air') – cf. the old conception in the *Lost Tales*,
      I. 216.

§79   The storing of the light of the Sun in vats and pools in Valinor
      reflects an idea found long before in Kulullin, the great cauldron of
      golden light in Valinor: the Gods gathered that light 'in the great vat
      Kulullin to the great increase of its fountains, or in other bright basons
      and wide pools about their courts, for the health and glory of its
      radiance was very great' (I. 181). Afterwards the idea emerged again in
      relation to the Two Trees: 'the dews of Telperion and the rain that fell
      from Laurelin Varda hoarded in great vats like shining lakes, that were
      to all the land of the Valar as wells of water and of light' (*The
      Silmarillion* p. 39).

The passage beginning 'Gods and Elves, therefore, look forward
yet . . .' has survived through S and Q from the earliest conceptions. In
the phrase 'the Elder Sun and Moon' the word 'Elder' is written over an
erasure, and the obliterated word was certainly 'Magic' – the last
occurrence of the old 'Magic Sun'. On the mysterious foretelling of
Ulmo see IV. 50.

The account of the raising of the mountain-wall and the reason for
not closing the Pass of Kôr is much enlarged from the corresponding
passage in Q.

It will be seen that at the time when my father began *The Lord of the Rings* the conceptions of the *Ambarkanta* were still fully in being, and that the story of the making of the Sun and Moon from the last fruit and the last flower of the dying Trees was still quite unshadowed by doubt of its propriety in the whole structure of the mythology.

## 7  OF MEN

§81   The Valar sat now behind the mountains and feasted, and all save Manwë and Ulmo dismissed the exiled Noldor from their thought; and having given light to Middle-earth they left it for long untended, and the lordship of Morgoth was uncontested save by the valour of the Gnomes. Most in mind Ulmo kept them, who gathered news of the earth through all the waters.

§82   At the first rising of the Sun above the earth the younger children of the world awoke in the land of Hildórien in the uttermost East of Middle-earth that lies beside the eastern sea; for measured time had come upon earth, and the first of days, and the long awaiting was at an end. Thereafter the vigour of the Quendi that remained in the inner lands was lessened, and their waning was begun; and the air of Middle-earth became heavy with the breath of growth and mortality. For there was great growth in that time beneath the new Sun, and the midmost lands of Middle-earth were clothed in a sudden riot of forest and they were rich with leaves, and life teemed upon the soil and in the waters. But the first sun arose in the West, and the opening eyes of Men were turned thitherward, and their feet as they wandered over earth for the most part strayed that way.

§83   Of Men* little is told in these tales, which concern the eldest days before the waxing of mortals and the waning of the Elves, save of those Fathers of Men who in the first years of Moonsheen and Sunlight wandered into the North of the world. To Hildórien there came no God to guide Men or to summon them to dwell in Valinor; and Men have feared the Valar, rather than loved them, and have not understood the purposes of the Powers, being at variance with them, and at strife with the world.

*Footnote to the text:* The Eldar called them Hildi, the followers; whence Hildórien, the place of the birth of the Hildi, is named. And many other names they gave to them: Engwar the sickly, and Fírimor the mortals; and named them the Usurpers, the Strangers, and the Inscrutable, the Self-cursed, the Heavyhanded, the Nightfearers, the Children of the Sun.

Ulmo nonetheless took thought for them, aiding the counsel and will of Manwë; and his messages came often to them by stream and flood. But they have not skill in such matters, and still less had they in those days ere they had mingled with the Elves. Therefore they loved the waters, and their hearts were stirred, but they understood not the messages. Yet it is told that ere long they met the Dark-elves in many places, and were befriended by them. And the Dark-elves taught them speech, and many other things; and Men became the companions and disciples in their childhood of these ancient folk, wanderers of the Elf-race who had never found the paths to Valinor, and knew of the Valar but as a rumour and a distant name.

§84   Not long had Morgoth then come back into the Middle-earth, and his power went not far abroad, and was moreover checked by the sudden coming of great light. There was little peril, therefore, in the lands and hills; and there new things, fair and fresh, devised long ages before in the thought of Yavanna, and sown as seed in the dark, came at last to their budding and their bloom. West, north, and south the children of Men spread and wandered, and their joy was the joy of the morning before the dew is dry, when every leaf is green.

§85   But the dawn is brief and day full often belies its promise; and now time drew on to the great wars of the powers of the North, when Gnomes and Dark-elves and Men strove against the hosts of Morgoth Bauglir, and went down in ruin. To this end the cunning lies of Morgoth that he sowed of old, and sowed ever anew among his foes, and the curse that came of the slaying at Alqualondë, and the oath of Fëanor, were ever at work: the greatest injury they did to Elves and Men. Only a part is here told of the deeds of those days, and most is said of the Gnomes, and the Silmarils, and the mortals that became entangled in their fate. In those days Elves and Men were of like stature and strength of body; but Elves were blessed with greater wit, and skill, and beauty; and those who had dwelt in Valinor and looked upon the Gods as much surpassed the Dark-elves in these things as they in turn surpassed the people of mortal race. Only in the realm of Doriath, whose queen Melian was of divine race, did the Ilkorins come near to match the Elves of Kôr. Immortal were the Elves, and their wisdom waxed from age to age, and no sickness nor pestilence brought death to them. Yet their bodies were of the stuff of earth and could be destroyed, and in those days they were more like to the bodies of Men, and to the earth, since they had not so long been inhabited by the fire of the spirit, which consumeth them from within in the courses of time. Therefore they could perish in the tumults of the world, and stone and water had power over them, and they could be slain with weapons in those days, even by mortal Men. And outside Valinor they tasted bitter grief, and some wasted and waned with sorrow, until they faded from the earth. Such was the measure of their mortality foretold in the Doom of Mandos spoken in Eruman. But if they were slain or wasted with grief, they died not from the earth, and their spirits went back to the halls of Mandos, and there waited, days or years, even a thousand, according to the will of Mandos and their deserts. Thence they are recalled at length to freedom, either as spirits, taking form according to their own thought, as the lesser folk of the divine race; or else, it is said, they are at times re-born into their own children, and the ancient wisdom of their race does not perish or grow less.

§86    More frail were Men, more easily slain by weapons or mischance, and less easily healed; subject to sickness and many ills; and they grew old and died. What befell their spirits after death the Elves know not. Some say that they too go to the halls of Mandos; but their place of waiting there is not that of the Elves; and Mandos under Ilúvatar alone save Manwë knows whither they go after the time of recollection in those silent halls beside the Western Sea. They are not reborn on earth, and none have ever come back from the mansions of the dead, save only Beren son of Barahir, whose hand had touched a Silmaril; but he never spoke afterward to mortal Men. The fate of Men after death, maybe, is not in the hands of the Valar, nor was all foretold in the Music of the Ainur.

§87    In after days, when because of the triumph of Morgoth Elves and Men became estranged, as he most wished, those of the Elf-race that lived still in the Middle-earth waned and faded, and Men usurped the sunlight. Then the Quendi wandered in the lonelier places of the great lands and the isles, and took to the moonlight and the starlight, and to the woods and caves, becoming as shadows and memories, such as did not ever and anon set sail into the West, and vanished from the earth, as is here later told. But in the dawn of years Elves and Men were allies and held themselves akin, and there were some among Men that learned the wisdom of the Eldar, and became great and valiant and renowned among the captains of the Gnomes. And in the glory and beauty of the Elves, and in their fate, full share had the fair offspring of Elf and Mortal, Eärendel and Elwing, and Elrond their child.

Commentary on Chapter 7

§82 *Hildórien* as the name of the land where Men awoke (replacing *Eruman* of Q) has appeared in the *Ambarkanta*: between the Mountains of the Wind and the Eastern Sea (IV. 239). The name was written into AV 2 (note 13): 'Hildórien in the midmost regions of the world' – whereas in QS it lay 'in the uttermost East of Middle-earth'. There is here only an appearance of contradiction, I think. Hildórien was in the furthest east of *Middle-earth*, but it was in the middle regions of the world; see *Ambarkanta* map IV, on which Hildórien is marked (IV. 249). – My note in IV. 257 that the name *Hildórien* implies *Hildor* needs correction: the footnote to the text in §83 shows that the form at this time was *Hildi* (cf. also the *Etymologies*, stem KHIL).

§83 The footnote on Elvish names for Men belongs with the original writing of the manuscript.

§85 There are some important differences in the passage concerning the fate of the Elves from that in Q (IV. 100) on which this is based. Q has nothing corresponding to the statement that Elvish bodies were then more like mortal bodies, more terrestrial, less 'consumed' by 'the fire of their spirit', than they afterwards became. Nor is there in Q the reference to the Doom of Mandos – which in any case does not in Q refer to the subject of Elvish mortality. This first appears in the account of the Doom in AV (annal 2993), where the phrase 'a measure of mortality should visit them' is used, echoed here in QS: 'Such was the measure of their mortality foretold in the Doom of Mandos'; see IV. 278–9. Another, and remarkable, development lies in the idea of the Elves, returning at length out of Mandos, 'taking form according to their thought, as the lesser folk of the divine race' (i.e. no longer as corporeal beings, but as spirits that could 'clothe' themselves in a perceptible form).

§86 The 'Western Sea' is here the Outer Sea, Vaiya. This may well be no more than a slip, for Q has 'his wide halls *beyond* the western sea'; my father corrected it at some later time to 'Outer Sea'.

§87 With 'the great lands and the isles' cf. Q (IV. 162): 'the great isles, which in the disruption of the Northern world were fashioned of ancient Beleriand' (retained in QS, p. 331, §26).

It is clear from the last sentence of the chapter that at this time Elros had not yet emerged, as he had not in *The Fall of Númenor* and *The Lost Road* (pp. 30, 74); on the other hand, he is present in the concluding portion of QS, p. 332, §28.

# 8 OF THE SIEGE OF ANGBAND

§88 Before the rising of the Moon Fëanor and his sons marched into the North; they landed on the northern shores of

Beleriand beneath the feet of Ered-lómin, the Echoing Mountains, at that place which is called Drengist. Thence they came into the land of Dor-lómen and about the north of the Mountains of Mithrim, and camped in Hithlum, the realm of mist, in that region that is named Mithrim, north of the great lake that has the same name. There a host of Orcs, aroused by the light of the burning ships, and the rumour of their march, came down upon them, and there was fought the first battle upon Middle-earth; and it is renowned in song, for the Gnomes were victorious, and drove away the Orcs with great slaughter, and pursued them beyond Eredwethion into the plain of Bladorion. This was the first battle of Beleriand, and is called the Battle-under-Stars.* Great was the valour of Fëanor and his sons, and the Orcs ever feared and hated them after; yet woe soon followed upon triumph. For Fëanor advanced unwarily upon Bladorion, pursuing the Orcs northward, and he was surrounded, when his own folk were far behind, but the Balrogs in the rearguard of Morgoth turned suddenly to bay. Fëanor fought undismayed, but he was wrapped in fire, and fell at length wounded mortally by the hand of Gothmog, lord of Balrogs, whom Ecthelion after slew in Gondolin. But his sons coming rescued him and bore him back to Mithrim. There he died, but was not buried; for so fiery was his spirit that his body fell to ash as his spirit sped; and it has never again appeared upon earth nor left the realm of Mandos. And Fëanor with his last sight saw afar the peaks of Thangorodrim, greatest of the hills of Middle-earth, that towered above the fortress of Morgoth; and he cursed the name of Morgoth thrice, and he laid it on his sons never to treat or parley with their foe.

§89    Yet even in the hour of his death an embassy came to them from Morgoth, acknowledging defeat, and offering terms, even to the surrender of a Silmaril. Then Maidros the tall, the eldest son, persuaded the Gnomes to feign to treat with Morgoth, and to meet his emissaries at the place appointed; but the Gnomes had as little thought of faith as had Morgoth. Wherefore each embassy came with greater force than was agreed, but Morgoth sent the greater and they were Balrogs. Maidros was ambushed, and all his company was slain, but he himself was taken alive by the command of Morgoth, and brought to Angband and tortured.

§90    Then the six brethren of Maidros drew back and fortified a great camp in Hithlum; but Morgoth held Maidros as hostage,

*Marginal note to the text: Dagor-nui-Ngiliath.

and sent word to Maglor that he would only release his brother if the Noldor would forsake their war, returning either to Valinor, or else departing from Beleriand and marching to the South of the world. But the Gnomes could not return to Valinor, having burned the ships, and they did not believe that Morgoth would release Maidros if they departed; and they were unwilling to depart, whatever he might do. Therefore Morgoth hung Maidros from the face of a precipice upon Thangorodrim, and he was caught to the rock by the wrist of his right hand in a band of steel.

§91   Now rumour came to the camp in Hithlum of the march of Fingolfin and his sons, and Inglor the son of Finrod, who had crossed the Grinding Ice. And all the world lay then in new wonder at the coming of the Moon; for even as the Moon first rose Fingolfin set foot upon Middle-earth, and the Orcs were filled with amazement. But even as the host of Fingolfin marched into Mithrim the Sun rose flaming in the West; and Fingolfin unfurled his blue and silver banners, and blew his horns, and flowers sprang beneath his marching feet. For a time of opening and growth, sudden, swift, and fair, was come into the world, and good was made of evil, as happens still. Then the Orcs dismayed at the uprising of the great light fled unto Angband, and Morgoth was afraid, pondering long in wrathful thought. But Fingolfin marched through the fastness of the realm of Morgoth, that is Dor-Daedeloth, the Land of Dread, and his foes hid beneath the earth; but the Elves smote upon the gates of Angband, and the challenge of their trumpets shook the towers of Thangorodrim.

§92   But Fingolfin doubted the wiles of Morgoth, and he withdrew from the doors of hell, and turned back unto Mithrim, so that Eredwethion, the Shadow Mountains, might shelter his folk while they rested. But there was little love between those that followed Fingolfin and the house of Fëanor; for the agony of those that had endured the crossing of the ice had been great, and their hearts were filled with bitterness. The numbers of the host of Tûn had been diminished upon that grievous road, but yet was the army of Fingolfin greater than that of the sons of Fëanor. These therefore removed and camped upon the southern shore of Mithrim, and the lake lay between the peoples. In this the work of the curse was seen, for the delay wrought by their feud did great harm to the fortunes of all the Noldor. They achieved nothing while Morgoth hesitated and the dread of light was new and strong upon the Orcs.

§93   Then Morgoth arose from thought, and seeing the

division of his foes he laughed. And he let make vast vapours and great smoke in the vaults of Angband, and they were sent forth from the reeking tops of the Iron Mountains, and afar off these could be seen in Hithlum, staining the bright airs of those earliest of mornings. The North shook with the thunder of Morgoth's forges under ground. A wind came, and the vapours were borne far and wide, and they fell and coiled about the fields and hollows, dark and poisonous.

§94     Then Fingon the valiant resolved to heal the feud. Of all the children of Finwë he is justly most renowned: for his valour was as a fire and yet as steadfast as the hills of stone; wise he was and skilled in voice and hand; troth and justice he loved and bore good will to all, both Elves and Men, hating Morgoth only; he sought not his own, neither power nor glory, and death was his reward. Alone now, without counsel of any, he went in search of Maidros, for the thought of his torment troubled his heart. Aided by the very mists that Morgoth put abroad, he ventured unseen into the fastness of his enemies. High upon the shoulders of Thangorodrim he climbed, and looked in despair upon the desolation of the land. But no passage nor crevice could he find through which he might come within Morgoth's stronghold. Therefore in defiance of the Orcs, who cowered still in the dark vaults beneath the earth, he took his harp and played a fair song of Valinor that the Gnomes had made of old, ere strife was born among the sons of Finwë; and his voice, strong and sweet, rang in the mournful hollows that had never heard before aught save cries of fear and woe.

§95     Thus he found what he sought. For suddenly above him far and faint his song was taken up, and a voice answering called to him. Maidros it was that sang amid his torment. But Fingon climbed to the foot of the precipice where his kinsman hung, and then could go no further; and he wept when he saw the cruel device of Morgoth. Maidros, therefore, being in anguish without hope, begged Fingon to shoot him with his bow; and Fingon strung an arrow, and bent his bow. And seeing no better hope he cried to Manwë, saying: 'O King to whom all birds are dear, speed now this feathered shaft, and recall some pity for the banished Gnomes!'

§96     Now his prayer was answered swiftly. For Manwë to whom all birds are dear, and to whom they bring news upon Taniquetil from Middle-earth, had sent forth the race of Eagles. Thorondor was their king. And Manwë commanded them to dwell in the crags of the North, and keep watch upon Morgoth; for Manwë still had pity for the exiled Elves. And the Eagles brought news of much that passed in these days to the sad ears of Manwë; and they hindered the deeds of Morgoth. Now even as Fingon bent his bow, there flew down from the high airs Thorondor, King of Eagles; and he stayed Fingon's hand.

§97   Thorondor was the mightiest of all birds that have ever been. The span of his outstretched wings was thirty fathoms. His beak was of gold. He took up Fingon and bore him to the face of the rock where Maidros hung. But Fingon could not release the hell-wrought bond upon his wrist, nor sever it, nor draw it from the stone. Again, therefore, in his pain Maidros begged that he would slay him; but Fingon cut off his hand above the wrist, and Thorondor bore them both to Mithrim.

§98   There Maidros in time was healed; for the fire of life was hot within him, and his strength was of the ancient world, such as those possessed who were nurtured in Valinor. His body recovered from its torment and became hale, but the shadow of his pain was in his heart; and he lived to wield his sword with left hand more deadly than his right had been. By this deed Fingon won great renown, and all the Noldor praised him; and the feud was healed between Fingolfin and the sons of Fëanor. But Maidros begged forgiveness for the desertion in Eruman, and gave back the goods of Fingolfin that had been borne away in the ships; and he waived his claim to kingship over all the Gnomes. To this his brethren did not all in their hearts agree. Therefore the house of Fëanor were called the Dispossessed, because of the doom of the Gods which gave the kingdom of Tûn to Fingolfin, and because of the loss of the Silmarils. But there was now a peace and a truce to jealousy; yet still there held the binding oath.

§99   Now the Gnomes being reunited marched forth from the land of Hithlum and drove the servants of Morgoth before them, and they beleaguered Angband from west and south and east. And there followed long years of peace and happiness; for this was the age which songs name the Siege of Angband, and it lasted more than four hundred years of the Sun, while the swords of the Gnomes fenced the earth from the ruin of Morgoth, and his power was shut behind his gates. In those days there was joy beneath the new Sun and Moon, and there was birth and blossoming of many things; and the lands of the West of Middle-earth where now the Noldor dwelt became exceeding fair. And that region was named of old in the language of Doriath Beleriand, but after the coming of the Noldor it was called also in the tongue of Valinor Ingolondë, the fair and sorrowful, the Kingdom of the Gnomes. And behind the guard of their armies in the North the Gnomes began now to wander far and wide over the land, and they built there many fair habitations, and established realms; for save in Doriath and in Ossiriand (of which more is after said) there were few folk there before them. These were Dark-elves of Telerian race, and the Noldor met them in gladness, and there was joyful meeting as between kinsfolk long sundered. And Fingolfin made a great feast, and it was held in the South far from the threat of Morgoth, in the Land of Willows beside the waters of Sirion. The joy of that feast was long remembered in later days of sorrow; and it was called Mereth Aderthad, the Feast of Reuniting, and it was held in spring. Thither came all of the three houses of the Gnomes that could be spared from the northern guard; and great number of the Dark-elves, both the wanderers of the woods, and the folk of the havens from the land of the Falas; and many also came of the Green-elves from Ossiriand, the Land of Seven Rivers, afar off under the walls of the Blue Mountains. And from Doriath there came ambassadors, though Thingol came not himself, and he would not open his kingdom, nor remove its girdle of enchantment; for wise with the wisdom of Melian he trusted not that the restraint of Morgoth would last for ever. But the hearts of the Gnomes were high and full of hope, and it seemed to many of them that the words of Fëanor had been justified, bidding them seek freedom and fair kingdoms in Middle-earth.

§100     But on a time Turgon left Nivrost where he dwelt and went to visit Inglor his friend, and they journeyed southward along Sirion, being weary for a while of the northern mountains; and as they journeyed night came upon them beyond the Meres of Twilight beside the waters of Sirion, and they slept upon his banks beneath the summer stars. But Ulmo coming up the river laid a profound sleep upon them and heavy dreams; and the trouble of the dreams remained after they awoke, but neither said aught to the other, for their memory was not clear, and each deemed that Ulmo had sent a message to him alone. But unquiet was upon them ever after and doubt of what should befall, and they wandered often alone in unexplored country, seeking far and wide for places of hidden strength; for it seemed to each that he was bidden to prepare for a day of evil, and to establish a retreat, lest Morgoth should burst from Angband and overthrow the armies of the North.

§101    Thus it came to pass that Inglor found the deep gorge of Narog and the caves in its western side; and he built there a stronghold and armouries after the fashion of the deep mansions of Menegroth. And he called this place Nargothrond, and made there his home with many of his folk; and the Gnomes of the North, at first in merriment, called him on this account Felagund, or Lord of Caverns, and that name he bore thereafter until his end. But Turgon went alone into hidden places, and by the guidance of Ulmo found the secret vale of Gondolin; and of this he said nought as yet, but returned to Nivrost and his folk.

§102    And even while Turgon and Felagund were wandering abroad, Morgoth seeing that many Gnomes were dispersed over the land made trial of their strength and watchfulness. He shook the North with sudden earthquake, and fire came from the Iron Mountains; and the Orcs poured forth across the plain of Bladorion, and invaded Beleriand through the pass of Sirion in the West, and burst through the land of Maglor in the East; for there is a gap in that region between the hills of Maidros and the outliers of the Blue Mountains. But Fingolfin and Maidros gathered great force, and while others sought out and destroyed all the Orcs that strayed in Beleriand and did great evil, they came upon the main host from the other side, even as it was assaulting Dorthonion, and they defeated the servants of Morgoth, and pursued the remnant across Bladorion, and destroyed them utterly within sight of Angband's gates. This was the second great battle of these wars and was named Dagor Aglareb, the Glorious Battle; and for a long while after none of the servants of Morgoth would venture from his gates; for they feared the kings of the Gnomes. And many reckoned from that day the peace of the Siege of Angband. For the chieftains took warning from that assault and drew their leaguer closer, and set such watch upon Angband that Fingolfin boasted Morgoth could never again escape nor come upon them unawares.

§103    Yet the Gnomes could not capture Angband, nor could they regain the Silmarils; and the stronghold of Morgoth was never wholly encircled. For the Iron Mountains, from the southernmost point of whose great curving wall the towers of Thangorodrim were thrust forward, defended it upon either side, and were impassable to the Gnomes, because of their snow and ice. Thus in his rear and to the North Morgoth had no foes, and by that way his spies at times went out and came by devious routes into Beleriand. And the Orcs multiplied again in the bowels of the earth, and Morgoth began after a time to forge in secret new weapons for the destruction of his enemies. But only twice in all the years of the Siege did he give sign of his purpose. When nearly a hundred years had run since the Second Battle, he sent forth an army to essay the northern ways; and they passed into the white North. Many there perished, but the others turning west round the outer end of the Iron Mountains reached the shores of the sea, and came south along the coast by the route which Fingolfin followed from the Grinding Ice. Thus they endeavoured to invade Hithlum from the rear. But Fingon fell upon them by the firth of Drengist, and drove them into the sea, and none returned to Morgoth. This was not reckoned among the great battles, for the Orcs were not in great number, and only part of the folk of Hithlum fought there.

§104   Again after a hundred years Glómund, the first of Dragons, issued at night from the gates of Angband, by the command of Morgoth; for he was unwilling, being yet young and but half-grown. But the Elves fled before him in dismay, and abandoned the fields of Bladorion, and Glómund defiled them. But Fingon, prince of Gnomes, rode up against him with horsed archers; and Glómund could not withstand their darts, being not yet come to his full armoury, and he fled back to hell. And Fingon won great praise, and the Gnomes rejoiced; for few foresaw the full meaning and threat of this new thing. But they had not seen the last of Glómund.

### Commentary on Chapter 8

§88   In the opening passage my father was closely following AV annal 2995 (virtually the same in the two versions). The account of the Battle-under-Stars, placing it in Mithrim, followed by pursuit of the Orcs into the plain of Bladorion, likewise derives from AV; in Q the battle was fought on the (still unnamed) plain itself. Comparison of the texts will show that in the story of the pursuit of the Orcs and the mortal wounding of Fëanor he had both Q and AV in front of him when he wrote it. I shall not point further to the way in which he used Q and AV, and then AB, in this chapter (while at the same time introducing new narrative elements), for these interrelations are readily traced.

The marginal note *Dagor-nui-Ngiliath* is contemporary with the writing of the manuscript. The earlier form *Dagor-os-Giliath* was corrected to *Dagor-nuin-Giliath* in AV 2 (note 12) and AB 2 (note 3).

Fëanor's death and fate as described here may be compared with what is said in §85; the meaning is no doubt that Fëanor was never reborn, nor ever left Mandos in the manner described in the earlier passage. – His cursing of the name of Morgoth as he died was transferred, or extended, from Túrin (IV. 172), who did the same after the death of Beleg in the *Lay of the Children of Húrin* ; but in the Lay Túrin cursed Morgoth thrice, as is not said of Fëanor in Q, and 'thrice' now reappears.

§89   The words 'and they were Balrogs', deriving from Q, show that at this time Balrogs were still conceived to exist in large numbers (see IV. 173); so also 'a host of Balrogs' in §143, and 'Balrogs one thousand' in the Battle of Unnumbered Tears (p. 310 §15).

§91   *Dor-Daedeloth* was altered from *Dor-Daideloth* ; this looks to be an early change (the same in AV 2, note 14).

§92   It is not said in the earlier sources that Fingolfin's host remained the greater.

§93   'The North shook with the thunder of Morgoth's forges under ground' reappears from S (IV. 22): 'The North shakes with the thunder under the earth'; it is not found in Q, nor in AB.

§§96–7   *Thorondor* was an early change from *Thorndor*; but *Thorondor* appears later in QS (§147) as the manuscript was originally written.

§98   Maidros' asking of forgiveness for the desertion in Eruman, his returning of the goods of Fingolfin, the waiving of his claim to the kingship, and the secret disavowal of this among his brothers, are all new elements in the narrative (see IV. 173).

§99   The entire passage that in Q (§9) follows 'beleaguered Angband from west and south and east', concerning the dispositions of the Noldorin lords in Middle-earth and their relations with the Dwarves, is omitted here in QS, where the text now jumps on to IV. 104, 'This was the time that songs call the Siege of Angband'; similarly no use is made here of the long passage in AB on this subject (annal 52). The reason for this is the introduction of the new chapter (9) in QS, *Of Beleriand and its Realms*.

In 'it lasted more than four hundred years of the Sun' the word 'four' was an early emendation over an erased word, obviously 'two'; see the note on chronology at the end of this commentary.

With the statement that Beleriand was a Doriathrin name cf. the passage added at the end of the *Lhammas* (§11): 'from Beleriandic is the name *Balar*, and *Beleriand*'. In an addition to Q (IV. 107 note 2) *Beleriand* was said to be Gnomish; and in the same place occurs *Ingolondë the fair and sorrowful*: see IV. 174 and the *Etymologies*, stem ÑGOLOD.

With 'Dark-elves of Telerian race' cf. the earlier passage in QS (§30): 'The Lembi were for the most part of the race of the Teleri, and the chief of these were the Elves of Beleriand.'

§100   This is the first occurrence (other than in corrections to AB 2) of the name *Nivrost* (later *Nevrast*). It was in fact written *Nivros*, here and subsequently, but the final *t* was added carefully in each case, clearly soon after the writing of the manuscript (so also in the annal for

the year 64 added in to AB 2, note 8; *Nivrost* in the *Etymologies*, stems
NIB and ROS²).

The story of the discovery of Nargothrond by Inglor and of
Gondolin by Turgon derives from AB (annal 50), but it is not said
there that they journeyed together and slept by Sirion, that the
foreboding dreams were laid on them by Ulmo, or that neither spoke
to the other of his dream.

§101   Though *Felagund* has several times been rendered 'Lord of
Caves' or 'Lord of Caverns', it has not been said that it was at first a
laughing nickname given to him by the Noldor.

On the date of Turgon's actual departure to Gondolin see the note
on chronology at the end of this commentary.

§102   QS adds to the account of the Dagor Aglareb in AB 2, annal 51:
the Orc-hosts came through the Pass of Sirion and through Maglor's
Gap (see the commentary on AB 2 annal 52), and Fingolfin and
Maidros defeated the main host as it was assaulting Dorthonion. Here
and subsequently the form first written was *Dorthanion*, but the
change to *Dorthonion* was made early. For the many forms preceding
*Dorthonion* see note 9 to AB 2.

§103   On the relation of Angband to Thangorodrim and the Iron
Mountains see the commentary on the *Ambarkanta*, IV. 260, where I
noted that 'Thangorodrim is shown on map V as a point, set slightly
out from the Iron Mountains.' See also the beginning of Chapter 9 in
QS (§105).

In 'When nearly a hundred years had run since the Second Battle', 'a
hundred' was an early emendation from 'fifty'; see the note on chronology below.

On the route of the Orc-army that left Angband by the unguarded
northern exit (described also in AB 2, annal 105) see the note on the
northern geography, pp. 270–2.

§104   Here again (as in §103) 'a hundred' was an early change from
'fifty'; see the note on chronology below.

It is not said in AB 2 (annal 155) either that Glómund's first issuing
from Angband was by Morgoth's command, or that he was unwilling
to venture forth.

*Note on the chronology*

This is a convenient place to discuss the chronology of the years of the
Siege of Angband in chapters 8 to 10.

In the chronology of AB 2 as originally written the Siege of Angband
lasted a little more than two hundred years; and important dates for the
present purpose are:

   50   Turgon discovered Gondolin
   51   Dagor Aglareb and the beginning of the Siege of Angband
   52   Turgon departed to Gondolin
  105   Orc-raid down the west coast

155    First emergence of Glómund
255    Battle of Sudden Fire and the end of the Siege

By corrections to the manuscript of AB 2 (given in parentheses in that text) these dates were changed as follows:

(50    Turgon discovered Gondolin; unchanged)
  60    Dagor Aglareb and the beginning of the Siege of Angband
  64    Turgon departed to Gondolin (additional annal, given in note 8 to AB 2)
155    Orc-raid down the west coast
260    First emergence of Glómund
455    Battle of Sudden Fire and the end of the Siege

Thus the Siege lasted nearly four hundred years; on this final extension of the chronology of the first centuries of the Sun, reaching that in the published *Silmarillion*, see IV. 319–20.

The dates in QS before emendation were:

–    The Siege of Angband 'lasted more than two hundred years' (§99);
–    The western Orc-raid took place 'nearly fifty years' after the Dagor Aglareb (§103) – which does not perfectly agree with the earlier chronology of the *Annals*, where 54 years elapsed between the two events);
–    Glómund's first emergence from Angband was 'again after fifty years' (§104).

These dates were all emended at an early stage, to give 'more than four hundred years' for the Siege, 'nearly a hundred years' from the Dagor Aglareb to the Orc-raid, and a further hundred years to Glómund's coming forth. This agrees, if not quite precisely, with the revised chronology in AB 2 (i.e. 60 to 455; 60 to 155; and 155 to 260).

In QS chapter 10 the new chronology was already in being as the manuscript was written; thus in §125 the Orc-raid that ended at Drengist is stated to have occurred in 155, and this was 105 years before the appearance of Glómund; and after that, i.e. from the year 260, there were 'well nigh two hundred years' of peace, i.e. till the Battle of Sudden Fire in 455. Here also it is said that the encounter of the Noldor with the Dwarves in the Blue Mountains took place about the time of the Orc-raid, agreeing with the altered dating in AB 2, where the meeting with the Dwarves, first given in the year 104, was changed to 154.

In QS therefore, though the date of Turgon's departure to Gondolin is not precisely indicated, he left Nivrost in 64, 'a few years' (§116) after the Second Battle, as in AB 2 revised.

## 9    OF BELERIAND AND ITS REALMS

§105    This is the fashion of the lands into which the Gnomes came, in the North of the western regions of Middle-earth, in the ancient days. In the North of the world Melko reared Ered-engrin

the Iron Mountains; and they stood upon the regions of everlasting cold, in a great curve from East to West, but falling short of
the sea upon either side. These Melko built in the elder days as a
fence to his citadel, Utumno, and this lay at the western end of his
northern realm. In the war of the Gods the mountains of Melko
were broken and distorted in the West, and of their fragments
were made Eredwethion and Eredlómin; but the Iron Mountains
bent back northward and there was a hundred leagues between
them and the frozen straits at Helkaraksë. Behind their walls
Melko coming back into Middle-earth made the endless dungeons
of Angband, the hells of iron, where of old Utumno had been. But
he made a great tunnel under them, which issued south of the
mountains; and there he made a mighty gate. But above this gate,
and behind it even to the mountains, he piled the thunderous
towers of Thangorodrim; and these were made of the ash and slag
of his subterranean furnaces, and the vast refuse of his tun-
nellings. They were black and desolate and exceedingly lofty; and
smoke issued from their tops, dark and foul upon the northern
sky. Before the gates of Angband filth and desolation spread
southward for many miles. There lay the wide plain of Bladorion.
But after the coming of the Sun rich grass grew there, and while
Angband was besieged and its gates shut, there were green things
even among the pits and broken rocks before the doors of hell.

§106   To the West of Thangorodrim lay Hithlum, the land
of mist, for so it was named by the Gnomes because of the clouds
that Morgoth sent thither during their first encampment; and it
became a fair land while the Siege lasted, although its air was cool
and winter there was cold. It was bounded in the West by
Eredlómin, the Echoing Mountains that march near the sea; and
in the East and South by the great curve of Eredwethion, the
Shadowy Mountains that looked across Bladorion, and across
the vale of Sirion. In the East that corner which lay between
Eredwethion and the Mountains of Mithrim was called the land of
Mithrim, and most of Fingolfin's folk dwelt there about the shores
of the great lake. West of Mithrim lay Dor-lómen, and was
assigned to Fingon son of Fingolfin. West again lay Nivrost*
beyond the Echoing Mountains, which below the Firth of
Drengist marched inland. Here at first was the realm of Turgon,
bounded by the sea, and Eredlómin, and the hills which continue

*Marginal note to the text: Which is West Vale in the tongue of
Doriath.

the walls of Eredwethion westward to the sea, from Ivrin to Mount Taras which standeth upon a promontory. And Nivrost was a pleasant land watered by the wet winds from the sea, and sheltered from the North, whereas the rest of Hithlum was open to the cold winds. To the East of Hithlum lay Bladorion, as has been said; and below that the great highland that the Gnomes first named Dorthonion.* This stretched for a hundred leagues from West to East and bore great pine forests, especially upon its northern and western sides. For it arose by gentle slopes from Bladorion to a bleak and lofty land, where lay many tarns at the feet of bare tors whose heads were higher than the peaks of Eredwethion. But southward where it looked towards Doriath it fell suddenly in dreadful precipices. Between Dorthonion and the Shadowy Mountains there was a narrow vale with sheer walls clad with pines; but the vale itself was green, for the river Sirion flowed through it, hastening towards Beleriand.

§107   Now the great and fair country of Beleriand lay on either side of this mighty river Sirion, renowned in song, which rose at Eithel Sirion in the east of Eredwethion, and skirted the edge of Bladorion, ere he plunged through the pass, becoming ever fuller with the streams of the mountains. Thence he flowed down south, one hundred and twenty-one leagues, gathering the waters of many tributaries, until with a mighty flood he reached his many mouths and sandy delta in the Bay of Balar. And the chief of the tributaries of Sirion were in the West: Taiglin, and Narog the mightiest; and in the East: Mindeb, and Esgalduin the enchanted river that flowed through the midst of Doriath; and Aros, with its tributary Celon, that flowed into Sirion at the Meres of Twilight upon the confines of Doriath.

§108   Thus Beleriand was bounded upon the North by Nivrost and Hithlum and Dorthonion; and beyond Dorthonion by the hills of Maidros, son of Fëanor; and upon the West it was bounded by the Great Sea; and upon the East by the towers of Eredlindon, the Blue Mountains, one of the chief ranges of the ancient world; and by Ossiriand between these mountains and the river Gelion. And in the South it was held by some to be bounded by Gelion, that turning westward sought the sea far beyond the mouths of Sirion. Beyond the river Gelion the land narrowed suddenly, for the Great Sea ran into a mighty gulf reaching almost to the feet of Eredlindon, and there was a strait of mountainous

*Marginal note to the text: Ilkorin name.

land between the gulf and the inland sea of Helkar, by which one might come into the vast regions of the South of Middle-earth. But the land between the mouths of Sirion and Gelion was little visited by the Gnomes, a tangled forest in which no folk went save here and there a few Dark-elves wandering; and beyond Gelion the Gnomes seldom came, nor ever east of Eredlindon while that land lasted.

§109    Following Sirion from North to South there lay upon the right hand West Beleriand, at its widest seventy leagues from river to sea: first the Forest of Brethil between Sirion and Taiglin, and then the realm of Nargothrond, between Sirion and Narog. And the river Narog arose in the falls of Ivrin in the southern face of Dorlómen, and flowed some eighty leagues ere he joined Sirion in the Nan-tathren, the land of willows, south of Nargothrond. But the realm of Nargothrond extended also west of Narog, even to the sea, save only in the country of the Falas (or Coast), south of Nivrost. There dwelt the Dark-elves of the havens, Brithombar and Eglorest, and they were of ancient Telerian race; but they took Felagund, lord of Nargothrond, to be their king. And south of Nan-tathren was a region of fair meads filled with many flowers, where few folk dwelt; and beyond lay the marshes and isles of reeds about the mouths of Sirion, and the sands of his delta empty of all living things save birds of the sea.

§110    But upon the left hand of Sirion lay East Beleriand, at its widest a hundred leagues from Sirion to Gelion and the borders of Ossiriand: first the empty lands under the faces of the southern precipices of Dorthonion, Dimbar between Sirion and Mindeb, and Nan-dungorthin between Mindeb and the upper waters of Esgalduin; and these regions were filled with fear by the enchantments of Melian, as a defence of Doriath against the North, and after the fall of the Gnomes they became places of terror and evil. Beyond them to the East lay the north-marches of Beleriand, where the sons of Fëanor dwelt. Next southward lay the kingdom of Doriath; first its northern and lesser part, the Forest of Neldoreth, bounded east and south by the dark river Esgalduin, which bent westward in the midst of Doriath; and then the denser and greater woods of Region, between Esgalduin and Aros. And Menegroth the halls of Thingol were built upon the south bank of Esgalduin, where he turned westward; and all Doriath lay west of Sirion, save for a narrow region of woodland between the meeting of Taiglin and Sirion and the Meres of Twilight. And this wood which the folk of Doriath called Nivrim, or the West-march, was very fair, and oak-trees of great beauty grew there; and it was included in the girdle of Melian, so that some portion of Sirion which she loved in reverence of Ulmo should be wholly under the power of Thingol.

§111  Beyond Doriath to the East lay wide woods between Celon and Gelion; here few folk dwelt, but Damrod and Díriel took it as their realm and hunting-ground; and beyond, between Gelion and the Blue Mountains, was the wide land of Thargelion,* where Cranthir dwelt of old. But in the southern corner of Doriath, where Aros flowed into Sirion, lay a region of great pools and marshes on either side of the river, which halted there in his course and strayed in many channels. This region the Elves of Doriath named Umboth Muilin,† the Twilight Meres, for there were many mists, and the enchantment of Doriath lay over them.

§112  For all the northern half of Beleriand sloped southward to this point and then for a while was plain, and the flood of Sirion was stayed. But south of Umboth Muilin the land again fell suddenly and steeply, though in no wise with so great a fall as in the North. Yet all the lower plain of Sirion was divided from the upper plain by this sudden fall, which looking North appeared as an endless chain of hills running from Eglorest beyond Narog in the West to Amon Ereb in the East, within far sight of Gelion. Narog came south through a deep gorge, and flowed over rapids but had no fall, and on its west bank rose into great wooded highlands, Taur-na-Faroth, which stretched far southward. On the west side of this gorge under Taur-na-Faroth, where the short and foaming stream Ingwil tumbles headlong from the highlands into Narog, Inglor established Nargothrond.

§113  But some seventy miles east of the gorge of Nargothrond Sirion fell from the North in a mighty fall below the meres, and then he plunged suddenly underground into great tunnels that the weight of his falling waters delved; and he issued again three leagues southward with great noise and smoke through rocky arches at the foot of the hills which were called the Gates of Sirion. But this dividing fall was named Andram, or the Long Wall, from Nargothrond to Ramdal, or Wall's End, in East Beleriand. And in the East the wall became ever less sheer, for the vale of Gelion sloped ever southward steadily, and Gelion had neither fall nor

---

*Marginal note to the text:* or Radhrost.
†*Footnote to the text:* But the Gnomish names were Hithliniath the pools of mist or Aelin-uial Lakes of Twilight.

rapids throughout his course, but was ever swifter than was Sirion. But between Ramdal and Gelion there stood a single hill, of great extent and gentle slopes, but seeming loftier than it was, for it stood alone; and this hill was named Amon Ereb, and Maidros dwelt there after the great defeat. But until that time all the wide forests of East Beleriand south of Andram and between Sirion and Gelion were little inhabited, and the Gnomes came there seldom.

§114    And east of this wild land lay the country of Ossiriand, between Gelion and Eredlindon. Gelion was a great river, and it arose in two sources, and had at first two branches: Little Gelion that came from the hill of Himring, and Greater Gelion that came from Mount Rerir, an outlier of Eredlindon; and between these branches was the land of Maglor, son of Fëanor. Then joining his two arms Gelion flowed south, a swift river but of small volume, until he found his tributaries some forty leagues south of the meeting of his arms. Ere he found the sea Gelion was twice as long as Sirion, but ever less wide and full; for more rain fell in Hithlum and Dorthonion, whence Sirion drew his waters, than in the East. From Eredlindon flowed the tributaries of Gelion. These were six: Ascar (that was after renamed Rathlóriel), Thalos, Legolin, Brilthor, Duilwen, and Adurant; they were swift and turbulent, falling steeply from the mountains, but going southward each was longer than the one before, since Gelion bent ever away from Eredlindon. Between Ascar in the North and Adurant in the South, and between Gelion and the mountains, lay Ossiriand, the Land of Seven Rivers, filled with green woods wide and fair.

§115    There dwelt the Danian Elves, who in the beginning were of Gnomish race, but forsook the march from Kuiviénen, and came never to Valinor, and only after long wanderings came over the mountains in the dark ages; and some of their kindred dwelt still east of Eredlindon. Of old the lord of Ossiriand was Denethor, friend of Thingol; but he was slain in battle when he marched to the aid of Thingol against Melko, in the days when the Orcs were first made and broke the starlit peace of Beleriand. Thereafter Doriath was fenced with enchantment, and many of the folk of Denethor removed to Doriath and mingled with the Elves of Thingol; but those that remained in Ossiriand had no king, and lived in the protection of their rivers. For after Sirion Ulmo loved Gelion above all the waters of the western world. But the woodcraft of the Elves of Ossiriand was such that a stranger might pass through their land from end to end and see none of them. They were clad mostly in green in spring and in summer, and hence were called the Green-elves; and they delighted in song, and the sound of their singing could be heard even across the waters of Gelion, as if all their land was filled with choirs of birds whose fair voices had taken thought and meaning.

§116    In this way the chieftains of the Gnomes held their lands and the leaguer upon Morgoth after his defeat in the Second Battle. Fingolfin and Fingon his son held Hithlum, and their chief fortress was at Eithel Sirion in the east of Eredwethion, whence they kept watch upon Bladorion; and their cavalry rode upon that plain even to the shadow of Thangorodrim, and their horses multiplied for the grass was good. Of those horses many of the sires came from Valinor. But Turgon the wise, second son of Fingolfin, held Nivrost until the Second Battle, and returned thither afterward, and his folk were numerous. But the unquiet of Ulmo increased upon him, and after a few years he arose and took with him a great host of Gnomes, even to a third of the people of Fingolfin, and their goods and wives and children, and departed eastward. His going was by night and his march swift and silent, and he vanished out of knowledge of his kindred. But he came to Gondolin, and built there a city like unto Tûn of Valinor, and fortified the surrounding hills; and Gondolin lay hidden for many years.

§117    The sons of Finrod held the northern march from the pass of Sirion between Hithlum and Dorthonion unto the eastern end of Dorthonion, where is the deep gorge of Aglon. And Inglor held the pass of Sirion, and built a great watchtower, Minnastirith, upon an isle in the midst of the river; but after the founding of Nargothrond this fortress he committed mostly to the keeping of his brother Orodreth. But Angrod and Egnor watched Bladorion from the northern slopes of Dorthonion; and their folk was not great for the land was barren, and the great highlands behind were deemed to be a bulwark that Morgoth would not lightly seek to cross.

§118    But east of Dorthonion the marches of Beleriand were more open to attack, and only hills of no great height guarded the vale of Gelion from the North. Therefore the sons of Fëanor with many folk, well nigh half of the people of the Gnomes, dwelt in that region, upon the Marches of Maidros, and in the lands behind; and the riders of the folk of Fëanor rode often upon the vast northern plain, Lothland the wide and empty, east of Bladorion, lest Morgoth attempted any sortie towards East

Beleriand. And the chief citadel of Maidros was upon the hill of Himring, the Ever-cold; and this was wide-shouldered, bare of trees, and flat upon the summit, and surrounded by many lesser hills. Its name it bore because there was a pass, exceeding steep upon the west, between it and Dorthonion, and this was the pass of Aglon, and was a gate unto Doriath, and a bitter wind blew ever through it from the North. But Celegorn and Curufin fortified Aglon, and manned it with great strength, and they held all the land southward between the river Aros that arose in Dorthonion and his tributary Celon that came from Himring. And between Celon and Little Gelion was the ward of Damrod and Díriel. And between the arms of Gelion was the ward of Maglor, and here in one place the hills failed altogether; and here it was that the Orcs came into East Beleriand before the Second Battle. Therefore the Gnomes held much cavalry in the plains at that place; and the people of Cranthir fortified the mountains to the east of Maglor's Gap. For Mount Rerir, and about it many lesser heights, stood out from the main range of Eredlindon westward; and in the angle between Rerir and Eredlindon there was a lake, shadowed by mountains on all sides save the south. This was Lake Helevorn, deep and dark, and beside it Cranthir had his abode; but all the great land between Gelion and Eredlindon, and between Rerir and the river Ascar, was called by the Gnomes Thargelion (that is the land beyond Gelion), or Dor Granthir the land of Cranthir; and it was here that the Gnomes first met the Dwarves.*

§119   Thus the sons of Fëanor under the leadership of Maidros were lords of East Beleriand, but their folk was in that time mostly in the north of the land; and southward they rode only to hunt, and to seek solitude for a while. And thither for like purpose the other Elflords would sometimes come, for the land was wild but very fair; and of these Inglor came most often, for he had great love of wandering, and he came even into Ossiriand and won friendship of the Green-elves. But Inglor was King of Nargothrond and overlord of the Dark-elves of the western havens; and with his aid Brithombar and Eglorest were rebuilt and became fair towns, recalling somewhat the havens of the Elves upon the shores of Valinor.

§120   And Inglor let build the tower of Tindobel upon a cape west of Eglorest to watch the Western Sea; and some of the folk of

---

*Marginal note to the text:* But Dor Granthir was before called by the Dark-elves Radhrost, the East Vale.

Nargothrond with the aid of the Teleri of the havens built new ships, and they went forth and explored the great isle of Balar, thinking here to prepare an ultimate refuge, if evil came. But it was not their fate that they should ever dwell there. And Inglor's realm ran north to Tolsirion the isle in the river aforesaid, and his brothers held Dorthonion and were his vassals. Thus his realm was far the greatest, though he was the youngest of the great lords of the Gnomes, Fingolfin, Fingon, and Maidros, and Inglor Felagund. But Fingolfin was held overlord of all the Gnomes, and Fingon after him, though their own realm was but the northern lands of Nivrost and Hithlum. Yet were their folk the most hardy and valiant, and the most feared by the Orcs and most hated by Morgoth.

§121     And in Doriath abode Thingol, the hidden king, and into his realm none passed save by his will, and when summoned thither; and mighty though the Kings of the Noldor were in those days, and filled with the fire and glory of Valinor, the name of Thingol was held in awe among them.

*Commentary on Chapter 9*

§105     This is the first occurrence of the final form *Ered-engrin* (for earlier *Eiglir Engrin*, IV. 220). The description of the Iron Mountains here agrees with the *Ambarkanta* map IV (IV. 249), where they are shown as a great wall across the North, slightly bowed southwards, and where, as stated in QS, they do not extend to the shores of either the Western or the Eastern Seas. I have discussed in IV. 258–60 the relation of the *Ambarkanta* map V to the description here of the changes in the northern mountains and of Angband and Thangorodrim.

§106     Hithlum is called 'Land(s) of Mist' in the *Lay of the Children of Húrin*, in Q, and in AB 1, 'realm of mist' in QS §88, but this explanation of the name has not been given before. It is interesting to look back to the original idea (I. 112): *'Dor Lómin* or the "Land of Shadow" was that region named of the Eldar *Hisilómë* (and this means "Shadowy Twilights") . . . and it is so called by reason of the scanty sun which peeps little over the Iron Mountains [i.e. the Mountains of Shadow] to the east and south of it.'

*Nivrost*, always early changed from *Nivros*, is now placed geographically in the previously unnamed region which appears already on the first Map (IV. 228), and it is here explicitly reckoned a part of Hithlum (but in §120 there is a reference to 'the northern lands of Nivrost and Hithlum'). The marginal note translating the name as 'West Vale' ('West-dales' in the *Etymologies*, stem NIB) is contemporary with the writing of the manuscript (in *The Silmarillion* the later form *Nevrast* is translated 'Hither Shore', p. 119). On Hithlum's exposure to the North see the note on the geography of the far North, pp. 270–2.

This is the first occurrence of *Taras*, but the great mountain was clearly marked out on the second Map as originally drawn, and before the name was inserted (p. 408, square D2).

The marginal note defining *Dorthonion* as an Ilkorin name (in agreement with the *Etymologies*, stem THŌN) looks as if it belongs with the original writing of the manuscript, although it contradicts the statement in the text: 'the great highland that the Gnomes first named Dorthonion.'

§108   At the first occurrence of *Eredlindon* in this paragraph there is a footnote to the text added after the writing of the manuscript:

Which signifieth the Mountains of Ossiriand; for the Gnomes called that land Lindon, the region of music, and they first saw these mountains from Ossiriand. But their right name was Eredluin the Blue Mountains, or Luindirien the Blue Towers.

I have not included this in the text printed, feeling uncertain of its date. In the passages of revision to the second version of *The Fall of Númenor* the name *Lindon* appears. I have shown that these revisions come from a time during the writing of *The Lord of the Rings* (see pp. 31–4) – although that does not necessarily imply that *Lindon* had not arisen earlier. Originally *Eredlindon* certainly meant 'Blue Mountains': see IV. 328, 341; and in the *List of Names* (p. 405) a word *lind* 'blue' is adduced (cf. the *Etymologies*, stem GLINDI).

With the account of the extent of Beleriand cf. the legend on the first Map (IV. 226–7). – The present passage is the first statement about the lower course of Gelion; on the *Ambarkanta* map V (IV. 251) the river (unnamed) is shown turning west and flowing into the sea in another great bay south of Balar. Also shown on map V is the 'Great Gulf', and 'the strait of mountainous land' (there called the 'Straits of the World') 'between the gulf and the inland sea of Helkar' (see IV. 258–9).

§109   *Nan-tathren* was changed from *Nan-tathrin*, as in AB 2 (note 5). – In AB 2 (annal 52) Fingolfin was 'Lord of the Falas or Western Shore, and overlord of the Dark-elves as far south as Eglorest and west of the river Eglor', while Felagund possessed the lands east of Eglor (between Eglor and Sirion). Changes made to that manuscript (notes 12 and 13) altered the text to say that it was Felagund who was 'held to be overlord of the Falas, and of the Dark-elves of the havens of Brithombar and Eglorest'; and here in QS the Elves of the Havens 'took Felagund to be their king'.

§110   Here is the first occurrence of the name *Dimbar*. Cf. AB 2, annal 52: 'between Sirion and the river Mindeb no one dwelt.' On *Nan-dungorthin* see IV. 222. Here also is the first occurrence of *Nivrim*, 'the West-march'. On the second Map, as on the first, the region is marked as 'Doriath beyond Sirion'; see IV. 224, 330.

§111    *Thargelion*, here first appearing, was an early change from *Tar-gelion* (but in §122 *Thargelion* is original in the manuscript). The marginal note 'or Radhrost' was probably a subsequent addition, but certainly belongs to the early period; see under §118 below. The second footnote is certainly original. While *Umboth Muilin* goes back to the *Lost Tales* (see II. 225, 349), neither *Hithliniath* nor *Aelin-uial* have occurred before.

§112    Here first appears the name *Taur-na-Faroth* of the highlands previously called in the *Lays of Beleriand* 'the Hills of the Hunters', 'the Hunters' Wold', and on the first Map *Duil Rewinion* (IV. 225), where these hills are shown extending far to the south of Nargothrond.

§113    This account of the Slope of Beleriand and the great dividing fall is entirely new, as are the names *Andram* 'the Long Wall' and *Ramdal* 'Wall's End' (both written at both occurrences over other names that were wholly obliterated). Ancient features of the rivers of Beleriand – the torrential Narog, the Pools of Twilight, the plunging of Sirion underground – are now related in a comprehensive geographical conception. The 'Gates of Sirion' are new both as name and conception (though marked and named on the second Map as originally drawn, p. 410): nothing has been said hitherto of the issuing of the river from its subterranean passage.

§114    The two tributary branches of Gelion are shown on the second Map but are here first named; and now occurs for the first time *Mount Rerir*, where Greater Gelion rose. The form *Himring* has already appeared in *Lhammas B*, p. 189 (but it was still *Himling* on the second Map as originally drawn).

At the name *Adurant* there is a footnote to the text added after the writing of the manuscript:

And at a point nearly midway in its course the stream of Adurant divided and joined again, enclosing a fair island; and this was called Tolgalen, the Green Isle. There Beren and Lúthien dwelt after their return.

Like the footnote to §108, I have not included this in the text because of uncertainty as to when the addition was made. The second Map does not show the island formed by the divided course of Adurant; on the other hand an addition to the stem AT(AT) in the *Etymologies* explains the actual meaning of *Adurant* precisely from the divided course (Ilkorin *adu*, *ado* 'double'). This is the first occurrence of the name *Tolgalen*, and of this precise placing of the dwelling of Beren and Lúthien after their return. On the first Map 'the Land of the Dead that Live' was moved several times, the final placing being in Ossiriand (IV. 224, 230), as in Q (IV. 133).

§115    With 'when the Orcs were first made' cf. QS §62: 'he brought into being the race of the Orcs' (i.e. when Morgoth came back to Middle-earth).

This account of the Green-elves ('Danian Elves') will be found to be in good agreement with the *Lhammas* §7. It is not told there that they were called Green-elves because they were clad in green in spring and summer (but 'the house of Denethor loved green above all colours'); and there is now the first mention of their singing, which led to their land being named *Lindon* (see the commentary on §108, but also the *Etymologies*, stem LIN²).

§116    From the beginning of this paragraph the text is derived, with much alteration and expansion, from AB 2, annal 52.

On the lapse of time between Turgon's discovery of the hidden valley of Gondolin and his final departure from Nivrost see pp. 257–8. In AB 2 he 'departed south', i.e. from Hithlum, later changed (note 8) to agree with QS, where he 'departed eastward', i.e. from Nivrost. This is the first mention of the likeness of Gondolin to the city of the Elves in Valinor, although, as I have suggested (II. 208), it was perhaps an old underlying idea.

§117    The name *Minnastirith* is written over a total erasure, but the obliterated name was clearly *Inglormindon*, which appears in an addition to AB 2 (note 14), changed there also to *Minnastirith* (and then to *Minastirith*).

Another element in the changed history of Orodreth now enters, an aspect of his association with Inglor Felagund rather than with Angrod and Egnor (see the commentary on §73): he no longer has land in the east of Dorthonion, near to his friends Celegorn and Curufin, but is the warden of Inglor's tower on Tol Sirion. This new story was introduced into AB 2 by later corrections (notes 10, 25, 29).

§118    The account of the defences of Beleriand in the North-east and the lands of the Fëanorian princes does not differ in essentials from that in AB 2, but is fuller and more precise in detail. The name *Lothland* first appears here, and this is the first time that Himring (Himling) has been described, or an interpretation given for either form. The territory of Damrod and Díriel is made more definite, and apparently more northward (earlier in this chapter, §111, its limits are 'between Celon and Gelion'). Lake *Helevorn*, beside which Cranthir dwelt, is now first mentioned (the name being written over an erasure, perhaps of *Elivorn*, see p. 405); it is not shown on the second Map as originally drawn.

The words 'by the Gnomes Thargelion (that is the land beyond Gelion) or Dor Granthir' were an addition, together with the marginal note on the Dark-elvish name *Radhrost*, but made very carefully at an earlier time. On *Granthir* beside *Cranthir* see the note on *Gorgoroth*, p. 298. The encounter of Cranthir's people with the Dwarves in Eredlindon is given in AB 2 under the year 104 (> 154), but the account of the Dwarves at this point in the *Annals* is in QS reserved for the new chapter that follows.

§§119–20    It is not said in AB 2 (annal 65) that Felagund aided the Elves of the Falas in the rebuilding of their Havens, nor that it was he who raised the Tower of Tindobel: for Fingolfin was still Lord of the Falas (see under §109 above). The name was first written here *Tindabel*, as also on the second Map: I read *Tindobel* on the assumption that this was an early change, a reversion to the form on the first Map and in AB 1 and 2.

### Note on the geography of the furthest North

I have remarked (IV. 259) when discussing the *Ambarkanta* maps that it is interesting to see how near Hithlum is placed on Map V to the edge of the world, the Chasm of Ilmen; and this is a convenient place to consider a further aspect of the matter. In QS §105 it is said:

> In the war of the Gods the mountains of Melko were broken and distorted in the West, and of their fragments were made Eredwethion and Eredlómin; but the Iron Mountains bent back northward and there was a hundred leagues between them and the frozen straits at Helkaraksë.

Though very cramped and hastily sketched in, Map V seems to agree well with this. I attempt here to enlarge and clarify the depiction of these regions on the map, adding letters to make reference to it plainer.

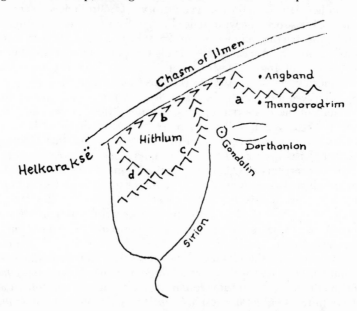

The western end of the Iron Mountains (marked *a* on the sketch) now turns in fairly sharply northwards to the Chasm of Ilmen; Eredwethion (*c*) and Eredlómin (*d*) are clearly identifiable. The herring-bone line (*b*) that runs along the edge of the Chasm is in pencil, whereas the other ranges are inked over pencil, but it is not clear whether this has any significance. The statement in QS just cited that there were a hundred leagues between the end of the Iron Mountains and the Helkaraksë suggests that there were no great heights between Hithlum and the Chasm – and cf. QS §106: 'Nivrost was sheltered from the North' (by Eredlómin), whereas 'Hithlum was open to the cold winds'.

On the other hand, earlier in QS (§103) the army sent out by Morgoth to test the defences of the Noldor 'turning west round the outer end of the Iron Mountains reached the shores of the sea', endeavouring 'to invade Hithlum from the rear'. This army came south along the coast and was destroyed by Fingon at the Firth of Drengist. Does this imply that the Orc-host could not invade Hithlum from the North owing to defensible heights between Hithlum and the Chasm of Ilmen? In which case some configuration after this fashion might be supposed:

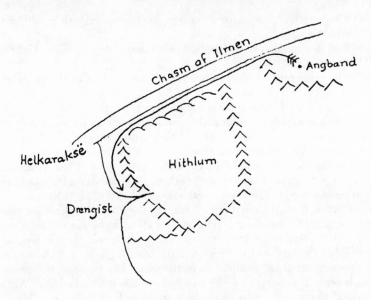

But the evidence does not seem to allow of a certain answer; and the second Map gives no help – indeed it presents a further problem in the representation of Thangorodrim (p. 409). Here the colossal triple peaks of Thangorodrim are surrounded by a closed circle of lesser heights, and there is no suggestion of the 'great curving wall' of the Iron Mountains from which 'the towers of Thangorodrim were thrust forward' (QS §103). I am at a loss to explain this; but in all the years during which my father used this map he never made any mark on it suggesting that the picture should be changed.

At this time Thangorodrim was conceived to be quite near: the second Map agrees closely with the *Ambarkanta* map V in this. In post-*Lord of the Rings* writing it is said that 'the gates of Morgoth were but one hundred and fifty leagues distant from the bridge of Menegroth' (*The Silmarillion* p. 96); whereas according to the scale of the second Map (see below) the distance was scarcely more than seventy.

## Note on distances

I list here the definitions of distance that are given in Chapter 9:

- 100 leagues between the end of the Iron Mountains in the West and the Helkaraksë (§105).
- Dorthonion stretched for 100 leagues (§106).
- The length of Sirion from the Pass to the Delta was 121 leagues (§107).
- West Beleriand at its widest was 70 leagues from Sirion to the sea (§109).
- The length of Narog from Ivrin to its confluence with Sirion was some 80 leagues (§109).
- East Beleriand at its widest was 100 leagues from Sirion to Gelion (§110).
- The great falls of Sirion were some 70 *miles* east of the gorge of Nargothrond (§113).
- Sirion flowed underground for 3 leagues (§113).
- The confluence of Ascar and Gelion was some 40 leagues south of the confluence of Greater and Little Gelion (§114).

A note on the back of the Map gives a scale of 50 miles to 3·2 cm. (the length of the sides of the squares). On this scale most of the distances given in QS agree well or very well with measurements on the Map (as might be expected). The rivers were measured in a straight line, in the case of Sirion from the northern opening of the Pass. But there are two statements in QS that do not harmonise at all with the Map. These are the length of Dorthonion (100 leagues) and the extent of West Beleriand at its widest (70 leagues from Sirion to the sea). A glance will show that Dorthonion was of far smaller extent than East Beleriand at its widest, though both distances are given in QS as 100 leagues, and that West Beleriand at its widest was virtually as great as East Beleriand. These statements are, I think, simply errors, without further significance; and they were in fact corrected (long after), the length of Dorthonion becoming 60 leagues, and West Beleriand at its widest 99 leagues, harmonising with the Map.

## 10    OF MEN AND DWARFS

§122    Now in time the building of Nargothrond was complete, and Gondolin had been raised in secret. But in the days of the Siege of Angband the Gnomes had yet small need of hiding places, and they ranged far and wide between the Western Sea and the

Blue Mountains in the East. It is said that they climbed Eredlindon and looked eastward in wonder, for the lands of Middle-
earth seemed wild and wide; but they did not pass the mountains,
while Angband lasted. In those days the folk of Cranthir came first
upon the Dwarfs, whom the Dark-elves named Naug-rim; for the
chief dwellings of that race were then in the mountains east of
Thargelion, the land of Cranthir, and were digged deep in the
eastern slopes of Eredlindon. Thence they journeyed often into
Beleriand, and were admitted at times even into Doriath. There
was at that time no enmity between Elves and Dwarfs, but
nonetheless no great love. For though the Dwarfs did not serve
Morgoth, yet they were in some things more like to his people than
to the Elves.

§123    The Naugrim were not of the Elf-race nor of mortal
kind, nor yet of Morgoth's breeding; and in those days the
Gnomes knew not whence they came. [But* it is said by the wise
in Valinor, as we have learned since, that Aulë made the Dwarfs
while the world was yet dark, desiring the coming of the Children
of Ilúvatar, that he might have learners to whom he could teach his
lore and craft, and being unwilling to await the fulfilment of the
designs of Ilúvatar. Wherefore the Dwarfs are like the Orcs in this,
that they come of the wilfulness of one of the Valar; but they were
not made out of malice and mockery, and were not begotten of evil
purpose. Yet they derive their thought and being after their
measure from only one of the Powers, whereas Elves and Men, to
whomsoever among the Valar they chiefly turn, have kinship with
all in some degree. Therefore the works of the Dwarfs have great
skill, but small beauty, save where they imitate the arts of the
Eldar; and the Dwarfs return unto the earth and the stone of the
hills of which they were fashioned.]†

§124    Iron they wrought rather than gold and silver, and the
making of weapons and of mail was their chief craft. They aided

*Marginal note against the bracketed passage: quoth Pengolod.
†Footnote to the text: Aulë, in his love of invention, devised a new
speech for the Dwarfs, and their tongues have no kinship with
others; in use they have made them harsh and intricate, and few have
essayed to learn them. In their converse with the Elves of old they
used according to their ability the language of the Dark-elves of
Doriath. But their own tongues they maintained in secret, and
they survive still in Middle-earth, and in some part certain of the
languages of Men are derived from them. Against this is written in the
margin: So, the Lhammas.

the Gnomes greatly in their war with the Orcs of Morgoth; but it is not thought that they would have refused to smithy also for Morgoth, if he had had need of their work, or had been open to their trade. For buying and selling and exchange was their delight, and the winning of wealth. But this they gathered rather to hoard than to use, or to spend save in commerce. Their stature was short and squat; they had strong arms and sturdy legs, and their beards were long. Themselves they named Khuzûd, but the Gnomes called them Neweg, the stunted, and those who dwelt in Nogrod they called Enfeng, the Longbeards, because their beards swept the floor before their feet. Their chief cities in those days were Khazaddûm and Gabilgathol, which the Elves of Beleriand called, according to their meaning in the language of Doriath, Nogrod, the Dwarfmine, and Belegost, the Great Fortress. But few of the Elves, save Meglin of Gondolin, went ever thither, and the Dwarfs trafficked into Beleriand, and made a great road, passing under the shoulders of Mount Dolmed, which followed thence the course of Ascar, and crossed Gelion at Sarn-athrad. There battle later befell, but as yet the Dwarfs troubled the Elves little, while the power of the Gnomes lasted.

§125   It is reckoned that the first meeting of Gnomes and Dwarfs befell in the land of Cranthir about the time when Fingolfin destroyed the Orcs at Drengist, one hundred and fifty-five years after the crossing of the Ice, and one hundred and five before the first coming of Glómund the Dragon. After his defeat there was long peace, and it lasted for well nigh two hundred years of the Sun. During this time the fathers of the houses of the Men of Beleriand, that is of the Elf-friends of old, were born in the lands of Middle-earth, east of the mountains; Bëor the Vassal, Haleth the Hunter, and Hador the Goldenhaired.

§126   Now it came to pass, when some four hundred years were gone since the Gnomes came to Beleriand, that Felagund journeyed east of Sirion and went hunting with the sons of Fëanor. But he became separated from his companions, and passed into Ossiriand, and wandered there alone. At a time of night he came upon a valley in the western foothills of Eredlindon, and he saw lights in the valley and heard from afar the sound of uncouth song; and he wondered greatly, for the Green-elves of that land lit no fires and sang not by night. And the language of the song, which he heard as he drew nigh, was not that of the Eldar, neither of the Dark-elves nor of the Gnomes, nor was it that of the Dwarfs. Therefore he feared lest a raid of the Orcs had escaped the leaguer of the North, but he found that this was not so. For he spied upon the camp beneath the hills, and there he beheld a strange people. Tall they were, and strong, and fair of face, but rude and little clad.

§127    Now these were the people of Bëor, a mighty warrior among Men, whose son was Barahir the bold that was after born in the land of the Gnomes. They were the first of Men that wandering west from far Hildórien passed over Eredlindon and came into Beleriand. After Bëor came Haleth father of Hundor, and again somewhat later came Hador the Goldenhaired, whose children are renowned in song. For the sons of Hador were Gumlin and Gundor, and the sons of Gumlin were Húrin and Huor, and the son of Húrin was Túrin the bane of Glómund, and the son of Huor Tuor father of Eärendel the blessed. All these were caught in the net of the fate of the Gnomes and wrought great deeds which the Elves remember still among the deeds of their lords and kings of old. But Haleth and Hador at that time were yet in the wild lands east of the mountains.

§128    Felagund drew nigh among the trees to the camp of Bëor and he remained hidden, until all had fallen asleep. Then he went among the sleeping men, and sat beside their dying fire, where none kept watch; and he took a rude harp which Bëor had laid aside, and he played music upon it such as mortal ear had never heard. For Men had as yet had no masters in such arts, save only the Dark-elves in the wild lands. Now men awoke and listened to Felagund as he harped and sang; and they marvelled, for wisdom was in that song as well as beauty, so that the heart grew wiser that hearkened to it. Thus it was that Men called King Felagund, whom they met first of all the Noldor, Gnome or Wisdom;* and after him they named his race the Wise, whom we call the Gnomes. At first they deemed that Felagund was one of the Gods, of whom they had heard rumour that they dwelt far in the West. But Felagund taught them true lore, and they loved him and became his followers; and thus Bëor the Vassal got his name among the Gnomes.

---

*Footnote to the text:* It is recorded that the word in the ancient speech of these Men, which they afterwards forsook in Beleriand for the tongue of the Gnomes, so that it is now mostly forgotten, was *Widris.* *Against this is written in the margin:* quoth Pengolod. *Added to this:* & Ælfwine.

§129 Bëor lived in the service of Felagund while his life lasted; and Barahir his son served also the sons of Finrod, but he dwelt mostly on the north marches with Angrod and Egnor. The sons of Hador were allied to the house of Fingolfin, and the lordship of Gumlin was in Hithlum; and there afterwards his son Húrin dwelt, whose wife was Morwen of the house of Bëor. She was surnamed Eledhwen, the Eflsheen, for her beauty was like unto the beauty of the daughters of the Eldalië. But Haleth and his folk took no service and dwelt in the woods upon the confines of Doriath in that forest that was called Brethil.

§130 In this time the strength of Men was added to the Gnomes, and the folk of the three houses grew and multiplied. Greatest was the house of Hador, and most beloved by the Elves. His folk were yellow-haired and blue-eyed for the most part; though Túrin was dark of hair, for his mother Morwen was from Bëor's people. They were of greater strength and stature in body than the Elves; quick to wrath and laughter, fierce in battle, generous to friends, swift in resolve, fast in loyalty, young in heart, the Children of Ilúvatar in the youth of mankind. Like to them were the woodland folk of Haleth, but they were not so tall; their backs were broader and their legs shorter and less swift. Less fiery were their spirits; slower but more deep was the movement of their thought; their words were fewer, for they had joy in silence, wandering free in the greenwood, while the wonder of the world was new upon them. But the people of Bëor were dark or brown of hair; their eyes were grey, and their faces fair to look upon; shapely they were of form, yet hardy and long-enduring. Their height was no greater than that of the Elves of that day, and they were most like to the Gnomes; for they were eager of mind, cunning-handed, swift of understanding, long in memory. But they were short-lived, and their fates were unhappy, and their joy was blended with sorrow.

§131 Bëor died when he had lived but eighty years, for fifty of which he had served Felagund; and it is said that when he lay dead of no weapon or sickness, but stricken by age, the Elves saw then for the first time the death of weariness, and they grieved for the short span allotted to mankind. Nonetheless these Men of old, being of races young and eager, learned swiftly of the Elves all such art and knowledge as they would teach; and in their skill and wisdom they far surpassed all others of their kind, who dwelt still east of the mountains, and knew not the Eldar of the West, ere ruin befell Beleriand.

## Commentary on Chapter 10

§122    The transient use in this chapter and subsequently of the plural form *Dwarfs* is curious (*Dwarves*, which goes back to the beginning, and was the form in *The Hobbit*, is used in the previous chapter, §118). In AB 2 *Dwarves* was at one occurrence only (note 41) changed to *Dwarfs*. The form *Naugrim* first occurs here; the Dwarves were *Nauglath* in the *Lost Tales*, *Nauglir* in Q. In the third Tree of Tongues (p. 196) their language is *Nauglian*.

In AB 2 (annal 104) 'the Dwarves had great mines and cities in the East of Eredlindon, *far south of Beleriand*, and the chief of these cities were Nogrod and Belegost', as in the direction on the first Map (Eastward Extension), IV. 231–2; but the Dwarf-cities are now placed in QS as they were to remain, in the mountains east of Thargelion, and AB 2 was corrected correspondingly (note 17). That the Dwarves 'were admitted at times even into Doriath' has not been said before, but the idea that they were already well-known to the Dark-elves of Beleriand when the Gnomes first encountered them in the Blue Mountains appeared in the second version of AB 1 (see IV. 332, 336), and their ancient road is there said to have extended to the river Aros, i.e. to the confines of Doriath.

It is remarkable that at this time the statement that the Dwarves were 'in some things more like to Morgoth's people than to the Elves' still survived from Q (IV. 104); but this is now palliated by what is said in §123, where the likeness of the Dwarves to the Orcs is represented only as an analogous limitation of natural powers consequent on their origins.

§123    This is the third account of the legend of the origin of the Dwarves, following those in AB 2 (annal 104) and in the *Lhammas* §9, both of which contain the remarkable assertion that the Dwarves have 'no spirit indwelling'; see the commentaries on those passages. Both versions were modified in respect of this; the *Lhammas* text was roughly emended with a specific direction to follow the passage here in QS beginning 'Yet they derive their thought and being after their measure from only one of the Powers . . .' But this passage in QS is itself written over something else wholly erased. Very likely, then, QS also had here a phrase concerning the absence of a 'spirit indwelling' in the Dwarves, and my father corrected both QS and the *Lhammas* at the same time, as he did elsewhere. Moreover, the account of the fate of the Dwarves given here, their return 'unto the earth and the stone of the hills of which they were fashioned', is taken from the same passage in AB 2 (it is absent from that in the *Lhammas*), and this is surely a concomitant of the conception that 'the Dwarves have no spirit indwelling'.

The square brackets enclosing this passage can be seen to belong with the writing of the manuscript; they evidently show to what portion of the text the marginal 'quoth Pengolod' refers. The question again arises (see §49) why Pengolod appears as annotator if he were the author, as he certainly appears to be in the preamble to the *Quenta Silmarillion* given on p. 201: 'This Account was composed first by Pengolod of Gondolin'. A possible explanation is to be found in the other forms of preamble on pp. 203–4. From the first of these it can be concluded that the reference is to 'The Silmarillion' in the larger sense (i.e. as including the *Annals* and the *Lhammas*), since it is said that Pengolod 'used much the writings of Rúmil . . . *chiefly in the annals of Valinor and the account of tongues*'. The second (typescript) form of this preamble makes the wording less precise: 'he used much the writings of Rúmil . . . concerning other matters than the wars of Beleriand'. Both versions also say that he used the accounts preserved in the Golden Book, though there is no indication of what matter the Golden Book contained. In either case there is no statement one way or the other specifically about the *Quenta Silmarillion*. It may be therefore that my father now regarded Pengolod as redactor or compiler rather than as author, at any rate in certain parts of the book, and in these Pengolod marked off his own contributions and named himself as authority for them – just as he did in the *Annals of Valinor* and the *Lhammas*. Thus here, as in the *Lhammas* §9, the passage concerning the origin of the Dwarves is an addition by Pengolod to older material (in this case writing by Rúmil).

The footnote on Dwarvish language, making specific reference to the *Lhammas*, certainly belongs with the original writing of the manuscript.

§124   *Khuzûd:* the first appearance of this name, or of any Dwarvish name for Dwarves. Cf. *The Lord of the Rings*, Appendix F: '*Khazad-dûm*, the Mansion of the Khazad; for such is their own name for their own race, and has been so, since Aulë gave it to them at their making in the deeps of time.'

*Enfeng:* cf. Q (IV. 104): 'those who dwelt in Nogrod they called Indrafangs, the Longbeards, because their beards swept the floor before their feet.' The name *Enfeng* here first appears. Originally the Longbeards were the Dwarves of Belegost (II. 247).

*Khazaddûm* is the first occurrence of the celebrated name. It is interesting to observe that it existed – but as the Dwarvish name of Nogrod – already at this time. Later the Dwarvish name of Nogrod was *Tumunzahar* (*The Silmarillion* p. 91); *Gabilgathol*, now first appearing, remained as the Dwarvish name of Belegost.

In this paragraph is the first reference to Meglin's association with the Dwarves. – *Dolmed* now replaces *Dolm* (and AB 2 was corrected correspondingly, note 17).

§125   In QS §103 it is said that it was Fingon who destroyed the Orcs at Drengist. – On the new dating, now present from the first writing of the manuscript, see the note on chronology, pp. 257–8.

§126   Parallel with the extension of the Siege of Angband by two
hundred years, the meeting of Felagund and Bëor, originally dated in
the year 200 in AB 2, undergoes a corresponding postponement.

§128   The footnote to the text is original. Whereas in *The Silmarillion*
the word in the language of the people of Bëor for 'Wisdom' was *Nóm*
(see IV. 175), here it is *Widris*, and it can hardly be doubted that this is
to be related to the Indo-European stem seen, for instance, in Sanskrit
*veda* 'I know'; Greek *idein* (from *\*widein*) 'to see' and *oida* (from
*\*woida*) '(I have seen >) I know'; Latin *vidēre* 'to see'; Old English
*witan* 'to know' and *wāt* 'I know' (> archaic *I wot*), and the words that
still survive, *wit, wise, wisdom*. Cf. the *Lhammas* §10: 'Yet other Men
there were, it seems, that remained east of Eredlindon, who held to
their speech, and from this, closely akin to Taliska, are come after
many ages of change languages that live still in the North of the earth.'
– On the abandonment of their own tongue by Men in Beleriand see
the *Lhammas* §10 and commentary; and on the ascription of the
footnote to Pengolod see commentary on §123 above.

'Thus Bëor the Vassal got his name among the Gnomes': in the
*Etymologies* the name *Bëor* 'follower, vassal' is a Noldorin name (stem
BEW), whereas in *The Silmarillion* (p. 142) it is said that 'Bëor signified
"Vassal" in the tongue of his people'.

§131   According to the original dating of AB 2 Bëor was born in the year
170 and died in 250; with the altered chronology he was born in 370
and died in 450.

## 11   OF THE RUIN OF BELERIAND AND THE FALL OF FINGOLFIN

§132   Now Fingolfin, King of the North, and High-king of
the Noldor, seeing that his folk were become numerous and
strong, and that the Men allied to them were many and valiant,
pondered once more an assault upon Angband. For he knew that
they all lived in danger while the circle of the siege was incomplete, and Morgoth was free to labour in the dark beneath the
earth. This counsel was wise according to the measure of his
knowledge; for the Gnomes did not yet comprehend the fullness
of the power of Morgoth, nor understand that their unaided war
upon him was without final hope, whether they hasted or delayed.
But because the land was fair and their kingdoms wide, most of the
Noldor were grown content with things as they were, trusting
them to last. Therefore they were little disposed to hearken to
Fingolfin, and the sons of Fëanor at that time least of all. Among
the chieftains of the Gnomes Angrod and Egnor alone were of like
mind with the King; for they dwelt in regions whence Than-

gorodrim could be descried, and the threat of Morgoth was present to their thought. So the designs of Fingolfin came to naught, and the land had peace yet for a while.

§133    But when the sons of the sons of the Fathers of Men were but newly come to manhood, it being then four hundred years and five and fifty since the coming of Fingolfin, the evil befell that he had long dreaded, and yet more dire and sudden than his darkest fear. For Morgoth had long prepared his force in secret, while ever the malice of his heart grew greater, and his hatred of the Gnomes more bitter; and he desired not only to end his foes but to destroy also and defile the lands that they had taken and made fair. And it is said that his hate overcame his counsel, so that if he had but endured to wait longer, until his designs were full, then the Gnomes would have perished utterly. But on his part he esteemed too lightly the valour of the Elves, and of Men he took yet no account.

§134    There came a time of winter, when night was dark and without moon; and the wide plain of Bladorion stretched dim beneath the cold stars from the hill-forts of the Gnomes to the feet of Thangorodrim. The watchfires burned low, and the guards were few; and on the plain few were waking in the camps of the horsemen of Hithlum. Then suddenly Morgoth sent forth great rivers of flame that poured, swifter than the cavalry of the Balrogs, over all the plain; and the Mountains of Iron belched forth fires of many colours, and the fume stank upon the air and was deadly. Thus Bladorion perished, and fire devoured its grasses; and it became a burned and desolate waste, full of a choking dust, barren and lifeless; and its name was changed, and ever after was called the Land of Thirst, Dor-na-Fauglith in the Gnomish tongue. Many charred bones had there their roofless grave. For many Gnomes perished in that burning, who were caught by the running flame and could not fly to the hills. The heights of Dorthonion and of Eredwethion held back the fiery torrents, but their woods upon the slopes that looked toward Angband were all kindled, and the smoke wrought confusion among the defenders. This was the Third of the great Battles, Dagor Vreged-úr, the Battle of Sudden Fire.

§135    In the front of that fire came Glómund the golden, the father of dragons, and in his train were Balrogs, and behind them came the black armies of the Orcs in multitudes such as the Gnomes had never before seen or imagined. And they assaulted the fortresses of the Gnomes, and broke the leaguer about

Angband, and slew wherever they found them both the Gnomes and their allies, Dark-elves and Men. Many of the stoutest of the foes of Morgoth were destroyed in the first days of that war, bewildered and dispersed and unable to muster their strength. War ceased not wholly ever again in Beleriand; but the Battle of Sudden Fire is held to have ended with the coming of spring, when the onset of Morgoth grew less. For he saw now that he had not assembled sufficient strength, nor rightly measured the valour of the Gnomes. Moreover his captains and spies brought him tidings of the Elf-friends, the Men of Beleriand, and of their strength in arms; and a new anger possessed his heart, and he turned to thoughts of further evil.

§136    Thus ended the Siege of Angband; and the foes of Morgoth were scattered and sundered one from another. The Dark-elves fled south and forsook the northern war. Many were received into Doriath, and the kingdom and strength of Thingol grew greater in that time; for the power of the queen Melian was woven about his borders and evil could not yet enter that hidden realm. Others took refuge in the fortresses by the sea, or in Nargothrond; but most fled the land and hid in Ossiriand, or passing the mountains wandered homeless in the wild. And rumour of the war and the breaking of the siege reached the ears of Men in Middle-earth.

§137    The sons of Finrod bore most heavily the brunt of the assault, and Angrod and Egnor were slain; and Bregolas son of Bëor, who was lord of that house of Men after his father's death, was slain beside them. In that battle King Inglor Felagund was cut off from his folk and surrounded by the Orcs, and he would have been slain or taken, but Barahir son of Bëor came up with his men and rescued him, and made a wall of spears about him; and they cut their way out of the battle with great loss. Thus Felagund escaped and went south to Nargothrond, his deep fortress prepared against the evil day; but he swore an oath of abiding friendship and aid in every need unto Barahir and all his kin and seed, and in token of his vow he gave to Barahir his ring.

§138    Barahir was now by right lord of the remnant of the folk of Bëor; but most of these fled now from Dorthonion and took refuge among the people of Hador in the fastness of Hithlum. But Barahir would not flee, and remained contesting the land foot by foot with the servants of Morgoth. But Morgoth pursued his people to the death, until few remained; and he took all the forest and the highland of Dorthonion, save the highest and inmost region, and turned it little by little to a place of such dread and lurking evil that even the Orcs would not enter it unless need drove them. Therefore it was after called by the Gnomes Taur-na-Fuin, which is Mirkwood, and Deldúwath, Deadly Nightshade; for the trees that grew there after the burning were black and grim, and their roots were tangled, groping in the dark like claws; and those who strayed among them became lost and blind, and were strangled or pursued to madness by phantoms of terror.

§139   At length only twelve men remained to Barahir: Beren his son, and Baragund and Belegund, sons of Bregolas, his nephews, and nine faithful servants of his house whose names are yet remembered by the Gnomes: Radhruin and Dairuin they were, Dagnir and Ragnor, Gildor and Gorlim the unhappy, Arthod and Urthel, and Hathaldir the young. Outlaws they became, a desperate band that could not escape and would not yield; for their dwellings were destroyed, and their wives and children captured or slain, save only Morwen Eledhwen daughter of Baragund and Rian daughter of Belegund. For the wives of the sons of Bregolas were of Hithlum, and were sojourning there among their kinsfolk when the flame of war broke forth. But from Hithlum there came now neither news nor help, and Barahir and his men were hunted like wild beasts, and Morgoth sent many wolves against them; and they retreated to the barren highland above the forest, and wandered among the tarns and rocky moors of that region, furthest from the spies and spells of Morgoth. Their bed was the heather and their roof the cloudy sky.

§140   So great was the onslaught of Morgoth that Fingolfin and Fingon could not come to the succour of Felagund and his brethren; and the hosts of Hithlum were driven back with great loss to the fortresses of Eredwithion, and these they hardly defended against the Orcs. Hador the golden-haired, prince of Men, fell in battle before the walls defending the rearguard of his lord Fingolfin, being then sixty and six years of age, and with him fell Gundor his younger son; and they were mourned by the Elves. But Gumlin took the lordship of his father. And because of the strength and height of the Shadowy Mountains, which withstood the torrent of fire, and by the valour of the Elves and Men of the North, which neither Orc nor Balrog could yet overcome, Hithlum remained yet unconquered, a threat upon the flank of Morgoth's attack. But Fingolfin was sundered by a sea of foes from his kinsmen.

§141   For the war had gone ill with the sons of Fëanor, and

well nigh all the east marches were taken by assault. The pass
of Aglon was forced, though with great cost to Morgoth; and
Celegorn and Curufin being defeated fled south and west by the
marches of Doriath and came at last to Nargothrond, and sought
harbour with their friend Orodreth. Thus it came to pass that the
people of Celegorn swelled the strength of Felagund, but it would
have been better, as after was seen, if they had remained in the
East among their own kin. Maidros the chief of Fëanor's sons did
deeds of surpassing valour, and the Orcs could not endure the
light of his face; for since his torment upon Thangorodrim his
spirit burned like a white fire within, and he was as one that
returneth from the dead, keen and terrible; and they fled before
him. Thus his citadel upon the hill of Himring could not at that
time be taken, and many of the most valiant that remained, both of
the folk of Dorthonion and of the east marches rallied there to
Maidros; and for a while he closed once more the pass of Aglon, so
that the Orcs could not enter Beleriand by that road.

§142  But they overwhelmed the riders of the folk of Fëanor
upon Lothland, for Glómund came thither, and passed through
Maglor's Gap, and destroyed all the land between the arms of
Gelion. And the Orcs took the fortress upon the west slopes of
Mount Rerir, and ravaged all Thargelion, the land of Cranthir;
and they defiled Lake Helevorn. Thence they passed over Gelion
with fire and terror and came far into East Beleriand. Maglor
joined Maidros upon Himring; but Cranthir fled and joined the
remnant of his people to the scattered folk of the hunters, Damrod
and Díriel, and they retreated and passed Rhamdal in the South.
Upon Amon Ereb they maintained a watch and some strength of
war, and they had aid of the Green-elves; and the Orcs came not
yet into Ossiriand or the wild of South Beleriand.

§143  For nearly two years the Gnomes still defended the west
pass about the sources of Sirion, for the power of Ulmo was in that
water, and Glómund would not yet adventure that way, for the
time of his full strength was not come; and Minnastirith withstood
the Orcs. But at length after the fall of Fingolfin, which is told
hereafter, Sauron came against Orodreth, the warden of the
tower, with a host of Balrogs. Sauron was the chief servant of the
evil Vala, whom he had suborned to his service in Valinor from
among the people of the Gods. He was become a wizard of
dreadful power, master of necromancy, foul in wisdom, cruel in
strength, mis-shaping what he touched, twisting what he ruled,
lord of werewolves: his dominion was torment. He took Min-

nastirith by assault, the tower of Inglor upon the isle of Sirion, for a dark cloud of fear fell upon those that defended it; and he made it a stronghold of evil, and a menace;* for no living creature could pass through that vale that he did not espy from the tower where he sat. And Morgoth held now also the western pass and his terror filled the fields and woods of Beleriand.

§144   *The death of Fingolfin.* It came to pass that news came to Hithlum that Dorthonion was lost and the sons of Finrod overthrown, and that the sons of Fëanor were driven from their lands. Then Fingolfin saw that the ruin of the Gnomes was at hand, and he was filled with wrath and despair, and a madness came upon him. And he rode alone to the gates of Angband, and he sounded his horn and smote upon the brazen gates and challenged Morgoth to come forth to single combat. And Morgoth came. That was the last time in these wars that he passed the doors of his stronghold, and it is said that he took not the challenge willingly; for though his might is greatest of all things in this world, alone of the Valar he knows fear. But he could not now deny the challenge before the face of his captains; for the rocks rang with the shrill music of the silver horn of Fingolfin and his voice came keen and clear down into the depths of Angband; and Fingolfin named Morgoth craven, and lord of slaves. Therefore Morgoth came, climbing slowly from his subterranean throne, and the rumour of his feet was like thunder underground. And he issued forth clad in black armour; and he stood before the king like a tower, iron-crowned, and his vast shield, sable unblazoned, cast a shadow over him like a storm cloud. But Fingolfin gleamed beneath it like a star; for his mail was overlaid with silver, and his blue shield was set with crystals; and he drew his sword Ringil, and it glittered like ice, cold and grey and deadly.

§145   Then Morgoth hurled aloft as a mace Grond, the hammer of the Underworld, and swung it down like a bolt of thunder. But Fingolfin sprang aside, and Grond rent a mighty pit in the earth, whence smoke and fire darted. Many times Morgoth essayed to smite him, and each time Fingolfin leaped away, as a lightning shoots from under a dark cloud; and he wounded Morgoth with seven wounds, and seven times Morgoth gave a cry of anguish, whereat the rocks shivered, and the hosts of Angband fell upon their faces in dismay.

*Footnote to the text:* And it became called Tol-na-Gaurhoth, the Isle of Werewolves.

§146    But at last the king grew weary, and Morgoth bore down his shield upon him. Thrice he was crushed to his knees, and thrice arose again and bore up his broken shield and stricken helm. But the earth was all rent and pitted about him, and he stumbled and fell backward before the feet of Morgoth; and Morgoth set his left foot upon his neck, and the weight of it was like a fallen hill. Yet with his last and desperate stroke Fingolfin hewed the foot with Ringil, and the blood gushed forth black and smoking and filled the pits of Grond.

§147    Thus died Fingolfin, High-king of the Gnomes, most proud and valiant of the Elven-kings of old. The Orcs make no boast of that duel at the gate; neither do the Elves sing of it, for sorrow; but the tale of it is remembered, for Thorondor, king of eagles, brought the tidings to Gondolin, and to Hithlum. For Morgoth took the body of the Elven-king and broke it, and would hew it asunder and cast it to his wolves; but Thorondor came hasting from his eyrie among the peaks of Gochressiel, and he stooped upon Morgoth, and smote his golden beak into his face. The rushing of his wings was like the noise of the winds of Manwë, and he seized the body in his mighty talons, and soaring suddenly above the darts of the Orcs he bore the Elven-king away. And he laid him upon a mountain-top that looked from the North upon the hidden valley of Gondolin; and Turgon coming built a high cairn over him. Neither Orc nor Balrog dared ever after to pass over the mount of Fingolfin or draw nigh his tomb, until the doom of Gondolin was come and treachery was born among his kin. Morgoth goes ever halt of one foot since that day, and the pain of his wounds cannot be healed; and in his face is the scar that Thorondor made.

§148    There was lamentation in Hithlum when the fall of Fingolfin became known; but Fingon took the kingship of the Noldor, and he maintained still his realm behind the Shadowy Mountains in the North. But beyond Hithlum Morgoth pursued his foes relentlessly, and he searched out their hiding-places and took their strongholds one by one. And the Orcs growing ever bolder wandered at will far and wide, coming down Sirion in the West and Celon in the East, and they encompassed Doriath; and they harried the lands, so that beast and bird fled before them, and silence and desolation spread steadily from the North. Great numbers of the Gnomes, and of the Dark-elves, they took captive and led to Angband, and made thralls, forcing them to use their skill and knowledge in the service of Morgoth. They laboured without rest in his mines and forges, and torment was their wage.

§149   Yet Morgoth sent also his spies and emissaries among the Dark-elves and the thrall-Gnomes, and among the free; and they were clad in false forms and deceit was in their speech, and they made lying promises of reward, and with cunning words sought to arouse fear and jealously among the peoples, accusing their kings and chieftains of greed, and of treachery one to another. And because of the curse of the kin-slaying at Alqualondë, these lies were often believed; and indeed as the times darkened they had a measure of truth, for the hearts and minds of the Elves of Beleriand became clouded with despair and fear. And most the Gnomes feared the treachery of their own kin, who had been thralls in Angband; for Morgoth used some of these for his evil purposes, and feigning to give them liberty sent them abroad, but their wills were chained to his, and strayed only to come back to him again. Therefore if any of the captives escaped in truth, and returned to their own people, they had little welcome, and wandered alone outlawed and desperate.

§150   *Of the Swarthy Men.* To Men Morgoth feigned pity, if any would hearken to his messages, saying that their woes came only of their servitude to the rebel Gnomes, but at the hands of the rightful lord of earth they would get honour and a just reward of valour, if they would leave rebellion. But of the Three Houses few men would give ear to him, not even were they brought to the torment of Angband. Therefore he pursued them with hatred, but he sent his messengers east over the mountains. And it is said that at this time the Swarthy Men came first into Beleriand; and some were already secretly under the dominion of Morgoth, and came at his call; but not all, for the rumour of Beleriand, of its lands and waters, of its wars and riches, went now far and wide, and the wandering feet of Men were ever set westward in those days. And Morgoth was glad of their coming, for he thought they would prove more pliable to his service, and that through them he might yet work great injury to the Elves.

§151   Now the Easterlings or Rómenildi, as the Elves named these newcomers, were short and broad, long and strong in the arm; their hair was black, and grew much also upon their face and breast; their skins were swart or sallow, and their eyes brown; yet their countenances were for the most part not uncomely, though some were grim and fierce. Their houses and tribes were many, and some had greater liking for the Dwarfs of the mountains than for the Elves. But the sons of Fëanor, seeing the weakness of the

Noldor, and the growing power of the armies of Morgoth, made alliances with these men, and gave their friendship to the greatest of their chieftains, Bór and Ulfang. And Morgoth was well content; for this was as he had designed. The sons of Bór were Borlas and Boromir and Borthandos; and they followed Maidros and Maglor, and cheated the hope of Morgoth, and were faithful. The sons of Ulfang the Black were Ulfast and Ulwarth and Uldor the Accursed; and they followed Cranthir and swore allegiance to him, and proved faithless.

§152   There was small love between the Three Houses and the Swarthy Men; and they met seldom. For the newcomers abode long in East Beleriand; but the people of Hador were shut in Hithlum, and Bëor's house was well nigh destroyed. Yet Haleth and his men remained still free; for they had been at first untouched by the northern war, since they dwelt to the southward in the woods by Sirion. There now there was war between them and the invading Orcs; for they were stout-hearted men and would not lightly forsake the woods they loved. And amid the tale of defeats of this time their deeds are remembered with honour: for after the taking of Minnastirith the Orcs came through the western pass, and would maybe have ravaged even unto the mouths of Sirion; but Haleth sent swift word to Thingol, being friendly with many of the Elves that guarded the borders of Doriath. And Thingol sent Beleg the bowman, chief of his march-wardens, to his aid with many archers; and Haleth and Beleg took an Orc-legion at unawares in the forest, and destroyed it; and the advance of the power of Morgoth southward down the course of Sirion was stayed. Thus the folk of Haleth dwelt yet for many years in watchful peace in the forest of Brethil; and behind their guard the kingdom of Nargothrond had respite and mustered anew its strength.

§153   It is said that Húrin son of Gumlin, son of Hador, of Hithlum was with Haleth in that battle, and he was then seventeen years of age; and this was his first deed of arms, but not his last. For Húrin son of Gumlin was fostered for a while in boyhood by Haleth, according to the custom of Men and Elves in that time. And it is recorded that in the autumn of the year of Sudden Fire Haleth took Húrin, then newcome from his father's house, and they went hunting northward up the vale of Sirion; and by chance or the will of Ulmo they came upon the secret entrance to the hidden valley of Tumladin, where Gondolin was built. But they were taken by the guards, and brought before Turgon; and they looked upon the forbidden city, whereof none of those outside yet knew aught, save Thorondor king of eagles. Turgon welcomed them; for messages and dreams had come to him up Sirion from the sea, from Ulmo, Lord of Waters, warning him of woe to come and foretelling that the aid of mortal men would be necessary, if he would save any of the Gnomes from their doom. But Turgon deemed that Gondolin was strong, and the time not ripe for its revealing; and he would not suffer the men to depart. It is said that he had great liking for the boy Húrin, and love was joined to policy; for he desired to keep Húrin at his side in Gondolin. But tidings came of the great battle, and the need of Gnomes and Men; and Haleth and Húrin besought Turgon for leave to go to the aid of their own folk. Turgon then granted their prayer, but they swore deep oaths to him, and never revealed his secret; and such of the counsels of Turgon as Húrin had learned he kept hidden in his heart.

§154    Turgon would not as yet suffer any of his own folk to issue forth to war, and Haleth and Húrin departed from Gondolin alone. But Turgon, rightly deeming that the breaking of the Siege of Angband was the beginning of the downfall of the Noldor, unless aid should come, sent secret messengers to the mouths of Sirion, and to the Isle of Balar. There they built ships, and many set sail thence, seeking for Valinor, to ask for help and pardon. And they besought the birds of the sea to guide them. But the seas were wild and wide, and shadow and enchantment lay upon them, and Valinor was hidden. Therefore none of the messengers of Gondolin came ever unto the West at that time; and many were lost and few returned; but the doom of Gondolin drew nearer.

§155    Rumour came to Morgoth of these things, and he was unquiet amid his victories; and he desired greatly to learn tidings of Felagund and Turgon. For they had vanished out of knowledge, and yet were not dead; and he feared what they might yet accomplish against him. Of Nargothrond he knew indeed the name, but neither its place nor its strength; but of Gondolin he knew naught, and the thought of Turgon troubled him the more. Therefore he sent forth ever more spies into Beleriand; but he recalled the main hosts of his Orcs and mustered again his forces. And it is said that he was dismayed to find how great had been their loss, perceiving that he could not yet make a final and victorious battle, until he had gathered new strength. Thus Beleriand in the South had a semblance of peace again for a few brief years; but the forges of Angband were full of labour.

§156  *Siege of Eithel Sirion and Fall of Gumlin.* Nor did the assault upon the northern strongholds cease. Himring Morgoth besieged so close that no help might come from Maidros, and he threw suddenly a great force against Hithlum. The Orcs won many of the passes, and some came even into Mithrim; but Fingon drove them in the end with heavy slaughter from the land, and pursued them far across the sands of Fauglith. Yet sorrow marred his victory, for Gumlin son of Hador was slain by an arrow in the siege of the fortress of Fingon at Eithel Sirion. Húrin his son was then new-come to manhood, but he was great in strength both of mind and body; and he ruled now the house of Hador and served Fingon.* And in this time also the outlaws of Dorthonion were destroyed, and Beren son of Barahir alone escaping came hardly into Doriath.

### Commentary on Chapter 11

§132  This paragraph is developed from the first part of annal 222 in AB 2 (there is nothing of it in the earlier sources).

§133  'The sons of the sons of the Fathers of Men' are the second generation after Bëor, Hador, and Haleth (Baragund, Belegund, Beren; Húrin, Huor; Handir), whose birthdates, according to the revised chronology in AB 2, fall between 424 (Baragund) and 444 (Huor).

§138  The application of *Mirkwood* to Taur-na-Fuin is interesting. Cf. the reverse case in *Unfinished Tales*, p. 281, where (long after) in a note to *The Disaster of the Gladden Fields* my father wrote: 'the shadow of Sauron spread through Greenwood the Great, and changed its name from Eryn Galen to Taur-nu-Fuin (translated Mirkwood).'

§139  The only names of the men of Barahir's band given in AB 2 (annal 257), other than his son and nephews, are Gorlim, Radros (> Radruin), Dagnir, and Gildor. – On the story that Morwen and Rian were of Hithlum, and were staying there at the time of the Battle of Sudden Fire, see AB 2 annal 257 and commentary.

§140  According to the revised dating, Hador was born in 390, and he died with Gundor in 456. As AB 2 was originally written, Gundor was the elder son, but he became the younger (note 20), born in 419 'beneath the shadows of Eredlindon' (i.e. before Hador crossed the mountains into Beleriand).

§141  *Celegorn*, not *Celegorm*, was here the form first written (see commentary on §41). – It is said in QS §117 that after the founding of

*Footnote to the text:* For he returned unto his own folk after the victory in the woods of Brethil, while the ways north to Hithlum were passable because of the defeat of the Orcs at that time.

Nargothrond Inglor Felagund committed the tower of Minnastirith to Orodreth; and later in the present chapter (§143) it is recounted how Sauron came against Orodreth and took the tower by assault (the fate of the defenders is not there mentioned). The statement here that Celegorn and Curufin 'sought harbour with their friend Orodreth' – rather than 'sought harbour with Felagund' – is found also in an emendation to AB 2 (note 25); the implication is that Orodreth reached Nargothrond before them, and that their friendship with him was the motive for their going to Nargothrond. This friendship survived the change of Orodreth's lordship from the east of Dorthonion ('nighest to the sons of Fëanor', AB 2 annal 52 as originally written) to the wardenship of the tower on Tol Sirion. The sentence 'the people of Celegorn swelled the strength of Felagund, but it would have been better . . . if they had remained in the East among their own kin' goes back to Q (IV. 106), though in Q Celegorm and Curufin came to Nargothrond together with Orodreth.

§142    The fortress on the west slopes of Mount Rerir is here first mentioned.

§143    On the shifting representation of the growth of the great Dragon to his full power and terror see IV. 181–2, 317–18. The statement in AB 2 annal 255 that Glómund was 'in his full might' at the Battle of Sudden Fire was not taken up in QS §135, and in the present passage 'the time of his full strength was not come'. In *The Silmarillion* (p. 151) Glaurung was again 'in his full might' at the time of the battle: this was taken from the final version of the *Annals* (the *Grey Annals*).

This is the first occurrence of the name *Sauron* in the 'Silmarillion' tradition; but its actual first occurrence (in a text as first written) is probably either in *The Lost Road* or in the second version of *The Fall of Númenor* (see the commentary on FN II §5). The statement that Morgoth suborned Sauron '*in Valinor* from among the people of the Gods' is notable. The implication must be that at this period my father conceived Sauron to have followed Morgoth when he fled to Middle-earth accompanied by Ungoliantë.

With the words 'a host of Balrogs' cf. the commentary on §89.

§§144–7    The account of the death of Fingolfin in QS was largely based on the *Lay of Leithian* Canto XII (see III. 293) – which in turn had followed the prose version in Q (IV. 176–8).

§147    In Q §9 (IV. 106) 'The Orcs sing of that duel at the gates', and in the *Lay of Leithian* (lines 3584–5) 'Yet Orcs would after laughing tell / of the duel at the gates of hell.'

The name *Thorondor* (for *Thorndor*) appears now in this form as first written (see commentary on §§96–7).

*Gochressiel*: this name (on which see the *Etymologies*, stem KHARÁS) was afterwards changed to *Crisaegrim*. In Q §15 Thorndor dwelt on Thangorodrim until the Battle of Unnumbered Tears, when he removed his eyries 'to the northward heights of the Encircling Mountains', and kept watch there 'sitting upon the cairn of King Fingolfin'. This goes back to S (§15; see IV. 66). Afterwards the *Crissaegrim* 'abode of eagles' were expressly stated to be the peaks to the south of Gondolin, and the name was so marked in on the second Map; but *Gochressiel* in QS need not have had this narrower significance.

In Q §9 it was Thorndor who 'set' Fingolfin's cairn on the mountain-top, just as in the *Lay of Leithian* (lines 3626–7) 'in mounded cairn the mighty dead / he laid upon the mountain's head'; but in QS, with the changed story of the foundation of Gondolin, it is Turgon who comes up from the city in the valley beneath and builds his father's tomb.

§150    The earlier sources have nothing of the content of this paragraph, in which first appears the important development that some of the Swarthy Men were already under Morgoth's dominion before they entered Beleriand (see IV. 179–80).

§151    In the description of the Swarthy Men, or *Rómenildi* ('Eastern Men', Easterlings) as they are called here, my father was following AB 2 annal 263 (463), the year of their first coming into East Beleriand. The form *Bór* was changed from *Bor* subsequent to the writing of the manuscript, as in AB 2 (note 33); but *Ulfang* and *Ulwarth* (appearing only by emendation in AB 2) are original.

§152    There is here the explicit assertion that the house of Bëor was 'well nigh destroyed'; earlier in this chapter (§138) it was said that after the Battle of Sudden Fire 'Barahir was now by right lord of the remnant of the folk of Bëor; but most of these fled from Dorthonion and took refuge among the people of Hador in the fastness of Hithlum.'

The passage concerning the people of Haleth and the destruction of the Orcs in Brethil by Haleth and Beleg with archers out of Doriath is derived from annal 258 in AB 2, and much expanded.

§153    The story of Húrin's sojourn in Gondolin is found in AB 2 (annal 256) in very much the same form as it is told here. The statement in the opening sentence of the paragraph that Haleth and Húrin (then seventeen years old) were 'in that battle' refers to the destruction of the Orcs in Brethil in the year 458; Húrin was born in 441. See note 32 to AB 2.

§154    The account of the vain attempt of Turgon to send messengers over the ocean to Valinor is developed from that in annal 256 in AB 2.

§156    The attack on Hithlum took place in the year 462, the year in which Beren fled from Dorthonion. – The name *Fauglith* was written *Dor-na-Fauglith*, but changed at the time of writing.

With the footnote (contemporary with the writing of the manuscript) cf. the addition to AB 2 annal 258 (note 32): 'Húrin of Hithlum was with Haleth; but he departed afterward since the victory [in Brethil] had made the journey possible, and returned to his own folk.'

## 12–15  OF BEREN AND TINÚVIEL

The *Quenta Silmarillion* came to an end not abruptly but raggedly. The textual history now becomes very complex, but since it bears strongly on the question of how matters stood when *The Lord of the Rings* was begun I give here an account of it. Since, as I believe, the story of what happened, and when, can be put together with a high degree of probability, I set it out on the basis of my reconstruction and in the order of events that I deduce, since this will be briefer and clearer than to give all the evidences first and only then to draw conclusions.

I have noticed earlier (p. 199) that there is now no trace of any rough drafts underlying the polished and beautiful QS manuscript (though they must have existed) until the tale of Beren and Lúthien is reached; but at this point they appear abundantly. The first of them is a very rough manuscript which I shall call 'QS(A)', or simply 'A'; this represents, I feel sure, the first essay at a prose version of the tale since the original *Tale of Tinúviel*, a prose 'saga' to be told on a far more ample scale than the brief account in Q (§10). The treachery of Gorlim, the surprising of Barahir's lair on Dorthonion, and Beren's recapture of the ring from the Orcs, are fully told; and in some two and a half thousand words this text only reaches the words of Thingol's people when the woods of Doriath fell silent (the *Lay of Leithian* lines 861–2).

On the basis of A (or perhaps of a further draft version now lost) my father then continued QS in fine script through chapter 12 and into 13, giving a general heading *Of Beren and Tinúviel* to both but entitling the individual chapters *Of the Meeting of Beren and Lúthien Tinúviel* and *The Quest of the Silmaril*. Here too the story was told very fully, but less so than in the rough draft A; for the story of Gorlim and the betrayal of Barahir is dealt with in less than a page, and Dairon is entirely excluded from the narrative. At the point where Inglor Felagund gave the crown of Nargothrond to Orodreth, the text ends. It is convenient to call this – just for the purpose of this discussion – 'QS I'.

QS I ends here because my father saw that it was going to be too long, overbalancing the whole work. He had taken more than 4000 words to reach the departure of Beren and Felagund from Nargothrond – and this did not include the story of Lúthien's imprisonment in the tree-house and her escape from it, which in the Lay precedes the account of Beren in Nargothrond. (That QS I was originally simply the continuation of QS is obvious from the fact that in the course of it there is the new chapter-heading numbered 13.) He therefore set it aside, and began anew on a less ample version, though still by no means severely compressed (this version reaches the departure of Beren and Felagund from Nargothrond in some 1800 words); but he retained the first page of QS I, which he considered to be sufficiently 'compressed'. This page takes the story to the words [*Beren*] *swore upon it an oath of vengeance* (*The Silmarillion* p. 163). For this reason QS I, as it now stands, has no beginning, but takes up at the head of the second page with the words *First therefore he pursued the Orcs that had slain his father.*

As a basis for the projected 'short' version of the tale, my father now made a draft version of the whole. This manuscript, 'QS(B)' or 'B', starts out clearly enough but rapidly declines into a scrawl. It begins, on page 1, with the words *First therefore he pursued the Orcs that had slain his father* – because the first page of QS I, extending precisely to this point, was retained for the new version.

From text B was derived the 'short' form of the story ('QS II') in the QS manuscript, written in the same fine script. This retains the chapter division 12/13 at the same point as it had been made in QS I, where Beren left Doriath; chapter 13 ends with the burial of Felagund on Tol Sirion; and chapter 14 is entitled *The Quest of the Silmaril 2*. Near the end of this chapter the script changes, slightly but noticeably, from one page to the next. The first script, extraordinarily uniform right through the manuscript from the beginning, ends at the foot of page 91 with the words *but the jewel suffered his touch (The Silmarillion* p. 181), and the new begins at the head of page 92 with *and hurt him not*, continuing to the end of chapter 14 a few lines down page 93 at *for the power of the Silmaril was hidden within him*. I feel certain that it was at the foot of page 91 that my father broke off when the QS manuscript went to Allen and Unwin on 15 November 1937.

But he was reluctant to set his work (the development of the rough text B into the finished narrative QS II) suddenly aside. He therefore at once began on an intermediate manuscript, 'QS(C)' or 'C', in a less fine and time-consuming form (intending to copy this into the QS manuscript when it came back to him). This I deduce from the fact that the first page of text C is numbered 92 and begins with the words *and hurt him not*, just as does the portion of QS II in the changed script.

When QS came back from the publishers on 16 December 1937 my father began immediately (see III. 366) on 'a new story about Hobbits', and I do not think that after that time he extended the narrative of the *Quenta Silmarillion* any further. But while the QS manuscript was away, he had extended the text C for a good distance, completing the story of Beren and Lúthien through a final chapter (15) entitled *The Quest of the Silmaril 3: The Wolf-hunt of Carcharoth*, writing a further chapter (16) *Of the Fourth Battle: Nírnaith Arnediad*, and commencing 17 *Of Túrin the Hapless*. By this stage the manuscript had as usual degenerated into a scrawl, and he left it at Túrin's putting on the Dragon-helm and becoming the companion of Beleg on the north marches of Doriath.

Still (if I am right) before the return of the QS manuscript, however, he followed text C in this leap-frogging fashion with a further and clearer manuscript, 'QS(D)' or 'D', which took up from C in the middle of chapter 16 (*Of the Fourth Battle*) at the point where it is told that Maidros was delayed by the machinations of Uldor the Accursed (*The Silmarillion* p. 190), and continued somewhat further into chapter 17 (here called *Of Túrin Turamarth or Túrin the Hapless*), as far as the words (referring to Túrin's outlaw band) *and their hands were turned against all who came in their path, Elves, Men, or Orcs* (*The Silmarillion* p. 200). Here the *Quenta Silmarillion* comes to a stop; and it may well be that these last words were written on the 16th of December 1937, and *When Bilbo, son of Bungo of the family of Baggins, prepared to celebrate his seventieth birthday* on the following day.*

When the short passage in changed script at the end of chapter 14 in the QS manuscript (see p. 293) was copied in from text C cannot be determined; my father may have put it in when the manuscript came back to him. But with the beginning of chapter 15 (*The Wolf-hunt of Carcharoth*) the writing in the manuscript changes again and strikingly, to a heavier, more ornate form with a thicker nib; this third script completes the chapter and the story of Beren and Lúthien, and this is effectively the conclusion of the manuscript (a small portion was added later in yet a fourth script).

In fact, chapter 15 was added to the QS manuscript long afterwards, in the time following the completion of *The Lord of the Rings*. I base this assertion on various evidences; in the first place on the script itself, which has close affinity with that of manuscripts undoubtedly belonging to the later time. Further, the draft text C, begun when the QS manuscript went to the publishers, received important additions and alterations which can be dated, for at the end of chapter 15 in C my father noted: 'revised so far, 10 May 1951'. Among these 1951 revisions is the phrase (*The Silmarillion* p. 187) 'the Two Kindreds that were made by Ilúvatar to dwell *in Arda, the Kingdom of Earth amid the innumerable stars*.' This phrase is found also in the later *Ainulindalë*, where a cosmology decisively different from that of the *Ambarkanta* had entered; moreover a note of my father's gives a brief list of 'Alterations in last revision 1951', which includes *Arda* ('Elvish name of Earth = our world'). On this list see p. 338. It was the text of C *with these revisions* that was copied into the QS manuscript; and thus he at last fulfilled (though only to this point) his intention of fourteen years before.

The story can be summarised thus:

(1) A rough draft 'A', in which the telling of the tale of Beren and Lúthien was very amply conceived, was soon abandoned.

(2) The QS-manuscript version of the tale was begun, again in a very full form but less so than in A, and was in turn abandoned quite early in the tale ('QS I').

(3) A rough draft 'B' for the whole story of Beren and Lúthien was completed, and this was the basis for:

---

*As will be seen subsequently (pp. 323–4) a rewriting of the end of the 'Silmarillion' narrative in Q also belongs to this time, and it is possible, though I think it less likely, that this was the last work that my father did before beginning 'the new story about Hobbits'.

(4) A second, more compressed version to stand in the QS manuscript ('QS II'); this was interrupted towards the end of the tale when the manuscript went to the publishers.

(5) An intermediate text 'C', taking up from this point, was continued as a substitute while the QS manuscript was gone, and this completed the story of Beren and Lúthien, extended through the chapter on the Battle of Unnumbered Tears, and went some way into the story of Túrin.

(6) When C became very rough, it was taken over by a text 'D', which beginning in the course of the chapter on the Battle of Unnumbered Tears extended somewhat further into the story of Túrin; this was abandoned when the QS manuscript returned in December 1937.

(7) In 1951 the conclusion of the tale of Beren and Lúthien (chapter 15) was at last added to the QS manuscript.

On a covering page to the 'fuller' version QS I my father wrote: *Fragment of a fuller form of the Geste of Beren and Lúthien told as a separate tale;* and in a letter of November 1949 he said:
The original intention was to tell certain of the included Tales at greater length, whether within the Chronicle [i.e. the *Quenta Sil-marillion*], or as additions. A specimen of what was intended will be seen in the Tale of Lúthien . . .
But, as I have shown, the 'fragment of a fuller form' only became so when it had been rejected as unsuitable in its scale to stand as the version of the story in QS. This is not to say, however, that my father never did really intend to tell the tale as a long prose 'saga'; on the contrary, he greatly wished to. The abandoned draft A and the abandoned QS I are testimony to his reluctance to compress: the story kept overflowing the bounds. When at the end of 1937 he had finally completed a prose version, he must still have felt that even if one day he could get 'The Silmarillion' published, the story would still not be told as he wished to tell it. Thus at the time when he turned again to the *Lay of Leithian* (see III. 390), *The Lord of the Rings* being finished but its publication very doubtful, he embarked also once more on a prose 'saga' of Beren and Lúthien. This is a substantial text, though the story goes no further than the betrayal by Dairon to Thingol of Beren's presence in Doriath, and it is so closely based on the rewritten form of the Lay as to read in places almost as a prose paraphrase of the verse. It was written on the verso pages of the text AB 2 of the *Annals of Beleriand*, and was not known to me when *The Silmarillion* was prepared for publication.

To present these texts would take many pages and involve a great deal of pure repetition in relation to the published version, and I restrict myself here therefore to remarking particular features and to indicating the genesis of chapter 19 in *The Silmarillion*. Essentially, the published text was based on the 'fuller' form, QS I, so far as it goes, and then follows the 'shorter', complete form, QS II. The story was also told, briefly, in the final version of the *Annals of Beleriand*, the *Grey Annals*, and some passages in the published version are derived from that source.

I have mentioned above that the opening page of QS I, the commencement of chapter 12, was retained as the opening of QS II, and I give here the text of that page, for it was much modified and expanded in the published work (pp. 162–3).

Among the tales of sorrow and ruin that come down to us from the darkness of those days there are yet some that are fair in memory, in which amid weeping there is a sound of music, and amid the tears joy, and under the shadow of death light that endureth. And of these histories most fair still in the ears of the Elves is the tale of Beren and Lúthien; for it is sad and joyous, and touches upon mysteries, and it is not ended.*

Of their lives was made the *Lay of Leithian*, Release from Bondage, which is the longest save one of the songs of the Noldor concerning the world of old; but here the tale must be told in fewer words and without song. When [Bëor >] Bregolas was slain, as has been recounted, Barahir his [son >] brother saved King Felagund, and received his ring in token of never-failing friendship. But Barahir would not forsake Dorthonion, and there Morgoth pursued him to the death. At last there remained to him only twelve companions, Beren his son, and the sons of Bregolas, and nine other men. Of these Gorlim son of Angrim was one, a man of valour. But Gorlim was caught by the guile of Sauron the wizard, as the lay tells, and Morgoth wrung from him knowledge of the hiding-place of Barahir; but Gorlim he rewarded with death. Thus Morgoth drew his net about Barahir, and he was taken by surprise and slain with all his companions, save one. For by fortune Beren was not with them at that time, but was hunting alone in the woods, as often was his custom, for thus he gained news of the movement of their foes. But Beren was warned by a vision of Gorlim the unhappy that appeared to him in sleep, and he returned in haste, and yet too late. For his father was already slain, and the carrion-birds arose from the ground as Beren drew near, and sat in the alder-trees, and croaked in mockery. For there was a high tarn among the moors, and beside it Barahir had made his lair.

---

*For the meaning of the words 'and it is not ended' (which should not have been omitted in *The Silmarillion*) see p. 304: the thought underlying the last sentence of the tale is much more explicit in the draft text B.

There Beren buried his father's bones, and raised a cairn of boulders over him, and swore upon it an oath of vengeance.

Gorlim's father Angrim now appears. The words first written 'When Bëor was slain . . . Barahir his son saved King Felagund' are puzzling. The original draft manuscript A had here likewise 'When Bëor and Bregolas were slain . . .' It was said in Q §9 that 'Bëor lived till death with Felagund', but in §10 that Bëor was slain in the Battle of Sudden Fire; this I took to be a (surprising) inconsistency within Q (IV. 179). In QS §131 (and in AB 2, annal 250) Bëor died of old age, five years before the Battle of Sudden Fire, and in his death 'the Elves saw for the first time the death of weariness, and they grieved for the short span allotted to mankind'; thus the inconsistency appears again and still more surprisingly in this version. But the corrections to QS here were made, almost certainly, at the time of composition.

It is said here that 'Gorlim was caught by the guile of Sauron the wizard, as the lay tells, and Morgoth wrung from him knowledge of the hiding-place of Barahir.' In the much fuller draft A the story was still almost exactly as in the *Lay of Leithian* (III. 162–4): Gorlim was all but caught as he looked through the window of the house at the figure of his wife Eilinel, he returned to his companions but said nothing, and finally, with a far more deliberate treachery than in the later story, yielded himself to the servants of Morgoth, who took him to Angband. A minor development is that whereas in the Lay the house in which he thought he saw Eilinel was not his own, it is now told that he went often to his own deserted home, and Morgoth's spies knew this (cf. the *Lay of Leithian Recommenced*, III. 337). More important, in A Morgoth 'revealed to Gorlim that he had seen but a phantom devised by the wizardry of Sauron to entrap him', which again advances the story to that of the rewritten Lay, where the phantom was expressly made by Sauron (III. 339, and see III. 348). I see no reason to think that the brief sentence which is all that is told of Gorlim in the QS version reflects a story different in any way from that in A. Years later, when as mentioned above (p. 295) my father once more attempted a full prose version of the story, he went back to A and emended it in preparation for this new work. The story now entered that Gorlim was captured on the first occasion that he saw the image of Eilinel through the window; but he was still taken to Angband, and addressed by Morgoth himself. This stage is represented in the first version of the rewritten Lay at this point (see III. 348). Finally, pencilled alterations to A changed Angband to Sauron's camp, and Morgoth to Sauron, and so reached the final story, as in the second version of the rewritten Lay.

When I composed the text of the opening of chapter 19 in *The Silmarillion* I did not at all foresee the possibility of the publication of the *Lay of Leithian*, and I wished to include the story of Gorlim, which is virtually excluded from QS. The second paragraph of the chapter, from

'Now the forest of Dorthonion rose southward into mountainous moors', was taken from the *Grey Annals*; and for the story of Gorlim that follows I used the text of A – in its final form, as just described.

In the story of Beren's solitary life on Dorthonion, his flight south over the Mountains of Terror, and his meeting with Lúthien – as far as 'though the time was brief', *The Silmarillion* p. 166 – the two QS versions are not in fact greatly different in length, and here I interwove some elements from the 'shorter' version, QS II; but from the point where Thingol learns of Beren's presence in the forest QS I was followed to its end at the words 'and Celegorm and Curufin said nothing, but they smiled and went from the halls' (*The Silmarillion* p. 170), for all of this narrative is in QS II compressed into two paragraphs. Thereafter QS II was followed to the end of the story.

The QS version(s) of 'Beren and Lúthien' are thus to be found in chapter 19 of the published work, and are not given here; but significant points in which the QS text(s) were altered editorially must be mentioned. I list these in order of their occurrence, with references to the pages of *The Silmarillion* (hardback edition).

*Tarn Aeluin* (pp. 162–3): introduced from later sources (*Grey Annals*, rewritten Lay, etc.)

*Rivil's Well* and the *Fen of Serech* (p. 163): introduced from later sources.

*Noldor* for *Gnomes* (p. 164 and throughout, wherever *Gnomes* appears in QS).

*Gorgoroth*, *Ered Gorgoroth* (p. 164). In QS I the latter is *Ered-orgoroth*, and in A and QS II *Ered-'orgoroth* (beside *Gorgoroth* standing alone). As I understand the matter, this variation is due to the phenomenon in 'Exilic Noldorin' (i.e. the language of the Noldor in Middle-earth, in exile from Valinor) called 'Initial Variation of Consonants', whereby a consonant at the beginning of the second element of a compounded word (or of the second word in two words standing in a very close syntactic relation, as noun and article) underwent the same change as it would when standing in ordinary medial position. For example, the original voiceless stops *p, t, k* remained in Exilic Noldorin unchanged initially before vowels, but were voiced to *b, d, g* medially; so *tâl* 'foot' but *i·dâl* 'the foot', or *Thorondor* (*thoron* + *taur* 'king'). Medially, original voiced stop -*g*- became 'opened' to -*ʒ*-, which then weakened and disappeared; in this case therefore the 'initial variation' is between *g* and nil, the lost consonant being represented by a sign called *gasdil* ('stopgap', see the *Etymologies*, stem DIL), transcribed as '. Thus *galaʒ* 'tree', *i·alaʒ* 'the tree'; *Gorgoroth*, *Ered-'orgoroth*. (This was an old linguistic conception, as is seen from forms given in the original 'Gnomish dictionary', as *Balrog* but *i'Malrog*, from an initial consonant combination *mb*- (I. 250).) In post-*Lord of the Rings* texts the form is *Ered Orgoroth* (-*ath*), beside *Gorgoroth* (-*ath*), but in a couple of cases the form after *Ered* was apparently emended to *Gorgoroth*.

*the rising of the Moon* (p. 164) is an error; all the texts have *raising*.

*Dungortheb* (p. 164): later form for QS *Dungorthin*; again on p. 176.

*Ungoliant* (p. 164): introduced for agreement with the occurrence of the name in *The Lord of the Rings*; QS *Ungoliantë*.

*And he passed through the mazes that Melian wove about the kingdom of Thingol, for a great doom lay upon him* (pp. 164-5). QS I has here: 'he could not have found the way, if his fate had not so decreed. Neither could he have passed the mazes that Melian wove about Doriath, unless she had willed it; but she foresaw many things that were hidden from the Elves.' QS II is similar. The reason for the change in *The Silmarillion* is Melian's earlier foretelling to Galadriel that 'one of Men, even of Bëor's house, shall indeed come, and the Girdle of Melian shall not restrain him, for doom greater than my power shall send him' (*ibid.* p. 144), a passage introduced from the *Grey Annals*; the sentence cited above was taken from the same source.

*in the Grey-elven tongue* (p. 165). QS I has 'in the speech of Beleriand', with a marginal note 'quoth Ælfwine'.

*But Daeron the minstrel also loved Lúthien, and he espied her meetings with Beren, and betrayed them to Thingol* (p. 166). As noticed earlier, Dairon was omitted from QS I (he appears in QS II but much later in the story). In view however of a pencilled note on QS I: *Dairon*, with a mark of insertion, I introduced this sentence (derived from the *Grey Annals*). QS I has here simply: 'But it came to pass that the coming of Beren became known to Thingol, and he was wroth'; similarly in QS II.

*'Who are you,' said the King* (p. 166). Here and subsequently throughout, 'you', 'your' is substituted for QS 'thou', 'thy' (and 'ye' plural), except in Lúthien's words to Sauron, p. 175.

*the badge of Finarfin* (p. 167): QS *the badge of Finrod*.

*the fate of Arda* (p. 167): QS *the fate of the world*.

*Talath Dirnen* (p. 168): later form for QS *Dalath Dirnen* – the first occurrence of the Elvish name of the Guarded Plain.

*Taur-en-Faroth* (p. 168): later form for QS *Taur-na-Faroth*.

*Finrod Felagund* (p. 169): QS *Felagund*; again on p. 174.

*and he knew that the oath he had sworn was come upon him for his death, as long before he had foretold to Galadriel* (p. 169). Added from the *Grey Annals*; the reference is to *The Silmarillion* p. 130, where Felagund said to Galadriel: 'An oath I too shall swear, and must be free to fulfil it, and go into darkness' (also derived from the *Grey Annals*).

*Celegorm* (p. 169): QS *Celegorn*, and subsequently.

*Finarfin's son* (p. 169): QS *Finrod's son*; again on p. 170.

*Then Celegorm arose amid the throng* (p. 169). In QS this is followed by 'golden was his long hair'. In the Lay at this point (line 1844) Celegorm has 'gleaming hair'; his Old English name was *Cynegrim*

*Fægerfeax* ('Fair-hair'), IV. 213. The phrase was removed in *The Silmarillion* text on account of the dark hair of the Noldorin princes other than in 'the golden house of Finarfin' (see I. 44); but he remains 'Celegorm the fair' in *The Silmarillion* p. 60.

*Edrahil* (p. 170). This name was taken from the *Grey Annals*; in QS the chief of those faithful to Felagund is *Enedrion*.

*Taur-nu-Fuin* (p. 170): later form for QS *Taur-na-Fuin* (and subsequently).

Citation from the *Lay of Leithian* (p. 171). QS (where the narrative is now only that of the 'shorter' version, QS II) has: 'Sauron had the mastery, and he stripped from them their disguise.' The introduction of a passage from the Lay was justified, or so I thought, by the passage cited later in QS (p. 178).

*Tol-in-Gaurhoth* (p. 172): later form for QS *Tol-na-Gaurhoth*.

*but she sought the aid of Daeron, and he betrayed her purpose to the King* (p. 172). An addition, derived like that on p. 166 from the *Grey Annals*; QS has only 'Thingol discovering her thought was filled with fear and wonder.'

*the mountains of Aman* (p. 174): QS *the Mountains of the Gods*.

*the fates of our kindreds are apart* (p. 174). In QS this is followed by: 'Yet perchance even that sorrow shall in the end be healed.'

*in Tol-in-Gaurhoth, whose great tower he himself had built* (p. 174) was an editorial addition.

*fairest and most beloved of the house of Finwë* (p. 174) was added from the *Grey Annals*.

*Ered Wethrin* (p. 175): later form for QS *Eredwethion*.

*unless thou yield to me the mastery of thy tower* (p. 175). In QS this is followed by: 'and reveal the spell that bindeth stone to stone.' A little further on, the words *and the spell was loosed that bound stone to stone* were an addition to the QS text. This rearrangement was mistaken. (The draft text B has here: 'Then lest he be forced from the body unwillingly, which is a dire pain to such spirits, he yielded himself. And Lúthien and Huan wrested from him the keys of the tower, and the spell that bound stone to stone.')

*and it was clean again* (p. 176). The passage following this in *The Silmarillion* was an editorial rewriting of QS, which has:

> and it was clean again, and ever after remained inviolate; for Sauron came never back thither. There lies still the green grave of Inglor, Finrod's son, fairest of all the princes of the Elves, unless that land is changed and broken, or foundered under destroying seas. But Inglor walks with Finrod his father among his kinsfolk in the light of the Blessed Realm, and it is not written that he has ever returned to Middle-earth.

Cf. the *Lay of Leithian* lines 2871–7; and for 'the trees of Eldamar' in the rewriting see the rewritten Lay, III. 358 lines 20–1.

*In that time Celebrimbor the son of Curufin repudiated the deeds of his father, and remained in Nargothrond* (p. 176). This was an editorial addition derived from a late note.

*Maedhros* (p. 176): later form for QS *Maidros*. After 'where Maidros their brother dwelt' QS has: 'In the days of the Siege the high road had run that way, and it was still passable with speed, since it lay close,' &c. I do not now recollect why this change was made. This is the first reference to a highroad running from East to West.

*Anfauglith* (p. 178): QS *Fauglith*.

*There Beren slunk in wolf's form beneath his throne* (p. 180): an addition, taken from the *Grey Annals*; cf. the Lay, lines 3939–43.

*She was not daunted by his eyes* (p. 180). QS has: 'she alone of all things in Middle-earth could not be daunted by his eyes.'

*with wings swifter than the wind* (p. 182). The draft text B (see p. 293) has at this point: 'Thorondor led them, and the others were Lhandroval (Wide-wing) and Gwaewar his vassal.' In the following text C, also of 1937, this became: 'Thorondor was their leader; and with him were his mightiest vassals, wide-winged Lhandroval, and Gwaewar lord of the wind.' This was emended (in 1951, see p. 294) to 'Gwaihir the lord of storm', and in this form the passage is found in the QS manuscript. It was omitted in *The Silmarillion* on account of the passage in *The Return of the King* (VI. 4): 'There came Gwaihir the Windlord, and Landroval his brother . . . *mightiest of the descendants of old Thorondor*, who built his eyries in the inaccessible peaks of the Encircling Mountains when Middle-earth was young.' At the time, I did not understand the nature and dating of the end of QS. It now appears that there was no reason to suppress the names; in fact, it seems that *Gwaewar* was changed to *Gwaihir* to bring it into accord with *The Lord of the Rings* – however this is to be interpreted.

*Gondolin the fair where Turgon dwelt* (p. 182). This is followed in QS by: 'But it is said in song that her tears falling from on high as she passed came like silver raindrops on the plain, and there a fountain sprang to life: the Fountain of Tinúviel, Eithel Nínui, most healing water until it withered in the flame.' This passage, found already in the draft text C, should not have been omitted.

*Crissaegrim* (p. 182). The draft texts B and C, and also the QS manuscript as it was written, have here *Gochressiel* (see QS §147 and commentary); in QS it was emended (as also in QS §147) to *Crisaegrim*.

*Daeron* (p. 183). *Dairon* (so spelt) here first appears in the QS version.

*and among the great in Arda* (p. 184). An addition, taken from the *Grey Annals*.

*Beren Erchamion* (p. 185): QS *Beren Gamlost; Beren Camlost* (p. 186): QS *Beren Gamlost;* but at the occurrence on p. 184, where the name stands alone, QS also has *Camlost*. The C/G variation is found also in the drafts B and C, and is another example of the 'initial variation of consonants' referred to in the note on *Gorgoroth* above (original voiceless stop *k* > *g* medially). But here also, as in the case of *Ered Orgoroth*, late changes altered *Beren Gamlost* to *Beren Camlost*. – *Erchamion* is original (and appears already in the draft B) at its occurrence on p. 183, and is the first appearance of the name other than by later emendation.

*They bore back Beren Camlost* (p. 186). At this point my father entered (later) a new chapter-heading in the QS manuscript: 16 *The Song of Lúthien in Mandos*. In C chapter 16 is *Of the Fourth Battle*.

*the Two Kindreds that were made by Ilúvatar to dwell in Arda, the Kingdom of Earth amid the innumerable stars* (p. 187). This is original, deriving from QS as revised in 1951 (see p. 294).

*Because of her labours and her sorrow* (p. 187): QS 'because she was the daughter of Melian, and because of her labours and her sorrow'; see pp. 304–5.

This is not an exhaustive list of all the alterations made to the QS version(s) in the published text, but it includes all changes in names, and all omissions and additions of any substance. I shall not here go into the question of the justifiability of constructing a text from different sources. I hope that it will be possible later to present the major texts from the post-*Lord of the Rings* period, on the basis of which and in relation to what has thus far been published almost every detail of the 'constructed' text will be determinable. The tale of Beren and Lúthien is only a small and relatively very simple element in that construction, and is far from providing sufficient evidence on which to judge either it or its justification. I will say, however, that I now regret certain of the changes made to this tale.

It is proper to mention that here as elsewhere almost every substantial change was discussed with Guy Kay, who worked with me in 1974–5 on the preparation of *The Silmarillion*. He indeed made many suggestions for the construction of the text (such as, in the tale of Beren and Lúthien, the introduction of a passage from the *Lay of Leithian*), and proposed solutions to problems arising in the making of a composite narrative – in some cases of major significance to the structure, as will I hope be shown in a later book. The responsibility for the final published form rests of course wholly with me.

The more important differences between the narratives of the *Lay of Leithian* and *The Silmarillion* have been sufficiently discussed in Vol. III, and I make no further general analysis here. Many other small divergences will be seen in a close comparison of the two works. There are however certain particular points in the QS version and the preparatory drafts that remain to be mentioned.

In QS I, Lúthien's song at the birth of spring (*The Silmarillion* p. 165) is likened to the song of the lark that 'rises from the gates of night and pours its voice among the dying stars, *seeing the sun behind the walls of the world*.' This self-evidently contradicts the *Ambarkanta*; but a possible explanation is that my father was in fact thinking, not of the *Ilurambar* beyond which is the Void, but of the Walls of the Sun, the mountain-range in the furthest East answering to the Mountains of Valinor in the West: see the *Ambarkanta*, IV. 236–7, 239, and the map of the world, IV. 249. The lark flying high in the early dawn sees the unrisen sun beyond the eastern mountains. On the other hand this is not the only place where the expression 'the Walls of the World' is used in a way that seems anomalous in relation to the *Ambarkanta*: see IV. 253, and the commentary on QS §9.

In Q (IV. 113), when the knife (unnamed) which Beren took from Curufin snapped as he tried to cut a second Silmaril from the Iron Crown, it is called 'the knife of the treacherous Dwarves'; cf. the Lay, lines 4160–1: 'The dwarvish steel of cunning blade / by treacherous smiths of Nogrod made'. The absence of this in QS may be significant, but it is more likely due merely to compression. In the draft B 'the knife of the Dwarfs snapped', which hints at the idea; C has simply 'the knife snapped'. – The name *Angrist* of the knife is found in B, but it is not there ascribed to Telchar; this is first found in QS (*The Silmarillion* p. 177), where also Telchar becomes a Dwarf of Nogrod, not of Belegost as in Q (named as the maker of the Dragon-helm, IV. 118).

Of much interest is the development of the conclusion of the tale (*The Silmarillion* pp. 186–7, from 'Thus ended the Quest of the Silmaril; but the Lay of Leithian, Release from Bondage, does not end.') The original draft B, written in a rapid scrawl, was already near to the final form as far as 'Manwë sought counsel in his inmost thought, where the will of Ilúvatar was revealed.' Text C, almost an exact copy of B to this point, was emended long after (1951) to produce the form in the QS manuscript, but a footnote to the sentence beginning 'But the spirit of Lúthien fell down into darkness' belongs to the earlier time (and was not taken up into the final text):

> Though some have said that Melian summoned Thorondor and bade him bear Lúthien living to Valinor, claiming that she had a part in the divine race of the Gods.

With this cf. S §10 (IV. 25): 'Some songs say that Lúthien went even over the Grinding Ice, aided by the power of her divine mother, Melian, to Mandos' halls and won him back', and Q §10 (IV. 115): 'though some songs say that Melian summoned Thorndor, and he bore [Lúthien] living unto Valinor.' – The text of B continues:

And this was the choice that he decreed for Beren and Lúthien. They should dwell now in Valinor until the world's end in bliss, but in the end Beren and Lúthien must each go unto the fate appointed to their kind, when all things are changed: and of the mind of Ilúvatar concerning Men Manwë kn[ows] not. Or they might return unto Middle-earth without certitude of joy or life; then Lúthien should become mortal even as Beren, and subject to a second death, and in the end she should leave the earth for ever and her beauty become only a memory of song. And this doom they chose, that thus, whatsoever sorrow might lie before them, their fates might be joined, and their paths lead together beyond the confines of the world. So it was that alone of the Eldalië Lúthien died and left the world long ago: yet by her have the Two Kindreds been joined, and she is the foremother of many. For her line is not yet extinguished, though the world is changed, and the Eldalië honour still the children of Men. And though these are grown proud and strong, and often are blind, but the Elves are diminished, they cease not to haunt the paths of Men, or to seek converse with those that go apart, for haply such are descended from Lúthien, whom they have lost.

We meet here the conception of the 'choice of fate' by Beren and Lúthien before Mandos. In the earlier accounts there was no choice. In the old *Tale of Tinúviel* – where Beren was an Elf – the fate of Beren and Lúthien was the simple decree of Mandos (II. 40); and in Q (IV. 115) it is the same, though the decree is different, since Beren was now a Man. I have discussed the meaning of these passages at some length (II. 59–60; IV. 63–4, 190–1). In the present text, if the first choice were accepted Beren and Lúthien must finally part, even though that parting is cast into a future indefinitely remote – the end of the world; and that parting would proceed from the different principles of their being, leading inevitably to a different final destiny or doom. Beren could not *finally* escape the necessity imposed upon by him his 'kind', the necessity of leaving the Circles of the World, the Gift of Ilúvatar that cannot be refused, though he may dwell – by unheard-of privilege, as an unheard-of reward – in Valinor until the End. The union of Beren and Lúthien 'beyond the world' could only be achieved by acceptance of the second choice, whereby Lúthien herself should be permitted to change her 'kind', and 'die indeed'.

In the following text C this passage was entirely recast, virtually to the form in which it was afterwards written into the QS manuscript. Here the choices are imposed on Lúthien alone (in the margin of QS is written *The Choices of Lúthien*), and they are changed; for the possibility of Beren accompanying Lúthien to the Blessed Realm is not open. The choice becomes therefore in a sense simpler: Lúthien may leave Beren *now*, and their fates be sundered for ever, *now*; or she may remain with him 'for ever', by becoming mortal, changing her nature and her destiny.

The form of the first choice begins in C: 'She, being the daughter of Melian, and because of her sorrow, should be released from Mandos', becoming in QS: 'She, because she was the daughter of Melian, and because of her labours and her sorrow, should be released from Mandos.' This takes up the idea in the footnote to C cited above (p. 303): Melian claimed that Lúthien 'had a part in the divine race of the Gods'. The words 'because she was the daughter of Melian' were regrettably omitted from the *Silmarillion* text.

One other point may be noticed in the passage cited from the B text (p. 303). It is said there that 'of the mind of Ilúvatar concerning Men Manwë knows not.' With this cf. QS §86: 'Mandos under Ilúvatar alone *save Manwë* knows whither they [Men] go after the time of recollection in those silent halls beside the Western Sea.' In the passage of Q from which this derives (IV. 100) it is said that 'Mandos under Ilúvatar knew *alone* whither they went.'

Text B continues on from 'Lúthien, whom they have lost' as follows:

But yet Beren and Lúthien abode together for a while, as living man and woman; and Mandos gave unto them a long span of life. But they dwelt not in Doriath, and taking up their mortal forms they departed and wandered forth, knowing neither thirst nor hunger, and came beyond the river into Ossiriand, Land of Seven Streams. There they abode, and Gwerth-i-Cuina the Gnomes named their dwelling, the Land of the Dead that Live, and thereafter no mortal man spoke with Beren son of Barahir.

In C this passage becomes the opening paragraph of chapter 16, *Of the Fourth Battle* (and is so treated in *The Silmarillion*, where it opens chapter 20, *Of the Fifth Battle*), but it was not altered from B in any significant way. In the QS manuscript it was entered on a final page, in yet a fourth script, careful but much less ornate, and here it is again the conclusion of the previous chapter and the end of the tale of Beren and Lúthien. In QS it takes this form:

It is said that Beren and Lúthien returned to the northern lands of Middle-earth, and dwelt together for a time as living man and woman; for taking up again their mortal form in Doriath, they went forth alone, fearing neither thirst nor hunger, and they passed beyond the rivers into Ossiriand, and abode there in the green isle, Tol-galen, in the midst of Adurant, until all tidings of them ceased. Therefore the Noldor afterwards called that land Gyrth-i-Guinar, the country of the Dead that Live, and no mortal man spoke ever again with Beren son of Barahir; and whether the second span of his life was brief or long is not known to Elves or Men, for none saw Beren and Lúthien leave the world or marked where at last their bodies lay.

The longer form that appears in *The Silmarillion* was 'integrated' with the text of the *Grey Annals*. In QS, chapter 16 then opens, with the title *Of the Union of Maedros* (despite the insertion of a chapter-heading 16 *The Song of Lúthien in Mandos*, p. 302); but after the words 'In those days Maedros son of Fëanor lifted up his heart' my father laid down his pen, and the manuscript ends there.

In B and C it is said, as it had been in Q (IV. 115), that the span of the second lives of Beren and Lúthien was long.* In the *Annals of Beleriand* the first death of Beren took place, according to the latest chronology, in 465, and the final departure of Beren and Lúthien is recorded under the year 503. This date is found again in post-*Lord of the Rings* versions of the *Tale of Years*; and on this account the words 'whether the second span of his life was brief or long is not known to Elves or Men' were omitted from *The Silmarillion*. But they should not have been. It is also said in the annal for 503 that *their deathday is not known*: the annal records as fact the coming of the messenger to Dior in Doriath by night, bearing the Silmaril on the Necklace of the Dwarves, but as surmise the saying of the Elves that Beren and Lúthien must be dead, else the Silmaril would not have come to their son. I think now that this is how the words of QS are to be interpreted; the belief that the coming of the Silmaril to Dior was a sign of their deaths is simply not referred to.

The name *Gwerth-i-Cuina* has appeared in later emendations to Q, and in an emendation to the Eastward Extension of the first Map (IV. 233). The placing of the dwelling of Beren and Lúthien after their return on the isle of Tol-galen in the river Adurant appears in an addition to QS §114 (see the commentary).

## 16  OF THE FOURTH BATTLE: NÍRNAITH ARNEDIAD

The two manuscripts of this chapter have been described on pp. 293–4: the first, QS(C), was the intermediate text begun while QS was away in November–December 1937, and this gives the whole of chapter 16, while the second, QS(D), of the same period, begins some way through it. To the point where D takes up, therefore, C (rough but legible) is the only text. As noted above, in C the chapter opens with the paragraph concerning the second lives of Beren and Lúthien, whereas the QS manuscript includes it at the end of chapter 15 and begins 16 with the Union of Maidros, breaking off after the first words. I recommence the paragraph-numbers here from §1.

### The Union of Maidros

§1  'Tis said that Beren and Lúthien returned into the lands of the North, and abode together for a while, as living man and

---

*In another passage of Q (IV. 134) the land where they dwelt after their return had only a 'brief hour of loveliness', just as in the *Tale of the Nauglafring* (II. 240) 'upon Beren and Tinúviel fell swiftly that doom of mortality that Mandos had spoken.'

woman; and the span of their second life was long. But they did not dwell in Doriath; for taking up their mortal form they departed thence and went forth alone, fearing neither thirst nor hunger. And they passed beyond the rivers into Ossiriand, the Land of Seven Streams, and dwelt among the Green-elves secretly. Therefore the Gnomes called that land Gwerth-i-Cuina, the Land of the Dead that Live; and thereafter no mortal man spoke with Beren son of Barahir.

§2   But in those days Maidros son of Fëanor lifted up his heart, perceiving that Morgoth was not unassailable; for the deeds of Beren and Lúthien and the breaking of the towers of Sauron were sung in many songs throughout Beleriand. Yet Morgoth would destroy them all, one by one, if they could not again unite, and make a new league and common council. Therefore he planned the Union of Maidros, and he planned wisely.

§3   For he renewed friendship with Fingon in the West, and they acted thereafter in concert. Maidros summoned again to his aid the Dark-elves from the South, and the Swarthy Men were gathered together, and he sallied from Himring in force. At the same time Fingon issued from Hithlum. For a while the Gnomes had victory again, and the Orcs were driven out of the northward regions of Beleriand, and hope was renewed. Morgoth withdrew before them and called back his servants; for he was aware of all that was done, and took counsel against the uprising of the Gnomes. He sent forth many spies and emissaries, secret or disguised, among Elves and Men, and especially they came to the Easterlings, the Swarthy Men, and to the sons of Ulfang. The smithies of Nogrod and Belegost were busy in those days, making mail and sword and spear for many armies; and the Dwarfs in that time became possessed of much of the wealth and jewelry of Elves and Men, though they went not to war themselves. 'For we do not know the right causes of this quarrel,' they said, 'and we favour neither side – until one hath the mastery.'

§4   Great and well-armed was the host of Maidros in the East. In the West all the strength of Hithlum, Gnomes and Men, were ready to his summons: Fingon and Huor and Húrin were their chiefs. Then Turgon, thinking that maybe the hour of deliverance was at hand, came forth himself unlooked for from Gondolin; and he brought a great army and encamped upon the plain before the opening of the western pass in sight of the walls of Hithlum. There was joy among the people of Fingon his brother, seeing their kinsfolk that had long been hidden.

§5   Yet the oath of Fëanor and the evil deeds that it had wrought did injury to the design of Maidros, and he had less aid than should have been. Orodreth would not march from Nargothrond at the word of any son of Fëanor, because of the deeds of Celegorn and Curufin. Thence came only a small company, whom Orodreth suffered to go, since they could not endure to be idle when their kinsfolk were gathering for war. Gwindor was their leader, son of Guilin, a very valiant prince; but they took the badge of the house of Fingolfin, and marched beneath the banners of Fingon, and came never back, save one.

§6   From Doriath came little help. For Maidros and his brethren, being constrained by their oath, had before sent to Thingol and reminded him with haughty words of their claim, summoning him to yield to them the Silmaril, or become their enemy. Melian counselled him to surrender the jewel, and perchance he would have done so, but their words were proud and threatening, and he was wroth, thinking of the anguish of Lúthien and the blood of Beren whereby the jewel had been won, despite the malice of Celegorn and Curufin. And every day that he looked upon the jewel, the more his heart desired to keep it for ever. Such was its power. Therefore he sent back the messengers of Maidros with scornful words. Maidros answered naught, for he had now begun to devise the league and union of the Elves; but Celegorn and Curufin vowed openly to slay Thingol and destroy his folk, if they came victorious from war, and the jewel were not surrendered of free will. For this reason Thingol fortified the marches of his realm, and went not to war, nor any out of Doriath save Mablung, and Beleg who could not be restrained.

§7   The treacherous shaft of Curufin that wounded Beren was remembered among Men. Therefore of the folk of Haleth that dwelt in Brethil only the half came forth, and they went not to join Maidros, but came rather to Fingon and Turgon in the West.

§8   Having gathered at length all the strength that he could, Maidros appointed a day, and sent word to Fingon and Turgon. Upon the East was raised the standard of Maidros, and to it came all the folk of Fëanor, and they were many; and the Dark-elves of the South; and of the Green-elves of Ossiriand many companies; and the tribes and battalions of the Easterlings with the sons of Bór and Ulfang. Upon the West was the standard of Fingon, and to it were gathered the armies of Hithlum, both Gnomes and Men; and Turgon with the host of Gondolin; to which was added such strength as came from the Falas, and from Brethil, and from

Nargothrond; and they waited upon the borders of Dor-na-Fauglith, looking for the signal of the advancing banners from the East.

[At this point the manuscript D takes up, and is followed here. It is a very close reworking of C, taking up the preparatory emendations made to the earlier text but scarcely developing it except in small stylistic detail.]

§9   But Maidros was delayed upon the road by the machinations of Uldor the Accursed, son of Ulfang; and continually the emissaries of Morgoth went among the camps: and there were thrall-Gnomes or things in Elvish form, and they spread foreboding of evil and the suspicion of treason among all who would listen to them.

§10   Long the armies waited in the West, and fear of treachery grew in their thoughts when Maidros tarried. The hot hearts of Fingon and Turgon became impatient. Therefore they sent their heralds forth upon the plain of Fauglith, and their silver trumpets were blown, and they summoned the hosts of Morgoth to come out.

§11   Then Morgoth sent a force, great and yet not too great. Fingon was minded to attack it from the woods at the feet of Erydwethion, where the most of his strength was hid. But Húrin spake against it. Therefore Morgoth, seeing that they wavered, led forth the herald of Fingon that he had wrongfully taken prisoner, and he slew him upon the plain, and sent back the others with his head. Thereupon the wrath of Fingon was kindled to flame, and his army leaped forth in sudden onslaught; and ere Turgon could restrain them, a great part also of his host joined in the battle. The light of the drawing of the swords of the Noldor was like a sudden fire kindled in a field of reeds.

§12   This was indeed as Morgoth designed; but it is said that he had not reckoned the true number of his enemies' array, nor measured rightly their valour, and almost his plan went astray. Ere the army that he sent forth could be strengthened, it was overwhelmed; for it was assailed suddenly from West and South; and that day there was a greater slaughter of the servants of Morgoth than had yet been achieved. Loud rang the trumpets. The banners of Fingon were raised before the very walls of Angband. It is told that Gwindor son of Guilin and the folk of Nargothrond were in the front of the battle, and they burst through the gates, and slew the Orcs upon the stairs of Angband, and fear came upon Morgoth on his deep throne. But in the end

Gwindor and his men were taken or slain, for no help came to them. By other secret doors in the mountains of Thangorodrim Morgoth had let issue forth his main host that he had held in waiting; and Fingon and the army of Hithlum were beaten back from the walls.

§13 Then in the plain there began that Battle which is called Nírnaith Arnediad, Unnumbered Tears, for no song or tale can contain all the grief of that day, and the voices of those that sing of it are turned to mourning. The host of Fingon retreated with great loss over the sands of Dor-na-Fauglith, and Hundor son of Haleth was slain in the rearguard, and with him fell most of the Men of Brethil and came never back to the woods. And Glorwendil, daughter of Hador and wife of Hundor, died of grief in that unhappy year. But the Orcs came between Fingon and the passes of Erydwethion that led into Hithlum; therefore he withdrew towards the vale of Sirion. Before the entrance of that valley, upon the borders of Taur-na-Fuin, there remained still in hiding a great part of the host of Turgon; and Turgon now sounded his horns, and came forth in might with help unlooked for, and many of the Orcs, being caught between the two armies, were destroyed.

§14 Then hope was renewed in the hearts of the Elves. And in that hour the trumpets of Maidros were heard coming from the East, and the banners of the Sons of Fëanor and their allies came up on the flank of the Enemy. And some have said that even now the Elves might have won the day, had all been faithful; for the Orcs wavered, and their onslaught was stayed, and already some were turning in flight.

§15 But even as the vanguard of Maidros came upon the Orcs, Morgoth let loose his last strength, and hell was emptied. There came wolves and serpents, and there came Balrogs one thousand, and there came Glómund the Father of Dragons. And the strength and terror of the Worm were now grown very great; and Elves and Men withered before him. Thus Morgoth hindered the joining of the hosts of the Elves; yet he would not have achieved this, neither with Balrog nor Dragon, had the captains of the Easterlings remained true. Many of these men now turned and fled; but the sons of Ulfang went over to the side of Morgoth, and they fell upon the rear of Maidros and wrought confusion. From that day the hearts of the Elves were estranged from Men, save only from those of the Three Houses, the peoples of Hador, and Bëor, and Haleth; for the sons of Bór, Boromir, Borlas, and Borthandos, who alone among the Easterlings proved true at need, all perished in that battle, and they left no heirs. But the sons of Ulfang reaped not the reward that Morgoth had promised them; for Cranthir slew Uldor the Accursed, the leader in treason, and Ulfast and Ulwarth were slain by the sons of Bór, ere they themselves fell.

§16   Thus the design of Morgoth was fulfilled in a manner after his own heart; for Men took the lives of Men, and betrayed the Elves, and fear and hatred were aroused among those who should have been united against him. And the host of Maidros, assailed in front and rear, was dispersed and was driven from the battle eastward; and the Gorge of Aglon was filled with Orcs, and the Hill of Himring garrisoned by the soldiers of Angband, and the gates of the land were in the power of Morgoth. But fate saved the Sons of Fëanor, and though all were wounded none were slain. Yet their arms were scattered, and their people diminished, and their league broken; and they took to a wild and woodland life beneath the feet of Eredlindon, mingling with the Dark-elves, bereft of their power and glory of old.

§17   In the west of the battle Fingon fell, and flame sprang from his helm when it was cloven. He was overborne by the Balrogs and beaten to the earth, and his white banners were trodden underfoot. But Húrin and Huor his brother, and the men of the House of Hador, stood firm, and the Orcs could not yet gain the pass of Sirion. Thus was the treachery of Uldor redressed. The last stand of Húrin is the most renowned of the deeds of Men among the Elves; for he held the rear while the remnant of the hosts of the West withdrew from the battle. Few came ever back over Eredwethion to Hithlum; but Turgon mustered all that remained of the folk of Gondolin, and such of Fingon's folk as he could gather; and he escaped down Sirion into the dales and mountains, and was hidden from the eyes of Morgoth. Neither Elf nor Man nor spy of Angband knew whither he had gone, nor found the hidden stronghold until the day of Tuor son of Huor. Thus the victory of Morgoth was marred, and he was wroth.

§18   But the Orcs now surrounded the valiant Men of Hithlum like a great tide about a lonely rock. Huor fell pierced with a venomed arrow, and all the children of Hador were slain about him in a heap, until Húrin alone was left. Then he cast away his shield and wielded his axe two-handed; and it is said that standing alone he slew one hundred of the Orcs. At length he was taken alive by Morgoth's command, for in this way Morgoth thought to do him more evil than by death. Therefore his servants grasped

Húrin with their hands, and though he slew them, their numbers
were ever renewed, until at last he fell buried beneath them, and
they clung to him like leeches. Then binding him they dragged
him with mockery to Angband.

§19   Great was the triumph of Morgoth. The bodies of his
enemies that were slain he let pile in a great mound in the midst of
the plain; and it was named Hauð-na-Dengin, the Hill of Slain.
But grass came there and grew green upon that hill alone in all the
desert that Morgoth made; and no Orc thereafter trod upon the
earth beneath which the swords of the Gnomes crumbled into rust.
The realm of Fingon was no more, and the Sons of Fëanor wandered as leaves before the wind. To Hithlum none of the men of
Hador's house returned, nor any tidings of the battle and the fate
of their lords. But Morgoth sent thither Men who were under his
dominion, swarthy Easterlings; and he shut them in that land and
forbade them to leave it, and such was all the reward that he gave
them: to plunder and harass the old and the children and womenfolk of Hador's people. The remnant of the Elves of Hithlum he
took to the mines of Angband, and they became his thralls, save
some few that eluded him and wandered wild in the woods.

§20   But the Orcs went freely through all the North and came
ever further southward into Beleriand. Doriath yet remained, and
Nargothrond was hidden; but Morgoth gave small heed to them,
either because he knew little of them, or because their hour was
not yet come in the deep purposes of his malice. But the thought of
Turgon troubled him greatly; for Turgon came of the mighty
house of Fingolfin and was now by right the lord of all the
Gnomes. And Morgoth feared and hated most the house of
Fingolfin, both because they had scorned him in Valinor, and
because of the wounds that Fingolfin had given him in battle.

§21   Húrin was now brought before Morgoth, and defied him;
and he was chained and set in torment. But Morgoth remembered
that treachery, and the fear of treachery, alone would work the
final ruin of the Gnomes, and he thought to make use of Húrin.
Therefore he came to him where he lay in pain, and he offered to
him honour and freedom and both power and wealth, if he would
accept service in his armies and would lead a host against Turgon,
or even if he would reveal where that king had his secret stronghold. For he had learned that Húrin knew the secret of Turgon,
but kept it silent under oath. But Húrin the Steadfast mocked
him.

§22    Then Morgoth devised a cruel punishment; and taking Húrin from prison he set him in a chair of stone upon a high place of Thangorodrim. There he was bound by the power of Morgoth, and Morgoth standing beside him cursed him with a curse of unsleeping sight like unto the Gods, but upon his kin and seed he laid a doom of sorrow and dark mischance.

§23    'Sit now there,' said Morgoth, 'and behold the working of the doom that I have appointed. For thou shalt see with my eyes, and know with my thought, all things that befall those whom thou lovest. But never shalt thou move from this place until all is fulfilled unto its bitter end.' As so it came to pass; for Morgoth kept life in Húrin. But it is not said that Húrin ever spoke in pleading, either for death or for mercy upon himself or his children.

### Commentary on Chapter 16

A comparison with Q §11 and AB 2 annal (272>) 472 will show that the present text is very largely derived from these two sources, which are interwoven. In the treatment of the part played by Turgon and the people of Gondolin in the Battle of Unnumbered Tears the result of this combination is (surprisingly) not entirely coherent, and this is discussed in a note at the end of the Commentary.

§1    On the development of this paragraph see pp. 305–6. In the sentence *dwelt among the Green-elves secretly*, the word *secretly* was struck out and replaced by *in Tol-galen the Green Isle*; and *Gwerth-i-Cuina* was changed to *Gwerth-i-Guinar*. These may have been much later changes preparatory to the inclusion of the paragraph as the final instalment of the QS manuscript (which has however *Gyrth-i-Guinar*).

§3    It is not said elsewhere that 'Fingon issued from Hithlum' during the initial period of warfare under the Union of Maidros in which the Noldor were victorious.

The passage concerning the cynical and calculating Dwarves derives closely from Q (IV. 116). Against it my father scribbled 'Not true of Dwarvish attitude'; this, I feel sure, was put in long after. The plural form *Dwarfs* associates the text with QS chapters 10 and 11 (see the commentary on §122). It was used also in the manuscript QS(B) of the tale of Beren and Lúthien (p. 303).

§7    The wounding of Beren by Curufin, not mentioned in the *Annals* in connection with the response of the Men of Brethil to the Union of Maidros, reappears (see IV. 180–1), and 'only the half' of Haleth's people came to the war, although in §13 (as in AB 2) 'most of the Men of Brethil' were slain.

§8    Neither in Q nor in the *Annals* are the Green-elves of Ossiriand mentioned among the forces of Maidros.

§11    That the heralds were sent back bearing the head of the one who had been executed is a new detail.

§13    The retreat of the western host towards the Pass of Sirion, and the destruction of the Men of Brethil in the rearguard, is derived from the *Annals*, not from Q.

An addition to AB 2 (note 22) gives a new annal: '436.   Hundor son of Haleth wedded Glorwendel daughter of Hador', and an addition to the annal describing the Battle of Unnumbered Tears states: 'Glorwendel his wife died in that year of grief.' These are the first allusions to this union between the House of Hador and the People of Haleth. In *The Silmarillion* Hador's daughter is *Glóredhel*.

§15    The number of a thousand Balrogs (found in both versions of the *Annals*) was still present (see the commentary on §89). – After 'all perished in that battle' the earlier text (C) has the addition 'defending Maglor against the assault of Uldor', but this was not taken up in D. It is not said in the *Annals* that Ulfast and Ulwar(th) were slain by the sons of Bór ('ere they themselves fell'), but the reverse.

§17    Text D has *Erydwethion* in §§11 and 13, but *Eredwethion* here; C has *Eredwethion* throughout.

§18    In Q the Dragon-helm, reappearing from the *Lay of the Children of Húrin*, is first described at this point in the narrative (for Húrin was not wearing it at the battle); but a note to Q postpones it to the tale of Túrin, as is done in this version.

§19    *Hauð-na-Dengin:* C had *Cûm-na-Dengin* (see note 37 to AB 2), changed to *Amon Dengin* (see IV. 146), with *Hauð na* written above *Amon*. This is the first occurrence of *Hauð-na-Dengin* (the form in text D); cf. *Hauð in Ndengin* in the *Etymologies*, stems KHAG, NDAK.

### Turgon's part in the Battle of Unnumbered Tears

As noted above, the combination of Q and the *Annals* produced here a most uncharacteristic incoherence. Turgon came forth from Gondolin unlooked for and encamped on the plain before the western pass in sight of the walls of Hithlum (§4); when the day was appointed 'Maidros sent word to Fingon and Turgon', and the host of Gondolin was arrayed under the standard of Fingon (§8); Turgon and Fingon became impatient and sent their heralds out onto the plain of Fauglith (§10). In all this my father was closely following Q as emended (IV. 120–1, notes 7 and 14), where, as I suggested (IV. 181), there seems to be a stage intermediate between the original story (in which Turgon was one of the leaders of the Western Elves from the beginning of the preparations for war) and that in *The Silmarillion*: 'Turgon now emerges from Gondolin already long since in existence, but he does not march up in the nick of time, on the day itself, as in the later story: he comes, certainly unexpected, but in time to take part in the final strategic preparations.'

Then, in the present account, 'a great part' of Turgon's host joined in the premature assault, though he would have restrained them if he could (§11). This is not in Q, which only further mentions Turgon as escaping down Sirion. But *then*, Turgon 'sounded his horns', and 'a great part' of his host that had remained in hiding before the Pass of Sirion and on the borders of Taur-na-Fuin came forth unlooked for, so that many Orcs were destroyed, caught between Turgon's army and that of Fingon retreating southwards (§13). It seems that at this point my father went over to the *Annals*; but they (both AB 1 and AB 2) tell a different story from that in Q. In the *Annals*, 'tidings came to Turgon' long before the battle, and 'he prepared for war in secret' (annal 465–70, according to the final dating); there is no suggestion of his playing any part at all until Fingon, cut off from the passes of Eredwethion, retreated towards Sirion – and then 'Turgon and the army of Gondolin sounded their horns, and issued out of Taur-na-Fuin': they had been 'delayed by the deceit and evil of the forest, but came now as help unlooked for.' There now took place, in the *Annals*, the joyful meeting between Turgon and Húrin (the story of Húrin's sojourn in Gondolin had not emerged when Q was written). This meeting does not take place in the present account; for they would have met again much earlier (when 'there was joy among the people of Fingon, seeing their kinsfolk that had long been hidden', §4).

This chapter appears in subsequent amanuensis typescripts, but my father never changed them or corrected them in any way.

## 17  OF TÚRIN TURAMARTH OR TÚRIN THE HAPLESS

The two manuscripts QS (C) and QS (D) continue into one further chapter, and D extends somewhat further in it than does C (see pp. 293–4). C is here extremely rough, and the text given is that of D, since it followed C very closely and scarcely deviated from it save in small points of expression. D was substantially corrected and added to, and the concluding pages struck out in their entirety, but I believe that all this belongs to a much later phase of work on the 'Túrinssaga', and I give the text as it was originally written.

This version of the story, so far as it goes, shows a huge expansion on the very brief account in Q §12 – and would have run into the same problem of length as did the QS version of the tale of Beren and Lúthien. The primary source for this chapter was in fact the *Lay of the Children of Húrin* in the section *Túrin's Fostering* (III. 8 ff., and in the revised form of the poem III. 104 ff.), which in turn derived quite closely from the original story, the *Tale of Turambar*. The later evolution of the 'Túrinssaga' is as tangled as Taur-na-Fuin, and need not be in any way considered here; but it may be noticed that the present chapter is not (apart from a few phrases) the antecedent of the opening of chapter 21 in

*The Silmarillion*. On the other hand, it will be found that much of the chapter is in fact preserved embedded in the *Narn i Hîn Húrin* in *Unfinished Tales* (from 'Now Túrin was made ready for the journey', p. 73), despite the introduction of several major new elements (the history of the Dragon-helm, Nellas the friend of Túrin's childhood, the changed story of Orgof/Saeros, etc.)

The dependence of the new version on the Lay is in places close, extending even to actual wording here and there; on the other hand some features of the Lay are changed (as for example the taunting of Orgof), reduced (as the account of Orgof and his character), or omitted (as the avenging wrath of Orgof's kinsmen and Thingol's placating gifts). But the comparison between the two is now easily made, and I restrict the commentary to a few particular points. The relation between the Lay and the *Narn* is in any case studied in the commentary on the Lay (III. 24–8).

§24　Rían, daughter of Belegund, was the wife of Huor. When no tidings came of her lord, she went forth, and her child Tuor was born of her in the wild. He was taken to nurture by Dark-elves; but Rían went to Hauð-na-Dengin and laid her there and died. But Morwen daughter of Baragund was wife of Húrin, and she abode in Hithlum, for her son Túrin was then seven years old, and she went again with child. With her there remained only old men, too aged for war, and maidens and young boys. Those days were evil; for the Easterlings dealt cruelly with the people of Hador and robbed them of all that they possessed and enslaved them. But so great was the beauty and majesty of the Lady Morwen that they were afraid and whispered among themselves, saying that she was perilous and a witch skilled in magic and in league with the Elves. Yet she was now poor and without aid, save that she was succoured secretly by her kinswoman Airin, whom Brodda had taken to wife. Brodda was mighty among the in-coming Men, and wealthy (such as wealth was reckoned in that time of ruin); for he had taken for his own many of the lands and cattle of Húrin.

§25　Morwen could see no hope for her child Túrin son of Húrin but to become a churl or a servant of the Easterlings. Therefore it came into her heart to send him away in secret and to beg King Thingol to harbour him. For Beren son of Barahir was her father's cousin, and had been, moreover, a friend of Húrin ere evil befell. But she herself did not at that time venture forth from Hithlum, for the road was long and perilous, and she was with child. Also her heart still cheated her with hope, and she would not yet leave the house in which she had dwelt with Húrin; and she listened for the sound of his feet returning in the watches of the night, for her inmost thought foreboded that he was not dead. And though she was willing that her son might be fostered in the halls of another after the manner of that time, if boys were left fatherless, she would not humble her pride to be an almsguest even of the King of Doriath. And thus was the fate of Túrin woven, which is full told in that lay which is called *iChúrinien*, the Children of Húrin, and is the longest of all the lays that speak of those days. Here that tale is told in brief, for it is woven in with the fate of the Silmarils and of the Elves; and it is called the Tale of Grief, for it is sorrowful, and in it are revealed the worst of the works of Morgoth Bauglir.

§26    It came to pass that on a day Túrin was made ready for the journey, and he understood not the purpose of his mother Morwen, nor the grief that he saw upon her face. But when his companions bade him turn and look upon the house of his father, then the anguish of parting smote him like a sword, and he cried: 'Morwen, Morwen, when shall I see thee again?', and he fell upon the grass. But Morwen standing on her threshold heard the echo of that cry in the wooded hills, and she clutched the post of the door so that her fingers were torn. This was the first of the sorrows of Túrin.

§27    After Túrin was gone Morwen gave birth to her child, and it was a maiden, and she named her Nienor, which is Mourning. But Túrin saw not his sister, for he was in Doriath when she was born. Long and evil was the road thither, for the power of Morgoth was ranging far abroad; but Túrin had as guides Gethron and Grithron, who had been young in the days of Gumlin; and albeit they were now aged, they were valiant, and they knew all the lands, for they had journeyed often through Beleriand in former times. Thus by fate and courage they passed over the Shadowy Mountains and came down into the vale of Sirion and so to the Forest of Brethil; and at last weary and haggard they reached the confines of Doriath. But there they became bewildered, and were enmeshed in the mazes of the Queen, and wandered lost amid the pathless trees, until all their food was spent. There they came near to death, but not so light was Túrin's doom. Even as they lay in despair they heard a horn sounded. Beleg the Bowman was hunting in that region, for he dwelt ever upon the marches of Doriath. He heard their cries and came to them, and when he had given them meat and drink he learned their names and whence they came, and he was filled with wonder and pity. And he looked with great liking upon Túrin, for he had the beauty of his mother Morwen Elfsheen and the eyes of his father, and was sturdy and strong of limb and showed a stout heart.

§28 'What boon wouldst thou have of King Thingol?' said Beleg to the boy. 'I would be a captain of his knights, and lead them against Morgoth and avenge my father,' said Túrin. 'That may well be when the years have increased thee,' said Beleg. 'For though thou art yet small, thou hast the makings of a valiant man, worthy to be the son of Húrin the Steadfast, if that were possible.' For the name of Húrin was held in honour in all the lands of the Elves. Therefore Beleg gladly became the guide of the wanderers, and he led them through the marches of the Hidden Kingdom, which no mortal man before had passed save Beren only.

§29 Thus Túrin came at last before Thingol and Melian; and Gethron spoke the message of Morwen. Thingol received them kindly, and he set Túrin upon his knee in honour of Húrin the mightiest of Men and of Beren his kinsman. And those that saw this marvelled, for it was a sign that Thingol took Túrin as foster-son, and this was not at that time done by kings. 'Here, O son of Húrin, shall thy home be,' said he; 'and thou shalt be held as my son, Man though thou art. Wisdom shall be given thee beyond the wit of mortals, and the weapons of the Elves shall be set in thy hands. Perchance the time may come when thou shalt regain the lands of thy father in Hithlum; but dwell now here in love.'

§30 Thus began the sojourn of Túrin in Doriath. With him for a while remained Gethron and Grithron his guardians, though they longed to return again to their lady, Morwen. Then age and sickness came upon Grithron and he stayed beside Túrin until he died; but Gethron departed, and Thingol sent with him an escort to guide him and guard him, and they brought words from Thingol to Morwen. They came at last to the house of Morwen, and when she learned that Túrin was received with honour in the halls of Thingol, her grief was lightened. And the Elves brought also rich gifts from Melian, and a message bidding her return with Thingol's folk to Doriath. For Melian was wise and foresighted, and she hoped thus to avert the evil that was prepared in the thought of Morgoth. But Morwen would not depart from her house, for her heart was yet unchanged and her pride still high; moreover Nienor was a babe in arms. Therefore she dismissed the Elves with her thanks, and gave them in gift the last small things of gold that remained to her, concealing her poverty; and she bade

them take back to Thingol the helm of Gumlin. And behold!
Túrin watched ever for the return of Thingol's messengers; and
when they came back alone he fled into the woods and wept; for he
knew of Melian's bidding and had hoped that Morwen would
come. This was the second sorrow of Túrin.

§31   When the messengers brought Morwen's answer, Melian
was moved with pity, perceiving her mind; and she saw that the
fate which she foreboded could not lightly be set aside. The helm
of Gumlin was given into Thingol's hands. It was made of grey
steel adorned with gold, and thereon were graven runes of victory.
A power was in it that guarded any who wore it from wound or
death, for the sword that hewed it was broken, and the dart that
smote it sprang aside. Upon this helm was set in mockery an image
of the head of Glómund the dragon, and oft had Gumlin borne it
to victory, for fear fell on those who looked upon it towering above
the heads of Men in battle. But the Men of Hithlum said: 'We have
a dragon of more worth than Angband hath.' This helm was
wrought by Telchar the dwarf-smith of Belegost, whose works
were renowned. But Húrin wore it not, in reverence of his father,
lest it should suffer hurt or be lost, so greatly did he treasure the
heirloom of Gumlin.

§32   Now Thingol had in Menegroth deep armouries filled
with great wealth of weapons; metal wrought like fishes' mail and
shining like water in the moon; swords and axes, shields and
helms, wrought by Telchar himself or by his master Zirak the old,
or by elven-wrights more skilful still. For many things he had
received in gift that came out of Valinor and were wrought by
Fëanor in his mastery, than whom no craftsman was greater in all
the days of the world. Yet he handled the helm of Gumlin as
though his hoard were scanty, and spoke courteous words saying:
'Proud were the head that bore this helm, which Gumlin bore,
father of Húrin.'

§33   Then a thought came into his heart and he summoned
Túrin, and he told him that Morwen had sent to her son a mighty
thing, the heirloom of his grandsire. 'Take now the Dragonhead
of the North,' he said, 'and when the time cometh, go wear it
well!' But Túrin was yet too young to lift the helm, and he heeded
it not because of the sorrow of his heart.

§34   For nine years Túrin lived in the halls of Thingol; and in
that time his grief grew less; for Thingol gained tidings of
Hithlum as he could, and messengers went at times between
Morwen and her son. Thus Túrin learned that Morwen's plight

was bettered, and that his sister Nienor grew in beauty, a flower among maidens in the grey North. Greatly he desired to see her.

§35   Meanwhile Túrin grew, until while yet a boy his stature was great among Men and surpassed that of the Elves of Doriath; and his strength and courage were renowned in the realm of Thingol. Much lore he learned, and was wise in word and crafty in hand; yet fortune favoured him little, and oft what he wrought went awry, and what he wished he did not gain. Neither did he win friendship easily, for sorrow sat upon him, and his youth was scarred. Now when he was seventeen years of age and upon the threshold of manhood he was strong of arm and skilled with all weapons, and in the weaving of words in song or tale he had a great craft, whether in the tongue of the Noldor or of Doriath; but mirth was not in his words or his works, and he brooded upon the downfall of the Men of Hithlum.

§36   Still deeper became his grief when after nine years tidings came no more from his home; for Morgoth's power was over the land of Hithlum, and doubtless he knew much of all the doings of Húrin's folk, and had not further molested them, so that his design might be fulfilled. But now in pursuit of this purpose he set a close watch upon all the passes in the mountains, so that none might come out of Hithlum or enter into it; and the Orcs swarmed about the sources of Narog and Taiglin and the upper waters of Sirion. Thus there came a time when the messengers of Thingol did not return, and he would send no more. He was ever loath to let any stray beyond the guarded borders, and in nothing had shown greater goodwill to Túrin than in sending his people through many perils to Morwen.

§37   Now the heart of Túrin grew grim and heavy, for he knew not what evil was afoot, or what dire fate had befallen Morwen and Nienor. Therefore he put on the helm of Gumlin, and taking mail and sword and shield he went to Thingol, and begged him to give him Elf-warriors for his companions; and he went to the marches of the land and made war upon the Orcs. Thus while yet a boy in years his valour was proved; for he did many daring deeds. His wounds were many by spear, or arrow, or the crooked blades of Angband; but his doom delivered him from death. And word ran through the woods that the Dragon-helm was seen again in battle; and Men said: 'Who hath waked from death the spirit of Gumlin, or hath Húrin of Hithlum indeed returned from the pits of hell?'

§38   One only was there mightier in war at that time than the boy Túrin, and that was Beleg the Bowman; and they became friends and companions in arms, and walked far and wide in the wild woods together. Túrin came seldom to the halls of Thingol, and he cared no longer for his looks or raiment, but was unkempt of hair and his mail was covered with a grey cloak stained with the weather. But on a time it chanced that Thingol summoned him to a feast, to do him some honour for his prowess; and Túrin came and sat at the table of the king. And at the same table sat one of the Dark-elves, Orgof by name, and he was proud and was no lover of Men, and thought that Túrin had slighted him; for Túrin would oft make no answer to words that others spoke to him, if sorrow or brooding were on him. And now as they sat and drank Orgof spoke across the board to Túrin, and Túrin heeded him not, for his thought was upon Beleg whom he had left in the woods. Then Orgof took out a golden comb and cast it towards Túrin, and he cried: 'Doubtless, Man of Hithlum, you came in great haste to this feast and may be excused thy ragged cloak; but there is no need to leave thy head untended like a thicket of brambles. And maybe if thy ears were uncovered thou wouldst hear somewhat better.'

§39   Then Túrin said nought but turned his eyes upon Orgof, and he being wroth was not warned by the light that was in them. And he said to one that sat nigh him: 'If the Men of Hithlum are so wild and fell, of what sort are women of that land? Do they run like the deer, clad only in their hair?'

§40   Then Túrin, unwitting of his growing strength, took up a drinking vessel and cast it in Orgof's face, and he fell backwards and died, for the vessel was heavy and his face was broken. But Túrin, grown suddenly cold, looked in dismay at the blood upon the board, and knowing that he had done grievous offence he rose straightway and went from the hall without a word; and none hindered him, for the king was silent and gave no sign. But Túrin went out into the darkness, and he fell into a grim mood, and deeming himself now an outlaw whom the king would pursue he fled far from Menegroth, and passing the borders of the realm he gathered to himself a company of such houseless and desperate folk as could be found in those evil days lurking in the wild; and their hands were turned against all whom came in their path, Elves, Men, or Orcs.

### Commentary on Chapter 17

In the title of the chapter (which has in fact no number in either C or D) *Turamarth* is emended from *Turumarth*; the same change in Q (IV. 131 note 12).

§24  *Hauð-na-Dengin:* C has here *Amon Dengin*; cf. the commentary on chapter 16, §19.

§25  In Q it is said that the fate of Túrin is told in the 'Children of Húrin', which is certainly a reference to the alliterative Lay, though that had been abandoned several years before; now the Lay is expressly mentioned, and given the Elvish name *iChúrinien*. This form is a further example of the phenomenon of 'Initial Variation of Consonants' in Exilic Noldorin (see pp. 298, 301). The original aspirated stops *ph, th, kh* were 'opened', and *kh* became the spirant [x] (as in Scottish *loch*), represented as *ch*; this sound remained medially, but initially was reduced to [h]. Thus *aran Chithlum* 'King of Hithlum' (*Etymologies*, stem TĀ-), *iChúrinien*. It may be noted here that later *iChúrinien* was replaced by *Narn i Chîn Húrin*, which is so spelt at all occurrences, but was improperly changed by me to *Narn i Hîn Húrin* in *Unfinished Tales* (because I did not want *Chîn* to be pronounced like Modern English *chin*).

§27  *Gethron* and *Grithron* as the names of Túrin's guides appear in AB 2, annal (273>) 473. See under §30 below.

§28  Of the words between Beleg and Túrin (preserved in the *Narn*, p. 74) there is no suggestion in the Lay.

§30  In AB 2 it was Gethron who died in Doriath, Grithron who went back (see the commentary on annal 273). – The gifts of Melian to Morwen are not mentioned in the old versions.

§31  It is curious that whereas in the tale of Beren and Lúthien in QS Telchar is of Nogrod (p. 303), he now becomes a smith of Belegost, as he had been in Q (IV. 118). – A new element in this passage is the statement that Húrin never wore the Dragon-helm, and the reasons for this; in Q he did not wear it 'that day' (i.e. at the Battle of Unnumbered Tears), and in the Lay he often bore it into battle (line 314). In the much enlarged account of the Helm found in the *Narn* Húrin's reasons for not wearing it are quite different (*Unfinished Tales* p. 76).

§32  Here first appear Telchar's master Zirak, and the story that Thingol possessed many treasures that had come from Valinor (both preserved in the *Narn*).

§34  On the 'betterment' of Morwen's plight see II. 127.

§35  *Dates in Túrin's early life.* According to the (later) dating of AB 2, Túrin was born in the winter of 465, and departed for Doriath in 473, when he was seven years old (as is said here in §24); in 481 all tidings out of Hithlum ceased, and he being 'in his sixteenth year' went to war on the marches (his sixteenth birthday fell in the winter of that year). In the present text, however, the dates appear to be different by a year. The reference in §35 to his being seventeen is presumably made because it was then that he went out to fight; and in §§36–7 the ending of news from Hithlum and his going to the marches took place 'after nine years' (i.e. from his coming to Doriath).

The supposition must be that Túrin had acquired a knowledge of the Noldorin tongue from the Noldor in Hithlum – or perhaps rather from his father and mother – while he was a child.

§38   In the Tale and the Lay Túrin's peculiar gloominess on that night was caused by its being the twelfth anniversary of his departure from Hithlum.

## THE CONCLUSION OF THE *QUENTA SILMARILLION*

There remains one further text to be considered within the framework of the *Quenta Silmarillion*. This is a clear manuscript very similar in style to QS(D), which has been followed to its conclusion in the last chapter, and may conveniently be called 'QS(E)' or 'E'. The first page is numbered '55', and it begins in the middle of a sentence: 'and they looked upon the Lonely Isle and there they tarried not', which will be found in the second version of Q (Q II) §17, IV. 153. The passage describes the voyage of Eärendel and Elwing to Valinor:

they came to the Enchanted Isles and escaped their enchantment; and they came into the Shadowy Seas and passed their shadows; [here page 54 of the Q II typescript ends and page 55 begins] and they looked upon the Lonely Isle and they tarried not there . . .

This manuscript E is in fact a further version of the conclusion of Q: and the question arises, when was it written? A note on a page found with Q provides, I think, a clear answer. This says: '36–54 is still included in main version, being unrevised.' Now on p. 36 of the Q typescript occurs the sentence (IV. 123):

He fled then the court, and thinking himself an outlaw took to war against all, Elves, Men, or Orcs, that crossed the path of the desperate band he gathered upon the borders of the kingdom, hunted Men and Ilkorins and Gnomes.

This is the antecedent of the sentence which ends the QS(D) version of the tale of Túrin (p. 321); and at this point on the Q typescript a line is drawn across, separating what precedes from what follows.

By 'main version' my father probably meant the *Quenta Noldorinwa*, the implication being that the narrative from Túrin's outlawry to the voyage of Eärendel to Valinor (i.e. pages 36–54 in the Q typescript) had not been rewritten, and so was absent from the *Quenta Silmarillion* (QS) and still only found in the *Quenta Noldorinwa* (Q). I think therefore that it is certain that the text QS(E) now to be given belongs to the same period (i.e. immediately before the commencement of *The Lord of the Rings*) as the other chapters (the end of 'Beren and Tinúviel', the Battle of Unnumbered Tears, the beginning of 'Túrin') that belong with the QS manuscript but were not written into it (or, in the case of the last part of 'Beren and Tinúviel', not till long after).* Why my father should have jumped to the end in this way, taking up in mid-sentence, I cannot at all explain.

It is seen then that at the period with which this book is concerned the missing parts of the QS narrative were the greater part of the tale of Túrin, the destruction of Doriath, the fall of Gondolin, and the earlier part of the tale of Eärendel. But my father never returned to these tales (in the strictly 'Silmarillion' tradition: the Túrin story was of course enormously developed later, and some slight elaboration is found elsewhere for the other parts. The *Grey Annals* were abandoned at the end of the tale of Túrin, and the later tale of Tuor (given in *Unfinished Tales*) before Tuor came to Gondolin).

The manuscript E was emended, frequently but not radically, at different times: some changes were made at or very near the time of its original composition (and these are adopted silently into the text); others, made very roughly in pencil, are clearly from long after (and these are not mentioned here).

The text is closely related to Q II, §§17–19, and for substantial stretches, especially towards the end, the earlier work was followed with unusual fidelity: thus for example the Second Prophecy of Mandos, with its mysterious elements, was repeated virtually without change. Of course, the later emendations made to Q II and given in the notes to that text were, according to my father's usual practice, preparatory to the present version, and very likely belong to this time: the amount of change is therefore, to appearance, diminished, as between the material given in Vol. IV and the present chapter. It would have been possible to restrict the text printed here to those passages which differ significantly from Q II (as revised), but I have thought it best to give it in its entirety. The very fact that the end of 'The Silmarillion' still took this form when *The Lord of the Rings* was begun is sufficiently remarkable, and by its inclusion in full a complete view of the Matter of Middle-earth and Valinor at that time is provided.

The numbering of the paragraphs begins again here from §1.

§1     And they looked upon the Lonely Isle and there they tarried not; and at the last they cast anchor in the Bay of Elvenhome upon the borders of the world; and the Teleri saw the coming of that ship and were amazed, gazing from afar upon the light of the Silmaril, and it was very great. But Eärendel, alone of living Men, landed on the immortal shores; and he said to Elwing and to those that were with him, three mariners who had sailed all the seas beside him, and Falathar, Airandir, and Erellont were

---

*The existence of the rewritten conclusion should have been mentioned in the footnote to III. 366.

their names: 'Here shall none but myself set foot, lest you fall under the wrath of the Gods and the doom of death; for it is forbidden. But that peril I will take on myself for the sake of the Two Kindreds.'

§2   And Elwing answered: 'Then shall our paths be sundered for ever. Nay, all thy perils I will take on myself also!' And she leaped into the white foam and ran towards him; but Eärendel was sorrowful, for he deemed that they would now both die ere many days were past. And there they bade farewell to their companions and were taken from them for ever.

§3   And Eärendel said to Elwing: 'Await me here; for one only may bear the messages that I am charged with'; and he went up alone into the land, and it seemed to him empty and silent. For even as Morgoth and Ungoliantë came in ages past, so now Eärendel had come at a time of festival, and wellnigh all the Elvenfolk were gone to Valinor, or were gathered in the halls of Manwë upon Taniquetil, and few were left to keep watch upon the walls of Tûn.

§4   These watchers rode therefore in great haste to Valmar; and all the bells in Valmar pealed. But Eärendel climbed the great green hill of Kôr and found it bare; and he entered into the streets of Tûn and they were empty; and his heart was heavy, for he feared that some evil had come even to the Blessed Realm. He walked now in the deserted ways of Tûn, and the dust upon his raiment and his shoes was a dust of diamonds, and he shone and glistened as he climbed the long white stairs. And he called aloud in many tongues, both of Elves and Men, but there were none to answer him. Therefore he turned back at last towards the shores, thinking to set sail once more upon Vingelot his ship and abandon his errand, and live for ever upon the sea. But even as he took the shoreward road and turned his face away from the towers of Tûn one stood upon the hill and called to him in a great voice, crying: 'Hail Eärendel, radiant star, messenger most fair! Hail thou bearer of light before the Sun and Moon, the looked for that comest unawares, the longed for that comest beyond hope! Hail, splendour of the children of the world, slayer of the dark! Star of the sunset, hail! Hail, herald of the morn!'

§5   And that was the voice of Fionwë son of Manwë; and he came from Valmar and he summoned Eärendel to come before the Gods. And Eärendel went to Valinor and to the halls of Valmar, and never again set foot upon the lands of Men. There before the faces of the undying Gods he stood, and delivered the errand of the Two Kindreds. Pardon he asked for the Noldor and pity for their great sorrows, and mercy upon unhappy Men and succour in their need. And his prayers were granted.

§6 Then the sons of the Valar prepared for battle, and the captain of their host was Fionwë son of Manwë. Beneath his white banner marched also the Lindar, the Light-elves, the people of Ingwë; and among them were also those of the Noldor of old who had never departed from Valinor, and Ingwiel son of Ingwë was their chief. But remembering the slaying at the Swan-haven and the rape of their ships, few of the Teleri were willing to go forth to war; but Elwing went among them, and because she was fair and gentle, and was come also upon her father's side from Thingol who was of their own kindred, they harkened to her; and they sent mariners sufficient to man and steer the ships upon which most of that army was borne east oversea; but they stayed aboard their ships and none ever set foot upon the shores of the Hither Lands.

§7 And thus it was that Elwing came among the Teleri, Eärendel was long time gone and she became lonely and afraid; and she wandered along the margin of the sea, singing sadly to herself; and so she came to Alqualondë, the Swan-haven, where lay the Telerian fleets; and there the Teleri befriended her. When therefore Eärendel at last returned, seeking her, he found her among them, and they listened to her tales of Thingol and Melian and the Hidden Kingdom, and of Lúthien the fair, and they were filled with pity and wonder.

§8 Now the Gods took counsel concerning Eärendel, and they summoned Ulmo from the deeps; and when they were gathered together Mandos spoke, saying: 'Now he shall surely die, for he has trodden the forbidden shores.' But Ulmo said: 'For this he was born into the world. And say unto me: whether is he Eärendel Tuor's son of the line of Hador, or Idril's son Turgon's daughter of the Elven-house of Finwë? Or being half of either kindred, which half shall die?' And Mandos answered: 'Equally was it forbidden to the Noldor that went wilfully into exile to return hither.'

§9 Then Manwë gave judgement and he said: 'To Eärendel I remit the ban, and the peril that he took upon himself out of love for the Two Kindreds shall not fall on him; neither shall it fall upon Elwing who entered into peril for love of Eärendel: save only in this: they shall not ever walk again among Elves or Men in the Outer Lands. Now all those who have the blood of mortal Men, in whatever part, great or small, are mortal, unless other doom be granted to them; but in this matter the power of doom is given to me. This is my decree: to Eärendel and to Elwing and to their sons shall be given leave each to choose freely under which kindred they shall be judged.'

§10   Then Eärendel and Elwing were summoned, and this decree was declared to them. But Eärendel said to Elwing: 'Choose thou, for now I am weary of the world.' And she chose to be judged among the Firstborn, because of Lúthien, and for the sake of Elwing Eärendel chose alike, though his heart was rather with the kindred of Men and the people of his father.

§11   The Gods then sent Fionwë, and he came to the shore where the companions of Eärendel still remained, awaiting tidings. And Fionwë took a boat and set therein the three mariners, and the Gods drove them away East with a great wind. But they took Vingelot, and they hallowed it, and they bore it away through Valinor to the uttermost rim of the world, and there it [*added:* passed through the Door of Night and] was lifted up even into the oceans of heaven. Now fair and marvellous was that vessel made, and it was filled with a wavering flame, pure and bright; and Eärendel the mariner sat at the helm, glistening with dust of elven-gems; and the Silmaril was bound upon his brow. Far he journeyed in that ship, even into the starless voids; but most often was he seen at morning or at eve, glimmering in sunrise or sunset, as he came back to Valinor from voyages beyond the confines of the world.

§12   On those journeys Elwing did not go, for she had not the strength to endure the cold and pathless voids, and she loved rather the earth and the sweet winds that blow on sea and hill. Therefore she let build for her a white tower upon the borders of the outer world, in the northern region of the Sundering Seas; and thither all the sea-birds of the earth at times repaired. And it is said that Elwing learned the tongues and lore of birds, who had herself once worn their shape; and she devised wings for herself of white and silver-grey, and they taught her the craft of flight. And at whiles, when Eärendel returning drew near again to earth, she would fly to meet him, even as she had flown long ago, when she was rescued from the sea. Then the farsighted among the Elves that dwelt most westerly in the Lonely Isle would see her like a white bird, shining, rose-stained in the sunset, as she soared in joy to greet the coming of Vingelot to haven.

§13   Now when first Vingelot was set to sail on the seas of heaven, it rose unlooked-for, glittering and bright; and the folk of earth beheld it from afar and wondered, and they took it for a sign of hope. And when this new star arose in the West, Maidros said unto Maglor: 'Surely that is a Silmaril that shineth in the sky?' And Maglor said: 'If it be verily that Silmaril that we saw cast into the sea that riseth again by the power of the Gods, then let us be glad; for its glory is seen now by many, and is yet secure from all evil.' Then the Elves looked up, and despaired no longer; but Morgoth was filled with doubt.

§14   Yet it is said that Morgoth looked not for the assault that came upon him from the West. So great was his pride become that he deemed that none would ever again come up with open war against him. Moreover he thought that he had for ever estranged the Gnomes from the Gods and from their kin; and that content in their blissful Realm the Valar would heed no more his kingdom in the world without. For to him that is pitiless the deeds of pity are ever strange and beyond reckoning.

§15   Of the march of the host of Fionwë to the North little is said in any tale; for in his armies went none of those Elves who had dwelt and suffered in the Hither Lands, and who made the histories of those days that still are known; and tidings of these things they learned long afterward from their kinsfolk, the Light-elves of Valinor. But at the last Fionwë came up out of the West, and the challenge of his trumpets filled the sky; and he summoned unto him all Elves and Men from Hithlum unto the East; and Beleriand was ablaze with the glory of his arms, for the sons of the Gods were young and fair and terrible, and the mountains rang beneath their feet.

§16   The meeting of the hosts of the West and of the North is named the Great Battle, the Battle Terrible, and the War of Wrath. There was marshalled the whole power of the Throne of Morgoth, and it had become great beyond count, so that Dor-na-Fauglith could not contain it, and all the North was aflame with war. But it availed not. The Balrogs were destroyed, save some few that fled and hid themselves in caverns inaccessible at the roots of the earth. The uncounted legions of the Orcs perished like straw in a great fire, or were swept like shrivelled leaves before a burning wind. Few remained to trouble the world for long years after. And it is said that all that were left of the three Houses of the Elf-friends, Fathers of Men, fought for Fionwë; and they were avenged upon the Orcs in those days for Baragund and Barahir, Gumlin and Gundor, Huor and Húrin, and many others of their lords; and so were fulfilled in part the words of Ulmo, for by

Eärendel son of Tuor help was brought unto the Elves, and by the swords of Men they were strengthened on the fields of war. But the most part of the sons of Men, whether of the people of Uldor or others newcome out of the East, marched with the Enemy; and the Elves do not forget it.

§17 Then, seeing that his hosts were overthrown and his power dispersed, Morgoth quailed, and he dared not to come forth himself. But he loosed upon his foes the last desperate assault that he had prepared, and out of the pits of Angband there issued the winged dragons, that had not before been seen; for until that day no creatures of his cruel thought had yet assailed the air. So sudden and ruinous was the onset of that dreadful fleet that Fionwë was driven back; for the coming of the dragons was like a great roar of thunder, and a tempest of fire, and their wings were of steel.

§18 Then Eärendel came, shining with white flame, and about Vingelot were gathered all the great birds of heaven, and Thorondor was their captain, and there was battle in the air all the day and through a dark night of doubt. And ere the rising of the sun Eärendel slew Ancalagon the Black, the mightiest of the dragon-host, and he cast him from the sky, and in his fall the towers of Thangorodrim were thrown down. Then the sun rose, and the Children of the Valar prevailed, and all the dragons were destroyed, save two alone; and they fled into the East. Then all the pits of Morgoth were broken and unroofed, and the might of Fionwë descended into the deeps of the earth. And there Morgoth stood at last at bay, and yet unvaliant. He fled into the deepest of his mines and sued for peace and pardon; but his feet were hewn from under him and he was hurled upon his face. Then he was bound with the chain Angainor, which long had been prepared; and his iron crown they beat into a collar for his neck, and his head was bowed upon his knees. But Fionwë took the two Silmarils which remained and guarded them.

§19 Thus an end was made of the power of Angband in the North, and the evil realm was brought to nought; and out of the pits and deep prisons a multitude of thralls came forth beyond all hope into the light of day, and they looked upon a world all changed. For so great was the fury of those adversaries that the northern regions of the western world were rent asunder, and the sea roared in through many chasms, and there was confusion and great noise; and rivers perished or found new paths, and the valleys were upheaved and the hills trod down; and Sirion was no more. Then Men, such as had not perished in the ruin of those days, fled far away, and it was long ere any came back over Eredlindon to the places where Beleriand had been.

§20 But Fionwë marched through the western lands summoning the remnant of the Noldor, and the Dark-elves that had not yet looked on Valinor, to join with the thralls released and to depart from Middle-earth. But Maidros would not harken, and he prepared, though now with weariness and loathing, to attempt in despair the fulfilment of his oath. For Maidros would have given battle for the Silmarils, were they withheld, even against the victorious host of Valinor and the might and splendour of the sons of the Gods: even though he stood alone in all the world. And he sent a message unto Fionwë, bidding him yield up now those jewels which of old Fëanor made and Morgoth stole from him.

§21 But Fionwë said that the right to the work of their hands, which Fëanor and his sons formerly possessed, had now perished, because of their many and merciless deeds, being blinded by their oath, and most of all because of the slaying of Dior and the assault upon Elwing. The light of the Silmarils should go now to the Gods, whence it came in the beginning; and to Valinor must Maidros and Maglor return and there abide the judgement of the Valar, by whose decree alone would Fionwë yield the jewels from his charge.

§22 Maglor desired indeed to submit, for his heart was sorrowful, and he said: 'The oath says not that we may not bide our time, and maybe in Valinor all shall be forgiven and forgot, and we shall come into our own in peace.' But Maidros said that, if once they returned and the favour of the Gods were withheld from them, then their oath would still remain, but its fulfilment be beyond all hope. 'And who can tell to what dreadful doom we shall come, if we disobey the Powers in their own land, or purpose ever to bring war again into their holy realm?' And Maglor said: 'Yet if Manwë and Varda themselves deny the fulfilment of an oath to which we named them in witness, is it not made void?' And Maidros answered: 'But how shall our voices reach to Ilúvatar beyond the circles of the World? And by Him we swore in our madness, and called the Everlasting Darkness upon us, if we kept not our word. Who shall release us?' 'If none can release us,' said Maglor, 'then indeed the Everlasting Darkness shall be our lot, whether we keep our oath or break it; but less evil shall we do in the breaking.' Yet he yielded to the will of Maidros, and they took counsel together how they should lay hands on the Silmarils.

§23 And so it came to pass that they came in disguise to the camps of Fionwë, and at night they crept in to the places where the Silmarils were guarded, and they slew the guards, and laid hands upon the jewels; and then, since all the camp was roused against them, they prepared to die, defending themselves until the last. But Fionwë restrained his folk, and the brethren departed unfought, and fled far away. Each took a single Silmaril, for they said: 'Since one is lost to us, and but two remain, and two brethren, so is it plain that fate would have us share the heirlooms of our father.'

§24 But the jewel burned the hand of Maidros in pain unbearable (and he had but one hand, as has before been told); and he perceived that it was as Fionwë had said, and that his right thereto had become void, and that the oath was vain. And being in anguish and despair he cast himself into a gaping chasm filled with fire, and so ended; and the Silmaril that he bore was taken into the bosom of Earth.

§25 And it is told of Maglor that he could not endure the pain with which the Silmaril tormented him; and he cast it at last into the sea, and thereafter he wandered ever upon the shores singing in pain and regret beside the waves. For Maglor was the mightiest of the singers of old, but he came never back among the people of the Elves. And thus it came to pass that the Silmarils found their long homes: one in the airs of heaven, and one in the fires of the heart of the world, and one in the deep waters.

§26 In those days there was a great building of ships upon the shores of the Western Sea, and especially upon the great isles which, in the disruption of the northern world, were fashioned of ancient Beleriand. Thence in many a fleet the survivors of the Gnomes, and of the companies of the Dark-elves of Doriath and Ossiriand, set sail into the West and came never again into the lands of weeping and of war. But the Lindar, the Light-elves, marched back beneath the banners of their king, and they were borne in triumph unto Valinor. Yet their joy in victory was diminished, for they returned without the Silmarils and the light before the Sun and Moon, and they knew that those jewels could not be found or brought together again until the world was broken and re-made anew.

§27 And when they came into the West the Gnomes for the most part rehabited the Lonely Isle, that looks both West and

East; and that land became very fair, and so remains. But some returned even to Valinor, as all were free to do who willed; and there the Gnomes were admitted again to the love of Manwë and the pardon of the Valar; and the Teleri forgave their ancient grief, and the curse was laid to rest.

§28  Yet not all the Eldalië were willing to forsake the Hither Lands where they had long suffered and long dwelt; and some lingered many an age in the West and North, and especially in the western isles and in the Land of Leithien. And among these were Maglor, as hath been told; and with him for a while was Elrond Halfelven, who chose, as was granted to him, to be among the Elf-kindred; but Elros his brother chose to abide with Men. And from these brethren alone the blood of the Firstborn and the seed divine of Valinor have come among Mankind: for they were the sons of Elwing, Dior's daughter, Lúthien's son, child of Thingol and Melian; and Eärendel their sire was Idril's son Celebrindal, the fair maid of Gondolin. But ever as the ages drew on and the Elf-folk faded upon earth, they would set sail at eve from the western shores of this world, as still they do, until now there linger few anywhere of their lonely companies.

§29  This was the doom of the Gods, when Fionwë and the sons of the Valar returned to Valmar and told of all the things that had been done. Thereafter the Hither Lands of Middle-earth should be for Mankind, the younger children of the world; but to the Elves, the Firstborn, alone should the gateways of the West stand ever open. And if the Elves would not come thither and tarried in the lands of Men, then they should slowly fade and fail. This is the most grievous of the fruits of the lies and works that Morgoth wrought, that the Eldalië should be sundered and estranged from Men. For a while other evils that he had devised or nurtured lived on, although he himself was taken away; and Orcs and Dragons, breeding again in dark places, became names of terror, and did evil deeds, as in sundry regions they still do; but ere the End all shall perish. But Morgoth himself the Gods thrust through the Door of Night into the Timeless Void, beyond the Walls of the World; and a guard is set for ever on that door, and Eärendel keeps watch upon the ramparts of the sky.

§30  Yet the lies that Melkor, the mighty and accursed, Morgoth Bauglir, the Power of Terror and of Hate, sowed in the hearts of Elves and Men are a seed that doth not die and cannot by the Gods be destroyed; and ever and anon it sprouts anew, and bears dark fruit even to these latest days. Some say also that Morgoth himself has at times crept back, secretly as a cloud that cannot be seen, and yet is venomous, surmounting the Walls, and visiting the world to encourage his servants and set on foot evil when all seems fair. But others say that this is the black shadow of Sauron, whom the Gnomes named Gorthû, who served Morgoth even in Valinor and came with him, and was the greatest and most evil of his underlings; and Sauron fled from the Great Battle and escaped, and he dwelt in dark places and perverted Men to his dreadful allegiance and his foul worship.

§31   Thus spake Mandos in prophecy, when the Gods sat in judgement in Valinor, and the rumour of his words was whispered among all the Elves of the West. When the world is old and the Powers grow weary, then Morgoth, seeing that the guard sleepeth, shall come back through the Door of Night out of the Timeless Void; and he shall destroy the Sun and Moon. But Eärendel shall descend upon him as a white and searing flame and drive him from the airs. Then shall the Last Battle be gathered on the fields of Valinor. In that day Tulkas shall strive with Morgoth, and on his right hand shall be Fionwë, and on his left Túrin Turambar, son of Húrin, coming from the halls of Mandos; and the black sword of Túrin shall deal unto Morgoth his death and final end; and so shall the children of Húrin and all Men be avenged.

§32   Thereafter shall Earth be broken and re-made, and the Silmarils shall be recovered out of Air and Earth and Sea; for Eärendel shall descend and surrender that flame which he hath had in keeping. Then Fëanor shall take the Three Jewels and bear them to Yavanna Palúrien; and she will break them and with their fire rekindle the Two Trees, and a great light shall come forth. And the Mountains of Valinor shall be levelled, so that the Light shall go out over all the world. In that light the Gods will grow young again, and the Elves awake and all their dead arise, and the purpose of Ilúvatar be fulfilled concerning them. But of Men in that day the prophecy of Mandos doth not speak, and no Man it names, save Túrin only, and to him a place is given among the sons of the Valar.

§33   Here endeth *The Silmarillion*: which is drawn out in brief from those songs and histories which are yet sung and told by the fading Elves, and (more clearly and fully) by the vanished Elves that dwell now upon the Lonely Isle, Tol Eressëa, whither few mariners of Men have ever come, save once or twice in a long age when some man of Eärendel's race hath passed beyond the lands of mortal sight and seen the glimmer of the lamps upon the quays of Avallon, and smelt afar the undying flowers in the meads of Dorwinion. Of whom was Eriol one, that men named Ælfwine, and he alone returned and brought tidings of Cortirion to the Hither Lands.

*Commentary on the conclusion of the Quenta Silmarillion*

[All references to Q are to the second version, Q II.]

§1    After 'landed on the immortal shores' my father wrote (following Q, IV. 153) 'and neither Elwing nor any of his three mariners would he suffer to go with him, lest they fall under the wrath of the Gods', but struck this out in the moment of composition and replaced it by the passage given. The three mariners were not named in Q, where it is only said that Eärendel had a 'small company'. Cf. *The Lost Road* p. 60 and note 8.

§2    The story here of Elwing's leaping into the surf in the Bay of Elvenhome, and (in §3) of Eärendel's command to her to stay by the shores and await his return, is changed from that found in revisions to the text of Q (IV. 156), where Elwing was sundered for ever from Eärendel (see IV. 197–8).

§6    It is notable that the Lindar are here (and again in §§15, 26) called the 'Light-elves', this being a reversion to the earlier application of the term. At the beginning of QS (§§25, 40) the Lindar are the 'High Elves', and 'the Lindar and the Noldor and the Teleri are named the Light Elves' (§29), thus distinguished from the 'Dark Elves' who never passed over the sea to Valinor.

The words 'and Ingwiel son of Ingwë was their chief' first appear in an addition to Q (IV. 156 note 19). I suggested (IV. 196) that what my father really meant was that Ingwiel was the chief of the Lindar, among whom went the Noldor of Valinor; not that Ingwiel was the leader of the Noldor themselves – that was Finrod (later Finarfin).

§§6–7    A new element in the story is the sojourn of Elwing among the Teleri; the implication is clearly that the Teleri were influenced by her in providing their ships and mariners. Elwing was the great-grand-niece of Elwë Lord of Alqualondë. In AB 2 (annal 333–43), following AB 1, none of the Teleri left Valinor, though 'they built a countless multitude of ships.'

§§8–11    Wholly new is the matter of the council of the Gods, the decree of Manwë declared to Eärendel and Elwing, their choices of fate, and the despatch of the three mariners eastwards with a great wind. – On 'the forbidden shores' and the Ban of the Valar see the commentary on *The Fall of Númenor I*, §4.

§9    It is to be observed that according to the judgement of Manwë Dior

Thingol's Heir, son of Beren, was mortal irrespective of the choice of his mother.

§11    As Q II was originally written, Elwing devised wings for Eärendel's ship, whereby he sailed into the sky bearing the Silmaril (§17), but *after* the Great Battle and the expulsion of Morgoth through the Door of Night, because Eärendel was scorched by the Sun and hunted by the Moon, the Gods took his ship Wingelot and hallowed it, and launched it through the Door of Night (§19). In view of the statement in Q here that Eärendel 'set sail into *the starless vast* . . . voyaging *the Dark behind the world*', and in view also of the very explicit account of the Door in the *Ambarkanta* (IV. 237) – it 'pierceth the Walls and opens upon the Void' – I have supposed (IV. 203) that 'this act of the Valar was to protect Eärendel, by setting him to sail in the Void, above the courses of the Sun and Moon and stars, where also he could guard the Door against Morgoth's return.' In the same passage of the *Ambarkanta* it is said that the Valar made the Door of Night 'when Melko was overcome and put forth into the Outer Dark', and that it is 'guarded by Eärendel'.

The passage in Q §17 was, however, revised (IV. 156 note 20), and the launching of Wingelot by the Gods introduced at an earlier point in the narrative, before the Great Battle, and so before the making of the Door of Night (according to the *Ambarkanta*). It is not said in this revised passage that Eärendel passed through the Door, nor is it made explicit into what high regions he passed: his ship 'was lifted even into the oceans of the air'. This revision is taken up here in the present text, and again (as originally written) the Door of Night is not mentioned: the ship 'was lifted up even into the oceans of heaven' – and Eärendel journeyed far in it, 'even into the starless voids'. One could therefore possibly accommodate the revised story of the launching of Eärendel in Vingelot to the *Ambarkanta* by supposing that it was no longer my father's thought that he passed through the Door of Night (which was not yet in existence): he did not pass into Ava-kúma, the Outer Dark, but remained within 'the starless voids' of Vaiya. But this theory is undone by my father's addition of the very words in question, 'passed through the Door of Night', to the account. (This addition was not one of those made at the time of the writing of the manuscript, but it was made carefully in ink and does not belong with the rough alterations made much later.) In any case the words 'as he came back to Valinor from voyages *beyond the confines of the world*' suggest that he sailed into the Void. It seems therefore only possible to explain this on the assumption that the *Ambarkanta* conception had in this point been abandoned, and that the Door of Night was already in existence before Morgoth's great defeat.

§12    On the history of the white tower whither all the sea-birds of the world at times repaired see IV. 197. In Q II as originally written it was Eärendel who built the tower; by the revision (IV. 156 note 20) it was built by Elwing, who devised wings for herself in order to try to fly to him, but in vain: 'and they sundered till the end of the world.' Now the story shifts again. Elwing still builds the tower, but it is added that she learns the tongues of the birds and from them the craft of flight; and she is not now parted for ever from Eärendel after his transformation into the Star: she rises to meet him from her tower as he returns from his voyages beyond the confines of the world.

§15    A substantial space is left in the text after §14, and §15 begins with an ornate initial, suggesting that my father foresaw the beginning of a new chapter here. This was in fact inserted at the time of the late, pencilled emendations: *Of the Great Battle and the War of Wrath*.

§§15–16    In the account of the Great Battle my father simply followed the opening of Q II §18, though the outline of a much fuller tale had appeared at the end of AB 2: the landing of Ingwiel at Eglorest, the Battle of Eglorest, Fionwë's camp by Sirion, the thunderous coming of Morgoth over Taur-na-Fuin (this, if not actually excluded, at least made to seem very improbable in Q and QS), and the long-contested passage of Sirion.

§16    In my view there is no question that the words (not in Q) 'save some few [Balrogs] that fled and hid themselves in caverns inaccessible at the roots of the earth' preceded by a good while the Balrog of Moria (there is in any case evidence that a Balrog was not my father's original conception of Gandalf's adversary on the Bridge of Khazad-dûm). It was, I believe, the idea – first appearing here – that some Balrogs had survived from the ancient world in the deep places of Middle-earth that led to the Balrog of Moria. In this connection a letter of my father's written in April 1954 (*Letters* no. 144, p. 180) is interesting:

> [The Balrogs] were supposed to have been all destroyed in the overthrow of Thangorodrim . . . But it is here found . . . that one had escaped and taken refuge under the mountains of Hithaeglin [*sic*].

On the words 'all that were left of the three Houses of the Elf-friends, Fathers of Men' see the commentary on *The Fall of Númenor I*, §1.

§18    On the retention of the motive of the birds that accompanied Eärendel (which arose from an earlier form of the legend) see IV. 203. Thorondor as the captain of 'the great birds of heaven' is not named in Q, which has here 'a myriad of birds were about him.'

§20    A further heading was pencilled in against the beginning of this paragraph (see under §15 above): *Of the Last End of the Oath of Fëanor and his Sons*.

§22    The debate between Maglor and Maidros is articulated further than it was in Q, with the last and wisest word to Maglor, though the outcome is the same: for Maidros overbore him.

§26    A final heading was pencilled at the beginning of this paragraph: *Of the Passing of the Elves*.

§28    On the earlier accounts of Elrond's choice see p. 23. Now there appears both his changed decision, 'to be among the Elf-kindred', and the choice of his brother Elros 'to abide with Men'. Elros has been named in emendations to Q (IV. 155) and in later alterations to AB 2 (commentary on annal 325), and though these additions say nothing about him he was obviously introduced into these texts after the legend of Númenor had begun to develop. This is shown by the fact that still in the second text of *The Fall of Númenor* it was Elrond the mortal who was the first King of Númenor and the builder of Númenos (§2), and Elros only appears in his place by emendation.

In view of the presence here of Elros beside Elrond – whereas Elros is still absent in QS §87 – and the respective choices of the Half-elven, it is perhaps surprising that in §16 my father made no mention of the land of Númenor made for the Men of the Three Houses (see §§1–2 in both FN I and FN II); still more so, that he followed Q so closely in features where the 'intrusion' of Númenor had already introduced new conceptions. Thus he still wrote here in §19 that after the Great Battle 'Men . . . fled far away, and it was long ere they came back over Eredlindon to the places *where Beleriand had been*', and in §26 of 'the great building of ships upon the shores of the Western Sea, and especially upon the great isles which, in the disruption of the northern world, were fashioned of ancient Beleriand.'

It is not easy to trace the evolution of my father's conception of the survival of Beleriand (especially in relation to the destruction wrought at the Downfall of Númenor, see pp. 153–4); but in the FN texts there is clearly already a somewhat different view from that in Q. In FN II (where as noted above Elros had not yet emerged and which must therefore have preceded the present text) the story of the Last Alliance was already developed (§14): Elendil the Númenórean, a king in Beleriand,

> took counsel with the Elves that remained in Middle-earth (and these abode then mostly in Beleriand); and he made a league with Gil-galad the Elf-king . . . And their armies were joined, and passed the mountains and came into inner lands far from the Sea.

While the passages cited above from the present text are not in necessary or explicit contradiction to this, they are hardly congruent with it. The fact that my father later pencilled against §28 the names *Gilgalad* and *Lindon* could indeed be taken at first sight as showing that the conception of the undrowned land west of the Blue Mountains, and the alliance between Men and Elves who dwelt there, arose after it was written; but the evidence is decisive against this being the case.

I cannot offer any convincing explanation of this situation. It might be suggested that my father had the conscious intent to represent different and to some degree divergent 'traditions' concerning events after the overthrow of Morgoth and the great departure of Elves into the West; but this seems to me improbable. (On the name *Lindon* of the undrowned land see pp. 31–4 and the commentary on QS §108.)

*Idril's son Celebrindal* is an old idiom = Idril Celebrindal's son.

§30  Notable, and disconcerting to the editor, is the form *Melkor* (instead of *Melko*), which is quite certainly original here. I have said in IV. 282 that '*Melkor* for *Melko* was not introduced until 1951.' The evidence for this lies in the note referred to on p. 294, which gives a list of 'Alterations in last revision [i.e. of 'The Silmarillion'] 1951': these include *Aman, Arda, Atani / Edain, Eä, Eru, Melkor*, and a few less significant names. This important scrap of paper provides an external date – rare good fortune in this study – by which pre- and post-*Lord of the Rings* texts can often be distinguished; and the checks furnished by it are in complete harmony with what may be more tentatively deduced on other grounds. I have found nowhere any reason to suspect that *Aman, Arda*, etc. were ever used in the pre-*Lord of the Rings* period; and I therefore too readily assumed that the same was true of *Melkor* (which differs from the others in that it is not an entirely new name but only a new form), not having observed that it occurred in the present passage as an original form. It is to be noted that *Melko* was changed to *Melkor* on the Q-text at the same point (IV. 166 note 1).

No doubt the explanation of my father's including *Melkor* as an alteration made in 1951 when he had used it long before is in fact quite simple: he decided on *Melkor* at this time, and when he returned to 'The Silmarillion' after *The Lord of the Rings* was finished he used it in his revisions and rewritings of QS, and it was therefore an alteration of 1951. This is a good example of the traps that he most unwittingly laid, and which I cannot hope to have evaded in more significant matters than this.

The difficult passage concerning Morgoth's 'surmounting' the Walls of the World survives from Q (IV. 164): see IV. 253.

*Gorthû:* thus the name *Thû*, compounded *Gorthû*, reappears as the name of Sauron in the Noldorin tongue (see the *Etymologies*, stem THUS). *Gorthû* has occurred in emendations to the *Lay of Leithian* (III. 232–3), and in a change to the typescript text of FN II (p. 33). – With the statement that Sauron served Morgoth in Valinor cf. QS §143 and commentary ('Sauron was the chief servant of the evil Vala, whom he had suborned to his service in Valinor from among the people of the Gods'). In Q here 'others say that this is the black shadow of Thû, *whom Morgoth made*', changed (IV. 166 note 3) to a reading close to that of the present text.

§33  *The quays of Avallon.* At this time *Avallon* was a name of Tol Eressëa: 'the Lonely Island, which was renamed Avallon', FN II §1. *The meads of Dorwinion* must be in Tol Eressëa. The name has previously occurred as a land of vines in 'the burning South' in the *Lay of the Children of Húrin*, in the wine of Dorwinion in *The Hobbit*, and as marked on the map made by Pauline Baynes; see III. 26, which needs to be corrected by addition of a reference to this passage.

# PART THREE

---

# THE
# ETYMOLOGIES

# THE ETYMOLOGIES

The mode of my father's linguistic construction, which as is well known
was carried on throughout his life and in very close relation to the
evolution of the narratives, shows the same unceasing movement as do
they: a quality fundamental to the art, in which (as I believe) finality and
a system fixed at every point was not its underlying aim. But while his
'language' and his 'literature' were so closely interwoven, to trace the
history of the literary process through many texts (even though the trail
might be greatly obscured) is of its nature enormously much easier than
to trace the astounding complexity of the phonological and grammatical
evolution of the Elvish languages.

Those languages were conceived, of course, from the very beginning
in a deeply 'historical' way: they were embodied in a history, the history
of the Elves who spoke them, in which was to be found, as it evolved, a
rich terrain for linguistic separation and interaction: 'a language requires
a suitable habitation, and a history in which it can develop' (*Letters* no.
294, p. 375). Every element in the languages, every element in every
word, is in principle historically 'explicable' – as are the elements in
languages that are not 'invented' – and the successive phases of their
intricate evolution were the delight of their creator. 'Invention' was thus
altogether distinct from 'artificiality'. In his essay 'A Secret Vice' (*The
Monsters and the Critics and Other Essays*, 1983, p. 198) my father
wrote of his liking for Esperanto, a liking which, he said, arose 'not least
because it is the creation ultimately of one man, not a philologist, and is
therefore something like a "human language bereft of the inconveniences
due to too many successive cooks" – which is as good a description of the
ideal artificial language (in a particular sense) as I can give.' The Elvish
languages are, in this sense, very inconvenient indeed, and they image
the activities of countless cooks (unconscious, of course, of what they
were doing to the ingredients they had come by): in other words, they
image language not as 'pure structure', without 'before' and 'after', but as
growth, in time.

On the other hand, the linguistic histories were nonetheless 'images',
invented by an inventor, who was free to change those histories as he was
free to change the story of the world in which they took place; and he did
so abundantly. The difficulties inherent in the study of the history of any
language or group of languages are here therefore compounded: for this
history is not a datum of historical fact to be uncovered, but an unstable,
shifting view of what the history was. Moreover, the alterations in the
history were not confined to features of 'interior' linguistic development:
the 'exterior' conception of the languages and their relations underwent

change, even profound change; and it is not to be thought that the representation of the languages in letters, in *tengwar*, should be exempt.

It must be added that my father's characteristic method of work – elaborate beginnings collapsing into scrawls; manuscripts overlaid with layer upon layer of emendation – here find their most extreme expression; and also that the philological papers were left in the greatest disorder. Without external dating, the only way to determine sequence (apart from the very general and uncertain guide of changing handwriting) is in the internal evidence of the changing philology itself; and that, of its nature, does not offer the sort of clues that lead through the maze of the literary texts. The clues it does offer are very much more elusive. It is also unfortunately true that hasty handwriting and ill-formed letters are here far more destructive; and a great deal of my father's late philological writing is, I think, strictly unusable.

It will be seen then that the philological component in the evolution of Middle-earth can scarcely be analysed, and most certainly cannot be presented, as can the literary texts. In any case, my father was perhaps more interested in the processes of change than he was in displaying the structure and use of the languages at any given time – though this is no doubt due to some extent to his so often starting again at the beginning with the primordial sounds of the Quendian languages, embarking on a grand design that could not be sustained (it seems indeed that the very attempt to write a definitive account produced immediate dissatisfaction and the desire for new constructions: so the most beautiful manuscripts were soon treated with disdain).

The most surprising thing, perhaps, is that he was so little concerned to make comprehensive vocabularies of the Elvish tongues. He never made again anything like the little packed 'dictionary' of the original Gnomish language on which I drew in the appendices to *The Book of Lost Tales*. It may be that such an undertaking was always postponed to the day, which would never come, when a sufficient finality had been achieved; in the meantime, it was not for him a prime necessity. He did not, after all, 'invent' new words and names arbitrarily: in principle, he devised them from within the historical structure, proceeding from the 'bases' or primitive stems, adding suffix or prefix or forming compounds, deciding (or, as he would have said, 'finding out') when the word came into the language, following through the regular changes of form that it would thus have undergone, and observing the possibilities of formal or semantic influence from other words in the course of its history. Such a word would then exist for him, and he would know it. As the whole system evolved and expanded, the possibilities for word and name became greater and greater.

The nearest he ever came to a sustained account of Elvish vocabulary is not in the form of nor intended to serve as a dictionary in the ordinary sense, but is an etymological dictionary of word-relationships: an alphabetically-arranged list of primary stems, or 'bases', with their derivatives (thus following directly in form from the original 'Qenya Lexicon' which I have described in I. 246). It is this work that is given here. My father wrote a good deal on the theory of *sundokarme* or 'base-structure' (see SUD and KAR in the *Etymologies*), but like everything else it was frequently elaborated and altered, and I do not attempt its presentation here. My object in giving the *Etymologies**\* in this book is rather as an indication of the development, and mode of development, of the vocabularies of the Elvish languages at this period than as a first step in the elucidation of the linguistic history; and also because they form an instructive companion to the narrative works of this time.

It is a remarkable document, which must be reckoned among the most difficult of all the papers containing unique material which my father left. The inherent difficulties of the text are increased by the very bad condition of the manuscript, which for much of its length is battered, torn, crumpled at the edges, and discoloured (so that much that was very lightly pencilled is now barely visible and extremely hard to decipher). In some sections the maze of forms and cancellations is so dense, and for the most part made so quickly, that one cannot be sure what my father's final intention was: in these parts he was working out potential connections and derivations on the spot, by no means setting down already determined histories. There were many routes by which a name might have evolved, and the whole etymological system was like a kaleidoscope, for a decision in one place was likely to set up disturbing ripples in etymological relations among quite distinct groups of words. Moreover, complexity was (as it were) built in, for the very nature of the 'bases' set words on phonetic collision courses from their origin.

The work varies a great deal, however, between its sections (which are the groups of base-stems beginning with the same initial letter). The worst parts, both in their physical condition and in the disorganisation of their content, are the central letters of the alphabet, beginning with E. As the text proceeds the amount of subsequent alteration and addition, and resultant confusion, diminishes, and when P and R are reached the etymologies, though rough and hasty, are more orderly. With these groups my father began to use smaller sheets of paper which are much better preserved, and from S to the end the material does not present serious difficulty; while the concluding section (W) is written out very legibly in ink (in this book the last section is Y, but that is not so in the original: see p. 346). These relatively clear and orderly entries are found also in the A-stems, while the B-stems are distinct from all the rest in that they were written out as a very finished and indeed beautiful manuscript. The entries under D are in two forms: very rough material that was partly overwritten more legibly in ink, and then a second, much clearer and more ordered version on the smaller sheets.

---

\*On a covering page to the manuscript is written *Etymologies*, and also *Beleriandic and Noldorin names and words: Etymologies*.

I have not been able to reach any certain interpretation of all this, or find an explanation that satisfies all the conditions in detail. On the whole I am inclined to think that the simplest is most likely to be right in essentials. I have little doubt that the dictionary was composed progressively, through the letters of the alphabet in succession; and it may be that the very making of such a dictionary led to greater certainty in the whole etymological system, and greater clarity and assurance in its setting-out, as the work proceeded – but this also led to much change in the earlier parts. Having reached the end of the alphabet, my father then turned back to the beginning, with the intention of putting into better order the sections which had been first made and had suffered the most alteration; but this impulse petered out after the entries under D. If this were so, the original A and B entries were subsequently destroyed or lost; whereas in the case of D both survive (and it is noticeable that the second version of the D-entries differs from the former chiefly in arrangement, rather than in further etymological development).

Turning now to the question of date, I give some characteristic examples of the evidence on which I think firm conclusions can be based.

The original entry ELED gave the meaning of the stem as 'depart', with a derivative *Elda* 'departed'. Since this was the interpretation of *Eldar* in the *Lhammas* §2 and in QS §23 as those works were originally written, and first appears in them, the original entries under E clearly belong to that time. This interpretation was replaced in both the *Lhammas* and QS by carefully made emendations changing the meaning to 'Star-folk', and introducing the term *Avari*, with the meaning 'Departing'. Now the meaning 'Star-folk' appears in a second entry ELED replacing the first (and to all appearance made not long after); while the stem AB, ABAR bore, as first written, the meaning 'depart', and the derivative *Avari* was defined as 'Elves who left Middle-earth'. Thus the original A-entries and some at least of the alterations under E belong to the phase of the earliest alterations to QS.

In QS the meaning of *Avari* was then changed to 'the Unwilling' (see p. 219), and at the same time the root-meaning of AB, ABAR in the *Etymologies* was changed to 'refuse, deny' and the interpretation of *Avari* to 'Elves who never left Middle-earth or began the march.' This change can be dated from the note of 20 November 1937 (given on p. 200) in which my father said that *Avari* was to replace *Lembi* as the name of the Elves who remained in the East, while *Lembi* were to be 'Ilkorin Teleri', i.e. the Eldar who remained in Beleriand (see QS §§29–30 and p. 219). These changes were incorporated in the typescript of QS, which seems to have been in being by the beginning of February 1938 (p. 200). (The additional entry LEB, LEM shows this development, since *Lembi* is there translated as 'Elves remaining behind = Telerin Ilkorins'.)

In the note dated 3 February 1938 (p. 200) my father said that while *Tintallë* 'Kindler' could stand as a name of Varda, *Tinwerontar* 'Queen of Stars' must be changed to *Elentári*, because '*tinwë* in Qenya only =

spark (*tinta-* to kindle).' In the entry TIN the names *Tinwetar* and *Tinwerontar* of Varda were struck from the original material, and in the margin was written: '*Tintanië, Tintallë* Kindler = Varda; Q *tinta-* to kindle, make to spark'. Original T-entries can therefore be dated before February 1938.

Under the stem MEN appears the form *harmen* 'south', which was not subsequently changed, and again under the (additional) entry KHAR, but in this case the base-stem was afterwards changed to KHYAR and *harmen* to *hyarmen*. The insertion of *y* in this word was one of the alterations required in the note of 20 November 1937.

Putting these and a number of other similar evidences together, it seems to me clear that despite their very various appearance the *Etymologies* were not spread over a long period, but were contemporary with QS; and that some of the additions and corrections can be securely dated to the end of 1937 and the beginning of 1938, the time of the abandonment of QS and the beginning of *The Lord of the Rings*. How much longer my father kept the work in being with further additions and improvements is another question, but here also I think that an answer can be given sufficient for the purpose. This lies in the observations that there are relatively few names that belong specifically to *The Lord of the Rings*; that all of them are quite clearly additions to existing entries or introduce additional base-stems; that almost all were put in very hastily, mere memoranda, and not really accommodated to or explained in relation to the base-stems; and that the great majority come from the earlier part of *The Lord of the Rings* – before the breaking of the fellowship. Thus we find, for example, *Baranduin* (BARÁN); the imperative *daro!* 'stop!' (DAR; this was the sentry's command to the Company of the Ring on the borders of Lothlórien); *Hollin* added under ERÉK; the scrawled addition of a base ETER with the imperative *edro!* 'open!' (the word shouted by Gandalf before the doors of Moria); *Celebrimbor* (KWAR); *Caradras* (RAS; replacing in the original draft of the chapter *The Ring Goes South* the name *Taragaer*, itself found in the *Etymologies* under the added base TARÁK); *Celebrant* (RAT); *Imladris* (RIS). The words *caras* (KAR) and *naith* (SNAS), both of them additions, probably argue the existence of *Caras Galadon* and the *Naith* of Lothlórien, and the added *rhandir* 'pilgrim' under RAN, taken with the added *mith* 'grey' under MITH, shows *Mithrandir*. Clear cases of names from later in *The Lord of the Rings* do occur (so *Palantir* under PAL and TIR, *Dolbaran* under BARÁN), but they are very few.

I conclude therefore that while my father did for two or three years more make rather desultory entries in the *Etymologies* as new names emerged in *The Lord of the Rings*, he gave up even this as the new work proceeded; and that the *Etymologies* as given here illustrate the development of the Quenya and Noldorin (later > Sindarin) lexicons at the decisive period reached in this book, and provide in fact a remarkable point of vantage.

The *Etymologies*, then, reflect the linguistic situation in Beleriand envisaged in the *Lhammas* (see especially the third version, *Lammasethen*, p. 194), with Noldorin fully preserved as the language of the Exiles, though profoundly changed from its Valinorian form and having complex interrelations in respect of names with 'Beleriandic' (Ilkorin), especially the speech of Doriath. Afterwards my father developed the conception of a kind of amalgamation between Noldorin and the indigenous speech of Beleriand, though ultimately there emerged the situation described in *The Silmarillion* (p. 129): the Noldor abandoned their own tongue and adopted that of the Elves of Beleriand (Sindarin). So far-reaching was this reformation that the pre-existent linguistic structures themselves were moved into new historical relations and given new names; but there is no need here to enter that rather baffling territory.

The presentation of such a text as this can obviously not be exact: in the most chaotic parts a degree of personal interpretation of what was meant is altogether inevitable. There is in any case a great deal of inconsistency in detail between the different parts of the manuscript – for example, in the use of marks expressing length of vowel, which vary unceasingly between acute accent, macron (long mark), and circumflex. I have only 'standardized' the entries to a very limited extent, and only in so far as I have felt confident that I ran little risk of confusing the original intention. In particular, I have done nothing to bring divergent forms, as between one part of the *Etymologies* and another, into accord, seeing that the evolution of 'bases' and derivative words is an essential part of the history; and indeed in the most complex parts of the manuscript (initial letters E, G, K) I have attempted to distinguish the different 'layers' of accretion and alteration, though elsewhere I have been very selective in pointing out additions to the original list. I have 'standardized' the entries to the extent of giving the 'bases' always in capitals, and of using the acute accent to signify long vowels in all 'recorded' forms (as opposed to 'hypothetical' antecedent forms), with the circumflex for long vowels in stressed final syllables in Exilic Noldorin and Ilkorin, as is largely done in the original. I use *y* for *j* of the original throughout (e.g. KUY, DYEL for KUJ, DJEL), since this is less misleading and was my father's own practice elsewhere (found in fact here and there in the *Etymologies*); the stems with initial J, becoming Y, are moved forward from their original place before K to the end of the list. I print the back nasal (as in English *king*) with a Spanish *tilde* (ñ), again following my father's frequent practice, though in the *Etymologies* he used special forms of the letter *n*. His grammatical abbreviations are retained, as follows:

| adj. | adjective | g.sg. | genitive singular |
|------|-----------|-------|-------------------|
| adv. | adverb | inf. | infinitive |
| cpd. | compound | intr. | intransitive |
| f. | feminine | m. | masculine |

| *pa.t.* | past tense | *q.v.* | *quod vide,* 'which see' |
| *pl.* | plural | *sg.* | singular |
| *p.p.* | past participle | *tr.* | transitive |
| *prep.* | preposition | | |

The sign † means 'poetic or archaic'. The abbreviations used for the different languages are as follows (there is no explanatory list of them accompanying the manuscript):

| *Dan.* | Danian |
| *Dor.* | Doriathrin |
| *Eld.* | Eldarin |
| *EN* | Exilic Noldorin (also referred to as 'Exilic', but most often simply as N) |
| *Ilk.* | Ilkorin |
| *L* | Lindarin |
| *N* | Noldorin |
| *ON* | Old Noldorin (i.e. the *Korolambë* or *Kornoldorin*, see the *Lhammas* §5) |
| *Oss.* | Ossiriandeb (the name in the *Lhammas*, where however the form *Ossiriandic* is also found) |
| *PQ* | Primitive Quendian |
| *T* | Telerin |

An asterisk prefixed to a form means that it is 'hypothetical', deduced to have existed from later, recorded forms.

My own contributions are always enclosed within square brackets. A question mark standing within such brackets indicates doubt as to the correctness of my reading, but in other cases is original. Where I have found words totally illegible or can do no better than a guess (a very small proportion of the whole, in fact) I have usually omitted them silently, and so also with scattered jottings where no meaning is attached to forms, or where no clear connections are given. I have kept my own notes to a minimum, and in particular have very largely eschewed the temptation to discuss the etymologies in relation to earlier and later Elvish forms published elsewhere. On the other hand, while my father inserted many internal references to other stems, I have substantially increased the number (those due to me being enclosed within square brackets), since it is often difficult to find an element when it had been greatly changed from its ultimate 'base'. The Index to the book is further designed to assist in the tracing of name-elements that appear in the *Etymologies*.

# A

**AB-, ABAR-**   refuse, deny, *\*ábārǒ* refuser, one who does not go forth: Q *Avar* (or *Avaro*), pl. *Avari* = Elves who never left Middle-earth or began the march; N *Afor*, pl. *Efuir, Efyr* (ON *abóro*). Cf. AWA.
[This entry as first written gave the root-meaning as 'go away, depart',

translated *ábārŏ as 'departer, one who goes forth', and defined *Avari* as 'Elves who left Middle-earth' (see p. 344). An additional entry seems to allow for both developments from the root-meaning: 'AB-retreat, move back, refuse'.]

**AD-** entrance, gate, *adnō: Q *ando* gate; N *annon*, pl. *ennyn* great gate, Q *andon* (pl. *andondi*).

**AIWĒ-** (small) bird. Q *aiwe*, N *aew*. Cf. *Aiwenor* 'Birdland' = lower air. [For *Aiwenor(ë)* see the *Ambarkanta* and diagrams, IV. 236 etc.]

**AK-** narrow, confined. *akrā: Q *arka* narrow; N *agr, agor*. Cf. N *Aglond*, *Aglon* defile, pass between high walls, also as proper name; cf. *lond, lonn* path [LOD]. Q *aksa* narrow path, ravine.

**AKLA-R-** See KAL. Q *alka* ray of light; *alkar* or *alkare* radiance, brilliance; *alkarinqa* radiant, glorious. N *aglar* glory, *aglareb* glorious.

**ÁLAK-** rushing. *álākō rush, rushing flight, wild wind: N *alag* rushing, impetuous; *alagos* storm of wind. Cf. *Anc-alagon* dragon-name [NAK]. Related to LAK[2].

*alk-wā swan: Q *alqa*; T *alpa*; ON *alpha*; N *alf*; Ilk. *alch*; Dan. *ealc*. Cf. *Alqalonde* Swan-road or Swan-haven, city of the Teleri [LOD].

**ÁLAM-** elm-tree. Q *alalme*, also *lalme*; N *lalf (lelf)* or *lalven*, pl. *lelvin*; Ilk. *lalm*, pl. *lelmin*; Dan. *alm*. The stem is perhaps LÁLAM, q.v., but some hold it related to ALA since the elm was held blessed and beloved by the Eldar. [The end of this entry, from 'but some hold it', was an addition. Probably at the same time a stem AL- was added, with derivatives *alma* 'good fortune', *alya* 'rich', etc.; but this entry was struck out. The same derivative words are found under GALA.]

**ÁLAT-** large, great in size. Q *alta* [. . .] *alat-* as in *Alataire* = *Belegoer* [AY].

**AM[1]-** mother. Q *amil* or *amme* mother; Ilk. *aman*, pl. *emuin*. (N uses a different word, *naneth*, hypocoristic [pet-name form] *nana* [NAN]).

**AM[2]-** up: usually in form *amba-*. Q prefix *am-* up; *amba* adv. up(wards); *amban* upward slope, hill-side; *ambapenda, ampenda* uphill (adj.); see PEN. N *am* up; *am-bend, amben* uphill; *amon* hill, pl. *emuin, emyn*; *am-rûn* uprising, sunrise, Orient = Q *ambaron* (g.sg. *ambarónen*) or *Ambaróne*.

**ANA[1]-** Cf. NA[1]. to, towards. *anta-* to present, give: Q *anta-* give; *anna* gift; *ante* (f.), *anto* (m.) giver. Cf. *Yav-anna* [YAB]; *Aryante* [AR[1]]. N *anno* to give; *ant* gift. [Added:] Q *anta* face.

**ANA[2]-** Cf. NA[2]. be, exist. [Added:] *anwa* real, actual, true.

**ÁNAD-, ANDA-** *andā long: Q *anda*; N *and, ann*. Cf. names *Andram* long-wall [RAMBĀ], *Andfang, Anfang* Longbeard, one of the tribes of Dwarves (pl. *Enfeng*) [SPÁNAG].

**ÁNAK-** Cf. NAK bite. Q *anca* jaw; N *anc*; cf. *Ancalagon* [ÁLAK].

**ANÁR-** sun; derivative of NAR[1]. *anār-: Q *Anar* sun; EN *Anor*.

**ANGĀ-** iron. Q *anga*; N *ang*. Q *angaina* of iron; N *angren*, pl. *engrin*.

**ANGWA-** or **ANGU-** snake. Q *ango*, pl. *angwi*; N *am-* in *amlug* dragon: see LOK.

**AP-** *apsa* cooked food, meat. N *aes*; Ilk. *ass*.

**AR¹-** day. *\*ari*: Q *are*, pl. *ari*; N *ar-* only in names of week-days, as *Arvanwe* [see LEP]. Cf. name *Aryante* Day-bringer [ANA¹], N *Eriant*. Q *arin* morning, *arinya* morning, early; *arie* daytime; *ára* dawn; *Arien* the Sun-maiden. N *aur* day, morning; *arad* daytime, a day (= Q *arya* twelve hours, day).

**AR²-** Q *ara* outside, beside; also prefix *ar-* as in *Arvalin* (= outside Valinor). In Q this is purely local in sense. So also in Ilkorin, cf. *Argad* place 'outside the fence', or *Argador* (in Falathrin dialect *Ariad*, *Ariador*) lands outside Doriath (in Ilkorin *Eglador*), especially applied to West Beleriand, where there was a considerable dwelling of Dark-elves. In N *ar-* developed a privative sense (as English *without*), probably by blending with *\*al*, which is only preserved in *Alchoron* = Q *Ilkorin* [LA]. Thus *arnediad* without reckoning, = numberless [NOT]. In this sense Q uses *ava-*, as *avanóte* (see AWA). Hence Q *ar* and.

**ÁS-AT-** Q *asto* dust; N *ast*.

**ATA-** father. PQ *\*atū*, *\*atar*: Q *atar*, pl. *atari*; hypocoristic *atto*. N *adar*, pl. *edeir, eder*; *ada*. Cf. *Ilúv-atar*. Ilk. *adar*, pl. *edrin*; *adda*.

**AT(AT)-** again, back. Q *ata* again, *ata-*, *at-* back, again, re-; N *ad*. Cf. TAT, ATTA = two; Q *atta* two, N *tad*. N prefix *ath-* on both sides, across, is probably related; *athrad* ford, crossing (see RAT). Ilk. *adu*, *ado* double; cf. *Adurant*, a river in Ossiriand which for a distance has divided streams. [Ilk. *adu*, *ado* 'double' and the explanation of *Adurant* was an addition; this shows the conception of the island of Tol-galen (see the commentary on QS §114). Other additions made at different times to this entry were Q *atwa* double, and N *eden* new, begun again.]

**AWA-** away, forth; out. Q *ava* outside; *Avakúma* [KUM] Exterior Void beyond the World; *au-*, *ava-* privative prefixes = N *ar* (see AR²), as *avanóte* without number, numberless [NOT]. [Added:] *Avalóna*, cf. *lóna* [LONO].

**AY-** *\*ai-lin-* pool, lake: Q *ailin* (g.sg. *ailinen*); N *oel*, pl. *oelin*; cf. *Oelinuial* Pools of Twilight [LIN¹; YŪ, KAL].

**AYAR-, AIR-** sea, only used of the inner seas of Middle-earth. Q *ear* (*earen*) and *aire* (*airen*); N *oear, oer*. Cf. *Earráme*, a Q name = Wings of the Sea, name of Tuor's ship. *Belegoer* 'great sea', name of Western Ocean between Beleriand and Valinor, Q *Alataire* (see ÁLAT).

**AYAK-** sharp, pointed. Q *aika* sharp, *aikale* a peak; N *oeg* sharp, pointed, piercing, *oegas* (= Q *aikasse*) mountain peak. Cf. N *Oeges engrin* Peaks of Iron, *oeglir* range of mountain peaks. ?Related is Q *aiqa* steep, cf. Ilk. *taig* deep (blended with *tára*, see TĀ).

**AYAN-**   See YAN. *\*ayan-* holy: Q *Ainu*, f. *Aini*, holy one, angelic spirit; *aina* holy; *Ainulindale* Music of the Ainur, Song of Creation.


# B

[On the distinctive manuscript of the B-entries see p. 343. The following entries were added in pencil: BAD, BARÁN, BARAT, BARATH, BEN, and at the same time certain changes were made to existing entries. In this section I give the original entries as they were written, and note the alterations.]

**BAD-**   *\*bad-* judge. Cf. MBAD. Not in Q. N *bauð (bād-)* judgement; *badhor, baðron* judge. [Pencilled addition.]

**BAL-**   *\*bálā:* Q *Vala* Power, God (pl. *Valar* or *Vali* = PQ *\*bal-ī* formed direct from stem, cf. *Valinor*); there is no special f. form, where necessary the cpd. *Valatári* 'Vala-queen' is used, f. of *Valatar* (g.sg. *Valatáren*) 'Vala-king', applied only to the nine chief Valar: Manwe, Ulmo, Aule, Mandos, Lorien, Tulkas, Osse, Orome, and Melko. The *Valatári* were Varda, Yavanna, Nienna, Vana, Vaire, Este, Nessa, Uinen. T *Bala.* ON *Bala*, and *Balano* m., *Balane* f.; EN *Balan* m. and f., pl. *Belein, Belen.* In Ilk. *tórin* 'kings' was used, or the cpd. *Balthor, Balthorin (\*bal'tar-).*

Q *valya* having (divine) authority or power; *valaina* of or belonging to the Valar, divine; *valasse* divinity. Q *Valinor*, for *\*báli-ndóre*, reformed after the simplex *nóre* 'land', also in form *Valinóre*, land of the Gods in the West; ON *Balandor (\*bala-ndore)*, EN *Balannor.* Cf. also ON *Balthil* one of the names of the White Tree of Valinor, usually named in Q *Silpion*; EN *Belthil*, but this was usually applied to the image of the divine tree made in Gondolin, the tree itself being called *Galathilion.* Related is probably the name *Balar* of the large island at Sirion's mouth, where the Ilkorins long dwelt who refused to go West with Ulmo; from this is named *Beleriand* which they colonized from the island in the dark ages. *Balar* is probably from *\*bálāre*, and so called because here Ossë visited the waiting Teleri. [The explanation of *Balar, Beleriand* given here is not necessarily at variance with the story told in QS §35 that the Isle of Balar was 'the eastern horn of the Lonely Isle, that broke asunder and remained behind, when Ulmo removed that land again into the West'; but it can scarcely be brought into accord with the story (QS §36) that 'the Teleri dwelt long by the shores of the western sea, awaiting Ulmo's return', and that Ossë instructed the waiting Teleri 'sitting upon a rock nigh to the margin of the sea.' Moreover, the 'colonization' of Beleriand from Balar seems to take no account of Thingol, and those of his people 'that went not because they tarried searching for Thingol in the woods': 'and these multiplied and were yet scattered far and wide between

Eredlindon and the sea' (*Lhammas* §6). More must be meant than simply that Elves from Balar removed to the mainland, for this 'colonization' from Balar is here made the very basis of the name *Beleriand*.]

**BAN-** \**bánā*: Q *Vana* name of the Vala, wife of Orome, and sister of Varda and Yavanna; ON and T *Bana*; in ON also called *Bana-wende*, whence EN *Banwend*, *Banwen* (see WEN). \**bányā*: Q *vanya* beautiful; EN *bein*. Cf. Q *vaṇima* fair; *Vanimo*, pl. *Vanimor* 'the beautiful', children of the Valar; *Úvanimo* monster (creature of Melko); EN *úan* (\**úbanō*) monster; *uanui* monstrous, hideous.

**BAR-** Original significance probably 'raise'; cf. BARAD, MBAR. Hence uplift, save, rescue(?). \**barná*: Q *varna* safe, protected, secure; [struck out: *varne* protection;] *varnasse* security. \**baryǎ-*: Q *varya-* to protect; EN *berio* to protect. [The removal of *varne* 'protection' was due to the emergence of BARAN 'brown' with the derivative Q *varne* 'brown'.]

**BARÁD-** [Added: is blended with BARATH, q.v.] \**barádā* lofty, sublime: [added: ON *barada*, EN *baradh*, steep;] Q *Varda*, chief of the Valatári, spouse of Manwe; T *Barada* [> *Baradis*]. [Struck out: ON *Bradil*, EN *Breðil* (\**b'radil-*).] \**b'randā* lofty, noble, fine: T *branda*; ON *branda*, EN *brand*, *brann* (whence *brannon* lord, *brennil* lady); cf. name *Brandir* (*brand-dīr*: see DER).

**BARÁN-** Q *varne* (*varni-*) brown, swart, dark brown. ON *barane*, EN *baran*. Cf. river name *Baranduin*, *Branduin*. *Dolbaran*. [Pencilled addition. On *Dolbaran* (probably a further addition) see p. 345.]

**BARAS-** Stem only found in Noldorin: \**barasǎ* hot, burning: ON *barasa*, *baraha*; EN *bara* fiery, also eager; frequent in masculine names as *Baragund*, *Barahir* [KHER], etc. \**b'rás-sē* heat: ON *brasse*, white heat, EN *brass*: whence *brassen* white-hot.

**BARAT-** N *barad* tower, fortress. [Pencilled addition.]

**BARATH-** Probably related to BAR and BARÁD. \**Barathī* spouse of Manwe, Queen of Stars: ON *Barathi(l)*; EN *Berethil* and *El-bereth*. Q *Varda*, T *Baradis* show influence of *barádā* lofty. [Pencilled addition. The application of the name *Elbereth* to Varda seems to have arisen in the hymn of the Elves to the Goddess in the original second chapter (*Three is Company*) of *The Lord of the Rings*, written early in 1938 (where in rough workings for the song the name appears as *Elberil*). Concomitant with this the Ilkorin names *Elbereth* (of different meaning) and *Elboron* were removed from the original entries BER and BOR. These were the names of Dior's sons in AB 1 and 2 (annal 206/306), replaced in AB 2 (note 42) by *Eldûn* and *Elrûn* (which were added also to Q §14); *Elrûn* appears in the *Etymologies* in an addition to stem RŌ.]

**BAT-** tread. \**bátǎ*: ON *bata* beaten track, pathway; EN *bâd*. \**battǎ-* (with medial consonant lengthened in frequentative formation): ON *batthó-* trample, EN *batho*. ON *tre-batie* traverse, EN *trevedi* (pa.t. *trevant*) [see TER]. Cf. Q *vanta-* to walk, *vanta* a walk.

**BEL-** strong. Cf. BAL(?). Stem not found in Q. T *belle* (physical) strength; *belda* strong. Ilk. *bel* (*belē*) strength; *Beleg* the Strong, name of Ilkorin bowman of Doriath. *bélek : *bélekā : ON *beleka* mighty, huge, great; EN *beleg* great (n.b. this word is distinct in form from though related to Ilk. name *Beleg*); cf. EN *Beleg-ol* [GAWA] = Q *Aule*; *Belegoer* Great Sea [AY], name of sea between Middle-earth and the West; *Belegost* Great City [OS], name of one of the chief places of the Dwarves. T *belka* 'excessive' is possibly from ON; ON *belda* strong, *belle* strength (EN *belt* strong in body, *bellas* bodily strength) are possibly from T. Cf. name *Belthronding* of Beleg's yew-bow: see STAR, DING.

**BEN-** corner (from inside), angle. N *bennas* angle [NAS]. [Pencilled addition.]

**BER-** valiant. *bérya- : Q *verya-* to dare; *verya* bold; *verie* boldness. ON *berina* bold, brave; *bértha-* to be bold; EN *beren* bold, *bertho* dare; cf. proper name *Beren*. Ilk. *ber* valiant man, warrior (*berō); *bereth* valor; [struck out: cf. Ilk. name *El-bereth*.] Danian *beorn* man; this is probably blended with *besnō : see BES. [On the removal of *El-bereth* see BARATH.]

**BERÉK-** *bérekā : Q *verka* wild; EN *bregol* violent, sudden, cf. proper name *Bregolas* fierceness; *breged* violence, suddenness; *breitho* (*b'rekta-*) break out suddenly. Cf. *Dagor Vregedúr* [UR] Battle of Sudden Fire (EN *bregedur* wild-fire). [See MERÉK.]

**BERÉTH-** T *bredele* beech-tree; Ilk. *breth* (*b'rethā*) beech-mast, but the beech was called *galbreth* [GALAD] in Falasse, and *neldor* in Doriath (see NEL). The beech-tree was probably originally called *phéren*, Q *feren* or *ferne* (pl. *ferni*), ON *pheren*; but in EN *fêr* pl. *ferin* was usually replaced by the Ilk. *breth* mast, whence EN *brethil* beech-tree; cf. *Brethiliand, -ian* 'Forest of Brethil' [see PHER].

**BES-** wed. *besnō husband: Q *verno*; ON *benno*, EN *benn* man, replacing in ordinary use the old word *dîr* (see DER); *hervenn, herven* husband (see KHER). Ilk. *benn* husband; Danian *beorn* man, blended with *ber(n)ō : see BER.

*bessē wife: Q *vesse*; ON *besse*, EN *bess* woman, replacing old words *dî, dîs* (see NĪ¹, NDIS); *herves* wife (see KHER). In the f. the shift of sense in ON was assisted probably by blending with *dess* young woman, ON *dissa*.

*besū dual, husband and wife, married pair: Q *veru*. Cf. Q *Arveruen* third day (of the Valinorian week of 5 days) dedicated to Aule and Yavanna [LEP].

*bestā : Q *vesta* matrimony; *vesta-* to wed; *vestale* wedding.

**BEW-** follow, serve. *beurō follower, vassal: ON *biuro, bioro*, EN *bior, beor*; cf. proper name *Bëor*. *beuyā- follow, serve: ON *buióbe* to serve, follow, EN *buio* serve, hold allegiance to. T *búro* vassal, *búa-* serve. [On the name *Bëor* see the commentary on QS §128.]

**BIRÍT-** Stem only found in Ilkorin. *\*b'rittē* : Ilk. *brith* broken stones, gravel. Cf. river name *Brithon* (whence is named *Brithombar*) 'pebbly'. Late Exilic *brith* gravel is from Ilkorin.

**BOR-** endure. Q *voro* ever, continually; prefix *vor*, *voro-* as in *voro-gandele* 'harping on one tune', continual repetition; *vorima* continual, repeated. *\*bóron-*: ON *boron* (pl. *boroni*) steadfast, trusty man, faithful vassal; EN *bór* and pl. *býr* for older *berein*, *beren*; Ilk. *boron*, pl. *burnin*. Cf. N names given to the 'Faithful Men': *Bór*, *Borthandos*, *Borlas*, *Boromir*. *Borthandos* = *Borth* (see below) [but this element is not further mentioned] + *handos* (see KHAN). *Borlas* = *Bór* + *glass* joy (see GALÁS). *Boromir* is an old N name of ancient origin also borne by Gnomes: ON *Boronmíro*, *Boromíro*: see MIR. [Struck out: 'Cf. also Ilk. *boron* in Dor. name *El-boron*.' On the removal of *El-boron* see BARATH.]

**BORÓN-** extension of the above (originally a verbal form of the stem seen in *\*bóron-* above). Q *voronwa* enduring, long-lasting; *voronwie* endurance, lasting quality; cf. name *Voronwe* = ON *Bronwega*, EN *Bronwe* [WEG]. ON *bronie* last, endure, survive; EN *bronio* endure, *brono* last, survive; *bronadui* enduring, lasting. *\*b'rōnā*: ON *brūna* that has long endured, old (only used of things, and implies that they are old, but not changed or worn out); EN *brûn* old, that has long endured, or been established, or in use.

**Brodda** Name of a man in Hithlum. He was not one of the Elf-friend races, and his name is therefore probably not EN or Ilkorin.

**BUD-** jut out. Cf. MBUD.

# D

[A very rough pencilled list was for most of its length overwritten in ink, and nearly all these entries appear in a second, pencilled list, the differences between the two being largely a matter of arrangement; see p. 343.]

**DAB-** give way, make room, permit, allow. Q *lav-* yield, allow, grant. N *dâf* permission.

**DAL-** flat (variant or alteration of LAD). Q *lára* 'flat' may derive from *\*dāla* or *\*lāda*. EN *dalw* flat; *dalath* flat surface, plane, plain [see TIR]. ON *dalma* (probably = *dal* + *mā* hand) palm of hand; EN *dalf*. Ilk. *dôl* flat, lowlying vale.

**DAN-** Element found in names of the Green-elves, who called themselves *Danas* (Q *Nanar*, N *Danath*). Cf. *Dan*, *Denethor* and other names. See NDAN?

**DAR-** stay, wait, stop, remain. N *deri*, imperative *daro!* stop, halt; *dartha* wait, stay, last, endure.

**DARÁK-** *\*d'rāk* : Q *ráka* wolf; EN *draug*; Dor. *drôg*.
**DARÁM-** beat, hew. EN *dramb, dram(m)* a heavy stroke, a blow (e.g. of axe); *dravo* to hew (pa.t. *drammen,* † *dramp*); *drafn* hewn log; *drambor* clenched fist, hence blow with fist (see KWAR); *gondrafn, gondram* hewn stone. [Cf. the name of Tuor's axe in the *Lost Tales* : *Drambor, Dramborleg*; see II. 337.]
**DAT-, DANT-** fall down. EN *dad* down, cf. *dadben* downhill (see PEN); *dath* (*\*dattā*) hole, pit, Q *latta*. Q *lanta* a fall, *lanta-* to fall; N *dant-* to fall, *dannen* fallen. Cf. *Atalante* 'the Fallen', and *lasselanta* 'leaf-fall', Autumn [see TALÁT].
**DAY-** shadow. Q *leo* (*\*daio*) shade, shadow cast by any object; *laime* shade; *laira* shady. EN *dae* shadow; cf. *Daeðelos* = Shadow of Fear. Dor., Ilk. *dair* shadow of trees; cf. names *Dairon* and *Nan-dairon*.
**DEM-** sad, gloomy. Ilk. *dimb* sad (cf. *Dimbar*); *dim* gloom, sadness (*\*dimbē*); *dem* sad, gloomy (*\*dimbā*).
**DEN-** hole; gap, passage. N *dîn* opening, gap, pass in mountains, as in *Din-Caradras, Din-Dûhir*, etc. [On the first list DEN was given the meaning 'hillside, slope', whence Q *nende* slope, *nenda* sloping; N *dend, denn,* sloping, *dadðenn* downhill, *amdenn* uphill. This entry was struck through and the material transformed and transferred to PEN (whence *dadbenn, ambenn*). Cf. AM²; the A-entries belong to the second phase, later than the first form of the D-entries (see pp. 343–4).]
**DER-** Adult male, man (elf, mortal, or of other speaking race). Q *nér*, pl. *neri*, with *n* partly due to NĪ, NIS woman, partly to strengthened stem *ndere* bridegroom, ON *daer* [see NDER]. ON *dîr*, EN † *dîr* surviving chiefly in proper names (as *Diriel* older *Dirghel* [GYEL], *Haldir, Brandir*) and as agental ending (as *ceredir* doer, maker). Owing to influence of *dîr* (and of strengthened *ndisi* bride) N goes the opposite way to Q and has *dî* woman (see NDIS). In ordinary use EN has *benn* (properly = husband) [see BES].
**DIL-** stop up, fill up hole, etc. EN *dîl* stopper, stopping, stuffing, cf. *gasdil* stopgap [GAS]; *dilio* to stop up. [The rather unlikely word *gasdil* is mentioned because it was the name of a sign used to indicate that *g* had disappeared; see p. 298, note on *Gorgoroth*.]
**DING-** Onomatopoeic, var. of TING, TANG, q.v. Ilk. *ding, dang,* sound; cf. name *Bel-thron(d)-ding* [BEL, STAR].
**DO3, DÔ-** Q *ló* night, a night; *lóme* Night, night-time, shades of night. ON *dogme, dougme, doume*; EN *daw* night-time, gloom; *dû* (associated with NDU) nightfall, late evening – in EN night, dead of night is *fuin*; *Dú(w)ath* night-shade; *dûr* dark, sombre; cf. Q *lóna* dark. Ilk. *daum* = N *daw*. Cf. N *durion* a Dark-elf = *dureðel*. Q *lómelinde* nightingale; N *dúlind, dúlin(n)*. Cf. *Del-du-thling* [DYEL, SLIG.]
**DOMO-** Possibly related to the preceding (and certainly in some derivatives blended with it); faint, dim. *\*dōmi-* twilight in Q fell

together with *doʒmē* from DO3 in *lóme* night. Ilk. *dûm* twilight; Q
*tindóme* starry twilight = Ilk. *tindum* = N *tinnu* (see TIN).
**DÓRON-** oak. Q *norno*; N *doron* (pl. *deren*); Dor., Ilk. *dorn*. Cf. Q
*lindornea* adj. having many oak-trees [LI].
**DRING-** Noldorin stem = beat, strike. EN *dringo* to beat. Cf. sword-
name *Glamdring*. [In *The Hobbit*, *Glamdring* is rendered 'Foe-
hammer', called by the Orcs 'Beater'.]
**DUB-** lie, lie heavy, loom, hang over oppressively (of clouds). Q
*lumna* lying heavy, burdensome, oppressive, ominous; *lumna-* to lie
heavy. N *dofn* gloomy.
**DUI-** Ilk. *duin* water, river; cf. *Esgalduin*. Cf. *duil* river in *Duilwen*.
**DUL-** hide, conceal. N *doelio*, *delio*, and *doltha* conceal, pa.t. † *daul*,
p.p. *dolen* hidden, secret. Cf. *Gondolind*, *-inn*, *-in* 'heart of
hidden rock' [see ID]. Related is *ndulna* secret: Q *nulla*, *nulda*;
N *doll* (*dolt*) obscure. Cf. name *Terendul*. [See NDUL, and for
*Terendul* see TER.]
**DUN-** dark (of colour). Dor. *dunn* black; Dan. *dunna*; N *donn* swart,
swarthy. Cf. Doriath place-name *(Nan) Dungorthin* = N *Nan Dongoroth*, or *Nann Orothvor* Vale of Black Horror [see ÑGOROTH].
**DYEL-** feel fear and disgust; abhor. EN *delos*, *deloth* (probably < *del*
+ *gos*, *goth*) abhorrence, detestation, loathing, cf. *Dor-deloth* Loathly
Land; *deleb* horrible, abominable, loathsome; *delw* hateful, deadly,
fell; cf. *Daedhelos* Shadow of Abomination, *Deldú(w)ath* Deadly
Nightshade, a name of Taur-na-Fuin, *Delduthling*, N name of Ungoliantë [DAY, DO3]. Q *yelma* loathing, *yelwa* loathsome, *yelta-* to
loathe.

# E

[The entries under E are particularly confused and difficult. A small
number of original and clear entries were mostly struck through and the
pages covered with faint pencilled notes often hard to interpret.]

**EK-, EKTE-** spear. Q *ehte* spear, *ehtar* spearman. N *aith* spear-
point, *êg* thorn, cf. *Egthelion*, *Ecthelion* [STELEG]. [This original
entry was retained, with change of EKTE to EKTI, Q *ehtar* to *ehtyar*,
and the following additions:] [N] *ech* spear, Q *ekko*. Cf. *Eg-nor*.
**EL-** star. Q poetical *él* star (*elen*). Dor. *el*; N only in names, as *Elwing*.
[This original entry received many changes:] **EL-** star, starry sky. Q
poetical *elen* (*ellen* or *elena*) star. Dor *el*; N only in names, as *Elwing*,
*Elbereth*. Cf. *Eled-* Starfolk, that is Elves. *Elrond* = starry-dome, sky
[ROD]. [Added in margin:] Q *Elerína* star-crowned = Taniquetil;
*Elentári* Star Queen = Varda; N *Elbereth* = Varda. [On *Elbereth* see
note to BARATH; on *Elerína* and *Elentári* see p. 200.]

**ELED-**   go, depart, leave. Q *Elda* 'departed' Elf; N *eledh*. Q *lesta-* to leave, pa.t. *lende*. [This original entry was replaced by the following, written as carefully and clearly as the first:] **ÉLED-**   'Star-folk', Elf. Q *Elda* (*Eldamar* or *Elende* = Elvenhome, *Eldalie*, *Eldarin*); N *Eledh*, pl. *Elidh*, cf. *Eledhrim*, *Eledhwen* [Elf-fair >] Elf-maid, *Elennor* (*Eledandore* > *Eleðndor*). Dor. *Eld*, pl. *Eldin*. Dan. *Elda*. [The Dor. and Dan. forms were subsequently struck through and the following added:] In Dor. and Dan. transposed > *edel-* whence Dor. *Egla*, *Eglath* (cf. *Eglamar*, *Eglorest*); Dan. *Edel*. *Eglador* = Doriath in Doriathrin; *Ariador* = lands outside of Eglador. Cf. *Eglor* (Elf-river), Ilkorin name of a river in W. Beleriand. [On the earlier and later entries ELED see p. 344. Further faint pencillings show my father doubtful of the derivation of *Eldar* from a base meaning 'star', and suggesting that, although the name was so interpreted, it was probably in fact altered from *edela* 'eldest' – *eðel*, *eðil* being found also in Noldorin. A base EDE-, EDEL- 'precede, come forward' is proposed, with derivative *edela* (= *eleda*) 'firstborn', but this is struck out.]

**EN-**   element or prefix = over there, yonder. Q *en* there, look! yonder. Adj. *enta* that yonder. *Entar*, *Entarda* (*Enta* + *harda* [3AR]) Thither Lands, Middle-earth, Outer Lands, East.

**ÉNED-**   centre. Q *endya*, *enya* middle; *ende* middle, centre. N *enedh*. [To this original entry was added:] *Endamar* Middle-earth. *Endor* centre of the world. [See NÉD.]

**ÉNEK-**   six. Q *enqe*; N *eneg*.

**ERE-**   be alone, deprived. Q *er* one, alone; *erya* single, sole; *eresse* solitude; *eressea* lonely. N *ereb* isolated (*\*ereqa*); *eriol* alone, single. Cf. *Tol-eressea*, *Amon Ereb*. Q *erume* desert, cf. *Eruman* desert N.E. of Valinor; N *eru* waste, desert.

**ERÉD-**   *\*eredē* seed: Q *erde* seed, germ; N *eredh*; Ilk *erdh*. [See RED.]

**ERÉK-**   thorn. Q *erka* prickle, spine; *erka-* to prick; *erkasse* holly. N *ercho* to prick; *erch* a prickle; *ereg* (and *eregdos* [TUS]) holly-tree, pl. *erig*. Cf. *Taur-nan-Erig* or *Eregion* = Dor. Forest of *Region*: Dor. *regorn* holly-tree (pl. *regin*, g.pl. *region*) [see OR-NÍ]. [Further addition:] *Regornion* = Hollin.

**ES-**   indicate, name. Q *esta* to name, *esse* a name.

**ESE-, ESET-**   precede. Q *esta* first; *esse* beginning; *essea* [?primary] *Estanesse* the Firstborn. [Neither of these two entries were rejected, though they are certainly mutually exclusive, but the second was marked with a query.]

**ESEK-**   Ilk. *esg* sedge, *esgar* reed-bed. Cf. *Esgaroth* Reedlake, because of reed-banks in west.

**ET-**   forth, out. Q prefix *et-*, N *ed-*. Cf. *ehtele* under KEL. [To this original entry was added:] *etsiri*: Q *etsir* mouth of a river, N *ethir* [SIR]. *ette* outside; *ettele* outer lands; *ettelen* [?foreign].

**ETER-** Cf. ET out. open (come out, of flowers, sun, etc.). *edro!* open!
**EY-** everlasting. Q *aira* eternal; *aire* eternity; *ia (\*eyā)* ever. Cf. *Iolosse* ever-snow, N *Uiloss (\*Eigolosse)*. N *uir* eternity, *uireb* eternal. [This original entry was struck out, the material reappearing under GEY. *Iolosse* was probably the form underlying the early emendation to *Oiolosse* in QS §13. *Oiolosse* arose with the further transformation of this base to OY, q.v.]
**EZDĒ-** 'rest', name of the wife of Lórien. Q *Este*; ON *Ezde*, *Eide*, *Ide*; N *Idh*. See SED.
**EZGE-** rustle, noise of leaves. Q *eske*; Ilk. *esg*; cf. *Esgalduin*. [This, which may be one of the original entries, was struck out. Cf. ESEK, and for *Esgalduin* see SKAL[1].]

# G

[The entries under G present much the same appearance as those under E: an initial layer of a few clear entries in ink, and a mass of changes and additions put in very roughly afterwards.]

**GAL-** shine; variant of KAL.
**GALA-** thrive (prosper, be in health – be glad). Q *'al* in the following forms which are not confused with *ala-* 'not': *alya* prosperous, rich, abundant, blessed; *alma* good fortune, weal, wealth; *almie*, *almare* blessedness, 'blessings', good fortune, bliss; *almárea* blessed. Cf. name *Almáriel*. N *galw*; cf. names *Galadhor*, *Galdor* (later *Gallor*) – though these may contain GÁLAD. N *galas* growth, plant; *galo-* to grow. Possibly related are GÁLAD, GALÁS. [*Almáriel* is the name of a girl in Númenor in *The Lost Road*, p. 59.]
**GALAD-** tree. Q *alda*; N *galadh*. Cf. *Galadloriel (Galagloriel)*, *Galathilvion*. [*Galadlóriel* and *Galathilion* (not as here *Galathilvion*) appear in very early emendations to QS §16. The form *Galagloriel* is found in an early draft for the chapter *A Knife in the Dark* in *The Fellowship of the Ring*. – This, one of the original entries, was not struck out or altered (apart from *Galathilvion* > *Galathilion*), but a new entry for the stem was made:] **GÁLAD-** tree. Q *alda*; N *galadh*. Cf. names *Galadhor*, *Galdor*, etc. Q *Aldaron* name of Oromë. *Aldalemnar*, see LEP. Dor. *gald*, cf. *galbreth* beech [BERÉTH].
**GALÁS-** joy, be glad. N *glas* joy; cf. names as *Borlas*. Q *alasse* joy, merriment.
**GAP-** N *gamp* hook, claw; Q *ampa* hook.
**GAR-** hold, possess. N *gar-*. [An original entry, struck out; see 3AR.]
**GAS-** yawn, gape. *\*gassā*: N *gas* hole, gap; *gasdil* stopgap [DIL]; Q *assa* hole, perforation, opening, mouth. [Cf. *Ilmen-assa*, the Chasm of Ilmen, IV. 240. – This original entry was retained, but the

following addition made:] *gāsa: ON *gása* = Q *kúma*; EN *gaw*, *Belego* the Void.

**GAT-** Q *atsa* catch, hook, claw; N *gad-*, *gedi* catch.

**GAT(H)-** N *gath* (*gattā*) cavern; *Doriath* 'Land of the Cave' is Noldorin name for Dor. *Eglador* = Land of the Elves. The Ilkorins called [?themselves] *Eglath* = Eldar. Rest of Beleriand was called *Ariador* 'land outside'. N *gadr*, *gador* prison, dungeon; *gathrod* cave. Another name is *Garthurian* = Fenced Realm = N *Ardholen* (which was also applied to Gondolin). [Added to this later:] Dor. *gad* fence; *argad* 'outside the fence', the exterior, the outside. Cf. *Argador*, Falathrin *Ariador*. [See AR², ÉLED, 3AR, LED.]

**GAWA-** or **GOWO-** think out, devise, contrive. Q *auta* invent, originate, devise; *aule* invention, also as proper name of the god *Aule*, also called *Martan*: N *Gaul* usually called *Belegol* (= great Aule) or *Barthan*: see TAN, MBAR. N *gaud* device, contrivance, machine.

**GAY-** Q *aira* red, copper-coloured, ruddy; N *gaer*, *goer*.

**GÁYAS-** fear. *gais-*: Q *aista* to dread; ON *gaia* dread; N *gae*. *gaisrā*: ON *gǣsra*, *gérrha*; N *gaer* dreadful.

**GENG-WĀ-** Q *engwa* sickly. N *gemb*, *gem*; cf. *ingem* 'year-sick' [YEN], suffering from old age (new word coined after meeting with Men). N *iaur* ancient [YA], *ifant* 'year-full' [YEN, KWAT] did not connote weakness. [*Engwar* 'the Sickly' is found in the list of Elvish names for Men in QS §83.]

**GEY-** everlasting. Q *ia* ever (*geiā*); *iale* everlasting; *íra* eternal; *íre* eternal [?read 'eternity']; *Iolosse* Everlasting Snow (*Geigolosse*) = Taniquetil. N *Guilos*, *Amon Uilos* (*guir* eternity, *guireb* eternity [read 'eternal']). N *Guir* is confounded with *Gui* = Q *Vaiya* (*wāyā*) [WAY]. [This note, replacing the rejected entry EY, was in its turn struck out and replaced by OY.]

**GIL-** (cf. GAL, KAL; SIL, THIL; GUL, KUL) shine (white or pale). *gilya*: N *gîl* star (pl. *giliath*). [This original entry was retained, with the addition to *gîl*: 'pl. *geil*, collective pl. *giliath*', and the following also added:] *gael* pale, glimmering; *gilgalad* starlight; *Gilbrennil*, *Gilthoniel* = Varda. Q *Ilma* starlight (cf. *Ilmare*), N [?*Gilwen*] or *Gilith*; *Ilmen* region above air where stars are. [On *Ilma* and *Ilmen* see the commentary on QS §4.]

**GIR-** quiver, shudder. N *giri* shudder; *girith* shuddering, horror.

**GLAM-** N form of LAM, also influenced by ÑGAL(AM). N *glamb*, *glamm* shouting, confused noise; *Glamhoth* = 'the barbaric host', Orcs [KHOTH]. *glambr*, *glamor* echo; *glamren* echoing; cf. *Eredlemrin* = Dor. *Lóminorthin*. *glavro* to babble, *glavrol* babbling.

**GLAW(-R)-** Q *laure* gold (properly the light of the Tree *Laurelin*); N *glaur* gold. The element *glaur* reduced in polysyllables to *glor*, *lor* appears in many names, as *Glorfindel*, *Glaurfindel*, *Galadloriel*. [This original entry was struck out and replaced by:] **GLAWAR-** N alteration of LAWAR, q.v.

**GLIN-** sing. Q *lin-*; N *glin-*. Q *linde* song, air, tune; N *glinn*. Cf. *Laurelin*. [Original entry, struck out. See LIN².]

**GLINDI-** pale blue. N *glind*, *glinn*; Q *ilin*. [Original entry, struck out. Cf. the original meaning of *Eredlindon*, Blue Mountains, commentary on QS §108, and see LIN².]

**GLING-** hang. Q *linga*; N *gling*. Cf. *Glingal*. [Original entry, struck out and replaced by:] **GLING-** N alteration of LING 'hang', q.v.

**GLIR-** N form of LIR¹ sing. N *glîr* song, poem, lay; *glin* to sing, recite poem; *glær* long lay, narrative poem. Q *laire* poem, *lirin* I sing.

**GÓLOB-** *\*golbā* branch: Q *olwa*; N *golf*. Cf. *Gurtholf* [> *Gurutholf*] [ÑGUR]. [For the form *Gurtholf* (earlier *Gurtholfin*) see p. 406.]

**GOLÓS-** Q *olosse* snow, fallen snow; N *gloss* snow. Cf. *Uilos*. N *gloss* also adj. snow-white. [An original entry, this was retained with alteration of Q *olosse* to † *olos*, † *olosse* and the note: 'poetical only: confused with *losse* flower, see LOS which is perhaps originally connected.' The stem in question in fact appears as LOT(H).]

**GOND-** stone. Q *ondo* stone (as a material); N *gonn* a great stone, or rock. [This original entry was retained, but the base was changed to GONOD-, GONDO-, and the following added:] Cf. *Gondolin* (see DUL); *Gondobar* (old *Gondambar*), *Gonnobar* = Stone of the World = Gondolin. Another name of Gondolin *Gondost* [OS], whence *Gondothrim*, *Gondothrimbar*. [Cf. *Gondothlim*, *Gondothlimbar* in the *Lost Tales* (II. 342).]

**GOR-** violence, impetus, haste. Q *orme* haste, violence, wrath; *orna* hasty. N *gormh*, *gorf* impetus, vigour; *gorn* impetuous. [Apart from the removal of the form *gormh* this original entry was retained, with these additions:] Cf. *Celegorn* [KYELEK]; and cf. *Huor, Tuor*: *Khōgore* [KHŌ-N], *Tūgore* [TUG].

**GOS-, GOTH-** dread. Q *osse* terror, as name *Osse*. Cf. *Mandos* (see MBAD). N has *Oeros* for *Osse* (\**Goss*). Cf. *Taur-os* [TÁWAR]. N *gost* dread, terror; *gosta-* fear exceedingly; cf. *Gothrog* = Dread Demon [RUK]; *Gothmog* [MBAW]. *Gostir* 'dread glance', dragon-name [THĒ].

**GŪ-** Prefix *gū-* no, not, as in Q *ū-* not (with evil connotation); *Úvanimor* [BAN].

**GUL-** glow, shine gold or red (cf. GIL); also *yul-* smoulder [YUL]. N *goll* red (\**guldā*). [This original entry was struck out. See KUL.]

**GWEN-** (distinguish WEN(ED)). Q *wenya* green, yellow-green, fresh; *wēn* greenness, youth, freshness (blended with *wende* maid). N *bein* fair, blended with BAN. Ilk. *gwên* greenness; *gwene* green; cf. *Duilwen* [DUI].

**GYEL-** [< GEL-] Q *yello* [< *ello*] call, shout of triumph. N *gell* joy, triumph; *gellui* triumphant; *gellam* jubilation. Cf. *Diriel* [DER]. *Gelion* merry singer, surname of Tinfang. [*Tinfang Gelion* occurs in the *Lay of Leithian*: III. 174, 181–2.] *Gelion* shorter name of a great river in E. Beleriand; a Gnome interpretation (this would have been

*Dilion* in Ilkorin); cf. Ilk. *gelion* = bright, root GAL. [This rather perplexing note seems certain in its reading.]

**GYER-** *gyernā* old, worn, decrepit (of things): Q *yerna* old, worn; *yerya* to wear (out), get old. N *gern* worn, old (of things).

# 3

[The few entries under the initial back spirant 3 were struck out and replaced more legibly.]

**3AN-** male. Q *hanu* a male (of Men or Elves), male animal; ON *anu*, N *anw*; Dor. *ganu*. (The feminine is INI.)

**3AR-** Stems 3AR have, hold, and related GAR, GARAT, GARAD were much blended in Eldarin. From 3AR come: Q *harya-* possess; *harma* treasure, a treasured thing; *harwe* treasure, treasury; *haryon* (heir), prince; *haran* (pl. *harni*) king, chieftain (see TĀ). N *ardh* realm (but Q *arda* < GAR); *aran* king (pl. *erain*). Dor. *garth* realm, *Garthurian* (Fenced Realm = Doriath), *garon* lord, may come from 3AR or GAR.

From GAR: Q *arda* realm – often in names as *Elenarda* 'Star-kingdom', upper sky; *armar* pl. goods; *aryon* heir; *arwa* adj. (with genitive) in control of, possessing, etc., and as semi-suffix *-arwa*, as *aldarwa*, having trees, tree-grown. N *garo-* (*gerin*) I hold, have; *garn* 'own', property.

**GARAT-** Q *arta* fort, fortress. N *garth*: cf. *Garth(th)oren* 'Fenced Fort' = Gondolin – distinguish *Ardh-thoren* = Garthurian. [This note is the final form of two earlier versions, in which the Qenya words are all derived from 3AR. In one of these versions it is said that N *Arthurien* is a Noldorinized form of *Garthurian*, *Arthoren* a translation; in the other that N *Arthurien* is 'a half-translation = N *Arthoren*'; see THUR.]

**3ARAM-** Dor. *garm* wolf; N *araf*. [Struck out. Another version gave also Q *harma*, Dan. *garma*.]

**3EL-** sky. Q *helle*, ON *elle*, sky. In Noldorin and Telerin this is confused with EL star. Other derivatives: Q *helwa*, ON *elwa* (pale) blue, N *elw*; cf. name of *Elwe* King of the Teleri [WEG]; and names as *Elulind*, *Elwing*, *Elrond*. Q *helyanwe* 'sky-bridge', rainbow, ON *elyadme*, N *eilian(w)* [YAT]. Dor. *gell* sky, *gelu* sky-blue. [A later note directs that *Elwe* be transferred to EL star. *Elrond*, *Elwing* are also given under EL.]

**3Ŏ-** from, away, from among, out of. This element is found in the old partitive in Q *-on* (*3ō* + plural *m*). Q *ho* from; Ilk. *go*; N *o* from. In Ilk. *go* was used for patronymics, as *go-Thingol*.

# I

[The single page of entries under I consists only of very rough notes.]

**I-** that (deictic particle) in Q is indeclinable article 'the'. N *i-* 'the', plural *in* or *i-*.

**I-** intensive prefix where *i* is base vowel. ITHIL- Moon (THIL, SIL): Q *Isil*; N *Ithil*; Dor. *Istil*. INDIS- = *ndis* bride; *Indis* name of the goddess Nessa (see NDIS, NĪ). [*Ithil* occurs in *The Lost Road* (p. 41) as the 'Beleriandic' name of the Moon – i.e. the name in a language (Noldorin) perceived by Alboin Errol to be spoken in Beleriand.]

**ID-** *\*īdī*: heart, desire, wish. Q *íre* desire; *írima* lovely, desirable. Q *indo* heart, mood; cf. *Indlour, Inglor* (*Indo-klār* or *Indo-glaurē*). N *inn, ind* inner thought, meaning, heart; *idhren* pondering, wise, thoughtful; *idher* (*\*idrē*) thoughtfulness. Cf. *Idhril*; *Túrin(n)* [TUR], *Húrin(n)* [KHOR]. [The Q word *írima* occurs in the song in *The Lost Road* (p. 72): *Toi írimar*; *Írima ye Númenor*; cf. also *Írimor* 'Fair Ones', name of the Lindar in the Genealogies, p. 403. – For the original etymology of *Idril, Idhril* see II. 343.]

**IL-** all. Q *ilya* all, the whole. **ILU-** universe: Q *ilu, ilúve*: cf. *Ilúvatar, Ilurambar* Walls of the World. *Ilumíre* = Silmaril. *ilqa* everything.

**ING-** first, foremost. *inga* first. Element in Elfin and especially Lindarin names. Cf. *Ingwe* prince of Elves. QL [i.e. Qenya-Lindarin] form is always used (*Ingwe*): not *ngw > mb* [i.e. in Noldorin] because the L form persisted and also the composition was felt *ing + wege* [WEG]. Cf. *Ingil*. [*Elfin* at this date is a strange reversion to old usage.]

**INI-** female. See NĪ: Qenya *ní* female, woman. Q *hanwa* male, *inya* female; *hanuvoite, inimeite*. N *inw* after *anw* [see 3AN].

**INK-, INIK-?** Q *intya-* guess, suppose; *intya* guess, supposition, idea; *intyale* imagination. N *inc* guess, idea, notion.

**IS-** Q *ista-* know (pa.t. *sinte*); *ista* knowledge; *istima* having knowledge, wise, learned, *Istimor* = Gnomes [cf. p. 403]. Q *istya* knowledge; *istyar* scholar, learned man. N *ist* lore, knowledge; *istui* learned; *isto* to have knowledge. Cf. *Isfin* (= *Istfin*) [PHIN].

# K

[The numerous entries under K are perhaps the most difficult in the work. A first layer of etymologies written carefully and clearly in ink was overlaid by a mass of rapid notes in pencil that are now in places almost invisible.]

**KAB-** hollow. Q *kambe* hollow (of hand); N *camb, cam* hand, cf. *Camlost* 'Emptyhand' [LUS] (= Dor. *Mablost*). *Erchamui* 'One-handed'. [An earlier version of this entry gives also *Cambant* 'full hand'; see KWAT.]

**KAL-**   shine (general word). Variant forms AKLA-, KALAR-, AKLAR-. Q *kala* light; *kalma* a light, lamp; *kalya* illuminate; *kalina* light (adj.). In N the variant GAL appears: *gail* (\**galyā*) bright light, *glaw* radiance (\**g'lā*, cf. Q *kala* < \**k'lā*). But in longer forms KAL also in N, as *aglar*, *aglareb*, see AKLA-R. Also *celeir* brilliant (\**kalaryā*); Q *kallo* noble man, hero (\**kalrō*), N *callon* (\**kalrondō*) hero; N poetical *claur* splendour, glory – often in names in form *-glor*. *gôl* light (\**gālœ-*) in *Thingol*. [Parts of this original entry were rejected: the etymology of *Thingol* (see THIN), and the idea that GAL was a Noldorin variant of KAL. It is not clear at this stage how these bases were related. The entry was covered with a maze of new forms, often rejected as soon as written. The following can be discerned:] N *calad* light (cf. *Gilgalad*); *calen* bright-coloured = green. Q *kalta-* shine; *Kalakilya*; *Kalaqendi*, N *Kalamor*; *Kalamando* = Manwe [see MBAD]. *Ankale* 'radiant one', Sun. *yúkale*, *yuale* twilight, N *uial* [YŪ].

**KALPA-**   water-vessel. Q *kalpa*; N *calf*. Q *kalpa-* draw water, scoop out, bale out. [Added entry.]

**KAN-**   dare. Q *káne* valour; N *caun*, *-gon* (cf. *Turgon*, *Fingon*). Q *kanya* bold. N *cann* (\**kandā*). *Eldakan* (name) = *Ælfnoþ*. [Added entry.]

**KÁNAT-**   four. Q *kanta-*, *kan-*; N *canad*. [Added entry.]

**KAP-**   leap. [Added:] N *cabr*, *cabor* frog.

**KAR-**   make, do. Q *kar* (*kard-*) deed; N *carð*, *carth* deed, feat. Cf. KYAR cause. Q *karo* doer, actor, agent; *ohtakaro* warrior. [This stem was very roughly rewritten thus:] **KAR-**   make, build, construct. Q *kar* (*kard-*) building, house; N *car* house, also *carð*. Q *karin*, *karne*, I make, build. Cf. **KYAR-** cause, do. Q *tyaro* doer, actor, agent; *ohtatyaro* warrior. N *caras* a city (built above ground).

**KARAK-**   sharp fang, spike, tooth. Q *karakse* jagged hedge of spikes; cf. *Helkarakse*, N *elcharaes* [KHEL]. [This entry was retained, with KARAK > KÁRAK and *elcharaes* > *helcharaes*, and the following faintly visible additions made:] Q *karka* tooth, *karkane* row of teeth. N *carag* spike, tooth of rock; *carch* tooth, fang (*Carcharoth*).

**KARÁN-**   red. Q *karne* (\**karani*) red; N *caran*. \**k'rannā*: N *crann* ruddy (of face), cf. *Cranthir* [THĒ], [?as noun] like Old English *rudu*, face, blush, the cheeks. [Added entry.]

**KARKA-**   crow. Q *karko*; N *carach*. [This stem was changed thus:] **KORKA-** crow. Q *korko*; N *corch*.

**KAS-**   head. Q *kár* (*kas-*); N *caw* top. [Added:] \**kas-sa*, \**kas-ma*: Q *cassa* helmet.

**KAT-**   shape. Q *kanta* shaped, and as quasi-suffix, as in *lassekanta* leaf-shaped; *kanta-* to shape; N *cant*. [The meaning 'outline' was attributed to *cant*, and the following added:] \**katwā*: ON *katwe* shaped, formed, N *cadw*, *-gadu*. \**katwārā* shapely: N *cadwor*, *cadwar*. N *echedi*, pa.t. *echant* (\**et-kat*) fashion. [Cf. *Im Narvi hain echant* above the Doors of Moria.]

**KAY-** lie down. Q *kaima* bed. N *caew* lair, resting-place; *cael* (Q *kaila*) lying in bed, sickness; *caeleb* bedridden, sick: cf. Q *kaimasse*, *kaimassea*.

**KAYAN-, KAYAR-** ten. Q *kainen*; N *caer*. [Added entry.]

**KEL-** go, run (especially of water). \**et-kelē* spring, issue of water: Q *ehtele*, N *eithel* (from metathesized [i.e. with transposed consonants] form \**ektele*). Q *kelume* stream, flow; N *celon* river; Q *kelma* channel. Cf. KYEL run out, come to an end; KWEL fade away. [These changes were made: 'N *celon* river' > 'Ilk. *celon* river, and as proper name, *kelu+n*'; 'N *celw* spring, source' added.]

**KEM-** soil, earth. Q *kén* (*kemen*). N *coe* earth (indeclinable), *cef* soil, pl. *ceif*. Q *kemina* of earth, earthen; [N] *cevn*. Q *kemnaro* potter. [Added entry.]

**KEPER-** knob, head, top [changed to 'ridge'. This entry consists of disconnected jottings, all struck out, but concerned with N *ceber* pl. *cebir* and *Sern Gebir*, of which the meaning seems to be 'lone stones'.]

**KHAG-** \**khagda* pile, mound; Q *hahta*; N *hauð* mound, grave, tomb (cf. *Hauð iNdengin*). [Added entry.]

**KHAL¹-** (small) fish. Q *hala*; cf. Q *halatir* 'fishwatcher', kingfisher, N *heledir*. [Added entry. The same origin of *halatir* is found under TIR; but here KHAL was changed to KHOL and the *-a-* of the Q forms to *-o-*, before the entry was struck out with a reference to base SKAL – which (a later addition to the S-stems) is clearly the later formulation.]

**KHAL²-** uplift. ON *khalla* noble, exalted (\**khalná*); *orkhalla* superior. N *hall* exalted, high; *orchel* [*e* uncertain] superior, lofty, eminent. [Added entry.]

**KHAM-** sit. Q *ham-* sit. [The other derivatives are too chaotic and unclear to present.]

**KHAN-** understand, comprehend. Q *hanya* understand, know about, be skilled in dealing with; *hande* knowledge, understanding; *handa* understanding, intelligent; *handele* intellect; *handasse* intelligence. EN *henio* understand; *hann*, *hand* intelligent; *hannas* understanding, intelligence. Cf. *Handir*, *Borthandos*. [Added entry.]

**KHAP-** enfold. N *hab-* clothe; *hamp* garment; *hamnia-* clothe; *hammad* clothing.

**KHARÁS-** (cf. KARAK). \**khrassē*: precipice: N *rhass* (*i-rass*, older *i-chrass*); Dan. *hrassa*. Cf. *Gochressiel* [< *Gochrass*] a sheer mountain-wall. [Added entry. For *Gochressiel* see QS §147 and commentary.]

**KHAT-** hurl. N *hedi*, pa.t. *hennin*, *hant*; *hador* or *hadron* thrower (of spears or darts), cf. *Hador*; *hadlath*, *haglath* a sling (see LATH). [Added entry.]

**KHAW-** (= KAY, q.v.) N *haust* bed. [This original entry was enlarged thus:] **KHAW-** rest, lie at ease (= KAY, q.v.) N *haust* bed (*\*khau-stā*, literally 'rest-ing'). In N associated with *hauð* mound (see KHAG). Cf. Q *hauta-* cease, take a rest, stop.

**KHAYA-** far, distant. Q *haira* adj. remote, far, [?also] *ekkaira*, *avahaira*. *hāya* adv. far off, far away. [Added entry.]

**KHEL-** freeze. Q *helle* frost; N *hell*. **KHELEK-** ice. N *heleg* ice, *helch* bitter cold; Q *helke* ice, *helk* ice-cold. [The base KHEL and derivatives were struck out, but KHELEK and derivatives retained.]

**KHEN-D-E-** eye. Q *hen* (*hendi*); N *hent*, pl. *hinn* >*hent*, *hint*, or *henn*, *hinn*. [N forms changed to *hên*, *hîn*.]

**KHER-** rule, govern, possess. Q *heru* master, *heri* lady; *héra* chief, principal. ON *khéro* master, *khíril* lady; N *hîr*, *hiril*. N *herth* household, troop under a *hîr*; cf. *Bara-chir* [BARÁS]. Cf. N *hervenn* husband, *hervess* wife [BES]. Q *heren* fortune (= governance), and so what is in store for one and what one has in store; *herenya* fortunate, wealthy, blessed, rich; cf. *Herendil* = Eadwine. [Added entry. '*Herendil* = Eadwine' derives from *The Lost Road*: Herendil is Audoin/Eadwine/Edwin in Númenor, son of Elendil. On the meaning of Old English *éad* see *ibid*. p. 46, and cf. IV. 212.]

**KHIL-** follow. Q *hilya-* to follow; *hildi* followers = mortal men (cf. *Hildórien*), also *-hildi* as suffix. In N *fir* was used [PHIR]. Cf. *Tarkil* (*\*tāra-khil*). [Added entry. Cf. *Rómenildi* in QS §151.]

**KHIM-** stick, cleave, adhere. Q *himya-* to stick to, cleave to, abide by; *himba* adhering, sticking. N *him* steadfast, abiding, and as adv. continually. Cf. N *hîw* sticky, viscous (*\*khīmā*); *hæw* custom, habit (*\*khaimē*) = Q *haime* habit. [Added entry.]

**KHIS-, KHITH-** mist, fog. *\*khīthi*: Q *híse*; N *hith*, cf. *Hithlum* [LUM]. *\*khithme*: Q *hiswe*; N *hithw* fog. *\*khithwa*: Q *hiswa* grey; N *hethw* foggy, obscure, vague; Dor. *heðu*. Cf. *Hithliniath* or *Eilinuial* = Dor. *Umboth Muilin*. [Added entry. For *Hithliniath* 'pools of mist' (LIN¹) see QS §111.]

**KHŌ-N-** heart (physical). Q *hōn*; N *hûn*. Cf. *Hundor*. *Khō-gorē*, Q *Huore*, N *Huor* 'heart-vigour', courage [GOR]. [Added entry.]

**KHOP-** Q *hópa* haven, harbour, small landlocked bay; *hopasse* harbourage. N *hûb*; *hobas*, cf. *Alfobas* or *hobas in Elf* = *Alqalonde* capital of the Teleri. [Added entry; see KOP.]

**KHOR-** set going, put in motion, urge on, etc. Q *horta-* send flying, speed, urge, *hortale* speeding, urging; *horme* urgency (confused with *orme* rushing [GOR]); *hóre* impulse, *hórea* impulsion. N *hûr* readiness for action, vigour, fiery spirit; *hortha-* urge on, speed; *horn* driven under compulsion, impelled; *hoeno*, *heno* begin suddenly and vigorously. Cf. *Húr-ind*, *Húrin* [ID]. [Added entry.]

**KHOTH-** gather. *\*khotsē* assembly: N *hoth* host, crowd, frequent in people-names as *Glamhoth*. Cf. *host* gross (144). Q *hosta* large number, *hosta-* to collect. N *hûd* assembly.

**KHUGAN-** Q *huan* (*húnen*) hound; N *huan*. [This entry was changed to read thus:] **KHUG-** bark, bay. *\*khugan* : Q *huan* (*húnen*) hound; N *Huan* (dog-name); Q *huo* dog; N *hû*.

**KHYAR-** left hand. Q *hyarmen* south, *hyarmenya* southern; *hyarya* left, *hyarmaite* lefthanded [MA3]. N *heir* left (hand), *hargam* lefthanded [KAB]; *harad* south, *haradren*, *harn* southern. [Added entry. The *-y-* in the base-stem was a further addition, and at the same time the Q forms were changed from *har-* to *hyar-*; see p. 345.]

**KHYEL(ES)-** glass. Q *hyelle* (*\*khyelesē*); ON *khelesa*, *khelelia*; N *hele*, cf. *Helevorn* 'black-glass' [MOR], lake-name. Cf. KHELEK. [Added entry. *Helevorn* is written over an erasure in QS §118.]

**KIL-** divide (also SKIL). Q *kilya* cleft, pass between hills, gorge. [The base SKIL is not found in the *Etymologies*. To this entry was added:] N *cîl*. Cf. *Kalakilya* 'Pass of Light', in which Kôr was built. N *Cilgalad*; *Cilthoron* or *Cilthorondor*.

**KIR-** Q *kirya* ship; N *ceir*. [Added:] *cirdan* shipbuilder [TAN].

**KIRIK-** Q *kirka* sickle; N *cerch*. Q *Valakirka*, N *Cerch iMbelain* [BAL], Sickle of the Gods = Great Bear. N *critho* reap (*\*k'riktā*).

**KIRIS-** cut. Q *kirisse* slash, gash; N *criss* cleft, cut. [Added:] *Cristhoron* – g.sg. of *thôr* eagle. N *crist* a cleaver, sword. Cf. RIS.

**KOP-** Q *kópa* harbour, bay. [This entry was struck out; see KHOP.]

**KOR-** round. *\*kornā* : Q *korna* round, globed; *koron* (*kornen*) globe, ball; *koromindo* cupola, dome. *Kôr* round hill upon which Túna (Tûn) was built. N *corn*, *coron*, *Côr* (*koro*). [*Côr* > *Caur*, and the following added:] [Q] *korin* circular enclosure [cf. I. 257]; N *cerin*. N *rhin-gorn* circle [RIN]. Cf. Ilk. *basgorn* [sc. *bast-gorn* 'round bread', loaf: MBAS].

**KOT-** strive, quarrel. *\*okta* strife: Q *ohta* war. N *auth* war, battle; *cost* quarrel (*kot-t-*), Q *kosta-* quarrel. [The base was changed to **KOTH**, and the following added:] Q *kotumo* enemy, *kotya* hostile. [N] *coth* enmity, enemy; cf. *Morgoth* – but this may also contain GOTH. [See OKTĀ.]

**KRAB-** press. N *cramb*, *cram* cake of compressed flour or meal (often containing honey and milk) used on long journey. [Added entry.]

**KŪ-** *\*kukūwā* dove; Q *ku*, *kua*, ON *ku*, *kua*, (= *kūua*); N *cugu*. [Added entry. The base-stem is not given but is taken from a later etymological note.]

**KUB-** Q *kumbe* mound, heap; N *cumb*, *cum*. [Added entry.]

**KU3-** bow. > *kuw* : Q *kú* bow; N *cû* arch, crescent; *cúran* the crescent moon, see RAN. [Added:] *\*ku3nā* : N *cûn* bowed, bowshaped, bent; but Ilk. *\*kogna* >*coun*, *caun*, Dan. *cogn*.

**KUL-** gold (metal). Q *kulu*, N *côl*; Q *kuluinn* of gold. **KULU-** gold (substance). Q *kulo*. [This entry was struck out and the following roughly substituted:] **KUL-** golden-red. Q † *kullo* red gold; *kulda*, *kulina* flame-coloured, golden-red; *kuluina* orange; *kuluma* an orange; N *coll* red (*\*kuldā*).

**KUM-** void. Q *kúma* the Void; *kumna* empty; N *cûn* empty. [The Q forms were retained, but the Noldorin altered to read:] ON *kúma*, N *cofn, caun* empty, void, but in EN [the Void was] called *Gast, Belegast* [cf. GAS].

**KUNDŪ-**   prince. Q *kundu*; N *cunn*, especially in names as *Felagund, Baragund*. [Added entry.]

**KUR-**   craft. Q *kurwe* craft. N *curw, curu*; *curunir* wizard; cf. *Curufin* [PHIN]. Cf. N *crum* wile, guile; *corw* cunning, wily. [Added entry. N *crum* was rejected; see KURÚM.]

**KURÚM-**   N *crum* the left hand; *crom* left; *crumui* left-handed (*\*krumbē, -ā*). [Added entry. Cf. KHYAR.]

**KUY-**   come to life, awake. Q *kuile* life, being alive; *kuina* alive; *kuive* (noun) awakening; *kuivea* (adj.) wakening; *kuivie* = *kuive*, cf. *Kuiviénen*. N *cuil* life; *cuin* alive; *echui(w)* awakening (*\*et-kuiwē*), hence *Nen-Echui* = Q *Kuiviénen*. [The following additions were made:] N *cuino* to be alive; *Dor Firn i guinar* Land of the Dead that Live.

**KWAL-**   die in pain. Q *qalme* agony, death; *qalin* dead; *unqale* agony, death. [Added entry. See WAN.]

**KWAM-**   Q *qáme* sickness; N *paw*; Ilk. *côm*. [Added entry.]

**KWAR-**   clutching hand, fist. Q *qár* hand (*qari*); N *paur* fist. [This stem was not struck out, but a second form of it was put in elsewhere in the list:] **KWAR-**   Q *qáre* fist; ON *póre*; N *paur, -bor*, cf. *Celebrimbor* Silver-fist.

**KWAT-**   Q *qanta* full; ON *panta*; N *pant* full, cf. *Cambant* [KAB]; *pathred* fullness; *pannod* or *pathro* fill. [Added entry.]

**KWEL-**   fade, wither. Cf. *Narqelion* fire-fading, autumn, N *lhasbelin* [LAS¹]. *\*kwelett-* corpse: Q *qelet, qeletsi*.

**KWEN(ED)-**   Elf. *\*kwenedē*: Q *qende* Elf; N *penedh*, pl. *penidh*; Dan. *cwenda*. Q *Qendelie*, N *Penedhrim*. The word *Eledh* is usually employed. [Added entry.]

**KWES-**   *\*kwessē*: Q *qesse* feather; Ilk. *cwess* down; N *pesseg* pillow (Q *qesset*). [Added entry.]

**KWET-** (and **PET-**)   say. *\*kwetta*: N *peth* word. *\*kwentā* tale: N *pent*, Q *qenta*; N *pennas* history. *\*kwentro* narrator: Q *qentaro*; N *pethron*; Dor. *cwindor*. [Added:] Q *qetil* tongue, language; *qentale* account, history; *lúmeqentale* history [LU]. N *gobennas* history, *gobennathren* historical. Q *avaqet-* refuse, forbid [AWA]. [For *go-* prefix see WO.]

**KWIG-**   Cf. KU3. *\*kwingā*: Q *qinga* bow (for shooting); N *peng*. [Added entry.]

**KYAB-**   taste. Q *tyavin* I taste.

**KYAR-**   cause (cf. KAR). Q *tyar-* cause.

**KYEL-**   come to an end. Q *tyel-* end, cease; *tyel* (*tyelde*) end; *tyelima* final. Cf. TELES. [Added entry.]

**KYELEK-**   swift, agile. Q *tyelka*; N *celeg*, cf. *Celegorn* [GOR].

**KYELEP-** and **TELEP-**   silver. N *celeb* silver; Q *telpe* and *tyelpe* silver; *telepsa* of silver = *telpina*, N *celebren*. Cf. *Irilde Taltelepsa* =

*Idhril Gelebrendal.* [*celebren, Gelebrendal* early changed from *celebrin, Celebrindal.* The entry was rewritten thus:] **KYELEP-** (and **TELEP?**) silver. ON *kelepe,* N *celeb,* silver; Q *telpe* and *tyelpe* silver; *telemna,* N *celefn, celevon* = *telpina,* N *celebren.* Cf. *Irilde Taltelemna* = *Idhril Gelebrendal.* T *telpe*; Ilk. *telf.* Q *telpe* may be Telerin form (Teleri specially fond of silver, as Lindar of gold), in which case all forms may refer to KYELEP. [For *Idril* (*Idhril*) see ID, and cf. *Irilde Taltelepta* in the *Lost Tales,* II. 216.]

# L

[The L-stems consist of lightly pencilled entries, in themselves hard to read, but not much changed subsequently.]

**LA-** no, not. Q *lá* and *lala,* also *lau, laume* (= *lá ume* [UGU]), no, no indeed not, on the contrary; also used for asking incredulous questions. As prefix *la-* > [vocalic] *l* > Q *il,* N *al,* as in *Ilkorin,* N *Alchoron,* pl. *Elcheryn.* Q *lala-* to deny. [See AR².]

**LAB-** lick. Q *lamba* tongue, N *lham(b).* Q *lavin* I lick, also *lapsa* to lick (frequentative). N *lhefi* (*lhâf*).

**LAD-** Cf. DAL, LAT. Q *landa* wide, N *lhand, lhann.* N *camland* palm of hand. Cf. *Lhothland, Lhothlann* (empty and wide), name of a region [LUS].

**LAG-** Q *lango* broad sword; also prow of a ship. N *lhang* cutlass, sword.

**LAIK-** keen, sharp, acute. Q *laike,* N *lhaeg.* Q *laike* acuteness, keenness of perception. Ilk. *laig* keen, sharp, fresh, lively (blended with *laikwa* [see LÁYAK]).

**LAK¹-** swallow; cf. LANK. Q *lanko* throat.

**LAK²-** swift (cf. ÁLAK). *\*lakra*: Q *larka* swift, rapid, also *alarka*; N *lhagr, lhegin.*

**LÁLAM-** elm-tree. Q *alalme*; N *lhalwen* (*lelwin*), *lhalorn*; D *lalm.* [See ÁLAM.]

**LAM-** Q *lamya* to sound; *láma* ringing sound, echo; *lamma* a sound; *lámina* echoing; *nallama* echo. Dor. *lóm* echo, *lómen* echoing. Thus Dor. *Lómendor, Lóminorthin,* Noldorinized > *Dorlómen, Ered Lómin*; pure N *Eredlemrin, Dorlamren.* See GLAM.

**LAN-** weave. Q *lanya* weave; *lanwa* loom; *lanat* weft; *lanne* tissue, cloth.

**LANK-** Q *lanko* throat; N *lhanc.* [This stem was first written LANG, with derivatives Q *lango* (*\*langwi*), N *lhang.* See LAK¹.]

**LAP-** Q *lapse* babe; N *lhaes.*

**LAS¹-** *\*lasse* leaf: Q *lasse,* N *lhass*; Q *lasselanta* leaf-fall, autumn, N *lhasbelin* (*\*lassekwelene*), cf. Q *Narqelion* [KWEL]. *Lhasgalen*

Greenleaf, Gnome name of Laurelin. (Some think this is related to the next and *lassē 'ear'. The Quendian ears were more pointed and leaf-shaped than [?human].)

**LAS²-** listen. N *lhaw* ears (of one person), old dual *lasū* – whence singular *lhewig*. Q *lár, lasta-* listen; *lasta* listening, hearing – *Lastalaika* 'sharp-ears', a name, cf. N *Lhathleg*. N *lhathron* hearer, listener, eavesdropper (< *la(n)sro-ndo*); *lhathro* or *lhathrado* listen in, eavesdrop.

**LAT-** lie open. Q *latin(a)* open, free, cleared (of land); cf. *Tumbolatsin*. Cf. *Tumladen* plain of Gondolin. N *lhaden*, pl. *lhedin* open, cleared; *lhand* open space, level; *lhant* clearing in forest. [Cf. LAD.]

**LATH-** string, thong. Q *latta* strap; N *lhath* thong of [?leather]; cf. *hadlath, haglath* sling (KHAT).

**LAW-** warm. *lauka* warm: Q *lauka*, N *lhaug*.

**LÁWAR-**, N **GLÁWAR-** *laurē* (light of the golden Tree *Laurelin*) gold – the metal was properly *smalta*, see SMAL; Q *laure*, N *glaur*, Dor. Oss. *laur*. Hence N *glor-, lor-* in names, as *Glorfindel* [SPIN], *Inglor* [ID]. Cf. *Laurelin*, N *Galad-loriel*; *Rathloriel* [RAT]. N *glawar* sunlight, radiance of Laurelin; † *Glewellin*. [See GLAW(-R). Cf. QS §16: 'Glewellin (which is the same as Laurelin song of gold)'.]

**LÁYAK-** *laik-wā*: Q *laiqa* green; N *lhoeb* fresh – 'green' only in Q *Laiqendi* Green-elves, N *Lhoebenidh* or *Lhoebelidh*. Ilk. *laig* is blended with *laika* [LAIK].

**LEB-, LEM-** stay, stick, adhere, remain, tarry. Q *lemba* (*lebnā*) left behind, pl. *Lembi* Elves remaining behind = Telerin Ilkorins; N *lhevon, lhifnir*. [See p. 344.]

**LED-** go, fare, travel. Cf. Q *lende* went, departed (*linna* go). ON *lende* fared; *etledie* go abroad, go into exile; N *egledhi* or *eglehio* go into exile, *egledhron* exile (ON *etledro*), *eglenn* exiled (ON *etlenna*). In N *egledhron* was often taken as the meaning of Ilk. *Eglath* = Eldar = Ilkorins [see ÉLED, GAT(H)].

**LEK-** loose, let loose, release. N *lhein, lhain* free(d); *lheitho* to release, set free; *lheithian* release, freeing. Q *leuka, lehta* loose, slacken. Ilk. *legol* nimble, active, running free; cf. *Legolin*, a river-name. [A note on a slip accompanying these etymologies gives: '*Leth-* set free (cf. LED); EN *leithia* to release, *leithian* release; cf. *Lay of Leithian*.' I have referred to this note in III. 154, at which time I overlooked the present entry.]

**LEP-, LEPET** finger. Q *lepse*; N *lhebed*.

Cf. **LEP- (LEPEN, LEPEK)** five. Q *lempe*; N *lheben*. Q *lemnar* week. The Valian week had five days, dedicated (1) to Manwe: *(Ar)Manwen*; (2) to Ulmo: *(Ar)Ulmon*; (3) to Aule and Yavanna: *(Ar)Veruen*, i.e. of the Spouses [BES]; (4) to Mandos and Lorien: *(Ar)Fanturion* [SPAN]; (5) to the three younger Gods, Osse, Orome, Tulkas, called *Nessaron* or *Neldion* [NETH, NEL]. The 73 weeks were divided into 12 months of 6 weeks. In the middle of the Year there was a separate week, Midyear week or week of the Trees, *Endien* [YEN] or *Aldalemnar*, N *Enedhim, Galadlevnar*.

N names: *Ar Vanwe*; *Ar Uiar* (Ulmo) [WAY]; *Ar Vedhwen* (*Bedū + ina*), or *Ar Velegol* (Aule [see GAWA]); *Ar Fennuir*; *Ar Nethwelein* = of the young Gods, or *Ar Neleduir* of the three kings.

[The dual form 'husband and wife' is given as *besū* in the entry BES 'wed', not as here *bedū*; similarly under KHER, NDIS and NĪ reference is made in the original to BED, not BES. There is however no suggestion of any alteration in the entry BES itself. – For the element *Ar* see AR¹. In the Quenya names of the days *Ae* is written above *Ar*, but *Ar* is not struck out. – For the 'young Gods' see p. 120.]

**LI-** many. Q *lie* people; *-li* pl. suffix, *lin-* prefix = many, as *lintyulussea* having many poplars [TYUL], *lindornea* having many oaks [DÓRON]. In N the ending *-lin* 'many' has been blended with *rhim* > *lim, rim*.

**LIB¹-** drip. Q *limba* a drop; cf. *helkelimbe* [KHELEK].

**LIB²-** **laibē*: Q *laive* ointment. N shows GLIB-: *glaew* salve. **libda*: Q *lipsa*; N [*lhúð* >] *glúð* soap.

**LILT-** dance. Q *lilta-* dance.

**LIN¹-** pool. Q *linya* pool; N *lhîn*; Ilk. *line*. Cf. *Ailin* [AY], *Taiglin*.

**LIN²-** (originally GLIN) sing. Q *linde* air, tune; N *lhind, lhinn*. Q *lindo* singer, singing bird: cf. *tuilindo* swallow, N *tuilinn* [TUY], Q *lómelinde* nightingale, N *dúlinn*. Q *lindele* music. Cf. *Laurelin* (g.sg. *Laurelinden*), but this also taken as 'hanging-gold' (g.sg. *Laurelingen*): see LING. *Lindon, Lhinnon* Ilk. name of Ossiriand: 'musical land' (**Lindān-d*), because of water and birds; hence *Eredlindon*, = Mountains of Lindon.

[*tuilindo* ('spring-singer'): cf. I. 269. On the origin of *Lindon, Eredlindon* see commentary on QS §108. – See GLIN.]

**LIND-** fair (especially of voice); in Q blended with *slindā* (see SLIN). Q *linda* fair, beautiful, cf. *Lindar*; N *lhend* tuneful, sweet; Ilk. *lind*.

**LING-, N GLING-** hang. Q *linga-* hang, dangle; N *gling*. Cf. *Glingal* [and see LIN²].

**LINKWI-** Q *linqe* wet. N *lhimp*; *lhimmid* moisten (pa.t. *lhimmint*).

**LIP-** Q *limpe* (wine), drink of the Valar. [The first appearance of *limpe* since the *Lost Tales*, where it was the drink of the Elves; for the old etymology see I. 258.]

**LIR¹-** sing, trill; in N *g-lir-* [see GLIR]. Q *lirin* I chant.

**LIR²-** ON *líre* row, range, N *lhîr* row. Cf. *oeglir* range of mountain peaks.

**LIS-** honey. Q *lis* (*lissen*); N *glî, g-lisi*. Cf. *megli* (*meglin* adj.) bear (**mad-lī* honey-eater [MAT], kenning for *brôg*, see MORÓK). Cf. *Meglivorn* = Blackbear.

**LIT-** Q *litse* sand; ON *litse* > *litthe*, N *lith*; cf. *Fauglith* [PHAU].

**LIW-** **liñwi* fish: Q *lingwe*; N *lhimb, lhim*; Dor. *liw*.

**LOD-** *londē* narrow path, strait, pass: N *lhonn* (cf. *Aglon*); cf. N *othlond, othlon* paved way (*ost* city + *lond*). Q *londe* road (in sea), entrance to harbour, cf. *Alqalonde*.

**LOK-** great serpent, dragon. Q *lóke* (-*ī*) dragon; *angulóke* dragon [ANGWA], *rámalóke* winged dragon [RAM], *urulóke* fire-dragon [UR], *fealóke* spark-dragon [PHAY], *lingwilóke* fish-dragon, sea-serpent [LIW]. Cf. N *lhûg, amlug, lhimlug*.

**LOKH-** Q *lokse* hair; N *lhaws, lhoch* (\**lokko*) ringlet.

**LONO-** *lóna* island, remote land difficult to reach. Cf. *Avalóna* [AWA] = Tol Eressea = the outer isle. [Added to this is *A-val-lon*. *Avallon* first appears in the second version of *The Fall of Númenor* (§1) as a name of Tol Eressea with the explanation that 'it is hard by Valinor'.]

**LOS-** sleep. Q *olor* dream, cf. *Lórien* = N *Lhuien*. Q *lóre* slumber, *lorna* asleep. N *ôl* dream, *oltha* [to dream]. [See óLOS.]

**LOT(H)** flower. Q *lóte* (large single) flower; *losse* blossom (usually, owing to association with *olosse* snow, only used of white blossom [see GOLÓS]). N *lhoth* flower; *gwaloth* blossom, collection of flowers [wo]. Cf. *Wingelot, Wingelóte* Foamflower, N *Gwingeloth* [WIG]; *Nimloth* [NIK-w] = Galathilion.

**LU-** Q *lúme* time (cf. *lúmeqenta* history, chronological account, *lúmeqentale* history, *lúmeqentalea* historical); *lú* a time, occasion. N *lhû*. [See KWET.]

**LUG¹-** \**lungā* heavy: Q *lunga*; N *lhong*; Dor. *lung*; cf. Dor. *Mablung* [MAP].

**LUG²-** \**lugni* blue: Q *lúne*; N *lhûn* (Dor. *luin* pale, Dan. *lygn*). Cf. *Lúnoronti* Blue Mountains, N *Eredluin* (also *Lhúnorodrim, Lhúndirien* Blue Towers) = *Eredlindon* Mountains of Lindon (= Ossiriand). [For an occurrence of *Lunoronti* see p. 32. *Luindirien* Blue Towers occurs in a footnote added to QS §108 (commentary).]

**LUK-** magic, enchantment. N *lhûth* spell, charm; *lhútha* to enchant; *Lhúthien* enchantress (Dor. *Luithien*). Q *lúke* enchantment; *luhta* enchant. [The etymology of *Lúthien* changed to read thus:] Doriath *luth*, whence *Luthien* (Noldorized as *Lhúthien*): \**luktiēnē*.

**LUM-** Q *lumbe* gloom, shadow; *Hísilumbe*, N *Hithlum* [KHIS]. In Q the form is usually *Hísilóme* by attraction of *lóme* night [DO3]. N *lhum* shade, *lhumren* shady.

**LUS-** N *lhost* empty, cf. [*Mablothren* >] *Camlost* [KAB], *Lothlann* [LAD]. Q *lusta* void, empty.

**LUT-** float, swim. Q *lunte* boat; N *lhunt*. N *lhoda* float.

# M

[The M-entries are faint and difficult to interpret, and some are very confused. My father made a beginning on a new list, writing the etymologies out afresh and clearly, but this petered out after he had treated the stems in MA- and a few others (MBAD, MBER, MEL).]

**MAD-** Q *marya* pale, fallow, fawn. N *meið, maið*, hence *Maidhros* (anglicized *Maidros*) = 'pale-glitter' [RUS].

**MAƷ-** hand. PQ *\*māȝ (maȝ-)* hand: Q *mā*; ON *mō* (pl. *mai*) usually replaced by *kamba* (N *camm*): see KAB. Hence *\*maȝiti* handy, skilled, Q *maite* (pl. *maisi*); ON *maite*, N *moed*. *\*maȝ-tā* to handle: Eld. *\*mahtā-*: Q *mahta-*, ON *matthō-be*, N *matho* stroke, feel, handle; wield (confused with *\*maktā*, see MAK).

Related is **MAG-** use, handle, in *\*magrā* useful, fit, good (of things): Q *mára*, N *maer*; *\*magnā* skilled: ON *magnā*, N *maen* skilled, clever, *maenas* craft, handicraft, art. [In the original form of this entry the name *Maidros* (see MAD) was placed under MAG: *Maedhros* < *Maenros*.]

**MAK-** sword, or as verb-stem: fight (with sword), cleave. *\*makla*: Q *makil* sword; N *magl, magol*. *\*maktā*: Q *mahta-* wield a weapon (blended with *maȝ-tā*, see MAƷ), fight: hence *mahtar* warrior = N *maethor*. N *maeth* battle, fight (not of general host but of two or a few), *maetha* to fight. Cf. *Maglaðûr* [cf. DOƷ?] or *Maglaðhonn* = Black-sword (as name). Q *Makalaure* = Gold-cleaver, name of fifth son of Feanor, N *Maglor*.

[In the original form of this entry the N forms of the noun 'sword' were *megil, magol*, and the name 'Black-sword' was *Megildur* (> *Magladhûr, Maglavorn*). If these forms were to replace *Mormakil, Mormegil* etc. as Túrin's name in Nargothrond they never appear in the texts.]

**MAN-** holy spirit (one who has not been born or who has passed through death). Q *manu* departed spirit; N *mān*. Cf. Q *Manwe* (also borrowed and used in N [see WEG]).

**MANAD-** doom, final end, fate, fortune (usually = final bliss). Q *manar, mande*. N *manað*. Cf. N *manathon*. In Q this stem is partly blended with MBAD, q.v. and cf. *Mandos, Kalamando*.

**MAP-** lay hold of with hand, seize. Q *mapa-* grasp, seize. ON *map-* seize, take away by force. Ilk. (Dor.) *mab* hand (*\*mapā*), cf. *Mablung* [LUG¹]. Ilk. *Ermab(r)in* one-handed (of Beren: cf. *Mablosgen* emptyhanded = N *Erchamron, Camlost*). [The forms *Ermab(r)in* and *Erchamron* are certain.]

**MASAG-** knead, make soft by rubbing, kneading, etc. *\*mazgā*: Q *maksa* pliant, soft; ON *mazga* > *maiga*, N *moe*, soft. *\*mazgē*: Q *makse* dough, N *moeas* dough. Ilk. *maig* dough.

**MAT-** eat. Q *mat-*; N *medi*. For *megli* bear see LIS.

**MBAD-** duress, prison, doom, hell. *\*mbanda*: N *band, bann* duress, prison; *Angband* Hell (Iron-prison) (Q *Angamanda*). Q *Mando* the Imprisoner or Binder, usually lengthened *Mand-os* (*Mandosse* = Dread Imprisoner, N *Bannos* [GOS]. Blended in Q with MAN –

hence *Kalamando* Light Mando = Manwe, *Morimando* Dark Mando = Mandos. MBAD is in turn related to BAD, q.v.

**MBAKH-**  exchange. Q *manka-* trade; *makar* tradesman; *mankale* commerce. N *banc, banga*; *bachor* pedlar; *bach* article (for exchange), ware, thing (*\*mbakhā*).

**MBAL-**  Q *malle* street; *ambal* shaped stone, flag.

**MBAR-**  dwell, inhabit. Q *a-mbar* (*ambaron*) 'oikoumenē', Earth; *Endamar, Ambarenya* Middle-earth. N *ambar, amar* Earth; *Emmerein, Emerin* (*Ambarenya*) Middle-earth. *Martan(ō)* Earthbuilder = Aule (N *Barthan*) [TAN]. *Gondobar, Findobar* [PHIN]. [With the use of the Greek word *oikoumenē* here cf. *Letters* no. 154, p. 197. – *Ambarendya* occurs in the *Ambarkanta*, IV. 241–3. – With *Martan* cf. I. 266, entry *Talka Marda*. – *Findobar* was the son of Fingon (p. 403).]

**MBARAT-**  Q *umbar* (*umbarten*) fate, doom; N *ammarth*. Q *marta* fey, fated; *maranwe* destiny; *martya-* destine. N *barad* doomed; *bartho* to doom. Cf. *Turamarth*, Q *Turambar* [apparently written thus over *Turumbar*].

**MBAS-**  knead. Q *masta-* bake, *masta* bread. N *bast* bread; *basgorn* loaf [KOR].

**MBAW-**  compel, force, subject, oppress. Q *mauya-* compel; *mausta* compulsion; *maure* need. N *baug* tyrannous, cruel, oppressive; *bauglo* to oppress; *bauglir* tyrant, oppressor; *bui* (*\*mauy-*) (impersonal); *baur* need. Cf. *Gothmog* (*\*Gothombauk-*) [GOS].

**MBER-**  Q *meren* (*merend-*) or *merende* feast, festival; N *bereth*. Q *merya* festive; *meryale* holiday. N *beren* festive, gay, joyous. [This stem was first MER, and the N words *mereth, meren*; but a new stem MER was then introduced and the former MER changed to MBER, the N words becoming *bereth, beren*. The name *Mereth Aderthad* was never changed in the texts.]

**MBIRIL-**  (compound of MIR and RIL, q.v.) Q *miril* (*mirilli*) shining jewel; *mirilya-* glitter. Ilk. *bril* glass, crystal; cf. *Brilthor* glittering torrent.

**MBOTH-**  Dor. *moth* pool, *umboth* large pool. Cf. Q *motto* blot, N *both* puddle, small pool. Cf. *Umboth Muilin* [MUY] = N *Elinuial* or *Hithliniath*.

**MBUD-**  project. *\*mbundu*: Q *mundo* snout, nose, cape; N *bund, bunn*. Cf. *\*andambundā* long-snouted, Q *andamunda* elephant, N *andabon, annabon* [ÁNAD].

**MEL-**  love (as friend). Q *mel-*; *melin* dear, *melda* beloved, dear; *melme* love; *melisse* (f.), *melindo* (m.) lover; *melima* loveable, fair, *Melimar* = Lindar. Irregular vocalism: *\*mālō* friend, Q *málo*. N *meleth* love; *mell* dear; *mellon* friend; *meldir* friend, f. *meldis*; *melethron, melethril* lover. *míl* love, affection; *milui* friendly, loving, kind.

**MEN-**  Q *men* place, spot; *ména* region. Cf. *Númen, Rómen, Harmen* [see KHYAR], *Tormen* [which is the form in the *Ambarkanta*, IV. 244–5, 248–9, changed later to *Formen* (PHOR).]

**MER-** wish, desire, want. Q *mere*, pa.t. *merne*. [See MBER.]

**MERÉK-** [This entry was struck out, and the stem MBERÉK written against it. It was the same as the entry BERÉK, q.v., except that the Q form was here *merka* 'wild' for *verka*, a N form *brerg* 'wild, fierce' was given, and *bregol* was translated 'fierce'.]

**MET-** end. Q *mente* point, end; N *ment* point; *meth* end (*\*metta*); *methen* end. Q *metya-* put an end to.

**MI-** inside. Q *mi* in, within; *mir* and *minna* to the inside, into; *mitya* adj. interior.

**MIL-IK-** Q *milme* desire, greed; *maile* lust; *mailea* lustful; *milya-* long for; *milka* greedy; *Melko* (*\*Mailikō*), N *Maeleg* (*\*-kā*). N *melch* greedy; *mael* lust; *maelui* lustful. [The stem vowel *ae* in the N words was changed to *oe*: *Moeleg*, etc. The Gnomish name *Moeleg* of Melko occurs in Q (IV. 79, 164).]

**MINI-** stand alone, stick out. Q *mine* one; *minya* first; *minda* prominent, conspicuous; *mindo* isolated tower. N *min* one, *minei* (*\*miniia*) single, distinct, unique; *minnas* tower, also *mindon* (*\*minitaun*, cf. *tunn* [see TUN]).

**MINIK-W-** Q *minqe* eleven.

**MIR-** Q, ON *míre*; N *mîr* jewel, precious thing, treasure. Cf. *Nauglamîr* (Doriathrin form). *Mirion* ordinary N name of the *Silevril* (*Silmarilli*), pl. *Miruin*; = N *Golo(ð)vir* or *Mîr in Geleið*, Dor. *Goldamir*. [The name *Borommíro* is scribbled in: see BOR.]

**MIS-** go free, stray, wander. Q *mirima* free; cf. *Mirimor* = the Teleri. *mista-* stray about. N *mist* error, wandering; *misto* to stray; *mistrad* straying, error. [In the long note to QS §29 giving names 'in song and tale' of the Kindreds of the Elves a name of the Teleri is 'the Free' (and another 'the Wanderers').]

**MISK-** Q *miksa* wet; N *mesg*, *mesc*.

**MITH-** N *mith* white fog, wet mist; cf. *Mithrim* [RINGI]. [Later addition: *mith* = grey.]

**MIW-** whine. Q *maiwe* gull, N *maew*. Q *miule* whining, mewing.

**MIZD-** *\*mizdē*: Q *miste* fine rain; N *mídh* dew; Dor. *míd* moisture (adj. *méd* wet, *\*mizdā*); Dan. *meord* fine rain. Cf. Dor. name *Dolmed* 'Wet-head' [NDOL]. [The stems MISK-, MITH-, MIZD- are evidently related, but it is scarcely possible to see from the changes on the manuscript what my father finally intended.]

**MŌ-** *\*mōl-*: Q *mól* slave, thrall; N *mûl*. Q *móta-* labour, toil; N *mudo* (pa.t. *mudas*). [Cf. *Lhammas* §8: *múlanoldorin* > *mólanoldorin*, language of the Noldor enslaved by Morgoth.]

**MOR-** *\*mori* black: Q *more* black (N †*môr*); *mordo* shadow, obscurity, stain; *móre* blackness, dark, night; *morna* gloomy, sombre; *morilinde* nightingale (Ilk. *murulind*, *myrilind*). N *maur* gloom; *moru* black. Ilk. *môr* night. *Meglivorn*: see LIS, MAT. *Morgoth* Black Foe

[KOT] = Melko. *Morimando* = Mandos [see MBAD]. *Moriqendi* Dark Elves = *Morimor*, N *Duveledh* or *Dúrion* [DO3]. [This entry is extremely confused through changes and afterthought additions, and I have tried to arrange the material more sequentially. It is not clear, however, that all the forms given were intended to stand.]

**MORÓK-** *\*morókō* bear: Q *morko*; N *brôg*; Ilk. *broga*. [See LIS.]

**MOY-** Q *moina* familiar, dear; ON *muina*, N *muin* dear. [See TOR.]

**MŪ-** not, no. [See UGU, UMU.]

**MUY-** Q *muina* hidden, secret; *muile* secrecy. Dor. *muilin* secret, veiled; *Umboth Muilin* veiled pool = N *Lhîn Uial* or *Eilinuial*. Dor. *muil* twilight, shadow, vagueness. (Not in N because it became identical with *moina* [MOY].)

# N

[There was no new start made on the N-entries, which remain in their extremely difficult original form. The stems with an initial back nasal consonant (followed by the stop *g*), represented in the manuscript by a special form of the latter *n*, are here printed Ŋ̄G-.]

**NĀ¹-** [Cf. ANA¹] Q *an*, *ana*, *na* to, towards, prefix *ana-*. N *na* with, by, prefix *an-*. Also used as genitive sign.

**NĀ²-** [Cf. ANA²] be. Stem of verb 'to be' in Q. Cf. *nat* thing, N *nad*.

**NAD-** Q *nanda* water-mead, watered plain. N *nand*, *nann* wide grassland; *naðor*, *naðras* pasture. Dor. *nand* field, valley. Cf. *Nandungorthin*, *Nan Tathren*.

**NAK-** [Cf. ÁNAK] bite. Q *nak-* bite; N *nag-*. Q *nahta* a bite; N *naeth* biting, gnashing of teeth [see NAY]. N *naew (\*nakma)*, Q *nangwa* jaw. Cf. *\*an-kā* jaw, row of teeth: Q *anka*, N *anc*; *Anc-alagon* 'Biting-Storm', dragon-name [ÁLAK].

**NAN-** N *nana* (hypocoristic) mother; *naneth*. [See AM¹.]

**NAR¹-** flame, fire. Q *nár* and *náre* flame, cf. *Anar* Sun; *narwā* fiery red. N *naur* flame; *Anar* Sun; *narw*, *naru* red. Cf. *Egnor* [EK], etc.; for *Feanor* see PHAY. Q *narqelion* 'fire-fading', autumn [KWEL]. [The N form *Anar* is clear. See ANÁR.]

**NAR²-** (Q *nyar-*) tell, relate. Q *nyáre* tale, saga, history, *lumenyáre* [LU]; *nyarin* I tell. ON *naróbe* he tells a story (pa. t. *narne*), *trenare* he recounts, tells to end (inf. *trenarie*). N †*naro* tell; *treneri (nennar)*, pa.t. *trenor*, *trener*; *trenarn* account, tale (ON *trenárna*); *narn* tale, saga (Q *nyarna*). [For prefix *tre-* see TER.]

**NÁRAK-** tear, rend (tr. and intr.). *\*narāka* rushing, rapid, violent: Q *naraka* harsh, rending, violent; N *narcha-* to rend, Q *narki*. N *Narog* river-name; *Nar(o)gothrond* [OS] = fortress of Narog; *Narogardh* = realm of Narog.

**NAS-** point, sharp end. Q *nasse* thorn, spike; *nasta-* prick, sting. N *nass* point, sharp end; angle or corner (cf. BEN); *nasta* prick, point, stick, thrust. Cf. SNAS, SNAT.

**NAT-** (cf. NUT) lace, weave, tie. Q *natse* web, net; N *nath* web; Dor. *nass*. N *nathron* weaver, webster; *gonathra-* entangle, enmesh, *gonathras* entanglement. [For prefix *go-* see wǒ.]

**NAUK-** Q *nauko* dwarf. N *naug*. Cf. *Nogrod* Dwarf-city [cf. ROD?]. Also in diminutive form *naugol* (*naugl-*). The name *Nauglamîr* is strictly Doriathric, in which genitive in *-a(n)* preceded. The true N idiom is *mîr na Nauglin* or *Nauglvir* > *Nauglavir*.
[N *naug* was struck out and replaced by: 'N *nawag* (pl. *neweig*, *neweg*); Dor. *naugol*, whence EN *naugl*'; but the rest of the entry was allowed to stand. The steam NÁWAK was written beside NAUK.]

**NAY-** lament. *naeth* (*nakt-*) 'biting' is associated in N with this stem, and gets senses of gnashing teeth in grief: cf. *Nírnaeth Arnediad* (or *Aronoded*) [NOT]. Q *naire* lament, *naina-* lament. N *noer* adj. sad, lamentable; *nae* alas, Q *nai*. Q, ON *noi*, *nui* lament (*\*naye*); *Nuinoer*, *Nuinor*, name of Túrin's sister.

**NÁYAK-** (or perhaps NAYKA-, elaboration of NAK, q.v.) pain. Q *naike* sharp pain; *naikele*; *naikelea* painful. N *naeg* pain; *negro* to pain.

**NDAK-** slay. ON *ndakie* to slay, pa.t. *ndanke*; *ndagno* slain (as noun), corpse; *ndakro* slaughter, battle. N *degi* to slay; *daen* corpse; *dangen* slain, cf. *Hauð i Ndengin*; *dagr*, *dagor* battle; *dagro* to battle, make war. *\*ndākō* warrior, soldier: ON *ndóko*, N *daug* chiefly used of Orcs, also called *Boldog*. [*Boldog* is an Orc-captain in the *Lay of Leithian* and in Q §10. The meaning here is that *Boldog* was used beside *daug*; see ÑGWAL.]

**NDAM-** hammer, beat. Q *namba* a hammer, *namba-* to hammer. *Nambarauto* hammerer of copper, sixth son of Fëanor, N *Damrod* [RAUTĀ]. N *dam* a hammer, *damna-* to hammer (pa.t. *dammint*).

**NDAN-** back. (Cf. *Danas*; N *Dân*, pl. *Dein*, *Daðrin*). Q *nan-* (prefix) backwards. Dor. *dôn* back (noun). Cf. Q *nā*, *nān* but, on the contrary, on the other hand, *a-nanta* and yet, but yet. [See DAN, and commentary on *Lhammas* §7.]

**NDER-** strengthened form of *der* man (see DER). *\*ndēro* bridegroom > Eldarin *ndǣr*, Q *nér* man (blended with *dér*); ON *ndair*, N *doer* bridegroom. Cf. *Ender* surname of Tulkas (*Endero*), as *Indis* (see NDIS) of his wife.

**NDEW-** follow, come behind. Q *neuna* (*\*ndeuna*) second; *\*ndeuro* follower, successor: Q *neuro*, cf. Dor. *Dior* successor (i.e. of Thingol). The stem is confused with NDŪ 'sink' in N.

**NDIS-** Strengthening (parallel to NDER of DER) of NIS 'woman', itself elaborated from INI.

**NDIS-SĒ/SĀ** Q *nisse* beside *nis* (see NIS, NĪ) woman. ON *ndissa* young woman (in N *dess* was blended with *bess*, properly 'wife'); *\*ndīse* bride > ON *ndîs*, N *dîs*. Intensive form *\*i-ndise* = Q *Indis* 'bride', name of the goddess Nessa.

**NDOL-**   Q *nóla* round head, knoll; N *dôl* (ON *ndolo*) head. Cf. Q *Andolat* hill-name, N *Dolad*. N *dolt* (pl. *dylt*) round knob, boss. Cf. Dor. *Ndolmed, Dolmed* = Wet Head, name of mountain in Eredlindon.

**NDOR-**   dwell, stay, rest, abide. Q *nóre* land, dwelling-place, region where certain people live, as *Vali-nóre (Valinor)*. The long vowel in Q is due to confusion with *nóre* clan (NŌ; ONO). N *dor (\*ndorē); dortho-* dwell, stay. Cf. *Endor = Endamar* Middle-earth. *Doriath* : see GATH. [Under ÉNED *Endor* is defined as 'centre of the world'. See IV. 254–5.]

**NDŪ-**   (see also NŬ) go down, sink, set (of Sun, etc). Associated in N with DO3 night, also with NDEW. Q *númen* west (see MEN), *númenya* western; *núta* set, sink (of Sun or Moon); *andūne (\*ndūnē)* sunset. N *dûn* west, beside *annûn* used as opposite of *amrûn* (see AM); also *dúven* [?southern].

[Scribbled marginal notes give: '*Númenóre* and *Andúnie* = Land of Great Men (after the Last Battle). NDUR, NUR bow down, obey, serve; *núro* sunset; cf. *-dûr* in name *Isildur*.' In FN I (§2) *Andúnie* was likewise the name of the land of Númenor, not (as in FN II) of its chief town.]

**NDUL-**   See DUL. *\*ndulla* : Q *nulla* dark, dusky, obscure; N *doll*, cf. *Terendul*.

**NÉD-**   See ÉNED. middle, centre. N *enedh* core, centre; Q *ende*. But N *nedh-* as prefix = mid-.

**NEI-**   tear. Q *níre, nie* tear; cf. *nieninqe* snowdrop [NIK-W], *Nienna*. N *nîr* tear, weeping; *nírnaeth* lamentation [NAY]; *nîn (\*neinē)* tear, *nínim* snowdrop (*nifredil*). Q *níte (\*neiti-)* moist, dewy; N *nîd* damp, wet; tearful. *\*neiniel-* : N *niniel* tearful.

**NEL-**   three. **NÉL-ED-**   three: Q *nelde*; N *neledh* later *neled* (after *canad* four). Prefix *nel-* tri-. *nelthil* triangle (*neltildi*) [TIL]. Doriathrin *neldor* beech. Cf. *Neldoreth* name of a forest in Doriath, properly name of *Hirilorn* the great beech of Thingol with three trunks = *neld-orn*? [see ÓR-NI]. The N name is *brethel*, pl. *brethil* (cf. Forest of Brethil); see BERÉTH [where *brethil* is given as the singular]. The proper Dor. name was *galdbreth* > *galbreth* [GALAD].

**NÉL-EK-**   tooth. Q *nelet, nelki*. ON *nele, neleki*; N *nêl, neleg*.

**NEN-**   Q *nén (nen-)* water; N *nen* (pl. *nîn*). Q *nelle (\*nen-le)* brook; *nende* pool; *nenda* watery, wet. N *nend, nenn* watery. Cf. *Ui-nend*, Q *Uinen* [UY].

**NEÑ-WI-**   nose. Q *nengwe, nengwi*; *nengwea* nasal. N *nemb, nem*; Dor. *nîw*.

**NĒR-**   Q stem for PQ *der-* man, derived from influence of *ndere* and *nī, nis* : see NĪ, DER, NDER.

**NÉTER-**   nine. Q *nerte*; N *neder*.

**NETH-**   young. Q *Nessa* goddess, also called *Indis* (bride): see NĪ,

NDIS. *nessa* young (*\*neth-rā*); *nése* or *nesse* youth; *nessima* youthful. N *nîth* youth (*\*nēthē*); *neth* young (*nethra*); *Neth* or *Dineth* = Indis Nessa.

ÑGAL- / ÑGALAM- talk loud or incoherently. Q *ñalme* clamour; N *glamb, glamm* (*\*ngalámbe*, influenced by *lambe* [LAB]) barbarous speech; *Glamhoth* = Orcs. See LAM, GLAM. [The stem was changed subsequently to ÑGYAL- and Q *ñalme* to *yalme*.]

ÑGAN-, ÑGÁNAD- play (on stringed instrument). Q *ñande* a harp, *ñandelle* little harp; *ñandele* harping; *ñanda-* to harp; *ñandaro* harper. N *gandel, gannel* a harp; *gannado* or *ganno* play a harp; *talagant* [> *talagand*] harper (*\*tyalañgando*), cf. *Talagant* [> *Talagand*] of Gondolin [TYAL]. Ilk. *gangel, genglin*. [*Talagant* appears in no literary source, but cf. *Salgant* in the tale of *The Fall of Gondolin*, the cowardly but not wholly unattractive lord of the People of the Harp: II. 173, 190–1, etc.]

ÑGAR(A)M- Dor. *garm* wolf; N *garaf*; Q *ñarmo, narmo*.

ÑGAW- howl. N *gaur* werewolf; Q *ñauro*. N *gaul*, Q *naule* wolfhowl. N *gaw-* howl; *gawad* howling.

ÑGOL- wise, wisdom, be wise. Q *ñolwe* wisdom, secret lore; *ñóle* wisdom; *ñóla* wise, learned; †*ingole* deep lore, magic (N †*angol*). N †*golw* lore, *golwen* (*\*ngolwina*) wise, learned in deep arts; *goll* (*\*ngolda*) wise; *gollor* magician; *gûl* magic. Dor. *ngol, gôl* wise, magical; *(n)golo* magic, lore; *durgul, mor(n)gul* sorcery.

ÑGOLOD- one of the wise folk, Gnome. Q *ñoldo*; ON *ngolodo*, N *golodh*, pl. *goeloeidh, geleidh*, and *golodhrim*; T *golodo*, Dor. *(n)gold*; Dan. *golda*. Q *Ingolonde* Land of the Gnomes (Beleriand, but before applied to parts of Valinor); N *Angolonn* or *Geleidhien*. *Golovir* (*Mîr in Geleidh*) = Silmaril; Dor. *Goldamir*; Q *Noldomíre* [MIR].

ÑGOROTH- horror (cf. GOR; GOS, GOTH). N *Gorgoroth* deadly fear (*\*gor-ngoroth*), cf. *(Fuin) Gorgoroth*, later name of Dorthanion, also called *Taur-na-Fuin* or *Taur-na-Delduath*. Cf. Dor. name *Nan Dungorthin* (Dor. *ngorthin* horrible, *dunn* black); Dor. *ngorth* horror = N *goroth, Nan Dongoroth* or *Nann Orothvor* [see DUN].

ÑGUR- ON *nguru, ngurtu*; N *gûr* Death, also *guruth* [see WAN]. Q *nuru, Nuru* (personified) = Mandos; *Nurufantur* = Mandos *Gurfannor* [SPAN]. Cf. *Gurtholv* [> *Gurutholf*] 'Wand of Death', sword-name [GÓLOB].

ÑGWAL- torment. Q *ungwale* torture; *nwalya-* to pain, torment; *nwalka* cruel. N *balch* cruel; *baul* torment, cf. *Bal-* in *Balrog* or *Bolrog* [RUK], and Orc-name *Boldog* = Orc-warrior 'Torment-slayer' (cf. NDAK).

ÑGYÕ-, ÑGYON- grandchild, descendant. Q *indyo*; T *endo*; ON *ango* (not in N). Cf. YÕ, YON.

NĪ[1]- woman – related to īNI female, counterpart to ƷAN male. In Q *ní* was archaic and poetic and usually replaced by *nis* pl. *nissi* or *nisse* pl. *nissi*. See NIS, NDIS. In Q, PQ *dēr* 'man' became *nér* (not *lér*) owing to blending with *ndœr* 'bridegroom' and to influence of *nī, nis* (see DER, NDER).

In ON *nî* 'woman' later > *dî* through influence of *dîr* [see DER]; but *dî* was only rare and poetical ('bride, lady'): it was replaced in sense 'woman' by *bess* [see BES], and in sense 'bride' by cpd. *di-neth* (see NETH). *Dineth* is also N name for the goddess *Neth* = Q *Nessa*, and *Indis*.

**NI²-** = I.

**NIB-** face, front. N *nîf* (*\*nībe*) front, face. Dor. *nef* face; *nivra-* to face, go forward; *nivon* west, *Nivrim* West-march, *Nivrost* West-dales [ROS²]. [*Nivrim* 'West-march' occurs in QS §110, and *Nivrost* 'West Vale' in QS §106.]

**NID-** lean against. *\*nidwō* bolster, cushion: Q *nirwa*; ON *nidwa*, N *nedhw*.

**NIK-W-** Q *niqe* snow; *ninqe* white (*\*ninkwi*); *nieninqe* 'white tear' = snowdrop [NEI]; *ninqita-* shine white; *ninqitá-* whiten; *ninqisse* whiteness. *Taniqetil(de)* = High White Horn = N *Nimdil-dor* (*\*Ninkwitil(de) Tára*). N *nimp* (*nim*) pale; *nifred* pallor, fear; *nimmid* to whiten (pa.t. *nimmint*); *nifredil* snowdrop; *nimred* (*nimpred*) pallor.

**NIL-, NDIL-** friend. Q *nilda* friendly, loving; *nildo* (and *nilmo*), f. *nilde*, friend; *nilme* friendship. In names *-nil, -dil* = Old English *wine*, as *Elendil* (*\*Eled-nil*) = Ælfwine; *Herendil* = Eadwine [see KHER].

**NIN-DI-** fragile, thin. Q *ninde* slender; N *ninn*.

**NIS-** Probably an elaboration of INI, NĪ; feminine counterpart to DER 'man'. Q *nis, nissi* (see NĪ).

**NŌ-** (cf. ONO) beget. Q *nóre* country, land, race (see NDOR). N *nûr* race; *noss* (= Q *nosse*) clan, family, 'house', as *Nos Finrod* House of Finrod. Q *onóro* brother, *onóne* sister. ON *wanúro*, N *gwanur* [wŏ].

**ÑOL-** smell (intr.). Q, L *holme* odour. N *ûl* odour (*\*ñōle*); *angol* stench.

**NOROTH-** Q *norsa* a giant.

**NOT-** count, reckon. Q *not-* reckon, *onot-* count up; *nóte* number. N *noedia* count; *gonod-* count up, reckon, sum up; cf. *arnoediad*, *arnediad*, beside *aronoded*, innumerable, countless, endless; *gwanod* tale, number [see WŎ].

**NOWO-** think, form idea, imagine. Q *noa* and *nó*, pl. *nówi*, conception; *nause* imagination (*\*naupe*). N *naw*, pl. *nui*, idea; *nauth-* thought; *nautha-* conceive.

**NŪ-** Cf. NDŪ. Q *nún* adv. down below, underneath; *no* prep. under. N *no* under, with article *nui* (*Dagor nuin Giliath*). *\*nūrā*, or separate stem NUR; Q *núra* deep; N *nûr*. Cf. *Nurqendi* = Gnomes; *Núron*, N name for Ulmo.

**NUT-** tie, bind. Q *nutin* I tie; *núte* bond, knot; *nauta* bound, obliged. N *nud-*; *nûd* bond; *naud* bound.

**NYAD-**  gnaw. *$nyadrō$ : Q *nyano* rat; N *nâr* (< *naðr*).
**NYEL-**  ring, sing, give out a sweet sound. Q *nyello* singer; *nyelle* bell; T *Fallinel* (*Fallinelli*) = Teleri [PHAL]. N *nell* bell; *nella-* sound bells; *nelladel* ringing of bells. Q *Solonyeldi* = Teleri (see SOL); in Telerin form *Soloneldi*.

# O

**OKTĀ-**  See KOT. Q *ohta* war. N *auth*. Ilk. *oth*.
**ÓLOS-**  dream. Q *olor* dream, *Olofantur* (*s-f* >*f*) = *Lórien*. N [*olt* >] *ôl* (pl. *elei*); *oltha-* to dream (*$olsa$-); *Olfannor* (= *Olo(s)-fantur*) [SPAN] = Lórien. [See LOS.]
**OM-**  Q *óma* voice; *óman*, *amandi* vowel.
**ONO-**  beget (see NŌ). Q *onta-* beget, create (pa.t. *óne*, *ontane*); *onna* creature; *ontaro* (*ontáro*) begetter, parent (f. *ontare*); *ontani* parents. N *odhron* parent (*odhril*); (*$onrō$) *ed-onna* beget; *ûn* creature.
**ORO-**  up; rise; high; etc. (cf. RŌ). Q *óre* rising, *anaróre* sunrise; *orta-* rise, raise. N *or* prep. above; prefix *or-* as in *orchall*, *orchel* superior, eminent (see KHAL[2]); ON *ortie*, *orie* rise, *ortóbe* raise; N *ortho* raise (*orthant*); *erio* rise (†*oronte* arose).
**ÓROT-**  height, mountain. Q *oron* (pl. *oronti*) mountain; *orto* mountain-top. ON *oro*, pl. *oroti*, beside *oroto*; N *orod* (pl. *ereid*, *ered*) mountain; *orodrim* range of mountains (see RIM). Dor. *orth*, pl. *orthin*. Cf. *Orodreth*; *Eredwethion*, *Eredlindon*, *Eredlemrin*, *Eredengrin*.
**ÓR-NI-**  high tree. Q *orne* tree, high isolated tree. N, Dor. *orn*. In Doriath used especially of beech, but as suffix in *regorn* etc. used of any tree of any size. In N used of any large tree – holly, hawthorn, etc. were classed as *toss* (*tussa*) bush [TUS]: thus *eregdos* = holly [ERÉK]. N *orn* has pl. *yrn*.
**ÓROK-**  *$órku$ goblin: Q *orko*, pl. *orqi*. ON *orko*, pl. *orkui*; N *orch*, pl. *yrch*. Dor. *urch*, pl. *urchin*. Dan. *urc*, pl. *yrc*.
**ORÓM-**  *$Orōmē$: Q *Orome*; ON *Oroume*, *Araume* > Exilic *Araw*, also called *Tauros*. See ROM.
**OS-**  round, about. N *o* about, concerning, *h* before vowel as *o Hedhil* concerning Elves; *os-* prefix 'about', as *esgeri* cut round, amputate (3 sg. *osgar*). Q *osto* city, town with wall round. N *ost*; *othrond* fortress, city in underground caves = *ost-rond* (see ROD). Cf. *Belegost*, *Nargothrond*.
**OT- (OTOS, OTOK)**  seven. Q *otso*; N *odog*. Q *Otselen* Seven Stars, N *Edegil*, = Great Bear or *Valakirka* Sickle of the Gods.
**OY-**  ever, eternal. Q *oi* ever; *oia* (*$oiyā$) everlasting; *oiale*, *oire* everlasting [?age]; *oira* eternal. *Oiolosse* 'Everlasting snow' = Taniqetil = ON *Uigolosse*, N *Uilos*, *Amon Uilos*; *uir* eternity; *uireb* eternal. Q *Oiakúmi* = *Avakúma*. [This entry replaced that under GEY, which itself replaced EY.]

# P

**PAD-**  Q *panda* enclosure. N in *cirban* haven; *pann* courtyard.
**PAL-**  wide (open). Q *palla* wide, expansive; *palu-*, *palya-* open wide, spread, expand, extend; N *pelio* spread. Q *palme* surface; N *palath* surface. Q *palúre* surface, bosom, bosom of Earth (= Old English *folde*), hence *Palúrien* surname of Yavanna. [Later addition:] *palan-* far, distant, wide, to a great extent; *palantir* a far-seeing stone.
**PALAP-**  Q *palpa-* to beat, batter. N *blebi* for *\*plebi*; *blâb* flap, beat (wing, etc.)
**PAN-**  place, set, fix in place (especially of wood). Q *panya-* fix, set; N *penio*. Q *pano* piece of shaped wood. *\*panō*: plank, fixed board, especially in a floor: ON *pano, panui*, N *pân, pein*; *panas* floor. Q *ampano* building (especially of wood), wooden hall.
**PAR-**  compose, put together. *\*parmā*: Q *parma* book, ON *parma*, N *parf* (*perf*). Q *parmalambe* book-language = Qenya. ON *parthóbi* arrange, compose.
**PÁRAK-**  Q *parka* dry; ON *parkha*, N *parch*.
**PAT-**  (cf. PATH) *\*pantā* open: Q *panta*, obsolete in ON owing to coalescence with *qanta* full. Q *panta-* to unfurl, spread out, open. N *panno* to open, enlarge; *pann* (*\*patnā*) wide.
**PATH-**  *\*pathnā*: ON *pattha*, N *path*; Q *pasta* smooth. *\*pathmā*: ON *pathwa*, N *pathw* level space, sward.
**PEG-**  mouth. Q *pē*.
**PEL-**  revolve on fixed point. Q *pel-* go round, revolve, return. *\*pel-takse*: Q *peltas*, pl. *peltaksi* pivot; ON *pelthaksa*, N *pelthaes* pivot (see TAK).
**PEL(ES)-**  ON *pele* (pl. *pelesi, peleki*) [Old English] '*tūn*', fenced field. N *pel*, pl. *peli*. Q *peler*; *opele* walled house or village, 'town'; N *gobel*, cf. *Tavrobel* (village of Túrin in the forest of Brethil, and name of village in Tol Eressea) [TAM]; *Tindobel* = starlit village [TIN]. [On this remarkable reference to Tavrobel see pp. 412–13.]
**PEN-, PÉNED-**  Q *pende* slope, downslope, declivity; *ampende* upward slope, *penda* sloping down, inclined. N *pend, penn* declivity; *ambenn* uphill; *dadbenn* downhill, inclined, prone [see AM², DAT]. N *pendrad* or *pendrath* passage up or down slope, stairway. [See note to DEN.]
**PER-**  divide in middle, halve. Q *perya, perina*; N *perin*, cf. *Peringol* = half-Elf, or Gnome. [Cf. *Beringol* and *Peringiul* 'Half-elven', commentary on AB 2 annal 325; also *Pereldar* 'Half-eldar', Danas, in QS §28. The puzzling words 'or Gnome' should perhaps be interpreted as if 'half-Elf, or rather half-Gnome (*perin* + *ñgol*)'.]
**PERES-**  affect, disturb, alter. N *presto* to affect, trouble, disturb; *prestannen* 'affected', of vowel [i.e. 'mutated']; *prestanneth* 'affection' of vowels. ON *persōs* it affects, concerns. [This entry is found on a detached slip.]

**PHAL-, PHÁLAS-** foam. Q *falle* foam; *falma* (crested) wave; *falmar* or *falmarin* (*falmarindi*) sea-spirit, nymph; *falasse* beach; *Falanyel*, pl. *Falanyeldi* = *Solonel*, name of the Teleri, also in Telerin form *Fallinel* (see NYEL). N *falf* foam, breaker; *faltho* (ON *phalsóbe*) to foam; *falas* (pl. *feles*) beach, shore, as proper name *i Falas* west coast (of Beleriand), whence adj. *Falathren*. The variant SPÁLAS is seen in *espalass* foaming [?fall]; T *spalasta-* to foam, froth. [With *falmarin* 'sea-spirit' cf. *Falmarini*, spirits of the foam, in the *Lost Tales*, I. 66. *Falmarindi* is used of the Teleri: p. 403.]

**PHAR-** reach, go all the way, suffice. Q *farya-* suffice (pa.t. *farne*); *fáre* sufficiency, plenitude, all that is wanted; *farea* enough, sufficient. EN *farn* enough; *far* adv. sufficient, enough, quite.

**PHAS-** Q *fasse* tangled hair, shaggy lock; *fasta-* tangle. ON *phasta* shaggy hair, EN *fast* (cf. *Ulfast* [ÚLUG]).

**PHAU-** gape. Q *fauka* open-mouthed, thirsty, parched; ON *phauka* thirsty, N *faug* thirsty; *Dor na Fauglith* (thirsty sand, see LIT).

**PHAY-** radiate, send out rays of light. Q *faina-* emit light; *faire* radiance; ON *phaire*. Cf. *\*Phay-anáro* 'radiant sun' > Q *Feanáro*, ON *Phayanór*, N *Feanoúr*, *Féanor*. Cf. N *foen* radiant, white. [See SPAN.]

**PHÉLEG-** cave. T *felga* cave; Q *felya*; ON *phelga*, N *fela*, pl. *fili*; cf. *Felagund* [KUNDŪ].

**PHEN-** Q *fenda* threshold; ON *phenda*, N *fend, fenn*.

**PHER-, PHÉREN-** beech. Q *feren* or *ferne* (pl. *ferni*) beech-tree; *ferna* mast, beechnuts; *ferinya* beechen. T *ferne*. ON *pheren* beech; *pherna* mast; Exilic *fêr* was usually replaced by *brethil* (see BERÉTH).

**PHEW-** feel disgust at, abhor. Q *feuya*; ON *phuióbe*, N *fuio*.

**PHI-** Q *fion* (*fioni, fiondi*) [. . . .] Cf. *Fionwe* son of Manwe [see WEG]. [The meaning of Q *fion* is unfortunately not certainly legible; the likeliest interpretation would be 'haste', but 'hawk' is a possibility.]

**PHILIK-** small bird. Q *filit*, pl. *filiki*; N *filig* pl., analogical singular *fileg* or *filigod*.

**PHIN-** nimbleness, skill. ON *phinde* skill, *phinya* skilled; *\*Phinderauto*, N *Finrod* [RAUTĀ]. Cf. Q *Finwe*, ON *Phinwe*, name of chief Gnome (Exilic *\*Finw* [see WEG]). *Find-* occurs also in names *Findabar* (*\*Phind-ambar*), *Fingon* (*\*Findekáno*) [KAN]; *phinya* or *-phini* occurs in *Fingolfin* (= *ngolfine* 'magic skill'), *Isfin* [IS], *Curufin* [KUR]; distinguish SPIN in *Glorfindel*. [On the absence of *Finw* in Exilic Noldorin see also the passage at the end of the *Lhammas* §11. – The name *Findabar* appears in the entry MBAR in the form *Findobar*, as also in the *Genealogies*, p. 403.]

**PHIR-** Q *firin* dead (by natural cause), *fírima* mortal; *fire* mortal man (*firi*); *firya* human; *Firyanor* = *Hildórien*; *ilfirin* (for *\*ilpirin*) immortal; *faire* natural death (as act). N *feir*, pl. *fîr* mortals; *firen* human; *fern*, pl. *firn* dead (of mortals). *Dor firn i guinar* Land of the

Dead that Live [KUY]. *Firiel* = 'mortal maid', later name of Lúthien.

**PHOR-** right-hand. Q *forya* right; *formaite* righthanded, dexterous [MA3]. *formen* north, *formenya* northern [MEN]. N *foeir, feir* right (hand); *forgam* righthanded [KAB]; *forven* north, also *forod*; *forodren* northern. Cf. *Forodwaith* Northmen, Northerland [WEG]; *Forodrim*. \**phoroti* : Q *forte*. N *forn* right or north. (Cf. KHYAR.)

**PHUY-** Q *fuine, huine* deep shadow; *Fui, Hui* Night. ON *phuine* night, N *fuin* ; cf. *Taur na Fuin* = *Taure Huinéva*.

**PIK-** ON *pika* small spot, dot; N *peg*. ON *pikina* tiny, N *pigen*.

**PÍLIM-** Q *pilin (pilindi)* arrow.

**PIS-** Q *pirya* juice, syrup. N *peich* ; *pichen* juicy.

**PIW-** spit. Q *piuta* ; ON *puióbe*, N *puio*.

**POL-, POLOD-** physically strong. Q *polda* strong, burly. Cf. *poldore*, adj. *Poldórea*.

**POR-** \**pori* : Q *pore* flour, meal.

**POTŌ-** animal's foot. ON *poto, poti*, N *pôd, pŷd*.

**POY-** \**poikā* clean, pure: Q *poika* ; N *puig* clean, tidy, neat.

**PUS-** stop, halt, pause. Q *pusta-* to stop, put a stop to, and intr. cease, stop; *pusta* (noun) stop, in punctuation full stop. N *post* pause, halt, rest, cessation, respite. [An added entry gives PUT-, with Q *putta* stop (in punctuation), *pusta-* to stop, *punta* a stopped consonant; but the entry PUS- was not cancelled or changed.]

# R

**RAB-** \**rāba* wild, untamed: Q *ráva*, N *rhaw* wilderness. [Q *ráva* and N *rhaw* with wholly different meaning are also derivatives from stem RAMBĀ, and N *rhaw* appears in a third sense under RAW.]

**RAD-** back, return. Dor. *radhon* east (cf. *nivon* forward = west [NIB]); *Radhrim* East-march (part of Doriath); *Radhrost* East-vale, land of Cranthir under Blue Mountains [ROS²]. \**randā* cycle, age (100 Valian Years): Q, ON *randa* ; N *anrand*.

**RAG-** \**ragnā* : ON *ragna* crooked, N *rhaen*.

**RAK-** stretch out, reach. \**ranku* : Q *ranko* arm, pl. *ranqi* ; ON *ranko*, pl. *rankui* ; N *rhanc*, pl. (archaic) *rhengy*, usually *rhenc*, arm. \**rakmē* fathom: Q *rangwe* ; ON *ragme*, N *rhaew*.

**RAM-** \**rāmā* : Q *ráma* wing, cf. *Earráme* 'Sea-wing' [AY], name of Tuor's ship. N *rhenio* (\**ramya-*) fly, sail; wander (cf. RAN); *rhofal* pinion, great wing (of eagle), pl. *rhofel* (\**rāmalē*); *rhafn* wing (horn), extended point at side, etc. (\**ramna*). [With *rhofal* cf. 'wide-winged Lhandroval' in QS (p. 301); for the first element see LAD.]

**RAMBĀ-** Q *ramba* wall, cf. *Ilurambar* ; N *rhamb, rham*, cf. *Andram* 'Long Walls' [ÁNAD] in Beleriand. Q *ráva* bank, especially of a river; N *rhaw* [see RAB, RAW].

**RAN-** wander, stray. *Ranā*: Q *Rana* Moon, N *Rhân*. Q *ranya-* to stray, N *rhenio* (cf. RAM); Q *ráne* straying, wandering, *ránen* errant; N *rhaun*, [added later:] N *rhandir* wanderer, pilgrim.

**RAS-** stick up (intr.). Q *rasse* horn (especially on living animal, but also applied to mountains); N *rhaes, rhasg*; cf. *Caradras* = Redhorn [KARÁN]. [This entry was an addition at the end of the list. The N words and the reference to *Caradras* were scribbled in still later.]

**RÁSAT-** twelve. [No other forms are given.]

**RAT-** walk. *ratā*: N *râd* path, track; *rado* to make a way, find a way; *ath-rado* to cross, traverse [AT(AT)]; *athrad* crossing, ford, cf. *Sarn Athrad*. *rattă*: ON *rattha* course, river-bed, N *rath* (cf. *Rathloriel*) [LÁWAR]. *ostrad* a street. [Added:] *rant* lode, vein; *Celebrant* river-name. Ilk. *rant* flow, course of river.

**RAUTĀ-** metal. Q, ON *rauta*; N *rhaud*, cf. *-rod* in names *Finrod*, *Angrod*, *Damrod* (see PHIN, ANGĀ, NDAM). [The original meaning of RAUTĀ was given as 'copper', changed to 'metal'; cf. *Nambarauto* (*Damrod*) 'hammerer of copper' under NDAM.]

**RAW-** *rāu*: Q *rá* (pl. *rávi*) lion; ON *ró* (pl. *rówi*), N *rhaw* (pl. *rhui*). [Cf. I. 260, entry *Meássë*. – Distinct N words *rhaw* appear under RAB and RAMBĀ.]

**RÁYAK-** Q *raika* crooked, bent, wrong; N *rhoeg* wrong.

**RED-** (Cf. ERÉD) scatter, sow. Q *rerin* I sow, pa.t. *rende*; N *rheði* to sow. *? reddā* 'sown', sown field, acre.

**REG-** edge, border, margin. Q *réna*. N *rhein, rhain* border; *edrein*.

**REP-** bend, hook. *rempa* crooked, hooked.

**RĪ-** Q *ríma* edge, hem, border. Dor. *rim* (as in *Nivrim* [NIB], *Radhrim* [RAD]); N *rhîf*.

**RIG-** Q *rie* crown (*rīgē*); *rína* crowned (cf. *Tinwerína*); ON *ríge*, N *rhî* crown. Cf. *Rhian* name of a woman, = 'crown-gift', *rīg-anna* [ANA¹]; N *rhîn* crowned; *rhîs* queen. [*Elerína*, which was substituted for *Tinwerína* in a note dated February 1938 (p. 200), appears in a marginal addition to entry EL.]

**RIK(H)-** jerk, sudden move, flirt. Q *rihta-* jerk, give quick twist or move, twitch. *rinki*: Q *rinke* flourish, quick shake. N *rhitho* jerk, twitch, snatch; *rhinc* twitch, jerk, trick, sudden move.

**RIL-** glitter (cf. SIL, THIL, GIL). Q *rilma* glittering light; *rilya* glittering, brilliance. Cf. *Silmarille, Silmaril* (pl. *Silmarilli*), N *Silevril* (*silimarille*).

**RIM-** *rimbā*: Q *rimba* frequent, numerous; ON *rimba*, N *rhemb, rhem*. *rimbē* crowd, host; Q, ON *rimbe*, N *rhimb, rhim* – often as pl. *-rim* [see LI].

**RIN-** Q *rinde* circle, *rinda* circular. N *rhind, rhinn* circle; *iðrind, iðrin* year [YEN]; *rhinn* circular; *rhingorn* circle [KOR].

**RINGI-** cold. Q *ringe*; ON *ringe*, N *rhing*; cf. *Ringil* name of one of the great Lamps (pillared on ice), also of Fingolfin's sword. Q *ringe* cold pool or lake (in mountains); Dor. *ring*, N *rhimb*, *rhim*, as in *Mith-rim*.

**RIP-**   rush, fly, fling. Q *rimpa* rushing, flying; N *rhib-*, *rhimp*, *rhimmo* to flow like a [?torrent]; river-name *Rhibdath*, *Rhimdath* 'Rushdown'. [This entry was a hasty scribbled addition at the end of the R-stems.]

**RIS-**   slash, rip. ON *rista-* rend, rip; N *risto*. Cf. *Orchrist* sword-name. [This entry was left unchanged, but a second form of it was added later without reference to the first:]

**RIS-**   Cf. KIRÍS; cut, cleave. *\*rista-*: Q *rista-* cut; *rista* a cut; N *rhisto*, *rhest*; Ilk. *rest*, cf. *Eglorest*, ghyll or ravine made by the river *Eglor* [see ELED] at its mouth, name of town there. *\*risse-*: N *rhis*, *rhess* a ravine, as in *Imladris*.

**RŌ-**   (form of ORO, q.v.) rise. Q *rómen* (see MEN) east, *rómenya* eastern; *róna* east; contrast NDŪ 'down'. ON *róna* east, N *rhûn*, *amrûn* (cf. *dûn*, *annûn*); †*rhufen* east. Cf. name *El-rûn*. [*El-rûn* was an addition. See note to BARATH.]

**ROD-**   cave. Q *rondo* cave; N *rhond*, *rhonn*, cf. *Nargothrond*, *othrond* (see OS). Dor. *roth*, pl. *rodhin*, as in *Meneg-roth* is probably from *rōda* > *rōdh* > *rōth*. Cf. ON *rauda* hollow, cavernous, N *rhauð*. ON *rostóbe* to hollow out, excavate, N *rosto*. In Ilkorin *rond* = domed roof, hence *Elrond* (vault of heaven) [EL], name of Eärendel's son.

**ROK-**   Q *rokko* horse; N *roch* horse.

**ROM-**   (Cf. ORÓM and *Orome*, *Araw*) loud noise, horn-blast, etc. Q *romba* horn, trumpet; ON *romba*, N *rhom*. Q *róma* loud sound, trumpet-sound; ON *rúma*, N †*rhû* in *rhomru* sound of horns.

**ROS¹-**   distil, drip. Q *rosse* fine rain, dew. N *rhoss* rain, cf. name *Celebros* Silver-rain of a waterfall. *Silivros* = Q *Silmerosse*, name of Silpion. [Both *Silivros* and *Silmerosse* are found in the list of the names of the Trees in QS §16. *Celebros* is translated 'Silver Rain' in AB 2 annal 299 (previously 'Foam-silver', 'Silver Foam').]

**ROS²-**   Dor. *rost* plain, wide land between mountains; cf. *Nivrost* [NIB], *Radhrost* [RAD].

**ROY¹-**   chase. *\*ronyō* 'chaser', hound of chase: Q *ronyo*, N *rhŷn*. Q *roita-* pursue; *raime* hunt, hunting; N *rhui(w)*.

**ROY²-**   (N GROJ-) ruddy, red. Q *roina* ruddy; N *gruin*. [This second stem ROY was put in very rapidly at the end of the R-stems and without any reference to the former.]

**RUD-**   *\*rundā*: Q *runda* rough piece of wood; ON *runda*, N *grond* club; cf. *Grond* name of Melko's mace, and name *Celebrond* 'Silver-mace'.

**RUK-**   demon. Q *rauko* demon, *malarauko* (*\*ñgwalaraukō*, cf. ÑGWAL); N *rhaug*, *Balrog*.

**RUN-**   flat of hand or sole of foot. Q *runya* slot, footprint; *tallune* (*\*talrunya*) sole of foot, N *telloein*, *tellen* [TAL]. N *rhoein*, *rhein* slot, spoor, track, footprint.

**RUS-**   flash, glitter of metal. Q *russe* corruscation, †sword-blade; ON *russe* polished metal (N †*rhoss* chiefly found in names as *Maedhros* [MAD], *Findros*, *Celebros* etc., owing to coalescence with ROS[1]).

**RUSKA-**  ON *ruska*, N *rhosc* brown.

# S

**S-**  demonstrative stem. *sŭ*, *sŏ* he (cf. *-so* inflexion of verbs); *sĭ*, *sĕ* she (cf. *-se* inflexion of verbs). Cf. N *ho*, *hon*, *hono* he; *he*, *hen*, *hene* she; *ha*, *hana* it; plurals *huin*, *hîn*, *hein*.

**SAB-**  Q *sáva* juice; ON *sóba*, N *saw* (pl. *sui*).

**SAG-**  *\*sagrā*: Q *sára* bitter; N *saer*. *\*sagmā*: Q *sangwa* poison; N *saew*.

**SALÁK-(WĒ)**  Q *salqe* grass; Ilk. *salch*. ON *salape* herb, green food plant, N *salab* (pl. *seleb*) herb.

**SÁLAP-**  lick up. Q *salpa-* lick up, sup, sip; ON *salpha* liquid food, soup, broth; N *salf* broth.

**SAM-**  unite, join. *samnar* diphthongs. [Hasty later addition; see SUD and SUS.]

**SAR-**  Q *sar*, pl. *sardi* stone (small); *sarna* of stone; *sarne* strong place. N *sarn* stone as a material, or as adj.; cf. *Sarnathrad*.

**SAY-**  know, understand. *saira-* wise; *sairon* wizard.

**SED-**  rest (cf. EZDĒ 'rest', Q *Este*, ON *Ezda*, wife of Lórien). Q *sére* rest, repose, peace; *senda* resting, at peace; *serin* I rest. N *sîdh* peace.

**SEL-D-**  daughter [see YEL]. Q *selde*. In N *iell* (poetic *sell* girl, maid) with *i* from *iondo* son [YŌ]; a change assisted by the loss of *s* in cpds. and patronymics: cf. *Tinnúviel* (*\*tindōmiselde*, Q *Tindómerel*), see TIN. [The meaning 'daughter' was later changed to 'child', with Q forms *seldo*, *selda* added.]

**SER-**  love, be fond of (of liking, friendship). Q suffix *-ser* friend; *sermo* friend (f. *serme*), also *seron*. Cf. name *Elesser* (*Eleδser*) = Ælfwine.

**SI-**  this, here, now. Q *sí*, *sin* now; *sinya* new. N *sein* (pl. *sîn*) new; *siniath* news, tidings; *sinnarn* novel tale [NAR[2]].

**SIK-**  Q *sikil* dagger, knife; N *sigil*.

**SIL-**  variant of THIL; 'shine silver'. These in Q cannot be distinguished normally, but Q *Isil* Moon, N †*Ithil* has *th*. *s-* appears in *\*silimē* 'light of Silpion', †silver, Q *silme* (cf. *Silmerosse*, N *Silivros*), N *\*silif*. *\*silimā* silver, shining white (adj.): Q *silma*, N *\*silef*, cf. *Silevril*, Q *Silmaril* (see RIL). In N *Belthil* (see BAL) *s* or *th* may be present. The Q name of the Elder Tree is *Silpion* (see below).

Cf. Dor *istel*, *istil* silver light, applied by the Ilkorins to starlight, probably a Q form learned from Melian. For *\*silif* N has *silith*, by assimilation to or from influence of †*Ithil*.

Related is **SÍLIP** whence Q *Silpion* (N *\*Silfion*, not used).

**SIR-**  flow. Q *sir-*, ON *sirya-*, N *sirio* flow. Q, ON *síre*, N *sîr* river (cf. *Sirion*); Q *siril* rivulet.

**SIW-** excite, egg on, urge. Q *siule* incitement; ON *hyúle*, N *húl* cry of encouragement in battle.

**SKAL¹-** screen, hide (from light). Q *halya-* veil, conceal, screen from light; *halda* (**skalnā*) veiled, hidden, shadowed, shady (opposed to *helda* stripped bare, see SKEL). ON *skhalia-, skhalla*; N *hall*; *haltha-* to screen. Ilk. *esgal* screen, hiding, roof of leaves. Dan. *sc(i)ella* shade, screen. Derivative name *Haldir* 'hidden hero' [DER] (son of Orodreth); also Ilk. *Esgalduin* 'River under Veil' (of [?leaves]). [There seems to be a query before the bracketed words at the end of the entry.]

**SKAL²-** small fish. Q *hala*; *halatir(no)* 'fishwatcher', kingfisher; N *heledir*. [This stem was a later addition; see KHAL¹, TIR.]

**SKAR-** **skarwē* : Q *harwe* wound; N *harw*. Cf. Ilk. *esgar*. **skarnā* : Q *harna* wounded; N *harn*; *harno* to wound (Q *harna-*). Root sense: tear, rend; cf. **askarā* tearing, hastening: N *asgar, ascar* violent, rushing, impetuous. Ilk. *ascar* (cf. river-name *Askar*).

**SKAT-** break asunder. Q *hat-*, pa.t. *hante; terhat-* break apart.

**SKEL-** **skelmā* : Q *helma* skin, fell. N *helf* fur, *heleth* fur, fur-coat. **skelnā* naked: Q *helda*; ON *skhella*, N *hell. helta* (*skelta-*) strip.

**SKWAR-** crooked. Q *hwarin* crooked; *hwarma* crossbar. Dan. *swarn* perverse, obstructive, hard to deal with.

**SKYAP-** **skyapat-* shore: Q *hyapat*; ON *skhapa*, pl. *skhapati*; N *habad* shore (pl. *hebeid*).

**SLIG-** **lignē, *slingē*: N *thling* spider, spider's web, cobweb. Q *líne* cobweb; N *thlingril* [*r* uncertain] spider. Q *lia* fine thread, spider filament (**ligā*); N *thlê*; Q *liante* spider. Cf. *Ungoliante* [UÑG], N *Deldu-thling* [DO3, DYEL].

**SLIN-** **slindi* fine, delicate. Q *linda* 'fair' is blended with **lindā* sweet-sounding [see LIND]. N *thlinn, thlind* fine, slender; *thlein* (pl. *thlîn*) = **slinyā* lean, thin, meagre.

**SLIW-** sickly. **slīwē* sickness: Q *líve*, ON *slíwe, thlíwe*, N *thliw* later *fliw*. **slaiwā* sickly, sick, ill; Q *laiwa*, ON *slaiwa, thlaiwa*, N *thlaew* [> *thloew*] later *flaew*.

**SLUK-** swallow. [No forms given.]

**SLUS-, SRUS-** whisper. N *thloss* (*floss*) or *thross* a whisper or rustling sound; Q *lusse* a whispering sound, *lussa-* to whisper.

**SMAG-** soil, stain. N *maw* (**māgā*) soil, stain, *mael* (**magla*) stain and adj. stained. [N *maw* and *mael* changed to *hmas* and *hmael*; see note to SMAL.]

**SMAL-** yellow. **smalinā* : Q, ON *malina* yellow, N *malen* (pl. *melin*). **smaldā* : Q *malda* gold (as metal), ON *malda*, N *malt*; N *malthen* (analogical for *mallen*) of gold. Cf. *Melthinorn*, older *Mellinorn*. **smalu* pollen, yellow powder: Q *malo*, ON *malo* (pl. *malui*), N *mâl*, pl. *meil* or *mely*. **smalwā* fallow, pale: Q *malwa*, N *malw*.

　**asmalē*, **asmalindē* yellow bird, 'yellow hammer': Q *ammale, ambale*; ON *ammale, ammalinde*, N *em(m)elin, emlin*.

[I give this entry as it was before it became confused by later changes in the phonology of initial *sm-* (ON retained *sm-*, and the N words have *(h)m-*); these were not carried through consistently. – *Melthinorn* 'tree of gold' is found in the list of names of the Trees in QS §16.]

**SNAR-** tie. Q *narda* knot; N *narð*.

**SNAS-, SNAT-** ? Q *nasta* spear-head, point, gore, triangle (cf. NAS); Dan. *snæs*. N *naith* (*natsai* pl. ?) gore. [Cf. the Naith of Lothlórien. The question-mark is followed by a drawing of an arrow-head.]

**SNEW-** entangle. Q *neuma* snare; ON *núma*, N *nû* noose, snare. [The N forms were changed to *sniuma* and *snýma*; *hniof* (pl. *hnyf*) and *hnuif*. See note to SMAL.]

**SNUR-** twist. N *norn* twisted, knotted, crabbed, contorted; *norð* cord.

**SOL-** Q *solor* (*\*solos*) surf, cf. *Solonel*, pl. *Soloneldi* = Teleri. This is a Telerin form, cf. *Fallinel*, and cf. pure Q *Solonyeldi* [see NYEL].

**SPAL-, SPALAS-** variants of PHAL, PHALAS, q.v.

**SPAN-** white. Q *fanya*, *fána* cloud. N *fein* white, *faun* cloud (*\*spāna*); T *spania*; Dan. *spenna*. Cf. *Fanyamar* upper air; *Spanturo* 'lord of cloud', Q *Fantur* surname of Mandos (*Nurufantur*, N *Gurfannor* 'lord of Death-cloud') and of his brother Lórien (*Olofantur*, N *Olfannor* 'lord of Dream-cloud'); N pl. *i-Fennyr* or *Fennir* = Lórien and Mandos [see ÑGUR, OLOS]. (Confused in N with PHAY, q.v.) [The beginning of this entry was first written *'fanya* cloud'; 'cloud' was struck through, and *fána* added, with meanings 'white' and 'cloud', but it is not clear how they are to be applied. – For *Fanyamar* see the *Ambarkanta*, IV. 236 etc. – I do not think that this association of the Fanturi with 'cloud' is found anywhere else.]

**SPÁNAG-** *\*spangā* : Q *fanga*; T *spanga*; ON *sphanga* beard; N *fang*, cf. *An(d)fang* [ÁNAD] Longbeard, one of the tribes of Dwarves (pl. *Enfeng*). Cf. *Tinfang* 'Starbeard', name of an Elvish piper; *Ulfang* [ÚLUG].

**SPAR-** hunt, pursue. ON *(s)pharóbe* hunt, *(s)pharasse* hunt(ing); EN *faras* hunting (cf. *Taur-na-Faras*); *feredir* hunter (pl. *faradrim*); *faro* to hunt. *Elfaron* 'star-hunter', Moon. [With *Taur-na-Faras* (the Hills of the Hunters or Hunters' Wold) cf. *Taur-na-Faroth* in QS §112, and with the name 'Star-hunter' of the Moon cf. QS §76.]

**SPAY-** despise, contemn. Q *faika* contemptible, mean. N *foeg* mean, poor, bad.

**SPIN-** *\*spindē* tress, braid of hair: Q *finde*, ON *sphinde* lock of hair; *sphíndele* (braided) hair; N *findel*, *finnel*, cf. *Glorfindel*. Cf. *spinē* larch, Q *fine*.

**SRIP-** scratch. N *thribi* to scratch.

**STAB-** *\*stabnē*, *\*stambē* : Q *sambe* room, chamber; *samna* wooden post. ON *stabne*, *sthamne*; N *thafn* post, wooden pillar; *tham*, *thamb* hall. Q *kaimasan*, pl. *kaimasambi* bedchamber [KAY]. N *thambas*, *thamas* great hall. *\*stabnō*, *\*stabrō* carpenter, wright, builder: Q *samno*; ON *sthabro(ndo)*, N *thavron*; Ilk. *thavon*.

**STAG-**   press, compress. *\*stangā*: Q *sanga* crowd, throng, press; N *thang* compulsion, duress, need, oppression; cf. *Thangorodrim* (the mountains of duress). Cf. *sangahyando* 'throng-cleaver' (sword-name), N *\*haðathang*, dissimilated to *havathang*, *haðafang* [see SYAD].

**STAK-**   split, insert. *\*stankā*, *\*staknā*: Q *sanka* cleft, split; ON *sthanka*, N *thanc*, cf. *Lhamthanc* 'forked tongue', serpent-name [LAB]. ON *nestak-* insert, stick in, EN *nestegi*, pa.t. *nestanc*.

**STAL-**   steep. Ilk. *thall* (*\*stalrē*) steep, falling steeply (of river); *thalos* torrent (also a proper name) [the river *Thalos* in Ossiriand].

**STÁLAG-**   *\*stalga* stalwart, steady, firm: T *stalga*; ON *sthalga*, N *thala*, cf. *thalion* (*\*stalgondō*) hero, dauntless man (pl. *thelyn*), especially as surname of Húrin *Thalion*.

**STAN-**   fix, decide. Cf. Q *sanda* firm, true, abiding; N *thenid*, *thenin*. Q *sanye* rule, law; *sanya* regular, law-abiding, normal.

**STAR-**   stiff. Q *sara* stiff dry grass, bent; N *thâr* stiff grass; *tharas* hassock, footstool; *gwa-star* hummock [wǒ]. ON *stharna* sapless, stiff, rigid, withered; N *tharn*; not in Q since it would coalesce with *\*sarnā* of stone [SAR].

**STARAN-**   Cf. Ilk. *thrôn* stiff, hard (*\*starāna*); cf. *thron-ding* in *Balthronding* name of Beleg's bow. [Under stems BEL and DING the name is written *Bel-*.]

**STELEG-**   N *thela* point (of spear); *egthel*, *ecthel*, cf. *Ecthelion* (see EK). [An illegible word after *ecthel* may read 'same', i.e. the same meaning as *thela*.]

**STINTĀ-**   short. Q *sinta*; ON *sthinta*, N *thent*. N *thinnas* 'shortness', name of mark indicating short quality of vowel.

**SUD-**   base, ground. *sundo* base, root, root-word. [A hasty later addition.]

**SÚLUK-**   Q *sulka*; ON *sulkha*, N *solch* root (especially as edible).

**SUK-**   drink. Q *sukin* I drink. N *sogo*, 3 sg. *sôg*, pa.t. *sunc*, *asogant* (*sogennen*); N *sûth* draught, Q *suhto*; N *sautha-* drain. *\*sukmā* drinking-vessel; Q *sungwa*; Ilk. *saum*.
Variant **SUG-** in *\*suglu*: Q *súlo* goblet, N *sûl*.

**SUS-**   hiss. *surya* spirant consonant. [Later addition with SUD and SAM.]

**SWAD-**   *\*swanda*: Q *hwan* (*hwandi*) sponge, fungus; N *chwand*, *chwann*, *hwand*.

**SWES-**   noise of blowing or breathing. *\*swesta-*: Q *hwesta-* to puff; *hwesta* breath, breeze, puff of air; ON *hwesta*, N *chwest* puff, breath, breeze.

**SWIN-**   whirl, eddy. Q *hwinya-* to swirl, eddy, gyrate; *hwinde* eddy, whirlpool. N *chwinio* twirl, whirl, eddy; *chwind*, *chwinn* adj.; *chwîn* giddiness, faintness; *chwiniol* whirling, giddy, fantastic.

**SYAD-** shear through, cleave. Q *hyarin* I cleave. *\*syadnō, \*syandō* 'cleaver', sword; cf. *\*stangasyandō* = Q *sangahyando* 'throng-cleaver' (sword-name) (see STAG). In N lost owing to coalescence with KHAD [a stem not given in the *Etymologies*], except in †*hǎð* [. . . .] (*\*syadā*), cf. *haðafang* (for *haðathang*) = Q *sangahyando*; *hasto* hack through, from *hast* axe-stroke (*\*syad-ta*). Cf. Q *hyatse* cleft, gash (*\*syadsē > syatsē*), and N *hathel* (*\*syatsěla*) broadsword-blade, or axe-blade. [The illegible word would most naturally be interpreted as 'throng', but this obviously cannot be the case (or cannot have been intended.).]

**SYAL-** *\*syalmā*: Q *hyalma* shell, conch, horn of Ulmo. N *half* seashell.

# T

**TA-** demonstrative stem 'that'. Q *ta* that, it; *tana* that (anaphoric); *tar* thither (*\*tad*), ON *tó*.

**TĀ-, TA3-** high, lofty; noble. *\*tārā* lofty: Q *tára*, ON *tára* absorbed in N by *taur* from PQ *\*taurā* (see TÁWAR, TUR). N poetic only or in ancient titles *taur*; often found in names, as *Tor-, -dor*. The latter was blended with *tāro* king and *turo* master: cf. *Fannor* [SPAN].

*\*tāro* king: only used of the legitimate kings of the whole tribes, as Ingwe of the Lindar, Finwe of the Noldor (and later Fingolfin and Fingon of all the exiled Gnomes). The word used of a lord or king of a specified region was *aran* (*âr*), Q *haran* [see 3AR]. Thus *Fingolfin taur egledhriur* 'King of the Exiles' [see LED], but *Fingolfin aran Chithlum* 'King of Hithlum'. Q *tár* (pl. *tári*). N †*taur*, Ilk. *tôr*, only used of Thingol: *Tor Thingol* = King Thingol.

*\*tārī* queen, wife of a *\*tāro*: Q *tári*, but especially used in Q of Varda (*Tinwetári* Queen of Stars) – but in cpds. and titles the sexless cpd. form *-tar* was used: *Tinwetar, Tinwerontar* Queen of Stars = Varda; *Sorontar* King of Eagles (name of a great eagle). The word survived in Ilk. only in form *tóril* = Melian. In N *rhien, rhîn* was used – 'crowned lady': see RIG.

Base stem TĀ appears in Q *Taniqetil* (see NIK-W, TIL), where N substitutes following adj.: *Nimdil-dor*. But the Q form is possibly reduction of *tān-nig* with adjectival *tāna < \*taʒna*. The latter is suggested by N *taen* height, summit of high mountain, especially in *Taen-Nimdil*, Manwe's hall. Cf. also *tarqendi* = Lindar, 'High-elves'; *tarqesta* = Lindarin, or Qenya 'high-speech'. [On *Tinwetar, Tinwerontar* see TIN and note.]

**TAK-** fix, make fast. Q *take* he fastens, pa.t. *tanke*; *tanka* firm, fixed, sure. N *taetho* fasten, tie; *tanc* firm; *tangado* to make firm, confirm, establish. Ilk. *taga* he fixes, constructs, makes; *tâch* firm, stiff, solid. *\*tankla* pin, brooch: Q *tankil*; Ilk. *tangol*; N *tachl, tachol*. *\*taksē* nail: Q *takse*; N *taes*; Ilk. *tass* pin. Cf. Q *peltas* (*peltaksi*) pivot, N *pelthaes* [PEL]. *\*takmā* 'thing for fixing': Q *tangwa* hasp, clasp; N *taew* holder, socket, hasp, clasp, staple; Ilk. *taum*. *\*atakwē* construction, building: Q *ataqe*; N *adab* building, house (pl. *edeb*).

**TAL-**   foot. Q *tál* (g.sg. *talen*); N *tâl*, pl. *teil*; Ilk. *tal*, pl. *tel*. Related is **TALAM** floor, base, ground: Q *talan* (*talami*) floor, ground; *talma* base, foundation, root (cf. *Martalmar*). N *talaf* ground, floor, pl. *teleif*; Ilk. *talum*, pl. *telmin*. *tal*- is often used for 'end, lower end': so *Rhamdal* 'Wall's-end', name of a place in East Beleriand [RAMBĀ]. – Q *tallune* (*\*talrunya*) sole of foot; N *tellein*, *tellen* (see RUN). [For *Martalmar* (also *Talmar Ambaren*) see the *Ambarkanta*, IV. 241–5.]

**TALÁT-**   to slope, lean, tip. Q *talta*- to slope; *talta* adj. sloping, tilted, leaning; *talta* an incline. N *talad* an incline, slope. *atland* sloping, tilted; *atlant* oblique, slanting; *atlanno* to slope, slant.

[The entry was first written thus. A first addition to it was 'Cf. *Atalante* (see LANT).' Subsequently the reference to LANT was changed to DAT (under which stem (DAT, DANT) are given Q *lanta* a fall, *lanta*- to fall, and *Atalante* the Fallen); but either at the same time or later this addition was made: '*Atalante* (*a*-prefix = complete) downfall, overthrow, especially as name of the land of Númenor.' Cf. the statement on this subject in my father's letter of July 1964, cited on p. 8 (footnote). – Other additions to this entry extended the meaning of Q *talta*- ('slope, slip, slide down') and added Q *atalta* 'collapse, fall in' and N *talt* 'slipping, falling, insecure.']

**TAM-**   (cf. NDAM) knock. *\*tamrō* 'woodpecker' (= knocker): Q *tambaro*; N *tafr* (= *tavr*), *tavor*, cf. *Tavr-obel* [PEL(ES)]. N *tamno* to knock (*\*tambā*); Q *tamin* I tap, pa.t. *tamne*; *tamba*- to knock, keep on knocking.

**TAN-**   make, fashion. *\*tanō*: Q *tano* craftsman, smith; *Martano* or *Martan*, surname of Aule (Earth-smith), N *Barthan* [MBAR]. Q *tanwe* craft, thing made, device, construction. Q *kentano* potter; N *cennan*. [*Certhan* >] *C(e)irdan* shipbuilder. *Tintánie* star-maker = Varda (Elbereth); N *Gilthonieth* or *Gilthoniel*. [The latter part of this entry, from Q *kentano*, was an addition. Under KEM a Q word *kemnaro* 'potter' is given. The form *Gilthonieth* appears in the first draft of the hymn to Elbereth in the original second chapter (*Three is Company*) of *The Lord of the Rings*.]

**TAP-**   stop. Q *tápe* he stops, blocks (pa.t. *tampe*); *tampa* stopper.

**TÁRAG-**   *\*targā* tough, stiff; Q *tarya*; ON *targa*, N *tara*, *tar*-; Ilk. *targ*. N *tarlanc* stiff-necked, obstinate; *tarias* [*s* uncertain] stiffness, toughness, difficulty. [There must be a connection between *tarlanc* 'stiff-necked' (LANK) and *Tarlang's Neck* (*The Return of the King* V.2), concerning which my father noted (*Nomenclature of The Lord of the Rings*, published in Lobdell, *A Tolkien Compass*, p. 193) that it was originally the name of a long ridge of rock but was later taken as a personal name.]

**TARÁK-** horn (of animals). Q *tarka* horn; N *tarag* horn, also used of steep mountain path, cf. *Tarag(g)aer* = Ruddihorn [GAY]. [This entry was additional to the main list. On *Taragaer* see p. 345.]

**TARAS-** ON *tarsa* trouble, N *tars*, *tass* labour, task. *trasta-* to harass, trouble.

**TATA-** (cf. ATA, ATTA). N *tâd* two, *tadol* double. Q *tatya-* to double, repeat; *tanta* double. [An earlier entry, struck out, was as follows: 'TAT- oldest form AT(AT)? two. Q *atta* again, *atta-* back again, re-'. See AT(AT).]

**TATHAR-** \**tathar*, \**tatharē*, \**tathrē* willow-tree: Q *tasar*, *tasare*; N *tathor* (= \**tathrē*), adj. *tathren* of willow; cf. *Nan-tathren*.

**TÁWAR-** wood, forest. \**taurē* great wood, forest: Q *taure*; N *taur*; Ilk. *taur*. N *Tauros* 'Forest-Dread' [GOS], usual N by-name of Orome (N Araw). \**tawar* wood (material): Q *tavar* wood, *taurina* of wood; N *tawar* often used = *taur*; *tawaren* wooden (pl. *tewerin*). Ilk. *taur* wood (place and material). \**tawarŏ/ē* dryad, spirit of woods: Q *tavaro* or *tavaron*, f. *tavaril* [cf. the old name *Tavari*, I. 66, 267.]
Note: N adj. *taur* mighty, vast, overwhelming, huge, awful, is blend of \**tārā* (= Q *tára* lofty), \**taurā* masterful, mighty (TUR). It affected the sense of *taur* forest (only used of huge forests).

**TAY-** extend, make long(er). Q *taina* lengthened, extended; *taita* to prolong; *taile* lengthening, extension. N *taen* long (and thin).

**TEƷ-** line, direction. Q *tie* path, course, line, direction, way (\**teʒē*), N *tê* line, way. Q *téra*, N *tîr* straight, right. [This stem was changed to TEÑ, and the ulterior form of Q *téra*, N *tîr* given as \**teñrā*. There is also a very rough additional entry TEÑ (see below).]

**TEK-** make a mark, write or draw (signs or letters). Q *teke* writes; *tehta* a mark (in writing), sign, diacritic – as *andatehta* 'long-mark'. \**tekla*: Q *tekil* pen. \**tekmē* letter, symbol: Q *tengwa* letter, *tengwanda* alphabet; *tengwe* writing, *tengwesta* grammar. N *teitho* write; *teith* mark (as *andeith*, ON *andatektha*); *tîw* letter (\**tekmē*); *tegl*, *tegol* pen. Q *tenkele* writing system, spelling; *tekko* stroke of pen or brush (') when not used as long mark.

**TEL-, TELU-** \**telmă*, *-ē* hood, covering. Q *telme* (cf. *telmello telmanna* from hood to base [sic], from crown to foot, top to bottom); *telta-* to canopy, overshadow, screen; *telume* dome, (especially) dome of heaven. Cf. *Telumehtar* 'warrior of the sky', name of Orion. N *telu* dome, high roof; *daedelu* canopy (see DAY); *ortheli* roof, screen above, *orthelian* canopy. [*Telumehtar* reappears from the *Lost Tales* (*Telimektar*, *Telumektar*).]

**TÉLEK-** stalk, stem, leg. Q *telko* leg, analogical pl. *telqi*; N *telch* (pl. *tilch*) stem.

**TELEP-** silver; see KYELEP.

**TELES-** elf, sea-elf, third tribe of the Eldar. Q *Teler*, pl. *Teleri*; *Telerin* Telerian; general pl. *Telelli*, *Telellie* 'Teler-folk'. Originally the sense was 'hindmost, tarrier'; cf. Q *tella* hindmost, last, *telle* rear (*télesā); N tele end, rear, hindmost part (pl. telei); adel behind, in rear (of). Some forms show blending with KYEL, q.v. [On the meaning of Teleri see the Lhammas §2 and QS §27.]

TEÑ-   N tî line, row (< *teñe); tær (*tenrā) straight. Q téma row, series, line; tea straight line, road. [See stem TE3 (changed to TEÑ), where the derivative words are different formations.]

TER-, TERES-   pierce. *terēwā piercing, keen: Q tereva fine, acute; N trîw fine, slender; Ilk. trêw. Cf. Q tere, ter through; N trî through, and as prefix tre-, tri; ON tre unstressed prefix, see BAT, NAR; prep. trí. *terēn(ē): Q teren (terene) slender; Terendul, name ('slender-dark') [DUL, NDUL]. [The name Terendul occurs in The Lost Road (p. 59).]

THAR-   across,   beyond.   Thar-gelion;   Thar-bad   [?Crossway]. [Scribbled additional entry.]

THĒ-   look (see or seem). N thîr (*thērē) look, face, expression, countenance; cf. Cranthir Ruddy-face [KARÁN], Gostir older Gorsthir 'dread-glance', dragon-name [GOS]. N thio to seem, thia it appears.

THEL-, THELES-   sister (cf. tor, toron- brother [TOR]). ON wathel sister, associate, N gwathel, pl. gwethil. N thêl, thelei sister, also muinthel, pl. muinthil [see MOY]. Q seler, pl. selli sister; ON thele, thelehi (thelesi); Q oselle [see wŏ] sister, associate. Usually used of blood-kin in Q was onóne, see NŌ, ONO; cf. ON wanúre kinswoman, N gwanur kinsman or kinswoman [wŏ].

THIL-   (variant of SIL, q.v.) N Ithil poetic name of the Moon (Rhân) = Q Isil 'the Sheen'; thilio to glister. Cf. Belthil, Galathilion, names of the Elder of the Two Trees – but these may contain the variant SIL.

THIN-   (cf. TIN). *thindi pallid, grey, wan: Q sinde grey. Sindo name of Elwe's brother, in Telerian form Findo, Ilk. Thind, later in Doriath called Thingol (i.e. Thind + gôl wise, see ÑGOL) or Torthingol [TĀ] King Thingol, also with title Tor Tinduma 'King of Twilight' [TIN], N Aran Dinnu. N thind, thinn grey, pale; Ilk. thind. Q sinye evening (N †thin); N thinna. Q sinta- fade (sintane), ON thintha.

THŌN-   Ilk. thôn pine-tree. N thaun pl. thuin is probably an early loan-word, with Ilk. ō treated as ON ō < ā. Ilk. Dor-thonion 'Land of Pines', name of mountainous forest N. of Doriath and afterwards becoming Taur-na-Fuin, a punning alteration of Dor-na-Thuin (Noldorin translation of Ilk. Dor-thonion).

THOR-, THORON-   Q soron (and sorne), pl. sorni eagle; N thôr and thoron, pl. therein – thoron is properly old gen. sg. = ON thoronen, Q sornen, appearing in names as Cil-thoron, or Cil-thorondor [KIL]. Ilk. thorn, pl. thurin. Q Sorontar (name of) King of Eagles, N Thorondor, Ilk. Thorntor = Torthurnion. [Added:] Cf. name Elthor(o)n = eagle of sky.

[The following was added in hastily above the entry THOR, THORON:

'THOR- = come swooping down; cf. *Brilthor.* Adj. *thôr* swooping, leaping down; *thórod* torrent.' I take this to be an indication of the root-sense of THOR eagle.]

THŪ- puff, blow. Q *súya-* breathe; *súle* breath. Cf. *Súlimo* surname of Manwe (wind-god). N *thuio* breathe; *thûl* breath.

THUR- surround, fence, ward, hedge in, secrete. Ilk. *thúren* guarded, hidden. Cf. Ilk. *Garthurian* Hidden Realm (= Doriath), sc. *garð-thurian*; Noldorinized as *Arthurien,* more completely as *Ar(ð)-thoren:* *thoren* (*\*tháurēnā*) pp. of *thoro-* fence [see ȝAR]. *Thuringwethil* (woman of) secret shadow, Doriathren name (N *Dolwethil*) assumed by Tinúviel as a bat-shaped fay [WATH]. [Cf. the *Lay of Leithian* line 3954, where a marginal note explains *Thuringwethil* as 'she of hidden shadow' (III. 297, 304). The present entry retains the story of the Lay: it was Lúthien who called herself by this name before Morgoth (see III. 306).]

THUS- (related to THŪ?) *\*thausā:* Q *saura* foul, evil-smelling, putrid. N *thaw* corrupt, rotten; *thû* stench, as proper name *Thû* chief servant of Morgoth, also called *Mor-thu,* Q *Sauro* or *Sauron* or *Súro* = *Thû.* [In the original draft for the chapter *A Knife in the Dark* in *The Lord of the Rings* Frodo (but not there called Frodo) cries *Elbereth! Gilthoniel! Gurth i Morthu!*]

TIK- (cf. PIK) Q *tikse* dot, tiny mark, point; *amatikse, nuntikse* [indicated in the manuscript to mean dots or points placed above (*amatikse*) or below (*nuntikse*) the line of writing. Added entry.]

TIL- point, horn. Q *tilde* point, horn; cf. *Ta-niqe-til* (g.sg. *tilden*); N *tild, till* horn. Q *Tilion* 'the Horned', name of the man in the Moon; N *Tilion.* Q *neltil* (*neltildi*), N *nelthil* triangle (see NEL). [Cf. QS §75: marginal note by Ælfwine to the name *Tilion:* '*hyrned*' (Old English, 'horned'). It is strange that Tilion is here 'the man in the Moon': in QS (as in Q, IV. 97) he was 'a young hunter of the company of Oromë'. Is the implication that in later ages the myth of Tilion became the story of the Man in the Moon? (see I. 202).]

TIN- (variant of (?) and in any case affected by THIN, q.v.) sparkle, emit slender (silver, pale) beams. Q *tine* it glints, *tintina* it sparkles; *\*tinmē* sparkle, glint: Q *tinwe* sparkle (star), [struck out: cf. *Tin-wetar, Tinwerontar* star-queen, title of Varda;] *tin-dóme* starlit dusk (see DOMO); *tingilya, tingilinde* a twinkling star (see GIL).

N *tinno* to glint; *tinw* spark, small star; *tint* spark; *gildin* silver spark (see GIL); *\*tindumh, tindu, tinnu* dusk, twilight, early night (without moon). Cf. *Aran Dinnu* King of Twilight, name given by Gnomes to Thingol, called by Ilkorins *Tor Tinduma.* Ilk. *tim* spark, star; *tingla-* sparkle; *tindum* starlight, twilight. Q *tinda* glinting, silver; *tinde* a glint.

N *Tindúmhiell, Tinnúviel, Tinúviel* = 'daughter of twilight', a kenning of the nightingale, Q *Tindómerel* (see SEL-D: *\*Tin-dōmiselde*), name given by Beren to Lúthien daughter of Thingol. N

ordinary name of nightingale is *dúlind*, *dúlin* [DO3, LIN²]; Q
*lómelinde*; Ilk. *mur(i)lind*, *myr(i)lind* (see MOR). N *moerilind*,
*merilin* was Noldorinized from Ilk. *murilind*, since *mori* did not =
'night' in N.
The 'twilight' sense was largely due to THIN, q.v.
[Against this entry is written in the margin: '*Tintanie*, *Tintalle*
Kindler = Varda; Q *tinta-* to kindle, make to spark': see pp. 344–5.
Other marginal notes are: 'cf. *Timbreðil*', which thus reappears from
Q, IV. 82 (see BARATH); '*Tindubel* twilit city' (see PEL(ES).]

**TING-, TANG-** onomatopoeic (cf. DING). Q *tinge*, *tango*, twang;
*tinga-*; N *tang* bowstring.

**TINKŌ-** metal. Q *tinko*; N *tinc*.

**TIR-** watch, guard. Q *tirin* I watch, pa.t. *tirne*; N *tiri* or *tirio*, pa.t.
*tiriant*. Q *tirion* watch-tower, tower. N *tirith* watch, guard; cf.
*Minnas-tirith* [MINI]. Cf. Q *halatir* (*-tirnen*), PQ *\*khalatirnŏ*
'fish-watcher', N *heledirn* = kingfisher; *Dalath Dirnen* 'Guarded
Plain'; *Palantir* 'Far-seer'. [For the etymology of 'kingfisher' see
KHAL¹, SKAL². – *Palantir* was a later addition, as also under
PAL.]

**TIT-** Q *titta* little, tiny; N *tithen* (pl. *tithin*).

**TIW-** fat, thick. *\*tiukā*: Q *tiuka* thick, fat; ON *túka*, N *tûg*; Ilk. *tiog*.
*\*tiukō* thigh: Q *tiuko*. Q *tiuya-* swell, grow fat; ON *tuio-*, N *tuio* to
swell (associated with TUY).

**TOL¹-OTH/OT** eight. Q *tolto*; N *toloth*.

**TOL²-** *tollo* island: Q *tol*, pl. *tolle*; N *toll*, pl. *tyll*; cf. *Tol-eressea*, N
*Toll-ereb*.

**TOP-** cover, roof. *\*tōp-*: Q *tópa* roof; *tópa-* to roof; *tope* covers (pa.t.
*tompe*). N *tobo* cover, roof over; *tobas* roofing.

**TOR-** brother (cf. THEL- sister). ON *wator* brother (*wa* = together),
especially used of those not brothers by blood, but sworn brothers or
associates; N *gwador* (*gwedeir*). ON *toron* brother, pl. *toroni*. N †*tôr*,
*terein*; usually used was the cpd. *muindor* with analogical pl. *muindyr*
(see MOY, *moina*). Q *toron*, *torni* brother; *otorno* sworn brother,
associate [wŏ]; *otornasse* brotherhood; but usually of the blood-
kinship was used *onóro* (*\*wa-nōrō* = of one kin, see wŏ, NŌ) = ON
*wanúro*, N *gwanur* kinsman.

**TOW-** Q *tō* wool; *toa* of wool, woollen; N *taw*.

**TUB-** *\*tumbu* deep valley, under or among hills: Q *tumbo*, N *tum*. Cf.
*Tumladen* 'the level vale' [LAT], the vale of Gondolin. *\*tubnā* deep:
Q *tumna* lowlying, deep, low; N *tofn*; Ilk. *tovon*. *\*Utubnu* name of
Melko's vaults in the North: Q *Utumno*; N *Udun*; Ilk. *Uduvon*; Dan.
*Utum*.

**TUG-** *\*tūgu*: Q *tuo*; ON *túgo*, N *tû*; Ilk. *tûgh*, *tû*; muscle, sinew;
vigour, physical strength. Cf. name *Tuor* (older *tūghor* = *tū-gor*
'strength-vigour', see GOR). *\*tungā*: Q *tunga* taut, tight (of strings,
resonant); N *tong*; Ilk. *tung*.

**TUK-** draw, bring. Q *tukin* I draw; N *tegi* (3 sg. *tôg*) to lead, bring; Ilk. *toga* he brings.

**TUL-** come, approach, move towards (point of speaker). Q *tulin* I come; N *teli* to come, *tôl* he comes. *\*tultā* make come: Q *tulta-* send for, fetch, summon; N *toltho* fetch; Ilk. *tolda* he fetches.

**TULUK-** Q *tulka* firm, strong, immoveable, steadfast; cf. *Tulkas* (*Tulkatho, Tulkassen*). *tulko* (*\*tulku*) support, prop. EN *tolog* stalwart, trusty. *tulu* (*\*tulukmē*, ON *tulugme*) support, prop. Tulkas was also called *Ender* (see NDER), EN *Enner*.

**TUMPU-** hump. Q *tumpo*; N *tump*.

**TUN-** *\*tundu*: Q *tundo*; N *tund, tunn* hill, mound. *\*tundā*: Q *tunda* tall; N *tond, tonn*; Ilk. *tund*. *\*Tŭnă̆*: Q *Tún, Túna* Elf-city in Valinor; ON *Túna*, N *Tûn*. Cf. N *mindon* isolated hill (*\*minitunda*), especially a hill with a watch-tower. [Under MINI N *mindon* is derived from *\*minitaun*. – I cannot explain why *Tún* appears here as a Q form: see QS §39, and commentary on §§39, 45.]

**TUP-** *\*tupsē*: Q *tupse* thatch; N *taus*; Ilk. *tuss*.

**TUR-** power, control, mastery, victory. *\*tūrē* mastery, victory: Q *túre*; N *tûr*. Cf. name *Turambar*, N *Túramarth* 'Master of Fate', name taken in pride by *Túrin* (Q *Turindo*) – which contains the same element *tūr* victory, + *indo* mood (see ID).

*\*tūrō* and in cpds. *turo, tur*, master, victor, lord: cf. Q *Fantur*, N *Fannor*. Q *turin* I wield, control, govern, pa.t. *turne*; N *ortheri*, 3 sg. *orthor* (*\*ortur-*) master, conquer; *tortho* to wield, control. *\*taurā*: Q *taura* mighty; N *taur* vast, mighty, overwhelming, awful – also high, sublime (see TÁWAR). [Added:] *Turkil*, cf. *Tarkil* = Númenórean [KHIL].

**TURÚM-** *\*turumā*: Q *turma* shield; *\*turúmbē*: T *trumbe* shield; Ilk. *trumb, trum*.

**TUS-** *\*tussā*: Q *tussa* bush, N *toss* low-growing tree (as maple, hawthorn, blackthorn, holly, etc.): e.g. *eregdos* = holly-tree. See ERÉK, ÓR-NI.

**TUY-** spring, sprout (cf. TIW grow fat, swell?). Q *tuia* sprouts, springs; N *tuio*. *\*tuilē*: Q *tuile* spring-time; also used = dayspring, early morn = *artuile* [AR¹]. Cf. *tuilindo* (for *\*tuilelindō* 'spring-singer') swallow, N *tuilind, tuilin* [LIN²]. *\*tuimā*: Q *tuima* a sprout, bud; N *tuiw, tui*.

**TYAL-** play. Q *tyalie* sport, play, game; *tyalin* I play. N *telio, teilio* (*\*tyaliā-*) to play. Cf. *tyalañgandō* = harp-player (Q *tyalangan*): N *Talagand*, one of the chiefs of Gondolin (see ÑGAN). N *te(i)lien* sport, play.

**TYUL-** stand up (straight). *\*tyulmā* mast: Q *tyulma*. *\*tyulussē* poplar-tree: Q *tyulusse*, N *tulus* (pl. *tylys*) [see LI].

# U

**UB-**   abound. Q *úvea* abundant, in very great number, very large; *úve* abundance, great quantity. N *ofr (ovr)*, *ovor* abundant (*\*ubrā*); *ovras* crowd, heap, etc.; *ovro* to abound.

**UGU-** and **UMU-**   negative stems: Q *uin* and *umin* I do not, am not; pa.t. *úme*. Q prefix *ú* (< *ugu*, or *gū*) not, un-, in- (usually with bad sense), as *vanimor* fair folk = (men and) elves, *úvanimor* monsters. Cf. GŪ, MŪ. [Under BAN the *Vanimor* are the Children of the Valar; see pp. 403–4. – This entry was first written, like all others in this part of the manuscript, in pencil, but then overwritten in ink; it was struck out, in pencil, but this may have been done before it was overwritten. Apparently later pencilled additions are: [Q] *úmea* evil, [N] *um* bad, evil.]

**ULU-**   pour, flow. Q *ulya-* pour (intr. pa.t. *ulle*, tr. *ulyane*); *ulunde* flood; *úlea* pouring, flooding, flowing. *\*Ulumō* name of the Vala of all waters: Q *Ulmo*; N *Ulu*, usually called *Guiar* (see WAY). N *oeil*, *eil* it is raining (*\*ulyā*); *\*ulda* torrent, mountain-stream, EN *old*, *oll*.

**ÚLUG-**   T *ulga*, Ilk. *olg* hideous, horrible; *\*ulgundō* monster, deformed and hideous creature: Q *ulundo*; T *ulgundo*, Ilk. *ulgund*, *ulgon*, *ulion*; N *ulund*, *ulun*. Also **ÚLGU**: cf. *Ul-* in *Ulfang*, *Uldor*, *Ulfast*, *Ulwarth*, names of Swartmen. [These names of the Easterlings were of course given to them by the Elves (as is specifically stated of those with the element BOR); but cf. the *Lhammas* §10, where this is not so.]

**UÑG-**   *\*uñgwē*: Q *ungwe* gloom; *ungo* cloud, dark shadow. Cf. *Ungweliante*, *Ungoliante* the Spider, ally of Morgoth (cf. SLIG). Ilk. *ungol* darkness, *ungor* black, dark, gloomy. In N not used except in name *Ungoliant*, which is really taken from Q. The name of the Spider in N is *Delduthling* (see DYEL, DO3).

**UNU-**   (cf. NŬ, NDŪ). *undu* a parallel form in Q made to equal *ama*, *amba* up [AM²]: down, under, beneath.

**UNUK-**   Q *unqe* hollow; *unka-* hollow out; *unqa* adj. hollow.

**UR-**   be hot. Q *úr* fire, N *ûr*. Q *Úrin* f. (g.sg. *Úrinden*) name of the Sun. Q *uruite*, *úruva* fiery. Cf. *Dagor Vreged-úr* Battle of Sudden Fire [BERÉK]. Q *urya-* blaze. [This entry was struck through, and beside it the following written very roughly:] **UR-** wide, large, great. *Úrion*. Q *úra* large; N *ûr* wide.

**USUK-**   *\*us(u)k-wē*: Q *usqe* reek; N *osp*; Ilk. *usc* smoke.

**UY-**   Q *uile* long trailing plant, especially seaweed; *earuile* seaweed [AY]; *Uinen (Uinenden)* wife of Osse, ON *Uinenda*, EN *Uinend*, *Uinen* (cf. NEN); [N] *uil* seaweed, *oeruil*.

# W

[The stems in W- form the concluding entries in the manuscript, and unlike those that precede were carefully written in ink, with some pencilled changes and additions.]

**WĀ-, WAWA-, WAIWA-** blow. Q *vaiwa, waiwa* wind; N *gwaew*; Ilk. *gwau.*

**WA3-** stain, soil. *\*waʒrā*: Q *vára* soiled, dirty; N *gwaur* (ON *wóra*); Ilk. *gôr.* \**wahtā-* to soil, stain: Q *vahta*; N *gwatho* (ON *wattóbe*); Ilk. *góda-.* \**wahtē* a stain: ON *watte*, N *gwath* coalescing with \**wath*, q.v. [WATH]; Ilk. *gôd* dirtiness, filth. \**wahsē*: Q *vakse* stain; ON *wasse*, N *gwass.* Cf. *Iarwath* 'Blood-stain' [YAR], surname of Túrin.

**WAN-** depart, go away, disappear, vanish. Q *vanya-* go, depart, disappear, pa.t. *vanne*; *vanwa* gone, departed, vanished, lost, past; *vanwie* the past, past time. This stem in N replaced KWAL in application to death (of elves by fading, or weariness): thus *gwanw* (\**wanwē*) death; *gwanath* death; *gwann* (\**wannā*) departed, dead. Note: *gwanw, gwanath* are the 'act of dying', not 'death, Death' as a state or abstract: that is *guru* (see ÑGUR). N *gwanno* (*wanta-*) depart, die. [The stem WAN was changed in pencil to VAN.]

**WA-N-** goose: Q *vān, wān* (pl. *vāni*) goose; N *gwaun*, pl. *guin.*

**WAR-** give way, yield, not endure, let down, betray. ON *warie* betray, cheat; *awarta* forsake, abandon. EN *gwerio* betray; *gwarth* betrayer; *awartha* forsake; *awarth* abandonment. Cf. *Ulwarth.* [This entry was an addition in pencil. On *Ulwarth* see ÚLUG and note.]

**WATH-** shade. ON *watha*, N *gwath*; Ilk. *gwath.* Cf. Ilk. *Urthin* (> N *Eredwethion*). [This entry was an addition in pencil. Above *Urthin* was written *Gwethion.*]

**WAY-** enfold. \**wāyā* envelope, especially of the Outer Sea or Air enfolding the world within the Ilurambar or world-walls: Q *w-* *vaia, w-* *vaiya*; ON *\*wōia, uia*, N *ui.* \**Vāyārō* name of Ulmo, lord of Vaiya: Q *Vaiaro*, N *Uiar* the usual N name of Ulmo. [The stem WAY was changed in pencil to VAY. Under ULU it is said that Ulmo was usually called *Guiar* in N.]

**WED-** bind. \**wedā*: ON *weda* bond, N *gweð*; Ilk. *gweð.* N *gwedi*, pa.t. *gwend, gwenn* later *gweðant*, bind. N *angweð* 'iron-bond', chain. \**wǣdē* bond, troth, compact, oath: Q *vēre*; ON *waide*, N *gwaeð.* \**wed-tā*: Q *vesta-* swear (to do something), contract, make a compact; *vesta* contract; *vestale* oath. N *gwest* oath; *gwesto* to swear; *gowest* contract, compact, treaty, Q *ovesta* [wǒ]. [The Q words derived from \**wed-tā* were struck out in pencil, with the note that they 'all fell with derivatives of BES'. These same words, with different meaning, are found under BES: *vesta* matrimony, *vesta-* to wed;

*vestale* wedding. The reference in the original here is to BES (not as previously to BED: see note to LEP).]

**WEG-** (manly) vigour. Q *vie* manhood, vigour (*wezē); *vea* adult, manly, vigorous; *veaner* (adult) man [NĒR]; *veasse* vigour. *veo* (*wegō) man. The latter in compound form *-wego is frequent in masculine names, taking Q form *-we* (< *weg*). This can be distinguished from *-we* (*-wē* abstract suffix) by remaining *-we* in N, from ON *-wega*. The abstract suffix occurs in the names *Manwe*, *Fionwe*, *Elwe*, *Ingwe*, *Finwe*. These names do not occur in Exilic forms *Manw*, *Fionw*, *Elw*, *Finw* – since Finwe for instance remained in Valinor [see PHIN]. These names were used even by Gnomes in Qenya form, assisted by the resemblance to *-we* in other names, as *Bronwe*, ON *Bronwega* (see BORÓN). In N otherwise this stem only survives in *gweth* manhood, also used = man-power, troop of able-bodied men, host, regiment (cf. *Forodweith* Northmen). *weg-tē [This entry, the last under W as the manuscript was originally written, was left unfinished. – Under PHOR the form is equally clearly *Forodwaith*.]

**WEN-, WENED-** maiden. Q *wende*, *vende*; N *gwend*, *gwenn*. Often found in feminine names, as *Morwen*, *Eleðwen*: since the latter show no *-d* even in archaic spelling, they probably contain a form *wen-*: cf. Ilk. *gwen* girl; Q *wéne*, *véne* and *venesse* virginity; N *gweneth* virginity. [Added:] Some names, especially those of men, may contain *gwend* bond, friendship: see WED. [The N noun *gwend* is not given under WED. – Against this entry is written: 'Transfer to GWEN'. – In the narrative texts (QS §29, AB 2 annal 245) the name *Eledhwen* was interpreted as 'Elfsheen' – and this survived much later in the *Grey Annals*; on the other hand under ELED the translation was changed from 'Elf-fair' to 'Elf-maid'.]

**WEY-** wind, weave. Q, owing to change *wei* > *wai*, confused this with WAY; but cf. *Vaire* (*weirē) 'Weaver', name of the doom-goddess, wife of Mandos: N *Gwîr*. N *gwî* net, web. [The stem WEY was changed in pencil to VEY.]

**WIG-** *wingē: Q *winge* foam, crest of wave, crest. Cf. *wingil* nymph; *Wingelot*, *Wingelóte* 'foam-flower', Earendel's boat (N *Gwingloth*) [LOT(H)]. N, Ilk. *gwing* spindrift, flying spray. [This entry was an addition in pencil. – With *wingil* cf. the old name *Wingildi*, I. 66, 273.]

**WIL-** fly, float in air. *wilwā air, lower air, distinct from the 'upper' of the stars, or the 'outer' (see WAY): Q *wilwa* > *vilwa*; N *gwelw* air (as substance); *gwelwen* = Q *vilwa*; Ilk. *gwelu*, *gwelo*. Q *vilin* I fly, pa.t. *ville*. N *gwilith* 'air' as a region = Q *vilwa*; cf. *gilith* = Q *ilmen* (see GIL). Q *wilwarin* (pl. *wilwarindi*) butterfly; T *vilverin*; N *gwilwileth*; Ilk. *gwilwering*. [The name *Wilwa* of the lower air is found also in the preparatory outline for *The Fall of Númenor* (p. 12), whereas *Wilwa* in the *Ambarkanta* was changed throughout to *Vista*, and so also on the accompanying world-diagrams (IV. 240–7). By subsequent pencilled changes the forms *wilwā, Q wilwa were changed to *wilmā, Q wilma; Q wilwa > vilwa was struck out; and Q vilin was changed to wilin. A new stem WIS with derivative Q vista (see below) was introduced, either at the same time or later, but the stem WIL was allowed to stand.]

**WIN-, WIND-** *windi blue-grey, pale blue or grey: Q vinde, N gwind, gwinn. *winyā: Q winya, vinya evening; N gwein, pl. gwîn; Ilk. gwini, gwine. *winta- fade: Q vinta-, pa.t. vinte, vintane; ON wintha it fades, advesperascit ['evening approaches'], N gwinna. [This entry was struck out, and 'see THIN' written against it. The following pencilled addition may have been made either before or after the original entry was rejected, since it is not itself struck through:] *windiā pale blue: Q win(d)ya, vinya; N gwind.

**WIS-**   Q vista air as substance. [See note to WIL.]

**WŌ-**   together. The form wŏ would if stressed > wa in Eldarin. In Q the form wō, and the unstressed wŏ, combined to produce prefix ŏ- 'together': as in o-torno (see TOR), o-selle (see THEL), and many other words, e.g. ovesta (see WED). In N we have gwa- when stressed, as in gwanur (= Q onóro) [TOR], gwastar (see STAR), and frequently, but only in old cpds. The living form was go-, developed from gwa- in unstressed positions – originally mainly in verbs, but thence spreading to verbal derivatives as in gowest (see WED). In many words this had become a fixed element. Thus not- count, nut- tie coalesced in Exilic *nod-; but 'count' was always expressed by gonod- unless some other prefix was added, as in arnediad [AR²]. In Ilk. owing to coalescence of gwo, ʒo (in go) this prefix was lost [see ʒŎ].

# Y

[As already mentioned (p. 346) I have changed the representation of the 'semi-vowel' j to y, and therefore give these stems here, at the end of the alphabet. The section belongs however among the entirely 'unreconstructed' parts of the work, and consists, like the I-stems, only of very rough and difficult notes.]

**YA-**   there, over there; of time, ago, whereas en yonder [EN] of time points to the future. Q yana that (the former); yá formerly, ago: yenya last year [YEN]; yára ancient, belonging to or descending from former times; yáre former days; yalúme former times [LU]; yasse, yalúmesse, yáresse once upon a time; yárea, yalúmea olden. N iaur ancient, old(er); io (ia?) ago. 'Old' (in mortal sense, decrepit) is ingem of persons, 'yearsick'; 'old' (decrepit, worn) of things is gem [GENG-WĀ]. See GYER.

**YAB-**   fruit. Q yáve fruit; N iau corn. Yavanna Fruit-giver (cf. ANA¹), N Ivann.

**YAG-**    yawn, gape. \**yagu-* gulf: N *ia*, chiefly in place-names like *Moria* = Black Gulf. \**yagwē* : Q *yáwe* ravine, cleft, gulf; N *iau*. Q *yanga-* to yawn.

**YAK-**    \**yakta-*: Q *yat* (*yaht-*) neck; N *iaeth*. Q *yatta* narrow neck, isthmus.

**YAN-**    Cf. AYAN. Q *yána* holy place, fane, sanctuary; N *iaun*.

**YAR-**    blood. Q *yár* (*yaren*); N *iâr*; *Iarwath* Blood-stained (see WA3), surname of Túrin. Ilk. *ôr* blood; *arn* red; cf. *Aros* (= N *iaros*) name of river with reddish water.

**YAT-**    join. \**yantā* yoke, beside \**yatmā*: Q *yanta* yoke; *yanwe* bridge, joining, isthmus. N *iant* yoke; *ianw* bridge (*eilianw* 'sky-bridge', rainbow, see 3EL).

**YAY-**    mock. Q *yaiwe*, ON *yaiwe*, mocking, scorn; N *iaew*.

**YEL-**    daughter. Q *yelde*; N *iell, -iel*. [This entry was removed with the change of etymology of N *iell*: see SEL-D and YŌ, YON. A new formulation of the stem YEL was introduced, but was in turn rejected. This gave:] **YEL-**    friend: Q *yelda* friendly, dear as friend; *yelme*; *-iel* in names = [Old English] *-wine* (distinguish N *-iel* derived from *selda*).

**YEN-**    year. Q *yén* (*yen-*); *linyenwa* old, having many years [LI]. Last day of year = *qantien*, N *penninar* [KWAT]; first year, first day *minyen* [MINI]. *Endien* Midyear [ÉNED] was a week outside the months, between the sixth and seventh months, [?dedicated] to the Trees: [also called] *Aldalemnar*, see LEP. N *în* year; *inias* annals; *iðrin* year (= *ien-rinde*, see RIN); *edinar* (*at-yēn-ar*) anniversary day; *ennin* = Valian Year; *ingem* 'year-sick' = old (mortally) [GENG-WĀ]; *ifant* aged, long-lived (= *yen-panta* > *impanta* > *in-fant*) [KWAT]. [The word *Inias* 'Annals' occurs in the title-pages given on p. 202.]

**YES-**    desire. Q *yesta* desire; N *iest* wish.

**YŌ, YON-**    son. Q *yondo, -ion*; N *ionn, -ion*. [The following was added when the entry YEL had been removed:] feminine *yēn, yend* = daughter; Q *yende, yen*.

**YŪ-**    two, both. N *ui-* twi-, as *uial* twilight [KAL]. Q *yūyo* both.

**YUK-**    employ, use. N *iuith* use, *iuitho* [?enjoy].

**YUL-**    smoulder. Q *yúla* ember, smouldering wood; *yulme* red [?heat], smouldering heat; *yulma* brand. ON *iolf* brand; *iûl* embers.

**YUR-**    run. ON *yurine* I run, *yura* course; N *iôr* course.

# APPENDIX

---

## THE GENEALOGIES

## THE LIST OF NAMES

### AND

## THE SECOND 'SILMARILLION' MAP

# I  THE GENEALOGIES

These belong essentially with the earliest *Annals of Beleriand*, but
though I knew of their existence (since they are referred to in the *List of
Names*) I presumed them lost, and only recently discovered this small
manuscript, after the work on Vol. IV was completed. It consists of
genealogical tables of the Elvish princes, of the three houses of the
Fathers of Men, and of the houses of the Eastern Men. There is no need
to reproduce these tables, but only to mention certain details that are not
found elsewhere. In the first of them are some additional persons:

Elwë, Lord of the Teleri (who is called 'Lord of Ships'), has a son
*Elulindo*;

Fingon has a son *Findobar* (this name, simply as a name, occurs in the
*Etymologies* under the stems PHIN (written *Findabar*) and MBAR);

Orodreth, in addition to his son Halmir, has a younger son *Orodlin*.

The genealogies of Men have dates of birth and death. These were a
good deal emended, changing them by a year or two, but in the result are
almost exactly as in the earlier version of AB 1. The following are
however not given in the *Annals* in any version (if they had been they
would of course have been extended in two steps, first by a hundred years
and then by two hundred years).

*Elboron* son of Dior born 192; *Elbereth* his brother born 195 (they
were thus fourteen and eleven years old at their deaths, AB 2 annal 306);

*Húrin* died in '?200' (in annal 200 in AB 1, repeated in AB 2, 'of his fate
no certain tidings are known');

*Ulfand the Swart* born 100, died 170; *Uldor the Accursed* born 125,
*Ulfast* born 128, *Ulwar* born 130;

*Bor the Faithful* born 120; *Borlas* born 143; *Boromir* born 145;
*Borthandos* born 147.

In addition to the genealogical tables there is also a table of the
divisions of the Qendi which is almost the same as that given with the
*Lhammas* on p. 197, and together with this table is a list of the many
names by which the Lindar, Noldor, and Teleri were known. This list is
a first form of that in QS §29 (note to the text), and all the names found
here are found also in the longer list in QS; but there are here also many
Elvish names which (apart from *Soloneldi*) are not found in QS:

The Lindar are named also *Tarqendi* 'High-elves', *Vanimor* 'the
Beautiful' [> *Írimor* 'the Fair Ones'], and *Ninqendi* 'White-elves';

The Noldor are named also *Nurqendi* 'Deep-elves', *Ainimor* [written
above: *Istimor*] 'the Wise', and *Kuluqendi* 'Golden-elves';

The Teleri are named also *Falmarindi* 'Foam-riders', *Soloneldi*
'Musicians of the shore', and *Veaneldar* 'Sea-elves'.

The name *Vanimor* is used in AV 2 of the lesser spirits of Valarin race,

among whom were 'later numbered' also the *Valarindi*, the Children of
the Valar (pp. 110, 121); the latter are the *Vanimor* in the *Etymologies*,
stem BAN, but under the negative stems UGU, UMU the name is
translated 'fair folk = (men and) elves'. Some other of these
names also appear in the *Etymologies*: *Tarqendi* (TĀ), *Nurqendi*
(NŪ), *Istimor* (IS), *Falmarindi* (PHAL), *Soloneldi* (SOL). With *Írimor*
cf. *Írima ye Númenor* in *The Lost Road* (p. 72), and see stem ID.

# II   THE LIST OF NAMES

During the 1930s my father began the task of making an alphabetic list,
with definitions, of all the names in his works concerned with the legends
of the Elder Days. A list of sources is attached to this list, and the entries
are accompanied by full references to sources (by page-number or annal-
date) – but these references are almost entirely confined to the *Annals of
Beleriand* and the *Genealogies* : the only others are a few to the first pages
of the *Qenta Noldorinwa* (Q) and two to the *Map*. In the list of sources
'Annals of Beleriand' and 'Genealogies' are marked with a tick; it is clear
then that my father had indexed these and made a beginning on Q when
he stopped.

As the List of Names was originally written the references are only to
the first version of AB 1 (but include additions made to that text
subsequently and given in the notes in IV. 310–13). But after the list was
abandoned as a methodical work of reference my father added to it more
haphazardly, without references, and these later additions show use of
the second version of AB 1, as well as some names that do not appear in
any of the texts; entries were also substantially modified and extended.

The majority of the entries do not in fact add anything in their
definitions to what is available in the sources, and it is quite unnecessary
to give the work in full. There follows here a small selection from the
material, this being restricted to those entries or parts of entries which
have some particular feature of interest (mostly concerning names or
name-forms).

*Aldaron*   The Noldorin equivalent is given as *Galaðon*, which does not
   appear elsewhere.
*Balrog*   is said to be an Orc-word with no pure Qenya equivalent:
   'borrowed *Malaroko-*'; contrast the *Etymologies*, stems ÑGWAL, RUK.
*Beleriand*   'Originally land about southern Sirion, named by the Elves
   of the Havens from Cape *Balar*, and Bay of *Balar* into which Sirion
   flowed; extended to all lands south of Hithlum and Taur-na-Danion,
   and west of Eredlindon. Its southern borders undefined. Sometimes
   includes Doriath and Ossiriand.' With this statement of the extent of
   Beleriand cf. QS §108; and with the derivation of the name *Beleriand*
   from Cape *Balar*, Bay of *Balar*, cf. the *Etymologies*, stem BAL. This is

the first occurrence of Cape Balar, which was however marked in on the second Map as originally drawn and lettered.

*Beren* The surnames of Beren were first given as *Mablosgen* 'Empty-handed' and *Ermabuin* 'One-handed' (as in AB 2 annal 232). The former was changed to *Mablothren* and then to *Camlost* (and in a separate entry *Mablosgen* > *Mablost*); the latter to *Erchamui* and then to *Erchamion* (again as in AB 2, note 22). From the *Etymologies* (stems KAB, MAP) it appears that the names containing the element *mab* are Ilkorin (Doriathrin) names, while those containing *cam*, *cham* are Noldorin.

*Cinderion* 'Gnomish name = Hither Lands'. This name has no reference to a source; it is found nowhere else, nor any form at all like it.

*Cristhorn* was emended first to *Cil-thorn* and then to *Cil-thor(o)ndor*, with the definition 'Eagle-cleft of Thorondor King of Eagles'. The forms *Cilthoron* and *Cilthorondor* are found in the *Etymologies* (stem KIL), as also is *Cristhoron* (KIRIS).

*Dagor Delothrin* 'The Last Battle, "the Terrible Battle", in which Fionwë overcame Morgoth.' The reference given is to AB 1 annal 250, where however no Elvish name is found. In a cross-reference in the list to the Last Battle it is called also 'the Long Battle' (for it lasted fifty years).

*Dagor Nirnaith* is given as a name of the Battle of Unnumbered Tears.

*Dark-elves* 'Translation of *Moreldar* (also called *Ilkorindi*, those who came not to Kôr), the name of all the Elves who remained wandering in the Hither Lands . . .' The term *Moreldar* is not found elsewhere. The nomenclature here is of course that of Q (§2), where *Eldar* = 'all Elves' and the *Ilkorindi* or Dark-elves are those who were lost on the Great March.

*Dor-deloth*, or *Dor-na-Daideloth* '"Land of Dread" or "Land of the Shadow of Dread", those regions east of Eredwethion and north of Taur-na-Danion which Morgoth ruled; but its borders were ever increased southward, and early it included Taur-na-Fuin.'

*Dorthanion* is stated to be a Doriathrin name: *thanion* = 'of pines' (*than*). See the *Etymologies*, stem THŌN.

*Dwarves* 'Called by the Dark-elves (and so by the Gnomes) *Nauglar* (singular *Naugla*).' *Nauglar* appears in an addition to AB 1 (IV. 311); the QS form is *Naugrim*.

*Elivorn* 'Lake-Black in Dor Granthir.' This was a latter addition to the list and has no source-reference. *Elivorn* may well have been the form erased and replaced by *Helevorn* in QS §118. *Dor Granthir* is found in the same passage in QS.

*Eredlindon* '"Blue Mountains" (*lind* blue), eastern bounds of Beleriand.' See the commentary on QS §108.

*Eredlúmin* '"Gloomy Mountains", mountains to east [*read* west] of Hithlum, overlooking the Seas.' As the list was originally made, *Ered-lómin* was at both occurrences written *Ered-lúmin*. I have noted (IV.

192–3) that both the meaning of the name and its application were changed, so that *Ered-lómin* 'Shadowy Mountains', to the east and south of Hithlum, as in Q, became *Ered-lómin* 'Echoing Mountains', the coastal range west of Hithlum; and at the same time the meaning of *Dor-lómin* changed from 'Land of Shadows' to 'Land of Echoes'. In the List of Names as originally made the new name for the mountains east and south of Hithlum, *Eredwethion* 'Shadowy Mountains', already appears (with the etymology *gwath* 'shadow'), and there is here therefore a halfway stage, when *Ered-lómin* (*-lúmin*) had become the name of the coastal range but did not yet have the significance 'Echoing'. There is no doubt an etymological halfway stage also, which I take to be the explanation of the *lúmin* form (found also in *Dor-lúmin* on the second Map): the source was now the stem LUM, given in the *Etymologies* as the source of *Hith-lum* (and of Q *Hísilumbe*, changed to *Hísilóme* under the influence of *lóme* 'night': Q *lumbe* 'gloom, shadow'). Hence the translation here 'Gloomy Mountains', which is not found elsewhere. Finally the interpretation 'Echoing' arose, with derivation of *-lómin* from the stem LAM.

*Fingolfin*    The cairn of Fingolfin is called *Sarnas Fingolfin*.

*Fuin Daidelos*    'Night of Dread's Shadow' or 'Deadly Nightshade' is given as a name of Taur-na-Fuin.

*Gothmog*    '= Voice of *Goth* (Morgoth), an Orc-name.' Morgoth is explained at its place in the list as 'formed from his Orc-name *Goth* "Lord or Master", with *mor* "dark or black" prefixed.' These entries in the List of Names have been discussed in II. 67. In the *Etymologies* the element *goth* is differently explained in *Gothmog* (GOS, GOTH) and in *Morgoth* (KOT, but with a suggestion that the name 'may also contain GOTH').

*Gurtholfin*    was subsequently changed to *Gurtholvin* and then to *Gurtholf*. *Gurtholfin* > *Gurtholf* also in AB 2, note 39; see the *Etymologies*, stems GÓLOB and NGUR.

*Hithlum*    is translated 'Mist-and-Dusk'; see the *Etymologies*, stems KHIS and LUM.

*Kuiviénen*    The Noldorin name *Nen Echui* is given; this is found in the *Etymologies*, stem KUY.

*Morgoth*    See *Gothmog*.

*Orcs*    'Gnomish *orch*, pl. *eirch*, *erch*; Qenya *ork*, *orqui* borrowed from Gnomish. A folk devised and brought into being by Morgoth to war on Elves and Men; sometimes translated "Goblins", but they were of nearly human stature.' See the entry ÓROK in the *Etymologies*.

*Sarn Athrad*    is translated 'Stone of Crossing'.

*Sirion*    The length of Sirion is given as 'about 900 miles' from Eithil Sirion to the Delta. In QS §107 the length of the river from the Pass of Sirion to the Delta is 121 leagues, which if measured in a straight line from the northern opening of the Pass agrees with the scale on the second Map of 3·2 cm. = 50 miles (see p. 272). But the List of Names and the original drawing of the second Map were associated, and two of the references given in the list are made to the Map, so that the figure of 900 miles (300 leagues) is hard to account for.

*Sirion's Haven*: '(*Siriombar*), the settlement of Tuor and the remnants of Doriath at *Eges-sirion*; also called *Sirion*.' The name *Siriombar* only occurs here; cf. *Brithombar*.

*Mouths of Sirion*: '(*Eges-sirion*), the various branches of Sirion at its delta, also the region of the delta.' Above the second *s* of *Eges-sirion* (a name not found elsewhere) is written an *h*, showing the change of original *s* to *h* in medial position.

*Sirion's Well*: '(*Eithil* or *Eithil Sirion*), the sources of Sirion, and the fortress of Fingolfin and Fingon near the spring.'

*Tol Thû*   is another name for *Tol-na-Gaurhoth*.

*Tulkas*  'The youngest and strongest of the nine Valar.' The reference is to Q, IV. 79, but it is not said there that Tulkas was the youngest of the Valar.

# III   THE SECOND 'SILMARILLION' MAP

The second map of Middle-earth west of the Blue Mountains in the Elder Days was also the last. My father never made another; and over many years this one became covered all over with alterations and additions of names and features, not a few of them so hastily or faintly pencilled as to be more or less obscure. This was the basis for my map in the published 'Silmarillion'.

The original element in the map can however be readily perceived from the fine and careful pen (all subsequent change was roughly done); and I give here on four successive pages a reproduction of the map *as it was originally drawn and lettered*. I have taken pains to make this as close a copy of the original as I could, though I do not guarantee the exact correspondence of every tree.

It is clear that this second map, developed from that given in Vol. IV, belonged in its original form with the earlier work of the 1930s: it was in fact closely associated with the List of Names – which in two cases (*Eglor* and *Eredlúmin*, although *Eredlúmin* is not marked on the map) gives 'Map' as the source-reference – as is shown by certain name-forms common to both, e.g. *Dor-deloth*, *Dor-lúmin*, *Eithil Sirion*, and by the occurrence in both of *Cape Balar* (see the entry *Beleriand* in the List of Names). Moreover the date in 'Realm of Nargothrond Beyond the river (until 195)' on the map associates it with the original *Annals of Beleriand*, where the fall of the redoubt took place in that year (IV. 305), as does the river-name *Rathlorion* (later *Rathloriel*).

The map is on four sheets, originally pasted together but now separate, in which the map-squares do not entirely coincide with the sheets. In my reproductions I have followed the squares rather than the

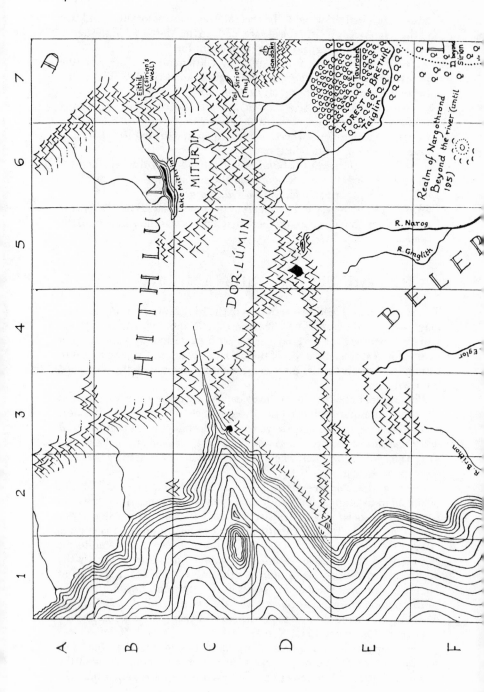

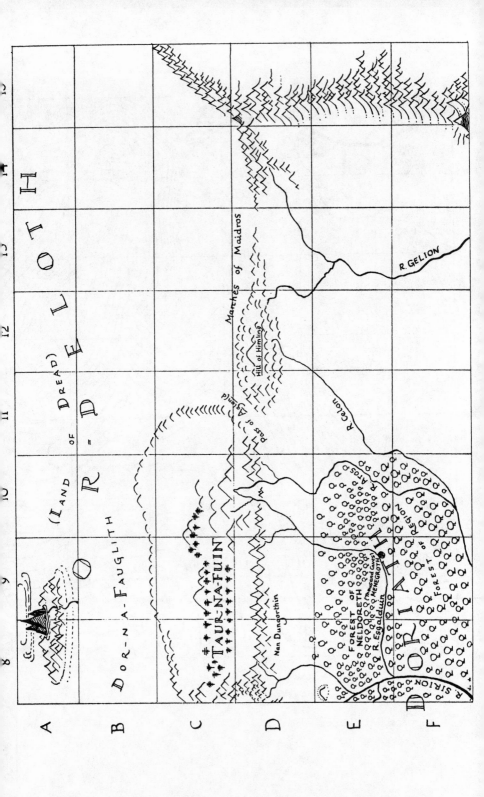

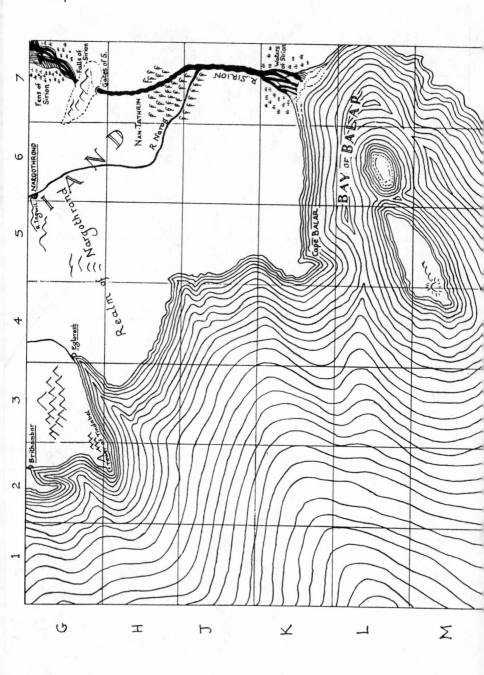

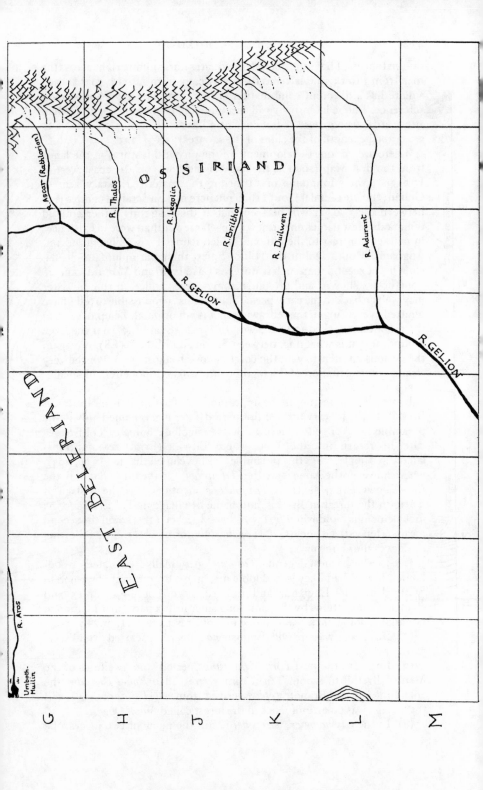

original sheets. I have numbered the squares horizontally right across the map from 1 to 15, and lettered them vertically from A to M, so that each square has a different combination of letter and figure for subsequent reference. I hope later to give an account of all changes made to the map afterwards, using these redrawings as a basis. The scale is 50 miles to 3·2 cm. (the length of the sides of the squares); see p. 272.

There are various developments in the physical features of the lands from the first Map (such as the large island lying off the coast west of Drengist; the Mountains of Mithrim; the eastern tributary arm of Gelion; the isle of Balar), but I shall not here make a detailed comparison between the two. It will be seen that at this stage my father entered remarkably few names on the new map – far fewer than were in existence, in marked contrast to the old one, which names Ivrin, Thangorodrim, Angband, Mount Dolm, the Hill of Spies, the great mountain-chains, etc. On the second map such features as Lake Ivrin and Mount Dolm are nonetheless shown, and of course some names added in roughly later may well go back to the early period; but as this is impossible to tell I have omitted everything in the redrawing that is not original. I cannot explain the mountain blacked-in to the west of Ivrin (square D5), nor the large mound, if that is what it is, between Sirion and Mindeb (E8), nor again the curious circular bay on the coast below Drengist (C3). On the very strange representation of Thangorodrim, isolated in a circle of smaller peaks, see p. 271.

Especially interesting is the appearance of Tavrobel in the Forest of Brethil. In the literary texts of this period Tavrobel is named only in the preamble to AV 1 (cited on p. 201), as Pengolod's home in Tol Eressëa 'after his return unto the West', where Ælfwine (Eriol) saw and translated the Annals; from this preamble was developed that to QS (p. 203), where however the name is written *Tathrobel*. On the other hand, in the *Etymologies* (stem PEL(ES)) *Tavrobel* is mentioned as the 'village of Túrin in the forest of Brethil, and name of village in Tol Eressëa'; the first element is Noldorin *tafr*, *tavor*, 'woodpecker' (TAM), and the second means '(fenced) village' (Qenya *opele*, Noldorin *gobel*). The following evidences thus appear:

(1) In the earliest legends *Tavrobel* (originally translated 'wood-home', I. 267) had likewise a double meaning: it was Great Haywood in Staffordshire in England, and it bore, according to complex and changing conceptions by this time long since lost, a particular relation to Gilfanon's home of the same name in Tol Eressëa (see II. 292–3, 310).

(2) *Haywood* was in Old English *hæg-wudu* 'enclosed wood' (II. 328).

(3) Later (in the post-*Lord of the Rings* period) the dwellings of the Men of Brethil to whom Túrin came were called *Ephel Brandir* 'the encircling fence of Brandir' (*ephel* derived from *et-pel* 'outer fence'), and this village was on an eminence in the forest called *Amon Obel*.

(4) In the *Etymologies*, *Tavrobel* is still the name of two places, the

village of the Woodmen in Brethil, and a village in Tol Eressëa, where (in the preambles to AV 1 and QS) Pengolod (successor, as I have argued in IV. 274, to Gilfanon) dwelt.

But there is no indication at all why Tavrobel should still be used twice in this way. It may be thought that my father did not wish finally to abandon this old and deep association of his youth; and it is tempting therefore to see his bestowal at this time of the name *Tavrobel* in this way and in this place as an echo of Great Haywood, and perhaps not entirely fanciful to wonder whether he was influenced by the confluence of the two rivers, Taiglin and Sirion, not wholly unlike, in their relative courses here, that of the Sow and the Trent at Great Haywood (I. 196).*

*Gilfanon's house, the House of the Hundred Chimneys, stood near the bridge of Tavrobel (I. 174–5), where two rivers, Gruir and Afros, joined (II. 284, 288). I noted (I. 196 note 5) the possibility that there was, or is, a house that gave rise to Gilfanon's; and it has been pointed out to me by Mr G. L. Elkin, Acting Director of the Shugborough Estate, who has kindly supplied me with photographs and a detailed map, that Shugborough Hall, the home of the Earls of Lichfield and now the property of the National Trust, is near the end of the old packhorse bridge (called the Essex Bridge) which crosses the rivers at their confluence, and that the chimneys of the mansion are a prominent feature. It seems very likely that it was my father's sight of the great house through the trees and its smoking chimneys as he stood on the bridge that lies, in some sense, behind the House of the Hundred Chimneys in the old legend. Mr Elkin has further suggested that the High Heath or Heath of the Sky-roof, where the great battle was fought, so that it became the Withered Heath (II. 284, 287–8), might be Hopton Heath (where a battle of the Civil War was fought in 1643), which lies a few miles to the North-west.

# INDEX

The vast array of forms contained in Part III of this book constitutes a problem in respect of the Index. In the first place, a large number of names found in the *Etymologies* do not occur elsewhere in the book, and in many cases names are registered in greatly varying forms according to the divergent phonetic development in the different languages. In the second place, discussion of the history of names and the isolation of their elements makes the distinction between 'name' and 'common word' unreal; for the purposes of this 'etymological dictionary' *Alqualondë* illustrates *alqua* 'swan' and *londë* 'harbour-entrance, roads'. But to list alphabetically even a proportion of these Elvish 'common words' in Part III would be preposterous, since (quite apart from the practical consideration of length) it would mean rewriting the 'dictionary' in such a way as to conceal the historical relation between words which it is the object of the work to display.

I have in fact excluded the whole content of the Etymologies from normal representation in the Index, but I have attempted to assist reference to them in the following ways. (1) In the page-references to names that do occur elsewhere in the book I include also pages in the *Etymologies* where these names are explained – all such references being printed in *italics*. As a general rule I restrict these references to actual occurrence in the *Etymologies* of the name in question, but I have departed from this rule where it seemed useful to provide a reference to an element in a name that only appears in the *Etymologies* as a 'common word' (e.g. *nyárë* 'tale, saga, history' under *Eldanyárë*). (2) Where the *Etymologies* give names for persons, peoples, or places that are different from those found elsewhere in the book these are mentioned in the Index but not given separate entries; e.g. the Noldorin names *Mirion* and *Núron* are given under *Silmarils* and *Ulmo*. By these means, the great majority of names in the *Etymologies* are at least indicated in the Index. But beyond this, the many curiosities of the work – such as the structure of the Valinorian year and the names of the days in the Valinorian 'week', or the etymology of *cram* – emerge only from the study of it.

From the large number of names that occur in or in association with *The Lost Road* I have excluded some of the more casual and insignificant. References are not given for names on the tables accompanying the *Lhammas* or on the reproductions of the second Map.

As before, I have adopted a single form of capitalisation and hyphenation for the purposes of the Index.

*High-elves* A name of the Lindar. 214, 218, 223, 334, 403 (see *Tarqendi*); in later sense, the Elves of the West, 7

*High Heath* Near Tavrobel. 413

*High Speech of the West* 190

*Hildi* The Followers, Men. 72, 245, 248, *364*; *Hildor* 248

*Hildórien* The land where the first Men awoke. 120, 245, 248, 275, *364* (another name *Firyanor*, *381*)

*Hill of Spies* East of Nargothrond. 412

*Hills of the Hunters* 268. See *Taur-na-Faroth*.

*Himring, Hill of* 'Ever-cold' (265). 145, 177, 189, 263, 265 (described), 268–9, 283, 289, 307, 311, (*364*, *383–4*); earlier form *Himling* 127, 132, 134, 145, 189, 268–9; the speech of Himring 177

*Hísilómë* Hithlum. 266, (*364*), 370, 406; *Hísilumbë* 370, 406

*Hithaeglir* The Misty Mountains. 336

*Hither Lands* Middle-earth. 118–19, 125, 170–2, 176–8, 184, 220–1, 326, 328, 332, 334, 405. See *Cinderion*.

*Hithliniath* 'Pools of Mist'. 262, 268, *364*. See *Aelin-uial*, *Umboth Muilin*.

*Hithlum* 19, 117, 127, 130–1, 133–40, 145, 147, 151–2, 239, 249–52, 255, 259–60, 263–4, 266, 269–71, 276, 280–2, 284–5, 287, 289, 291, 307–8, 310–14, 316, 318–23, 328, *364*, 370, 404, 406; *Men of Hithlum* 19, 311, 319–21; *King of Hithlum* (Fingolfin) 128, 146, *Aran Chithlum* 322; northern edge of Hithlum 270–1; origin of the name 'Land of Mist' 259, 266

*Hobbits* 98, 199, 293–4

*Hollin* 345, (*Regornion 356*)

*Holy Elves* A name of the Lindar. 215

*Holy Mount* Taniquetil. 234

*Hopton Heath* In Staffordshire. 413

*House of the Hundred Chimneys* The house of Gilfanon at Tavrobel. 413

*Hroald* Viking leader. 80

*Hrothgar* King of the Danes in *Beowulf*. 93–4

*Huan* The Hound of Valinor. 135, 151, 300, *364–5*

*Hundor* Son of Haleth. 130–1, 136, 146–7, 275, 310, 314, *364*

*Hunters' Wold* 268. See *Hills of the Hunters*.

*Huor* 64, 131, 136–8, 140, 179, 191, 275, 289, 307, 311, 316, 328, *359*, *364*

*Húrin* Called 'the Steadfast' (131, 312, 318, sc. *Thalion*, *388*). 30, 131–2, 134–8, 141, 147, 150, 275–6, 287–9, 291, 307, 309, 311–20, 322, 328, 333, *361*, *364*, 403

*Hy Bresail* See 81

*Ialassë*, *Iolossë* Earlier forms for Oiolossë. 210, *357–9*

*I·Chúrinien* The Lay of the Children of Húrin (q.v.). 317, 322. See *Narn i Hîn Húrin*.

*Ingwëa*   The 'noble dialect' of the speech of the Lindar (= *Ingwelindarin, Ingwiqen(d)ya*). 183, 195
*Ingwelindar*   The house and people of Ingwë. 171, 183 (see *Ingwi*); *Ingwelindarin* = *Ingwëa*, 185, 195
*Ingwemindon*   The tower of Ingwë. 222, 225, *373*, *395*. See *Ingwë*.
*Ingwi* = *Ingwelindar*. 171, 183
*Ingwiel*   Son of Ingwë. 144, 326, 334, 336
*Ingwil*   River flowing into the Narog at Nargothrond. 262
*Ingwiqen(d)ya*   A tongue whose relations are differently described (see 195). 172, 184–5, 193–5
*Inias Valannor* or *Inias Balannor*   The Annals of Valinor. 202; *Inias Veleriand* or *Inias Beleriand*, the Annals of Beleriand, 202; *400*
*Inner Lands*   Middle-earth. 245
*Inner Sea*   The Great Sea of the West. 209. *Inner Seas* (of Middle-earth) 25, 161
*Inscrutable, The*   An Elvish name for Men. 245
*Insula Deliciarum*   80–1
*Inwë*   See *Ingwë*
*Inwir*   The house of Inwë in the *Lost Tales*. 183
*Ireland*   39, 80–2, 84, 103; see *Erin*. *Irish, Irishmen* 39, 78, 81–2
*Irimor*   'The Fair', a name of the Lindar. *361*, 403–4. See *Fair-elves*.
*Iron Crown*   125, (135, 144), 154, 233, (284), 303, 329
*Iron-forest*   12, 23
*Iron Mountains*   251, 254–5, 257, 259, 266, 270–2; *Mountains of Iron* 125, 280; *Mountains of Morgoth* 127, *of Melko* 259, 270. See *Eiglir Engrin, Ered-engrin*.
*Isfin*   Sister of Turgon, mother of Meglin; called 'the White' (223). 136, 139, 152, 223, *361*, *381*
*Isil*   'The Sheen', name of the Moon. 41, 56, 72, 240, 243, *361*, *385*, *392*. See *Ithil, Rana*.
*Isildur*   71, *376*
*Isle of Balar*   See *Balar*; *Isle of Werewolves*, see *Tol-na-Gaurhoth*.
*Istar*   Queen of Númenor. 15–16, 27. (Replaced by *Tar-Ilien*.)
*Istimor*   'The Wise', a name of the Noldor. *361*, 403–4; cf. 215
*Italy*   54–5, 91; Old English *on Eatule* 55
*Ithil*   Name of the Moon in Noldorin. 41, 56, 243, *361*, *385*, *392* (another name *Elfaron* 'Star-hunter' *387*, cf. 241). See *Isil, Rana*.
*Ivrin*   260, 272, 412; *Falls of Ivrin* 261
*Ivrineithel*   Ivrin's Well. 139

*Kalakilya*   The Pass of Light. 168, 173, 185, 223–4, 242, *362*, *365* (also *Cilgalad*). See *Kôr*.
*Kalamor*   Light-elves. 197, *362*
*Kalaqendi*   Light-elves. 197, *362*; *Calaquendi* 197
*Kay, Guy G.*   302

222, 300; *Mountains of the West* 64; *encircling mountains* 222; *mountains of defence* 241

*Múlanoldorin* Language of the slave-Noldor. 177, 189, *373*

*Musicians of the Shore* A name of the Teleri. 215, 403. See *Soloneldi*.

*Music of the Ainur* 155–60, 163–4, 204, 207, 212, 217, 232, 247; *Second Music of the Ainur* 157, 163, 166


*Naith of Lothlórien* 345, *387*

*Nameless Land, The* (poem) 82, 98–100

*Nan-dungorthin* 261, 267, *355, 374, 377* (also *Nan Dongoroth, Nann Orothvor*); *Dungorthin* 299; later form *Dungortheb* 299

*Nan-tathren* 145, 261, 267, *374, 391*; earlier form *Nan-tathrin* 126, 140, 145, 267. See *Land of Willows*.

*Nargothrond* 18, 29, 126, 128–9, 133, 135–6, 138–41, 146–7, 150–2, 177, 189, 254, 257, 261–2, 264–6, 268, 272, 281, 283, 287–8, 290, 292, 301, 308–9, 312, *374, 379, 384*, 407; speech of Nargothrond 177

*Narn i Hîn Húrin* 316, 322, *374*; see especially 322, and *i·Chúrinien, Lay of the Children of Húrin*.

*Narog, River* 128, 139, 152, 254, 260–2, 268, 272, 320, *374*; *caves of Narog* 126, 254; *realm of Narog* 139, (*Narogardh 374*); *King of Narog* (Felagund) 128

*Nauglamír* 141–2, *373, 375* (also *Mîr na Nauglin, Nauglavir*).

*Nauglar, Nauglath, Nauglir* Earlier forms of the Elvish name of the Dwarves. 277, 405. See *Naugrim*.

*Nauglian* Languages of the Dwarves. 197, 277. See *Aulian*.

*Necklace of the Dwarves* 306; *Dwarf-necklace* 141. See *Nauglamír*.

*Necromancer, The* 23

*Nefantur* Mandos. 207. (Replaced by *Nurufantur*.)

*Neldoreth* The forest forming the northern part of Doriath. 126, 148, 261, *376*

*Nellas* Elf of Doriath, friend of Túrin in his boyhood. 316

*Nen-Echui* Waters of Awakening, *Kuiviénen*. *366, 376*, 406

*Nen-girith* 'Shuddering Water'. 140, *358*

*Neorth* Early name of Ulmo. 97

*Nerthus* 'Mother Earth', goddess worshipped in antiquity in the islands of the Baltic. 97

*Nessa* Wife of Tulkas. 110, 206, *376–8* (also *Neth, Dineth*; Nessa was also named *Indis* ('bride'), *361, 375*)

*Nevrast* Later form for *Nivrost*. 256, 266

*Neweg* 'Stunted', Gnomish name for the Dwarves. 274, *375*

*New Lands* In the World Made Round. 16; *New World* 17, 28

*Nienna* 110, 113, 206–9, 227, 241, *376*; *Fui Nienna* 207, *382*

*Nienor* 138 ('the Sorrowful'), 139–40, 317 ('Mourning'), 318, 320 (cf. *Nuinoer, Nuinor* as the name of Túrin's sister, *375*).

(language) 8, 56. *Númenóreans* 12–30 *passim*; 56, 71, 74, 76, 79, 149; *Lie-númen* 12, *Númenórië* 12, 19; language 30, 149; stature 25; aging 71

*Númenos* (1) Númenor. 11. (2) The chief city of Númenor. 14, 19, 30. (3) The high place of the king. 25, 30, 337. See *Númar*.

*Nurqendi* 'Deep-elves', a name of the Noldor. *378*, 403–4. See *Deep-elves*.

*Nurufantur* Mandos. 205, 207, *377, 387* (also Noldorin *Gurfannor*). (Replaced *Nefantur*.)

*Nyarna Valinóren* The Annals of Valinor. 202 (see *Yénië Valinóren*); *Nyarna Valarianden*, the Annals of Beleriand, 202; *374*

*Oath of the Fëanorians* 115–17, 142–4, 234, 237, 239, 246, 252, 308, 330–1, 336

*Ohtor* Viking leader. 80

*Oiolossë* 'Everlasting Whiteness', Taniquetil. 209–10, *359, 379*. See *Amon Uilos, Ialassë*.

*Old English*. 38–9, 53–5, 80, 84–5, 91–6, 103, 120–1, 123, 202–3, 209, 243, 279, 300, 412; see also *Anglo-Saxon(s)*.

*Old World* (after the Cataclysm) 12, 16–18, 21, 28

*Olofantur* Lórien. 205, *379, 387* (also Noldorin *Olfannor*).

*Olwë* Later name of Elwë (1), brother of Thingol. 217

*Ondor* Earlier name of Gondor. 33–4

*Orcs* 24, 29, (65, 74), 114, 117–51 *passim*, 161, 177–9, 190–1, 212, 216, 233, 238–9, 249–94 *passim*, 307, 309–12, 315, 320–1, 323, 328, 332, 404, 406. Origin of the Orcs 24, 29, 114, 122, 125, 148, 212, 216, 233, 238–9; numbers 137; language 177–9, 190–1, 404, 406; etymology *379*, 406. See *Glamhoth, Goblins*.

*Orgof* Elf of Doriath, slain by Túrin. 138, 316, 321. (Replaced by *Saeros*.)

*Orodlin* Son of Orodreth. 403

*Orodreth* Son of Finrod (1) = Finarfin. 116, 119, 127, 132–3, 135–6, 138–9, 145–7, 150, 223, 226, 234, 237, 239, 264, 269, 283, 290, 292, 308, *379*, 403; see especially 239

*Oromë* 110–13, 120, 122, 168–9, 175, 180–3, 186, 192–3, 205–8, 212–14, 216–19, 221, 223, 225, 230–1, 240, *379, 384* (also Noldorin *Araw*); *Lord of Forests* 168. See especially 110, 120, and see *Aldaron, Galaðon, Tauros*.

*Oromian* Languages derived from Oromë's instruction of the Elves (= *Quendian*). 168, 178, 193–5

*Orontor* Númenórean. 62, 71

*Orquin, Orquian* Language of the Orcs. 178

*Ossë* 11, 14, 24, 110, 113, 120, 161, 171, 186, 205, 208, 221–2, 224–5, 233, 236, 239, *359* (also Noldorin *Oeros*).

*Ossiriand* 32, 34, 112, 114, 119, 126, 128, 135, 141, 146, 153–4, 175–80, 182, 186, 189, 193–4, 196, 253, 260–1, 263, 265, 267–8, 274,

*Qendi, Quendi* (1) The First Kindred of the Elves (replaced by *Lindar*). 107, 122, 180–1. (2) All Elves. 119, 122, 168, 171, 174, 178, 180, 182–3, 197, 212–14, 218–19, 225, 246, 247, *366* (also *Qendië*, Noldorin *Penedhrim*), 403

*Qenta, Quenta* (References in the texts themselves) 119, 171, 180, 185, 191, 201–2, 226, *366*. See *Pennas.*

*Qenya, Quenya* 'The Elvish Tongue'. 8, 56, 75, 172–5, 180, 184–6, 188, 192–5, 200, 217, 343–5, 404, 406, 412; *Qendya* 185. See *Elflatin, Parmalambë, Tarquesta.*

*Quendian* Languages derived from Oromë (= *Oromian*). 168, 181, 188, 192–7, 205, 207, 342, 347; *Quendian race* 178

*Radhrost* 'East Vale', Dark-elvish name of Thargelion. 262, 265, 268–9, *382, 384*

*Radhruin* Companion of Barahir. 147, 282; *Radruin* 147, 289. (Replaced *Radros.*)

*Radros* Companion of Barahir. 133, 147, 289. (Replaced by *Rad(h)ruin.*)

*Ragnor* Companion of Barahir. 282

*Ramdal* 'Wall's End' in East Beleriand. 262–3, 268; *Rhamdal* 283, *390*

*Rana* 'The Wayward', the Moon. 56, 240, 243, *383* (also Noldorin *Rhân*). See *Isil, Ithil.*

*Rathloriel, River* 'Bed of Gold'. 141, 263, *368, 383*, 407; earlier form *Rathlorion* 407

*Region* The forest forming the southern part of Doriath. 126, 148, 261, 356 (also *Eregion, Taur-nan-Erig*)

*Rerir, Mount* Outlier of Eredlindon, on which was a fortress of the Noldor. 263, 265, 268, 283, 290

[*Rhibdath, Rhimdath* River Rushdown. 384. This name only appears in the *Etymologies*, but it should have been mentioned there that the Rushdown is the river that flowed from the Misty Mountains to join Anduin north of the Carrock.]

*Rian* Mother of Tuor. 131, 133, 136–7, 151, 282, 289, *383* (*Rhian*); *Rían* 316

*Ringil* (1) The Sea of Ringil, formed from the fall of the Lamp Ringil. 32, *383*. (2) Fingolfin's sword. 284–5, *383*

*Ring of Doom* The council-place of the Valar. 209, 229

*Rivil's Well* 298

*Rome* 55; *Roman(s)* 39, 91–2; Old English *Walas, Rūm-walas* 92

*Rómenildi* Easterlings. 286, 291, (*364*)

*Rómenna* Haven in the east of Númenor. 74

*Rosamunda* Wife of Alboin the Lombard. 37, 54

*Rúmil* 113–14, 116, 122–3, 155–6, 164, 167, 178, 191–2, 203–4, 278; called *the sage of Kôr, of Tûn* 167, *the Elf-sage of Valinor* 123, 203–4

*Saeros* Elf of Doriath, slain by Túrin. 187, 316. (Replaced *Orgof.*)

*Sailors, The* A name of the Teleri. 215

150–1, 404–5; *Taur-na-Thanion, -Thonion, -Donion* 145, (*392*). See *Dorthonion*.

*Taur-na-Faroth* The Hills of the Hunters. 262, 268, 299, *387* (*Taur-na-Faras*); later form *Taur-en-Faroth* 299

*Taur-na-Fuin* 'Forest of Night' (133). 133–6, 139, 144, 153, 282 (translated 'Mirkwood'), 289, 300, 310, 315, 336, *382* (also Quenya *Taurë Huinéva*), *391–2*, 405–6; with reference to Greenwood the Great 289; later form *Taur-nu-Fuin* 289, 300. See *Deldúwath, Fuin Daidelos, Gwathfuin-Daidelos*.

*Tauros* Name of Oromë. 206, *359, 391*

*Tavrobel* 201, 203, *380, 390*, 412–13; *Tathrobel* 203, 412

*Telchar* Dwarf smith of Belegost, or of Nogrod. 303, 319, 322. [The statement in the Index to Vol. IV that Telchar was 'originally of Nogrod' is an error; see IV. 182.]

*Teleri* 112–13, 115–16, 119, 122, 143, 161, 168–71, 173–4, 178, 180–4, 186, 193, 197, 200, 214–15, 218, 221–6, 231, 233, 235–6, 239, 242, 256, 266, 324, 326, 332, 334, 344, *391* (also *Mirimor 373, Fallinelli, Falanyeldi 379, 381*), 403; language of the Teleri 171, 173–4, 180, 184, 222, 224, 226; meaning of the name 168, 183, 214, 218, *391–2*; in old sense, the First Kindred, 165, 182; other names 215, 403

*Telerian* (of language) 175, 181, 184, 187; (with other reference) 125, 148, 169, 176, 182, 187, 194, 218–19, 253, 256, 261, 326

*Telerin* Language of the Teleri. 172, 188–9, 193–5, 347; adjective to *Teleri* 344

*Telperion* A name of the White Tree of Valinor. 209, 211, 244

*Terendul* 'Slender and dark', derisive name given to Herendil son of Elendil. 59, 70, *355, 376, 392*

*Terrible Battle* See *Great Battle*.

*Thalos, River* 128, 263, *388*

*Thangorodrim* 117–18, 125, 132, 137, 144, 249–51, 254, 257, 259, 264, 266, 271, 279–80, 283, 290, 310, 313, 329, 336, *388*, 412; see especially 259, 271

*Thargelion* The land of Cranthir, 'Beyond Gelion'. 262, 265, 268–9, 273, 277, 283, *392*; earlier form *Targelion* 268. See *Dor Granthir, Radhrost*.

*Thingol* 112–14, 119, 125–6, 134–5, 138, 141–2, 148, 168, 174–6, 181, 186–7, 189–90, 194, 215, 217, 220–1, 225, 253, 261–3, 266, 281, 287, 292, 295, 298–300, 308, 316–22, 326, 332, 362, *389*, *392–3* (also *Tor Thingol; Tor Tinduma* 'King of Twilight', Noldorin *Aran Dinnu*); *the hidden king* 266; *Thingol's Heir*, see *Dior*.

*Third Battle of Beleriand* The Battle of Sudden Fire. 130, 280. See *Dagor Húrbreged, Dagor Vregedúr*.

*Third Kindred (of the Elves)* 182, 217; *Third Host* 217. See *Teleri*.

*Thorondor* King of Eagles. 145, 251–2, 256, 285, 288, 290, 298, 301, 303, 329, 336, *392* (also *Thorntor, Torthurnion*), 405; earlier *Thorndor* 126, 132–3, 142, 145, 256, 290–1, 303. See *Sorontur*.